"COME INSIDE, HUMAN CHILD."

Joanna drank the wine and began to feel warm and unafraid. "Why do you call me 'Human Child'?"

"It is what you are."

"And you?"

Cormac said, very gently, "My dear, you must have seen that I am not entirely human." The dark eyes flicked over her and flared into golden life, and Joanna felt a strange delight. "Do not trust me," he said softly, "for I am of wolf blood, Joanna."

"Is that . . . possible?"

"Oh yes. You see?"

He touched his eyes, and Joanna had the impression that his face was sharpening, becoming crueler. "How do you know I will not leap on you, Joanna? How do you know I will not devour your soul, Human Child?"

WOLFKING

Bridget Wood

A Del Rey® Book

BALLANTINE BOOKS • NEW YORK

A Del Rey ® Book
Published by Ballantine Books
Copyright © 1991 by Bridget Wood

Library of Congress Catalog Card Number: 92-90199

ISBN 0-345-38328-1

Manufactured in the United States of America

First Ballantine Trade Edition: July 1992
First Mass Market Edition: July 1994

10 9 8 7 6 5 4 3 2 1

CHAPTER ONE

BEFORE THE APOCALYPSE Joanna would not have had to draw water from the well and carry it in pails to the kitchen. There would have been levers that you turned, and there the water would have been. Some of the legends even said you could have the water hot if you wanted, but this was not generally thought correct. Joanna's father said if all the stories about the Letheans were true, they ought to have been able to fight the Apocalypse and destroy it before it destroyed them. They certainly ought to have been able to stop it from stalking the world and laying waste and burning up cities wholesale. It was only a pity, said Joanna's father, that a bit more of the Letheans' fabled learning had not survived, and then Joanna would not have to pull up pailfuls of water, and her mother would not have to wrestle with the cauldron of clothes on wash days, and he himself could have travelled to every corner of the farm in a machine that drove itself, like the Letheans were said to have done.

The Letheans. The Forgotten Ones. Named after the River of the Underworld—the Lethe—whose waters made the souls of the dead forget their lives on earth. And, what was so terrible to Joanna, they had been given the name because so little of them had survived that no one now knew for sure what they had been called.

"Ah, it's a grand old name for them," said Flynn O'Connor. "And aren't they truly the forgotten ones, anyway? In some lands they call them the Quondam!"

Joanna asked what that meant.

"That which once was, but is no longer."

1

You could not altogether trust Flynn's information, because like most Irishmen he could spin a good tale if he thought he could get away with it, but you could not entirely dismiss it either. The O'Connors were honoured in Tugaim. "Old Stock," said Joanna's aunt Briony reverently, but then Aunt Briony's information could not really be trusted either, because she had once been betrothed to be conjoined to Flynn's great-uncle Diarmid, and was apt to be sentimental about the family. Joanna's father said that Diarmid O'Connor had deliberately disappeared one night, rather than face conjoining with Aunt Briony, but Joanna did not believe this either.

Aunt Briony was inclined to promote a conjoining between Joanna and Flynn because it was a tradition, and a linking of two great Irish families. "The land marches along—well, we know that. And Joanna would like marrying Flynn. He has books," said Aunt Briony reverently, "from before the Apocalypse. Not the thin rubbishy stuff your father reads, my dear, but real books. Paper like satin and printing so clear you wouldn't believe it. Remarkable things." She had read one once, she said. "All the way through, and not one word in ten did I understand, which just shows you. A great city it was, with desperate criminals and horses drawing the finest contraptions to carry folk about. And a man who wore an odd hat solving the crimes, and a doctor helping him. A fine old tale it was, but it was nothing like we have in the world today."

There was not very much crime in Tugaim of course, unless it might be Seamus Flaherty carrying off Fingal O'Dulihan's pigs, and swearing it was a wild bull got them.

You were not really supposed to possess anything from before the Apocalypse, although of course people did. But if you had anything that your ancestors had salvaged, you were supposed to take it along to the People's Museum in Dublin, so that everyone could see how the Letheans had lived. Everyone thought that was a fine idea, but nobody ever donated much, because, as Joanna's mother said, hadn't they all sufficient to do all day without digging up the fields to see had the Letheans buried anything there before Devastation? Joanna knew all about Flynn's books and the maps and the copper pans and the pewter jugs, and she did not see why Flynn's family should not keep these things for themselves if they wanted to.

But nobody really owned very much from the Letheans'

time. Except land, of course, and anyone could have land. There was so much of it. But it was usually a problem to find land where crops would grow properly, and land that did not glow in the dark.

"Never," said Joanna's mother, "never *ever* live on land that does that, acushla."

"Why not?"

But Joanna's mother did not know. It was one of the legends, an old wives' tale, some kind of ancient warning handed down from the survivors of the Letheans' Great Battle. It was sometimes extremely irksome, because it meant that acres of good flat land could not be built on. But no one had ever risked going against the warning, and so no one had ever really found out why the Glowing Lands were unsafe. One day Joanna was going to coax Flynn to take her to Tara's Hill, where a soft incandescent light sometimes showed, and picnic there by moonlight and find out what happened. She thought she would do it quite soon, but she thought she would have to be feeling extra brave, because she had once seen the great ruined city of Cork glowing like a massive furnace against the night sky, though it was generations since the Apocalypse had stalked Ireland and everywhere else in the world. Had it come to Ireland first? Or last?

"No one knows," said Flynn, lying down on the hillside, his hair tossed into wild disarray, his eyes bright blue and his thin cheeks whipped to colour against the sky. "Oh, it was a shocking thing, Joanna. The Last Battle . . . the world in flames. But they say that the Letheans were so weakened by their dissolute way of life, and so flabby from generations of soft living and greed and arrogance, that they hadn't the backbone to put up a fight."

"I don't see them as greedy and arrogant." Joanna picked out an apple from their lunch basket and prepared for a good argument. "I see them as sad. Misguided. Hadn't they missed the point of life somewhere—the stories all tell that over and over. Weren't they so taken up with their machines and their fine cities that they forgot about the important things? They were children," said Joanna, her grey eyes black-fringed and enormous in her little pointed face. "Children with huge machines they failed to master."

"They were heedless children," said Flynn, his eyes sparkling, for Joanna, the darling girl, always gave a man a great old argument. "They deserved to be punished." He rolled over on to his back. "But if the Apocalypse came back today, wouldn't he find a different story! Oh wouldn't he just! We'd give the creature a fight for his impudence, Joanna! We'd skin the ruffian and tweak his tail and send him to the rightabout!"

Flynn visualized the Apocalypse as something between a mischievous boy and an enraged pig, but Joanna knew that the Apocalypse had been something so huge and so incredibly powerful that your mind would never grasp it. An immense evil, a vast spirit conjured up from another world. It had destroyed the Letheans and their marvellous world so completely that only the thinnest of memories of them were left.

The Letheans. The Lethe. The Forgotten Ones.

It was achingly sad to Joanna that a race, a culture, a whole world, could have so cruelly and so comprehensively disappeared.

"We have nothing of them," she said.

"We have a little," said Flynn.

But it was so little that all it did was tantalise you.

"If," said Joanna, lying back on the springy turf at Flynn's side, "if I could work magic, I believe I should go back to their time."

"And meet up with the Beast? Girl dear, he'd huff his scorchy breath on to you and you'd be frizzled up in a minute! He'd have you for breakfast and spit out the bones. Much better to stay here."

"It'd be before the Apocalypse came," Joanna replied, suddenly warm inside at Flynn's soft cajolery, "when the Letheans lived in their great glittering cities, and had machines to take them everywhere, and got water from levers and fire from pressing buttons. They could fly—did you know that? Oh wouldn't that have been grand. Flynn, you're not listening."

Flynn said, "But there was once a much better time, acushla." And Joanna shivered and delight ran all over her, because when Flynn looked at her like that and called her acushla, which was a very privileged word indeed, it sent rivulets of pleasure trickling down beneath her ribs. It would not do to admit it of course. Conjoining was meant to be strictly practical. It was a weighty undertaking. Her father often said so. The Kin Book had to be consulted, so that people did not conjoin with near relations—which might bring forth idiots; the joining up of land had to be considered, so that Glowing Lands were not farmed or built on—which might bring forth anything at all.

"A business arrangement," said Joanna's mother, explaining it to Joanna. "And all very sensible."

The Letheans had conjoined freely and wherever they chose. "Too freely," said Joanna's mother. "They were like animals."

"And look where it got them," said Joanna's father. And taking her quietly aside, he explained that there was nothing particularly wonderful about conjoining, as so many of the young people seemed to think. "A simple physical process. Something to be done to bring children into the world. Be guided by me."

Even so, Joanna thought her mother sometimes looked a bit wistful, almost as if she was thinking: is this all there is? And what about the soft look on Aunt Briony's face when she talked about Diarmid O'Connor. And what about her own delight when Flynn smiled at her and called her acushla, which was such a very old and very precious word? She thought she could easily be envious of the Letheans who had known about conjoining with whoever you wanted; who had known, as well, about indulging their every appetite. "Overindulging it," said Joanna's father. "That's where they went wrong. We shall do better."

The Letheans had done disastrously, of course, everyone knew that, but even so, they had married whom they liked and conjoined where they pleased, and had not had to bother about Kin Books and land registrations.

But, since you were not supposed to care about such things, Joanna did her best to conform. Even, said her mind, even when Flynn lies beside you on the hillside, and even when you ache with wishing he would just reach out and touch your face, your neck, your breasts . . .

Even then. It did not do to be different. And even these days, even with the Great Devastation so far behind them, non-conformity was still looked at askance. The coming of the Apocalypse had produced so many odd things, that to begin with, there had been laws about certain people being let to conjoin at all. There had been a word: mutation. Joanna had never seen a mutation. "Of course not," said Aunt Briony. "They had died out by the time you were born."

"Had they?" said Joanna's mother, and sent a wary look through the window to where the great grim bulk of the Gealtacht, the terrible House of Mutants, stood on its hill overlooking Tugaim. Everyone tried to pretend that the Gealtacht was empty these days, and that it had been empty for years, but everyone knew that lights still showed there sometimes, and that dreadful screams could be heard if you went near to the hill. Hardly anyone ever did go near to the hill of course, because it was sinister and repellent, and because the very thought of being out there alone on the cold hillside in the dark was enough to send most people scurrying to the safety and the comfort of their firesides. Some of the older people occasionally hinted at terrible things; monsters, deformities, all shut away inside the House, but no one really believed this. And no one Joanna knew had ever actually seen a Mutant.

Even so, the idea of something not quite as other people had remained like a tender spot on a good many consciences. You had to be absolutely the same as everyone else, otherwise you might find you were crossed from the Kin Book altogether, and not allowed to own land, except the Glowing Lands, which nobody wanted anyway.

And so, although Joanna often lay awake and imagined how Flynn's hands would feel caressing her body, and how his mouth would taste, she could not let anyone know. When Flynn said, "There was once a much better time," and smiled, she moved back a little and said, "Tell me about the better time," and tried not to know that he smelt of masculine skin and clean hair, and the wild strawberries they had been eating for their lunch. His mouth would taste of the strawberries, sweet, tender, and quite beautiful and you could drown in the delight of it . . .

Flynn smiled at Joanna, and thought: what would she do if I reached for her now? Dare I? Would she go running off to Grady the Landgrabber, shrieking "rape"? Oh, but her mouth would be soft and sinless, and I could lay her down on the hillside and take her innocence, my sweet lovely girl, because for sure she'll be innocent . . .

He would not do it. He would abide by the unwritten laws that permitted of no conjoining before marriage, and he would slake his hungers on the women of Peg Flanagan's, whose business that sort of thing was. But none of it stopped him lying wakeful and alone in the yellow and white bedroom beneath the eaves, and none of it stopped him aching with longing, because he would never really want anyone other than Joanna.

He turned away, rolling on to his front so that he could throw stones down the hill and see them splash into the Sidh Pool far below, and Joanna at once felt a sense of loss—a withdrawal. He had been looking at her and smiling, and there had been something so tender and so full of promise . . . I am on the brink of something wonderful, she had thought.

But she had been reared in a stern school, and so she put the thought of Flynn's mouth and his hands on her body from her mind, and said, "Tell me about the better time."

Flynn sat up, his eyes sparkling, reached for the wild strawberries again and began to talk about an ancient Ireland, an Ireland of long ago.

Neither of them had ever heard those magical words "once upon a time" for the art of story-telling, like so many of the other arts, had been lost. For the last three hundred years, men and women had been too taken up with rebuilding a shattered burnt-out world to think of such mundane things as telling stories. But some things never quite die, and both Joanna and Flynn were imaginative; both were Irish, with the true Irish gift for telling and hearing a story. If Flynn did not say "once upon a time" he did not need to, for the magic was in his voice and in his eyes, and Joanna was immediately and wholly enthralled.

"So LONG AGO, that it was nearly the beginning of time, Ireland was ruled by a great and wonderful Court," said Flynn softly. "The Court of Tara, where the High Kings sat on the throne of Dierdriu of the Nightcloak, and of Niall of the Nine Hostages.

"It was a time when the land was ruled by sorcery and heroism and intrigue; when men were better than human and when women lay with the beasts of the forest, and gave birth to strong and cruelly beautiful children who had the blood of the wolves and the eagles and the lions in their veins. Did you ever see a Bible, Joanna? An immense book, very greatly honoured by the Letheans at one time in their history. In one place, it says 'There were giants on the earth in those days.' Giants, Joanna. Creatures better than human. Near-gods. The people of the old, old Ireland were that, acushla. Beautiful mystical beings. Creatures to revere and serve, and perhaps fear. Yes, I think one would be a little frightened of them, but one would never be able to resist them. Half human and half animal, so that they had power over the animals, so that they could call them, summon them to their side in battle. Did you ever hear of the Battle of Cormac of the Wolves? The Wolfram, they called him. He was exiled from the Court, but he swore to return, and he stood on Tara's Hill and sent out a call to his brothers, the wolves. And they came, they obeyed him, they came streaming out of the forest, down the valley, and converged on the hill at his side.

"Remarkable," said Flynn, his eyes faraway.

"It's there I'd go if you could work your magic, Joanna. To the Old Ireland: the land of half-humans, magic and wars, princes and enchanted beings, and great battles, mist-shrouded forests. Do you know we've never seen mist, Joanna? The Apocalypse burned us up so that all the moisture went from the world. But they had mists then—like great smoky clouds they were. They called Ireland the blue and green, misty island. Beautiful. Men sailed the seas just to catch glimpses of it, for tales of it had spread half across the world. It was beautiful, acushla. Not the dry arid place it is now. We have the Hard Rain, but once there was a soft gentle rain in Ireland, so soft that it shrouded the land in blue and purple mist." He sat up. "Would you come with me, Joanna? Follow me into a land so old that its memories are lost in the beginnings of time? So old that the Letheans had forgotten it, just as we have forgotten the Letheans. Would you do it, acushla?"

It was impossible to resist Flynn when he talked like this; absurd extravagant nonsense that you did not quite believe, but that you could not quite disbelieve either. For a moment, just for the briefest second, Joanna had seen it all quite clearly; the beautiful cruel faces of the children, and the slant-eyed intelligence of people who would not obey human laws, and who might not obey the laws of the animals either.

"Oh," said Joanna, her hands clasped tightly together, her eyes shining, "oh, if only we could go back, Flynn. If only we could."

"Would you come with me?"

All my fortunes at thy foot I'll lay and follow thee my lord throughout the world . . . ?

The beautiful tragic words were lost for all time, but even so, an echo lingered. Joanna looked at Flynn and said slowly, "I believe I would.

"Yes, I believe I would."

JOANNA'S FATHER KNEW himself for a reasonable man. Everyone said he was. "John Grady's as reasonable a man as you'd find in a week's search," they said.

He was part of the ruling body of Tugaim, one of its Elders. He had a say in the entering up of the Kin Book, and he was almost always asked to make one of any inquiries that were set up when laws were broken. He hoped he was not guilty of the Letheans' sin of complacency, but he thought he could be just the smallest bit proud of himself. A reasonable man. One of the Elders of Tugaim, and a Grady, a member of that grand old Irish line. Not everyone could boast of possessing that coveted second, family name these days; names, memories, and lineages, like so much else, had been lost during Devastation. The surviving families had not always known who they were when they crawled back up into the light after the Apocalypse had at last exhausted its strength. But the Gradys had kept their name, and everyone knew that the Gradys of Tugaim had been a highly thought of family before Devastation.

"Utter rubbish," said Seamus Flaherty, stinging from John Grady's stern sentence after the unfortunate episode of Fingal O'Dulihan's pigs. "He's no more a Grady than O'Dulihan's pigs. He might be a *graibéir*." And then several people had to be reminded that a *graibéir* was a landgrabber. "That's where the famous 'Grady' comes from," reiterated Seamus, pleased with himself, carrying Fingal off to Peg Flanagan's wine shop where they could both drink poteen and cry destruction on the Elders and lasting death to the Apocalypse, and confusion to the Landgrabbers. It was a sorry thing when a man could not do that, and you might thank whichever god you paid homage to that one of the things the Apocalypse had not destroyed was the secret of making poteen.

John Grady was not a landgrabber, of course, the very idea was absurd. Everyone knew that Seamus Flaherty was the biggest romancer in Tugaim, and everyone knew that you could not trust a word he said. Of course there had been *graibéirs* after Devastation; of course people had taken what land they could, started up little farms, and then bigger ones. Land had been there for the asking anyway, and no one had needed to do any grabbing. He would deal with Flaherty more sternly the next time the ruffian came up before the Elders, and the man would certainly not be left free to go off drinking poteen with his arch enemy and lifelong friend O'Dulihan. John Grady disapproved of Peg Flanagan's wine shop and the poteen that Peg made; he did not hold with becoming intoxicated any more than he held with frivolity. Too much poteen gave people ideas, and you had only to go back three hundred years— probably more like two hundred and fifty—to see where intoxication and getting ideas got people.

It was to be hoped that Seamus did not spread his nonsense about *graibéirs* too far. John Grady remembered a word that the Letheans had used: snob. It had signified someone who thought he or she was better than anyone else. The Letheans had set a lot of store by that kind of thing; possessions and standing in the world. John Grady knew the worthlessness of such things, of course. Even so, you had to have standards, you had to remember that there were always those who led and those who followed. John was glad to think himself a leader, and he was very glad indeed to know himself above *snobbishness*. You did not often hear the term nowadays, but it was descriptive, nevertheless. It did not, naturally, describe John Grady, although he had his standards. It would not do for people in Tugaim to be saying his ancestors had been one of those unprincipled marauding gangs who had roamed the desolate wastes that were all the Apocalypse had left to mankind, taking land and plundering people's homesteads. Everyone knew about them; everyone knew, as well, about the courage and the determination of the survivors. A terrible time it must have been, and the pity was that the *graibéirs*—the real ones—had succeeded, so that even in Tugaim there were descendants of them. He dared say that Seamus Flaherty was one.

You could not be too careful whom you allowed your family to conjoin with these days. He was going to be very careful indeed about Joanna. The child had been given some ridiculous Lethe notion about love and romance and suchlike; she was off with the wild O'Connor boy whenever the opportunity presented itself, and that was one of the things that was going to be stopped. Briony, foolish old woman, had encouraged her in her nonsense, but then Briony had always been more or less witless. Small wonder that Diarmid O'Connor had disappeared rather than be conjoined. Not that conjoining needed any particular degree of intimacy, of course. John himself had never been especially intimate with Joanna's mother, it was a silly Lethe idea to think you had to live like that. The business of bed and board, and of day to day life could be done quietly and without fuss. There was a certain amount of messiness about conjoining, of course, he'd known that before he did it, but he'd gone through with it staunchly, because in these times it was every man's duty to beget good sturdy children for the world.

Joanna was certainly not going to be conjoined with Flynn O'Connor. Doubtless the boy had his worth, but John Grady did not think that Flynn had anything in his head other than daydreams and Lethean nonsense. As for the O'Connor land, well, there was certainly a lot of it, but John did not think it was so very marvellous. He had looked at the maps carefully. Mostly fruit, of course. Some wheat and maize and a few sheep as well. And that treacherous belt of Glowing Land on its southeast boundary.

"A grand spot," Michael O'Connor, Flynn's father, had told him. "Can't you see the Mountains of the Morning from there. The finest sight in all Ireland."

Grady had been surprised. He had said, "You have actually walked across Glowing Land? Actually stood on it?" and a strange look had come into Michael's eyes.

He'd replied, "Well now, wouldn't any man be tempted?" and Grady had hardly been able to believe his ears, for didn't everyone know, quite certainly, that the Glowing Lands were absolutely and finally forbidden?

O'Connor had said gently, "But do you know why they're forbidden, John Grady?" and John had had to admit that he did not. But then no one did.

"Do they not?" said Michael softly. "Oh, do they not, indeed." And John had taken himself off grumpily.

Joanna was certainly not going to be given into such an impractical family. John would not be at all surprised to find a hidden Mutant or two in the O'Connor background. You were not supposed to conceal Mutants, although people did, you were supposed to take the poor creature to the House of Mutants where it could be looked after and kept with its own kind. You had, as well, to enter the Mutant in the Kin Book, and if a Mutant was born into your family, you could not breed again. The line had to die out. Mutants had pretty well ceased to be born now, but occasionally you came across one . . . terrible creatures. Ah, when you were an Elder, you had to see some shocking things. You had to make some hard decisions. John was very thankful that the Gealtacht stood a little apart from Tugaim, remote on its high hill—a dreadful thing indeed if normal, whole people had to mingle with those deformities!

Joanna should be conjoined with Brian Muldooney. The Muldooneys were what was called New Stock; John did not think they had owned any land before the Apocalypse—you could nearly always tell when people were not accustomed to owning and possessing and having; but of course, this was not something which had to be taken too much into account. It certainly did not have to be taken into account when the land in question marched so neatly alongside Grady land, although John would not, of course, allow this to influence his decision.

Joanna should be conjoined with Brian Muldooney and that was all there was to it. The Muldooneys were scrupulous about keeping the laws, which was a thing to be considered; they paid their dues and they did what they should, and if they had ever harboured a Mutant, it would be a very great surprise. Which was more than you could say about Flynn O'Connor and his father.

The Muldooney farmlands would round off John's own acres very nicely. It had been ridiculous of anyone to seriously consider Flynn, what with his impractical ways and his daydreaming family and his blend of arrogance and disinterest. John, who knew his own worth, and who knew, as well, that he himself was a natural leader of men, did not always care for Flynn O'Connor's air of calling no man master. All men were equal, and that was what everyone today believed. It had not been what men believed before the Apocalypse, of course, they all of them knew that. There was even an ancient, carefully preserved book which the Letheans had thought well of, which said that all men were equal but that some were more equal than others. John had seen a copy of it in the People's Museum, and had been very much shocked to see such a sentiment actually written down for all to read. He thought it told you a good deal about the Letheans.

Anyway, Joanna was going to Muldooney.

CHAPTER TWO

MICHAEL O'CONNOR WAS feeling altogether great. Life was grand if you made it so; life was a fine old thing for a man these days. To be sure, his ancestors had bargained with the devil, and they had lost, so that the devil had walked in to the world and gobbled most of it up—the memories were not so many, but they were there, and people knew a little of that time. But weren't there grand compensations at times. Wasn't O'Connor land as safe as ever it had been, and didn't they do well enough with their fruit orchards and their sheep rearing, which was as yet modest, but would not always be. And wasn't the square stone farmhouse as snug a home as you'd find anywhere in Ireland?

Best of all, wasn't it the finest thing in the world to be keeper of a secret so immense and so breathtaking that a man might be pardoned for feeling a touch arrogant now and then; he might be pardoned for feeling just the smallest bit superior to the likes of Grady the Landgrabber when he came poking his long nose, asking questions, actually sizing up an O'Connor for conjoining with his lovely daughter. Michael liked Joanna very much; he would have been very glad for Flynn to have Joanna; he thought Flynn would be glad as well. But wasn't it as plain as a cowpat that the Landgrabber had no notion of Flynn for the child? A very great pity, and if there was anything Michael could do, he would do it, but Grady was a hard man, an inflexible man. He was suspicious, as well; would you only look at how he'd quizzed Michael about the Glowing Lands, and drawn in his prim mouth and looked disdainful. They could well do without the likes of John Grady in Tugaim.

The secret of the Glowing Lands was safe, of course. Michael would never betray it, not even when he had drunk Peg Flanagan's poteen; certainly not when he had taken Peg or her sister, or both, off to bed for the night.

To be appointed one of the Keepers of the Secret had been the most tremendous honour. Michael's father, initiating Michael when he was twenty-one, had said it was only because of the accident of geography; the Glowing Lands were on their territory and the thing had been preordained. A modest man he'd been. But Michael's grandfather, who'd been a grand old ruffian and whose memory was still green in Tugaim today, had winked and grinned at his grandson, and said hadn't the Keepers been chosen with great care throughout the world?

"Throughout the world?"

"There'll be one or two in every land, even in England, although that's always been known for a terrible dull place. Cold-blooded the English. Weren't we for ever at war with them?"

"Were we?"

"Even the English will have Keepers," said Michael's father. "For there'll be Glowing Lands in every corner of the world—the Apocalypse made sure of that, may he rot in hell for ever."

But the Apocalypse, wherever he was now, had done the world a curious favour. "Although," said Michael's father seriously, "if he'd known it, he'd have found a way of avoiding it. He intended destruction, you see; he brought down War, Plague, Famine, and Death. He left the Glowing Lands as a permanent reminder. They say he touched them with his scorching breath as he passed through the world, and that they will glow for ever. Some people call them Gateways to Hell."

"But of course," said Michael's father, "they are no such thing."

MICHAEL O'CONNOR THOUGHT wasn't it remarkable the way life moved in a circle. Twenty years ago he had stood on this very spot, his father at his side, and looked down the hillside to the ovoid below them that was one of Ireland's Glowing Lands. Now he stood here with Flynn at his side, and felt excitement and fear mingle in exactly the way his father must have done. Would Flynn understand? Could he be trusted with the Secret? Had his own father wondered these things? And in twenty years' time, would Flynn stand here with his own son? Michael hoped so. In any case, it had to be an unbroken line. Father to son. The first Keepers had been firm about that. Continuity. Father to daughter might be permitted, or perhaps father to grandson or nephew, but a special Council would have to sit, and the Keepers were always cautious about meeting together more than was absolutely necessary.

"We dare not," the first Keepers had said, "draw attention to ourselves."

Nor had they. They met when required; when one of them was admitting a son into the Secret. Or when no son existed, they met to consider who in that Keeper's family might be handed the trust. They met stealthily, carefully, nearly always at night. Michael had attended perhaps three assemblies of Keepers since his own admission twenty years earlier. They were solemn gatherings, and they were not to be lingered over. There was a prescribed ritual to be followed.

"For," said the first Keepers, "anyone adjudged indiscreet; anyone who it is considered will not keep absolute and total silence about the reality of the Glowing Lands, cannot be allowed to live."

It was a harsh law but it was a necessary one. Even so, twenty years earlier, the young Michael, brought before the Keepers, had stammered, "But I cannot take a vow of silence until I know what the Secret is." And then, with a spurt of anger, "In any case, how would any of you know if I broke my vow?"

"We would know," said the Keepers.

Flynn would be trustworthy, Michael thought he could be sure of that. The boy was a bit wild, he was a dreamer—still, I trust him, thought Michael, glancing at the silent figure at his side. And wondered was that an odd thing to think about your own son.

Flynn was amused and intrigued by this midnight meeting; he was also intensely curious. No one, or at least no one Flynn could think of, went up Tara's Hill after nightfall, and no one ever stood on its summit and looked down on the Glowing Lands.

"Haunted," said the villagers and shuddered, but Flynn

thought that if the Hill was haunted, it was not haunted by anything you could put a name to. Several tales of hauntings had survived from the Letheans' time, but Flynn knew that Tara's Hill was not haunted by anything the Letheans would have recognised. There was a tremendous sense of anticipation tonight; there was a feeling of someone (something?) existing on the Hill, just out of sight and just out of hearing. Something that tried ceaselessly and tirelessly to make itself seen and heard. Flynn mentioned this to Michael as they began to ascend the hill, but Michael only said, "Perhaps. There are some odd things in the world since Devastation," and fell silent.

Flynn was aware, as never before, of the immense stillness of Tara's Hill, and of a queer thrumming note on the night air. He tilted his head listening, for surely his father could hear it as well. But Michael, appealed to, said, "I hear nothing."

"Yes ... listen. Surely it is music ..."

But no music he had ever heard the like of. Few of the Letheans' music-making machines had survived, but some had. People had lately begun to rediscover these machines' secrets; there was a little more time now from the healing of the land, there was not quite such a need to be endlessly tilling and planting and reaping. People were learning how to relax just a little. A family in Donegal had found music notation in an old tin trunk; someone had fathomed the principles of it. Flynn and his father had actually heard the most marvellous sounds made by something called a violin, and something else called a piano, played at a gathering of O'Connor families. Remarkable. The music had been written long before the Great Devastation, hundreds of years, it was thought. A German, someone said.

But van Beethoven's music had been nothing like the music Flynn was hearing now. He thought: I am not just hearing it, I am feeling it. The someone or the something that is just out of sight is pouring it into my soul, as easily as pouring water from one jug to another. He felt himself filling up with the music, until it spread to every pore of his body, and he wanted to shout aloud with delight and he wanted, as well, to turn and run away, because there was besides something cold and inhuman and rather cruel. I think, said Flynn to himself, that to listen to this for too long might drive a man insane.

He glanced at his father again. "Do you truly not hear it?"

he said, and Michael replied, "I hear nothing," so that Flynn fell silent, for his father's tone was dismissive.

They had crested the summit of Tara's Hill now, and below them, Flynn could see clearly the incandescent light. The Glowing Lands. There were many belts of them throughout Ireland; throughout the world, it was believed. They were known to be dangerous, although no one knew why, and they were thought to have been cursed. They were feared and avoided and they were never built on. "*Never* build on Glowing Lands," said the old warning, and no one ever had.

"Are we going down there?" said Flynn.

"We are."

"To the Glowing Lands?"

"Yes." Michael looked at his son out of the corners of his eyes. "Afraid?"

"Terrified," said Flynn, and grinned. "Will I lead the way?"

"If you wish."

And then Flynn saw the hooded and cloaked figures waiting for them.

THEY WERE WELCOMED courteously, but rather solemnly, into the circle of dark figures; Flynn thought afterwards that there was an air of glancing over the shoulder about them. He thought they were not exactly afraid, these unseen faces, but they were very, very wary.

There were not very many of them; were there ten? Perhaps eleven or twelve. Certainly not more. One of them stepped forward and handed Flynn a cloak.

"You must put this on."

"Why?"

"You will blend better into the night. We do not want to be seen."

Flynn considered rebelling, but only for a second. His imagination was stirred and his curiosity aroused. As well as that, his sense of humour was awake. Were they all to caper goat-like on the damp grass and invoke the Old Gods? I'm not missing any of this, thought Flynn, and donned the cloak and a sober mien, and waited to see what came next.

The men drew round him in a circle, and the one who had given him the cloak looked at him intently. Flynn thought, he is attempting to see into my soul, and felt at once uneasy.

The man said, "Flynn O'Connor. Son of Michael, son of Liam, son of Patrick, son of Seamus, son of Donal, the First Keeper of the O'Connors. Listen. And listen carefully. Do not interrupt.

"When the Great Devastation nearly killed the world and the Apocalypse stalked the land, many things died. Many things the world knew then will never be known to the world today.

"But when the Apocalypse left his paw marks on the world, he did not know that in doing so he had disturbed something very ancient and very dangerous."

A pause. Michael glanced at Flynn, but Flynn was silent.

"Ours is not the only world," said the speaker, his eyes in shadow. "There have been many other worlds; there are still many other worlds, and there will be many worlds that will come after us. We cannot know of them, nor they of us. Ever since time began, they have been hidden from us, for the Gods who made the world drew down the Time Curtain, so that there should be no passage between these many and varied worlds."

Again the pause, as if he was listening to Flynn's reactions. He appeared satisfied; he gave a small nod, and continued.

"Imagine, if you can, Flynn O'Connor, son of the unbroken line of an old Irish family, the men and women who lived through the Great Devastation. Think of those ancestors of ours, think of what they endured. They were Letheans—the last of those extraordinary people, and yet they were the first of a new race as well. They had lived in the Lethe world with all its marvels and its learning and its luxuries. Its decadence, also, for we know that the Letheans, towards the end, had become very decadent. They had been born into it, those ancestors of ours, and they had never known any other world.

"And then the Apocalypse came. We do not know what sort of warning they had, but we can assume there was some. Think of them, terrified, powerless, visualising the horrors about to be unleashed on them, for whatever else they may have lacked, we know they did not lack imagination.

"And when the Apocalypse came, there would have been unimaginable terrors. Fiery walls of light. Blazing furnaces. Cities burning and floods and earthquakes. And afterwards, when the Apocalypse had gone, there would have been disease and hunger and thirst. People dying by the thousands. It has been said, and perhaps truly, that the unfortunate ones were those who survived . . .

"The world was a burnt-out graveyard, Flynn, but the people who survived were courageous beyond description. They were survivors in the truest and oldest sense of the word. An extraordinary people. They were strong and they were fearless.

"They rebuilt the world, Flynn, and they tried to explore all of its possibilities, and they took on tasks that we would perhaps shrink from.

"The Glowing Lands fascinated them. They knew the dangers—they knew they were the stigmata of the Great Devastation, but they still explored them. This is perhaps the greatest example of their courage, for we know that the Glowing Lands were very much brighter than they are now, and they would have been frightening places. They are dimming, you see, Flynn. With every generation that passes, the Glowing Lands—and their powers—are fading. A little each year. It may be that one day in the future, there will be no such things as Glowing Lands, and then there will be no need for Keepers of the Secret."

He stopped speaking and appeared to wait. Flynn said cautiously, "But what is the secret? And why does it need—all of this?"

"The secret is a vast one," said the man. "When it was discovered, it was thought by our ancestors to be too vast and widely reaching for it to be made generally known. Only the people who had Lands on their own territories . . ."

Again the pause. "Yes?"

The speaker seemed to hesitate, choosing his words.

"When the Apocalypse stalked the world he did something to it that no one could have thought possible. I have not the learning to explain it to you fully; none of us has. The Letheans, with their scholars and their men of science and their philosophers might have done, but even then we cannot be sure. There are no recorded instances . . ."

Once again Flynn said, "Yes?"

"It is simple enough," said the man.

"The Apocalypse tore the Time Curtain, Flynn. The Glowing Lands, every one of them, are gateways to the past."

At once there was an air of relief about the silent figures; a feeling of: at last it is out in the open again! Now we can talk, even if only for a short while; for a short while we can relax our guard and share with our own kind the marvellous, terrible inheritance of Devastation.

Flynn did not speak. His mind was tumbling with new ideas, struggling to adjust to something he had never before thought about. Or had he? Did so much not now become clear? The other-world feeling of Tara's Hill. The strong sense of something pressing close to him whenever he was there. And the music—oh yes, above all, the cold beautiful music. And then above that, of course, above everything, the knowledge that Tugaim had of the past. Not the near past; not the Letheans and their terrible battle, which had been only eleven—was it eleven?—generations ago; not that.

The Deep Past—everything remembered and written and preserved. Every ancient book hoarded and jealously guarded by Flynn's family. "For," had said Flynn's grandmother, "this is our heritage, and we must keep it so that it can be handed on." And there had been firelit evenings when the family would gather in the long low-ceilinged room of the farmhouse and weave stories and tell legends, and there had been long drowsy afternoons in the apple orchard when they would sing some of the old old songs, old before the Letheans' time, of the Ancient Ireland.

The Ancient Ireland—the misty beginnings of time when creatures not quite human but not quite animal had ruled; when the Court of Tara had sat in unguessed-at splendour on this hill—oh dear God yes, thought Flynn, this very hill—and when Ireland had been ruled by sorcery and enchantment and by cunning and strength and intrigue. The Plain of the Fál, the Stone of Knowledge, phallus-shaped and giving voice when touched by the destined High King. The people of legend: Niall of the Nine Hostages, and the Twelve Chariot Warriors, and the Couch of Conchobar. Mab the Intoxicating One and Cormac mac Airt, Cormac of the Wolves, who had been exiled from Tara. Flynn sat and stared and listened and all the time thought: of course it is true! Of course we know it all. *We were there.* In the lost past of Ireland. In the mist-shrouded days when there were High Kings and sorcerers and battles.

People were there. Recently. Since Devastation. The Apocalypse tore the Time Curtain and people have been back. That is why it has been so important to preserve the past. That is why the past is so important to us. A great sense of awe filled him, and he leaned forward, anxious to hear, eager not to miss anything.

The discussion had become general now; the hooded figures were seated in a tight little circle on the grass, words tumbling from them, clearly keen to welcome him into their ranks, delighted to give the newcomer as much knowledge as they had.

There were Glowing Lands throughout the world, said one; there were Keepers of the Secret in every country the Apocalypse had visited.

Flynn asked: was the Great Devastation after all so widespread? What of the rumours that a few lands had escaped? Was that only a myth?

"We do not believe any part of the world escaped," said the man sadly. "Devastation was total. The Apocalypse was merciless, for although in other lands he is called by a different name, the results of his wrath are exactly the same."

Flynn was at once intrigued by the idea of knowledge filtering in from other lands, and the man, sensing this, said, "We have occasionally met Keepers from far-off countries. From time to time, the journey has been undertaken, for although it is arduous and long to travel such immense distances, still we have done it in order to learn and in order to gain a little understanding."

"Everywhere, it is the same," said another. "The Great Devastation. War, plague, famine, and death. In some lands, the Apocalypse is called the Armageddon. In others he is called by a name we could not pronounce. But everywhere it is the same."

"And everywhere has belts of Glowing Land," said yet another. "In every country, the Time Curtain has been torn."

"But what happens? How does it work?"

There was a sudden silence, and Flynn thought: I should not have said that. They are shocked.

But they considered his question courteously; they glanced uneasily at one another, until, at length, the man who had told the story, and who appeared to be some kind of leader, said, "That is one of the things we do not know. It is one of the things you must promise, Flynn. Never to test the power of the Lands. Never to try to go back."

If you break the vow, we shall know ... Michael, quietly

listening, contributing little to the discussion, remembered his own initiation, twenty years earlier. If you break the vow, we shall know ... of course they would know.

"We know the power of the Lands," said the leader, "for it is one of the things the first Keepers discovered, and one of the things they have handed down to us. We know that some of them did go back."

"And returned?"

"Yes," said the leader, carefully, "yes, they returned. But as each decade passed, it was a little more difficult for them to do so. It is easy to travel back, but it is not so easy to return."

And the power of the Glowing Lands is dimming ... No one said it, but the words hovered. Flynn thought: to go back there, to find undreamed of wonders and terrors, but perhaps never to return ...

"Eventually," said the leader, "it was agreed that to test the power of the Gateways must be strictly forbidden. That is one of our two laws, Flynn. The other is absolute secrecy. You must never speak of what you have learned tonight, and you must never, under any circumstances whatsoever, try to go through the Time Curtain."

"BUT OF COURSE, people have gone through it," said Michael, walking slowly back to the snug stone farmhouse, where fires would still burn for them, and where they would pour themselves tots of Peg Flanagan's poteen and probably talk until first light of what had happened.

"Of course they have gone back," said Michael again. "It is how we in Tugaim have acquired our knowledge of Ancient Ireland."

Flynn said, "But why only Ancient Ireland? Why just that one time?"

"If I had the learning," said Michael, who was, in fact, a gentle, scholarly man when he had not taken poteen, "if I had the learning, I could explain it all clearly. As it is, I can tell you best by saying that each piece of Glowing Land is like a doorway. It opens on to one part of the past, and one part only. There are Tunnels of Time, great echoing caverns, which go on and on, and where a man might wander forever in the dark, searching for the doorways that would lead him into the Past. They say that there are endless winds in the Tunnels," said Michael, his eyes staring ahead unseeingly now. "And wouldn't that be a terrible thing to find yourself trapped in one of those Tunnels.

"But the tears in the Time Curtain are not where the Tunnels are," he said, "therefore, we do not have unlimited access to the Past. We cannot get into the Tunnels and walk along them until we reach the doorways we want. Whole centuries are still sealed.

"But each of us who owns Glowing Land, has a gateway into a portion of the past. A direct doorway, you see. The English have a chink through to the days of the druids, and another to the time of a chieftain they revered—Arthur. And there are many others I wouldn't know about. The Keepers are reticent. Each guards his Gateways jealously."

They had reached the farmhouse now. Normality! thought Flynn. And was glad to see the place again. Wasn't he? And then he remembered that strange, beckoning, other-world music on Tara's Hill, and wondered if he was glad. He lit lamps from the embers of the fire on the hearth, and tugged off his boots. There was a basket of sweet-scented applewood logs in the fender, and he tipped several of them on to the dying fire. Yes, normality. Perhaps after all it was safest.

"Tell me about the Keepers."

Michael sat down and stretched his legs to the blaze. It was good to be home. It was very good indeed to be able to talk to Flynn about the Secret.

"The Keepers came into being after Devastation. When people who owned Glowing Lands began to discover the truth. No one knows how they did discover it, and to be sure, the Lands themselves were nothing to take much notice of. They were always blackened and arid. Nothing ever grew there. But there were reports of odd visions; strange lights, creatures that did not fit into any known category. That, of course, was not so very remarkable then; you have heard of the Mutants—"

"Yes. Oh yes."

"Well, they were not Mutants, of course. No one knows quite what they were. Little by little, our ancestors pieced together the truth. As you heard our leader say tonight, they were brave people. Some of them must have gone through the Time Curtain."

"And?"

"They brought back tales. Those who came back."

Those who came back . . . There it was again, the chill suggestion that once beyond the Time Curtain, one might not be able to return. Flynn shivered, and went quickly to the built-in oak cupboard for the poteen. They'd have a pinch of spice in with it, to warm them.

"At length," said Michael, taking the glass from Flynn and sipping it gratefully, "there was consternation. Our ancestors began to be worried by what they had found. There was too much to be done here; there was too much rebuilding of a world nearly destroyed to worry about other worlds. Mankind could not be allowed to escape to the past. The idea of guardians was put forward; people who owned Glowing Lands to be admitted to the truth, but no one else. Absolute secrecy to be demanded. And careful rumours to be spread that the Lands were dangerous."

Flynn said softly, "Never build on Glowing Lands."

"Yes." Michael leaned back, savouring the warmth of the fire and of the wine. "It was decreed that the Secret was to be kept within the Keepers' families—handed on to the eldest son when he reached the age of twenty-one. And the two laws: secrecy at all costs, and the promise never to go through the Time Curtain." He looked at Flynn. "The penalty for breaking either law is death."

"But why? Why is it so strictly forbidden? Could we not learn from these other worlds? Find out about our beginnings?" Once again, Michael heard the echo of his own self, twenty years earlier.

"The reason is twofold, Flynn. The first Keepers did not want people escaping their responsibilities here. It would have been a harsh cold world then; even harsher to the Letheans who had lost everything.

"But there is also the undoubted fact that Time cannot be tampered with. The Time Curtain exists for a purpose. Think. If you or I or anyone went back into the past, think of what might happen. We would become involved; we would meddle, for mankind is an inquisitive species. Events that shaped our history might be altered. Supposing our ancestors were killed before they had founded our line . . . whole families might become unborn.

"And so the two laws were made. No journeys through the

Time Curtain. And the knowledge to be guarded by the Keepers. It was not thought that the knowledge would have to be guarded for ever, anyway.

"The Glowing Lands are dimming, Flynn. The tears in the Time Curtain are healing. It may be that we shall only have to guard the secret for another generation or two. You may have to admit your son, as I admitted you tonight, but he may not have to admit his in turn. The Glowing Lands will cool and they will become one of our myths. Even so, the Keepers are strict. They brook no flouting of the laws.

"Anyone betraying the Secret, or attempting to go through the Curtain is put to death."

JOANNA COULD NOT believe it when her father took her into the small front parlour of the farmhouse, which was only used for special occasions and which smelt rather cold and stuffy, and asked her to sit down and then told her of the match arranged for her.

Muldooney! Brian Muldooney the pig farmer! Muldooney who was fat and oily. Joanna knew him—not very well—but she knew him. He was gross. His skin was coarse and it was pink like his pigs. He had small eyes and a tight small mouth. People said the eyes were the windows of the soul, that you could read a person's character from his eyes, but Joanna thought that mouths were a much better indication. Muldooney's mouth was tight and mean; it folded itself into a prim puckered line and looked as if it had never uttered a generous word in its life.

Flynn's mouth . . . ah no, she must not think of Flynn.

"This is quite an honour," said her father, watching her in what Joanna suddenly thought was a rather unpleasant way. A glittery, sly, sort of way. "Brian Muldooney is a very fine fellow, Joanna. You are very lucky."

And Brian Muldooney's farmlands are very extensive, which is even luckier . . . It would not do to say it, but Joanna thought it anyway.

She said slowly, "So you are going to conjoin me to Muldooney . . ."

"A very minor matter," said her father, in what Joanna could not help thinking of as a rather too careful voice. "Over very quickly."

And when it is over, I shall be left with a fat, oily pig farmer whose farmhouse is miles from anywhere, and miles from Flynn. I shall be without Flynn! thought Joanna in sudden panic. I can't do it! I *can't*!

"But," said Joanna's mother, when appealed to, "you will have your own household. You will like that."

Joanna would not like it the smallest bit.

"Miles from anywhere," said Aunt Briony, with that curious habit she sometimes had of picking up one's thoughts. "Of course, it has to be . . ." She continued with her mending, not looking up. *"Pigs,"* she said, rather meaningfully.

"I don't—oh I see. The smell."

"The *least* of Joanna's problems will be the smell of the pigs," said Aunt Briony, biting off a length of cotton viciously, and Joanna thought: oh *please* don't let her mention Flynn. I shall be all right if only she doesn't mention Flynn.

"What about Flynn?" said Aunt Briony, and Joanna remembered that your wildest pleas were never really answered.

"What about him?" That was Joanna's father, frowning at Aunt Briony, and drumming his fingers on the table in the way he did when anything displeased or discomfited him.

"Joanna was intended for Flynn."

"Not really. Not seriously."

"It's a tradition," said Aunt Briony. "John Grady, you're a hard man."

"It's a matter of business."

"You're selling Joanna to a pig-man."

"Joanna go to bed. This is not for your ears."

It was the ritual that worried her most. She thought she could get used to living on Muldooney's farm, because you could make even the most dismal of places quite comfortable if you put some thought into it. She could probably get used to the pigs as well. Pigs were pleasant creatures. Placid. And piglets were rather sweet. Also, you did not need to concentrate solely on them. She could have chickens which would run about the farmyard and cluck and produce nice golden eggs. There was an old Lethe dish in which you beat up the eggs with butter and milk over a slow heat. Delicious. Yes, she would certainly want to keep chickens.

But along with the made-comfortable farmhouse and the nice homely chickens and the eggs would be Muldooney himself. And the ritual. And Flynn would be beyond her reach. He would only be a mile away to the east, but he would be as far from her as if he was on the other side of Ireland, or on the other side of the world, or on another world altogether.

Perhaps if she did not think about Flynn it would be all right. And to disobey her father was unthinkable (wasn't it?). I shan't think about Flynn, said Joanna firmly, but she did think about him. Aunt Briony was right, she *had* been intended for Flynn.

SHE WAS DRIVEN over to Muldooney's farm by her father in the cart, with Bess jogging over the ruts and the potholes. In some places they had made good smooth roads, but the road that led to Muldooney's farm had not been smoothed at all. Perhaps Muldooney had not thought it was necessary to make the road easier for his guests. Perhaps he did not have many guests. If this was the only road to his farm, Joanna was not surprised.

The outing was so that she and Muldooney could become better acquainted.

"And to see the house, of course," said her mother, and Joanna caught a look between her mother and father, and felt excluded.

"The house is a fine place," said her father, but as they approached it now, Joanna found that her heart was sinking. It was bleak. It was in the middle of nowhere, and it was bleak and gaunt and comfortless. It did not look as if it would be as comfortable as the Grady house, which had been built by Joanna's ancestors shortly after Devastation—Landgrabbers, said Flynn's father—and which was square and large and modern. It was definitely not as nice as the O'Connor house which was very old.

"Pre-Devastation," said Flynn, grinning. "Stone, you see. It stood up to the Apocalypse quite well. Or perhaps the Apocalypse never wanted it."

Joanna loved the O'Connor farmhouse with its low ceilings and beams, and the huge fireplace and bright copper pans in the kitchen, which Flynn's ancestors had buried in the garden when they knew the Apocalypse was coming.

"So that they could cook a meal when he had gone," said Flynn solemnly. "My great-great—oh, several times great-grandmother was frying bacon and eggs as he disappeared over the horizon in a cloud of smoke."

Muldooney's farmhouse did not look as if anyone had ever done anything so homely as fry bacon and eggs there. It certainly did not look as if anyone made a joke or laughed in it. It looked what it was; a place where pigs were reared and where drab plain meals were cooked and eaten. You could not imagine people enjoying a glass of poteen, or gathering round the fire to tell stories, like they did at the O'Connor house when neighbours called at harvest time; or even having huge family gatherings like Joanna's parents did, when the kitchen was filled with the scent of baking for days, and Joanna's mother could not be appealed to on any subject that did not concern the preparation of food.

Still, they were made welcome enough by Muldooney, who had dignified the occasion by donning his best moleskin breeches and by having scrubbed his large face until it shone. They were given a glass of wine—"Just this once," said John Grady, frowning slightly—and Joanna was taken to see the house by Muldooney himself.

"While your father takes a look at the yards," said Muldooney looking at Joanna in a way that made her feel uncomfortable. She looked to her father for guidance and saw a look of—understanding was it?—pass between the two men, as if a question had been asked and answered. And so there was nothing to be done but to go with Muldooney and be shown the parlour, and the office where he saw to the ordering of stock and the selling of his pigs, and the rather cold scullery. And the bedrooms.

The bedrooms were cold and rather sparsely furnished— Muldooney had no time for prettifying, but Joanna would alter all that, wouldn't she? He knew that ladies like to primp and fuss and prettify a room. Not that there was money to spare for unnecessary things, of course; she must not think him a wealthy man, for he was no such thing.

"This is our room," said Muldooney, his face suddenly close to hers, his small brown eyes hot. They were pig's eyes. Muldooney was a pig. Joanna would not be surprised to discover he had little pink trotters instead of feet. She would certainly not be surprised to find out that he grunted when he was asleep and snorted when he ate. Cold panic seized the pit of her stomach.

"We'll be here together," said Muldooney, his hands on her arms. "For the conjoining. Have they told you about that?"

Joanna was certainly not going to let him think she was ignorant. "Oh that. Oh, I know all about that."

"Do you now? Do you indeed?" He was standing very close and he was fidgeting in an embarrassing fashion, and his eyes were glittering. Horrible man. She could not possibly live here in this cold, comfortless house with a man who grunted and snorted and glittered at her. She definitely could not go through with the conjoining . . . whatever it turned out to be.

"Will we have a bit of a taste of it, then?" said Muldooney, and quite suddenly, his hands were on her body, fumbling at buttons and fastenings, thrusting inside her gown until they found her breasts.

Joanna backed away, her eyes huge, crossing her hands over her breasts protectively. "Don't—"

"Oh, 'tis always done, and no harm in it—come on to the bed my pretty dear—oh, you shan't escape me, never fear, my little dearie . . ."

It was dreadful. It was so dreadful that Joanna felt sick. He was pulling at her clothing and at his own; she did not dare look, it was quite unspeakably embarrassing.

"Let me go," said Joanna furiously, but she said it in a low voice, because it was unthinkable to scream and bring her father running up the stairs. "Let me *go*!"

Her struggles seemed to make him even more determined.

He had her by the arms now, and he was pinning her down to the bed. His fingers were thick, repulsive, they were biting into her flesh. As if I am one of his pigs, thought Joanna. Dare I scream? Would Father hear?

Muldooney said softly, "For one who knows all about conjoining, you're mighty reticent, my dearie. So you know what's expected, do you?" He was pressing his warm fat body close to hers and Joanna bit back a shudder. "By the gods, if John Grady's sold me damaged goods . . ." The small eyes bored into hers. "Was it the O'Connor boy? Did he put it to you, my pretty? Well now, you'll see what a real man's like . . . Wait, 'til I show you."

He was fumbling with his trouser fastenings, reaching inside and tugging at something. Joanna was horrified; she knew, of course, that men were different to women—"All to do with making babies," her mother had said—but she had not been prepared for anything quite like this.

She had certainly not been prepared for this ugly swollen stalk of flesh protruding from Muldooney's trousers, or for the leering of his sweaty, red face as he watched her.

"D'you see it then, my pretty dear? A grand sight, isn't it? You'll not find a better. I'll wager the O'Connor boy never had a one like that now."

"Let me go," said Joanna again, torn between a wish to burst into tears, and another to bring her nails raking down across the face so close to hers.

"A foretaste of what you'll be getting," said Muldooney. And then, slyly, horribly intimate, "Y'can touch it, my dearie. Give me your hand—he likes being touched by a pretty lady's hand."

Joanna snatched her hand back as if it had been burnt, and scrambled from the bed, pulling the torn bodice of her gown about her.

"Well now," said Muldooney softly, "well now, so the pretty little dear thinks herself too good for me, does she?" He moved across the bed, and Joanna thought wildly: he is ridiculous. He is *comical*. You could not be afraid of a man who lunged at you with his trousers wide open and that, that *thing* hanging and flopping. I am not afraid of him, said Joanna backing into a corner, looking about her for something to use as a weapon.

He grabbed her roughly, and half dragged, half threw her on to the bed. "So, the pretty dear would escape me, would she? Oh, that will never do, and me having paid your father what I did pay. An investment, my little one, that's what you are. Any man who knows me, will tell you Muldooney makes the most of his investments. Did the O'Connor boy put it to you, then? Did he do this, and this . . ." His hands were pulling aside her gown, reaching up between her legs, probing, stroking, fingering. Joanna thought: I believe I am going to be sick. If he does not stop, I shall be sick in his face.

Muldooney was panting and grunting now, a slick of sweat on his face, his breath rather sour as he blew it into her face.

"That's more like it, isn't it . . . oh my, you're a soft tender little piece, aren't you . . . oh my, I'm going to enjoy you—"

"Please—let me go . . ."

"In a minute, my dearie. I'm not done yet—Oh, Muldooney isn't one of your two-minute merchants, as you'll see—a proper man, Muldooney is. You just let me show you. You let me put him here where he wants to be . . ."

There was a sudden convulsive movement, and a snorting grunt, and something glutinous and warm spurted across Joanna's thighs. Muldooney sagged across her, still half on top.

Joanna lay very still: I am not bearing any of this. It is dreadful. It is the most dreadful thing that has ever happened to me. I think I shall be sick. I think I might faint. Would it be better to faint and not know what came next, or would it be worse? It would serve him right if I was sick all over him. What was it he did? It's all over my legs. It's disgusting. If he doesn't move in a minute, I really will be sick.

Muldooney stirred. He sat up and pulled his trousers together, not looking at Joanna. His face was blotchy now, the redness fading in patches. When he was dressed he stumbled from the room, still not looking at her.

IN THE DOWNSTAIRS room, John Grady and Brian Muldooney looked at one another. There was no need for words, of course, between men it was understood what had happened. Decent men did not refer to such things. But John Grady knew that Muldooney had just done to Joanna what John himself did to Joanna's mother from time to time. It was nothing to make a fuss over; men occasionally had the need to do it, rather in the way they needed to empty a full bladder, although not, of course, as often. Joanna's mother was always very good about it, and Joanna would learn to be the same. She would have to, for the price Muldooney had paid was a good one, and John had no intention of returning any of it.

The women, of course, never knew about this side; they were flattered to think themselves sought; they were pleased to believe they had been requested for conjoining. There was no need for them to know about the purely business side; women did not understand these things, John had always known that. The Letheans had allowed women to meddle in business, and look what had happened to the Letheans.

Still, there was a code of good manners to be followed, and John Grady said, "Everything satisfactory?"

No man ever admitted to another that an excess of excitement or a lack of self-control had brought matters to a precipitate conclusion. Muldooney had his pride, and he thought: admit to John Grady that I shot my load before I got within sight of target! Not likely! And the girl would soon learn obedience, she could be taught her duty. He would rather enjoy doing that. He would certainly enjoy dismissing the woman who had cooked and cleaned for him in desultory fashion these last ten years. Joanna could do all that now, and a sight cheaper as well! Muldooney was very pleased with his bargain.

He said, "Perfectly satisfactory."

"In that case, I'll be off," said John, because there was no sense in prolonging the stay. The deal was concluded; Joanna had been conjoined and he could go back to his own home and see to the apple harvest. There was a good crop this year, damsons as well. Joanna's mother would bottle the damsons; the apples would be stored under the roof where they would scent the house until next spring. He turned to go, and then bethought himself of something else.

"Since you're satisfied, Joanna may as well stay here. I'll send her things over." No sense in making a double journey.

"Yes. Oh yes, you leave the pretty dear here," said Muldooney, and a slow smile creased his face.

CHAPTER THREE

JOANNA WAS IN despair. She had managed to sponge away the sticky fluid with water from the ewer, and had scrubbed at her gown where it was stained. While replacing the ewer on the washstand beneath the window, she had seen her father drive away, clicking to Bess to pick up her feet, holding the cart's reins with his left hand as he always did when he was feeling jaunty.

He was leaving her. He was leaving her with a man who grunted like one of his own pigs, and who could not remember her name.

That was the part that hurt most. Throughout the dreadful intimacy, Muldooney had not once called her Joanna. He had said "my pretty dear," "my little dear," "my pretty one." Exactly as he would to a child or a plaything. Joanna, horror rising in her like sickness, thought: I am shut away with a man who will look on me as a plaything.

She had the dreadful thought that in this house, conjoined to Muldooney, the real Joanna would eventually disappear; she would shrivel up and die for lack of recognition; so quietly that no one would notice, and in her place would only be Muldooney's woman, nameless, rarely speaking, called upon to cook and clean and do with Muldooney the things they had done a short time ago. Every night, perhaps. In this room and on that bed. And he would have the right. He would own her. Joanna stared out through the windows to where her father was only a tiny moving speck on the cart track, and thought: I can't do it.

She could not. She could not stay here, shut away in this

34

cold house with a man who would never use her name. She would do anything rather than stay here. Even though there was nowhere to run, still she would run away.

The thought brought an overwhelming relief. I have decided that I cannot bear it. I have decided not to bear it. She would not ever again be called on to face Muldooney's proddings and probings. She would not have to stay here in the comfortless bleak farmhouse.

Where would she go? Home? No, for her father would certainly make her return and her mother would support him. Through Joanna's mind there flickered the thought of Aunt Briony. An ally? Yes, Aunt Briony might just possibly be an ally. Only I must not involve her unless I have to, thought Joanna. Even so, the thought of Aunt Briony brought a faint far-off comfort. Aunt Briony understood. She knew that Joanna was meant for Flynn.

Flynn.

A smile curved Joanna's lips. She reached for her cloak and unlatched the bedroom door.

THE TWILIGHT WAS thickening as she slipped from the house, a silent shadow, unheard, unnoticed. The dusk was lilac-scented; Flynn's father called it the Purple Time, this half-light, this odd mysterious dying of the day and emerging of the night. "A time when magic may be abroad," he had said, and smiled, and Joanna had never been quite sure whether he was serious.

She slipped across the fields of Muldooney's lands and on to the track that would lead to Flynn's house.

She had hardly ever been out at night before, and she had certainly never been out at night by herself. The men went out; they went to Peg Flanagan's to drink poteen, or they went farther afield into Cork, but the women were expected to stay at home.

"Men's business," her mother had said, and Joanna had known a moment of rebellion. Had the Lethe women sat meekly at home while their men went off into the cities? Not for a moment! thought Joanna.

Even so, it was a bit frightening to be out like this by herself. She thought she would not give in to the feeling of nervousness, because there was really nothing to be nervous

about. If she said it several times, very firmly, she would begin
to believe it.

Tara's Hill loomed to her left, a dark secretive mound, sprin-
kled here and there with trees and thickets which had escaped
the Apocalypse's blast. When Joanna had been very small she
had thought Tara's Hill was an enchanted place, a place where
you might see anything in the world. But . . .

"Fairy story nonsense," her father said indulgently. "Not for
little girls to waste their time on. You will do better to help
your mother with the butter making."

But Joanna had never quite lost the feeling that Tara's Hill
was a magical place, that there were other worlds to be discovered there, and even now, fleeing from Muldooney—oh would
he have found her gone yet?—even running helter-skelter
through the dusk, even like this, she could spare a glance for
the Hill and its lure. Easy to imagine other worlds locked inside it; easier still to imagine those magical half-beast, half-
human creatures Flynn had talked about. Had they existed,
those beautiful cruel beings, or was it only a story?

The countryside looked quite different at night. It felt different and it sounded different. Once an owl—or was it?—flew
from a tree and hooted softly overhead. Once something
moved in the bushes a little ahead of her, and went scurrying
through the undergrowth in search of its supper or its mate.
Joanna thought about the Hill coming alive, waking, and the
night creatures coming out. The animals and the forest creatures had nearly all disappeared during the Great Devastation,
but not quite all. Sometimes you saw them, if you were very
quiet and looked very hard. Badgers and moles who would
have been underground when the Apocalypse walked. Owls
and bats and creatures of the night, and other creatures whose
names had been lost, but who had somehow secreted themselves away from the Apocalypse's fury.

The countryside was beautiful. People said, "Oh, but it
would have been breathtaking before Devastation." But Joanna
liked it now. There were still portions of the forest that had
once sprawled half up Tara's Hill, and within it huge patches
of undergrowth. Not everything had died. Things had survived.
Joanna would survive. Even out here, even in the dusk, with
Muldooney and probably her father raising the alarm for her?
Yes, even then. And I am going to Flynn, thought Joanna, and

a tremendous delight began to well up inside her. It suddenly seemed completely right that she should be going through the lilac-scented dusk to Flynn. Ahead of her she could see the lights of the O'Connor farmhouse, oblongs of warm yellow colour. Then I am nearly home, thought Joanna, and smiled at her choice of word. But yes of course it was home. Flynn was there and it was home.

It came as no surprise, as she rounded the curve in the path, to see Flynn coming towards her, his face pale in the dim light, his hair windswept, and his eyes glowing. How often had she come running like this, down the path with the briar thicket and the wild hedge rose in summer; past the great lilac bushes, and up to the wicket gate, only to see Flynn coming to meet her. She thought: he knows. Not *what* has happened, only that *something* has. He knows.

I always will know, my love . . .

Joanna quickened her pace, until she was flying over the rough ground, her hair streaming behind her, her mind alight and alive with delight. Oh how, sharing this with Flynn, this oneness, this *awareness*, how could I possibly have stayed with Muldooney?

The wind stirred the lilac and the scent came round her like an embrace.

Flynn held out his arms and Joanna ran straight into them.

FLYNN HAD NO defence against Joanna's distress. The longings so firmly banked down and sternly quenched for so many years—"For," he had thought, "they will never let me have her, and I would not cause her pain."—rose up now to betray him, so that he pulled her against him, and began kissing her hungrily. An immense delight closed over him, of *course* this is how it is meant to be! *This* is what is missing with the girls down in the village, satisfactory for a half hour's release, for a night's drinking and bedding, forgotten as soon as they are out of sight. *This* is what the Letheans knew about, and what the survivors of Devastation tried to stamp out. And he cupped Joanna's face between his hands and kissed her searchingly, but with such love and with such infinite longing that the night blurred about him.

In Joanna's mind there was no kinship between what had happened with Muldooney a few hours earlier, and what was happening now with Flynn. The cold, comfortless bedroom and Muldooney's soft fat body had no place in this safe secret warmth where Flynn's arms held her, and where the dusk was scented with its own magic—the Purple Hour! Oh yes, *now* I believe!—and where Flynn's lips were soft and demanding and exciting, and where his body was hard and strong and gentle.

When he drew away a little, she thought, oh no! He cannot stop now! I shall not bear it! But then Flynn was scooping her up in his arms, and after all they were still together, and the bond that had proved itself out here was not breaking. Then Flynn carried her into the farmhouse. The scents and the familiar feeling of the house closed about Joanna; old oak and polish and stored apples. The scents of welcoming. Of safety. Flynn murmured something; Joanna thought it was to do with his father being out in the barns with a sick animal, but she barely heard, because the blood was singing in her veins, and the world was slowing down to a soft slow heartbeat, and there was no one in the world but herself and Flynn, and there was nothing in the world to fear, and nothing to bother about, except this soft slow melting, this merging of one person with another.

The windows of Flynn's bedroom were open to the night air, and the lilac was there again, and the soft liquid notes of some night bird in the tree outside . . .

The nightingale or the lark. . . ? No, no, my love, it is yet the nightingale, and we have the entire night before us . . .

She heard Flynn laugh softly, and then the sheets were brushing her skin, cool, scented linen on warm living skin; Flynn's body was against hers, warm and insistent, and the nightingale was singing somewhere inside her head now . . .

There was a moment of swift, secret pain, and then there was a whirlpool of delight, and the most complete sense of sharing, and Joanna took Flynn's face in her cupped hands, and kissed him, because like this, like this, he was strong and gentle and infinitely precious, and he was somehow dreadfully vulnerable as well, and she could bear him being strong and gentle, but somehow she could not bear his vulnerability . . .

And then the whirlpool took them on, upwards and inwards, and they clung to each other; Joanna thought she was crying but she could not be sure, and Flynn moved convulsively and cried out. Just as Joanna felt the world splinter into a cascade of purest delight that descended on them in a soft blanket.

JOANNA AWOKE IN the yellow and white bedroom and lay watching the oblong of dark grey sky, star-spattered still, begin to lighten. Odd how the new light gave you courage. Hadn't there been a race, long ago, certainly before people began to record history, who had worshipped the sun, and who had believed that men drew strength from the dawn? It was a belief that Joanna found easy to understand. There you were, in the dark, somehow confused and unsure, and *frightened*, and then you saw the sky begin to lighten and become streaked with grey and then with pink, and you drew strength. There was something immeasurably comforting about its inevitability. After the dark the light. Had the people who had lived through Devastation found that? Or had the light disappeared altogether for a time? Endless darkness . . . I won't think about it, said Joanna.

Beside her, Flynn still slept, easily and noiselessly, his black hair falling across his forehead, a faint sheen on his eyelids. Tenderness welled up in Joanna, so strong that for a moment it hurt, and she wanted to reach out and pull him to her, and she wanted to shut out the world for ever.

It could not be done, of course. The world was waiting to be faced; her father and Muldooney were waiting to be faced. And I must do it, thought Joanna, drawing confidence from the dawnlight. It is something I must certainly do.

She thought she could do it now. Now; warm and safe and drowsy from Flynn's love-making, her mind and her body still singing with delight—"I shall never want to leave," she thought, and smiled, because that was what she had said to Flynn, somewhere between dusk and dawn:

I shall never want to leave . . .

And I shall never let you go, my love.

She need never go. She could stay here with Flynn in the comfortable whitewashed farmhouse, and nothing else could be contemplated.

I shall never let you go . . . And I shall never want to go . . .

There had been no need to say any of it because Flynn had known. *He always will know* said a voice in her head, and Joanna smiled.

Muldooney and her father would certainly come after her. Probably they would come quite soon, because it was pretty certain that Muldooney had already raised the alarm. They would come here first. To the place where she had always fled as a child. Would they? Yes, she thought they would. She turned her head on the pillow again and regarded the sleeping Flynn. Not to be thought of that she should bring Flynn into danger. Not to be contemplated that through her Flynn—and his father—should suffer. Flynn could outface anyone, of course, and he could certainly outface her father and Muldooney. "With one hand tied behind my back, acushla," he would have said. But it was not just those two that Joanna was worried about.

Supposing her father invoked his powers as an Elder of Tugaim? Supposing—just supposing—that he rallied the men of the village to search for her? Joanna thought that this was very likely indeed. John Grady was not especially popular—"Too prosperous!" he would have said with one of his complacent smiles—but he had his supporters. You might call them flatterers—Joanna did call them flatterers—but put them all together and rouse them up a bit and they would form quite a considerable bunch. And daughters, such useful pawns, were valuable.

"Grady's girl?" they'd say. "By God, has Grady's girl disappeared? Won't we go out at once to search for her?" And off they'd go.

And worse.

"Conjoined?" they'd say. "Isn't that a terrible way to behave? Every man out and start the search!"

Joanna could visualise it all very clearly. She could certainly visualise that the first place any of them would think of to search would be the O'Connor household.

"Michael O'Connor's farm," they'd cry. "For isn't the Grady girl forever with Flynn O'Connor, and the pair of them as close as sheep in a fold! If she's anywhere, she'll be there!" And out they'd come, a loud shouting mob, not violent, because nobody in Tugaim—well anywhere really—was violent these days. Violence was something that the survivors of Devastation had stamped out, and there would be no thought of it in the minds of the mob that John Grady would summon.

The violence would be in John himself.

And Flynn might be hurt.

Joanna lifted herself cautiously on one elbow and looked at Flynn again. Unbearable to think of Flynn in the hands of an angry crowd of men, led by her father, who was certainly capable of violence, who had a side of him that nobody but Joanna had ever guessed at.

What I must do, thought Joanna, is hide away, just for a day or two, just until everything has died down. Just so that when they come here, as they surely will, they will not find me. It would not be difficult. She could manage it all quite easily. Food and water. Her warm cloak. Yes, she could do it.

As to where she should go—a smile curved her lips again. Where in all of Tugaim was the one place where no one, and least of all John Grady, and Brian Muldooney, would venture?

"Never build on Glowing Lands" said the old warning. And alongside the warning, ran a fear, a superstitious, deeply buried, race-memory dread of the Lands.

But I shall be perfectly safe, thought Joanna, and went quietly down the stairs into the silent scullery.

She thought that neither Flynn nor his father would mind her taking food—only enough for a couple of days—a fresh loaf and a rich round cheese. There were some slices of cold meat—ham, was it? Yes. Very sustaining. There were dishes of apples and early pears from the O'Connor orchards. She would take those as well. And one of the large leather water sacks. She could fill it from the pump if she was very quiet. Or perhaps milk would be easier—there were two large covered jugs of milk sitting on the cold marble slab. She tipped one up carefully and heard it run into the leather sack.

Last of all was a note for Flynn. "Only until the fuss and flurry has died down . . . they will search here first, and I could not bear to bring such violence into your house . . ." Oh yes. "This way is safer," wrote Joanna, "and they will not think to look for me where I am going . . ." Would Flynn guess where that was? Joanna smiled and slid the note under the nearer of the milk jugs where it could not possibly be missed, and then she was ready.

THE COUNTRYSIDE WAS grey and silver in the dawnlight; it was scented in a way she had never noticed before. From here you could see nearly all of Tugaim spread out below you like one of the old tapestries she had read about. There was Flynn's farmhouse, and over to the west was her father's. No lights burned. Then I am still safe.

Just ahead was the belt of Glowing Land. Then she was still on O'Connor land, the thought was comforting. The important thing now was to summon up her courage to actually go into the centre of the Lands. Did she dare? In the farmhouse kitchen with the new sunlight filtering in it had seemed quite an easy thing to do. It had seemed rather trivial to worry about the Lands. Out here, in the thin raw dawn, it was not trivial at all. Joanna hesitated, watching the incandescent light that rose into the sky. The Lands were beautiful, but they were frightening as well. You felt a great power emanating from them. People said they would glow like that for a thousand years, but other people, older people, said they were dimming, and that in another few generations they would be like everywhere else.

Did she dare? Joanna stood watching the light, uncertain, trying to summon up the courage. "Never build on Glowing Lands" said the old warning. Most people would not even walk on them.

But I expect people do cross them, Joanna thought now. I expect they do. It was not in human nature not to go where you were forbidden. It was certainly not in human nature to leave places unexplored. The Letheans had been great explorers, they had known every corner of the world . . . And the Letheans had died, said a small warning voice in her head.

I don't care, said Joanna defiantly. This is the safest place for me to be, and I don't think anything very terrible is going to happen to me. I don't think anything is going to happen to me at all, really. I shall just be here, and I shan't look at anything. I shall just be quietly hiding, I might even fall asleep. There had been little sleep to be had during the night . . . Oh Flynn, Flynn, please don't come after me. Not yet.

The edges of the Glowing Lands were not so very different from anywhere else to begin with. Joanna's confidence rose. It was all a pretence, a nothing. Perhaps there had once been something here; perhaps after Devastation there had been something very terrible indeed. Perhaps—this was rather a dreadful thought, but—perhaps the Apocalypse had not vanished from the world, but had stayed behind, lurking and skulking in a patch of Glowing Land. Joanna did not really believe this, and she certainly did not believe it now, standing here summoning up courage to step on to the Lands. But it would account for all the stories, and it would certainly account for all the old warnings. But now, the Lands would be like everywhere else. Of course they are, thought Joanna, taking the first step out.

And with the first few steps her confidence came back. Nothing happened. There was no growling sound, no flashing light. Fairy-tale nonsense, said Joanna, remembering her father's words.

Even so, it was curious that the nearer she got to the centre of the light, the stranger she began to feel. She thought she could hear sounds and then she thought there was a soft rich scent. But she could not be sure of any of it.

The sound was like nothing she had ever heard in the whole of her life. Sweet and soft and rather cold. The louder it got, the nearer she got to it, the colder it became. Something from the bottom of the ocean, or from the other side of the sky. Something that might crawl out from beneath the caves and tap at your windows in the night. Icicle-fingers on glass. Joanna was dreadfully afraid, but she could not resist . . .

A beckoning. *Come to us Joanna . . . come through the Time Curtain . . . we are fishers of souls, Joanna, and we will take you to worlds you did not dream existed . . .*

Joanna stood stock-still at the centre of the light, and thought she was surely going mad.

There was a ripple of amusement. *Not mad, not mad, let her not be mad, sweet heaven keep her sane . . .* A thousand voices pressed in on her. *We can quote your poets, Joanna. They died before your world began, but still we can quote them . . . Come into the music, Joanna . . . we are fishers of souls and we will gather up your soul for our master . . .*

The most extraordinary part about the whole thing was how safe she felt. How secure and warm. As if, after a long journey, a wearisome journey of a thousand years, she was coming home. This is where I belong. In here, in the music, in the steady glow of the Light, in the rich warm scent. I know this place.

Of course you know it, Joanna . . . it is the end of all journeying and the beginning of delight . . . you belong here, as you always belonged . . . COME NEARER, JOANNA . . .

Joanna took a few hesitant steps forward. She thought: of course, none of this is happening. I have fallen asleep—yes, that is it. I have fallen asleep on Tara's Hill, and I am dreaming all of this ... Quite soon I shall awake ...

Awake and find you here upon the cold hillside ...

There was a deeper light ahead of her, and Joanna had the sense of thin green and blue arms reaching out to draw her towards them. She thought: of course, I am not believing any of this; even so, it is all very curious. But I am not really experiencing any of it.

Oh yes you are, Human Child, oh yes you are ...

Beyond the light was a mist, and beyond that the shapes of trees and mountains. The blue and green, misty island ... I am coming home, thought Joanna, and something triumphant rose up inside her. There are other worlds, and I am about to see one. There are creatures of mist and magic and wild woodland blood, and I am about to meet them.

And if a man should dream and go to Paradise, and pluck there a rose ... and if, on waking, he should find himself still possessed of that rose—what then? Come into the light, Human Child, and we will show you wonders that your poor bleak world never dreamed existed ...

Pluck the rose?

And wake finding you are still possessed of it ... And what then, Human Child ...

I suppose, thought Joanna, that it will be all right. After all, I can always come back.

FLYNN STOOD IN the farmhouse kitchen and broke eggs on to the stove for breakfast, began to slice bread. His mind and his heart were warm, still upstairs in bed with Joanna, and he was intensely happy. He had half woken when she slipped from his bed, and then had drifted back into sleep, lulled by the warmth of the bed and the lingering scent of her that still was with him. He had vaguely thought that she must have gone out for a breath of early morning air. He had certainly not thought any more than that.

For I will never let you go, my love ...

He smiled as he set the table and put out the earthenware mugs for the milk they would drink with breakfast. The Letheans had drunk steaming beverages; beans that you ground up and steeped in boiling water and which had a scent so strong and so sweet that it had embodied the essences of the hot far-off lands where they grew. And there had been some kind of plant as well, dried and seasoned in some way, that was served from a spouted utensil and taken with milk or lemon. Flynn thought he would have enjoyed both, but the secrets were lost like so much else. They drank milk at breakfast and at the midday meal. In the evenings there was often poteen or homemade wine from the apples and plums in the orchard; if the weather was particularly cold they heated the wine and sweetened it with honey. Once or twice, he had tasted a strong, distilled drink called brandy—it had been like drinking liquid fire—but there was only a very small supply of it left in the world, and it was believed that it took a very long time to mature and that even then it was enormously expensive to produce.

He stood for a moment longer, enjoying the sunshine that was pouring in, making the dish of honey transparent and warming the old pearwood chest that stood by the window and always soaked up the sun, so that by the afternoon you could smell the fragrant wood and the beeswax that generations of Flynn's ancestors had used to polish it.

Probably Joanna would appear at any moment. Flynn smiled at the thought. They would eat breakfast together, just the two of them, for his father would still be outside somewhere, and in any case, he would understand at once what had happened and he would be tactful. Flynn stood in the warm sunlit kitchen and all the years ahead when he and Joanna would eat breakfast here stretched out before him, and all the mornings when they would smile at one another over this table rose up to delight him. They would each have their own chair, and there would be warm honey, just as there was today, and fresh bread and butter from the churn, and they would discuss the day's plans, happy and peaceful and at home. A feeling of deep contentment settled over him as he opened the pantry door to fetch the milk from the settle.

As Flynn read Joanna's note, he experienced a sudden cold hollowness, as if something inside him had fallen down a huge bottomless hole.

Nothing had changed and everything had changed.

An image of Joanna came strongly into his mind, so that he

saw her with swift startling clarity. Joanna, with her cloudy dark hair and her wide-apart eyes and her little pointed face that a man would ache to take between his hands and kiss until solemnity dissolved.

I shall never want to leave you . . .

And I shall never let you go, my love . . .

And with the coming of the day she had gone, running into hiding to protect him.

Flynn knew at once where she had gone. He did not know how he knew it, but he did know. Some kind of link between them, was it? Better to say nothing of it in any case. Mutants were looked at askance; they were outlawed and sent to live in the grim grey building on the edge of Tugaim. They were made comfortable enough, but they were not allowed to mingle with people who were normal. They were certainly not allowed to conjoin or even, Flynn believed, to form ordinary friendships. They were looked on as freaks, and it was considered very shameful indeed to have a Mutant born into your family. How would people view it if it was known that an O'Connor was so far from being ordinary that he knew about events before they happened, or that he could pick up the feelings and the fears of people he was close to? Flynn thought he was very close to Joanna now, but he thought that such a power—could you call it a power?—would be looked at strangely, and so he had always kept silent about it. Had his father guessed? Yes, probably. Quite often, Flynn had found Michael looking at him in a strange intent way; quite often, Michael himself had known what Flynn was thinking, or what he was going to say before he said it. Some kind of sharing gift? Best to say nothing anyway.

After what had been between him and Joanna last night he thought he could feel her thoughts and her emotions very clearly indeed. And oh my love, my love, you are in some terrible danger, and I must somehow save you.

For a few minutes he pretended that it was only a physical danger, even though it sent his mind into agony to think of Joanna lying injured somehow, crying from the pain of a splintered bone, unable to crawl for help. It was perfectly possible, of course.

But it was not like that. Flynn did not know how he knew—

only that you could not be hurt, my darling girl, and I not suffer with you—but he did know it.

Joanna had gone to the Glowing Lands so that she would be safe from her father and Brian Muldooney. She would be at the centre of the light now, Flynn knew this quite definitely, and unless they were very quick she would have gone, or been taken, through the Time Curtain.

And the Lands are dimming, and the Curtain is re-sealing itself, and once beyond Time it is not always possible to return . . .

That was the agony now, and Flynn flinched.

But if Joanna had truly gone through the Time Curtain, then there was only one thing to be done.

He would have to go in after her.

The idea of following Joanna, of doing the absolutely forbidden thing, the thing that his ancestors had warned against for several generations, did not strike into him the terror it ought to have done. There was a tremendous excitement: a feeling of awe, a feeling of *at last I shall see and at last I shall know!*

The Glowing Lands were quiet when he reached them; they were quiescent and bland, and they were not in the least sinister or threatening. But Flynn knew them; he knew that they were neither quiescent nor bland. They could change in a breathspace, they could become strong and awesome and they could beckon. Had they beckoned to Joanna? Had she in her headlong flight from Muldooney stumbled into their centre, and had she heard that other-world music, cold and distant, and been tempted, or taken, through the Time Curtain?

Flynn stood irresolute on the boundaries, watching the soft light, thinking that the stories were true at least, the Lands were dimming, they were dying. Panic swept over him. Supposing he went in and could not get back. It was his old nightmare; the thought of being trapped in a far-off, long-forgotten land, unable to return to everything that was familiar and safe.

But then supposing he could not get through anyway? Suppose, just suppose, that the gap was closing, that it had closed already, that Joanna had somehow slipped through the final chink?

I won't think about it, said Flynn. But he did think about it, he sat down on the ground and stared at the Lands, and thought about Joanna carried far beyond his reach, in some merciless half-human world. I must get her out, he thought. It can be done, surely. Others have gone through the Curtain. There is nothing whatsoever to be afraid of. My father said others have done it, and that is why we know so much about the deep past. Despite himself, he felt his senses stir at the thought of seeing that ancient lost Ireland, the world he had so often heard about and dreamed about.

At last he moved forward, feeling the ground warm beneath him. He thought there was a soft thrumming in the air, and then he was not so sure. He certainly thought there was an echo of the music he had heard on the night he met the Keepers, but he was not certain about that either. It was like something heard from a long way off; an echo down a long dark tunnel, the briefest of glimpses of dark forests and mist-shrouded plains; the suspicion of creatures with long flowing hair and slanting eyes and beautiful cruel mouths.

He thought, I am missing something, I am here at the wrong moment, or else it is the right moment but the wrong place. Or I am saying the right words, all but one, or perhaps adding one that is not needed.

Oh open up to me, let me through for if I lose Joanna I have lost everything!

There was a moment of silence so complete that for a second he thought he had succeeded. The air seemed to waver, and he thought he saw a huge silver blue sheet that stretched up and up, as far as he could see, and down into the core of the earth, and away on each side to all the horizons. The Time Curtain! He took a deep breath and waited. For an instant, the dark misty forest came a little more sharply into focus, and then it blurred and seemed to slip back. Flynn had the sensation of something infinitely precious and infinitely beautiful slipping through his grasp, and he could have wept. There were dreams in the forest, and there were moving figures and red eyes gleaming, and prowling creatures that sometimes went on all fours and sometimes walked upright like men.

And then there was nothing. He was alone, sitting on the damp grass, a little breathless, a little dazed, and the Glowing Lands were as they had always been.

Joanna was as far from him as ever.

* * *

JOANNA HAD NOT been aware of passing through the silver blue light, but she had seen, at the edge of her vision, an immense flare of something intangible as the Time Curtain parted and she was pulled through.

For a moment, she stood, unable to think or see, blinded by the flare, dazzled by the sight that met her eyes.

The blue and green, misty island ... the Dark Forests of Flynn's tales, and the extravagant vegetation of a world not yet scorched into arid barrenness by the Apocalypse's anger. I have gone back, thought Joanna in awe. Somehow I have gone back to the deep past. I am not believing any of this, but still it is happening.

The music was still with her, but distantly, a little way off. As if—absurd thought that it was—but as if someone was playing a song and beckoning her to follow. *Over the hills and far away* ... yes, *and over hill, over dale, through bush, through briar* ... *through flood and fire* ... *there is a bank whereon the wild thyme blows* ... *there dwells the Master* ... *come farther in, Human Child* ...

Joanna thought: is this the world of all the stories? Has someone—something?—taken me back? Or will I awake and find me here upon the cold hillside ... *And if he should awake and find himself still possessed of the rose* ... Where had those words come from?

From out of the past, Human Child, and from out of the future for past and future are all one to those who come through the Time Curtain ...

Joanna turned in the direction of the sound, but there was nothing. I am alone in an alien world, I am alone in the past, and I have escaped from Muldooney more completely than I hoped was possible.

She was very much afraid, but she was a child of the New World, of the devastated world brought to near ruin by mankind's folly and greed, and she had had to work and struggle. In her veins ran the blood of the men and women who had survived a disaster greater than had ever been envisaged by anyone at any time: she was a survivor.

I am afraid, thought Joanna, but at least I can pretend not to be. Pretend and the pretence will become reality ... Yes, that was a good maxim.

The music was still reaching out to her, and through the

trees she began to make out shadowy figures. Flowing creatures of green and blue and silver, never quite still, never quite staying in one place, constantly changing and flowing with the music. Were they the music makers?

Yes we are, Human Child, we make the music of the world, we scoop up the rivers and the forests and the skies and turn them into music ... And you must come with us, you must follow us, for there is no resisting the music ... there is no fighting the music ...

Long fingers, twined about with slender birch twigs beckoned to her, and here and there she caught the curve of a cheek, the fall of a curtain of hair. Creatures never fully seen. Beautiful but with something strange about them. Were these the half-human beings of the old stories?

We are not human at all, Joanna, we are the sidh, *and in our veins runs the icy blood of the seas and of the worlds beyond the skies ... But our music is the music that has lured Men to their fates ever since Time started, and perhaps before that ... We are the sirens who sit on the rocks and we are the mermaids who draw sailors down to the worlds beneath the seas ... We sat at the side of the Thracian poet Orpheus and gave him the power to call up the trees and the waters, and to play his magical lyre that has lived on in men's memories ... And we sat on the shoulder of the rat-catcher of Hamelin when he drew the rats from the City ... Temptation we are and Desire ... Sin we are and Lust ... But we are beautiful, Human Child, and we serve our master, and there is no resisting us ...*

They were drawing her through the forest now, but so gently, so subtly, that she was barely aware of it. And yet, there were pine needles beneath her feet, thick as any carpet, and there were sounds overhead that would be birds, but no birds that she had ever heard. Beautiful, thought Joanna, afraid and excited and enchanted as she was.

Yes, our land is beautiful, Human Child ...

The *sidh* were still with her, flowing about her, pulling at her with their slender arms, and binding her with their soft flowing hair. Once or twice she caught again the glimpse of translucent skin, of slender arched feet, but the *sidh* kept to the edges of her vision, so that she never quite saw them.

The forest was quite unlike anything she had ever seen. There *were* blues and purples and there *were* gentle mists. To one accustomed to vast barren stretches of fields and burnt-out rock faces, it was beyond everything.

She moved on, half mesmerised by the music, fascinated by everything she saw. There were rustlings all about them, so that Joanna looked about her, hoping to see the creatures that had disappeared before her world began. Badgers and squirrels, and otters and beavers. Had they really existed? Would she see them now? Oh I do hope so, thought Joanna.

The trees were thinning now, and ahead of them was a great rearing building, darkly outlined against the sky, its turrets and towers clearly limned. Was this one of the Letheans' huge marvellous cities? Had she after all only gone back to their time, or had she truly in some incomprehensible way gone back to Flynn's magical ancient Ireland?

There were lights in the building—might it be some kind of fortress?—and Joanna was reminded of the tales of light-houses; huge towering constructions with lights glowing from the topmost windows to guide sailors through dangerous coast-lines. Joanna thought that the lights from the fortress were guiding her now.

The fortress was dark and forbidding. From the edges of the forest, Joanna could see that it had a massive, iron-studded door, and that the windows were narrow slits. As she came out of the forest, she saw that it stood on the other side of some kind of ravine, so that you had to walk along a little bridge to get to it. Someone lives there who does not want the world to get in, she thought. Or who wants to keep the world out . . . There is something in there that someone wants to keep very well hidden, she thought, and knew a sudden chill. But, I am not frightened, she thought, and clung to that thought, because it was a good thought to have when you were standing on the edge of a dark forest with a huge grim fortress directly ahead of you.

The mist was thicker here, so that the fortress swam in and out of her sight. Then that is settled, thought Joanna, relieved. I shall not need to go up to it, because I shall not be able to find it. The mist will hide it. But should she go back? Could she go back? Grope her way back through the blue and green lights, into the unfriendly world of Tugaim, to Muldooney waiting with his hot pig eyes and his thick fingers that prodded? What had those mist creatures said? A Time Curtain?

How remarkable, thought Joanna. Perhaps I should at least see a bit more before I go back.

And although Flynn's books had certainly included a fairy tale or two, salvaged from the world of the Letheans, Joanna had never really given them much credence. She thought she would not do so now. She thought it was quite important not to remember that strange sinister world, brimming with giantish castles approached by means of a narrow bridge, where doors swung open at a touch, and a deep soft voice from the darkness said, "Come inside, my dear." It was very important indeed not to remember ogres who could smell the blood of humans at ten leagues, or of their cooks who made man-pies, or of witches who put children in cages and fattened them.

It was certainly sensible not to recall silly foolish girls who wore brave red cloaks and who went skipping through forests, heedless of danger, and who followed creatures such as wolves in the most ridiculously trustful way imaginable. In any case, there were no wolves left anywhere in the world.

THERE WERE NO wolves left anywhere in the world, but there were wolves directly ahead of her. Lean grey creatures, who guarded the entrance to the narrow bridge, and who were watching her unblinkingly. The *sidh* drew back and there was a hiss of anger, but the wolves stood stock-still, only their eyes showing they were alive. Then the leader licked his lips, and Joanna caught the gleam of white pointed teeth.

All the better to eat you with, my dear . . .

She hesitated, uncertain of what to do next, for strange as the *sidh* were, there was at least a sense of safety about them. They might be luring her to all kinds of dreadful fates, but Joanna, child of the Brave New World, could not imagine anything worse than being made to lie in a bed with Muldooney. Or could she? Was there not, after all, some remnant of race memory, some thin vein of atavism remaining in the corners of her consciousness, so that fear awoke at the sight of the thin grey creatures, and she wanted to turn and run?

The *sidh* had vanished, dissolving into the forest, blue and green streaks melting into the trees and the rocks. The music had gone as well, so that Joanna felt suddenly cold and very much alone. Should she turn and go back? Her mind shuddered away from the thought. Back into the forest where there might be badgers and squirrels, but where there would almost certainly be other things as well? The thread of atavism strengthened; Joanna did not know that the forest held dangers, but she sensed that it did.

Onwards then? Up to the iron-studded door, to request admittance? Cross the narrow bridge in the company of the lean watchful animals? Surely the person who lived there could not refuse her hospitality for the night? thought Joanna, accustomed to the ways of her own world, where men might perhaps be a bit unimaginative, but where there had existed, ever since Devastation, a strong comradeship, and an obligation to help one another. It did not occur to Joanna that the owner of this awe-inspiring place might refuse to give her shelter.

She moved forward and the wolves moved with her, as if, she thought afterwards, they were forming some kind of guard. She could feel the warmth of their bodies, and she thought they were curious and wary of her, but she still had to remind herself that she was not frightened.

The bridge was longer than she had imagined, and it was very much narrower. Joanna stopped once and peered down into the ravine. It was a terribly long way down. It was so long that you could not see the bottom. Some kind of moss grew up the steep sides of the ravine, and here and there, there was movement, as if tiny unseen creatures scuttled in and out of the crevices. Joanna shuddered and looked up.

The castle was very much bigger than it had seemed from the comforting depths of the forest. It reared up out of the rock, a massive, towering edifice of grey and black. Once, she hesitated and almost turned to run, because it seemed as if the turrets were toppling over on to her. Once, the flickering light from the wall sconces, burning on each side of the great door, flared wildly into life so that you imagined a huge breath had blown on them. Once, she had the feeling that the slitted windows were eyes, watching unblinking, and that nameless things moved behind them. Joanna took a deep breath; she reminded herself that she had never seen anything like the castle before (or had she seen it in her dreams?) and that anything unfamiliar was always a bit frightening. Not that she was frightened. Well, not very much.

There was a ring handle on the great door. Well, she thought, I cannot go back. I cannot go back into the forest, not now it is night. I may as well go forward. She reached out and grasped the handle.

The handle turned and the door swung open quickly and easily. As if, thought Joanna, it had been waiting for her.

She was standing at the top of a flight of steps, looking down on to a huge stone-flagged floor, lit by firelight and by the glow of the torches in the wall brackets high up. There was a scent of woodsmoke and warmth, and Joanna thought it was like going down into a warm dark cave.

The fire burned at the centre of the hall, and glancing up, Joanna saw, far above her, some kind of chimney hole in the dim vaults of the roof. There were fur rugs on the floor, and there was a long table set with dishes, as if for supper. She remembered that she was hungry.

At the far end was a dais, with a massive carved chair on it, and more of the thick skin rugs. He was sitting quietly in the chair, watching her, and the wolves were lying at his feet, their eyes calm, their fur sleek. Joanna paused, unsure of what to do next, certainly unsure of what to say.

"Come inside, Human Child."

To a child of the age called Lethean, the words would have struck instant terror; but Joanna, child of the New World, heard nothing threatening. She only thought: well, at least I have not been turned away, and stepped farther in.

The young man on the dais was like no one she had ever seen before. He sat, quite calmly, watching her approach, and after a moment, he smiled. Joanna caught her breath, for surely no one had ever conveyed so much by a smile. Strength and arrogance and ruthlessness and a queer inverted beauty. I am very much afraid, she thought, but I am also very much excited.

The man got up and moved from the dais to where she stood, and she saw that he was not quite as tall as she had guessed. He was dark and very slim, but despite the slimness, there was no suggestion of weakness. There was a whipcord strength about him that suggested it would be dangerous to make an enemy of him. Joanna thought: oh my! wouldn't he be at your throat in an instant! and then was rather shocked at the thought. Even so, she received the impression of a tightly coiled spring, and she eyed him warily. His features slanted in his face, and his skull was high and rather pointed, covered with thick glossy hair that resembled an animal's pelt. His lips were thin and exquisitely modelled, but they looked as if they could be cruel. Even so, thought Joanna staring, even so, I believe he is looking at me with gentleness.

The man smiled again; he said, "I can be gentle, Human Child. That was perceptive of you," and Joanna jumped, because he had seemed to pluck the thought from her head.

I can hear your thoughts, Human Child. To do so is the blessing and the curse of Tara.

"So," he said aloud, "you have found your way here, have you?"

Found? Or been brought?

He caught that as well, for he said, "The *sidh* are not my people, but they owe some allegiance to me. They wait at the doorways that sometimes open between your world and this one and they lure with their music the souls of Men."

"A doorway?"

"Yes. There are such things." And said in such a normal, not-to-be-questioned tone, that Joanna thought: well, yes. Of course there are doorways.

"Do I frighten you, Human Child?"

"No," said Joanna much too loudly, and then, more quietly, "No. But I should like to know where I am."

The man regarded her again. At length, "You are inside Scáthach," he said. "That is, the Castle of Shadow."

"I see," said Joanna carefully, not seeing at all. "And—if it is not impolite to ask—who are you?"

Again the pause. At last, "I am Cormac mac Airt," said the man. "Whom some call Cormac Starrog." He moved nearer, and Joanna saw how his features slanted. Like a wolf's.

Cormac Starrog . . . Cormac of the Wolves . . . so, Flynn told the truth . . .

"Yes," said the man softly, "yes, I have another name, Joanna. It is Cormac of the Wolves.

"I am the exiled High King of Tara, and the last of my line."

JOANNA SAT IN the firelit hall, at the long oak table opposite to Cormac mac Airt. She was wearing a fur-trimmed robe over her clothes. "For," said her companion, "it will have been cold in the Forest of Darkness, and perhaps the *sidh* will have touched you with their icy breath."

"What are they?"

"They are the most purely magical beings in Ireland. They live beneath the seas and in the rocks, and they are the scavengers of the world, for they are greedy for human souls. But they are also constrained to serve the High Kings at times, and their music is the strongest enchantment that has ever been known. For that reason they are tolerated, and for that reason our sorcerers have never tried to drive them out."

"What do they look like?" For there had been the briefest glimpses of strange blue and green creatures, slipping from one shape to another, never quite materialising. And there had been a rippling light that soothed your eyes and hurt your mind with beauty.

"That I cannot tell you. But our scholars say that to look on the *sidh*, to look on their cold inhuman faces, would ruin your mind. You would never speak or see again." He drank from the wine goblet at his side. "They are insatiable for the seed of Men, but once a man has been drained of his seed by them; once he has known their cold fingers and their icy lips caressing his phallus, and felt himself empty into their wombs, he is no longer able to love his own kind." He studied her. "Your cheeks colour when I say these things."

"It is only that—"

"It is that our worlds are different. I had forgotten."

"You know my world?"

"A very little," said Cormac. "There have been wayfarers from time to time. Men and women who have travelled through the Time Curtain. Eat your supper."

The food was hot and had been served to them, silently and very efficiently, by small, dark-featured people who came and went in the fireglow; who placed dishes on the table and bowed to their master as they retreated. Joanna had been fascinated, but Cormac smiled, and said gently, "Our ways are different to yours."

"Better?"

"Different."

The food was very good. There were peculiar, unfamiliar things cooked in rich spices, served with fruit and nuts; huge platters of meat cut into cubes and bowls of some kind of grain that she could not identify. There were no forks, but there were small sharp knives, made of what looked like bone. She noticed that Cormac ate with great fastidiousness, cutting the meat into small portions before conveying it to his mouth.

Once he spoke, "This is bear meat. Prepared with the juices of autumn apples and with wild honey. It is very good."

A little later, he said, "On feast occasions, such as Samain or the Great Feast of Dagda, the father-god, we would eat the flesh of the white stag which we had hunted by night, or of the great king-bulls who had been brought out to fight for our entertainment."

"Fighting for entertainment?" said Joanna, child of a world that looked askance on all forms of violence.

Cormac smiled. "It is sexually arousing to the men, and usually to the women as well."

There were dishes of wild mushrooms: "Agaric and Amethyst," said Cormac; and bowls of the tiny, sweet, wood strawberries she had gathered with Flynn in another life.

Joanna drank the wine and began to feel warm and content and unlike herself, and began, as well, to feel entirely unafraid.

"Why do you call me 'Human Child'?"

"It is what you are."

"And you?"

As always, there was the pause, as if he was considering his reply. Then he said very gently, "My dear, you must have seen that I am not entirely human." The dark eyes flickered over her, and flared into golden life, and Joanna felt a strange secret delight stir. "Do not trust me," said her companion softly, "for I am of wolf blood, Joanna."

"Is that—possible?"

"Oh yes. You see?" He touched his eyes, and Joanna had the impression that his face was sharpening, becoming crueller. "How do you know I will not leap on you and do to you what men in your world call rape, Joanna? How do you know I will not devour your soul, Human Child?"

Come into the music, Joanna, for we are fishers of souls, and we would gather up your soul for our master . . .

Yes, but *supposing a man were to enter Paradise, and there pluck a rose. . . ?*

Joanna said loudly, "I don't know it," and her companion smiled.

"If I had not been of wolf blood, I could not have ascended to the Ancient Throne of Tara," he said, and setting down his wine, reached across the table for her hand. "Tara can never belong to the humans, Joanna. For a pure-bred human ever to occupy the High Throne would mean that Tara would crumble." A frown touched his brow and anger glittered in his eyes for a moment. "And I shall never allow that to happen," said Cormac.

Joanna, utterly and completely fascinated now, said, "Will you tell me?" and Cormac smiled at her and turned her hand over in his, so that it lay palm uppermost.

"Tara is cursed," he said. "It was cursed many hundreds of years ago by a very powerful and very evil sorceress who had been defeated in battle by the first High Queen of all—Dierdriu." He released her hand gently and reached for the wine again, lifting it to his lips, so that the red glow cast a shadow over his eyes. "In the ages to come," he said quietly, "I believe it is the one thing that will be remembered about Tara. That it was for ever cursed." For a moment, his eyes took on the inward-looking expression again, and then he looked back at her. "Curses can never be destroyed, you see. They can never be killed. They can only be set aside."

"Deflected," said Joanna, and Cormac smiled.

"Yes. And because the curse was directed at a human, our own sorcerers wove a very strong and very subtle enchantment so that humans could lie with Beasts." He smiled the slanting smile again and reached for her hand.

"My ancestors lay with the wolves, Joanna, and so I am part wolf. I have the best and the worst of both sides in me."

And do not trust me, my dear, do not trust me . . .

Joanna said cautiously, "It is a—rather a difficult idea for me to believe in." And looked at him again, and thought: but of course, I *do* believe in it. He is partly wolf . . .

"By lying with the Beasts, we were able to produce what is called the Bloodline," said Cormac. "The Ancient Royal Houses of Tara. The six families upon whom was bestowed the Enchantment of the Bloodline. It is a very great honour and a very rare and precious thing to belong to one of those families." Again the smile. "And so because the Royal Houses of Ireland are no longer pure-bred Human, the curse cannot work against them. It can only work against a Human. That is why a Human must never occupy Tara's High Throne."

Joanna said, "Tell me about the six."

"They are my people," said Cormac, and again there was the fierce possessiveness in his voice. "The Six Ancient Houses of the Bloodline. The Wild Panther People of Gallan. The Eagles. The White Swans and the Deer. The Chariot Horses." A pause. "And the Lions," he said, and Joanna looked up, because there had suddenly been a great bitterness in his voice. But he only said, "And there are lesser Houses now; families who have been admitted into the Enchantment as a reward for some special service usually. The Beavers and the Hares and the Red Foxes of the forest." Again the pause and the flicker of anger. "But it was the Lions who betrayed me," he said, and his fingers curled involuntarily, and Joanna flinched, and thought that he would be a very dangerous enemy indeed, but thought as well that he could be hurt.

"Of course I can be hurt," said Cormac at once. "It is three generations since my ancestors lay with the wolves, and so the Human side of me is strong. It will probably be my grandchildren who will invoke the Enchantment and lie with the wolves, but that will be a matter for the sorcerers and the appointed judges to decide." He looked at her. "There is a very exact balance to be maintained, you see."

"Yes. Yes of course," said Joanna, and Cormac smiled, and caressed the hand that lay in his, turning it over. Joanna thought: if I do not speak, perhaps he will go on talking. He has the most beautiful voice I have ever heard. Warm honey and firelight and deep soft velvet. What would it be like to lie beside him, to feel his hands on my bare skin . . . An exiled High King. I wonder how long he has been in exile? I wonder if I can ask him about Tara?

He caught that at once, of course, and rose from his seat, taking her with him. "Let me show you what I have lost," he said. "Come." He drew her to the narrow windows and stood looking down. "Do you see it? Over there, across the Forest of Darkness where the *sidh* sometimes dwell, and beyond the Plain of Fál. Do you see it, Human Child? The lights and the splendour of Tara?"

Tara, the Bright Palace . . .

Almost directly in line with the window, across a great valley, was a blaze of light and colour, and as Joanna blinked and stared, the lights seemed to shift and merge, prisms of hard brilliance, blending and blurring, pinks and blues and lilacs.

There were pinnacles and spires and steep slender towers, and she was not at all sure that what she was seeing actually existed.

"It does exist," said Cormac softly. "The Ancient Court of the Manor of Tara. Beautiful beyond bearing. Where every man and woman must have an art, for it is written that without an art, no one may enter Tara." He looked down at her, and Joanna blinked, because it was a wolf smile, it was tremendously frightening, and it was also dreadfully exciting.

"I could show you it all, Human Child," said Cormac, his lips close to her. "I could show you the wonders of my Court, Joanna." He was standing very near to her, and he reached out and traced a line across her cheek and over her neck and shoulders. Joanna closed her eyes and thought: I am shivering. Is it from delight or from fear? I want him to stop and I wish he would go on.

He drew her back to the table and seated himself again, pouring more wine, leaning an arm on the table and watching her. The light threw shadows across his face, so that his eyes gleamed, and Joanna lowered her gaze.

"Tell me about Tara."

"There are no words," said Cormac, and again there was the aching sadness.

"You cannot bear to have lost it," said Joanna softly, and was at once conscious of the inadequacy of her words.

His hand came out to her again. "Not inadequate, Human Child. Your mind conveys to me what your words cannot." He sipped his wine. "Your ancestors lost much when they lost the art of the Mindsong. Words are restricting, language is finite. True emotions and true meanings cannot always be conveyed. That is why we have developed the Mindsong. The *Samhailt*."

The Mindsong . . . the art of reaching the thoughts of others . . . The art of hearing the feelings of those to whom you are close.

"There is not a day, nor yet an hour when I do not miss Tara," said Cormac. "There is not a day when I do not stand at the window and look out across the valley, for it was a part of the Council's punishment that I should still be in sight of that which I had lost." He drank wine. "In every age and at every Court there are plotters, you see. There are those who wish to replace the rightful ruler with their puppets, their straw kings. I was the High King by right of blood and by right of battle and by right of conquest. I ruled by power and intrigue and by sorcery."

"Sorcery . . ."

"Child of a cold and barren future, there is much magic in the world. Even in your world it is still there, it is only that men have lost the knowledge. To serve the High King by sorcery is a coveted honour. I used sorcery, but I did not use the dark magic. I ruled my people well and I fought their battles and made safe the ramparts of the cities, and I drove back every enemy who tried to take Tara. But there were plotters at my Court; there were people who bore me a grudge and who harboured vengeance." The thin beautiful lips took on a cruel line. "They replaced me with another of the Bloodline," said Cormac. "Eochaid Bres—that is Eochaid the Handsome. He is of lion blood, and it is thought that fits him to occupy the High Throne. But he is ruled by his clever, sly Councillors, and by his mother, who is ambitious and also what your world once called a whore."

He paused, and again there was the sudden inward slant of his eyes. "Yes, she is a whore, the Queen Mother," said Cormac softly.

"And so for the moment it is Eochaid Bres who rules from the Seat of the High Kings, and I was brought across the Plain and through the Forest of Darkness, and I have been here for five years, Joanna, and I shall not bear it any longer." He looked at her, and his eyes glowed. "I am caged here by the enchantment woven by my own sorcerers," he said softly, "and I cannot break out by myself."

But with your help, Human Child, I could . . .

Joanna, hanging on to the remnants of sanity, said, "But you are—quite comfortable here."

"Yes. I was allowed to bring my servants."

"The people who brought our supper?"

"Yes, the Cruithin. They are human, the oldest of all the Irish races. They have served the High Kings faithfully since Tara first sprang from the rocks, and since Dierdriu ruled. When I was exiled, I was permitted to take with me those who would come." Again the sardonic smile. "A small following for one accustomed to riding at the head of vast and powerful armies. But they came with me, and they serve me, and they are loyal, and so I am grateful." He studied her. "You bear traces of their blood, Joanna: small, elfin, dark. Eyes that see more than most people. A mixture of fragility and great strength. Have you come from the future to break my exile, or have you only come to rejoin your people?" He smiled. "You *could* rejoin them, Joanna. They would accept you without questioning you, for the old race, the true Irish race, have the great gift of hospitality." He moved in his chair. He is restless, Joanna thought. He cannot bear to be confined and caged out here. I wish he would touch me again.

Cormac had risen and begun to pace the hall, so silently and so gracefully that Joanna glanced involuntarily at the wolves, silent and watchful before the fire.

"Eochaid Bres will bring about the ruin of Tara," said Cormac. "He is handsome, and for the moment he rules. But he is stupid and he is only kept at Tara by the strength of his Councillors and by his mother, and already they are plotting to topple him and bring in those enemies from the north that I fought so hard to keep out. Soon I shall have to raise an army and join with Eochaid's people in battle."

Joanna said, "Shall you? I mean do you have to?" and Cormac turned on her, his eyes glittering so that she shrank. "I only meant . . . you are very comfortable here. You have your own Kingdom. Everything you could wish—"

"Everything I could wish!" He came to sit close beside her, and Joanna thought—his face, his voice, his sheer *presence* is like no one else's I ever knew in my life.

"Listen," said her companion. "I am the last true Prince of an old old line, and Tara is my inheritance. The *sidh* sang on the night I was born, and the wolves of Tara awoke and banded together and swore to be my liegemen. The Great Stone of Fál, which cries aloud under the hand of the destined King shrieked in pain and ecstasy for nine days and nights when I touched it. Until I return, Tara can never be again the great and powerful Court it was in my father's day. Eochaid is not strong enough to bind the people to him. His Councillors and his mother, the Queen, rule him."

He paused, and Joanna thought; there is something in his voice when he mentions her. Hatred? Or something equally powerful but softer?

Cormac said, "Eochaid does not know it, but I know that his

Councillors are sending out secret messengers to Tara's enemies in the north. To the powerful, evil sorcerers who would gobble up Tara and rule the land by bloodshed and terror and the darkest magics known to Ireland. My family stamped them out and sent them back into the mountains and into the caves, but they are still there. Eochaid will not be strong enough. But I can do it, Joanna. I can lead the armies again; I can ride out at the head of the great legions once more and I can defeat the evil that Eochaid's Councillors and his mother are inviting back." His eyes were glowing, and Joanna thought that in anyone else the words would have been arrogant. In him, they seemed statements of truth.

"Tell me," she said, only half understanding, but swept along by his enthusiasm.

"There are those among the Council who wish to trade with the Old Ireland. The Dark Ireland."

"Why?"

"For power. For the dark magic that lives in the caves and the mountains. Eochaid's mother, the Queen, will do so for the power it will give her over men. The Councillors will do it for power over men's minds.

"I must stop them, Joanna. Eochaid is weak and vain, but he is my cousin and he is not evil. He is being betrayed.

"They are waking the terrible sorceresses of the north; The Morrigna, a trio of hell sisters who feed on the corpses that rot in battlefields, and who lure victims into their house and cage them.

"They are waking the most terrible figure of all the old stories. The Erl-King."

Cormac paused, and Joanna felt a great listening silence descend on them. Had it been when he had said that last name? A cold stillness touched her heart, and she thought: now I am *really* afraid.

At length, she said, very softly, "How do you know all this? What is going to happen?"

"I know it because the wolves go into the forest and listen to the other creatures. The Councillors are using the hares as their messengers."

"And you can—the wolves can . . ."

Cormac smiled. "Yes, Human Child, we can understand each other. Did I not tell you of the Mindsong? I can talk with the Beasts, with the creatures who listen and wait and know what happens at Tara, the Foxes and the Deer and the Wild Panthers of Gallan.

"As for the Erl-King ..." He paused, and a tremor went through him, so that Joanna thought—in purest astonishment—he is afraid.

"Yes, I am afraid," said Cormac, taking her hand once more. "I am very much afraid of the Erl-King."

"What does he do?"

Cormac looked back at her, the firelight reflected in his eyes.

"He eats the children," he said.

CHAPTER FOUR

FLYNN WAS IN an agony of despair. He knew that Joanna was in some terrible danger; he could feel her thoughts and her emotions soaking in through his skin and searing his soul, and he felt as weak and as impotent as a kitten.

He had sat at the centre of the Glowing Lands until his limbs were cramped and aching, and his eyes dry and sore from trying to pierce the shifting mists of the Time Curtain.

To no avail. The Curtain had closed and Joanna was sealed in some fragment of the past, and she was as far from him as she could be. He stumbled home as the night sky was beginning to streak with the rose and grey of a new day; uncaring of his appearance, heedless of anyone who might see him.

The old farmhouse closed about him like a blessing; he thought: there is a great sanity here. My ancestors lived here for hundreds of years; they weathered the terrors of Devastation here, and the appearance of the Apocalypse, and they survived. If I can find a way to reach Joanna, then I shall do so.

He thought he was drawing a strength from the old walls of his home, and he was obscurely comforted. Joanna would be reached. There would be a way. And she is not dead, he thought. I *know* she is not.

He poured milk into the jug, added a spoonful of honey, and laid twigs beneath the stove for the eggs and potato cakes that would constitute his and his father's breakfast.

"For," said Flynn, to Michael in the sun-filled room that his ancestors had called a morning room, "for, if we are to penetrate the Time Curtain, we must be well fed. Strong."

Michael looked up. He said, "Flynn, we cannot. We are not permitted. It is the unbreakable law of the Keepers."

"Pain of death? I should not care," said Flynn. "I should not mind dying if by doing so I saved Joanna."

"Lethe emotions, Flynn. You will incur the Elders' displeasure."

"Fuck the Elders," said Flynn, and grinned at his father. "A Lethe word." He helped himself to more of the potato cakes and drank some milk.

At length Michael said, "The Glowing Lands failed you?"

"Yes."

"Have you tried any of the others?"

"No." Flynn was heartened by his father's words, and by Michael's frown of concentration. He thought: the old man is not dismissing it. He is going to help.

Aloud, he said, "To try the other Lands would be difficult, I thought. It would mean venturing on to other people's property. A journey. And I should probably be seen and caught."

"Yes, there is the risk, and the Secret must be kept."

"Also," said Flynn, eating and discovering that he was hungry, "also, is it not true that each Land is its own Gateway? Our own Lands lead us to the Ancient Court of Tara—that is the legend. But others might lead to other places. To find Joanna, I must take the path she took."

"Yes, of course. Forgive me," said Michael, "I am not thinking properly. But, Flynn, the Secret *must* be kept. For another two or three generations anyway."

For the Time Curtain is healing and the Lands are dimming . . .

Neither man said it; both were aware of it. Flynn thought: I dare not believe that the gap has closed for ever. I dare not.

Michael was eating his breakfast abstractedly. Flynn waited.

"There is only one thing to do."

"Yes?"

"We must summon the Keepers."

THE MYSTERIOUS ALCHEMY that works in times of trouble, the unseen network of communication that all races and all ages have developed, regardless of time or technology, worked for Flynn now. He did not know and he did not ask how his father had reached the Keepers so quickly; he was only thankful that he had reached them. Twenty-four hours—two hours even— might make all the difference.

The Keepers in their hooded robes were solemn and silent. But they listened; they stood on the dark hillside, their heads bent courteously, their whole attitude that of people listening and thinking. Flynn thought: they cannot refuse to let me go back! They cannot! And then— Even if they do, I shall do it, he thought. The Lands are on my father's property.

The leader spoke, and Flynn remembered his voice. Authority: absolute and unblurred, as impossible to mistake as it was to question.

"Our laws do not allow us to go back through the Time Curtain," said the leader. "But, as with all laws, there are contingency arrangements."

"Yes?"

The leader stood deep in thought, his hands clasped, and Flynn noticed the dull gleam of the heavy, rather ornate ring he wore. Was it some kind of precious stone? He remembered the stories of the Letheans' priceless stones, all of them with fascinating names: sapphires, emeralds, topazes, and amethysts.

At length, the man said, "There is a way." He looked at Flynn with the direct stare Flynn remembered. "But it will be unpleasant and it may be dangerous."

"That would not weigh with me."

"No, the girl must certainly be rescued." He studied Flynn, and Flynn knew what was coming.

"You have kept the Secret?" said the Leader.

"Yes."

"The girl is not there by her own wish or will?"

"No."

The man looked at Flynn for a moment longer. Then, "Very well," he said, "in these conditions we are permitted to break our laws. Perhaps we are constrained to do so. Are you willing to go through the Time Curtain, Flynn?"

"Yes."

"And to risk not being able to return?"

The old nightmare . . . But Flynn said, "Yes. Yes I will risk that." For I would be with Joanna, no matter what world we lived in. "Yes," he said again, more firmly.

"Good." A pause. "You should not go alone," said the leader, and Michael moved forward at once. "No," said the man. "We dare not allow you to go, Michael. Two from the same family—you know our laws."

"The Secret must be handed on."

"Yes. To occupy a place on the Council of the Keepers is hereditary." He turned back to Flynn. "The first Keepers decreed it, and it is a good law, Flynn. Secrets within families are always safer. And so we cannot permit your father to go into danger. But his willingness to do so is praiseworthy." He smiled and touched Michael's arm, and the heavy carved ring caught the thin light again. Flynn waited, and the man turned back. "Flynn, would you accept me as your travelling companion?"

Flynn was surprised, but he thought: I believe there is no one I would rather have. How extraordinary. I barely know him and yet I am trusting him with my life. "I should accept with gratitude, sir."

"My name is Amairgen."

"That is an unusual name."

"Not really. After the Great Devastation, many of the survivors found that they had lost not only their homes and their possessions, but also their names. The Apocalypse had wiped clean their memories. That is one reason why we have so little knowledge of the Letheans. When the truth was discovered about the Glowing Lands, my ancestors were appointed as Leaders of the Council of Keepers. As with the Council itself, the office of Leader is hereditary. Father to son. They took their names from a great leader and traveller and scholar of Ancient Ireland: Amairgen, son of Míl, who journeyed from a distant land with companions into 'the blue and green mists to bring peace to Tara.' You see?" In the darkness, Flynn felt the man smile. "In view of what we are to undertake, my name would seem appropriate. And your own name is probably a derivation of Finn, from the young warrior who was the High King Cormac's champion and who formed the ancient and honourable and most formidable brotherhood of the *Fiana*. That also is appropriate."

"Yes, I see."

Amairgen said softly. "You know that we are constrained to return?"

"I don't—"

"And that in no circumstances other than death or mutilation are we permitted to remain in whatever world we may find beyond the Time Curtain?"

Flynn said, "I know it." And thought: damn! Why is my voice sounding too loud? He said again, "Yes, I do know. I understand." But he thought that Amairgen looked at him rather searchingly, as if he knew very well that Flynn's whole mind and soul and body had often yearned to go back, to find the blue and green mists. Had someone truly written that of Tara? But it is so familiar, thought Flynn, and was not surprised to find it so.

Amairgen lifted the hand that bore the great carved ring. "The symbol of the Leader," he said. "To be given to my son if I should have one, or to whomever I may appoint if I do not." Again there was that disconcerting study, and Flynn thought: I believe I know what he is thinking. And at once knew a shaft of panic. Oh, no, I don't want that . . . Or do I? And he looked afresh at the silent watchers with their shadowed faces, and he felt again the faint, far-off stir of music that he had always felt lay hidden just beyond hearing on this hill. To control such a Secret; said his mind . . . To lead these men who guard what is surely the greatest and most awful Secret that ever man had to guard . . .

Amairgen spoke in a brisker tone, "Well, we must leave at daybreak, I think. You should dress warmly but plainly, for we dare not call attention to ourselves on this side of the Time Curtain, or beyond it. And you should bring a weapon of some kind—something easy to carry but capable of defending you."

Weapons were almost totally unknown in Tugaim, or anywhere else, for that matter, for the Letheans had bequeathed a strong and deeply rooted aversion to violence. But Flynn thought that of course Amairgen was right. A knife of some kind perhaps? A wood axe? And felt amusement, for was he to undertake the most perilous journey imaginable armed with a bread knife? But, "Yes," he said again. "Yes, I understand." And paused, and waited.

In the dim light, Amairgen watched him. "Tell me," said Flynn at length, "where is it we go; to break through the Time Curtain?"

Amairgen paused, as if reluctant to speak. "It is not far," he said. "The boundaries of Tugaim.

"To the House of Mutants. To the Gealtacht."

* * *

IN THE COLD dawnlight, Amairgen was very much younger than Flynn had thought. He was of medium height, fair, grey-eyed, and slender. Even so, Flynn thought he would be a worthy ally and a dangerous opponent.

Amairgen smiled. He said, "You are right, Flynn. I can fight if I have to."

Flynn turned to look. "You knew my thoughts?" This was so interesting as to be compelling. It was almost as compelling as what lay ahead.

"Yes. I have a little—a very little—of what is called the Samhailt. The gift—or the curse—of Tara." He glanced at Flynn. "That is how I knew you spoke the truth. I knew you had kept faith and not betrayed the Secret. The Leaders of the Council of Keepers must always possess the Samhailt. I think you possess it yourself, a little." And then, as Flynn did not answer, Amairgen said gently, "Flynn. Don't be surprised or frightened by what is ahead, you and I are entering other worlds: ancient worlds. Tell me, do you think your Joanna is still alive?"

"Yes," said Flynn.

"Ah," said Amairgen, and Flynn thought: well at least he understands.

"Of course I understand," said Amairgen, and grinned.

Flynn recovered himself enough to say, "It's a difficult thing to possess at times."

"It is." Amairgen pointed to the hill in front of them. "The Gealtacht."

"Why do we have to come here?"

Amairgen stood for a moment, surveying the great grim building far above them. "Because," he said, "the Gealtacht is a place of asylum for the Mutants. But you know that, of course. Mutants are able to control the Lands. They have within them the same taint and the same damage that the Glowing Lands have: the paw mark of the Apocalypse who tore the Time Curtain. They are able to strengthen the doorway that will lead us back to the Court of Tara. You could not go through it, Flynn, not by yourself, because you had not sufficient power. Perhaps your Joanna possesses some strange power we do not know. Perhaps . . ." He stopped and Flynn said, "Yes?"

"Nothing. Only a legend I once heard . . ."

"Tell me."

"The return of the High Queen," said Amairgen in a whisper. "She would come from the future. But, no, it cannot be so. Joanna simply stumbled across the Time Curtain. In some way she parted it.

"The Mutants have a great power, you see. They also can part the Time Curtain and allow us to go through.

"And so we shall have to chain one of them and take him to Tara's Hill and force him to draw aside the Time Curtain."

THE CLIMB TO the Gealtacht was longer and more arduous than Flynn had expected. The hill was more barren than anything he had ever seen in Tugaim. The effects of Devastation? Or simply that this was a place so utterly abandoned by men that the land had lost heart. Ridiculous! said Flynn to himself, but the feeling of a desolation so total, a loneliness so dreadful, persisted.

The track was narrow and difficult, here and there it was rutted by some great upheaval.

"It is hardly ever used," said Amairgen. "Once you are inside the Gealtacht, you are not expected ever to come out. There are no recorded instances of anyone ever having done so."

Several times on the upward climb, Flynn stumbled and each time Amairgen was there with a hand outstretched to catch him. As they climbed higher, and the air became colder, Flynn found himself doing the same, anticipating Amairgen's missteps.

"The Samhailt?" he said, grinning.

"Of course. A difficult possession, but useful at a time like this. Without it, I should have been at the foot of that ravine."

But even with such good company, Flynn found the hill rather menacing. It was a long way from the warmth and the security of Tugaim, of course; there was a brooding air that chilled his inmost thoughts. To be brought up here, to know from the beginning that you were deformed, maimed, that you were not like others, and must be shut away in this terrible prison. Had they intelligence, these Mutants? Were they able to feel pain at their outcast state?

"Oh yes," said Amairgen. "That is the pity of it. But it is thought that they are made quite comfortable up here."

As they climbed even higher, Flynn found himself remembering that even today there were bands of fierce greedy men who would not work their own lands, but preferred to roam the hillsides and the forests, preying on solitary travellers, occasionally making raids on the more isolated farmhouses. To Flynn, violence was a totally abhorrent concept, and he thought it was to most of Tugaim. Even so, he recognised that it was not so for everyone. Violence had survived in the world. "The old order changeth not . . ." Where had he heard of, read, or dreamed that?

They stopped to break their fast when the sun was high. "For," said Amairgen, "it won't help if we arrive fainting from hunger and speechless from fatigue. Did you bring food? Oh good. Shall we share what we have?"

It was a curious meal they ate together, sheltering from the cold thin wind in the lee of some boulders, the bulk of the Gealtacht still far above them. Flynn looked up at it, and thought there was an air of patience about it, and an air of watchfulness. He thought it was looking down on Tugaim, waiting until its next victims were brought to it. He shook his head to clear the thoughts, and turned to unpack the food made up in the farmhouse early that morning.

"Cold chicken is it?" said Amairgen. "Excellent. And I have pigeon pie and potted mushrooms."

Flynn had brought fruit as well; crisp apples and velvet-skinned plums from the orchard. There were honey cakes and a small flask of the rich damson wine which Flynn's mother had always brewed, and which Flynn, remembering only a shadowy, rather beautiful lady, always thought tasted of happiness and sadness in equal portions.

"Life is happiness and sadness both," said Amairgen. "But not always in equal portions." And then he brushed the crumbs from his cloak and set about packing away the remains of their food and corking the wine flask, so that Flynn thought Amairgen himself was compounded of curiously unequal portions.

The sun had reached its zenith and was moving downwards over the Mountains of the Morning as they neared the Gealtacht. Flynn shivered in the cold raw air, thinking that few living things would ever come here. But no, here were tracks of some kind of animal; there against the hill face was the nest of some flying creature, too large for a hawk, too small for an eagle. He turned up his collar against the cold, and thought: even like this, even with the afternoon sun on it, the Gealtacht is a terrible place. How must it be to be up here at night, perhaps without even the light from the moon; to be close to the creatures inside the House, as cut off from the light as they were from the rest of humanity?

There was a scent of hawthorn and moss now, and the walls of the Gealtacht were rearing up against the sky. High walls. "Oh yes, they have to be high," said Amairgen.

"Are they—the Mutants—dangerous?"

"Some of them."

Even so, there were splashes of life and colour against the walls; gentians and star flowers and rowan. Rowan, the age-old protection against witches . . . But how near to the house itself did it grow?

Before them were the iron gates that shut away the Gealtacht, the House of Mutants, from the rest of the world. The gates were locked, secured with immense iron padlocks, and lined with sheets of steel, so that no one could look in. And no one could look out . . .

"Over the wall," said Amairgen. "You first. I'll follow."

THE BRAVE NEW World created by the Great Devastation did not admit (or not often) to flaws or taints. Devastation had been a purging, said the survivors determinedly; it had been tragic and terrible, but it had swept away all of the old imperfections and all of the old weaknesses; only the strong had come through, and it was the strong who would rebuild the world.

But not even those remarkable men and women who had lived through the Apocalypse's reign of terror and pain could hide the dreadful and pitiable creatures who had been directly touched by the Apocalypse's fire.

To begin with, they did not want to hide them. When the world settled, and the fires cooled, there had been a wave of love and friendship so tremendous that the scarred and the deformed had not mattered. The world was scarred and deformed, said the survivors staunchly; people must live and work side by side, never mind that some were hurt and mutilated. No one must hide, or shudder away from the poor maimed creatures who had borne the brunt.

But the Mutants did not conform. They did not slot into this splendid new world that was so carefully and so eagerly being rebuilt. They were bitter and withdrawn: "Understandably so," said the survivors, still buoyed up by the marvellous new feeling that was sweeping mankind, stimulated by the great task ahead.

But the Mutants suffered; they were prone to sickness, vomiting, and purging. They sometimes rolled in agony on the floor from the pains in their bones and organs. They could not be expected to work, and they could not really be left alone. No one had any palliatives to give, but everyone agreed that they must be gently treated, made as comfortable as possible. However much pity there might be for the damaged, the world must somehow struggle back into the light; this new wonderful sense of love and friendship must not be lost. It must be cherished and let to grow. It was not that they had not time to spare on the Mutants, said the survivors firmly, or that they had not pity for them, it was simply a question of practicalities. It was, in fact, a little irritating to have to break off to tend the Mutants when there was so much else to be done. Nobody came out and said so, but the Mutants were rather a problem. They were certainly a distraction.

The Houses were opened. People who had medical knowledge left from the old days ventured their services. It was exactly like the old wars, the really old ones. The Crimea had it been? And the First World War? Distant memories, ancient history, and really rather milk-and-water battles to people who had come through days and nights and weeks of terror. Even so, the Houses, the volunteers, provided a solution to the problem of the Mutants. They could be put together; there were enough old infirmaries still standing, enough old asylums. Built for exactly these purposes, said the survivors, pleased. The Mutants would be cared for. It need not be a problem.

The problem had not been the original Mutants.

It had been the Mutants' descendants.

"THEY OUGHT NOT have been allowed to breed," said Amairgen, jumping down beside Flynn into the gardens of the

House. "But no one guessed . . . And it seemed kindly to give them the comfort of sexual release if they wanted it."

The comfort of sexual release, so tolerantly bestowed, had very nearly destroyed the splendid new sense of love in the world.

"They bred from one another," said Amairgen, pausing in the still afternoon, his eyes surveying the great House ahead of the trees. "And they bred the most dreadful travesties of humanity."

The first Mutants, pitiable and maimed, had been possible to cope with; the survivors had been able to feel kindly towards them, and the people who tended them had been able to bring genuine compassion to their task. Wasn't everyone struggling to live again, and wasn't it only the luck of the draw that some were for ever tainted and some left whole? They dug deeply into the old knowledge for remedies: draughts to halt the terrible vomiting and purging; painkilling potions to dilute the bone agony of their charges; cooling lotions to help the dreadful weeping abscesses that broke out on the scorched skins. And there were what were called remissions; times when the Mutants could enjoy life a little, eat normal foods, carry on conversations . . . feel sexual arousal.

They were tended and allowed to do whatever they wished. Poor creatures, said those who had the care of them. Surely one could spare time and compassion on them. It would only be for a few years anyway.

It was not for a few years at all. The Mutants could somehow still breed. "Mankind fighting for rebirth," said the survivors sagely. But the women brought forth creatures such as no one could have imagined.

"Many were near-monsters," said Amairgen, one hand on Flynn's arm; so alert and so watchful that Flynn thought he might almost be sniffing the air.

"And so the Mutant strain was strengthened. Just as close cousins have never been supposed to breed from one another if there is any weakness that may be doubled, so the Mutant strain was made far worse than anyone could have foreseen. Since those days, we have had the Kin Book which must be strictly kept, and in which all Mutants born must be registered. Not," said Amairgen, "that so many are born now, but it still occurs occasionally."

"But people do not always admit to having produced a Mutant. They conceal, they send the child away to where the laws are not so strictly upheld."

Amairgen replied "Of course they do. Human nature has not changed so very much despite Devastation, Flynn."

The grounds of the Gealtacht were overgrown, but there were attempts at grassy banks and a few flower beds. There were dark shrubberies and laurel bushes, and towering oak and beech trees.

"Sheltered," said Amairgen. "Yes, I believe these are from the days before Devastation. Yes, for that tree must be at least two hundred years old, if not more. And the house itself escaped the worst of the fires."

It was curious and slightly eerie to see growing things which were largely unknown in Ireland now. Flynn stared at the immense trees, their branches interlacing overhead, making patterns against the sky, and thought: *what* did they do, our ancestors, to unleash on the world so great a power that it could destroy things like this? In a way, it was like entering a part of the past; Flynn thought that here was a world within a world; the Gealtacht did not need Tugaim, it did not need any of the outside world. It was complete in itself, and once the iron doors had clanged shut, escape from the House would be impossible.

They approached the building through a thick shrubbery, avoiding the gravel paths. Flynn thought that despite the bleak air, despite the deserted grounds, someone did tend the gardens a little. The lawns were roughly cut, the gravel paths had at some time been raked. The bushes were clipped into a kind of order.

Seen at closer range, the house looked as if it might be deserted. Windows were barred, and there was no sign of life anywhere. But ...

"Look," said Amairgen softly. "Smoke from the chimneys."

"Yes. And a smell of cooking. That would be the kitchen section."

It was difficult to escape the feeling of hidden watchers, of unseen eyes peering from the topmost windows, and of calculations being made. *Another two? Oh, for sure we can house them. There are cells, there are windowless prisons with chains and locked doors. Once inside the Gealtacht they will never get out.* Terrible thoughts. How many poor maimed creatures, damaged from the scorching fires, had been brought here and had those thoughts?

Amairgen found a side door, nearly covered by a thick mat of ivy, but unlocked. He turned to Flynn and placed a finger on his lips. Flynn nodded. They did not dare to be caught by those who had the care of the Mutants; they could not possibly explain their mission.

Capture and chain one of them . . .

It was a cold thought to have to contemplate chaining and binding another human creature. But, "Many are near-monsters," Amairgen had said. Flynn thought: I must bear it. If I can think of these creatures as simply sick human beings, perhaps I can manage. He remembered an old Lethe belief that the sins of people could be visited on their descendants, perhaps that was the explanation. The sins of those greedy, fool-hardy beings who burned the world and called up the Apocalypse were still punishing their descendants. It would explain a good deal; it might even explain why some had been left whole and others had not.

Inside the Gealtacht it was rather dark and there was a dank smell. Rats! thought Flynn, and repressed a shudder, for everyone knew the tales of how rats had run unchecked amidst the rubble of the burning cities, bringing plague and sickness with them. Everyone knew how the rats had eaten the dead bodies, and even of how, in desperate cases, survivors had eaten the rats. Not to be thought of, any of it.

They moved cautiously along a narrow corridor to their left, the clatter of crockery and pots and the hum of conversation coming faintly to them. Amairgen threw out a thought and Flynn picked it up at once. *At least they do not trouble to keep any kind of silence, these tenders of monsters. At least we should hear them coming, and have time to hide.*

Amairgen moved forward, his head tilted to catch the slightest sound, his eyes searching the shadows. Flynn thought: he is using the Samhailt to its utmost limits; he is trying to pick up the thoughts and the emotions of the people in here.

"But of course I shall not be able to," said Amairgen, and Flynn grinned despite himself.

"No?"

"The Samhailt can only really exist between people who are

in sympathy one with the other," said Amairgen. "And even then, it is possible to close your thoughts to the other." He stopped and put out his hand to Flynn, and Flynn stopped as well, because he had felt, just for a brief moment, a ripple of something on the air. Desperation, was it? Certainly a cry for help. He looked at Amairgen, and Amairgen said, "It could not be. Surely no creature in here could possess the Ancient Gift." But his voice was uncertain.

And then from somewhere at the very top of the house there was a muffled clang; iron against iron—a heavy door closing to. There was a squeal of rage or pain, or both, which died on the air, leaving only the brooding silence once again. The thread of thought that had seemed, so fleetingly, to come from somewhere inside the Gealtacht, vanished, and Flynn thought that perhaps after all they had imagined it.

They saw the first Mutant as they rounded a corner where two corridors converged. At first, Flynn thought it was just another echoing empty passage; he saw the twists of cable dangling from the ceilings that he had seen in Lethe-built buildings elsewhere, the bloom of condensation on the walls and the puddles of damp on the stone floor—or was it simply damp? There was a pile of clothes at the far end . . .

But the pile of clothes was moving. Both men stopped; *be careful!*

Amairgen moved forward, and Flynn thought: he does not hesitate, ever. He does not even have to think about being brave, or summoning courage. He has instinctive courage. He moved to Amairgen's side.

You do not need to prove anything, Flynn. You will have courage and to spare before we are done, and perhaps at a time when I shall not.

The creature ahead of them made a quick scuttling movement that reminded Flynn of an insect. And then it moved from the shadows, and dismay held both men motionless.

The creature was certainly a girl, for there were breasts and a certain softness of feature. There was an oval body with the head set at one side. But instead of two arms and two legs, three pairs of limbs protruded at regular intervals, jointed and gristly with sinew, neither quite arms nor legs, but a mixture of the two. The fingers at each end were thick and splayed so that the creature could grip and walk.

Flynn and Amairgen froze, and the girl looked at them. Flynn saw comprehension in her eyes and intelligence as well, and the pity of it burst like a fire inside his chest.

"Intruders?" said the girl, moving back and forth, and the two men saw that she used all six limbs to support herself, exactly as a spider, or a beetle, scurrying to and fro does. "Intruders," she said again, rearing up slightly, her upper limbs waving at them uncertainly.

"We intend you no harm," said Flynn softly.

"You have come to view us?"

"No. To ask for your help."

"Are you some kind of lookout?" said Amairgen warily.

"No. But they do not chain me as they chain the others. I am free to come and go as I please. But I keep to the shadows," said the girl. "You will understand why."

Flynn said, very gently, "But you have a gentle face—"

"And a repulsive body. The men make use of me when they wish to. I do not really mind." *I do not really mind anything,* said her tone, and Flynn felt the pity well up again, like sickness inside him.

"Forgive us, but we must search the house. There will be—one of your kind who will help us."

Again there was understanding. "Through there," she said, and moved away from them, dropping back on to her six legs, watching them wordlessly from the dark corner where she had been crouching. As the men moved away, they heard her say softly, "The strongest are chained. But it will be the strongest who will give you most help."

They moved away towards the intersection of the passages.

Down here?

Yes.

To begin with, it was some kind of instinct that drew them in that direction, but after a few moments, they both became aware of a noise, and as they drew nearer, both wanted to turn and run. Flynn thought it was like the cries of souls in hell, and then he thought that it was souls shut out of hell. His skin prickled and sweat started out on his brow.

Courage, said Amairgen silently. *Do not lose your sense of proportion, Flynn. These poor creatures are a very tiny section of mankind.*

Is that a consolation to them?

Amairgen sent him a quick look of understanding. "But you have a skin short, Flynn," he said, and took his arm as they saw, ahead of them, a great iron door.

The noise was deafening now. It echoed and reverberated around the old stone mansion, and as they stood before the door, Flynn saw in the dim light, a printed notice fixed to the wall, its surface pitted by fire and time, but readable still.

. . . and no attempts should be made to touch the Lunaticks, for although the Diet is extraordinary Good and Proper, yet they may be subject to Scurvy and Other Disease . . . the Lunaticks may not be viewed on Sundays . . .

Viewed, thought Flynn. *Viewed.* "You have come to view us," she had said. What long-ago Lethe put up that notice, beautifully printed by one of their machines, as cold and unfeeling in its wording as the machine that made it. The babble of cries on the other side of the door grew momentarily louder.

Amairgen took a deep breath and reached down to turn the iron handle. The door slid soundlessly open and Flynn and Amairgen stepped inside.

The Mutants were kept in a long windowless chamber, divided into sections by iron bars—like cages! thought Flynn. The walls and floors ran with damp, and there was some kind of fungus on the underside of the faraway roof. Straw was thrown down on the floor and there were troughs of water, and metal buckets containing some kind of coarse-looking meal. The walls had brackets with burning torches thrust roughly into them, so that the light burned continuously, lending an eerie glow to the scene before their eyes.

The Mutants were chained; every one of them had leg manacles attached to long chains embedded deeply in the old walls, which slithered and clanked every time they moved, with a cold, steel-on-wet-stone sound that made Flynn's nerve endings shudder. The chains were long; the Mutants could move about freely; they could reach the water trough and the meal buckets.

The Mutants were not all as physically deformed as the spider girl in the corridor. Some were only twisted or hunched, or were lacking a leg or an arm. Nothing so very terrible. But as Flynn looked, they seemed to become more terrible: nightmarish. There were men with one eye or with three; women with no necks, but heads growing from a shoulder; creatures covered with hair, with warts, with scaly growths. One man had neither neck nor shoulders, but a huge, completely smooth, egg-shaped torso with the facial features crammed into one end of the egg, and tiny useless-looking arms growing halfway down.

In one corner were beings so hideously deformed, that it was impossible to tell if they were one person or several; there were creatures with extra arms growing from their shoulders; creatures with two sets of shoulders and two heads on one trunk; single faces with two separate sets of features squashed into them; bodies that began normally but divided at the waist into two sets of legs, each with perfectly formed genitals between them, one male and one female. There were feet growing from shoulders and from thighs. In another corner was a Mutant with no head at all, just a body with a thick stump-like neck that had a gash for its mouth and great bulbous eyes at the top of the stump that twitched and protruded.

In every terrible face, there was a cunning, an evil, and such a complete absence of humanity, that Flynn was sickened. He thought he could have coped with monsters; he certainly thought he could have coped with ordinary malformed human beings.

But such travesties as these were not people, they were barely human. Both men thought as one: *we could not possibly take any of these.*

"Dear God," groaned Amairgen, and at the soft words, the nearest Mutant, a male covered in thick scaly skin and with massive ears, turned and saw them, and let out an animal screech of glee. In a moment, the Mutants had turned and were hurling themselves at Flynn and Amairgen, tearing frantically at their chains, reaching with hands for the two strangers.

Flynn and Amairgen backed away until they found themselves backed up against the great door.

"We cannot possibly—none of these poor things could be taken—they would never understand . . ." Flynn gasped.

"Nevertheless, we must try," Amairgen took a step forward. He held up a hand for silence, and the Mutants' tumult subsided a little, they were watching him slyly, chattering to themselves like animals.

Amairgen said, "Please—we mean you no harm. We want your help."

There was a silence and Flynn felt the puzzlement in the room. The word itself was alien to them.

"We would ask one of you to come with us," said Amairgen. "To the Glowing Lands. To help someone in danger."

Again the silence. The Mutants watched and considered the strangers and then began to move back to their corners.

Flynn said despairingly, "It's no use. I don't think they understand."

"They must ... Look at me, damn you!" cried Amairgen. "Look at me, you poor deserted things!" He strode into their midst. "Listen to me."

The Mutants were on him in an instant, tearing at his clothes, thrusting themselves up against him.

Flynn did not hesitate—"You will have courage and to spare before we are done," Amairgen had said—he snatched up an iron bar from the floor and laid about the Mutants until he had cleared a path to where Amairgen half sat, half lay, dazed and bruised, one arm raised to shield his face.

"Come on!" shouted Flynn furiously, and dragged his companion back to the door.

They fell through it together, gasping and choking, and pushed it to, breathing heavily, neither able to speak. Behind the iron barrier the Mutants had set up a terrible wailing, dragging their chains backwards and forwards across the stone floor in a frenzy.

At length, Amairgen straightened up and wiped the sweat from his face with the back of his hand. "We dare not stay here," he said. "The attendants will come running at any minute. The noise those creatures are making—"

"I'm going to be sick."

"Then go and do it in that corner as quietly as you can manage."

Flynn moved blindly and leaned over, retching for several minutes, feeling his insides scoured by the cold sourness of the place, his eyes streaming with sickness and pity.

Amairgen silently handed him the flask of damson wine and Flynn gulped several mouthfuls gratefully.

"I didn't know you had a squeamish stomach," said Amairgen.

"I haven't," said Flynn, and dredged up a smile. "Where now?"

"I think the upper floors."

"Are there other floors?" But of course there must be, the Gealtacht could not rear up against the night sky unless there were higher floors than this. And the Letheans had built high towering places, everyone knew that.

"There are several," said Amairgen. "The Letheans' class system operates here. What we saw in there were the poor creatures whose families have entirely abandoned them. The paupers," said Amairgen, using a word unfamiliar to Flynn.

"And the upper floors?"

"Will house the elite. The Mutants whose families do not mind paying for extra comforts, and for a degree of privacy."

Even so, there was little in the way of comfort to be found in the dank narrow cells under the Gealtacht's roof.

"Of course there is not," said Amairgen sadly. "The attendants pocket the money and feed these Mutants exactly as they feed the wretches downstairs."

"Can they? I mean can they do so without being discovered?"

"It's an old custom," said Amairgen. "And who comes here to check?"

The upper floor was bisected by yet another soulless passage, which they reached by means of a wide shallow-treaded staircase. Flynn touched the wooden balustrades: when the Letheans built, they built well. The balustrade was a strong solid oak; it was dull and scarred by neglect, but the grain was still beautiful; the delicately carved fir cones and oak leaves that decorated the hand rail were still lovely.

These cells opened off the corridor; each had a tiny grille and a name written on a card outside it. Each cell was firmly locked.

The cries were louder up here; they were of the same quality as those in the paupers' chamber, they conveyed the same unmistakable madness. But Flynn thought there was a terrible desolation about them now; an immense and aching loneliness. At least the Mutants downstairs had company. The Mutants up here had nothing.

Locked away in tiny windowless cells, without light, without warmth, barely knowing the comfort of another human being's presence ... These were indeed the damned, the ones shut out of hell, thought Flynn. I don't think I can bear this. But they have to bear it, said his mind. There is no running away for them. This is all their life consists of, and this is all it will ever consist of. What did they do, our ancestors, when they unleashed the beast Apocalypse on the world? He wanted to fling wide the doors of this great gloomy Lethe mansion, and see sunlight pour in and hear voices raised cheerfully, and feel warmth and friendship soak through the stone walls. He could do none of it. He could not even unlock the cell doors.

Apprehensive and fearful Flynn and Amairgen peered into the cells. "We have glimpsed worlds we did not suspect existed," said Flynn afterwards.

"I suspected," Amairgen replied sadly. "But I hoped I was wrong."

In the cell at the far end of the corridor a girl crouched in one corner, her knees drawn up, her feet wide apart. Between her thighs lay the almost unrecognisable remains of a baby. Flynn looked and then turned away at once, but not before he had seen the girl reach down with absorption into the bloodied mess and lift up a portion of skin and flesh. In the jellied lump, he thought he saw a tiny hand, five fingered but webbed.

Flynn snapped the grille shut and leaned back against the wall, his eyes closed.

"What was it?"

Flynn said, "She was eating—a dead child. I think she had just given birth ..."

"How do you know?"

"I saw the afterbirth," said Flynn, who had helped deliver calves and foals ever since he could remember, and who thought he had seen some odd things, but had never seen anything quite like this. He opened his eyes and looked at Amairgen. "Animals sometimes do it," he said. "If the offspring is deformed. They eat it ..."

Amairgen said slowly, "Eating the children," and frowned. "Inhuman."

"No," said Amairgen, "it was not that. Just for a moment, I thought there was something familiar ..." He shook himself.

"It does not matter. We must go back, Flynn. There is nothing here that can help us."

They returned cautiously to the lower floors, both of them conscious of having failed, each conscious of a great anger and an aching grief.

The spider girl was still sitting in her corner, staring at nothing with the patience of a sick animal.

Flynn stopped; his hand came out to Amairgen's, and again a thought was shared.

Why not this one? She is not the strongest, and it is the strongest who will most easily draw aside the Time Curtain. But she is a Mutant; she may have some power. And she is not mad like the others; they have not chained her or locked her away.

They started forward.

"You would take me out of here?" she said.

"Yes."

"You would do that?"

"Yes. But you must come quietly and you must come now."

"I would do anything . . ." The girl touched Flynn's hand. "I would serve you both, anything you asked, I would do. To be out of here . . ." She looked from one to the other. "And I am agile. I can climb to places you could not reach. I could be of help in all kinds of ways. Oh, take me with you."

Flynn and Amairgen straightened up; they looked at each other, and Amairgen gave a tiny nod.

"Come then. Have you things you wish to bring?"

"My cloak. It is here. I have nothing more."

"Quickly then. They will be searching for us now. They must have heard the Mutants screech."

"The Mutants always screech," said the girl. "But it is true; they will be serving supper soon."

"Tell us your name," said Flynn kindly.

"It is Portan."

"Ah," said Amairgen. "And your real name, my dear?"

A smile touched her lips. "In my family, I was called Maura. But names change inside the Gealtacht. I am always called Portan. It is an old Gael word, meaning—"

"The spider-crab," said Amairgen, gently. "This way, and let us be as quiet as we can."

* * *

IT WAS RATHER like having an obedient child, having Portan with them. She did not speak very much, but both men were strongly conscious of an unquestioning fidelity. Once she halted and sniffed the dusk; once she said, "I had forgotten how large the world was," but for most of the journey back down the hill, she said nothing, padding easily and silently at their side, usually on all six limbs, but occasionally raising up a little.

When they stopped, halfway down, she curled at Flynn's feet and accepted the food they shared out; watching them eat, copying how they did so with a faithfulness that Flynn found moving. He gave her the remains of the chicken, and peeled and sectioned an apple for her.

"This is a feast," said Portan. "I had forgotten there were such things."

"How long have you been in the Gealtacht?"

"Many years. I am not sure."

She appeared to possess the unusual gift of being able to live for the moment, and to be only too able to forget the years in the House of Mutants.

"But my family I do not forget," she said, and there was an ache of longing in her voice now. "I do not forget how I was taken to the House by nightfall and left there on the doorstep to be found or to die, as the gods chose. I do not forget that I cried and clung to my father and begged not to be left there." A tiny pause. "It was a terrible time," said Portan.

"Your family abandoned you?"

"It is how it should be," said Portan. "But it was hard, sometimes. And I should have liked to see my mother again."

Flynn said carefully, "But there is surely nothing shameful about having a Mutant born into the family—"

"Oh yes, it is a very shameful thing," said Portan, and there was no trace of bitterness in her voice. "People do not wish to admit that we still exist, you see. They do not like it known that they cannot breed normal healthy children. And my father was an important man. It would not have done. But I missed my mother," she said, and now there was such wistfulness in her voice, that Flynn felt his eyes burn with unshed tears.

Portan smiled up at him. "But I was luckier than most," she

said. "I was not disabled by my deformities, and they learned that I was not insane like so many were."

She had been entrusted with small tasks; carrying food, cleaning. "There were several of us who could do such things. They did not lock us in. And it made for a friendship between us." She laid down the remains of the chicken. "We had to wait on those who had us in their care," she said. "And in the summer we were made to attend to the gardens. That I enjoyed—to see the food growing—there is a satisfaction in that. But mainly I was alone."

"What did you do?"

"I waited," she said. "And I hoped," and Flynn, liking her and admiring her, was suddenly reminded of a trustful animal, abandoned by its master, but still watching the door for that master's return.

He smiled and reached out to take her hand. "I am glad you came with us, Portan," he told her.

"I hope I will be able to do what you want," said Portan.

Flynn hoped so as well.

CHAPTER FIVE

JOANNA AWOKE TO bright sunlight pouring in through the half-curtained windows of her bedchamber, and was hazily aware of a warm contented drowsiness.

And then, quite suddenly, of something else.

I am not alone.

Delight tinged with apprehension washed over her, and she turned her head across the deep soft bed and saw him.

He was still asleep, sprawled across the bed in unconscious grace—*animal* grace, thought Joanna, fascinated and terrified: *I have lain with a wolf.* And she knew only an immense, heart-stopping joy.

She lay quietly, watching him, the bed soft and warm, memories of the previous night flooding back.

They had sat before the fire talking, drinking wine; Cormac's eyes had been hard and slanting, golden in the firelight, and Joanna had thought: *I believe he is in some way casting an enchantment on me,* frowning, because the concept of such a thing was alien. Even so—*I believe he is* she thought, and discovered a wish to be enchanted wholly and for ever. All about them, the great Castle of Shadow settled into silence, and through the deep slit-like windows the winking lights of the forest dwellers went out one by one. They might have been the only people left in the world . . .

"WE ARE THE only people," said her companion softly, and Joanna jumped, because for a moment she had forgotten his trick of picking up a thought. Would he then know everything she thought?

"Not your deepest thoughts," he said, and smiled. "Those of us who possess the Samhailt are charged to use it honourably." He took her hand. "I possess it, because I could not be a Prince of Tara unless I did. But I must never probe too deeply." He held her hand a little more firmly. "Are you thinking, Human Child, that I have drawn you into my lair and kept you there for my own purposes?" The cool sharp wolfnails of his hand dug into her skin. He moved so that he was seated on the floor, in front of the great hearth, and his face and his limbs were bathed in the red light from the fire.

"Joanna, I am aching with desire for you," he said, and Joanna felt the delight and the fear run all over her. For an instant, the memory of Muldooney's fat soft body against hers swam into her mind, and for a truly terrible moment, the memory of Flynn's grey eyes and wide mobile mouth was there as well. But, "I am aching with desire," he said, and his face and his voice *were* like no one's Joanna had ever met in her life, and the reality of Flynn and Muldooney and that other world that she might never see again, was slipping away.

Cormac said softly, "There has been one who misused you, Human Child. You may forget him. And there has been one who loved you. You may forget him, also." He pulled her down to the floor beside him, and his face was close to hers, and she could smell the warm golden wolf scent of him, and desire cut through her from breast to womb, so fiercely and so sweetly that the room tilted and spun.

"I have the strength of Men to love you, Joanna, and I have the strength of Beasts, as well. I can love you like a human, Joanna, but I can love you like a wolf too. Your pure-bred humans could never love you like I can, Joanna."

He had risen and was looking down at her, and so beautiful and so strange was he that Joanna felt dizzy and sick, and was filled with delight and fear, and wished to wake up and find it all a dream, and wanted it to go on for ever.

"Contrary child," said Cormac gently, and pulled her to her feet, and drawing her close, kissed her slowly and lingeringly, his lips open and warm and tasting of wine and love. Joanna leaned against him, she thought she could not have stood by herself anyway by this time, and she felt the strong thighs and hips, and the powerful shoulders, and felt, as well, the hard hot masculine arousal between his legs.

"You see?" said Cormac softly. "You feel?" He slid the fur-trimmed robe from his shoulders, and stood naked before the flickering fire, and Joanna drew in a breath, and thought: beautiful! Animal and frightening, but so beautiful a creature that no one could resist him. *Is he going to do to me what Muldooney tried to do and failed?*

"I *shall* hurt you," said Cormac softly, and Joanna knew he had sensed her fear. "But you will not mind."

He reached for the robe she wore and slid it from her shoulders, his sharp nails brushing her skin, leaving rivulets of pleasure wherever they touched.

"Ever since you walked into my castle I have wanted you," he said.

Come inside, my dear . . . all the better to seduce you . . .

Joanna had never heard the old nursery stories; she had never absorbed, as children of an earlier age had, the primeval fear of wolves; of soft caressing voices that soothed and excited all in one; of slender and beautiful young men who were not quite what they appeared to be. To a child from the age known as Lethe, Cormac's behaviour and his words would have been sinister indeed; a Lethe child would have remembered that creatures with wolf blood in them had a way of suddenly changing, so that evil, hungry beings looked out of their eyes; that creatures with wolf blood in them had a taste for human flesh and human skin. *All the better to eat you with, my dear . . .* But a child of the Lethe age would never have found itself in this situation either, and even then, would not have believed in it, for the Letheans, whatever else they may have done, had found a way to solve the world's problems. They knew, or thought they knew, the solution to all the mysteries and they thought that their science had drawn aside all the veils, so that their knowledge had penetrated the dark secrets of the world. But perhaps, as well as all of this, they had lost something. Perhaps they had lost the sense of wonder. They had certainly lost the belief in magic and in other worlds.

And so, Joanna, child of an austere destroyed world but child also of an age who had known the Apocalypse and who therefore knew that anything in the world was possible, believed in this remarkable enchanted world and fell a little deeper into Cormac's bewitchment. She sat and listened and looked, and allowed herself to be seduced very fully, very completely.

Once lost, she was lost indeed. There was no thought of Flynn left in her mind, for Cormac was already spinning about her an old, old enchantment. There was absolutely no thought of Muldooney with his soft fat body and the obscene things he had done to her.

Cormac's hands on her body felt like nothing she had ever imagined; when he drew her hands down between his thighs so that she felt the strong dark tangle of hair and the warm hard arousal of his body, she did not think—I am betraying Flynn— for she had no memory of Flynn left. She pulled Cormac closer, exploring him, cupping him between her hands, trembling with pleasure when the warm silky seed began to spill on to her hands. There was nothing left in the world but this warm firelit room and this lithe lean being who was sending her body spinning into such delight that she thought she would surely faint.

He laid her on the floor, the soft skin rugs beneath her, and lowered himself on to her so that she felt his gentle weight, and smelt again the dark golden wolf scent. As he entered her, smoothly and strongly and yet somehow gently, she cried out, and there was a dark sweet flood of joy that came spinning outwards until it engulfed her entire body. She did not see Cormac's sideways glance at her, and she did not feel the satisfaction that coursed through his mind. She thought only: I am being loved by a wolf! And the pleasure soared.

Dawn was streaking the skies when he at last carried her up to his bedchamber and laid her on the great soft bed. He sent for warm wine and poured it for her, and drank with her, sharing the wine chalice, smiling at her, his eyes unfathomable, his mouth tender.

And I loved it all, she thought, stretching now, watching the sun travel slowly across the floor. At her side, Cormac slept still, sprawled with that peculiar grace, dark hair falling across his eyes. Joanna turned in the bed and watched him, and there was no memory left of another young man who had lain at her side, and who had dark hair that fell untidily across his brow, and who had loved her certainly as strongly and as passionately as Cormac.

* * *

A THOUGHT, ONCE voiced aloud, sometimes makes you realise with a shock that the thought has been there for a long time.

When Cormac said, "Come with me to Tara," Joanna stopped short in the middle of eating her breakfast, and thought: he has planned this. He has intended all along to wage war on the usurper, Eochaid Bres, and on Eochaid's mother. He has known all along he will do it, and he has known since last night that he will take me with him.

"I have known for longer than that, Human Child," said Cormac. "I have known ever since I was cast out of Tara, that I could only be released from Scáthach by a human. I have been waiting for you."

Joanna stared at him, round-eyed, and he smiled and reached for her hand in the gesture that was becoming familiar.

"Scáthach is not a prison with bars and locks," said Cormac. "For were you not able to turn the handle and walk in?

"It is a prison of enchantment. For when I was driven from Tara, the sorcerers wove the spell that would keep me here." He smiled at her. "But my people believe in the strength of pure-bred humans," he said, "and I have always known that it would be a human who would release me." He made a quick gesture with one hand. "Legend says it was a pure-bred human—Dierdriu of the Nightcloak—who was Tara's first High Queen. And although the High Throne must never be occupied by a human, we know that it is the humans who are the Kingmakers." He leaned closer. "It is only with your help that I shall break out of Scáthach, and it is only with your help that I shall regain Tara, Joanna."

A Kingmaker. A pure-bred human. Joanna thought: it all sounds too far-fetched. But she could not but be stirred by it all.

She could not but respond to him.

"Help me," said Cormac softly, his skin warm against hers. "Come to Tara with me."

"To—wage war?"

"Yes. On Eochaid Bres and his Councillors. On Bricriu of the Poison Tongue, and on Eochaid's mother. I cannot let them give Tara into the power of the Erl-King, Joanna. I dare not. Ireland would run with blood, and the skies would be for ever dark." His eyes were glowing with unnatural life now, and Joanna could not look away. "Come with me, Joanna. Ride at my side, at the head of my armies. Be with me when we turn back the Dark Magic. Help me to defeat them all." His eyes held hers. "Well?"

Joanna thought, confusedly, I do not trust him. Do I? But I do not think I can deny him. She said, a little breathlessly, "Would it work? Could you walk from here?"

"If you were with me I could."

"Your exile would be ended?"

"Yes."

"Then," said Joanna, "then I will do it."

"You will come with me?"

"Yes."

"It will be dangerous."

"Yes."

"You will not mind?"

"Yes," said Joanna. "Yes, I shall mind."

"Remarkable child." He released her hand. "Very well, then. But you must leave me now. You must leave me, for I am going down into the depths of Scáthach to send out the Mindsong."

"To your—your supporters?"

"To the Wolves," said Cormac, and smiled. "And if the Wolves answer my call, then I shall know that my exile is over. I shall know that you have broken the enchantment that held me here, Joanna."

IN THE BRIGHT morning, the forest was a very different place indeed. Joanna walked delightedly across the narrow bridge and skirted the trees.

There was delight everywhere.

Because I am happy? Because of what happened last night? I don't love him, thought Joanna, seating herself against a massive oak and leaning her head back. At least, I don't think I do. But I think I must follow him. I think I must ride at his side, as he has asked me to, and release him from the years of exile. And I think I must stay with him until he regains his kingdom. I suppose I ought to be afraid, thought Joanna, not in the least afraid at all. I certainly ought to worry about returning to Tugaim.

But if, when he awakes, he finds himself still in possession of that rose. . . ? I believe I should be for ever homesick for this place, she thought. Have I then truly fallen asleep and dreamed I have gone to Paradise? And if so, how shall I bear it when I do wake up?

I have fallen through a chink in Time, a half-open door, but I feel as if I was never meant to be anywhere else.

She leaned back lazily, watching the branches high above her. I could stay here for ever, thought Joanna sleepily, and frowned, because there was some very good reason why she should not stay here, and there was some very good reason why she should not want to stay here. Something she had left behind? Someone she had left behind? Her family? But they would not miss her. They would make a grand show of being grief-stricken at her disappearance; her father would certainly turn all of Tugaim upside-down to find her, but he would not really mind.

Muldooney would not mind either, although he would be annoyed because he would be made to appear silly. Joanna smiled, because the thought of Muldooney, flabby obscene person, being made to look silly was rather pleasant. But he would not miss her.

Wasn't there someone else ... Joanna frowned, because there was certainly someone on the edges of her vision, someone she ought to remember more strongly than the rest of them. Someone who ought to mean rather a lot to her.

It was no use. The face, the person, the memory had slithered from her grasp.

And probably I dreamt it, thought Joanna, blinking sleepily in the warm sunlight, falling a little deeper into enchantment. Yes, for sure it had been a dream.

She did not know that she was indeed more than halfway to being bewitched, or that she was caught in a gentle strong magic spun by her wolf-lover from the moment she had entered Scáthach.

But Cormac, with the inherited power of the Samhailt running through his veins, had been able to reach into Joanna's mind, far beyond the ancient code that bound those who possessed the Mindsong. It was utterly and absolutely forbidden, of course, for it was decreed that those who had the art must never overlook the deepest thoughts of another without their consent, and until now, Cormac had used the Samhailt honourably and carefully.

But the years inside Scáthach had wearied him; he ached for Tara, and he knew a great sense of fear when he thought of Eochaid Bres being manipulated by the greedy unscrupulous men of the Court. The human child, Joanna, must be bound to him utterly and for as long as it took him to regain Tara, and for that time there could be no divided loyalties. And so he had taken her hand and he had reached into her mind, and he had seen the image of Flynn that Joanna carried with her. There had been a surprising twinge of jealousy as well: she is mine! he had thought fiercely, and then he had summoned an old, old enchantment that would blur Joanna's memories of Flynn. Joanna must belong to him completely. The belief that the humans were the Kingmakers was bred in him, and the *sidh* with their unearthly chill music had long lain in wait on the edges of the Time Curtain. They had brought him Joanna, and she would ride at the head of the Wolves with him.

IT SEEMED TO Joanna, forgetful of her own world, certainly forgetful now of Flynn, that the forest was coming alive. There was an alertness in the air, a listening. A sense of something powerful and commanding and seductive. A beckoning.

Joanna thought: of course, it is the Mindsong, the Samhailt. He is sending out the summons to his half-brothers. He is calling up the Wolves of Tara.

And if the Wolves obey, then he will know that the years of his exile are nearing an end.

The forest thickened and thrummed with the feeling, and Joanna felt herself being borne forwards. "For," she said afterwards, "although it did not call to me, although I was Cormac's, body and soul, by then, and he did not need to use his sorcery on me, still I was drawn along by it."

It was like being swept into a whirlpool, only that you were not afraid, and it was like being blown forward by a huge wind, only that the wind was warm and infinitely sweet, and there was a tingling excitement and an anticipation in it.

A beckoning. The Mindsong. Cormac Starrog's Wolfsong.

She paused at the edge of the forest, unsure of whether she should go back across the ravine, not wanting to intrude. For, said Joanna to herself, I must not be a nuisance to him.

As she came into the open, she saw the Wolves, Cormac's creatures, streaming down the hillside and across the valley. He

has done it, thought Joanna, and knew a swift exultant pride.
He has summoned the Wolves, and he has broken the enchantment, and he will ride upon Tara. And mingled in with all of
this, was the singular feeling of vicarious triumph. She wanted
to say: See? See how powerful and remarkable is the man who
owns me? She did not say it, because there was no one to say
it to, and because a tiny part of her was still not quite under
the enchantment. Nobody owns me, the old Joanna would have
said. I am no one's.

She stayed where she was, watching the Wolves pouring
down into Scáthach, thinking they were swift and cruel and
wild, but thinking they were darkly beautiful as well.

And then, because there was no point in day-dreaming, she
brushed her skirt free of bracken, and moved forward. I suppose I am rather unsuitably dressed for a war, thought Joanna,
half amused, half serious. What ought one to wear?

"THE CLOAK OF the first High Queen," said Cormac, throwing
it about Joanna's shoulders. "Dierdriu's Cloak of Nightmares."

He stood back and looked at her, and Joanna said, "Oh!"
and felt the soft light folds fall about her. "Should I? I
mean—is it allowed?" The cloak was rich and full; it ought to
have felt heavy and cumbersome and stifling, but it was like a
cobweb, like a spider's gauze. Joanna felt it brush her skin, silk
and satin smooth. "Is it allowed?" she said, huge-eyed with apprehension and delight.

"It is for humans," said Cormac. "I cannot wear it. I cannot
even touch it for very long."

But the cloak was velvet-soft and Joanna stroked it with
pleasure. "Is it magical?"

"It is thought to be. It was woven by the *sidh* from the
dreams of Dierdriu, and it is believed to possess immense
power. In case of extreme danger it will summon up the creatures of Dierdriu's nightmares."

"Oh," said Joanna, and then in quite a different voice, "Oh!"

"It is a fearsome weapon," said Cormac, watching her. "It
has only ever been used twice in the history of Tara. And there
is a rule which must not be broken: the cloak can only ever be
used once against an enemy; it may not be used more than
once against the same person. But it is my right to give it and

your right to wear it. It is a heavy responsibility and a woman's weapon."

The dreams of the first Queen of Tara . . . Joanna wondered whether she would ever dare to use it.

But the cloak gave her a feeling of confidence. It was a shield, a charm against what might lie ahead. Joanna stood before the gilded looking glass in Cormac's bedchamber and thought it was not entirely vanity to think that the cloak became her, that it made her look different. She was taller, stronger-looking. She was certainly not the waif-like creature who had fled from Muldooney and tumbled through a doorway into the Dark Forest, and crossed the narrow bridge to Scáthach. She thought that Dierdriu's cloak gave her dignity and grace; her cheekbones slanted upwards intriguingly, and her mouth was wider and redder, her hair swung about her face and shone like ebony.

"You are becoming Cruithin again," said Cormac. "Your body is remembering, even if your mind does not."

It was a curious feeling to know herself sprung from the same root as the small, finely-boned Cruithin who came and went silently about the castle, and who were now busy in the kitchens, preparing food for the journey ahead. From the courtyard, Joanna could hear the whinnying of horses, and the jingle of spurs. The Wolves roamed everywhere.

"But they will not harm you," said Cormac.

The Cruithin were to accompany them on the journey, "although we shall travel quietly," said Cormac, and Joanna caught the longing in his voice. She thought that he must be remembering how he had once ridden out with all the trappings and all the ceremony of a High King, and felt a pity for him.

"Do we go straight to Tara?" For surely Tara, the Bright Palace, the Shining Fortress must be their destination.

"No. When I ride into Tara, I must do so as the acknowledged King. I must enter with the pennants of my family fluttering in the breeze, and with the Wolves of Tara preceding me. There must be cheering and dancing, triumphant music." He turned away. "Before that happens, I must depose Eochaid Bres and Bricriu, and before that I must raise an army greater than has ever been known."

"The Wolves—"

"Yes, they will be my lieutenants. But I must have far more. I must have the people of the Mountain sorcerers from the north; I must have the Wild Panther people of Gallan who are ruled by my cousin, Cait Fian." He sent her a glance. "He is dark and strong and beautiful, but he is subtle and unprincipled, and you should trust him even less than you should trust me, Joanna. I must wake the sorcerers of the Morne Mountains who served my ancestors, for Eochaid will have his own magic, and we must be ready for him. Shall you be afraid?"

"A little," said Joanna. She pulled Dierdriu's cloak more tightly about her.

"First we shall go through the Land of Sleeping Trees," said Cormac, "where we can gather the berries which yield the slumber-inducing juice. That will be useful. And if the trees awake, some of them may join us. But the trees have slept the Enchanted Sleep for centuries now, and no one knows how to wake them. We shall leave the army camped on the edges of Muileann, for I must cross the land of the Giant Miller to get to Cait Fian and the crossing must be as inconspicuous as possible."

"The Giant Miller . . ." Joanna said. "Is he one of Bricriu's people?"

"No," said Cormac. "He is the Erl-King's servant. He has giant mill wheels and millstones and his people fear him greatly."

"He makes bread?" said Joanna uncertainly.

"No. His mill is for men," said Cormac and looked down at her. "And the men are for the Erl-King's banqueting table."

DIERDRIU'S CLOAK WAS Joanna's protection and her comfort in the days that followed. She was not exactly frightened—or not very much—because Cormac seemed to her so strong and so invincible. But the cloak still felt like a shield; it was warm and light and strong. She thought: I have the dreams of the High Queen all around me. I am wrapped in magic and enchantment, and I can summon up the most terrible beings. I have only to concentrate, and the creatures of Dierdriu's nightmares will come tumbling out.

What would they be? Did people have the same kind of dreams? Joanna, child of an age that had never known monsters and giants, had dreamed of practical, tangible horrors;

even so, there was a vein of atavism. She could just about visualise the sort of things a High Queen from the ancient past might have dreamed of, and she found the visions very terrible.

Now and again, she felt the warm sweet breath of Dierdriu all about her, and at those times she glimpsed visions that were wild and beautiful: courtiers with hawklike faces and catlike eyes, little, finely-boned, dark people who prepared scented baths and sewed satin and brocade gowns, hunting parties and feasts and the music of the *sidh*. The deep past, thought Joanna, entranced, and clutched at the visions even as they shimmered and dissolved.

The exodus from Scáthach was impressive. "But we must travel more quietly later on," said Cormac.

He rode a coal-black horse, and Joanna a white one, and the Wolves padded silently behind them, with the Cruithin bringing up the rear, laden with the packs, weapons, and other trappings of their journey. Some of them carried poles in horizontal bearer-fashion, with provisions slung from them. A few rode or drove carts pulled by sturdy shaggy ponies. Some carried the braziers, fringed canopies, and pointed tents which would make their camp. "Although we shall find caves where we can," said Cormac. "And when we reach Muileann we must leave the wolves and the Cruithin behind for a time."

The days were golden and green and the nights were blue and misty. They lit fires, and the Cruithin prepared meals, and sometimes sang in their soft Irish voices, which were unlike any Joanna had ever heard.

"Of course they are not," said Cormac. "The Cruithin speak the Old Irish, the true Irish, and everything else is a travesty." And he pulled her against him in the fireglow of the supper fires, and told her how the Cruithin had come to Ireland after the great ice sheets had melted, and how they brought wonderful and hitherto unknown implements into the barren land Ireland had then been; items of jewellery and tools for the hunters and fishermen. There had been torques of twisted gold; gorgets of sheet gold; swords and vessels and cups.

"It is the age known to men as the Bronze Age," said Cormac, "but to Ireland, it was the Golden Age."

He slid an arm about her and leaned back against the rocky hillside, and spoke of the ancient trade routes, of Tarshish and Tyre, who had traded with Ireland, and he recounted, in his soft caressing voice, the words of an ancient seer, which were believed by the first High Kings to have been written of Tara.

"Thou that art situate at the entry to the sea and carry on merchandise with many lands. Thou who has said 'I am of perfect beauty; thy borders are in the midst of the seas, thy builders have perfected thy beauty.'" He paused, and Joanna recalled that first night—"Nothing that is not beautifully perfect or perfectly beautiful can enter into Tara."

All about them the night was silent and still. A little below, the Cruithin slept by the fires they made, small dark shapes. Joanna was comforted by them.

Cormac said, "They are a remarkable race, Joanna."

"Yes." Joanna moved away from him, into the cave where they would sleep that night. It was dark and the roof was low. A wolves' lair. Someone—the Cruithin?—had arranged animal skins into a bed.

Cormac had followed her. He stood at the cave's entrance, watching as she moved about, his features slanting, his teeth gleaming.

"Tell me, Human Child—"

"Yes?" Joanna turned, because there was something in his voice she had never heard before. The slightest hint of a snarl? "Yes?" said Joanna, and felt the warmth of Dierdriu's cloak brush her skin.

Be careful Joanna . . .

"Yes?" said Joanna, rather loudly.

Cormac came closer and there was a warm musk scent rising from his skin. "Do I frighten you?" he said, and this time the snarl was a little more defined.

Joanna stood quite still. She thought: yes, you do frighten me. You frighten me and you excite me and I think I have no choice but to follow you . . . *throughout the world, my lord . . .*

But it is not the man who frightens me, because for most of the time I can think of you as a man, a human. Only then something happens, like it has happened now, and I remember you are not entirely human. I am not afraid of the man, but I think I am afraid of the wolf.

You do well to be afraid, Joanna, child of my blood . . . The cloak stirred a little, as if there had been a breath of wind from outside the cave.

Cormac came a little closer. "For most of the time I *am* human," he said. "But ahead is danger, and ahead is certainly a battle, and that excites me. It wakes the wolf—" He stood for a moment longer. Then, "Go to sleep, Joanna," he said abruptly.

"Are you—are you going out?"

He turned his head, and Joanna saw that his lips were drawn back in a snarl.

"Are you—not coming to bed?"

"No. There is another hunger I must satisfy tonight."

HE RETURNED AT dawn, moving stealthily but waking her despite it and stood watching her from the cave entrance, his eyes glittering, the wolf-look sharpening the planes of his face.

Joanna was still half asleep. She raised herself on the bed of animal skins and stared at him.

Another hunger I must satisfy . . .

He was naked and the curling pelt between his thighs and on his stomach was wet and matted with blood. His shoulders and chest were splashed with gore and there was a sleek satiated look about him . . . *Another hunger . . .*

He walked lazily to the cave opening and stood, quite unselfconsciously, urinating. From inside the cave, Joanna could smell the acrid tang of it, mingled with the barely dry blood on him. *More wolf than man. He is more wolf than man. He has killed something—oh God, let it only have been a sheep—and he has devoured whatever he has killed.*

Cormac turned then, as if he had picked up her thought, and his eyes glinted in the dawnlight. The animal scent rose from him in the confined space of the cave, and he gave a low growl and moved forward.

He was on her before she realised his intention, biting and clawing, the victim's blood still wet on his skin so that it smeared Joanna's arms and shoulders. He forced her legs apart, thrusting himself between them, and Joanna cried out in pain and fear. Cormac pinned her to the floor of the cave, and the stench of the blood was like tin in her nostrils, so that she felt her stomach lift with nausea. She pushed at him, but he seemed not to notice. His head was thrown back and as his climax approached, his thrusts became harder and more uncontrolled, and he gave a long drawn-out groan that almost, but not quite, turned into a howl.

Joanna's arm was outstretched; she felt the back of her hand brush Dierdriu's cloak, and there was the faintest crackle of something from the silky folds.

Help me . . . cried Joanna silently, and felt at once the invisible presence of someone—something?—in the cave with them. Cormac hesitated for the fraction of a second, and Joanna grasped a fold of Dierdriu's cloak more firmly.

Help me . . .

There was no question about the response now. Forks of icy light shot from the cloak, illuminating the cave, sending tingling sparks along Joanna's hand. For a moment she saw, quite clearly, the underside of the cave roof with its centuries of accreted dirt. Beneath their feet . . .

Beneath their feet, the cave floor heaved and pulsated, throwing them both off balance. There was a dreadful wet squelching, a sucking sound, and the ghost of a bubbling chuckle. The cave floor tilted, and Joanna screamed.

Thin morning light filtered in through the entrance to the cave, showing up the floor quite clearly. And where there had been a solid dry, rather warm floor, there were dozens upon dozens of huge lidless eyes, swivelling in invisible sockets, jellylike and viscous against Joanna's bare feet. She screamed again and backed into a corner shuddering uncontrollably. Her foot slipped in the wet mess breaking open one of the eyes, and at once a dreadful glutinous substance oozed out, splashing her leg. She sank ankle deep into the ruptured eye, and felt the slimy fluid on her skin.

Cormac had fallen in a huddle in the opposite corner, and through her panic, Joanna heard him snarl and whip round, one hand reaching across to her.

The broken eye sucked her a little more deeply in, and there was a throaty evil laughter again, echoing round the cave, bouncing off the walls.

All the better to see you with, my dear . . .

Joanna thought: I think I am going to die. Oh somebody help me . . .

Cormac was inching his way to her, his hands stretched out—"Hold on, my love," and Joanna, through her terror, thought: he called me "my love." He is trying to save me. The man is in the ascendant again.

The eyes were like dead fish, they were like raw liver. She

tried to crawl across them, to where Cormac stood unflinching, but the eyes held her, they swivelled and turned, clammy and mucous, pulling her into their depths.

All the better to see you with, my dear ...

Someone very close by was screaming, or was it someone inside her head ... oh God let me get free, oh God, make it go away ... help me somebody ...

Cormac had reached her now, and Joanna thought he said, "The cloak—Dierdriu's cloak—" but she could not hear properly because of the person so close to them who was screaming, and she could not think properly because of the wet sucking eyes ... In another few minutes, I shall have been swallowed by them ... oh God, *let me wake up ...*

And at once, two quite separate things happened.

The wet fishlike eyes vanished, leaving the warm dry earth floor. And there was a sudden, achingly beautiful picture of herself—or was it herself?—waking in a blue and silver room with sunlight pouring in. And then the room also vanished, and Joanna gasped and sat up in the dawnlit cave.

Cormac wiped the blood of a bitten lip from his mouth with the back of his hand and looked at Joanna without speaking.

"Has it—has it gone?" said Joanna, thinking how strange her voice sounded. But the cave was empty—yes, there were only the two of them in it now. "What was it?" said Joanna at length.

"One of the nightmares. You invoked the power of the cloak against me." A rueful smile. "I do not blame you. Forgive me, Human Child, for being what I cannot always help."

"One of Dierdriu's dreams?"

"A nightmare."

"Is that what will happen if I use the cloak again? Will that—that thing, those eyes—will they come back?"

"I don't know," said Cormac. "Dierdriu must have dreamed many dreams and many nightmares. Some of the creatures of the cloak may be twice as terrible."

"Oh," said Joanna in rather a small voice, but she thought: well, after all, it is only a nightmare. Not real. Even if it comes again, I could banish it. All I had to do was ask to wake up ... nothing so very terrible about it at all when you think.

"It was more than just a nightmare, Joanna," Cormac said. "I do not know a very great deal about the Ancient Ireland—

our bards, the *filid*, would tell you more eloquently than I ever could, but I know a little for it is every High King's birthright. I know, as my ancestors knew, of the dread sorcerers of the North."

"The Erl-King."

"And his servants. Dierdriu would have known them, for at the very beginning, the Erl-King and his minions were forever waging battle on Tara. There were many wars—oh, the *filid* could tell you tales for a year and still not have told the whole. The battles of Mag Tuired; the magical Fomoire led by the Son of Goll the One-Eyed and by the Son of Garb. The Crusade Wars of the followers of Crom Croich—the god-idol who is a being of pure gold, and who eats the living hearts of his victims and must have a hundred sacrifices on the night of Samain. And of course, the famous Battle for the Trees, which was won by neither side, but where the sorcery was so powerful that it sent the Trees into a slumber from which they will probably never awake. Dreadful battles, Joanna.

"Dierdriu would have known many of them, for the Erl-King sent out his dark servants to Tara for countless years, and it fell to Dierdriu to turn them back . . ." He paused, and his eyes were far away. "They tell, our poets and our music makers, of how she rode out at the head of her armies, her hair so long it was like a black curtain falling to her knees. She rode a black stallion, a Barbary brought from the East by the people of Tarshish, and she never went into battle without wearing the *sidh*'s Nightcloak about her shoulders."

And the man with black-fringed blue eyes was at her side . . .

"She defeated the Erl-King and his minions," said Cormac, "and they were banished to their mountain halls. But the sight of them must have been a terrible one, for it is said that the Erl-King himself rode at the head of his armies in the final battle, and it is certain that Dierdriu saw him face-to-face.

"She saw his servants as well. The Giant Miller of Muileann who grinds human bones in his mill to make bread for the Erl-King's banqueting table. And the Morrigna, the sinister and destructive trio of women who have always served the Erl-King, and who haunt battlefields. She defeated them all, but she would not have been able to forget them, Joanna. They would have lived on in her dreams. They would have become part of the Nightcloak."

It brought Dierdriu suddenly and startlingly close to think that she had been haunted by the faces of her vanquished enemies. It softened the image of the strong and mighty Queen, so that for the first time, Joanna saw Dierdriu as a real person. Someone who could be victorious, but who could suffer nightmares afterwards.

"The thing we saw tonight . . . the eyes . . ."

Cormac hesitated. "She was one of the Morrigna. The dread trio who scavenge the earth for their master. Their leader is Morrigan—that is Queen of Phantoms. She is the strongest, and she is one of the most powerful sorceresses to come out of the Dark Ireland. She is the seductress of the three; she lures her victims into a web, by presenting herself to them in the light best calculated to soothe and lull. They say she is possessed of a voracious and perverted sexual appetite and that she will have women, as well as men, in her bed. Like the Erl-King she eats human flesh and bathes in human blood, and it is said that the two of them dine in his Citadel by firelight in an immense stone banqueting hall, and that their banquet is human meat and their entertainment is to bring up from the dungeons the poor wretches they have imprisoned. They have cages and pincers and red-hot needles, and there is no torture too cruel for them, and no perversion too warped for them.

"The middle one of the trio is Macha, who is bald and ugly and who is called the Mother of Monsters. She has a great army of misshapen creatures at her command, and they will tear a man to shreds. She can call up the hags and the harpies and the crones and the banshees and she is formidable in battle for that reason.

"But it is the third one that we saw tonight, Badb, which translates as Scald-Crow. She is a shape-changer, and she is a being of many forms, which she can don at an instant, each one more terrible than the last . . . She can swallow up whole armies with her Eyes or her Mouths." He looked at Joanna. "What we saw, was Dierdriu's last memory of Scald-Crow," he said. "Dreadful.

"But pray to whatever gods you hold dear that we never have to face the Morrigna in the flesh, Joanna."

"WHO ARE YOUR gods?" said Cormac, as they rode through the waking day, the Cruithin and the Wolves padding behind them.

"There were very few," said Joanna, relaxing a little now, enjoying the warm sun on her face, liking the scents of the countryside all around them. Ahead lay the Forest of Sleeping Trees. Cormac had said she would like that. "It is very beautiful," he had said. "And it is a place for renewal."

"There was never much time for gods," said Joanna who was finding, truth to tell, the preoccupation of Cormac's people with gods a bit unusual. In Tugaim you did not think very much about gods. As her father had always said, gods did not help you a great deal when the harvest had to be gathered or the well ran dry in the drought. Gods were all very well in their place, said John Grady, but their place was in the fairytale nonsense of the Letheans. In real life you concentrated on the tasks you had to do, and there was not very much time to spare for gods. Whatever gods might be anyway.

"You see," said Joanna carefully, "there was always so much to do." And then, because this might have sounded a bit disrespectful, "For quite a long time there was so much to do," she said, and looked at Cormac to make sure he understood about this.

But he only smiled at her rather thoughtfully, and said, "Tell me," and Joanna was heartened.

"Our world was nearly destroyed," she said. "Although a great deal of our history was lost to us, we have the accounts of Devastation from those who survived it. And we know that whole cities were burned; we know that people lay dead for years beneath the ruins, rotting and breeding disease. Stories are told of lone survivors eking out existences in tunnels and in cellars. Eating the rats before the rats ate them. Surviving the Apocalypse, but living in total solitude until hunger or thirst or disease killed them anyway. There were people who left diaries," said Joanna, her face solemn, her eyes far away. "We have them preserved in the People's Museum in one of our towns. And they tell a truly terrible tale, Cormac. It is something that we have never been able to forget. So much suffering."

"But the people who survived the Devastation," said Cormac, "were they not strong? Warriors?"

"I don't think," said Joanna, "that they were, really. I think they were just people who survived, because they were lucky or because they fought a little harder to stay alive. I don't think it was anything more than that." And she smiled at Cormac, who was probably visualising great heroes and warriors.

Cormac said softly, "And even if the people who lived in your world before Devastation had gods, those gods did not help them so very much."

But Joanna did not think that the Letheans had had any sort of god. "Theirs was rather a—a greedy world, I think," she said. "They did not have very much religion. And even if they did, even if they had a god or gods, those gods were not able to hold back the Apocalypse." She frowned. "Perhaps that is unfair." And thought that perhaps it was. "There is a belief that our ancestors summoned the Apocalypse and then failed to control it. Perhaps God—their God—allowed Devastation as a punishment."

"Gods frequently punish," said Cormac. "And never quite as one would expect. Had those ancestors—the ones who burned the world—had they forms of worship at all?"

Joanna hesitated, not because she did not know how to answer, but because just for a moment she had been back in Tugaim, back in the rather small, rather badly lit People's Museum, turning over the brittle mildewed pages of the famous diaries, left by the survivors, jealously and rigorously guarded. "For posterity," had said the men and women who ran the Museum. "So that we shall not ever forget," but Joanna thought that people would never forget Devastation.

"The stories vary so much," she said to Cormac. "We know that the Letheans had gods, for the legends tell of them. The diaries mention them. We know that there was a book which was called the Bible, and portions of that have survived. It is quite strange that that survived when so much else was lost. But the parts that we had, did not tell us a great deal, because it was all a jumble of stories and people, and is, was, all so—so unconnected, that no one ever made any sense of it. I think it was old before the Letheans' time anyway."

"Tell me about the Letheans," said Cormac, and Joanna looked quickly at him, in case he was only being polite. But he laughed, and said, "I am never polite and rarely diplomatic."

He took her hand. "I want to know about you," he said. "I want to know about your world, Joanna," and Joanna smiled rather warily, because when he said her name like that, when he turned his voice into a caress—and really, it was truly remarkable the caress that Cormac could get into his voice when he wanted to—the delight ran all over her, and she had to look away in case her expression gave her away.

"Their worship—if that is what it was—was not at all self-less," said Joanna. "The fragments of their Bible warn against the adoration of graven images—that is, carved reproductions. But the legends all suggest that the Letheans did worship those things. There were objects, possessions, they must all have. It is there, in the diaries. How they must always own better machines than their neighbours; how they must never be seen to own inferior ones. They travelled about in machines, you see," explained Joanna. "The secret has been lost, but we know that they never walked, or not very often.

"And there are descriptions of the houses that were destroyed by the Apocalypse. Rich furnishings and complicated machinery for cooking. The diaries sometimes refer to them, and describe what was lost. They liked their comfort, the Letheans," said Joanna, and then hoped she had not sounded bitter.

"Had they festivals?" asked Cormac. "Feastings?" and Joanna remembered the rather scrappy drawings preserved with the diaries.

"There were huge halls," she said, "vast high-ceilinged buildings with rows of seats and a raised platform at one end. But I do not know the purpose of the halls, although they could seat hundreds of people.

"And there are references to centres where food could be bought. They flocked there, the entire family, and bought the food, in greater quantities than you or I could imagine. After I read about those centres in the diaries," said Joanna, "I used to dream about it. And it was a—rather a disturbing dream. Great brightly lit places with rows upon rows of food; meat and fruit—oh, everything! Bread already baked—think of it. You just picked it up and carried it away. In the dream it is always very noisy—the Letheans were a noisy people I think. And the light so glaring. In the dream, the Letheans are running up and down, rather like squirrels, gathering up all they want—gathering up more than they need—and then taking it to their homes. It's rather an unpleasant dream," said Joanna. "There is always such a greed and such a complacency in the faces. And there is surely laziness as well, for all they have to do to be fed is stretch out a hand and take what they want."

"Greed and complacency are the most self-destructive of all the faults," said Cormac. He smiled at her. "Perhaps their god allowed the Apocalypse to teach them to be less selfish."

"It was a hard lesson," said Joanna.

THE FOREST OF Sleeping Trees was as beautiful as Cormac had said. Joanna, rested now, refreshed by a breakfast of lake fish and wild honey prepared and served by the Cruithin, thought she had never seen anywhere so perfect in her life.

"Yes, it is one of our hallowed places," said Cormac.

The Sleeping Trees grew close together—"for company," said Cormac quite seriously—and the great velvet-skinned berries hung down in clusters.

"Shall we be able to ride in between the trees?" asked Joanna, lowering her voice to a whisper.

"Yes. There is a path. But we must not stray far from it. To be lost here would be to be lost forever. You would sink deeper and deeper into slumber until you could not be roused."

There was a soft golden light among the trees, and Joanna could not decide where it came from. She thought it came from the sky, but that did not seem quite right, and then she thought it came from the trees themselves. "But I never really discovered," she said afterwards.

The light moved with them, like reflected waterlight rippling against old stone walls. There was a rich warm scent, and a faint drowsy hum.

They gathered the berries cautiously, reaching up to the laden branches, bringing down armfuls. "Be careful not to break open any of the berries," said Cormac, "for we should be overcome at once."

But Joanna could not resist burying her head in the velvet-skinned fruit, feeling the warm dark folds of sleep reach out for her, so that she backed away at once, and shook her head to clear it.

None of them wanted to leave the calm forest. "Although we shall come back," said Cormac.

"Shall we?"

"When the battle is won," he said. "This is a place for renewal. My people have always come here after a war has been fought. It cleanses the mind of horrors, and sometimes it eases the pain of wounds. But its air is strong, and one has to take only small draughts of it. But we will come back, Joanna; we will lie beneath the trees, and sleep and wake, and be whole again.

> " 'Unknown is wailing and treachery
> In the familiar cultivated land:
> There is nothing rough or harsh
> But sweet music striking in the ear.
>
> Without grief, without sorrow, without death.
> Without sickness, without debility.' "

He stood looking down at her, his eyes gentle, and Joanna thought: how could I ever have been afraid of him?

"You could and you will again, Human Child, for I cannot be other than I am. It is only here, where the air is filled with peace and with enchanted slumber that you trust me completely. But we are beginning to understand one another, I think." He gave himself a shake and turned to the waiting Cruithin. "Have we the berries?"

"Yes Sire," said one of them. "Purple berries for the Deep Slumber, red berries for the Slumber of Life, and golden berries for the Slumber of Love."

Cormac said, "I see black berries."

"Yes Sire. The berries of Death."

"Then gather them also."

The man regarded him. "That would be against the ancient code of Your Majesty's ancestors," he said, and Joanna noticed that although he spoke quite politely, there was no trace of subservience in his voice.

"Do it," said Cormac rather sharply.

"No," said the man, still quite respectfully. "For if you use the Death Berries without the permission or knowledge of the Sleeping Trees, you violate the code of all the High Kings, ever since Dierdriu . . . Sire," he added as an apparent afterthought. "Your Majesty knows that, of course." Joanna thought he did not say any of this as if he was threatening Cormac, or even as if he was annoyed with him, or worried; he said it as one stating a plain fact. "Your Majesty has surely not forgotten the Law," said the man, whose name was Gormgall.

Cormac frowned and his eyes glinted. "Remind me of it," he said, the hint of a growl in his tone.

"Certainly Sire," said Gormgall, who had served Cormac and Cormac's father, and who was not in the least bit intimidated by black frowns and growls. "But Your Majesty knows it well enough." He paused, and then said, in a sing-song voice, "No enchantment, magic, sorcery, spell, or beguilement of any kind whatsoever, may be used in times of war, battle, or peace, in any manner whatsoever without the full knowledge and consent of the one who created the enchantment, magic, sorcery, spell, or beguilement." He eyed Cormac. "But Your Majesty remembers very well the oath he took when ascending to the High Throne." He put his head on one side and waited, and Joanna thought he was treating Cormac a bit like a wayward child.

Cormac said, "You are right, of course," and frowned again, because no one, and certainly no one who has once occupied a throne, likes to be corrected.

"We may take the berries of Sleep," said Gormgall. "They will not keep for very long, of course, but we can take them because they are not really magical. They will put guards and sentries to sleep, but they are no more than a kind of herb. But the berries of Death are a powerful magic, and unless Your Majesty likes to consider waking one of the Sleeping Trees to ask permission—"

"Don't be ridiculous," said Cormac crossly. "The Trees have not been woken for centuries. Nobody knows how to."

"No," said Gormgall gravely. "And I cannot think of anything more annoying than to be woken up to ask if an enchantment could be borrowed for a week or so. The tree you chose would very likely not be best pleased, Sire, even if you were to choose a holly, who are reputed to be particularly good natured."

There was a short silence. "Gormgall," said Cormac ominously, "are you being impudent?"

"Your Majesty!" said Gormgall, shocked. "I wouldn't dare."

"Yes, of course you would," said Cormac. "Go away before I lose patience with you." But he grinned as he said it, and

Joanna thought that he and Gormgall understood each other very well, and in fact rather liked one another.

"He's an impudent old devil," said Cormac, as they rode on through the trees. "He's served my family for a long time, and so he thinks it gives him special privileges. I don't pay him any attention of course, although he likes to think I do."

"The King pays a great deal of attention to me really," said Gormgall to Joanna that night as they made camp. "Only it doesn't do for him to admit to it, of course." Joanna was helping to ladle stew into the wooden pannikins. "That's not for you to do," Gormgall said, shocked. "You're the King's Lady. His Majesty won't be best pleased if he comes back and finds you helping with the work."

But Joanna had not been used to being waited on. "And anyway," she said, "His Majesty is helping."

"Hunting," said one of them. "Night hunting."

"Which he enjoys," said another.

"But it's contributing," said Joanna. "It's providing food for us all. And anyway, I'm enjoying helping to cook supper. What is this, Gormgall?"

"Venison," said Gormgall, in the sort of tone that might just as easily have said poison. "Shot by His Majesty earlier today."

"And none the worse for it," put in somebody. "I said we'd be glad we'd carried the carcass with us."

Several people said rather crossly that it was all very well to say so if you hadn't had the carrying.

"And it ought to have been hung for at least a week," said Gormgall.

But the simmering cauldron of stew smelt and tasted very good. Joanna had never eaten venison before. "There are no such animals in my world," she explained.

"And won't be in this one if we hunt them in the wrong season," said Gormgall, and several people nodded agreement.

"When His Majesty deposes Eochaid Bres," said Gormgall, "he'll have to restrict the hunting a bit. Not but what this isn't a very good stew, but it's not the season to be shooting deer. Deer should be let to breed for at least three Beltanes. Anyone knows that."

"I suppose," said Joanna, eating her portion with enjoyment and rather liking talking to Gormgall and his people, "that His

Majesty does know it really. But I suppose he thought we ought to eat fresh meat where we could. Until he gets us some more." And glanced over her shoulder into the darkening forest, and hoped that Cormac would get them some more, and hoped as well that he would return before dawn.

"There's the thing," said Gormgall. "Although you won't tell him that it isn't the season to kill deer. You can't tell him anything, any more than you could tell his father. They're all the same, the Wolfline. They can be led but not driven. It comes of not being quite human and not quite beast. That isn't to say we aren't all the King's men, body and soul, my lady."

"Of course not," said Joanna.

"We'd follow him anywhere," said Gormgall, and several heads nodded firmly. "Well, we followed him into exile, as you know, and my word, that hasn't been all bull-feasts and Beltane revelries."

"More like cattle-raids and *ceilidh*."

"But," said Gormgall, "he's the High King, and we're his people. We'll follow wherever he takes us."

"We wouldn't follow Eochaid Bres," said one of them—Joanna thought he was called Dubhgall. "Not in a pig's eye we wouldn't."

"I should think not indeed. As for the Queen Mother, well, if she's any more morals than the *sidh* I've never heard tell of them," said Gormgall, and the heads wagged in agreement. Someone lit a clay pipe and the woodsy scent of it drifted pleasantly across the clearing.

"Eochaid Bres is stupid," said Dubhgall. "He's not wicked, but he's very stupid."

"Conceited," said another.

"Obstinate," said a third.

"He'd lead us straight into the clutches of the Giant Miller *and* the Erl-King," said Dubhgall and was promptly shushed.

"It's bad luck to even speak the name," said the one who had said Eochaid Bres was obstinate.

"It's very nearly death to speak it after dark," said the one who had called him conceited.

Dubhgall begged pardon.

Joanna said, "You are all very loyal to—to the King."

"Of course," said Gormgall. "We've served the High Kings down the ages. Our ancestors swore allegiance to the first

Lady of Tara—Dierdriu of the Nightcloak—and vowed to serve her descendants. A little more stew, my lady?"

"Thank you," said Joanna, passing her dish. "This is very good, Gormgall."

"It would have been even better if the deer had been hung for a week," said Dubhgall, but was not paid any attention.

"Ever since the Oath of Allegiance was taken to Dierdriu, we have always served the High Kings," said Gormgall.

"The true line, of course," put in another.

"Well yes," said Gormgall. "That's what I meant. Her ladyship knows that. You knew that, my lady, didn't you? Traitors and usurpers find no support here. Not if Dierdriu herself were to come back, as our people believe she will one day and command us, not even then would you find us bending the knee to Eochaid Bres or Bricriu the Fox."

"Especially not to Bricriu the Fox," said Dubhgall.

"There's a belief—" began Gormgall, and stopped, and Joanna leaned forward, and said, "Yes?" and Gormgall continued, "Well, I daresay you won't wish to hear of it," and Joanna said, "But I love legends and stories." And then, as Gormgall still looked doubtful, she said, "So much was lost when my ancestors fought the Apocalypse, my own world is very short of folklore."

Dubhgall, who liked battles, particularly if somebody else had the fighting of them, wanted to hear about the Apocalypse, but Joanna said it would keep.

"For another night," she said. "For now, won't you tell me about Dierdriu?"

"It is part of our folklore," explained Gormgall, almost as if he thought he ought to apologise. "Our ballad-makers and our storytellers, the *filid*, sing about it, well, I daresay your ladyship has heard them while we've been travelling."

"A little," said Joanna. "They were singing only the other night, I think."

"Ah, that's the younger ones," said Gormgall tolerantly. "They don't think, you see. They're a bit rowdy. They see all of this as a grand adventure more than anything, well it is an adventure of course," he added. "To be sure it is. But they see the glory and the excitement and forget the dangers and the discomforts. Also, of course, they're perhaps in the habit of taking a drop too much of His Majesty's wine now and again, well aren't we all—"

"I'm not," said Dubhgall rather crossly. "Not when I'm in the train of His High Majesty, I'm not. But even if I was, I wouldn't make such a noise. I know what's right and it's not right to hold a *ceilidh* in the middle of a battle march. Anyone at all might have heard us, and then where should we be, I wonder. This is a serious undertaking," he said looking very serious indeed. "And there's a great deal too much flightiness about some of the younger ones. I wonder His Majesty allows it."

"I think he enjoyed the singing," said Joanna, who had enjoyed it herself, but was trying to be polite. "He was telling me about some of your legends, and about the first Cruithin."

"Well," said Dubhgall, "I take that very kindly of him, for we've served the High Kings long and well. But there's no call for the younger element to go drawing attention to themselves. Time and to spare for singing. Gormgall, if you're going to tell the story of Dierdriu, I wish you'd get on with it. That's always supposing her ladyship really wants to hear it, and isn't just being polite."

"I do want to hear it," said Joanna. "I'm not just being polite. Gormgall, do tell me."

Gormgall leaned forward, his rather lined face lit up by the camp fire. "My people tell of it," he said, and quite suddenly, as if some kind of signal had been given, everyone fell silent. Dubhgall clamped his teeth down on his pipe, and sat cross-legged.

"It was when the Great Queen lay dying," said Gormgall, "with the Court all about her and the countryside hushed. Everyone was weeping, for she had been greatly loved and greatly respected, and she had led her people through many wars and turned back many enemies.

"She is said to have spoken to them before they took her to the Plain of Delight, which is where all the High Kings and Queens must go to die. She told them not to weep for her, but to turn their minds to the future and the one who should succeed her. 'For,' she said, 'I am on the edge of the greatest journey anyone ever makes, and to enter eternity is surely the finest adventure we can have.'

"And the courtiers wept afresh, but they tried to hide it from her.

"But Dierdriu knew her people and she sought to comfort them.

" 'I shall be with you again,' she said. 'You must look for me in the good things of life. In the things you love. I shall be there. In the woodsmoke of a twilight fire, and in the moonlight over the Morne Mountains, and in the golden sunrise over Tara. You will hear me laughing in the Purple Hour, for that is the most magical time of all. I shall be in the wine you drink, and when you hold feasts, I shall be among you still. You will never quite lose me.'

"They say she fell into a great weakness then, for she was sinking deeper into death.

"But at the end, as her litter was carried to the Plain of Delight, she opened her eyes and spoke again, and her voice was young and strong once more, so that the older courtiers heard the voice of the warrior queen who had led them through so many battles and emerged victorious. They saw her again as the beautiful, rather wild Dierdriu who had ridden out at the head of Tara's armies.

"Her words are with us still, for the ballad-makers wove them into their songs, and the Lay of Dierdriu has ever been sung at our feasts.

" 'If the Darkness of the Necromancers should ever dim the Bright Palace again,' she said, 'you may be sure I shall return in reality, for eternity is a place from which one may sometimes return.

" 'I have many lives yet to live, but Tara will always be the place to which I shall return, and I shall be forever homesick.

" 'Farewell. Do not mourn me, but remember me.'

"They did mourn," said Gormgall, staring ahead of himself thoughtfully, "it is written that they mourned for a year and a day, and even then, they would gather round their fires and tell tales of her bravery and her beauty. And they never ceased to hope for her return, just as my people today hope for it." He fell silent, and all about them the Cruithin were silent also. At length, Joanna summoned up her courage to speak, for although she did not want to break the silence, she knew they were waiting for her to do so.

She said, very softly, "It is a very moving story, Gormgall.

And is it still the belief among your people that the Queen will return?"

"It is something of a sacred belief, my lady," said Gormgall. "We have kept her memory alive for centuries, and we have always obeyed the laws she made when she ruled us. It is told that she will return in Tara's time of greatest need, and it is told, as well, that she will not come as a great and mighty Queen, but that she will be recognised by her own people."

I shall return ... I shall be forever homesick until I come back ...

"I daresay," said Gormgall knocking out his pipe against the side of the iron stew pot, "I daresay there are similar beliefs amongst your own people?"

Joanna said slowly, "My ancestors once revered a man who lived among them for a time, and who taught a way of life which was to be followed by thousands. And yes, his return was always promised."

"Did he come back?" one of them, not Gormgall, asked.

"Well," said Joanna, "I don't think he did. Or if he did, the story of his return was lost, along with so much else. My ancestors burned the world and called up the beast Apocalypse, and so much was lost to us."

"Perhaps he did return," said Gormgall, "but perhaps it was too late."

"Yes. Or perhaps," said Joanna, "my ancestors had to be given a punishment for their greed and their selfishness." She looked up and smiled. "But it was a harsh punishment!"

"Even worlds must sometimes die," said Gormgall. "Your own world will do one day. Do you not miss it, my lady?"

"No," said Joanna and smiled. "No, for I never felt I had a place there."

This is my place ...

"Do you not miss your people?" asked another.

"No," said Joanna. "No, I cannot think of anyone I miss." She smiled again. "And for sure there is no one who is missing me."

CHAPTER SIX

FLYNN THOUGHT THAT without Amairgen and Portan he would have been very nearly out of his mind with worry for Joanna. He thought he would certainly have despaired.

"Never despair," said Amairgen sharply. "To do so is a very old and very serious sin."

Flynn had stared, for "sin" was not a word often heard. He thought it was a Lethe word, although he could not be sure.

"It was a word old before the Letheans," said Amairgen. "The Letheans were not very aware of the severity of sinning, Flynn; they knew about the great teacher and leader who had lived among them—oh, centuries earlier, perhaps more than two thousand years—but they had grown arrogant. They knew about the laws that leader had left them, but save for a few isolated people, they did not pay them any attention. They had their own laws, and they were far more comfortable than any left by a half-forgotten foreigner."

Flynn said, "You know so much. You have so many memories of the past."

"My people were preservers," said Amairgen. "They revered the past and they were afraid for the future. They kept what they could." He regarded Flynn. "Even so, what they did keep was little enough, although I am grateful for what there is. But I do know that in the days when religious sects still existed, when men and women voluntarily forswore the world and its comforts to follow the ruling of that long-ago leader, then to despair was considered the gravest sin there was. They called it *accidie*, and they taught that it was the ultimate giving up of hope; the rejection of a higher power. Once you have despaired, Flynn, truly despaired, you are lost indeed." He paused, and Flynn had a sudden, startlingly clear image of a great aching void; a nothingness so complete that his mind reeled. That, then, was true despair, the real thing. A belief that there was nothing, ever again, anywhere.

"Yes," said Amairgen softly, "yes, you understand. Never give up, Flynn, for there will always be something." He glanced to where Portan was curled up, listening intently. "I think Portan understands me very well," he said.

"Yes. I might have despaired when I was in that place. I think I nearly did despair when my father took me there and left me, and when I thought I should never see the outside world again. But there was something—I do not know what it was, but something that said: there is more. There will be more. You will see. And so there was," said Portan simply. "You came."

They had descended the hill of the Gealtacht easily enough, and a cold dawn was glistening the sky as they saw the scattered farm buildings of Tugaim ahead of them.

Flynn had wanted to go straight to the Glowing Lands, but Amairgen had said it would be better to wait until nightfall. "We should be seen," he said. "And the task of breaking through the Time Curtain may require all our concentration, Flynn. Also, there is Portan to be considered."

Standing in the thin light, both men felt the shiver that went through Portan, but when they looked at her, she smiled, and said, "Yes, I am afraid, but also I am so very happy. To see the world again . . ." And then was silent, but Flynn thought it was the silence of deep contentment, and he thought that she was absorbing the scents and the sights and the sounds of the countryside. He thought that she was so intensely happy that she could hardly bear to speak.

Amairgen said, "As well as that, we are both tired and dispirited. The things we saw inside the Gealtacht . . . We should all rest before any attempt is made to go through the Time Curtain."

"Yes." Flynn tried not to sound ungracious, and knew that Amairgen was right. "Yes, of course. Will you both come to the farmhouse?" he said, and felt again the shiver of apprehension go through Portan. He smiled at her and said, "You may trust my father with your life and more, my dear," and Portan looked at him gratefully.

"But even so," she said, "it would be better for no one to know that you have taken a Mutant from the Gealtacht."

"People are not always kind," said Amairgen rather brusquely, "and you are right. But there is no reason why we could not shelter in an outbuilding of some kind. Flynn?"

"The Dutch barn?" said Flynn. "One of the original buildings, watertight and snug." He grinned. "We are rather proud of the Dutch barn, my father and I. Lethe arrogance. But you would be quite comfortable there, and I could bring out food and blankets."

"Admirable," said Amairgen when Flynn showed him the barn. "We will stay here, Portan and I. Will you come back at the Purple Hour?"

Flynn smiled at the words. "My father's own expression," he said. "I had not thought to hear anyone else ever use it."

"It is a very old term," said Amairgen. "Another of the things my family salvaged, perhaps. But it was always thought to be a very magical time of day. If we are to break through the Time Curtain, then we may as well use all the magic we can." He said this in a matter-of-fact way, and Flynn and Portan both stared.

At length, Flynn said, "Do you—I beg your pardon—but do you believe in such things?"

Amairgen had been surveying the inside of the Dutch barn. "This will do excellently," he said. "How very fortunate you are to still possess such things, Flynn. And the farmhouse itself is pre-Apocalypse, I think? Yes, of course it is. No one today builds half so well. As for magic . . ." He broke off and the thin, sweet, rather austere smile lifted the corners of his lips. "People did once believe," he said. And then, looking to where Portan was quietly listening, "Portan believes," he said.

"Do you?" Flynn was at once interested, because no one—or no one he had ever met—really did believe. And then he remembered that Joanna had believed; Joanna had listened to the legends and drunk in the enchanted creatures of myths, and she had believed, wholly and for ever. He put the thought from him, because he did not think he dared remember Joanna, at least not until they were setting out to bring her back.

Portan said cautiously, "Inside the Gealtacht there were a few of us—"

"Yes?"

"We had brought with us some of the old stories," said Portan. "I think that not all of us had been taken to the Gealtacht at birth, and so we could share memories of early childhood." She smiled at them. "The best time of all, early childhood," said Portan. "Fairy tales and legends. And you believe in it all then, quite unquestioningly."

Flynn said, "But surely the law says—"

"That Mutants must be taken to the Gealtacht at birth? Oh yes," said Portan, "but people do not always obey laws. And there were several of us whose mothers tried to cheat the law. We had been hidden away until the Elders discovered us."

"Did that happen to you?"

"Yes," said Portan softly. "Yes, that happened to me, and then my father, who was not brave, took me to the Gealtacht by night—perhaps because he could not bear to perform such an act by daylight—and I was left there. But you have brought me out now," she said, "and although I do not quite believe in magic any longer, I think I do not quite disbelieve." She looked at Amairgen. "I should like to know those old legends to be true."

Amairgen said, "You see, Flynn? People do still believe, if only a very little." He dropped a hand lightly on Flynn's shoulder. "If you could sleep for a few hours it would help you," he said. "Portan and I will be here. And a few hours could not make very much difference now."

But Flynn could not sleep. He was achingly tired, but he was also restless and strung up.

"Try to work," said Michael, who had been anxiously watching for their return, and who was secretly horrified at the sight of Flynn, white-faced, dark-eyed with fatigue, but also with a kind of wild determination about him. "You could gather up some of the apples," said Michael. "Flynn, you have to be strong for what is ahead of you." He said no more, but prepared a huge platter of eggs and ham and newly baked bread, which he persuaded Flynn to eat before taking a second platter out to the Dutch barn.

"I will not intrude," he said before he went, "for I can

imagine—just a very little—of how it must be for that poor creature you have brought out. This is a terrible world, Flynn."

"She will be very wary of you," said Flynn, but Michael only smiled and balanced the tray carefully as he crossed the yard to the Dutch barn.

"But I *was* shocked," he said afterwards to Flynn. "Truly we live in a dreadful world. Dear God, what did our ancestors do to mankind?"

But Portan, still cautious and certainly unsure of the world, had been able to meet Flynn's father calmly, and to thank him for the food. Michael had stayed with them for a little while, discussing what might lie ahead of them, wondering could they make any kind of contingency plans.

"But I do not think you can," he said. "For there is no knowing what you will meet." And he picked up the tray and the plates, and stood looking at them for a long moment. "I wish I could come with you, Amairgen. You know that I would do so if you had not forbidden it."

"Not forbidden," said Amairgen. "It is only that I do not think it would be prudent."

"Well," said Michael, "I expect you are right. And I shall be here waiting when you return. You will be constantly in my thoughts." He went quietly out and Portan, who was curled into a corner, said, "He is very like Flynn."

"Yes." Amairgen thought that there was a strange affinity and a strong similarity among all of the Keepers in fact. He had noticed it more than once. It was not always there to begin with, but it developed over the years. He wondered whether it was strength, and then he wondered whether it was courage. Or was it just that the sharing of a Secret so immense and so awful brought out the qualities necessary?

Portan said, "He is strong, Flynn's father," and Amairgen looked up, startled, because although he had had no indication that Portan might possess the Samhailt, she had caught his thoughts exactly.

"Yes, I believe he is."

"But he has not Flynn's—I am not sure of the word. Recklessness?"

"Flynn would take on the world," said Amairgen, and Portan smiled.

"I am so grateful to him," she said. "And to you. Inside that place—I do not think I should have stayed for very much longer."

"What would you have done?" Pity twisted Amairgen's throat as he remembered her life inside the Gealtacht, and a deep and bitter anger rose up in him at the people who had incarcerated her there.

"Perhaps I should have run away," said Portan, sitting up now, her eyes bright. "We talked of it sometimes—those of us who were only deformed in body and not in mind."

"You were able to do so?" said Amairgen, and was glad to think that at least she had been able to find a friend or two, kindred spirits in the Gealtacht.

"We talked of it often, at night, after we had been locked in," said Portan, and the shiver Amairgen had noticed earlier went through her again. "They locked us in every night, you see. And the sleeping chambers were terrible places. We slept on the floor—there were blankets, but they were old blankets. Not always very clean. And it was often cold, so that we would huddle together for warmth. And perhaps for comfort as well, for we were directly above the Paupers' Chamber—which you saw, I think—and the Mutants there would howl after dark." Again the shiver racked her. "It was terrible to hear, but for me more terrible was the sound of the door closing on us, and the key turning in the lock. It was every night, but I never got used to it." She looked at him. "We would not have harmed anyone."

"No. Go on."

"We would talk then, of how we would run away. How we would somehow steal out after nightfall. That was important, somehow. To leave as most of us had arrived, under cover of darkness. We pretended that we would be able to make our way to a place in the world where Mutants were not outlawed. We thought that there might be such a place somewhere. We needed to think that, perhaps," said Portan, and Amairgen, understanding this, nodded.

"We thought there would be somewhere where we could be accepted. Where we could work and be a part of the community. Share things." A half grin. "We knew, deep down, that it was only a pretence, but it was an escape for us. For a while we could imagine ourselves outside, in the real world. We had memories of the world, all of us, and we shared our memories.

We built our own world out of the memories we had brought and cherished," said Portan, her eyes faraway now. "And it became very real, that world we built. Houses we would live in. Tasks we would perform. Farming and cooking and gardening. Growing fruit." She looked at him. "I do not know if it exists, such a world," said Portan. "Where Mutants could be equal."

She looked at him again, and Amairgen heard the note of query in her voice, and said gently, "I do not know either, my dear," and wished he could have lied and said: yes it exists, and yes you will find it, you and those other pitiable creatures.

Portan said softly, "Thank you for not pretending, Amairgen," and Amairgen felt again the faint ripple on the air that was so like the Samhailt, but was not the Samhailt. "I wish," said Portan, "that it had been possible to bring the others out. I wish I could have done that."

She looked at him, and again he understood and said at once, "It was not possible."

"I know it was not."

Amairgen reached for her hand. "To have done so would have drawn attention to us all. We were in very great danger as it was. If you had brought your friends out, we would certainly have been caught and you would have been captured. Perhaps they would have chained you this time. And in the end, no one would have been free."

"Shall I ever go back?" said Portan, her eyes wide with fear, and Amairgen's hand tightened on hers.

"No," he said quietly, and Portan looked at him with deep gratitude.

"I promise," said Amairgen, "whatever else happens to us, Portan, we will never let them take you back to the Gealtacht."

FLYNN WORKED DOGGEDLY in the orchard, sick with fatigue, his mind tortured by images of Joanna alone and helpless in some long-dead world; at the mercy of the half-human, half-bestial creatures who had inhabited Ancient Ireland. He had always been interested in the legends and the folklore of his country and now his vivid imagination betrayed him; it turned about and presented him with terrible hurting pictures of Joanna in pain and frightened; thrown into some deep dungeon, raped and bleeding and starving.

Even so, in the warm afternoon sun, the orchard was a restful place, and Flynn, gathering the ripe apples and tipping them into baskets, found an unexpected comfort in the place where his ancestors had once worked. There was a drowsiness about the scent of the fruit, and there was a sleepiness in the very warmth of the trees. Once or twice, he found himself almost thinking that the trees were sleeping, dozing in the afternoon sun, and he thought he would just sit down for a moment. He thought he would certainly not be able to sleep, but he closed his eyes—just for a moment he thought—and leaned his head back against the bark of the tree. The sunlight was heavy on his eyelids—but I won't be able to sleep, thought Flynn. I shall be more or less awake really. I shall certainly be able to hear if anything happens.

But the sunlight lulled him and the apple-scent calmed him, and the sun was already sinking over the Mountains of the Morning when he awoke.

He sat there for a while longer, feeling himself rested and refreshed, thinking that his father—wily old devil!—had known what he was doing when he sent him out here.

"It's an old, old, orchard," Michael had said gravely. "And there has always been something about the scent of the fruit. Our family has always found it a peaceful place, Flynn."

Now, leaning back, watching the light turn to pink and then to lilac, knowing he must soon stir himself to go along to the Dutch barn, Flynn thought: something magical? Of course not! Even so, I feel stronger. I think I could tear the Time Curtain aside with one hand and bring Joanna out by myself.

In a moment, he would get up and get together some provisions for them to take, and then it would be time.

As he stood up, he saw the two figures making their way across the orchard towards him.

JOHN GRADY AND Brian Muldooney had formed a rather unlikely alliance. Neither man particularly liked the other; John thought Muldooney coarse and rough; Muldooney was finding John overfussy and pompous. What could it matter how many people got to hear of Joanna's disappearance, or how many of the villagers were called in to help with the search?

But John Grady, who knew his world, was adamant. No one, he said frowning, should know that Joanna had gone. Did

Muldooney want the whole of Tugaim to know that a girl, a little bit of a thing with more hair than muscle, had run away rather than be conjoined with Muldooney himself? Did he think that he, John Grady, one of the Elders of Tugaim, wanted everyone to know how a mere daughter had flouted his wishes and shown herself capable of disobedience such as no one in Tugaim had ever heard of? The story would spread; it would be exaggerated. Before they knew it, the pair of them would be held up to ridicule and contempt, and if Muldooney wanted that to happen, John certainly did not!

This was unanswerable. Muldooney scratched his head and could not think why he had not seen it for himself. But there, Grady had ever been a man for the intelligence; wasn't he an Elder, and it a terrible responsibility. Muldooney would not have taken on such a thing, even if he had been asked to, which he had not, but he did know you were not elected an Elder without you had some wits about you. He looked at the other man with respect, and said wouldn't they keep it as quiet as a midnight fog to be sure, and not a soul should hear tell of the girl's disappearance. To himself he thought: just as well to hush it up, for a different reason altogether. He had not forgotten how he had given a less than excellent performance with Joanna that night, well, afternoon it had been really if you wanted to be exact. It had not been his usual form, of course, good lord of course it had not! Many a one could have testified to that. Even so, it was not the sort of story a man wanted spreading all over Tugaim. He would say nothing about it.

He listened to Grady outlining their plan, and nodded in agreement at the idea of going to the O'Connor farmhouse. There could not be any harm in just going along there. John Grady said, rather portentously, that Joanna and Flynn had been close friends. He had never really trusted Flynn of course, he said, and now that Muldooney came to think about it, neither did he. There was something a bit wild about the boy; something too smooth and too satisfied. Condescending. Yes, that was the word for it. Flynn O'Connor was condescending to his neighbours, and as far as Muldooney could see, had no cause to be any such thing. He trod heavily along at Grady's side, listening while the man told how females had occasionally to be suitably chastised. They would find Joanna of course, said John, to whom any other notion was incomprehensible. They would find her, and Muldooney must do as he thought best. Doubtless, the silly child had been homesick for the familiar surroundings of her home. Certainly she had panicked. You could not blame her, said John Grady, that cold unsexed man, who had only conjoined because it was expected of him, and not very enthusiastically then. Even so, he hoped that Muldooney would not be too severe on Joanna; pig farmers could sometimes be rough, and it would be very uncomfortable for an Elder of Tugaim to be pointed out as the man who handed his only daughter over to a man who had treated her harshly.

In this rather divided frame of mind, the two of them approached the O'Connor farmhouse, both hoping, neither admitting, that Flynn would be found to be at the back of Joanna's disappearance. That insolent boy! I should like to have him before the Council one day! Grady thought. Muldooney, still smarting from Joanna's rejection of him, remembered Flynn's air of casual confident virility and experienced an impotent man's jealousy.

But Flynn, rested and refreshed from his long sleep in the apple orchard, filled with confidence about what lay ahead, treated the visitors in a cavalier fashion. He was politely welcoming; he asked would they step inside the house and take a glass of wine; but he said, "Missing is she?" and seemed more interested in transporting baskets of apples to the apple store than in anything else.

John Grady was stung by Flynn's attitude. "We have a very good idea of where she is, Mr. O'Connor," and Flynn turned, studying Grady with narrowed eyes.

"Do you indeed?" he said, and John heard, or thought he heard, the amused arrogance again. He remembered that he was an Elder—it was something he did not often forget—and he remembered as well that he could invoke all kinds of useful powers. Search the house? Make a tour of the outbuildings? And what about that useful law, not often invoked, but allowing that a man accused of a crime must, if found guilty, forfeit his lands and his goods to the one making the accusation? John hoped he was above such acquisitive ways—look where being acquisitive had got the Letheans!—but he could not forbear to just look about him and see the good prosperous lands that Michael O'Connor and his son owned. He could not help casting rather covetous eyes on the long white farmhouse, bathed in a rosy glow from the rays of the setting sun, solid and comfortable, and surprisingly spacious once you got inside. He noticed that the windows had very good quality glass in them; that they were what was called latticed—Lethean nonsense of course, but it looked very nice. The floors were of old oak planks, polished and buffed to a soft mellow shine, and the furniture had quite certainly seen the light of day well before the Apocalypse. Comfortable, as well, thought John Grady, seating himself on a deep sofa covered with some kind of elaborate floral-patterned cover. Of course, Michael O'Connor's wife had brought a deal of fine things with her from the West Coast, and didn't everyone know that Galway had missed most of the Apocalypse's blast. Yes, a very nice little farmhouse, this, and one that John Grady would be pleased to add to his property. A pity about that belt of Glowing Lands on the southeast boundary, but you could not have everything. He could easily overlook the Glowing Lands.

Muldooney was not thinking about Glowing Lands, or about acquiring other men's properties, but he did think that a man who had such unnecessary frivolities as geraniums growing in stone tubs at his front door and beaten brass jugs on oak chests in his hall might be capable of anything at all. O'Connor had also, for some reason, thought it necessary to whitewash the entire outside of the farmhouse, and Muldooney had clucked his tongue at the wanton extravagance, for didn't everyone know the price of good whitewash these days! He found himself disliking Michael and Flynn afresh, and he thought it would be very gratifying indeed if they could be found guilty of Joanna's disappearance.

Flynn's tiredness had fallen from him like a sloughed skin. He felt more alive than he had ever felt in his life, and he thought that he could outwit these two without any difficulty at all. Of course they thought he had hidden Joanna away somewhere, and of course they would be waiting their chance to search the entire place.

He listened, outwardly courteous, to the tale of how Joanna could not be found anywhere, and he smiled inwardly when John Grady asked could they search the O'Connor lands.

"Certainly," said Flynn, standing up. "Will I fetch my father?" Michael might be anywhere at this time of day, but

Flynn was fairly sure he had seen the men arrive and gone straight to the Dutch barn to warn Amairgen and Portan. Aloud, he said, "Joanna is not here, you know."

Again there was the cool note of arrogance in his voice, so that both men instantly thought: I was right! This boy has had her! This boy knows where she is! John Grady thought it was only what he would have expected; Muldooney thought you could never trust a Landgrabber not to sell you damaged goods. "We'll take a look," he said, standing up and glaring at Flynn, and Flynn smiled back. This is the most repulsive creature I have ever seen. He smells, and his skin is greasy and spotty. Oh Joanna, my dear love, is this the one your father would have given you to? And Flynn thought too that even had he not loved Joanna himself, he would have been sickened at the idea of her in Muldooney's bed. But he remained polite, and when Muldooney said, "We'll take a look," and John Grady added, "We will indeed," he said, "For sure, gentlemen. Will you come out now?"

John and Muldooney were puzzled. John thought that perhaps after all they'd made a mistake, young O'Connor had not the manner of one with anything to hide. Muldooney, less nimble-witted, thought wasn't the boy walking straight into their trap, lamb to the slaughter. Not that Muldooney had ever slaughtered a lamb, nor yet a sheep of course, for properly speaking it was not a pig farmer's job. Still, they'd set out to catch Flynn O'Connor, and it seemed as if they were going to do just that. Here was the boy leading them amiably through the square stone-flagged kitchen—Muldooney spared a look about him, and thought it was just as he had suspected, all manner of Lethe nonsense here, there was! Bunches of herbs set to dry, and dishes of brown eggs in a basket—a *basket* would you believe it!—and a smoke hole for hams and a side of bacon. There was nothing wrong with having a smoke hole, of course; in fact there were a good many people who argued that it was a prudent thing to possess, for how else would you keep a bit of bacon or a side of nice loin pork by you? But there were other things about this large sunny kitchen which would surely make a man contemptuous; there were gleaming brass pans neatly arranged along the length of a piece of furniture which Muldooney believed was called a Welsh dresser, but which he himself would not have given house room to, for didn't everyone know the Welsh for no better than watered-down Irishmen, and didn't any decent Irishman properly despise anything that smacked of Wales!

At the centre of the room stood a long polished oak table, and who in the name of all the gods at once had time to set to and polish a table only for the look of the thing! The table was all set out with plates and cutlery and with a flagon of wine as well. Muldooney had seldom seen the likes, for if the two of them, father and son, hadn't been intending to sit down at the table and eat their meal in what was a very Lethe fashion indeed, Muldooney did not know anything any more! A plain wooden platter with everything mixed up in it ought to be good enough for any man. But here was a separate plate for the bread, and a crock for the butter; there was a plate of baked potatoes decorated with parsley sprigs; there was another dish of broad beans, lying in some nonsensical sauce; there were glasses set out to pour the wine into! All to go with some slices of ham! Muldooney had never witnessed such sights before and hoped not to again!

John was not particularly concerned with the way in which Michael O'Connor and his son took their evening meal, although he had marked the flagon of wine, and thought it all of a piece with the latticed windows and the chintz covers and the copper jugs in the hall.

He was becoming very concerned about Flynn, however, for the boy was positively purring with affability and with what John supposed must be Lethe hospitality. The suspicion that they had, after all, made a mistake, solidified, and he was framing a careful explanation in his mind (not an apology certainly) when Flynn said, "And now for the search, gentlemen," and he found himself swept along outside. But he thought he could be fully as polite as Flynn, because he knew the rules, and one of them was that you did not insult a man under the man's own roof. But he thought he would wait his chance.

Muldooney was not watching his chance; he was suspecting Flynn of making game of them now, for nobody called you "gentlemen" in quite that way these days, and he was stung in his dignity, which is a place where no man—and certainly not a pig farmer—cares to be stung. He thought that it was all John Grady's fault that they were being insulted like this, and he thought that John Grady could certainly forget about having cheap bacon in the future.

Flynn, a little aware of his companions' thoughts, and rather amused, was as bland as buttermilk. "Come through this way, gentlemen . . . No indeed, it is not the smallest trouble . . . And there is no saying that she mightn't be here. People who are injured have been known to crawl for miles. And of course, our lands stretch rather far." He smiled guilelessly at John Grady as he said this, and thought: start measuring up the acres, Mister Landgrabbing Grady! But you shall not have an inch of my family's land!

He led them through the cluster of outbuildings, throwing out a warning to Amairgen in the Dutch barn as he did so, listening hard for Amairgen's response. It came, just as they turned into the square courtyard where the milk churns stood. *Yes Flynn, we hear! We understand. Do not worry.* Flynn relaxed. All would be well. They had heard him. They knew that Grady and Muldooney were on a tour of the outbuildings, and Amairgen would go straight to the Glowing Lands, Portan with him. All Flynn had to do was to get rid of the two half-wits who were dogging his footsteps, and join them.

But he gave no sign of any of this. He opened doors into hen coops and fruit stores; he picked out an apple to munch as they walked across the yard, and offered one to each of his guests.

"Or there are some very good pears if you prefer. The crop was especially good this year. Did you ever try the wine the Letheans made from apples over in England? Cider, they call it, and there's a grand powerful brew. You've never tasted the like in your life!" He grinned at Grady who looked prim and at Muldooney who could not be doing with all this frivolity and preoccupation with food and drink and the way you took meals, and so led the way to the Dutch barn.

John Grady, led hither and thither, scarcely given time to catch his breath, wondered after a time whether it mightn't in the end have been a good thing to let Joanna go to the O'Connors. Seen on the map, the O'Connor farm had been just a jumble of miscellaneous outbuildings; a farmhouse and several acres mainly laid down to fruit. And there was that sinister belt of Glowing Lands to the southeast. He'd always been wary of that. But seen properly, seen at the hands of Flynn

O'Connor, the place told a very different tale indeed. There were orderly rows of apples and pears and damsons; preserving sheds where the women of the village—and occasionally the men—worked to bottle the fruit to be later sold in Tugaim market. And sheep too! Everyone knew that you got a two-fold yield from sheep; there were the fleeces and the skins which could be sold for wool and for rugs and warm winter jackets. And everyone enjoyed roast spring lamb. Walking in Flynn's wake, nudging Muldooney to keep up with them, John Grady, that cautious careful farmer, saw that this was a prosperous concern.

He still did not trust Flynn; he still thought the boy had Joanna secreted somewhere. Why else was he being so open? Why else was he letting them search where they chose? Oh, Flynn O'Connor was a wily one, but John was wilier still! You had to be up very early to catch Grady.

But he kept silent, he was polite and courteous; he took Flynn's hand when the boy offered it, and he permitted himself to be escorted to the gates.

As they reached the curve in the roadway that took them just out of sight of the farmhouse, Grady closed his hand about Muldooney's fat forearm, and said, "Now for it! Back the way we came, and follow the boy wherever he goes!"

He thought he had managed it rather well.

FLYNN THOUGHT HE had managed it rather well, even so, he thought they had precious little time left to them. Amairgen and Portan would be at the Glowing Lands waiting for him, for if ever dusk had fallen, it had fallen now. There was time to bid Michael farewell—"And there is an old Lethe blessing that says 'God be with you,' " said Michael. "I daresay it means little nowadays, but I will say it anyway."

"God be with you also," said Flynn, and embraced his father quickly and roughly.

There was time to snatch up the small shoulder packs prepared earlier. "All the things I could think of that will not quickly spoil," said Michael. "The best I could do." Flynn thought it would do very well. There were two small, corked flagons of wine, tucked in, and a finely honed knife. "For," said Michael, "you do not know what you may meet with."

There was a final look round the farmhouse for, thought

Flynn, it is anyone's guess when I shall see it again, or if I shall see it again, and it is the only home I have known. And then he was through the door, not allowing himself time to think too much about anything, not bearing to look again at the bright welcoming sitting room with its time-worn beams and the deep warm hearth.

He stepped across the yard and was at once swallowed up by the shadows.

JOHN AND MULDOONEY had crept back through the farm gates, and had lain in wait for Flynn in the shadow of the dairy. Muldooney had been querulous, saying he couldn't see the point, and saying he was not used to skulking about in other people's farmyards. John was not used to it either, but he thought they were doing quite well. He explained to Muldooney—who was sulking—that the boy, Flynn, had been misleading them all along, and Muldooney, who had not real-ised this, rubbed his hands together, and said, "Oh-hoo. So the boy will lead us to the pretty little dear, will he?" in rather a nasty gloating voice which John did not altogether care for.

But Muldooney was docile enough as they waited for Flynn, although he began to fidget after a while, standing on first one foot and then the other. John nudged him sharply—they dare not be heard—and after a moment, Muldooney unbuttoned his breeches and relieved himself, copiously and rather noisily, against the dairy wall.

"Hasn't a man the need in this cold weather?" he said when John looked at him in disgust. "An' it does no good to hold it in for hours like some people. I'm not standing here bursting my breeches for you or anyone. Be thankful I missed your boots, for it's as dark as a bag out here."

He stumbled after John as they followed Flynn, both of them keeping their distance. "Although," said John softly, "I daresay he'll never see us in this light."

Flynn walked ahead of them purposefully and quickly, and John Grady's hopes rose. Hadn't the boy the very air of one going to meet a lover. Wouldn't they have him on a charge of abducting another man's conjoined property, and mightn't they also have him on a charge of holding back pre-Devastation goods? The copper pans and the chintz-covered furniture of the farmhouse had made their impression. Yes, John would have

Flynn O'Connor and his father on both charges before the week was out, and then wouldn't the fine O'Connor lands and the fine O'Connor farmhouse fall into the Gradys' lap as sweet as sweet.

Ahead of them were the Glowing Lands, and John stopped, Muldooney beside him, because both of them knew all of the stories, and now, faced with the reality of the Lands by night, faced with the gentle powerful spell of the Purple Hour, they hesitated. You could not, of course, quite believe in the old tales (monsters and half-men, all rubbish, thought John) but out here you could not quite disbelieve them either. John Grady, who had never been out alone in the dark before, because you could not count Flynn and you could not really count Muldooney either, began to feel unsure of himself.

The Lands seemed to him to become dreadfully alive. They shimmered and hummed and the light strengthened and deepened, so that at times it seemed to breathe with a life of its own. Standing there, the night sky behind them, John Grady, a man of scant imagination, thought, and was not the first to think, that the light almost seemed to both contain and conceal all those creatures of the myths.

He gave himself a shake, because it would not do to lose Flynn now. Beside him, Muldooney said in a whisper, "Did you see that? He's going straight to the centre of the light." And then, as both men stood watching, "There's somebody in there waiting for him."

"I see it," said John. And then, in a much louder voice, "After them!"

FLYNN HAD NOT been aware that he had been followed; there was no reason for him to think it, and Grady and Muldooney had been quiet. In any case, Flynn's mind had been moving ahead, to where Amairgen and Portan waited, and to where the light had become alive again.

He felt as if it was a tangible thing, Amairgen's welcome come out to meet him, and he felt as well the gentle shy presence of Portan. He thought: these people care about me! and he knew a great wave of affection and strength. They would do it, between them they would tear down the Time Curtain. They would go through the barrier erected by the gods at the dawn of the world, and they would find Joanna and bring her back.

Buoyed up by this immense determination, Flynn began to run across the last patch of ground, and as he did so, he heard John Grady's voice. He hesitated for the barest fraction of a second, and then his mind had taken in and swallowed whole what had happened. They thought he was going to Joanna—well, so he was—and they must have lain in wait and crept after him. He heard them start after him, and he flung himself over the terrain, his lungs rasping, bright streaks of red and gold and silver before his eyes. The muscles of his legs were protesting and he thought he would surely fall if he could not snatch just one breath before they caught him. But he must not, and he dare not, and he must go on until he reached the others.

Amairgen was running forward to catch him, a dark silhouette against the bright light of the Lands, and Portan was with him, galloping along, anxious and eager.

Flynn thought: I can do it ... only a little farther ... I can do it, I *can* ... And then for one terrible moment thought he could not.

Amairgen caught him as he fell, and half carried, half dragged him the rest of the way.

"Quickly Flynn, quickly! Are they pursuing you?"

Flynn, gasping, said, "Joanna's father ... and her ..."

"Ah," said Amairgen. "Come then." And drew Flynn towards the warm, scented, heart of the light.

"We should join hands," said Portan, and Flynn, feeling hands take his, knew again the rush of strength and the certainty that they would succeed. These two will not fail me, he thought, and at once came the response.

Never!

They were at the very centre of the light now, and the rich warm scent grew stronger. Flynn was blindingly aware of an endless sheet of silver blue light, beaded with brightness as if it had been trailed through dew; he thought there were figures in the light, but could not be sure.

And then Amairgen was saying, "It is yielding! Do not lose hold," and Flynn felt a shiver of pure power go through Portan. He tightened his grasp—they dare not become separated now—and as he did so, he felt sucked nearer to the light, and heard again the achingly beautiful music.

The horizon expanded in the pure clear light for as far as he could see, and there was a humming in his ears, so that he thought: I am going to faint.

And then the bright light seemed to part and yield and they caught sight of the dark misty forests of legend and felt themselves drawn nearer.

There was a shout from behind and a rush of movement, and as the Time Curtain opened more fully, John Grady, Muldooney at his heels, fell into the circle, and the Time Curtain drew back, and all five of them tumbled through into the deep past of Ireland.

CHAPTER SEVEN

JOANNA AND CORMAC stood at the edge of the forest and looked down into the valley. The sun was high and the hillside was lush and green. Behind them, a little deeper into the forest, they could just make out the camp; the to-ing and fro-ing of the Cruithin and of the Wolves; the cooking fires and the tents that someone had put up in a clearing. There was the cheerful clatter of pots and there was a splash of colour from the banners of the Wolf that someone had raised. Beneath them, the township of Muileann sprawled across the valley floor; the houses and the tall chimneys huddling together, a glint of light from a windowpane somewhere at the centre. Joanna caught the rather comfortable sound of carts rumbling across cobblestones.

"Muileann," said Cormac softly, and Joanna shivered and looked across the valley to the great rearing outline of the Giant Mill.

The people of the Miller . . .

"*Must* we go through the streets?" said Joanna.

"Yes. To reach Gallan and Cait Fian we have to cross the valley. From there we shall go through the Mountains of Morne." He looked down at her. "I must raise as great an army as I can."

"You have the Wolves."

"Eochaid will have the Lions." He smiled. "Would you trust a wolf against a lion's strength, Joanna? I dare not take any chances. If I am to regain my throne, I must ride against Eochaid Bres and Bricriu with the greatest army that has ever been seen since the days of Dierdriu."

The greatest army ... the Cruithin and the Wolves of
Cormac Starrog and the Wild Panthers of Cait Fian. Joanna
frowned, because just for a moment, the image of Cormac, armies streaming out behind him, the pennants of the Wolf and
the Panther fluttering in the breeze, was startlingly clear. She
could hear the cheering and see the flowers thrown from the
windows of the houses. She could hear the triumphant music.
The horses wore brilliantly coloured caparisons, and the emblem of the Wolf rode higher than the rest.

"The Cruithin and the Wolves will remain in the forest,"
said Cormac, looking about him. "It may be several weeks before we rejoin them, but that will not matter. The camp is well
hidden, and they will spend the time gathering information
about the Court, which may be of use to us. They know we'll
come back as soon as we can." He frowned. "But we must go
quietly, and as inconspicuously as possible. Even so, I believe
we should take Gormgall and Dubhgall with us."

The High King, exiled and outcast, but still traveling with a
retinue ... Joanna smiled. "Do we go right away?"

"At the Purple Hour," said Cormac, and Joanna thought how
suddenly familiar that sounded, and tried to remember why it
should be familiar, and could not.

"Will the journey be dangerous?" she said, and Cormac
looked at her for a long moment.

"Yes," he said. "But we shall go cautiously, and we ought
to be able to mingle with the townsfolk of Muileann."

Joanna thought this sounded a good idea. "Because you can
pass unnoticed much more easily in a crowd of people," she
said, and Cormac smiled at her.

"So we can, Human Child. And if we are very careful, and
if the gods are kind, we shall not be caught.

"But if the Miller or one of his jackals sees us, the alarm
will be raised, and if we are captured, we shall be thrown into
the Miller's cages.

"And then he will send word to the Erl-King."

THEY WORE DARK cloaks with hoods: "To appear as much like
the people of Muileann as possible," said Cormac. And they
each carried a wide flat basket. The men's held food and provisions, because Gormgall said they had to eat, hadn't they?
But Joanna's carried Dierdriu's cloak, carefully folded. "We

dare not leave it behind," said Cormac, "and we don't know when it may be of help to us," but Joanna would not have left it anyway.

"I should think not," said Gormgall, shocked.

"The very idea," said Dubhgall, and was moved to recount the cloak's history insofar as he knew it.

"Which," Gormgall said in an aside to Joanna, "is not so very much, my lady. But he likes to spin a tale or two."

"No I do not," said Dubhgall, who had been listening.

Gormgall had been efficient and philosophical about the journey—"I expect His Majesty knows best"—and Dubhgall had been efficient and lugubrious: "We'll be lucky if we're not caught and put between the Millstones," he said. "But there, it isn't my place to question the High King. But if we aren't all bread on the Erl-King's supper table by tomorrow night, it'll be a remarkable thing. And if we do escape, there'll be the sorcerers of the Morne Mountains to contend with.

"Now there's a thing I *don't* like to think about." Though he actually rather enjoyed thinking about gloomy things, and enjoyed even more sharing the gloom.

"It's all very well to say they'll be on our side," he added solemnly, "but what I say is, will they? You never know which way a sorcerer's going to jump."

"Let's not think about that," said Joanna, who was trying very hard not to think about the Miller or the Erl-King, and who was trying even harder not to think about the sorcerers. "Let's look forward to reaching Gallan instead. At least we can be sure of a warm welcome there, can't we? Can't we?"

"Well," said Gormgall, "if your ladyship will excuse me for saying it, it won't be a very peaceful time at Gallan."

"Always supposing we ever get there," said Dubhgall, never one to miss an opportunity.

"Because," said Gormgall, raising his voice, "we never do have a peaceful time at Gallan. Dear me, in all the years I've been in attendance on His Majesty I don't remember ever having a peaceful time at Gallan ... It's lively, of course."

Dubhgall said it depended on what you called liveliness, "Some people would say it was mayhem."

"It's Cait Fian, you see," explained Gormgall. "He and the High King don't get on at all well. Not at all. Well, not to put too fine a point on it, your ladyship, they fight."

"But isn't Cait Fian the King's liegeman?" said Joanna, who had picked this expression up from Cormac, and rather liked it. "Isn't he sworn to aid the King at all times?"

"Oh yes," said Gormgall, "oh for sure, he'll do that, well, won't we all? But they'll fight, my lady, oh dear me, I can see it coming already. Cat and dog, my lady, if that isn't an irreverent way to speak of the High King and one of the Bloodline. He's very high nobility, Cait Fian, of course, well, he's a Prince of Ireland really."

"And," said Dubhgall, "he's the King's second cousin. If you recall, it was the King's grandfather's brother who married one of the Pantherline. Of course, I said at the time no good would come of it, and now we see. I daresay Cait Fian would lay down his life for the King, but they still can't meet without fighting."

"What's worse," said Gormgall, "is that their *followers* can't meet without fighting either." And then, as Joanna looked startled, "Wolf and Panther, my lady," said Gormgall, and jerked his thumb in the direction of the camp, where the Wolves lay. "Cat and dog. They'll band together all right when we meet Eochaid Bres's armies, but we shall see the fur flying before that happens, my word we will. There'll be some rare old fights when we reach Gallan."

"If we reach Gallan," said Dubhgall. "Because if we don't set off soon, we shan't reach Muileann before midnight anyway. Is it today's Purple Hour or tomorrow's His Majesty means, do you suppose? Oh there you are, Sire. I was only saying we ought to—"

"Set off at once. Are we all ready? Very well then. On with it!"

Joanna thought, as they descended the hillside, using a rough narrow track, that it was a pity they could not have uttered some kind of battle cry. Wasn't this, after all, the first real battle? There ought to be something to mark it. Something to rouse them up a bit. And then, because she found she was rather frightened of what lay ahead, she searched her mind for a suitable cheer they might have used. It was extraordinary how battle cries echoed down the ages, when so much else had been lost, but there it was, they did echo, and she could think of several from the ancient wars.

"Up Guards and at 'em!" had been a very famous one. And

"God for Harry, England, and St. George!" whoever Harry and St. George had been. She went on thinking about it, because it was a calming thing to do, and because it concentrated your mind which was helpful if you were going into something nasty, and also because it stopped her from speculating on what was ahead.

"To the lanterns with the aristos" was another one which was very mysterious, and then there was "Death or Glory" which was much less mysterious, but not very appropriate to their present circumstances. You could not very well race down the hillside shouting "The Millstones or Glory." Well, you could, but it wouldn't have the right ring to it, and anyway, it would attract attention which they did not want.

I wonder, am I becoming feverish? thought Joanna, feeling cool and reasonably calm. They were almost on the valley floor now, and ahead of them were the great city walls of Muileann.

"Put there to keep people out?" wondered Gormgall.

"Put there to keep prisoners *in*," said Dubhgall.

As they went deeper down into the valley with the houses of Muileann looming ahead of them, Joanna began to remember an old old poem. Something that glorified and yet vilified war. One particular war it had been, she thought; not the Letheans' last Great War, but one that had been fought a long time before that. How did it go? Something about riding into the Valley of Death was it? And then something else about going knowingly into the jaws of Death, and into the mouth of Hell. Rather dreadfully evocative, thought Joanna, following the others up to the great brick wall of Muileann.

They stopped and looked at each other, and Joanna sensed for the first time the true depth of the immense loyalty that bound Gormgall and Dubhgall to Cormac. They quarrel with each other, she thought, and they reprove Cormac in a half-affectionate, half-servantish way, but they would follow him anywhere.

Into the Valley of Death . . . ?

Oh yes, thought Joanna, standing a little apart, watching them. Oh yes, they would follow him into the Valley of Death and into the mouth of Hell. I had better stop remembering those old expressions, thought Joanna, and gave herself a shake.

The scaling of the city wall had bothered them all a good deal for, as Cormac said, it was fully forty feet high, and as smooth as eggshell. Joanna had heard Gormgall and Dubhgall discussing grappling irons, and she hoped there would be another way found to get over the wall.

They did not need ladders or grappling irons. They did not even need to be especially agile. The city gates swung open when Cormac touched them, and they walked into the Miller's township of Muileann unchallenged.

"I don't like this," Cormac said. "It could be a trap," but Gormgall, ever practical, said that you could not expect them to have sentries posted all the time.

"And they are accustomed to innocent travellers, Sire. People have to pass through Muileann to reach the Mountains of Morne."

"True enough." But Cormac's brows were drawn down in a frown and when he walked forward, he did so as if he was walking on glass.

But no one came running out and no one called out to ask their business, and they moved at first warily and then a little more easily towards the first straggling houses. Joanna thought: I think it will be all right. We'll walk like this, slowly and quietly, and perhaps it will be all right.

Even so, the sight of the Giant Mill on the far side, a little apart from the town, gave her a cold sick feeling. She began to wish she had not come.

There was a heavy darkness in the air, and there was a perpetual noise in their ears; a dull grinding sound that made Joanna feel small and vulnerable.

"The Millwheels are turning," said Cormac, his eyes unreadable, his hair whipped into disarray by the wind. "Someone will be devoured tomorrow."

Joanna's sick feeling grew worse. "Inside the Mill?"

"Inside the Citadel of the Erl-King," said Cormac. He glanced at her. "It means the Miller has caught some poor wretched enemy or spy, and the Erl-King will hold a feast tomorrow night."

" 'Silver platters for human bones,' " muttered Gormgall softly.

" 'And golden goblets for human blood,' " said Dubhgall.
And someone will be devoured tomorrow . . .

Joanna reached furtively into the basket, and brushed the soft folds of the Nightcloak with the tips of her fingers. A charge of something—courage? strength?—passed from the silk through her skin.

Courage, Joanna. You have faced the Miller before ... There was a brief feeling of strong sweet light, an upsurge of power, and then darkness closed about her again.

"Do we go through the streets?" said Joanna.

"Yes. Yes, for if you look straight ahead, you can see that to do so brings us out on the other side of the valley, a little way up the hill. Gallan is over the hill and—oh, several leagues west. You cannot see it for the Morne Mountains, but it is there."

But it is over the hill and far away, and it is over hill and over dale, and before we reach it we must pass through Muile-ann and we must pass into the shadow of the Giant Mill ...

"Must it be the town, Sire?" That was Gormgall, of course, deferential as always, but not hesitating to question Cormac.

"It must," said Cormac. "It is safer. If we take the open road across the plain, we should be very noticeable. And the Miller will have his spies out. We should be man-pies on the Erl-King's banqueting table within a day."

Silver platters for human bones ...

"By going through the streets on foot," said Cormac, "by appearing to be nothing more than ordinary travellers, we may melt into the crowds of Muileann."

"*Is* it safe, Sire?" Dubhgall wanted to know.

"No," said Cormac. "But we must do it." He looked at them all. "Before we go any farther," he said, "I must have you remember that for my true identity to be learned here would mean instant death at the hands of the Miller, and immediate sacrifice to the Erl-King."

Golden goblets for human blood ...

"Do not," said Cormac, "under any circumstances at all, use my name or my title." But he knew they would not always remember his warning.

"Oh dear me, I don't like that," said Gormgall frowning, and Cormac said sharply, "I would rather be a live serf than a dead High King," and Gormgall begged pardon at once.

It seemed to Joanna as they walked towards the lights of Muileann—"Cautiously but not furtively," Gormgall said—that the silhouette of the Mill leaned nearer to them. It is watching us, thought Joanna. It is brooding over the countryside and it is picking its victims. The ones it will put between its grindstones.

Someone will be devoured tomorrow . . .

It has seen us, thought Joanna. It has seen us approach, and it is considering what we are and whether we would be grist for its stones. What a nasty word "grist" was. It made you think of gristle and bone and fat frying in a pan: all to be ground up for the Erl-King's table.

Silver platters for human bones . . .

Stop it! said Joanna to Joanna. There is absolutely no need to be afraid!

And you have faced the Miller before . . .

Oh yes, I had forgotten that, she thought, and fell into line between Gormgall and Dubhgall, with Cormac a little ahead of them.

"Just as it should be," said Gormgall.

"Oh hush!" said Joanna worriedly.

"I know what's due to a High King," said Gormgall, but he said it quite quietly.

The houses on the outskirts of the town were dark, rather gloomy buildings, surrounded by trees that made a sh-sh-shushing noise in the wind. No lights burned at any of the windows.

"But there will be look-out posts," said Cormac, and Joanna suddenly had the feeling of being watched by dozens of unseen eyes.

"Remember that we are ordinary travellers," said Gormgall.

"Going to visit our kin on the foothills of the Morne Mountains," added Dubhgall. "Not that anyone of any sense would live there, of course. It's as damp as a swamp."

"Oh do hush," said Joanna, who had caught a movement at one of the windows that might have been someone darting out of sight.

"Well, my lady, I believe Dubhgall's in the right of it for talking," said Gormgall. "For we wouldn't look natural if we were to plod along these streets in complete silence. A nice bit of conversation's needed," he added, and began to talk to Dubhgall about the houses they were passing, and how long their journey might be expected to take them, and what they would be finding at the end of it.

Dubhgall entered into the spirit of this with mournful glee, discussing the various ages and degrees of ill health of his kin, speculating on which of them might have died, or recovered, and inventing several great aunts and uncles with improbable names and astonishing life histories.

Joanna listened, and smiled occasionally, and tried to shut out the sight of the Mill and the dreadful sounds of the wheels grinding together. It was a truly terrible sound; it set your teeth wincing and made you think all over again about gristle and fat and blobs of bone in a mincing machine.

The houses were built closer together in the heart of the town, as if they had been planned that way, or perhaps as if they had clustered together since for comfort or safety. They passed down a narrow cobbled alleyway with a high brick wall on each side, and came out into a square with shops that had timber-framed frontages and jutting bow windows, and where the upper floors overhung the street, so that you felt as if they were toppling forward on to you.

Their footsteps rang out on the cobblestones loudly, and Joanna began to play games in her mind. If we can reach that warehouse on the corner without being seen, we shall be all right. And then, as they did reach the warehouse—one more hurdle behind us, she would think. Now, if we can get past the fourth house on the left, we shall be safe.

They had come through the square, and had turned into a side street, and Joanna was just saying, "If we can get to the house with the high wall and the iron gates—" when Cormac stopped, and said, "Listen," and Dubhgall, who had been looking back over his shoulder, walked into him, and for a moment there was confusion and Gormgall dropped his basket and had to be helped to find the apples that had rolled all over the street.

"Hush," said Cormac. "What do you hear?"

"Nothing," said Joanna. "What's the—" And then stared, because that was the exact truth. They could hear nothing.

Cormac looked at her, his eyes slanting upwards.

"The Millwheels have stopped," he said. "Be ready to run."

"It may mean nothing at all," said Gormgall, as they began to walk cautiously on again.

"On the other hand, it may mean that the Miller's servants are coming down from the Mill to catch us," said Dubhgall. "It may mean that they are watching us now, this very moment. Well, there's one thing to be said, Your Majesty, if we're caught by the Miller, we shan't have to worry about the sorcerers any more."

Gormgall said that Dubhgall was showing the wrong spirit entirely, but Dubhgall said he was trying to find a bright side. "And I'm a practical fellow, for all you others laugh at me. If you had to say anything about me, you'd say I was practical, wouldn't you now?"

"Practical's all very well in its way," began Gormgall, but Joanna broke in impatiently, and said, "Do stop it, you two. Look, there's a light. Isn't it? Behind those houses, a little to the left."

"There is a light of a sort," said Gormgall after a pause. "Is it coming towards us, would Your Majesty say?"

"It's certainly moving," said Cormac, frowning in an effort to see, and Joanna, standing on tiptoe and peering over his shoulder, saw that the light was bobbing up and down, as if it was being carried by someone.

"I daresay it will be someone off to his home," said Gormgall hopefully. "Perfectly in order."

"It's no more in order than anything else in this unnatural place," said Dubhgall crossly. "This place reeks of evil, if Your Majesty will pardon me for saying so. The sooner we all get out of here, the happier I shall be. As for bobbing lights, when everything else's been pitch black for the last two hours—well, I wouldn't trust them, Your Majesty. Not by the breadth of a mouse's whisker, would I trust them."

"Dubhgall's right," said Cormac. "Although I should feel happier if I knew who was carrying that light and coming towards us."

In the dark, his hand went to his sword, and Joanna said, "Oh please let's get on. The houses are thinning out here—we must be quite near to the other city wall. If we can just reach that alleyway—"

"There's a light up in the Mill," said Gormgall in rather a strangled voice. "And look! There's another behind those houses. I don't like this, Sire."

"And there's another at the end of the alley," said Dubhgall. "Gormgall's right, Your Majesty. This bodes ill."

"We must keep walking quite naturally," said Cormac. "As if we have nothing to hide. If we begin to behave suspiciously, we shall be lost."

It was harder than any of them would have believed possible to walk casually through the cobbled streets, keeping up a light conversation. Dubhgall resurrected the story of his fifth cousin, to whose house they were supposedly going, and related the tale of some mythical great-uncle's gout. Gormgall contributed his mite by saying "Oh really?" and "Is that so?" at intervals. Joanna clung to Cormac's hand, and tried not to see the lights that flared and then died all around them, as if they were signals of some kind. Had that blaze of light from the Mill been the sign? A single sudden flare, and everyone down in Muileann had seen it and known what it meant, and said: aha! and oh ho! so there are enemies amongst us! Out and after them!

The lights were not the solid, comforting yellow squares of candlelight that Joanna had known in Tugaim. They were not, either, the warm, faintly scented flares used by Cormac and the Cruithin. Joanna liked those; they had a red glow and made you think of log fires and applewood burning, and of safely bolted doors, and mulled wine, and tales told round the hearth.

The lights of Muileann were dull and rather smeary-looking. They burned up and then died quickly, but they showed you brief glimpses of narrow cul-de-sacs and dark corners, and Joanna began to have the impression that every time a light flared, it just missed showing you a *something* that had been lying hidden. It was particularly horrid to think of all those unseen *somethings*. But perhaps I am only imagining it, thought Joanna. Then she saw the gleam of red eyes from the shadows: she heard claws pattering across the cobblestones. Once there was the slither of a long tail across the stones, and once there was a sound that was like something scaly and damp creeping away to their right.

And then the whispering began.

Gormgall clapped his hands to his ears and said, "This is dreadful," and Dubhgall turned white. Cormac set his jaw, and took Joanna's hand and Joanna thought that even in the dull light, even dressed in a borrowed cloak and carrying a rush bas-

ket, he looked exactly what he was. The Wolfking of Tara . . . .
Oh God, don't let him be recognised. Oh God, let us escape.
Just as far as the next row of houses.

The voices seemed to come from out of the shadows; they
were on all sides of the travellers, first coming from the left,
and then the right. Several times, the company turned sharply,
expecting to see the Miller's men rushing down on them, but
each time the street behind was empty.

The whispers had horrid hissing voices, they were malevolent and greedy and cold. You could easily imagine that the
owners of such voices would be thin bony people with hard
soulless faces and cold flat eyes. They would put you in a cage
and prod you with their hard bony fingers to see if you had fattened up enough for the banquet . . . Someone will be devoured tomorrow night . . . No, no! I won't listen! cried Joanna
to herself and gripped Cormac's hand harder.

But it was impossible to shut the voices out, they echoed
about the four travellers' heads and ran slyly in and out of the
tall warehouses on each side of the street.

This-s-s one—this-s-s one for the Master's table—A fine fat
feas-s-st—that one we'll mince and that one we'll stew and
that one we'll cut into cold collops-ss—oh, a fine fat feast—set
the Millwheels up my dears—turn the handles and open the
gates—grind the bones and there'll be silver platters for human
bodies and there'll be golden goblets for human blood—stew
and mince and roast, my dears-s-s—that one first and that one
next—fetch the cages, my dears, and lay the table . . .

Joanna said, "Oh God, this is unbearable."

"With respect, Sire, shouldn't we make a run for it now—"

"We're within sight and sound of the dark lands on the other
side of Muileann, Sire."

Cormac said, "Yes. Yes, you're right. All hold hands. On no
account become separated." And Joanna drew a great lungful
of breath for the run and searched for Gormgall's hand.

". . . . and sharpen the knives-s-s," said the voices. "Grease
the pans and heat the fat—that's the way, my dears . . ."

"Ready?" said Cormac.

> " 'Light the fires and heat the pots
> Sizzle the fat in the waiting vats.

Mince and stew and roast and batter,
Pour the juice in the Erl-King's platter.' "

Cormac shouted "Run!" and Joanna felt Gormgall start forward. And then two things happened at once. The bobbing light they had spotted earlier came round a curve in the road; a dark shape barred their way. And the whispers shut off as abruptly as if a door had been slammed on them.

The four travellers stopped and Joanna felt Cormac's thoughts flow outwards to them.

Steady. Behave as if we have nothing to hide. On no account make a run for it now. Courage.

The blessed darkness that lay beyond the city wall was suddenly as remote as the stars. Joanna felt a great wave of despair. Had they then come this far only to be caught on the very edge of the Miller's territory?

They moved forward, walking quite normally, and the figure with the lantern came nearer.

Cormac laid a restraining hand on Joanna; he called out, *"Tráthnona maith agat,"* and Joanna whispered to Gormgall, "What is he saying?"

"He's bidding the person good evening."

"There's precious little that's good about it," said Dubhgall, but he said it in a mutter, so that the stranger would not hear.

Cormac said, "You are as late abroad as we are." And there was the smallest pause. Joanna thought: we are being inspected. To see if we are of interest? And waited, hardly daring to breathe.

Quite suddenly there was a low feminine chuckle, and a soft voice said mischievously, "Oh, I am up to no good, or so the people of Muileann would tell you," and Joanna thought: a woman! and heard Gormgall draw in his breath sharply.

Cormac said, quite smoothly, "We are on our way to our kin in the Morne Mountains, and must pass through the valley. But for sure, this is strange countryside. Tell me, Lady, what do they call this place?" and Dubhgall, who was bringing up the rear of the party, muttered to Joanna, "Oh ho, so he's using that trick, is he? Making her tell us what she's up to, instead of waiting for it to be the other way about. My word, he's his father's son and no mistake." He rubbed his hands gleefully, and Joanna, who wanted to hear the conversation properly, snapped, "Be quiet."

The lady had lowered the lantern so that the light fell across her face, and they saw that she was tall and slender and rather pale. But her mouth is greedy, thought Joanna, and felt a prickle of wariness.

There was the pause again, as if the lady was considering how best to answer Cormac. Then, "This is Muileann," she said. "They call it the town of the Giant Miller, but of course, that is just an old legend."

"Is it?" said Gormgall.

"Well," said the lady, drawing closer. "I've never seen any Miller." She smiled, and Joanna found herself thinking that after all she was rather attractive. It was only that her lips were too full and too red.

All the better to eat you with . . . ? No, of course not!

"You have a long journey ahead of you," said their new companion. "And you will surely not reach the Morne Mountains before the morning."

"It is a long journey," said Cormac equably.

"And that being so, we'd best get on with it," put in Gormgall.

"Of course. But you are surely going in the wrong direction for the mountain path?"

"This looked to be the best way," said Cormac, and the lady smiled rather engagingly.

"It *will* get you there, of course. And you cannot miss the mountains. But you could take a quicker route. Would you allow me to be your guide? As far as the city gates? I am not of Muileann, but I know its highways."

"Thank you, but I believe we must not trouble you," said Cormac with exquisite courtesy, and Joanna breathed a sigh of relief.

"Then I will walk with you if I may," said the lady, "for my house is on the edges of Muileann and I should be glad of some company." She drew a little nearer, and said in an amused voice, "Truth to tell, I have been visiting a gentleman, and it would not do for it to be known." A grin and a shrug. "People are so narrow, you understand. And I believe our ways lie together."

It was, of course, impossible to refuse. In Joanna's world, as well as in this one, there was a kind of unwritten law of chivalry amongst travellers. Company could be sought and offered; a person travelling alone could be given the protection of a larger party. A lady travelling alone could expect such protection almost as a right. Joanna wished she could rid herself of the feeling that their companion neither sought nor needed protection.

The lady was watching them, waiting, an amused look on her face. Cormac said the only thing he could say: "We should be glad of your company," and she smiled, her eyes crinkling up at the corners.

"I am rather unprincipled," she said. "But I promise you I am not an enemy."

At the back of the party, Dubhgall murmured, "I wonder is that meant to make us feel better?" but nobody heard him.

"This is an odd township," said Cormac, as they walked through the now silent streets, their footsteps ringing out on the cobblestones. Joanna noticed that he was keeping the lady a little apart from them. In case there was some kind of attack from her? So that three of them at least should escape? No, surely that was ridiculous. Even so, Joanna wished that their companion had not that greedy red mouth.

"Muileann is rather odd," agreed the lady. "It has a gruesome history, of course. You have heard of the Miller? Yes, I can see you have. He must have been a terrible figure."

"Does he no longer exist?" queried Gormgall.

"I don't think he has existed for many years," she said. "Although I believe his people preserve his memory. To keep unwanted strangers out, you understand. No more than that." She hesitated. "Tell me," she said, drawing a little closer to them, "did you have the misfortune to stray into the Street of the Whisperers?"

For a moment no one answered, then Cormac said, "We heard something we could not entirely explain. But it may have been a trick of the night. The wind, perhaps . . ."

"It is no trick," said the woman and looked about her. "Men say it is the echo of a dark and evil race who once lived here and served the Miller. Many have heard the Whisperers. I too, once—" Her voice broke off. "It is a frightening experience," she said. "I beg you, do not let us speak of it any more, for it is said that the echo can sometimes hear . . . But I daresay it is all only fancy." She smiled at them.

Presently Gormgall said, "I see the city wall directly ahead of us," and Joanna saw it as well, and felt a rush of thankfulness. The city wall. Nearly there. Nearly through this strange sinister place. If we can once reach the wall and be through the gates.

"Yes, that is the wall that girdles Muileann," said their companion. "A little beyond it lies my house." She hesitated and looked at them all one by one. "I wonder—would you step inside and rest for a while? You have been kind enough to bear me company—"

"I think we should continue our journey," said Cormac, and Joanna felt Gormgall and Dubhgall each give a sigh of relief.

"Of course," said the lady. "You are making for the house of your kin. No doubt you are expected. Forgive me." She appeared to lose interest, turning to point out to Cormac some ancient tower or other that could be seen against the sky, and Joanna thought: perhaps after all she is only a chance-met traveller. Perhaps she is no more and no less than she appears.

They walked through the great north gate of Muileann unchallenged, as they had been when they came into the town. "Oh, there are no sentries or guards now," cried the lady, amused. "People come and go all the time. Travellers and pilgrims . . ." She smiled in the flickering light of the lantern. "I have given many of them hospitality," she said. "For I like to talk with people from other lands. One should always listen and learn, do you not agree? It keeps the mind alert and young, and it is my belief that where the mind is young, so is the body." She grinned, gamine fashion. "I freely confess that there have been one or two gentlemen kind enough to tell me that my philosophy has worked for me."

Cormac said with instinctive gallantry, "I am sure it is not kindness that prompted them, madam," and in the rear Dubhgall sneezed disgustedly.

They walked on down the road, and Joanna wondered whether it was only her fancy that it was a much darker road than any they had travelled. There was a rather disturbing feeling of hidden watchers again, of shapeless, nameless *things* that waited.

Presently their companion lifted her lantern and pointed, the wide cloak falling back a little to reveal a slender white arm. "My house. You see? Behind the trees. Lights are always burning at my windows for weary travellers, and inside there is always a good meal prepared, roaring fires in the rooms, and comfortable beds." She stopped and looked at them, and for a moment it seemed as if the narrow green eyes slanted and grew larger, and as they did so, the four travellers, who had all been feeling quite reasonably fresh and well, became abruptly aware of extreme fatigue.

Joanna, who was nearest to the lady, thought: a comfortable bed! and tried to remember when she had last slept in one. It did not matter, of course, not really, because she had become quite at home with Cormac's people and with the rigours of marching and camping. She had rather enjoyed it. But now, quite unexpectedly, the idea of a comfortable bed that you sank into and that welcomed you with a feather-stuffed base and perhaps feather-lined pillows as well, was overpoweringly seductive. She could almost feel the thin cool sheets brushing her skin . . . she could certainly feel how the fatigue would smoothe out from her aching limbs. But she thought they ought not to enter anyone's house without seriously considering what they were doing, and she thought they definitely ought not to enter anyone's house in Muileann, because Muileann was where all the dangers were . . . For a moment, she thought that the Nightcloak stirred and then she thought it had only been a breath of wind. For another second, she thought there was something familiar about the lady—or had that been in another life somewhere?—and then the feeling vanished, and the fatigue was back, and really, it would be so wonderful to surrender to sleep, to sink into that deep soft bed . . .

Gormgall and Dubhgall, were aware of fatigue as well, although Gormgall was also aware of hunger, and was thinking, rather guiltily, how very good it would be to sit down to a meal, properly cooked, piping hot, where you did not have to remember that you were on the march, and that rations had to be shared. Dubhgall, who felt the cold, even with an extra jerkin, and whose chilblains had been troublesome at nights, dwelled hopefully on the idea of roaring fires so fiercely hot that you had to back away from them. And surely, surely, it could not matter to accept an hour or two's hospitality from this really very ordinary, chance-met traveller, and even though they were inside Muileann where the dangers might be, even then, surely it could not matter . . .

Cormac was the last to surrender to the drowsiness that had overcome the others. He had been the most alert since they entered Muileann, because he, of them all, knew the tales and the dreadful legends that surrounded Muileann and the Miller. He had known that they would almost certainly be the victims of some kind of attack, and when the lady had appeared, friendly and welcoming, every sense had responded, and he had thought: *is this it?* Is she a friend, or is she something quite different? And thought that for sure it would be a strange thing indeed to meet a truly friendly soul in Muileann.

He had opened his mind to its utmost, and he had used the Samhailt to its greatest limits, and he had been able to read nothing at all from the lady's mind. There had been a brief blur of greyness and coldness, and then there had been nothing at all. He thought she had deliberately set up a barrier so that he should not see her thoughts, and he thought that after all that in itself was not sinister, because people who did not possess the Samhailt themselves were often aware of it. A ripple on the air. A feeling that their minds were being pierced. But there was that coldness and there was certainly the blurred greyness, and Cormac, summoning up every drop of wolf-blood, thought: I do not *know* she is evil, not logically or sensibly. But I *smell* that she is.

The lady smiled, and appeared to concentrate all her attention on him, and Cormac, looking at the narrow green eyes, thought that after all she was not so very frightening. She was only one woman on her own. And they were all of them tired . . . He shook his head to clear it of the sleepiness, and he thought: but she is walking round us *in a circle*, and fought against the heavy drowsiness, because every enchantment ever woven by the sorcerers called for a circle in some form or another. The circle was the most powerful of all the spells . . . I do *not* trust her, thought Cormac, feeling his eyelids become heavy, we must be very careful indeed . . . we must not fall into any traps . . . It is only that I am so tired, and the others as well . . .

Joanna said, as if she was fighting something very strong, "We should be continuing our journey . . ."

Cormac said, "Yes, so we should." And neither of them moved.

Joanna remembered again about being aware of danger, and frowned and tried to identify the tug of memory. Cormac, struggling against the suffocating fatigue, found himself remembering only that they were all cold and tired, and that after all, this was only a lady on her own. He found that he was looking to where the house stood, half hidden by trees, and he caught a glimpse of warm lights in the windows and the leaping flare of firelight in one of the downstairs rooms, and he almost fancied he could smell the savoury aroma of cooking meat. He remembered that it was a long while since any of them had had a proper night's rest in a proper bed; he remembered that Joanna, unquestionably the frailest of their company, had often looked tired and pinched, but that she had never once complained, that she had always been cheerful, amusing them with tales of her own world, teaching them songs to sing as they marched, learning some of their own songs. Joanna deserved a good meal and a warm fireside and a deep soft bed for a few hours.

The lady said, as if the outcome did not matter to her either way, "You are most welcome to a bite of supper and a glass or two of wine. My house is always kept ready for travellers. And if you should care to sleep here tonight and set out for the Mountains by first light . . ."

It was the "set out by first light" that succeeded in dissolving the last of Cormac's fears. He thought: of course I am not the victim of any spell, and of course she did not walk round us in that circle earlier on. She is offering us no more than a night's lodging, and we shall be on our way in the morning. By first light we shall be on our way.

He said, "If it would in truth be no trouble to you?" and she smiled and said warmly, "No trouble at all, I promise. Will you come through the gates? That's right. Close them to and drop the latch."

They followed her along a tree-lined path to the white house, and although Joanna thought briefly that it was much farther from the road than it had seemed, and rather larger than it had looked, she was too tired to worry. There was an air of unreality about everything now, thought Joanna. It would be because they were all so tired. That was all. There was nothing to worry about.

"There is nothing to worry about," said the lady, and the

four travellers nodded and said, "There is nothing to worry about."

"You will come willingly into my house," said the lady softly, and again they nodded and said yes, they would come willingly into her house.

Joanna hesitated at the last minute, and turned on the threshold, thinking she had heard something—a voice?—in the trees that clustered thickly about the house. But then the wind made a faint shushing sound in the leaves, and a small hooting night creature flew out of a branch, and Joanna thought: well, perhaps it was only an owl, and turned back again.

The house had a massive studded oak front door with a huge brass handle; their companion stepped forward to turn it.

"And now come inside," she said, standing outlined against the warmly lit hall for a moment, and there was something subtly different about her voice. A gloating? A satisfied purring? But there was no time to identify it, for they were all over the threshold and into the house before they quite knew how it had happened.

"That's right," said the lady. "All of you. All of you safely inside my house at last. Close the door and shut us all in together.

"My two sisters will be *so* pleased to see you."

As THE LIGHT from the wall sconces flared, the heavy enchantment fell from the minds of the four travellers, and Joanna saw that Cormac had turned very white. Then he moved to the door, and the lady let out a peal of laughter. "Locked and barred, traveller, locked and barred. Or should I perhaps say 'Your Majesty'?" She moved round, so that the light fell fully across her face, and Joanna shivered, and felt again something stir within the depths of her mind.

"Dimbrim an t-aibhirseoir . . ." Begone, banish, adversary . . .

An old old language, once learned, once known so well, never truly forgotten . . .

She looked again at the creature before them, and saw that the lady was smiling, a forked tongue licking and darting between her lips. A sense of familiarity, the feeling that this was all an old, old battle that had been fought and won, and fought again, began to grow within her.

"Dimbrim, an t-aibhirseoir . . ."

The lady was not looking at Joanna. She was watching Cormac, and a sly, satisfied smile was on her lips. "So easily lured," she said. "So easily enchanted by the *Draiocht Suan,*" and Cormac, whose eyes had never left the lady, said softly, "The Enchanted Slumber. Of course," and the lady laughed again.

"The Enchanted Slumber, indeed, Cormac. The very spell that your ancestress Dierdriu summoned to send the Trees into their Great Sleep. And still you did not suspect!" She studied him. "Cormac of the Wolves," she said. "And the exiled High King of All Ireland. I salute you, Sire, and I am very glad to have you in my house. But then, you knew that one day I should do?"

Cormac was standing very still, his eyes never leaving her. "Yes, I knew it, for it is bred in to all the High Kings, madam. You are Ireland's enemy and you are the adversary of all who rule from Tara."

Adversary . . . Banish adversary . . . Joanna frowned, and then turned her attention back to the others.

"I know you very well indeed," said Cormac, and the lady laughed again, and Joanna shivered and thought: yes, she is very beautiful and yes, she is quite dreadfully evil.

"I and my sisters live in your folklore and your legends. Am I not the hag your old men whisper of, and the sorceress your mothers protect their children from?" the lady said. She moved closer and looked into his face. "I fought your ancestress, the High Queen Dierdriu, and I vowed to be avenged on her line for ever." She paused. "But truly, Sire, am I so ill-favoured? Could your loins not harden for me, and could you not spill your seed for me?" She pressed against him, her hips writhing, and a look of the purest revulsion flickered across Cormac's face.

He did not move, but screamed, in a voice Joanna had never heard him use, "Get from me, filth!" The lady laughed again, a cascade of delight that sent icy trickles of terror down Joanna's spine.

"Oh, you will be in my bed soon enough, Wolfking. You *will* obey my bidding." She leaned closer, the forked tongue flickering in and out. "And then I shall cut out your heart and your kidneys and cook them. I shall ladle your blood into a golden goblet and drink it. I shall quaff you and devour you, Wolfking, and your puny kingdom will be my Master's for ever!"

As she moved away, a red glint showed in Cormac's eyes. His teeth gleamed white, and a snarl broke from him. He leapt for her, claws curved, eyes slitted and blazing, and for a moment, Joanna thought he would reach her, that he would rake those cruel nails across her flesh, and sink his teeth into her white skin.

And he is capable of doing that, thought Joanna, caught between horror and a wish to see Cormac succeed. He is capable of it . . .

But the lady was gone before he reached her. There was a hiss, as if cold water had been dashed into a blazing fire, and there was a wisp of thick, sour smoke, and all that was left were peals of mocking laughter echoing round the room.

Cormac remained motionless for a moment, as if unable to believe what had happened. Then he turned. "I have led you into the most dreadful danger," he said, and there was such a humility and such a defeat in his voice, that a knife twisted in Joanna's heart. She went to stand beside him, not liking to show emotion before Gormgall and Dubhgall, but wanting to reach out and take him in her arms and somehow take away the hurt look from his eyes.

"You could not know. None of us could know." And she thought: oh damn! Why can I not be more articulate. Will he know what I am thinking? Yes, of course he will.

Gormgall and Dubhgall were nodding their agreement. "It was the enchantment, Sire," said Gormgall. "The *Draiocht Suan*. Dear me, I never thought I'd succumb to *that* one."

Dubhgall said it just went to show you should never trust strangers. "I knew how it would be," he said. "The minute we set foot in Muileann, I knew how it would be."

Joanna said, "But surely we couldn't know, not really, what would happen?" And struggled to come to terms with a place where enchantments were there for the weaving, and people could be sent into drowsiness so profound, that they followed enemies and were lured into traps.

"I did know," said Cormac. "I knew with my heart and my guts that it was wrong to follow her."

"But you were the victim of a *spell*, Sire," said Gormgall, as if that excused everything. "We were all of us victims of a spell."

Dubhgall said he had never trusted spells—nasty unpredictable things. "Mark my words, Sire, we won't get out of *this* in the flicker of a gnat's eyebrow," he said, and stumped over to the window to see could they get out that way.

"It's bolted and barred," said Gormgall, who had tried it himself not ten minutes before.

"I *know* it is," said Dubhgall crossly. "I'm only making sure."

Cormac sat down and looked at them all. "I did succumb," he said. "I ought to have known what she was doing. I did know, really, deep down. It was only that—"

"It was the mention of the fireside and the comfortable beds," said Gormgall.

"And the supper and being able to set off early tomorrow morning," said Dubhgall. "That was clever of her."

"It was the *Draiocht Suan*," said Gormgall firmly. "We all know what it was."

"I wanted Joanna to have a night's rest. I wanted us all to have a good supper." Cormac looked at Joanna as he said this, and Joanna wanted to cry.

"The thing is," said Gormgall, "if the *Draiocht Suan* had failed, she'd have tried something else. She'd have got us all in here by some means or other. Your Majesty knows that. She's been the enemy of all the High Kings and Queens, ever since Dierdriu. She swore revenge all those centuries ago, and she has never stopped trying to find a way back to Tara."

"She will never rest until she has brought down the Royal House, Sire," Dubhgall said.

"Yes." Cormac looked at them all. "And so I am face-to-face with her at last," he said, and Joanna drew in her breath sharply.

"You always knew that you would one day be confronted with her, Sire," said Gormgall.

"Yes." Amusement lifted Cormac's lips briefly. "At least she has not sought out the usurper. At least she recognises me as the true King."

"Begging your pardon, Sire, but I shouldn't think *that's* going to be much comfort to us before the night's out," said Dubhgall.

Joanna, looking at them bewildered, said, "But what does any of it mean?"

Cormac moved from the hearth and seated himself on a deep window seat. "She is the leader of the dread Morrigna," he said. "The Three Sisters. And she is one of the most feared of all my family's enemies. My ancestors have fought her down the generations, and although they have kept her at bay, they have never quite managed to destroy her."

Gormgall said, "Your own father, Sire, believed her to be indestructible."

"Yes." Cormac frowned, and the firelight fell across his face, so that pinpoints of red light danced in his eyes. "I never agreed with him. I believe that one day she will be destroyed." The grin lifted his face again. "I would very much like to go down in our history as the King who made an end to her but she is the Queen of Phantoms, and she is very powerful and very clever."

"Tell me about her," said Joanna, who was extremely frightened, but trying hard not to be. She thought it might be worse, rather than better, to know more about Morrigan, but she thought that at least it might give them an insight into the creature's nature. Insights into your enemy were useful things to have.

Cormac rearranged himself on the window seat, and Joanna thought that everything he did, every movement he made was just very slightly wolfish. Surely if anyone could get them out of here, he could.

"At the beginning of Tara's history, Morrigan and her two sisters, Macha and Scald-Crow, came out of the wild desolate northern isles," Cormac began.

"The people of those isles always coveted Tara," explained Gormgall in an aside to Joanna, "and it is countless centuries since they gave allegiance to the Erl-King who promised them that he would one day rule from the Sun Chamber."

"Oh," said Joanna, "I see. Thank you."

"There were many battles in those days," said Cormac, "for Tara was not then the invincible palace it is now, and the first High Queen Dierdriu had to repel many invaders.

"The Morrigna were the most powerful of all the invaders, for they had at their beck and call a truly fearsome army. The Dark Ireland," said Cormac, his lips thinning in fastidious disgust. "Hags and crones and harpies: Macha's family of monsters—numberless and endless, nourished on the filth of graveyards and suckled on the rotting flesh of battlefield corpses. Scald-Crow's ability to become anything she chose, to suck whole armies into her eyes, and to swallow entire battalions with her maw. And Morrigan's strong evil sorcery. Among them the Sisters summoned every dark enchantment ever known, so that their Master, the Erl-King, could possess Tara and crush Ireland.

"But Dierdriu's people beat them back. They fought long and dreadful wars—for Morrigan had no scruples about using her dread powers, and a war where sorcery is used is a terrible thing. But she was beaten back, and although she was not destroyed, in the end she retreated.

"But before she did so, she cursed Dierdriu," said Cormac. "Vilely and venomously she cursed her. It is from that curse that the founding of the Bloodline—the half-human, half-beast rulers—springs."

He stopped, and Joanna, scarcely daring to breathe, said, "Tell me."

"Morrigan could not injure Dierdriu," said Cormac, "for Dierdriu was protected by the wisest and most scholarly sorcerers of Ireland. She had, as well, the Druids on her side, and although it is many centuries since the Druids swore allegiance to anyone other than themselves, they did swear allegiance to Dierdriu at the beginning.

"Between them all, they created for the Queen the enchantment known as the Girdle of Gold—the strongest and most potent protection that has ever been known. It can encircle an entire City and render that City safe from any form of attack, and although it has long since been lost to my family, in those days Dierdriu possessed it and because of that, Morrigan could not harm her. They say she hovered over the battlefield in the last and most famous battle—the Battle for the Trees—and that the skies darkened and the air was filled with the screeching of her dark armies and with the beating of wings. But Dierdriu rode through them and they could not touch her.

"Morrigan towered above the Queen herself then, her hair a mass of writhing snakes, her eyes molten, and sent out a curse that splintered the skies and brought drops of blood raining from the heavens. She cursed Dierdriu's line for a hundred generations; she said, "Your line shall end with you, madam, and your children will die in the womb. Your seed shall never occupy Tara's Throne, for it is destined for my Master.'

"But Dierdriu bargained with the sorcerers, until at length a new enchantment was written into the Book of the Academy of Necromancers—and that," said Cormac, "is something which can only be done when the Bright Palace itself is in the utmost peril.

"The enchantment allowed the Royal Line of Ireland to lie with the animals, and to produce half-human, half-beast people who would rule from Tara and be immune to Morrigan's curse. For," said Cormac, "Morrigan's curse was that of a sorceress cursing a pure human, and Dierdriu knew that if her descendants could become other than purely human, the curse would not touch them."

"That is why," said Gormgall, as Cormac fell silent, "no pure-bred human can ever occupy Tara's Throne. That is why the Enchantment of the Bloodline is kept alive by our sorcerers, so that every third or fourth generation—"

"Or when the Judges decide it is necessary," put in Dubhgall.

"Yes, or when the Judges decide it is necessary, the Great Ritual is celebrated, and the Enchantment invoked."

Joanna, listening, fascinated and absorbed, received a sudden fleeting impression of a forest at night, and a solemn procession, torch-lit and formal, converging on the forest's heart, the Wolves waiting there, their eyes bright, their fur sleek.

The *Draiocht Prionsa den Fhiorfhuil* ... The Enchantment for the Princes of the Blood ... And once I knew it so well ... Once I stood at the forest's heart and welcomed that torch-lit procession, and once I stood and watched as the first Bloodline of all was created. Strength welled up inside her, and with it the beginnings of a very great anger.

Begone Morrigan ... banish, adversary ...

Dubhgall was explaining about the curse placed on Tara by Morrigan. "And once a curse is uttered," he said, "properly uttered, with full knowledge and full understanding, it's very nearly impossible to kill it. You can turn it aside if you are very clever—as Dierdriu did—but you can't unmake it. Nasty soulless things, curses. Personally, I wouldn't touch one."

"Morrigan has never ceased to hate Dierdriu's line," said

Cormac. "She vowed to seek out every descendant of Dierdriu who occupied the Ancient Throne and kill them, by trickery or sorcery, or ordinary human violence." He looked at Joanna as he said this, and Joanna felt again the implacable anger against Morrigan.

Cormac said softly, "My friends, we are in the hands of one of Ireland's greatest enemies, and if we do not outwit her, then Tara will fall into the hands of Morrigan's master."

"Her master?" said Joanna.

"The Erl-King," said Cormac, and for a moment a terrible silence fell.

Then Dubhgall, who believed in being as practical as you could, no matter the difficulties, and who was, in fact, usually at his best in dangerous situations, said, "Well, Sire, I'm a plain man, and I don't know much about magic, pure *or* the other sort. I always left that to the people whose business it was. But can't we just outwit the Morrigna, Sire? By ordinary human cleverness?"

"Would the cloak not help us?" asked Joanna hesitantly, who did not want to put forward any suggestion that might be thought silly, but thought they ought to consider every possibility.

Cormac said slowly, "The cloak can only be used once against an enemy. I believe we should wait until we are in the severest danger before we use it against Morrigan and her sisters."

"*Could* there be a severer danger than this?" asked Gormgall, and Cormac replied at once. "Oh yes. Oh yes, Gormgall, there could." Gormgall looked a bit white around the mouth, and relapsed into silence.

"Remember that we must not be separated," Cormac said, pacing the room restlessly. "Not for an instant. To lose each other now would be unthinkable."

"I suppose," said Gormgall, "that the door *is* locked?"

"Locked and bolted from the other side," said Dubhgall, who had been trying it at intervals, alternately checking on the window.

"What about the chimney?"

"What about it?"

"Couldn't we climb out that way?" said Gormgall, and Cormac smiled for the first time.

"My poor friends, did you truly suppose I would let you go up the chimney?" He pointed to the fire that blazed in the hearth.

"We could damp down the fire," said Dubhgall.

"What with?"

"If we hadn't a lady present I could tell you," said Dubhgall primly, and Joanna laughed, despite her fear of the Morrigna, because it was so like Dubhgall to remember the courtesies at such a moment.

She said, "If you think it will do any good, please don't worry about me. I've been travelling with the army for a number of days now."

"Ah, that'll be the younger ones," said Dubhgall with disapproval. "Weak bladders and no manners."

Cormac said, "Hush, I believe . . . yes, someone is coming." He urged them: "Remember that under no circumstances must we separate."

He took Joanna's hand firmly, and Joanna, who was still trying to pretend that she was not afraid, said, "Have we a chance of escaping?"

"There is bound to be one," said Cormac. "But we must watch carefully for it."

The door opened and Morrigan and her two sisters stood on the threshold.

THE SMALL AMOUNT of folklore that had survived Devastation told of many strange things. Joanna believed there were a number of tales—all of them horrid—about trios of evil women. But she thought there could never have been a stranger tale, or three more evil women, than the three in the room with them now.

There was a dreadful white stringy substance flowing between the sisters—"The Bonds of the Hag," said Cormac, softly. "Do not touch it if you value your sanity."

The Bonds had a life of their own; they flowed and pulsated, snakelike, and strands of them curled about Morrigan's head as she stood watching, a smile on her full wet lips. The other two stood a little behind. They are subordinates, thought Joanna; they are pawns to her. Even so, they are very terrible.

Macha, whom Cormac had called the Mother of Monsters, was a white sluglike creature, with fishlike eyes and tapering arms and legs that were webbed. But she was perceptibly female, and Joanna shuddered at the sight of the dozen or so breasts that protruded from Macha's body. Then she remembered that Macha's family was suckled by battlefield corpses. Macha caught Joanna's eye, and gave a sly calculating look, as if she was sizing her up, and saying: oh yes, this one will do very nicely.

Badb, whom Cormac had called Scald-Crow, was by far the ugliest of the three. She was bald and her skin was withered and puckered like an old apple. She looked at Joanna very directly, and Joanna said aloud, without realising it, *"The wet eyes in the cave."*

At once Badb grinned, "Like this, you mean, madam?" and became a huge single eye on scaly legs, waddling towards Joanna. She backed away, thinking: this is truly terrible. It is laughing at me. Can eyes laugh? Can one single eye laugh like that and look as if it might eat you . . .

"Sister behave," Macha said, in a low wet bubbling voice that made them all want to clear their throats and swallow, and Scald-Crow resumed her normal shape and scowled.

"Only a little fun, Sister."

"A waste of valuable energy," said Macha.

"Spoilsport!"

"Show-off!"

Scald-Crow sucked in a huge breath, and drew one eye back into her head, while the other stood out huge and red, dangling on to her cheek. Her mouth twisted, distorted into an impossibly wide grin, until it reached her ears, and they could see down inside her throat. A thick column of dark solid blood rose from the centre of her head like the mast of a ship.

Joanna gasped and Cormac's hand tightened over hers, and Scald-Crow changed back again.

"A little amusement," said Morrigan, her voice a purr. "They are excited at what lies ahead." She studied Cormac. "I hope, Your Majesty, that you do not intend to try to savage me again? It would avail you nothing. My powers are far greater than any puny sorcerer you may have at Tara." But for all her scorn her voice licked the name greedily, and Joanna knew that Cormac had been right: Morrigan had never ceased to want his kingdom.

Morrigan said, "You know what will happen to you all?"

"I know what you will try to achieve," said Cormac, and Morrigan smiled.

"You will be taken down to the Miller's cages that lie below this house—"

"Down below below," said Scald-Crow.

"And then I shall summon the Miller," said Morrigan, and at once Cormac seemed more alert.

"Summon? Does he not then wait for us?"

"He has to be summoned," said Morrigan, and Joanna, whose thoughts were already racing ahead, thought: summoned! So he is not yet here! Is there a chance somewhere that we might escape?

"You will be chopped and skinned and minced," said Macha leaning forward, the Bonds wreathing her head.

"Your blood will bathe us," said Scald-Crow, and at once became a gaping mouth.

"And then you will be eaten," said Morrigan with satisfaction. "A fitting end, Wolfking." She stood before him, her eyes raking him. "But first, a little pleasure, Your Majesty?

"Come now, am I so ill-favoured? Is not your reputation such that it is said you can have any woman? You can have me, Sire. Your final act before going to the Miller. But . . ." a shrug, "if you are unwilling, I have sufficient spells to harden you, Sire." Her eyes narrowed. "And I *will* harden you, Cormac. I *will* have you in my bed." She laughed, and Cormac snarled and reached for her. Morrigan moved deftly away and the snake-tongue flickered, and as it did so, something began to uncoil in Joanna's mind, and something that had been long asleep and deeply asleep, began to wake.

Banish, adversary . . . begone, Morrigan . . . The anger that she had experienced earlier began to rise up, and she thought: how *dare* this wicked, greedy, repulsive creature speak to Cormac like that! How *dare* she!

Morrigan was still regarding Cormac, hands on hips, his eyes slitted. "Snarl away, Wolfking. It will do you not the smallest good. I have you at last, and you will go to the cages, and then to my Master's table. Silver platters and golden goblets . . . we are going to eat you, Cormac, and your precious kingdom will be ours at last!"

Morrigan laughed again and so contemptuous was her laughter, that Joanna forgot about feeling sick now, and stood very still and allowed the overwhelming anger, and the sudden and immense strength to pour into her, as easily as pouring water from one jug to another. She thought: it is filling me up, this anger that is not mine and this strength that is someone else's. And she broke from the others, and walked to stand before Morrigan, her eyes blazing.

Morrigan did not exactly flinch, but looked startled, and Joanna felt a tremendous surge of power. She looked straight into Morrigan's eyes—after all, I am easily as tall as she is, thought Joanna, surprised—and saw that Morrigan's eyes were cold and old and colourless.

And after all, filth, I have defeated you once before . . .

The thought brought no surprise with it. The heat of the battlefield, the air dark with Morrigan's sorcery, the stench of the Army of Corpses summoned by Macha . . . oh yes, I was there, thought Joanna, and knew a swift exultation.

I have defeated you once before, Morrigan . . . I shall do so again . . .

Morrigan was watching Joanna, and there was something behind her eyes now that was not quite fear, but that was certainly not triumph.

Joanna felt the scalding power again, and heard her own voice speaking.

"Tóg ort! Bi a shiúl! Gread leat!"

For a moment there was a silence so profound that no one seemed even to breathe.

Then Morrigan said, very softly, *"Cé hé thusa?* Who are you?"

"Is me Dierdriu de shiúl oiche," said Joanna, and a flame of the purest terror flared in Morrigan's eyes. She backed away, and behind her, Macha whimpered and cowered, and Scald-Crow hissed and undulated, wisps of smoke curling from her nostrils.

Standing a little apart, Cormac said in a low voice, "Gormgall . . . Dubhgall . . . Is not that a very old form of Gael?"

Gormgall, whose eyes had never left Joanna, replied, "The oldest, Sire, and the purest. Her . . . your lady, has bidden the Morrigna begone, and when Morrigan asked who she was, said, 'I am Dierdriu of the Nightcloak.' At least, Sire, that's as near as I can get."

The Morrigna quickly recovered from their horrified surprise. Macha was standing by the door, her arms folded across her repulsive breasts, and Scald-Crow had taken on the form of a great leprous worm, and was squirming and hissing and chuckling evilly.

Morrigan said slowly to Joanna, "So it is true. All of the old prophecies ... the High Queen returned ... Madam, you travel more inconspicuously than once you did. And in strange company."

"I travel with my own. Get thee gone, Morrigan!"

"But we have an old, old score to settle first, Your Majesty," said Morrigan, and walked thoughtfully round Joanna. Cormac, watching, saw that Morrigan was walking in a circle again, and knew a pang of fear. But he knew that to interrupt now would break the tenuous strength that Joanna was drawing on, and he knew that if this was, indeed, the High Queen returned, then Joanna would be struggling to keep Dierdriu's presence within her. And despite his fear of Morrigan and the sisters, he felt a great exultation: Dierdriu returned to Ireland!

Morrigan was still studying Joanna. "A pretty bird for the plucking," she said, and reached out to stroke Joanna's cheek. "Oh, yes, a very pretty bird. So you lie with the wolves, do you my lady, just as you did all those years ago, just as you did when you commanded the sorcerers to weave the Enchantment of the Bloodline." She moved closer, her face level with Joanna's. "Do you enjoy them, Dierdriu, those wolves, with their cruel natures and their sharp pricks? Do they spear you, Dierdriu? And did you really create the Enchantment to save Tara, or to pleasure your own lusts?" She smiled, and Joanna looked coldly at her.

"The Enchantment was woven to cheat your curse, Morrigan. To save my people."

"Curses can never be cheated," said Morrigan, "because curses can never be unmade, Dierdriu. We both know it. I shall be revenged on you at last, as I always promised you." A pause, then, "I wonder how your wolf lover will feel towards you after I have had my fill of you?" And then, nodding to her sisters, "Take the Wolfking and his servants to the cages, and make ready to call up the Miller. But the High Queen take to my bedchamber."

CHAPTER EIGHT

FLYNN AND AMAIRGEN sat up and looked about them. It was not quite dark, but it was very nearly so. There were thickening shadows everywhere, and the heavy unmistakable scent of twilight.

Twilight. The Purple Hour.

Amairgen called, "Portan?" and at once there was a response.

"I am here."

Flynn, still dazzled and dazed by the Time Curtain, thought: we are truly here. We have travelled through many hundreds of years. We are in the ancient past. And felt his blood stir and his emotions fire.

Amairgen stood up and brushed his cloak clean. "There is no time for being emotional, Flynn. We are here, where we wanted to be, but I am afraid we have been followed. Do either of you know what happened to the two men who were chasing us?"

Flynn said slowly, "Yes. They are here. I can feel it . . . A kind of dark muddy anger. They are annoyed at us, but they are not quite sure what has happened."

Amairgen said, "Oh they of little imagination." And then, quite lightly, "Your powers are heightened, Flynn." Flynn realised with surprise that Amairgen was right. He could feel and he could sense in far greater strength than ever before. He could feel Portan's fear of this unknown world, but he could also sense her devotion and her gratitude flowing like a great golden river. He could feel as well Amairgen's concern and the man's determination.

Amairgen sent Flynn one of his rare sweet smiles, and Flynn said at once, "Should we try to find them? Joanna's father and Brian Muldooney?"

"They will find us soon enough. And is it not those two whom Joanna was fleeing?"

Flynn had very nearly forgotten this. He was horrified to realise it: "How could I? Amairgen, those were the men—"

"I do wish, Flynn, you were not so volatile." Amairgen was standing up looking about them. Flynn thought: as if he is sniffing the air, and then discovered that he, too, was sniffing the air. And he thought that there were things here that he had never encountered in his life, and he was both frightened and exhilarated.

Amairgen moved from the shelter of the trees on to a kind of highroad that unravelled before them, and Flynn and Portan followed. Flynn thought: "the blue and green misty island." *At last.* And looked about him and saw that the forest fringing the road was indeed mist-shrouded, and that the forest colours were so soft-hued as to be almost turquoise, and the shadows were purple tinged.

"The island of mist and mystery, where men lay with beasts and Magic was alive ..." Flynn did not know where the words came from, and he did not very much care. And it was twilight, it was the Purple Hour, but it was like no Purple Hour he had ever known before. Heady and heavy and laden with enchantment.

The Deep Past. The Old Ireland. *We are here.*

A great and painful longing swept over him, an only-now-recognised homesickness. This is where I belong. This is where I was meant to be. I feel it and I sense it. Not a part of the bleak struggling world that was left to the survivors of Devastation; not an Irish farmer, tilling the land and gathering the fruit harvest and shearing the sheep. *Here.* Here is my rightful place. In this strange misty land of dark forests and tall mountains and beckoning woodland paths. Here, where humans lie with beasts and give birth to strange half-humans who rule the land by powerful magic. This is what I have always yearned for, what I have ached for. I was born homesick, thought Flynn, but now I have come home, and a great joy unfolded in his breast. I was born in the wrong time and in the wrong world, but this is my time and this is my world, and I have come home.

And never once, in all the days and weeks and nights that followed, did he ever feel the loss of Tugaim, or miss its people. Never once did he lose the almost unbearable feeling of belonging.

They did not know it, but Flynn and Amairgen had broken through the Time Curtain in a slightly different place from Joanna. The great dark outline of Scáthach, the Fortress of Shadow where the Wolfking had sat out the days of his exile, lay across the valley from them, a distant shape. Before it was the hillside down which the Wolves of Tara had streamed in answer to the High King's call. Sprawled across the valley was the silent sinister Forest of Darkness, the dwelling place of the *sidh* with their eerie temptings. Directly ahead of them . . .

"Oh!" said Flynn softly, and for a brief space almost forgot about finding Joanna.

Ahead of them was the great, legendary Palace of Tara; the Shining Palace itself, brightly lit and blazing against the night sky; the Glittering Fortress, the Ancient and Magical Seat of the High Kings of Ireland; the Bright Castle, the shimmering City. Tara, with its soaring spires and its sparkling pinnacles, bastioned in colour and turreted in gilt and bathed in its own iridescence. Invulnerable and impregnable and beautiful beyond imagining and beyond bearing. Gramarye and the Gates of Paradise and the Isle of Avalon all bound up in one great radiant mansion.

And in my Father's House there are many such mansions . . .

Flynn thought: where did those words come from? The past? Or the future? How lovely it is. Dare we approach it?

For a long time no one spoke, and they were to think afterwards that it was as if they had been feasting on the splendour of Tara and drawing renewed strength from it. And then, Amairgen, who of the three had perhaps been a little more prepared, said as if repeating an incantation, "Nothing that is not beautifully perfect or perfectly beautiful could ever enter into Tara."

"Can we enter? Dare we?" said Flynn, but his whole body ached to go up to the great portcullis and gain entry.

"Joanna is days ahead of us," said Amairgen thoughtfully. "If she came this way, she would surely have gone to Tara."

Or been taken there? thought Flynn, but he did not say it, because to say it aloud might give substance to the thought.

Portan said hesitantly, "If we travel on this road, we may meet other wayfarers. People who could give us news."

"Yes, we need all the knowledge we can acquire," said Amairgen. "And not only of Joanna. We need to know about the people of this world. Most of all, we need to know about the people of Tara itself." He glanced at Flynn. "It is drawing you, Flynn. It is stretching out its enchantment to lure you inside. Well, that may be no bad thing. But were you imagining the people of Tara to be benevolent and kindly? Were you thinking that our ancestors were gentle and benign? I promise you they will be no such thing, Flynn. They will be beautiful and cruel and wild and totally unlike anything you have ever encountered." He smiled. "The world before Devastation was very different, Flynn. Even then, people were greedy and selfish. How much more so will these people be?" He looked at them both. "But we can be cruel and wild if we have to," said Amairgen. "Certainly we can be cunning." He touched Flynn's arm and laid a hand on Portan's head. "The Letheans had a saying, 'When in Rome, behave as a Roman.' I think we must do that now. I think we must walk up to the gates of Tara and request admittance, as if it is the most natural thing in the world. As if we have no thought of a refusal. That way we may get inside."

"And once inside?"

"Once inside it is up to us," said Amairgen.

"What explanation do we give?" asked Flynn. "Who do we say we are?"

"Travellers seeking shelter. No more and no less." Again there was the brief sweet smile. "Somewhere in Lethe history was a famous man who said one should never explain or apologise. His name is lost, but his words have survived and they are good words. So whoever he was, let us follow his philosophy."

"All right. Yes."

"Come then. If we are to find Joanna we must not lose any time."

THE ROAD THEY now travelled was like no road any of them had ever seen. "And yet," said Flynn once, "I believe I could almost identify parts of the countryside. Perhaps after all we have not come so very far."

"Ten thousand years, or half a league," said Amairgen.

The landscape was strange and wild. "But it is the blues and the greens of the true Ireland," said Amairgen in deep content. "The Old Ireland."

They walked on, neither tired nor hungry, "Although," said Flynn, "we should stop to eat and rest from time to time, don't you think?"

They met no one, although several times both Flynn and Amairgen had whisked round, hands on the knives thrust into their belts, only to be confronted with the long empty road. Once, Portan scuttled into the undergrowth at the side of the road as if to take cover.

"A feeling," she said. "Nothing more. I am sorry. Imagination." But the two men knew that Portan had not imagined it, and they became warier.

Even so, the road was smooth and easy to travel, and the brief stops they made were refreshing. Flynn was glad he had been able to bring all the food so carefully packed by Michael. Amairgen and Portan had gathered fruit from the orchard at the farm while they waited for him, and there was plenty for all.

"I climbed to the topmost branches," said Portan. "The sweetest fruit is always at the top. I remember that from—oh from somewhere in the world. I do not know. And I saw the countryside spread out below me. A marvellous thing for me. You cannot imagine how marvellous."

But both men thought they could realise a little what it must have been like for her. "And it was worth it for these pears," said Flynn, grinning.

They washed in the streams that ran alongside the path and then disappeared, silver, snakelike and silent into the great forest that fringed the road. They rested beneath the trees and talked, or were silent, and Flynn felt tireless and so charged with energy that he could have torn down the trees and marched up to Tara and battered down the doors single-handed. He felt that he was riding out at the head of a fearsome army and that he was invincible.

At his side, Amairgen spoke softly, "Finn of the *Fiana*. It is returning to you, my friend."

Flynn said, "What?" rather sharply, because he was not always entirely sure that he liked his thoughts being plucked wholesale from his head.

"Finn mac Airmall, the great warrior who served the High Kings and founded the ancient and honourable Order of the *Fiana*, the fighting young men of the old families who swore to defend the High King, and who must undergo stringent tests before they could be admitted to the brotherhood." He smiled. "They were strong and fearless, but they had also to be educated and cultured. They had to forswear their families and go wherever their leader took them."

"Harsh," said Flynn.

"Perhaps. But they were young men of adventure and imagination. They fought battles and routed the High King's enemies and there was a tradition that no girl of good family could be given in marriage until she had first been offered to the *Fiana*. I daresay it was not so bad a life," said Amairgen blandly, and Flynn laughed and was sorry he had been brusque. He took Amairgen's arm, and began to sing a song he could not remember ever having been taught.

The sun was sinking as they rounded the last curve in the road, and there, against the sky, was Tara, blood red in the glow of the dying sun, every window afire with light ... Waiting for them.

Flynn drew in a great breath. "Well?" he said, looking at Amairgen. "Do we in truth go up and request admittance?"

"We do."

"And if they refuse?"

Amairgen said slowly, "They will not refuse. I cannot tell why that will be or how I know. But I do know. It is preordained this, Flynn, and we must go on and play our parts."

"Very well then," said Flynn. "Here we go."

EOCHAID BRES HAD not really wanted to be King. He had much preferred to leave all that kind of thing to Cormac who, after all, had been brought up to it, and he had not really understood why Mother and Bricriu had thought it necessary to depose Cormac in the first place. He had not, truth to tell, been entirely comfortable about deposing Cormac, because wasn't Cormac the true King? Wasn't he a direct descendant of the first rulers of Ireland? Eochaid knew how it worked, because Mother and Bricriu had explained it to him. It was father to son and so on, all down the generations. Well, down the centuries really, because it was certainly hundreds of years since Dierdriu of the Nightcloak had ruled Ireland with her special blend of charm, strength, and sorcery. They had never had a High Queen to match her since, although it did not do to say so in Mother's hearing, of course. Mother called herself the Queen Mother now—"Quite correct," Bricriu said with one of his sly smiles—and liked to think that she would make as strong a mark on history as Dierdriu had. Eochaid thought glumly that she probably would, but for different reasons, and wished that he could close his ears to the sniggers of his courtiers. The Queen Mother would send for, and tire out a dozen men in a night, they said. Absolutely insatiable. Bricriu the Fox was thinking of setting up a detachment of the army especially for her, they said. Six months' secondment to the Queen Mother. Six months' *service* to the Queen Mother, added the younger ones, and grinned, and told how you'd be reduced to half an inch within the week. She'd devour you, they said, and spit out your bones in the morning.

Eochaid tried not to hear the talk, because it made you feel a bit of a fool, well, more than a bit, to know such things about your own mother. It lessened your dignity, and dignity was important if you were a High King. Cormac had never bothered of course, but Cormac had been brought up to it all, and in some mysterious way did not need to bother. Eochaid wondered whether it was perhaps because Cormac had not bothered about dignity that people had obeyed him. You could call Cormac a lot of things, but dignified was not one of them.

Eochaid had not been very happy about the revolution which Mother and Bricriu had mounted. Well, he had been very unhappy about it indeed, if he was to be truthful. And it had all been a bit tedious in the beginning, because there had been meetings, at which he usually fell asleep, and there had been Strategy and Tactics, and it had all been a touch boring.

But Mother had been insistent; the Wolfline must be deposed, she had said, and Bricriu, called up from Tara to be their guest, had nodded and smiled in his foxy way, and said: yes, to be sure they must, and wasn't this to be the Grand Revolution that would free the people of Ireland from tyranny. Eochaid had not previously considered Cormac in the light of a tyrant, and found it difficult to do so now, but he did not say this, in case he was wrong. It would not have done, especially not when they were going to make him High King. He would quite like to be High King—well he would like it a lot, really.

And so they had raised an army—several people had said with a smirk that Mab had enjoyed doing that, but Eochaid had pretended not to hear—and they had ridden down to Tara from the north which was where they lived. "In squalor," Mother had said, and made one of her grand gestures, but Eochaid had quite liked living in the north, where life was quite peaceful and where he knew everybody. He would not know everybody at Tara, and he would probably forget people's names and it would all be very worrying.

He had asked why they had to depose Cormac, and Mother had said impatiently, "Because he is a tyrant and because the Wolfline has ruled for too long," and Eochaid had said, "Oh. I see." And gone away more puzzled than before.

He had quite enjoyed riding out at the head of the army, with the lion pennants fluttering in the breeze (Bricriu's idea), although he had not really enjoyed beating Cormac's men, because he had had the dreadful suspicion that Cormac had only been beaten because Tara and the soldiers had been taken by surprise.

"Unprepared?" Bricriu had said, suave and smooth as butter from the churn. "Why, Your Majesty *knows* I sent two Marshals of the Lists to issue the challenge."

They all knew, of course, that Bricriu had done no such thing, and Eochaid had mulled this over and had wondered whether it might not have been outright treachery, although he had not liked to say so.

He had been allowed to appear at the battles, "But not to fight," said Bricriu firmly. "We dare not risk Your Majesty being wounded."

This had been a pity, because he would have enjoyed a good fight, although he had not really wanted to fight Cormac particularly, and he had been secretly relieved when they told him to stay behind the lines. And of course, it had been grand to come riding triumphantly into Tara after Cormac had been taken to Scáthach; Eochaid had had a new white palfrey for the occasion, and worn his best robes.

There were endless Council Meetings which he had to attend, with rambling discourses which he did not understand, all about taxes and levies and the paying of Senboth's Pence and Partholon's-geld, and feu and scutages and bondages, and other unpronounceable things, which all seemed to relate to money. "So sordid," Mother said with one of her grimaces and one of her wonderful airy waves of the hand. But, "Necessary," said Bricriu firmly, and tried to drill Eochaid into understanding about venery rights and the proper maintenance of the northern borders, and the bestowing of lands to people who had done the High King a service.

There were delegations, as well; visits from people who wanted tasks performing, towns rebuilding, or City Gates manning.

Eochaid went along with it, and was gracious to visiting chieftains, and tried hard to distinguish between people who ought genuinely to be helped and those who were out for a few cheap acres, but he thought it all a great waste of time. But Bricriu said no, they must do it; the chieftains in particular had to be kept happy because they would ride out to defend the King, they could whip up an army in no time at all, a massive and truly terrifying force which, added to Eochaid's own Royal Guard, could repel all invaders. Tara was invincible, of course, everyone knew that, but Eochaid must never forget that this would not deter enterprising enemies from launching attacks now and again. Far better, said Bricriu, far safer to be able to call on the chieftains to ride out. All they had to do was to get Conaire, who had a goodish vein of eagle blood in him, to send out a call to the birds, and the message would be with the chieftains inside an hour.

Eochaid had seen the force of this, of course; even so, it all got a bit tiresome. Nor did he altogether trust Conaire, who had been a drinking crony of Cormac's.

There was so much to remember. The chieftains from the north liked a bit of life: bull-feasts and jousts and hunting the white stag. They usually visited Tara on the feast of Dagda the Father-God, when flares were lit the length and breadth of Ireland, and of course, on Beltane and Samain, which meant bonfires, which was all very well if you did not have to consider the restrictions on tree felling.

The chieftains from the south were not nearly as wild as their northern counterparts. They were smooth and courteous; they considered themselves men of culture. They consid-

ered themselves widely read, which meant that Sean the Storyteller, Eochaid's official *ollam*, had to ransack the great library
for something they would not have heard. It was all very well
to tell the northern chieftains the tried and trusted tales about
Amairgen the Traveller, and Bran the Voyager; or to recite the
famous and magical *Táin Bó Cualinge* which was so hedged
about with rule and ritual that no one dared to speak during the
recital for fear of saying the wrong thing and spoiling the spell,
and during which Eochaid nearly always fell asleep. The
southern chieftains knew all about Amairgen and Bran; they
knew about the *Táin* as well, and they knew all of the side rituals to it, and they had to be given something a bit more up-
to-date. They liked the company of young girls, and Sean the
Storyteller was usually despatched to round up as many of the
village girls as could be persuaded to yield their virtue which
was not, properly speaking, Sean's job, but which he usually
volunteered for, because he could sample the wares for himself
on the way.

And so what with one thing, and what with another, the visits were apt to be bothersome. They were certainly expensive,
because you could not give a bull-feast without a pretty generous supply of bulls, which did not come cheap these days, and
village girls nearly always had venal fathers who would not be
letting Kate or Ethne or Niamne come along up to the feasting
without an earnest of payment, which generally meant a field
or two, if it did not mean a fully built house.

Eochaid found it all very tedious, although he did not say so
to Mother, who had worked so hard to put him here—"With
my life's blood, Eochaid Bres"—or to Bricriu, who would look
shocked and fix Eochaid with his queer colourless eyes, and
say, "But Your Majesty *knows* that to be a High King of Ireland is the greatest honour that can befall a man."

Eochaid knew it was an honour, but it did not stop him from
wondering how to pay for bull-feasts, or trying to find out
whether the trees were truly dead or only snoozing to fool everyone, or falling asleep during the recital of the *Táin* and nodding off in Council Meetings.

"His Majesty's dozed off again," they said when he did that.
"Oh well, let him be, for he contributes little enough to the
discussions anyway."

He knew he did not contribute very much, but he thought they might at least have pretended.

He was going to assert himself tonight.

Eochaid was going to let them all see he was the King. It was all very well for Bricriu and Mother to plot their plots and manipulate their pawns; Eochaid was not a pawn and he was not going to be manipulated and plotted with, and that was that.

He dressed carefully in the tawny velvet that he always fancied became him best. It was not that he precisely emphasised his antecedents, although he did not see why he should not, because lions were as good as and better than wolves any day. No, it was simply that he liked wearing golds and bronzes and rich ambers.

He trimmed his beard because he did not want to appear unkempt and he combed his thick springy golden hair, and dabbed a touch of scented oil behind his ears and then he was ready.

TARA WAS *en fête* tonight, eager to entertain a minor chieftain—who was not so minor that he could not command a degree of respect and a not inconsiderable army—and to pay compliments to his lady, who was not so aloof that she could not be judiciously wooed by the younger men. The vast Sun Chamber, built for Dierdriu of the Nightcloak, and angled so precisely that it caught the first dawnlight every morning and the last starlight every night, glittered and sparkled with life. It gave Eochaid a headache even to look at it. What gave him a worse headache (and had, in fact, even kept him awake at nights) was the way in which the people of the ancient Bloodlines had taken to clustering together every evening. There they were now, all seated around a table at the far end, apparently talking and laughing quite openly; some of them ostensibly eyeing the women. They made Eochaid vaguely uneasy. He could not forget that they had all been Cormac's friends and extremely loyal to Cormac; he could not rid himself of the idea that they might be plotting in secret to bring Cormac back from Scáthach.

He had, greatly daring, put this notion to Bricriu, and Bricriu had looked startled, and said, "Oh no, Sire, I don't think they're planning a Restoration. We'd surely know if they were." He smiled the fox-smile. "We have our own spies, remember."

Eochaid knew all about Bricriu's spies, who were rather unpleasant, slightly rat-faced people, given to scuttling out of the way when you approached them.

"Ratblood," said Mother, with the shrug of one to whom such things are beneath notice. "Bricriu makes use of some *nasty* little tools at times." But even she had added, "Although, if they are loyal, I do not think it matters what they are."

Loyalty was very important in a spy, Eochaid quite saw that. You could not have spies turning about and selling secrets to the other side, especially when the other side might consist of Cormac and of people who wanted him back at Tara.

"Oh, the Bloodline are not plotting Cormac's restoration," said Bricriu. "Dear me, Sire, we know all about the Bloodline and their little plans."

Eochaid asked how did they know.

"Because," said Bricriu, surprised, "the spies listen to everything they say." And then, as Eochaid frowned, "That is what spies are for, Sire."

Eochaid had not liked to point out that the problem was not what the Bloodline were saying that they could all hear, but what was being said that could not be heard. Speech without words. The Samhailt. *That* was the real problem.

"But," said his mother, when Eochaid carried this weighty problem to her, "the Samhailt has been outlawed."

Eochaid had pretended to have forgotten about this, but to himself he thought that to outlaw a thing did not necessarily banish it entirely. He thought there were probably a good many people at Court who possessed the Samhailt quite strongly, and he felt a bit wistful about this, because it was something he would very much have liked to have had himself.

"And there is the difficulty," Bricriu had said, wrestling with creating a whole new set of laws which could be made to fit Eochaid's accession. "Traditionally, Sire, the Samhailt is the privileged gift of the High Kings and the Bloodline."

"I *know* that," said Eochaid Bres, in what was very nearly a growl.

"But you do not possess it," said Bricriu, and Eochaid wished that Bricriu would not be quite so blunt. But because he could not think of anything to say, he relapsed into silence and waited. Bricriu went on, "We dare not have a High King who does not have the Samhailt, not while there are others who do have it, you see? To do so might argue that there are others at Court with a claim to the throne that is as strong as— nearly as strong as yours. It had better be outlawed," he had decided. "Made punishable by death. That will solve it, Sire, you will see." And he had gone away and written the new law that banished the Samhailt, although as Mother had pointed out, rather caustically, it was going to be extremely difficult to prove or disprove it either way. You could not actually see the Samhailt unless you had it yourself, and if you had it yourself, you were not going to admit to it if it was outlawed.

All of which had been so complicated, that Eochaid developed another headache and had to lie down and have a soothing draught brought to him.

But there had been a few cases of discovery, and the culprits had been dealt with smartly, because you could not risk having people communicating without speaking. You did not know what they might be plotting. You certainly had to suspect that anyone with the Samhailt might well be a supporter of Cormac.

"To the Miller with them!" cried Bricriu, and managed to make it sound almost gay, as if he were sending the victims on some kind of pleasant holiday. Eochaid spent quite a long time trying to forget what the Giant Miller of Muileann did to his prisoners.

Silver platters and golden goblets ... He'd had a nurse, a half-human, who had chanted that to him in his nursery, until Mother found out and dismissed her. He had only Cruithin nurses after that; the Cruithin were apt to be annoyingly stubborn in their allegiance to the Wolfkings, said Mother crossly, but at least they did not chant frightening verses to babies.

But he would not think about any of it tonight. He would remember about being assertive, and he would certainly remember about showing them all that he was the King.

He sat down at table, and felt profoundly depressed. He refused a dish of fresh wood gazelle—"Your Majesty's favourite!" cried the head cook, almost in tears—and he asked had they not plain honest roast boar in their sculleries. He wrinkled his nose at the wine and called for a flagon of best mead, wondering audibly whether there was a deliberate attempt at discourtesy to his guests that night.

He listened to the music being played and danced in a rather ponderous fashion with the visiting chieftain's lady, indulging himself in a little portly flirtation, causing the lady, no slouch, to preen herself afterwards and inform her particular crony that she had found the King quite charming.

"They say he's rather stupid and slow," said the crony, who had not been sought to dance and did not see why dearest Mugain should give herself airs.

"Oh not in the least!" cried Mugain. "I found him delightful. I fancy I made no small impression, my dear," and the crony thought it was as she had always suspected; poorest Mugain was a dear soul, but there was no *breeding*.

Bricriu and Mab watched the stately intimacy with disquiet. "For," said Mab to Bricriu, "Eochaid simply is not interested in that sort of thing as a rule."

"No. He's his father's son," said Bricriu rather daringly, but recalling that he had once shared Mab's bed for a night or two; an experience which Mab had long since forgotten, but which Bricriu had not.

"Oh, his father was never interested either," said Mab and sent Bricriu one of her brief blinding smiles, which made him wriggle inside his robes, and recall the young Mab who twenty years earlier had been called the Intoxicating One. He quelled an incipient heartburn, along with an incipient rush of heat between his legs, and thought he would have to partake sparingly of the feast tonight. He would have to summon one of the chambermaids to his bed later to relieve his body, and he never performed well when he had indigestion. It would not do to have it blabbed all over the Court that he could not get it up any more, which might very well prove the case if he ate too much roast boar . . .

Eochaid had returned Mugain to her lord's side, and was eyeing the Court impatiently. Well come on, you clever ones, where is my entertainment tonight? What is the good of being the High King at the most dazzling Court in the western world if I am to be bored and bejaded after my dinner every night? Several of the more impressionable courtiers remembered the King's ancestry, and told each other that he resembled an angry lion at the mouth of a cave, and several more found them-

selves regretting Cormac's exile rather more strongly than
usual. Wolves might be a bit unpredictable; they might certainly be erratic, but no one had ever been bored when the
Wolfkings reigned, and, rather curiously, no one had ever been
frightened either. A number of the Court remembered that
Cormac had had a sense of humour, and if Eochaid Bres possessed such a thing, he was keeping it very well hidden. He's
a tricky one, thought the courtiers; yes, he's very tricky. A
weak man's obstinacy. And certainly a stupid one's vanity.

Cormac had laughed and quarrelled, seduced the women and
got drunk with the men, and made up the rules as he went
along, and then broken them if he had felt like it. But he had
been a *King*, thought Eochaid's Court rather dismally. He had
been arrogant and brilliant and impatient, but he had been a
King. Eochaid was handsome and strong, but he was dull,
thought those who could remember the dazzling years of
Cormac's rule. Oh dear yes, he was as dull as he could be. Just
a heavy handsome animal, thought the courtiers, horrified at
their own disloyalty, and those who possessed a streak of the
Mindsong quenched it at once, lest it should be picked up and
orders given for their immediate despatch to the Miller. *Silver
platters and golden goblets* ... Everyone knew the old rhyme
and no one wanted to test its veracity.

The Sun Chamber turned with relief to the message sent up
from Phineas on the West Gate that two travellers had requested admittance, and shelter, and waited resignedly for, it
went without saying, the usual dismissal. It would come, of
course, as it always did, and Phineas on the West Gate knew
it as well as everyone else. But he would not have dared sup-
press the travellers' visit, because Bricriu the Fox had to know
everything that happened at Tara.

Cormac had been famous for his hospitality; he had delighted in gathering to the Court the travellers and the scholars,
the musicians and the poets, and in the days of the Wolfking,
Tara had become the great and glittering Court that would live
on in Ireland's legends. In Cormac's time you went down into
the Sun Chamber every evening in the knowledge that gathered there would be a glorious cornucopia of rich talent and
beauty and life, sometimes oddly matched but somehow never
jarring, because Cormac had had the rare gift of being able to
blend together any assortment of people. No one had ever been

turned away; everyone had been brought in, welcomed, given food and drink and a bed for the night. Tara was big enough for them all, Cormac had said, with regal disdain for the problems it had sometimes created for his household who often had to play put and take with the sleeping arrangements. Although to be fair, that had frequently been rather enjoyable as well.

Eochaid, ruled by the Fox, permitted no one to enter Tara's portals without an exhaustive inquiry into that person's antecedents, probable loyalties, and likely degree of treachery. You could not entirely blame him, said the courtiers, trying to be fair. Any usurper was prone to attacks from the former occupant of his throne and it was not to be expected that Cormac would stay quiescent for long out at Scáthach. Eochaid was surely entitled to his insecurity. Several people remembered the really shocking story of an entire army being sneaked inside an enemy's city hidden inside a huge wooden horse. Somewhere in the East had it been? Anyway, Eochaid Bres must be allowed his caution, but it was a great pity that the Court could not, as a result, enjoy the company of travellers, who usually had a few interesting tales to tell, and of pilgrims and men of other cultures. They turned to wait for the King's usual dismissal of the travellers who were at the West Gate.

Eochaid Bres said loudly and defiantly, "Bring the travellers in." And, as the gasp went round the Sun Chamber, "Lay places at the table for them."

FLYNN AND AMAIRGEN had not wanted to leave Portan behind, but she had been immovable.

"No," she had said, her eyes never leaving Flynn's face. "It is better I do not come."

"But we cannot leave you here," Flynn said.

"Why not? It is a mild night. I have warmth and food." She hugged about her the thick woven cloak Flynn had brought from the farmhouse, and touched their food sack.

Amairgen said gently, "But my dear, it is not to be thought of that you should remain out here in the forest by yourself," and in the dim light they saw her smile.

"I think I am safer here than inside the House of Mutants," said Portan. "I think I am certainly more comfortable. Freedom. And to listen to the trees and to the wind in the trees . . . You could not know the joy that is for me." She looked at

Flynn again. "And here there is a—I have not the words, but there is a sense of homecoming for me." She paused. "We all feel that."

"Yes," said Flynn slowly. "Yes, we are all of us at home here." *And this is my rightful place in the world.* Aloud he said, "My dear, if you are quite sure—"

"I am quite sure, Flynn. Inside there," she nodded in the direction of the glittering shape of Tara, "I should be an object of curiosity. I should be stared at and pointed at. It is a beautiful place and there will be beautiful men and women inside it. There would be the comparison ... Out here with you I do not mind, but there I should. And it is safer for you. There should be nothing about you to cause comment." She said this entirely without bitterness, and Flynn felt pity twist his guts again.

"We will leave you the large knife and the food. And—yes, look, there is a place over here. At the base of these trees, half cut into the bank, almost a cave. You would be quite warm and snug. And if you light a fire—"

"I shall not need a fire. The trees will not harm me. And I have your cloak. That is warmth and safety enough. I will be here waiting for you. Tomorrow?"

"Tomorrow or the next day," say Amairgen. "No longer, I promise. But if we are not back then—"

"Then I will find a way to come into Tara," said Portan, "I will come in and get you out."

FLYNN WAS DAZZLED and bewitched by Tara. From the moment they approached the great West Gate and sent in their request—"Food and a night's rest for two weary travellers"—to the moment when the doors of the Sun Chamber swung wide to admit them, he was intoxicated and charmed and held in thrall. How beautiful. How right. Oh yes, this is where I was meant to be.

Their welcome was cautious, for the Gatekeeper, used to the Wolfkings and only paying the most cursory of respect to Eochaid Bres, was voluble in his explanations.

No travellers to be admitted under any pretext at all, said Phineas, and wouldn't that give a man a dismal face from here to next Beltane's Eve? Not that he wasn't the King's man, of course, well weren't they all of them the King's men? But a

fine dismal time Eochaid Bres was giving them, and didn't all
Ireland know how he was under the thumb of Bricriu the Fox,
and didn't all Ireland know that Bricriu was under the thumb
of the Queen Mother, always supposing that she wasn't under
his, and the Gatekeeper didn't exactly mean thumb neither, although it wouldn't do to be more specific.

"You can't be sure who might be listening," he said. "And
you can't be sure the *sidh* aren't in Bricriu's pay, neither. Well,
I put it to you, what creature makes a better spy than an invisible one? And Bricriu isn't the one to be choosy; he'd have
half a dozen *sidh* inside Tara before you could say Dagda, for
all some people believe they've sworn allegiance to the Erl-
King. But that's another story again. And as for allegiances—
well," said the Gatekeeper, "we all know how binding *that* sort
of thing is nowadays. Look at the sorcerers—well you can't
look at them, of course, because they hardly ever come out
into the light of day—immersed in the Sorcery Chambers from
dawn to dusk, and if *they're* any more loyal to His Majesty
than the stable cat, it'll be a matter for comment. I wouldn't
trust a sorcerer from here to that door. Greedy. They'll spin an
enchantment for anyone who'll pay them enough.

"You'll take a drop of wine while we wait, I daresay, although I can tell you now that you'll be sent on your way.
Quite politely it'll be done, of course.

"Here you are, sirs, you'll forgive the discourtesy of poking
the mugs through the grille to you as if you were no better
than common tinkers, which any man can see you're not.

"Ah, that's the stuff, isn't it? Yes, it does make you cough
just a touch, doesn't it? I don't notice it myself, but they tell
me it's a mite strong. That's the King, ordering in the young
wine because it's cheaper. No breeding. Well, did you ever
hear of a High King who inspected the household accounts?
No, and no more did anyone else. Give me the Wolfkings any
day. Cormac now, there was a King. Snarl and snap at you he
would, but it was all over in a minute, and everyone the best
of friends after it. Now this one's prone to sulks, and if there's
one thing you can't be having in a High King, it's—

"Ah, there you are Sean, and is it the dismissal you've
brought us?"

But the man called Sean, who was bright-eyed and bowlegged, and had a face like seamed oak, had not brought any such thing.

They were to go along with him that very minute, he said, right up to the Sun Chamber and the High King, and the Gate-keeper, who had rearranged himself into a more comfortable position and refilled the mugs, was caught in mid-sup and swallowed several draughts down the wrong way. He had to be thumped on the back by Sean, who said it was a terrible waste to see all that grand wine being spat out on the floor, and hadn't Phineas any better respect for his drink? To which Phineas wiped his mouth, sneezed a couple of times, and re-torted that it was all very well for those up in the fine Sun Chamber, drinking the King's best mead and it a proper strong brew such as a man would never dream of choking on, but down here they had thin sour stuff you wouldn't call fit for the cat.

"You'll be forgiving Phineas for any irreverencies, I expect," said Sean, as they were led through echoing corridors and a great high-ceilinged chamber with inverted windows and doors. There was a rich unfamiliar scent—or have I tasted it before? wondered Flynn. That night on Tara's Hill? When I learned of the Time Curtain? When I became forever homesick for this place? Perhaps . . .

"We pay Phineas no attention at all," said Sean, scurrying along ahead of them with surprising agility. "He'll have talked a lot of treason, no doubt, it'll be better if you don't tell me. Well, it'll be better if you don't think about it either, for the King's very strict about the Samhailt, he won't have the small-est whiff of it within an archer's range of Tara, and I shouldn't be surprised to learn you both possess it. I wonder are you of royal blood at all? No, I'd rather not know, because if I did know I'd have to tell the King. I'm his *ollam*, you see, and I took the Vow to serve him, not that there was much option at the time, because who'd want to go out to Scáthach with Cormac? Nasty gloomy place, Scáthach. It's kept for traitors and pretenders, of course, not that there've been many pretend-ers, although some people still look on Eochaid Bres as a pre-tender really. You won't repeat that I daresay? Or that I've mentioned the Wolfking? They don't like his name mentioned here any more.

"Anyway, I took the Vow," said Sean, preceding them down

a flight of steps, "and that means I'm constrained to report any treason. You never know who might be listening these days either, so it doesn't do to let the smallest morsel of treason go unreported. Well, Eochaid Bres hasn't the strongest of rights to the Ancient Throne, you see, and they have to be very careful. You didn't hear me say that though."

"No," said Flynn and Amairgen, half mesmerised by the rapid flow of information.

"And when you remember that they send all traitors straight to the Miller—well it's a nasty end," said Sean. "It's one I don't care to think about. I ignore anything unpleasant," he said seriously. "And of course, we all know what being sent to the Miller means."

"Yes," said Flynn and Amairgen, who did not.

"You'd think they'd want to put it out of their minds," said Sean, leading them across a deserted hall with mosaic floors and symbols etched in gold on the walls. "You'd think they'd be glad to ignore the Miller. But no! Every Beltane Eve and every Samain there they are, wanting plays and masques and all manner of things about him. It's my belief," said Sean severely, "that they like being frightened. But if you've ever tried to make entertainment out of a subject like the Miller, you'll know it's no bed of roses. Well, it's an impossibility really, but there it is, Bricriu commands and we all have to obey." He bent to unlock a door. "Bricriu *says* it's the King's wishes," said Sean, "but of course, we all know it isn't."

Flynn said, "Isn't it?"

"Oh dear me no," said Sean. "Oh, rentless land to us all, no!" He pushed the doors open and led them into a kind of antechamber, silk-hung and studded with low couches. Skin rugs lay on the floors. "Wolfskin," said Sean with a gesture of disassociating himself. "Eochaid's idea of supremacy over the Wolfking. Myself I think it's petty.

"Anyway," said Sean briskly, "here we are. The Sun Chamber. You'll remember to keep the Mindsong quenched, won't you? *I* know you're not traitors—at least you don't look like traitors and you don't smell like traitors either. But the King's very acute now and again. Remarkable really. But I mustn't say that. People do gossip and I wouldn't put it past Bricriu to have the *sidh* in his pay. It would be easy to secrete them into the palace wouldn't it? And you know what *sidh* are; they'll do anything to get into a man's bed for a night. We all know where *that* leads! Not that there aren't some who'd argue that it's a preferable end to the Miller's cages and the Erl-King's banqueting table.

"Well, here it is, my friends. The Sun Chamber of the High Kings of Ireland. *Medchuarta*. The heart of the Manor of Tara." He swung the doors wide and a blaze of light streamed before their eyes.

To FLYNN AND Amairgen, coming from the darkness of the Forest and the comparative dimness of the Gatekeeper's room, that first glimpse of the great Sun Chamber was a massive assault on their senses. Blinded and made breathless, they were sent gasping and helpless into a whirling maelstrom of living colour, breathing light, and pulsating beauty. Flynn thought: I am drowning in a sea of brilliance. I am smothering in light.

He took a deep breath and the world steadied, and although his eyes were still dazzled and sunspots and starbursts danced against black velvet in his mind; although his senses were still intoxicated and reeling, he managed to square his shoulders and look about him.

The Great Sun Chamber of Tara had been built when Tara was raised out of the rock by the sorcerers. It was told how Dierdriu of the Nightcloak had somehow bargained with them to create for her a Hall of Light, a marvellous glittering banqueting hall, a *Grianan* which would dazzle and bewitch everyone who ever entered it, and which would make Tara into a palace so brilliant that its fame would spread half across the world.

The sorcerers had been loyal and earnest in those days; Ireland's magic had still been young, and Dierdriu's sorcerers had willingly bent their minds to the task and had woven the spell that had finally and marvellously given birth to the Bright Palace.

"And," Dierdriu had said, knowing that the sorcerers served her loyally, "Tara must be the most perfectly beautiful and the most beautifully perfect seat in the world, and travellers in far-off lands must tell stories of it, so that people of all the creeds and all the cultures will come to it."

And at the end, when the sorcerers had taken the Queen by

the hand and led her to the shimmering radiance that was Tara, Dierdriu had stood motionless and speechless, her eyes drinking in the beauty and her mind soaking in the brilliance.

"At the heart, is *Medchuarta*," said the sorcerers. "The living breathing core."

"A *Grianan*," said Dierdriu, her eyes glowing. "The Sun Chamber."

The Sun Chamber was strong magic now; the Court sometimes said that it was impossible to spend more than a few hours a day in it, for the light could hurt your eyes and the beauty could sear your soul. But they told, with pride, how Dierdriu had been able to stand it for days and nights together, and how she would stand at the crystal windows, looking down on the countryside. The Sun Chamber drew down the sunlight and the starlight; it absorbed it and reflected every sliver of sunlight and every flicker of candlelight. The old men of the Court told how it had looked in Cormac's day when the Samhailt had been unchecked. Marvellous days. And now they had Eochaid Bres, the usurper, who was frightened of the Samhailt and who could not be inside the Sun Chamber for more than a couple of hours without getting a headache. Oh dear.

Flynn and Amairgen, knowing none of this, stood helplessly in the doorway, their eyes adjusting, their senses ravished. At length, Flynn became aware of Sean still at their side, prodding them forward.

"To the High King," he said. "And don't let him see that you are dazzled by anything. That would never do."

Flynn, recovering a little, murmured, "But how could we not be dazzled?"

Sean shushed him and said crossly, "That's the trouble. People won't be told. They all think they know best. Well I can't do anything about it," and took himself off.

It seemed a very long journey across the shining silver floor to where the High King sat, half sprawled at the head of the banqueting table, watching them with unblinking tawny eyes. Flynn looked at him and felt a stab of the purest disappointment. *This* was to be the master of such glory! This handsome stupid beast to be overlord of such magnificence! He looked away quickly—"Quench the Mindsong," Sean had said—and began to study the people who lined the long oak banqueting table. They had all stopped eating and talking, were all seated motionless in their chairs, every eye on the two travellers. Flynn, whose every sense was alert and alive and whose every nerve ending was stripped and exposed, thought: they are beautiful. They are the most beautiful creatures I have ever seen. And they are the wildest and the most unscrupulous and the strangest as well. I wouldn't trust any one of them.

The people of Tara, gathered in the *Grianan* of Dierdriu, feasting and paying court to their High King, were wild and beautiful and just very faintly sinister. There were faces that had a three-cornered, pointed-eared look, and some that had slender, hawklike profiles, and others that were rounded and soft, but a bit sly. There were creatures with tawny eyes and russet hair, with sleek black pelts and sensuous limbs; there were others with eagle faces and jutting aquiline noses. They wore silks and velvets and fur-trimmed robes, and they had been daintily eating the feast set out for them. They had a thin veneer of civilisation, but Flynn and Amairgen, staying very close to each other, thought they were not civilised in the least. There was something in the slant of their eyes, in the curve of their fingernails, in the thin smiles they wore. Velvet gloves concealing iron fists; silk gowns covering greedy talons; velvet cloaks over cruel claws and teeth. Flynn caught the tail end of a thought from Amairgen: don't trust a one of them, Flynn! We are in very great danger! And then they were approaching the head of the table.

Eochaid Bres watched them without once moving, and Flynn thought: I was right, he is stupid. He is certainly no ruler for these untamed lovely creatures—I wonder are they entirely human? And remembered in the same moment the old old legend, never quite believed, of how humans could never own Tara.

He had time to notice that the High King was richly dressed and time too to notice that the figure at the King's side was reddish of hair and beard, and clever-looking and a bit cunning.

And then he looked at the lady on the King's right. Mab the Queen Mother, *Medb*, who twenty years earlier, at the Court of Cormac Starrog's father, had been named the Intoxicating One, and who was said to have had every single man at Court in her bed.

Mab was looking at Flynn with the sudden alertness of a predator scenting a new and interesting victim.

CHAPTER NINE

JOANNA HAD PASSED from being frightened into a kind of mesmerised dream where nothing seemed quite real.

She had stood, white-faced and motionless, as Macha and Scald-Crow summoned servants to bind and make helpless Cormac and the two Cruithin, and she had shuddered at the sight of those servants, who were little goblin men, no more than two feet high, but with dark hungry faces and slitted red eyes, and bald pointed skulls. They overcame their three captives easily, chanting and hissing and prodding at them with long bony fingers.

"Oho," they said. "Oho, here's a fine fat feast for our Master. A grand sizzling dish to set before the Erl-King. Light the fires, my dears, and heat the pots." They linked hands and danced round Cormac who snarled and lashed out at them.

"Oho, a fine strong dish," said the goblins, dodging out of the way. "A rare good feast. This one for the ovens, my dears. Oh there's nothing so fine as the sound of human fat sizzling. To the cages, my dears, and then to the ovens, and to the millwheels with the bones." And they grinned at Joanna who was trying very hard not to shudder. "There's nothing so fine as flour made with the bones of humans," they said. "Light the fires, my dears."

Cormac was growling and clawing, and Gormgall and Dubhgall were laying about the goblin men with their bare fists.

"Catch us if you can," cried the goblins, leaping and darting out of reach. "Catch us if you can. Spin the Bonds, Mistress, spin the Bonds." And they surrounded Morrigan, and stood watching eagerly as strings of saliva issued from her mouth, solidifying in the air. The goblins seized on the strings and ran about with them, pulling and twisting and braiding until they had long sticky ropes which they bound about their three captives.

"Bind them tight and string them strong," cried the goblins, running this way and that, spinning three cocoons. "That's the way, my dears. No escape for these. Oho, there'll be rich pickings from the Erl-King's table tomorrow, my dears. There'll be bones to suck and ribs to gnaw. To the cages, my dears, and then to the ovens, and then to the Millwheel. Human bones to human flour, my dears."

Cormac and the two Cruithin were bound so tightly now that they could not move, although Joanna believed that Cormac had clawed one of the goblins rather severely, and Dubhgall had certainly winded another. But the goblin men were too strong and too many; they danced and cavorted, never quite close enough to be caught, and they made obscene gestures and several times they turned their backs and bent their knees and broke wind loudly and horridly in their captives' faces.

"That's our opinion of High Kings," they said. "That's what we think of High Kings," and Joanna shuddered.

"Squeamish, my little bird?" said Morrigan, smiling. "Do you not care for my servants? Perhaps I should give you the opportunity to know them a little better."

At once the goblin men ran up to Joanna and unfastened their breeches, thrusting their little jutting penises at her, and Morrigan laughed again.

"You see, my pigeon? They are eager to get to know you.
"Well, my little men?"

"She's a pretty one, this," said the goblin men. "Oho, we'll have fun with this one. Prick up your appetites, my dears, and rub up your pricks. A plump pigeon for the plucking. A fat fantail for the fucking. Rub up your pricks, my dears, and prick up your appetites."

"You see how friendly they are?" said Morrigan in a slimy purr. "Well, when I have done with you we shall see." She parted her lips and the snake-tongue flickered. "They deserve a reward for bringing you to me. They live in the Street of the Whisperers, you know, and they are ever on the lookout for victims. But they have brought me a rare prize this time. They are loyal servants," said Morrigan, "and they have voracious appetites. As you see." The goblin men laughed and one or two rubbed themselves suggestively, and several more turned round and farted again.

From the other side of the room, Cormac snarled and tore at the white cocoon.

"Once I am free of this filth, Morrigan, you and I will settle all our scores!"

"Dear me," said Morrigan in a light amused voice. "I have scarcely begun yet, Wolfking. Sister, show him a little taste of real filth."

At once Scald-Crow drew in one of her immense breaths and began to dissolve, until a column of thick white slime stood before them. There was a low bubbling chuckle, and the column slid to the floor and oozed towards Dubhgall who was nearest.

Joanna screamed and thrust a fist into her mouth, because she would not give these creatures the satisfaction of seeing how repulsive she found all this. Dubhgall stood, unable to break free of his bonds, and the thick white liquid that was Scald-Crow slithered across the floor with a soft wet squelching sound and covered his feet.

Cormac said through his teeth, "Madam, if you have any shred of decency—"

"Not the merest rag, Wolfking. Watch."

The glutinous fluid flowed silently upwards, over Dubhgall's knees and between his legs, and Joanna thought it was not just her imagination that made her fancy that white stringlike fingers caressed his thighs and what lay between them.

Gormgall said urgently, "Morrigan—direct your filth to me!"

Morrigan laughed and said, "Chivalry! And I had thought it long since dead! No, son of servants, you shall watch your companion suffer! Onwards, Sister!"

The stuff oozed higher, surrounding Dubhgall's waist, and Joanna saw him become so pale that his skin took on a greenish tinge. "Oh dear God, this is unbearable—Morrigan—" and at once Morrigan smiled, and said, "Sister, leave him be."

Scald-Crow slid away and stood grinning at the prisoners.

"You favour her above me always," said Macha sullenly.

"Because I am more powerful," said Scald-Crow.

"All outside show," said Macha. And then, to Morrigan, "Let me call up the Hags and the Harpies, Sister. Let them fasten their claws into the flesh of our prisoners and scoop out their living eyes to devour, and nibble away their faces."

"All in good time, Sister," said Morrigan. "There is sufficient for us all to feast on."

Dubhgall, whose colour had gone from green to grey moaned, "I'm going to be sick," and leaning forward, he vomited into the fireplace. "Forgive me, Your Majesty—" Another bout of retching seized him.

"Oh *poor* Dubhgall," said Joanna. "Can't we do something—"

"He will recover himself," said Morrigan. "And my sister Macha will care for him."

Macha moved to Dubhgall and reached out her long plump white arms and Dubhgall said, "If you come near me, madam, I shall be sick all over you. My aim is very good."

"Shall I not wipe your fevered brow, poor human, and give you suck from my breasts?"

"Begging your pardon," said Dubhgall, faintly but determinedly, "and if it's all the same to you, I'd rather be comforted by a giant slug."

Joanna said, "Oh Dubhgall, don't give her the idea—"

"Easy!" said Scald-Crow, and there, as they looked, was a great black glistening slug, six feet in length, and with great sinews of iron in its haunches.

"How childish and effete," scoffed Macha. "Wars are not won by such cheap tricks."

"Kingdoms are not taken by armies of crones," retorted Scald-Crow, turning back into herself. "We shall see who is the better by and by."

"I recall that it was your peacocking ways that lost us the Battle for the Trees."

"And *I* recall that it was your harpies who were so concerned with the corpses left by Dierdriu's armies, that they failed to hold the Plain of the Fál against the *Fiana*."

"Enough!" said Morrigan. "Do you not see—we are boring our guests."

"I'm not bored," said Gormgall. "Are you bored, Dubhgall?"

"No. I feel sick, but I'm not bored."

"Nevertheless," said Morrigan in a soft slimy purr, "nevertheless, I believe we are guilty of discourtesy. And my little men are very eager." She moved closer to Joanna, and ran a finger across her cheek and down into the bodice of her jerkin.

Joanna stood very still and touched in her mind the golden core of anger she had felt earlier: still there. While I have this I am safe. She said, icily, "Do not touch me, Morrigan," and Morrigan smiled the snake smile.

"I will touch you, my little bird, my pigeon for the plucking; I will touch you in places you never dreamed anyone would touch you. There are nine openings to a human's body, Dierdriu, and I shall enter into every one. I shall spin the Bonds of the Hag, and they will fill you until you are bloated and begging for mercy. Until you are spilling and leaking with the fluid of my Bonds.

"We have an old old debt to settle, Dierdriu, and this time I shall be victor. I shall humiliate you, madam, and I shall explore you, and I shall sate myself on you. And when I have done, I shall give you to the goblin men for their entertainment—and heed me, Dierdriu, they have an insatiable desire for the bodies of humans.

"And then when they have had their fill, I shall take you down below to the cages and my sisters and I will call up the Giant Miller of Muileann, and no one looks upon that terrible creature and lives, Dierdriu.

"You will share your wolf lover's fate, madam, and you will end up on silver platters and in golden goblets on my Master's table.

"This way, Your Majesty."

THE NOT-TO-BE-QUENCHED FURY that had filled Joanna earlier—*"Is me Dierdriu de shiúl oiche"*—"I am Dierdriu of the Nightcloak"—she had said, was still with her. She thought it came from somewhere outside of herself, and then she thought it came after all from within. But it is someone else's fury, she thought, and it is someone else's courage. No matter, she would make use of it.

It sustained her throughout the dreadful hour when Morrigan and her sisters taunted their prisoners; Scald-Crow hissing and undulating and changing shape every few minutes; Macha quieter and more watchful.

The goblin men seized Joanna last, and with many sly pinches and nips drove her to Morrigan's bedchamber at the heart of the house. The anger flooded her again. How dare these loathsome creatures try to humiliate her! And within the anger was a glowing centre of immense courage. A world within a world. Courage inside anger. Strip away the anger and there is the courage. Strip away the courage and there is a heart, a core, a centre, and within that centre I am hiding, thought Joanna. I am at the centre and I am surrounded by courage and anger. I am distanced from this creature and her servants, thought Joanna; I am protected and armoured. She touched the courage in her mind as a soldier going into battle will touch his armour. A carapace?

She was able to stare coldly at Morrigan who was watching the goblin men. "Spread her legs, chaps, that's the way. Let the Mistress in. A plump pigeon, this one"—and she was able to look haughtily at the goblin men as they finished their work.

Even so, thought Joanna, looking back to Morrigan, even so, she is very terrible. I wonder if I shall be able to outwit her.

In the dim light, Morrigan might easily have been eight feet tall. She might certainly have possessed giant blood.

But the real Joanna was safely at the centre of the courage, and the real Joanna could not possibly be touched or harmed by anything that Morrigan might do. I am quite safe, said Joanna to Joanna firmly. I have a carapace. Presently, Joanna's voice said calmly, "Do to me what you must, Morrigan. I see you have still not learned to control your own body. How weak you are, my dear."

Morrigan hissed and the snake-tongue darted out, but Joanna saw that the taunt had hit home.

The voice that was Joanna's but did not use Joanna's words said, amusedly, "So you still give way to tantrums, as well, do you Morrigan? Do you recall how you truly lost the Battle for the Trees? Childish rage, Morrigan, that is all."

Morrigan reared up to her full height—ten feet, thought Joanna, horrified. "It was not lost," said Morrigan. "The Trees still sleep."

"But you did not gain control of them. Well, you poor ineffectual creature, your rages and your sick passions have lost you a throne more than once, they will do so again. You will not have Tara, you know. Not for your evil master, and not for yourself."

Morrigan said, "For that, High Queen, I will skin you alive with my own hands and cut your flesh into cold collops for the Erl-King's table."

"And I will summon the mighty armies of Finn mac Airmall and his *Fiana*, and the bewitchments of the Sorcerers of Tara," said Joanna's voice, in the sort of voice one might use when saying, "You silly child, I am a grown-up with a grown-up's strength." There was a low blurred laugh. "You will never vanquish me, Morrigan."

For a moment Morrigan did not speak. Then, "Dierdriu," she said in a voice filled with loathing. "I promise you that this is the final battle. *You will not escape.*"

"But I have escaped before, Morrigan. I escaped you before and I shall do so again. I promise you that." The voice that was Joanna's and yet not Joanna's became yet more menacing. "I also promised that if ever the Darkness should again threaten Tara, I would return. Did you ever know me to break a promise or forget a vow?"

"Human chivalries!" said Morrigan contemptuously. "And where have they brought you, Your Majesty? Into my house and into my power, and into the Miller's cages! Your wolf lover is bound and chained and your followers have deserted you!" Confidence was coming back into her voice. "Where are your armies and your famous *Fiana* now?" said Morrigan jeeringly. "Where is your beloved Finn mac Airmall? Where are the sorcerers you once ruled with your wonderful powers?" She leaned forward and hissed into Joanna's face, her breath sour and dry. "You are alone, Dierdriu, you are abandoned, and this will be the last battle of them all!"

Joanna's voice said, "We shall see!" And then, with a touch of irritation, "Oh let us get this over with. Do to me what you must. Relieve your itch on me if that is your pleasure, Morrigan." Joanna felt the impatience course through her. "Well?" she said. "What you waiting for?" and Morrigan turned to light the candles.

DIERDRIU'S ANGER AND Dierdriu's unfailing courage stayed with Joanna in the hours that followed. She could not move from the bed however much she struggled; Morrigan had her firmly pinned down.

Joanna thought: I shall bear it. It will come to an end. I shall free Cormac and the others. I shall find the Nightcloak, and *then* I shall be able to rout this filth. The thought of the cloak, still somewhere inside the house, was immensely comforting, and Joanna felt at once better. She raised her head to look about her.

Morrigan's bedchamber was dark and smelt of evil magic and of old dark enchantments. There were no windows, and the only light was from the black stumplike candles. There was a stale sour smell and Joanna thought it was like being in a worm's earthhole. This was how it would feel if you had been captured by a giant worm who had brought you back to its lair, and this was how you would feel as you lay waiting for the worm to come slithering in, blind and boneless, to crush you and eat you with its wet, toothless mouth.

There was a smeary kind of light in the room, and there were dull red bed hangings, and it was chokingly hot. Joanna's throat began to close and she had to fight very hard to be calm and she had to cling very tightly to the courage that did not belong to her.

The floor of the bedchamber was strewn with rugs made from some kind of skin. Joanna had had to walk across them with bare feet and they had felt rather nasty. They were not the thick luxurious pelts of animals Cormac had had at Scáthach, nor were they the strong furry hides that they had taken with them for sleeping during the march to Muileann. And I could not have borne it if they had been wolfskins, thought Joanna. But these were thinnish, rather smooth and very pale skins, and they felt cool and leathery to the touch. The soles of Joanna's feet had contracted in an instinctive horror.

"Silver platters and golden goblets," Morrigan had hissed, grinning. "But what do we do with the hides, my dear?"

The bed was hung with silk and brocade, but it felt cold to the touch, and a bit slimy. There was an overripe scent on the air, so that Joanna was reminded of rotten fruit—luscious and juicy on the outside, but with a decayed stench to it, so that you knew the minute you bit into it, it would be soft and squelchy and liquid, so that your teeth would sting and the water would rise in your mouth.

Morrigan was removing Joanna's clothes now, and Joanna thrashed and felt again the anger and the contempt surge up, so that she turned a look of such fury on her, that Morrigan hissed, and hatred glittered in her eyes.

"Still as haughty as ever, Your Majesty? Well, let us see how you react to this!" She ripped the jerkin from Joanna's breasts, and tore off the wide warm leggings that had been donned in Scáthach for the journey.

A hundred days ago had it been? Or a hundred years? And hadn't it been another person who had put on leggings and a jerkin and ridden from Scáthach with Cormac? Dierdriu is very close to me now, thought Joanna. Is she sharing this unspeakably dreadful experience? Joanna waited, and began to feel the ruffle of sweet strength.

Of course I am sharing it, my dear, and we shall defeat the filth, we shall banish the Adversary together . . .

Then I can bear it, thought Joanna. I believe I can bear it.

But it felt unbearably vulnerable to have to lie there flat on her back, entirely naked now, her legs stretched apart. And there was something so unclean about the room that Joanna felt as if its decay and its stench might soak into her skin: I shall never be clean again; if I take a thousand hot baths, I shall never again feel clean.

For she is filth and she is decay and all things loath-some . . .

Yes! thought Joanna gratefully. Yes, she is!

And always was, my dear . . .

Joanna thought that without Dierdriu's strength and without Dierdriu's steadfast anger against Morrigan, she could not have endured any of it. She had thought she would certainly break down and weep, and beg for mercy, and cry to be set free. But now she knew she would not give Morrigan the satisfaction of seeing her beaten and defeated; she certainly would not let Morrigan see how frightened she was. If she did not think about what might be ahead, she would probably be able to bear this. If she did not think about them all being flung into the cages and cut into collops and served up to the Erl-King, it might be possible to appear quite brave.

And Dierdriu was still with her. That was the thing that weighed most of all. Even so, thought Joanna, even so, I believe it is up to me. I believe I must watch my every chance for escape. And at least this cannot be much worse than the things that Muldooney did . . . can it?

With the memory of Muldooney the horrid pigman, his fat greedy face and his prodding sausage-fingers, there came another faint, far-off memory. Not Muldooney but someone connected with that world. Someone with black-fringed, blue eyes, who would sack cities and topple empires to save her . . . Someone infinitely sweet and entirely strong and wholly precious . . . And—*I am coming to you, Joanna,* said a distant, barely heard voice, so that Joanna frowned and half sat up and tried to hear more.

For the splinter of a second there was another memory— eating wild strawberries on a windy hillside, and then an even older vision, herself riding out at the head of an army with someone at her side, and an enveloping security and an all-enduring love . . . What had Morrigan said? "Where is your beloved Finn mac Airmall now?"

The moment passed, for Cormac's spell still held Flynn's memory at bay, and Joanna looked at Morrigan.

Morrigan pushed her back on to the bed and climbed on top of her.

THERE ARE A good many things which men and women can do to one another with their bodies in the name of love, or even only in the name of lust. Most of them are exciting and some of them are unexpected; nearly all of them are pleasant. But there are only a few things that women can do to other women with their bodies alone, and unless a woman is so made that she enjoys that, none of them are in the least bit pleasant.

Joanna was not so made. She found Morrigan's touch and Morrigan's cold, now naked body utterly repulsive. She found even more repulsive the array of artifacts and accessories ranged before them at the side of the bed.

Joanna had thought herself prepared for anything and everything Morrigan might do to her, she had thought herself braced for all manner of twisted practices. The nights with Cormac had opened her eyes, she thought hopefully; he had taught her all there was to know, and he had done to her all there was to do, and surely nothing this creature could do would be so very terrible.

But Cormac, wild and wolvish, had been, in part at least,

human. Morrigan, daughter of an old and corrupt line, was not human at all. Some stories told how she was the result of a union between giants and snakes, others said she came from a curious little-known breed of sea creatures, that she was part *sidh* with their merciless sexual appetites, and part fish with cold colourless fishblood in her. Still others whispered that she was directly descended from the evil Hags of the North, and this, perhaps, came closest to the truth.

Her skin, once she had shed her clothes (like a snake shedding its skin? No! Don't think of it!) was cold and dry and rough. There were scales between her legs, grey and faintly luminous. The hands that caressed Joanna were boneless, the fingers that slid between Joanna's legs had no knuckles.

Cormac had laughed and teased and been strong and gentle and exciting. He had poured wine over Joanna's bare skin for the pleasure of licking it off again; he had been warm and alive, and he had sometimes hurt her and he had sometimes made her do things that she had never dreamed humans could do. But there had been a warm masculine scent about him; there had been bones and eyes and skin and hair, and there had been a soaring delight and a sharing. When he woke in the mornings he had been drowsily passionate, and lying in bed with him had been secret and safe and exciting.

Lying in Morrigan's bed, with Morrigan naked beside her was like lying in a snake's nest, and feeling the snake crawl over your bare flesh. Joanna's skin shivered and she struggled uselessly against Morrigan's relentless hold.

Then she felt the snake-tongue, and a wave of such disgust engulfed her, that despite her vow of fortitude, she cried out and shuddered uncontrollably, and strained back in the bed, away from the sorceress. No! Not this! This is too terrible for anything. I cannot possibly endure this and still live! But she did endure it and she did live, and Morrigan raised her head to look at Joanna, eyes glittering, face filmed with sweat, lips stretched in a smile that held a real intimacy, and Joanna felt sick all over again.

"Not enjoying it, my pigeon?" said Morrigan.

Joanna knew that surely now was the time to act, now, when the creature was made vulnerable by her own disgusting passions. She turned her head on the pillow, seeking a weapon. What? Joanna snatched up a two-pronged phallus object that

lay near the bed and brought it smashing down across
Morrigan's face. Bone splintered and tore, and flecks of blood
and matter spattered Joanna's bare skin. (Dreadful. Don't think
about it. You can wash away somebody else's blood quite easily.) Morrigan screamed and put up a hand to ward off further
blows, and Joanna thought: at any minute, oh dear God, at any
instant, she will summon her sisters and they will work some
dreadful enchantment and then I shall be lost and Cormac will
be lost, and we shall all be in golden goblets and on silver
platters . . .

But there was no sound of running footsteps, there was no
dark gathering in the air which might indicate the presence of
evil magic. Morrigan was cowering in a corner, her hands covering her face, and Joanna felt a tremendous surge of power.

*I have you in my power, filth! I have you at my mercy at
last! THAT for Cormac and THAT for all the evil you have
wrought, and THAT for your reign of terror and all your merciless killings!*

She hit Morrigan again and again, and all the time she could
feel the enchantress's strength ebbing and all the time she
could feel her own power flowing. I am invincible, I am unstoppable. I can do anything and I need fear no one. But the
tears were streaming down her face, and somewhere deep inside her was a tiny appalled core of feeling. I cannot really be
doing this; I cannot really be inflicting these wounds and I
cannot possibly be enjoying it.

Morrigan fell back on the floor, barely conscious, and
Joanna saw with revulsion that the blood oozing from her
wounds was a thick whitish fluid. Fishblood!

THERE WAS NOT very much time to spare. Morrigan was rendered incapable, but it would only be a temporary thing. She
would recover, she would summon her sisters, and she would
invoke her terrible enchantments, and Joanna would die more
horribly and painfully than bore thinking of. At any minute,
Morrigna might burst in, and at any minute the goblin men
might come running. I must get out quickly, thought Joanna,
scrambling into her jerkin and leggings, for she would not go
running naked through the house, not even if all the spells in
the world and all the goblin men in Ireland were chasing her.
And I *must* find the cloak.

The house was in darkness and there was a brooding quiet about it. Quickly! cried Joanna silently, oh quickly! Let me find the Nightcloak, and then I may save Cormac and the others! And then we shall be out of here, over the hills and far away, into the safety of the Morne Mountains, into the realm of Cait Fian of Gallan. She sped from room to room, throwing open doors, heedless now who heard, expecting every minute to see Morrigan barring her way, certainly expecting to be confronted by the jeering goblin men.

She could feel a "something" stirring somewhere in the house now, a kind of clotting coalescing malevolence. Morrigan recovering from her wounds? Yes, certainly. She is not human, thought Joanna, and shuddered at the memory of the cold, whitish fishblood; she is not human, but she is sufficiently human to feel pain. This comforted her rather more than she had expected, because it showed a chink in Morrigan's armour.

I hurt her, thought Joanna, fascinated and appalled. Did I really smash that—that object—into her face? It *hurt* her, thought Joanna, and managed a rather sickly grin, just for reassurance. If you could smile at something, even when you were on your own, things were never quite so bad. She dredged up another smile, just to be sure of this.

The Nightcloak was lying discarded and dismissed on a chair in the room where they had been taken earlier on. Joanna snatched it up and swung it about her shoulders, fastening the clasp firmly. The thick soft folds settled about her, and there was a soft sigh of relief. Now I am safe. Dierdriu, is your courage still with me? *Yes, and the strength, my dear, onwards now.* All right, thought Joanna, taking a deep breath, here we go. Now for Cormac and the others.

She descended into the bowels of the house, opening a door into a scullery, pausing in the doorway to look about her. Morrigan's scullery smelt horrid—silver platters and golden goblets? oh please no!—and Joanna wasted precious seconds in being truly horrified at the sluttish mess. But in an odd way, the greasy pans and crusted plates and discoloured ovens strengthened her thin flow of confidence. You could not be frightened of a person who left burnt soup splashes on the top of a stove. You certainly could not be frightened of somebody who did not put a good pinch of woodash into the washing up water to remove egg stains from plates. Somebody had break-fasted off cooked eggs, and somebody had lunched off soup, and the stains were still all there. I hope they are only soup splashes, and I hope they are only egg stains, thought Joanna. Oh Cormac, Cormac, please be somewhat nearby!

She snatched up the half of a candle that someone had stuck into a pewter stick—the wick needed trimming of course; were Morrigan's servants truly so slovenly!—and turned to confront the two doors that led from the scullery.

And now it was very important indeed to remember that she was not afraid, and it was very important indeed to remember that Dierdriu's courage and strength were still with her.

Two doors . . . Joanna looked upwards, and felt sick all over again . . . Huge, a huge wide door, the iron handle so far up that she would only reach it if she stood on the tips of her toes. A giant's door, a door so massive that surely there could not be anyone in the world who would ever need to use it.

But the Giant Miller of Muileann is not just a legend, Joanna . . . He is fifteen feet high, and he wears seven league boots that can stride across the land . . . Be more careful of him than you have been of anything yet, Joanna . . .

Set deep into the wall, very nearly unnoticeable, was a low door, and Joanna looked at it and paused, because there was a vein of ancestral memory here; there was something comforting and quite magical about it. Joanna's ancestors, before they blew up the world, had known about symbolism and about imagery. "The low door in the wall" had been a key and a symbol, and Joanna, suddenly feeling very much better, thought: of course they will be down here, they will be through this door. Of course they will. I am going to find them. It is going to be all right.

She stepped through the door, and felt her way cautiously along a dark rather narrow passage. Not a giant's passage at all. A human-sized passage. And a dim light ahead of her. Nothing has happened to me yet, thought Joanna, and because this was a good thought to have, she fixed it firmly in the forefront of her mind.

The passageway widened abruptly, and the uncertain light brightened just the smallest bit. Joanna stepped on to cold stone flags that ran downwards and curved, and reached out a hand to steady herself, because the stone was uneven and it was damp and looked as if it might be slippery. The walls were rough and felt old and pitted. Joanna withdrew her hand and shuddered, because the walls felt dry and crumbly, and you could easily imagine that they might fall down all around you at any minute.

Ahead of her were steps, winding down and down, as far as she could see, away into some dreadful subterranean darkness.

Joanna gasped, and the sound echoed rather horridly in the enclosed atmosphere. The steps were more huge than any she had ever seen, they were giant steps, cut for giant feet—she had come out into the Miller's stairs (seven league boots? oh dear God, yes!). But I won't notice it, she said to herself, I'll just climb down them as well as I can, and I won't notice that each step is at least two feet deep. I'll go down on my bottom and I won't even notice.

She steadied herself against the cold wall again, and the light from the candle flared up in the raw air, making her shadow a massive, fantastic thing that danced and flickered as she descended.

It was a very long way down. "Down, down to hell and say I sent thee thither" . . . Yes, and "Come, my dear, let us away and down and away below" . . . "I am going into the soft underbelly of the Axis and I am going into the underground of the world" . . . Yes, but beneath it all are the Everlasting Arms . . .

And Cormac will be there, thought Joanna, and moved on even farther down.

CHAPTER TEN

CORMAC CAME UP out of a leaden cold sleep, and for the briefest second did not remember where he was. And then sleep receded, and memory came flooding back, and he knew a terrible loneliness.

I am in the Miller's cages, and I am entirely alone, and Joanna is in the hands of Morrigan.

He grasped at the shreds of sleep, willing himself back into the unaware darkness a little longer. Perhaps none of it really happened. Perhaps when I open my eyes, I shall still be in the cave on the outskirts of Muileann with Joanna at my side and the Cruithin and the Wolves within call.

Or shall I be still inside Scáthach, grim comfortless Scáthach, which I hated and which represented my defeat, but which I would now gladly trade my kingdom for?

Or shall I open my eyes and find I am back at Tara, beautiful incomparable Tara, with Eochaid Bres and Mab nothing more than irritants on the western boundaries? Mab an irritant? said his mind, and he smiled in the darkness. You did not regard Mab as something so minor as an irritant. You loved her or you hated her—and Cormac had done both—but you did not regard her as merely an irritant.

He allowed himself to pretend for a few moments longer, but the memory of Tara, his beautiful Bright Palace, his family's legacy, was like a deep and unhealed wound, and he dragged his mind from it. Useless to remember and pointless to ache. He would never be whole until he had regained Tara and he would never cease to long for it, but he no longer believed he would ever see it again. I shall die here, in the dark,

208

and I shall die alone, and if I am remembered at all, it will be as the last Wolfking. The defeated and exiled King. A failure. The thought was wormwood and gall to one who had ridden out triumphantly at the head of vast armies, who had beaten back the marauding Fomoire, the tainted line of the north. It was bitter to one who had held Court in the Sun Chamber and gathered about him the brilliant minds and the gifted artists and the musicians and ballad-makers of half the world.

He opened his eyes to the cold dark cage, and his vision of Tara vanished instantly. He was lying on the stone floor, and he was cramped and curled into a tight huddle, every bone of his body ached with cold and every muscle hurt with the enforced inactivity of his prison. At his head was a wooden pannikin of water, and at his feet a handful of straw. He remembered how the goblin men had jeered when they thrust his head in the water: "The Erl-King does not like his meat dried out, Wolfking. Drink your fill." He supposed the straw was for the relieving of bladder and bowels, and the fastidious, unwolfish part of him was disgusted. He thought: a High King to lie in his own ordure! Whatever it cost him, he would try to avoid that, at any rate. And then he remembered that he would probably die quite soon and it ceased to matter.

The cage was unlit, for the Miller did not need light to go about his gruesome work, and a man—even a High King— may as easily die by rushlight as by a hundred bright candles. But—I could wish there was some light, thought Cormac, and the memory of the Sun Chamber rose up to torment him again.

He rolled on to his side, wrapping his arms around his body in an effort to keep warm, feeling his limbs knotting with cramp, for it was one of the cage's subtler forms of torture that no man could quite stand upright inside it, nor quite sit, nor lie. Cormac, who had been used to riding and marching for hours on end, and who had hunted and jousted and been tireless, was beginning to find it unbearable. And then he remembered that it must be borne, for there was no other choice.

He wished he could have seen Joanna again. Just for a moment. Just to see her little pointed face with the too-wide mouth, and just to hold the fragile little body, and just to smell the sweet clean Joanna-scent. He thought it was something that pure-bred humans missed; that indefinable scent of another. He could smell enemies at twenty paces, just as he could smell friendship or lust.

He would not see Joanna again. Morrigan would have done her worst and Joanna would soon be dead, if she was not dead already. Cormac would not shed tears, but a grief and a loneliness so immense gripped him that he nearly cried out with pain.

She would have fought to the last, indomitable child, but she could never have overcome Morrigan and the hag-sisters, and she could never have overcome the goblin men. But she would have fought, and that was a good thought. It was a thought to hold on to.

Gormgall and Dubhgall would have fought as well; they would have considered anything else unthinkable.

"*Give in*, Your Majesty?" Gormgall would have said, shocked. "Not by a long way, Sire!"

Dubhgall would have said at least they would go down fighting—it wouldn't do any good, Your Majesty—but they would fight to the end.

Cormac would fight to the end as well, because anything else was as unthinkable to him as it would be to Gormgall and Dubhgall. He would fight for Tara and he would fight for his people and for Joanna. Yes, he would fight for Joanna. If only he could have seen her again. Just once. If only he could stand up and shake off this creeping cold there might be a chance of overcoming the Miller. If only they had not come to Muileann.

So many "if onlys." In his mind he saw them all, neatly stacked, each one holding up its neighbours, so that if you could have pulled out just one of them, the entire pile would fall down.

If only I had not left Scáthach. If only Eochaid Bres had stayed in the west. And . . .

If only I had never loved Mab.

He turned on to his side, staring into the impenetrable dark. Yes, and if only I had never loved Mab, if only I had never afterwards lost control and let the wolfish part take me over . . . If I had not loved Mab, she would not have sworn to be avenged on me for betraying her. She would not have intrigued to put Eochaid Bres on the throne, and I should not be here now.

* * *

HE HAD BEEN eighteen; "helplessly romantic," he had said afterwards, but "incurably lascivious" said his courtiers, half shocked, half proud. Wasn't it a great thing to have this wild, headstrong, heartstrong boy as their King, instead of the ailing old man that Cormac's father had become? There was not a one of them who had not loved Cormac's father, and there was not a one who would not have laid down his life for Cormac's father, but say what you would, life at Court towards the end had been *dull*. When the period of grief was officially over, and all the proper sacrifices had been rendered up to Dagda, and the dead King's soul duly sent to the place beneath the Roof of the Ocean, the Court had turned delightedly to Cormac. They loved him for what he was, as much as for what he was not; they flattered him and wooed him and would not hear a word said against him.

And therein lay my downfall, thought Cormac, moving restlessly on the cold straw. I was given everything I asked for, and quite often I was given things before I even knew I wanted them. I was spoilt and overindulged, my every wish was anticipated, and I was arrogant and frequently selfish.

And there at the centre of it all had been Mab. The Intoxicating One. The Wanton. Nearly twice his age, certainly fifteen years his senior, forbidden to him by the rules of society that frowned on a very young man lusting after a much older woman, but still the most fascinating woman he had ever seen.

Even then, her reputation had been legendary. Even then, the men sat up and eyed one another when she entered a room, preening a little, more alert, vying for her attention. The gossips said she broke the rules and blatantly, but the wise said that she bedded where she chose and was outside of the rules.

Cormac had known at once that both had been wrong. He had not known how he knew, but he did know. Mab was not any man's for the asking, not by a long way, nor was she altogether outside the rules. Was it that she had her own set of rules? Perhaps.

She had come to Court for his coronation, bringing with her a train of maidservants and menservants and cupbearers, and *ollam* and *filid*, bringing as well the young Eochaid Bres, pugnacious and shy, determined not to be overawed by the grandeur of Tara, but overawed by it anyway. Cormac, welcoming them with the ceremony that their high rank within the Bloodline demanded, had thought that he would have liked Eochaid the better if the boy had admitted to his shyness, if he had allowed himself to be dazzled and bewitched. He would have respected Eochaid's dazzlement and he would have helped him. He would have remembered that the Lionline was an ancient and honourable Bloodline, that it was nearly as old as the Wolfline, and he would have taught Eochaid Bres all the things he had himself been taught at Eochaid's age. He would certainly have preferred shyness to the self-opinionated obstinacy the boy displayed.

Mab had swept into the Sun Chamber that first night, clothed in vivid green from head to foot, a huge billowing black velvet cloak about her shoulders, her long slanting eyes drinking everything in. And Cormac had sat very still and thought: oh yes, that is what I want. And then, with more assurance: that is what I intend to have.

Mab the Wanton, her eyes brilliant with desire, her skin luminescent with allure. Irresistible.

It had been as inevitable as the phases of the moon, as unstoppable as the tide, that Cormac and Mab should come together. Hadn't it? The wayward, uncontrollable Wolfprince and the reckless aristocratic harlot, who had once boasted that she would lie with all the High Kings, and that no King of Ireland should ever wear his crown until he had worn it in her bed.

And yet—could I have resisted? thought Cormac. Just a little? Could I have turned back, held off desire, not allowed my eyes to catch and hold those narrow brilliant green eyes? And if I had done so, would Mab have shrugged her lovely shoulders and turned away also, and let her roving eye fall on the next man? And would desire have then subsided and life gone quietly on as before? And would I still be in Tara, the Bright Palace, and would the Miller's cages have remained empty?

And would I then not have met Joanna?

He thought it would not have happened; Mab had vowed to have him, she would not have considered her reputation complete unless she had lain with the arrogant unruly Wolfking, and she would have had him by human trickery or by sorcery. Cormac grinned. Yes, she knew about the sorcerers' arts, Mab. But so did I, my dear, so did I.

He could remember vividly the day they had finally set aside pretence. It had been the culmination of weeks (or had it only been days?) of the forest-fire blaze that had ignited between them. There had been looks, smiles, backs of hands brushing. There had been the knowledge of wanting between them. He had hung about in the corridors near her room, hoping for a glimpse of her; he had contrived to place her next to him at banquets.

"Sire, you do me too much honour." "Your Majesty, you put me in a position of such proximity to you." And all the while, her eyes said: Go ahead, Cormac, *do* me too much honour. Do me as much honour as you like until we are both exhausted. *Put* me in a position of proximity to you. Put me in any position you care to. And Cormac had sat out innumerable banquets, struggling with a lust that was as hard and as high as the beech trees that stood sentinel on the drive to Tara's West Gate.

There had been a ceremony at Court, a huge and vast and colourful ceremony, such as only Tara could mount, and such as only the Irish could enjoy. Cormac had been invested with the Orders and the Vows that had finally pledged him as a Prince of Tara, a High King; there had been speeches and presentations and jousts and pageants; he had been full with and spilling over with energy and he had been as wild and as riggish as the wolves his ancestresses had lain with. Yes, the Wolfblood had been in the ascendant on that day.

A group of them had gone riding into the forest to hunt the white stag, and then had swaggered back to Tara in time for supper in the Sun Chamber, hungry and thirsty and furiously randy from the hunt. Skirts would be lifted tonight, breeches unfastened; hands would stray and breasts and beds would bounce. The gilt corridors of the Bright Palace would be filled with night-garbed figures going from their own bedchambers to the bedchambers of their lady loves, and Tara would echo with the creaking of furtively unlatched doors and with muffled giggles. There had once been a hoary old joke that on the night following a hunt, you might stand in the upper corridors of the Bright Palace and meet everyone you knew between midnight and dawn. Sean the Storyteller, who had been Cormac's official *ollam*, but was now Eochaid Bres's, had written a wildly funny, blatantly bawdy ballad about the corridors of Tara on the night after a hunt. He had sung it to a roomful of men after the ladies had retired to bed, and Cormac could still remember the shouts of laughter that had greeted it. How had it gone? It had started with the riding home of the huntsmen—something about the Uprighting of the Pricks as they passed the High Hayricks. And then it had gone on to relate the events of the afternoon and the evening, each verse saucier than the last. There had been the Lifting of the Supper Table by the Pricks that were Strong and Able, and then there had been Gambling on the Chance that your Partner might prefer the Bugger-Dance.

"And the dangling of the balls
All in Tara's marble halls;
The furtive to and fro and the mighty cries of woe
When the stubbing of a toe
Means the rapier's shrivelled small.

The Councillors' cautious tread
As they go to someone's bed
With their nightcaps all awry
And their weapons t'wards the sky;
Shoulder-glancing, goatlike prancing,
Masked and muffled, tiptoe shuffled,
Joints a-creaking, softly sneaking,
Pussyfooting, hypocriting.

The squeaking of the doors and the laying of the whores;
The groaning of the groins and the languishing of loins.
When the day's at last a-breaking
Not a prick's around but's aching."

He smiled in the darkness. Remarkable Sean. And remarkable years. Golden, exciting, bawdy years. I was flown with the ceremonies that day and I was bursting with sheer rampant lust, and rather than being bowed down with the weight of my new powers, I was buoyed up with them. I had met with the sorcerers earlier, and I was charged with all the magic and all the force of every enchantment ever spun. I was overflowing with being a Prince of Tara, and I was any woman's for the asking.

He had been Mab's that night, and there had been no asking and no answering. There had been the long banqueting table, laden with food and flagons of wine; there had been the warm rich scent that was the heart and the centre of Tara—the place Cormac's ancestors had called *Medchuarta*—and there had been that immense feeling of power. He had looked down the table to where the sorcerers sat, for once present in the Sun Chamber, for they had formed an integral part of the ceremony of Cormac's Investiture. They were shadowy, rather remote creatures in the main, but tonight they were eating and feasting with the Court. Cormac thought: if I asked them, asked them properly and approached them seriously, would they weave an enchantment that would bind Mab to me? And then he looked to where Mab sat, and thought, with a blend of mischief and white-hot desire: but is any sorcerer's enchantment really needed? Doesn't she want me as much as I want her? And then—I am the High King, he thought, I can do anything I want.

Mab was sitting quite close to him; as a Princess of the Bloodline, she was permitted a high place at table. Cormac's eyes narrowed as he considered her, and dwelled on her ancestry. Lionblood. It would be several generations now since Mab's ancestor's had lain with the lionesses of Tara, and Cormac thought it was probably nearly time for them to strengthen the Lionline. The Judges would be convened and it was almost certain that the Enchantment would be invoked. He thought: so Mab is nearly human, but she is not quite human. And watching, saw the way she arched her back and smiled, and saw, as well, the sudden slitting of the narrow eyes and the curve of her hands. Lionblood . . . She would purr like a cat under my hands . . . And then she looked up at him without warning, and their eyes met, and in that moment, all of the power and all of the energy rushed to Cormac's loins, so that, like many another eighteen-year-old, he was instantly charged and stiff. ("The Lifting of the Supper Table . . ." Oh yes, Sean, how right you were!)

They had all sensed it, of course. The Mindsong had shivered and thrummed on the air all round the feasting Court, for Cormac, in his wildly aroused, frantically sexual state, had been as unable to control the Samhailt as he was unable to control his lust. Word had gone round the Sun Chamber: the King will lie with Mab tonight.

The Court had dispersed, going quietly away in twos and

threes, going to their beds—quite often to other people's beds—and the sorcerers had taken their leave of Cormac, bowing gravely, and returning to the great Sorcery Chambers below the Bright Palace. Cormac had thought: an enchantment to bring her to my bed? And laughed inwardly, for no such enchantment would be necessary. Mab would be his tonight, as surely as the dawn would touch the Sun Chamber to rose and gold life tomorrow morning. And shall I be hers in turn? I do not think I shall ever want another woman quite as much as I want this one.

They were alone now, seated at the vast banqueting table, the Sun Chamber dimming into its own purple and lilac twilight. It had been the curious half time between daylight and the Purple Hour, and Cormac, his mind still alight and alive, had felt the air heavy with twilight magic. He had studied Mab, and thought: she is not in the least beautiful. I am not sure if she is not ugly, but I have never known anyone like her. She will spoil me for any other woman.

She had caught that, of course, for the Samhailt was strong between them now, and Cormac's desire was white-hot.

Mab had laughed. She said, "A pity to waste so much energy on the Mindsong, Sire. Should we not put it to better use?" And then she had stood up and held out her hands.

And I nearly took her there, he thought, stirring restlessly in the dark cave. I nearly swept aside the remains of the banquet and forced her back on to the table and pushed aside her gown and did it to her there.

Somehow he had contained himself, and somehow he had walked with her to her bedchamber, hands interlocked, her skin cool and soft and intimate against his.

He smiled. So cool we were, so in command. But when we reached her bedchamber . . .

It had been like the bursting of a dam. His desire had reached scalding point and she had caught his mood at once, and they had flown at one another, like animals, tearing aside clothes, biting and clawing. Her teeth, her hands, her lips had been everywhere; his nails had torn her skin and she had arched her back like a cat and cried out, pulling him closer. A lioness aroused and hungry . . .

He had taken her again and again, quite unable to help himself, slaking his hunger over and over. Neither of them had slept until daylight, when the servants, who always knew what went on, had tactfully left trays of breakfast outside the door. There had been fresh warm bread and honey and fruit, and they had fallen on the food ravenously, and then Cormac had pulled her back into bed.

"Again, Sire?" And there had been the amusement, the intimacy, the look that said of course you are going to do it again, and of course I am going to enjoy it.

I was very nearly exhausted, I was rubbed and raw, but still I took her that last time.

And there had been a tired triumph, for just for a fleeting second, Mab's eyes had widened in surprise, and Cormac had thought: she believed I was spent. The knowledge sent the heat between his legs again, and the respect in Mab's eyes had lent him one final surge of energy.

He had slipped from her bed at last, and stood looking down at her, seeing her body as slender and as unmarked as a young girl's. Impossible to think she was twenty years his senior, and that those twenty years had been strongly lived. But—I could tame her, thought Cormac. I could subdue her and master her and together we could make Tara into something so truly great that its splendour will echo down the years. Every other empire and every other kingdom ever planned, ever conquered, ever dreamed about, would pale in comparison.

For a while he had believed it could be; he had been prepared to outface the Councillors and the Court; he had been ready to defy convention and set her beside him. And if there should be a child . . . His own blood stirred at the thought. Yes, we could make something exceptional, Mab and I. Children of light and fire and strength. Little elfin-faced girls with Mab's dark hair and wayward eyes and curving smile. Boys with the Wolf strain in them, tempered with the human part of me. And Ireland would be always and forever great.

His mind filled with brilliant images, his body drugged and replete, the morning sun streaming into his own bedchamber, Cormac had slept.

WHEN HE AWOKE, the bright warm bedchamber of Tara had vanished and he was again in the Miller's cage, cold and numb, thirsty and hungry, and the despair that engulfed him was like a huge black, iron band. See how I can douse your dreams, Wolfking. You may slip in and out of reality, and you may dream of your triumphs and your splendours and your lost kingdom, but I am here waiting for you. I am Despair and Anguish and Loss of Hope. I am going to triumph and you have no escape.

He thought that some sound from above had pulled him back to his surroundings, and he lay listening. Yes, there was a faint noise from somewhere over his head, a rather hesitant, rather cautious sound. Footsteps coming nearer.

Cormac was not the least bit afraid; the footsteps were too light and too wary for them to belong to Morrigan and her sisters, and in any case, Morrigan did not need footsteps. She could vanish and reappear wherever she chose. And the footsteps certainly did not belong to the Miller, for the Miller, when he finally came, would come stamping out to the cages, sniffing the air for the smell of human blood, and tying his leather apron. They said he wore boots which could stride seven leagues in one pace, and that he could smell the blood of humans at fifty paces . . .

Cormac, his every sense alert, knew that the footsteps, soft and gentle, did not belong to the Miller, and a great hope welled up inside him. He half sat up, leaning against the far wall, his eyes fixed on the direction of the stairs.

There was a flicker of candlelight, a whisper of silk, and Joanna, clad in Dierdriu's cloak, came into the cellars.

HE CRIED THEN, as he had not done earlier, tears streaming down his face, unable to speak, his hands gripping Joanna's through the bars of the cage, knowing he must be hurting her, unable to help himself.

She was quite dreadfully pale and her hair was tousled and there was a terrible knowledge in her eyes, so that he thought: oh yes, Morrigan has used her. And he wanted to fold her in his arms and ensure that nothing would ever hurt her again, and at the same time wanted to tear down the bars of his cage and go bounding up the stairs to Morrigan, to claw and rip and lacerate the creature.

At length, Joanna said softly, "You must let me go. At any minute they will be here—and I have not the keys to release you—"

"I thought you were dead!" Damn! he thought: cannot I even trust my own voice now?

Joanna smiled, and said, "Nearly. But I am here. And I have the cloak." As she spoke, there was a whisper of silk and Cormac and Joanna both felt their senses stir and a tremendous sense of adventure began to fill them. Cormac thought: to come face-to-face with the Miller is surely the greatest adventure of them all. And why should we not somehow defeat him? The power and the confidence that had filled him on the day of his coronation poured into him, and he stood for a moment, unmoving, feeling it flow into his veins.

And Joanna thought: why should we not defeat the Miller? We have got this far without being killed. I have injured Morrigan and disabled her. And I have the Nightcloak. Aloud, she said, "What of Gormgall and Dubhgall?"

"Somewhere here. We were separated. But I am sure they are still alive. I can feel them still alive. And we can—" He stopped and lifted his head, looking towards the stair, and in the uncertain light, Joanna saw him tilt his head, listening.

"What is it?"

Cormac said, "Someone's coming."

"Morrigan?"

"No. Listen. Cannot you feel?"

And then Joanna did feel. Footsteps. Great hungry heavy footsteps somewhere above them. A pounding and a thundering that made your bones shiver and froze your marrow. Seven league boots and a voracious bloodlust. *Something evil this way comes* . . .

Cormac, his eyes on her, said softly, "If you go now, you can escape. Up the stairs and out into the night. You would be a little dark shadow slipping out of the house, and no one would see you. You could be over the hills and far away. Cait Fian would help you."

And Joanna smiled, and said, "Don't be absurd," and Cormac smiled back, and the golden glow of power surged even higher.

"Then you must hide. You must snuff the candle and conceal yourself and watch your every opportunity. Use the cloak. Quickly now. He is coming nearer."

There was not really a proper hiding place in the dungeons, but Joanna scurried into a corner where the shadows were thickest, and where a jutting stone half-wall gave a little concealment. The cloak fell silently about her, and settled into close dark folds. There was nothing to do now but wait and seize whatever opportunity presented itself.

She could see the dungeons quite clearly from here. She could see the faint shape that was Cormac, and now she could hear the Miller's approach. Great heavy footsteps coming nearer. And then, without warning, a great booming voice, a terrible deep-chested roar that made Joanna want to clap her hands over her ears, and certainly made her want to turn and run.

"Where is the human child who injured my mistress, and where is the Wolfking who snapped at my servants? Mince and stew and roast, and someone will be devoured tomorrow night—oh yes, my poor scuttling humans, someone will be devoured.

"Hoho and aha, where are you? We'll polish the platters and we'll shine the goblets. We'll hone the knives and set the Millwheels grinding, for there's nothing my master likes so well as his bread made with the flour of human bones. And I shall find you out, my little ones, I shall scoop you up and you will be devoured and you will be quaffed."

Joanna was both burning hot and icy cold now, with fear and excitement and anticipation.

To confront the Miller is surely the greatest adventure yet . . .
Yes, and to die will be the greatest adventure of all . . .

Where had that thought come from? Something written long ago, or something not yet written? A faint dying echo of some thought not yet born? Or—and this was very sinister indeed—or something inside the house with them? Was it Morrigan stirring in the darkness, unable yet to use her full strength to damage them, but working on their minds? I won't listen, said Joanna firmly.

She pressed her burning cheek against the cold stone. I don't want to die. Don't let these creatures harm us. Don't let them kill us. Let us outwit them. Don't let us have come this far only to die. Let us escape to Gallan. Gallan! She thought, and delight unfolded at once. Yes, they would get to Gallan, somehow they would. Don't let us end up on silver platters and in golden goblets.

Yes but, *to die will be the greatest adventure of them all . . .*

"I won't listen!" said Joanna and closed her mind to everything except the Miller's approach and how they might outwit him.

The footsteps were shaking the dungeons now, and the floor was vibrating beneath their feet. There was a booming voice from above, and from her stone alcove, Joanna saw a thick smeary light spill down the stairs. The Miller was coming, he was nearly here. She hugged the cloak about her—Oh Dierdriu if you would help me, then help me now!—and the light came nearer. Joanna saw Cormac tense and saw his muscles bunch and ripple, a wolf ready to spring. She thought: he will leap straight for the Miller's throat, and felt a great rush of exhilaration. The greatest adventure would not be dying, but living: triumphing over the Miller. She straightened up and caught the flash of a thought from Cormac, and for the first time she saw the Samhailt form: a thin pure shaft of light, so brilliant that it sliced across the darkness, so dazzling that it stayed on the edges of Joanna's vision long after it had died. With the seeing came the receiving—courage, Joanna! This is the greatest adventure so far! She drew a deep breath, and fixed her eyes on the descending light.

Round the curve in the stairway, into the cold dank dungeons, there came a figure so terrible, so nightmarish, and yet so dreadfully familiar, that Joanna nearly cried out, and had to thrust a fist into her mouth to stifle the sound. She thought: I have never seen him. I have never imagined him. But I know him and I recognise him, and he is the embodiment of all the fears I knew as a child, and he is the nightmares I fled from through countless slumbers.

Her many-times ancestors, who had lived through the age called Victorian, would have known the Miller instantly; the Edwardians and the early second-Elizabethans would have recognised him as well, for it was the children of those eras who had been given to read the quite staggeringly unsuitable fairy tales of Austrian and German and Middle-European origin, and it was in those dark and frightening stories that the Giant Miller of Muileann had his place.

Race-memory awoke in Joanna again, as it had awoken on the night she approached Scáthach, and a primitive fear filled her. She knew nothing of Gargantua or Goliath; she had certainly never heard of Brobdingnag nor Blunderbore, nor of

Pantagruel the ever-thirsty, nor Cyclops the angry-eyed. And yet she did know these creatures, not with her eyes or with her mind, but with her heart and with her blood. Huddled into her corner, ancestral memory reared up to torment her; it raced through her veins, until the fearsome tales gathered by Jacob and Wilhelm Grimm and Hans Andersen, illustrated with the brilliant grisly perception of Arthur Rackham, tumbled into her mind. She was a child in a clean white pinafore, her hair plaited, seated before the nursery fire, and she was turning the pages of her storybook slowly and fearfully, because at any moment would come the picture of *him*, and she could feel the thick linen feel of the paper, and she could smell the slightly musty, slightly foxed smell of the book . . . it had been grand-mamma's and grandmamma had said you must treat it carefully because it was quite old and you were only let to look at it on Sundays as a special treat, and you had to say thank you to grandmamma and pretend you were pleased, and not let grandmamma know how much you were frightened of the terrible figure of the Giant . . .

Joanna blinked and swayed and the dungeon closed about her again.

Standing in the cold greasy light from his lantern was the Miller of Muileann. Fifteen feet high and massive, with a huge brutelike shape. He wore a leather apron and a jerkin and leather boots rolled down at the tops. He carried a cleaver and a great wooden club, and his hands were huge meaty hams hanging from his sides. His face was brutish and possessed of a sly greedy cunning. His eyes were small and piglike, and evil, and his nose was bulbous. There was a thatch of hair and a coarse redness about him, and Joanna felt again the unfamiliar pinafore and plaits and the thick damp-smelling storybook that grandmamma always brought out as a treat on Sunday afternoons . . .

There was a rumbling laugh, a sound fetched up from the bowels of hell, and Joanna shuddered and pressed back into her corner. Light streamed into Cormac's cell and the shadow of the Miller fell across the stonework.

Cormac did not waver; "So, Miller, you have come."

"To prepare you for my Master's table, Wolfking. My Master is partial to a morsel of wolfmeat." The dark bulk bent over. "And so am I, Wolfking. A choice bone to gnaw on. A little well-flavoured broth spiced with wolfblood. Are you ready to feel your bones ground to pulp between my Millwheels? Shall we begin?"

Cormac did not flinch. He said steadily, "Quite ready, Miller," and in that moment Joanna acted.

SHE HAD STOOD motionless, her senses shaken and her mind reeling at the sight of the Miller, but on his first words, she had thought: after all he is only ordinary flesh and blood. Giant flesh and giant blood, but there is no magic in him. There are no vile ancient arts in his veins. He can be defeated, thought Joanna. He can be defeated by ordinary human trickery and by the ancient enchantment of the High Queen Dierdriu. She felt the cloak tremble with eagerness, like an animal will quiver to be let off a leash.

All right, said Joanna silently, and taking a tight hold of the Nightcloak's soft folds, she closed her eyes and dredged up every ounce and shred of concentration.

Dierdriu ... Help us ... Send down your nightmares ... call up your dreams ... Help us ...

For a moment there was the most profound silence that Joanna had ever known, and a terrible doubt assailed her. Was the cloak useless? A burnt-out shell? And—fearful notion!—did I burn out its powers when I called upon it that night in the cave with Cormac? Was that the last flicker of a dying magic?

And then, in the uncertain light, Joanna saw the Miller turn his head as if he had caught a sound, and strength and hope returned to her. There is something, an immense fear, in him. Something he knows about, and something that he only acknowledges in his dreams. And she was at once afraid, for what kind of monster, what dread being summoned from the fast keep of the world of dreams could strike fear in the terrible Miller of Muileann? Had they called up the Miller's adversary only to find it their adversary as well?

And then into the dungeons, appearing from nowhere at all, came the slight figure of a young man, curiously and unfamiliarly dressed. His face was both beautiful and cruel, and his eyes were hard and golden like a cat's. In his hand he held a set of reed pipes, and as Joanna and Cormac stared, he seated himself cross-legged on a stone bench, and lifting the pipes to his lips, began to play.

Rats streamed into the dungeons . . .

The effect on the Miller was instantaneous and absolute. He fell back from the cage and threw up a hand to shield his eyes. There was fear and horror and disbelief on his face, and Joanna, not understanding, still concentrating on the cloak's power for all she was worth, moved out of her corner to see better.

The music was filling the dungeon now, and the young man was still seated, very straight-backed, the pipes still held to his lips. His eyes watched the scene before him emotionlessly, and there was a flicker of contemptuous amusement as if he might be thinking: Lord what fools these mortals be! His hair curled tightly to his head, and his skin had the pale faintly translucent quality of one who is unwell or unreal, or not quite human. His music was soft and cool, but beneath it all, ran an insidious command: *Follow me!*

The rats were still coming, squeaking in their eagerness, tumbling over one another, their hard little claws ringing out on the bare stone floor, their eyes red and greedy. Their long tails twitched and slithered after them, and they made darting, scuttling, little movements across the floor.

The Miller gave a great bellowing cry, and sagged at the knees, and at once the rats were upon him, swarming up his body, clinging to him with bared teeth, clawing and scratching. Joanna stood transfixed with astonishment, because although she did not like rats—nobody could like them—she was not especially afraid.

Cormac was not afraid of the rats either, although he glanced uneasily at the young man with the reed pipes, and memories of the old gods of the Greeks stirred in his mind. He reached through the bars of the cage to where the keys lay, dropped in fright by the Miller, and he unlocked the cage and stood for a moment, flexing his entire body, exulting in the freedom after confinement. He made no attempt to touch Joanna or to speak to her, and Joanna knew that Cormac understood about the cloak. The creatures before them had been summoned by the cloak's magic; only by the strongest of concentration could Joanna keep that magic alive, and only by sheer force of will could she keep the young man and the music and the rats there with them.

The Miller had backed into a corner now; he was blubbering

with fear and he was disgusting and revolting and not the least bit pitiable. The rats made a concerted lunge for him, and the Miller fell again to his knees, and then curled himself into a tight ball, covering his head with his hands. Joanna thought: I don't understand this. Why does he not simply use his great strength to throw them off? He could pick them up one by one between his fingers and hurl them against the wall. And although her stomach lifted at the thought, and although she could imagine with a shudder how the plump furry bodies would feel and the dreadful soft squelch they would make when they hit the wall, still she thought she could have done it. Anything other than be clawed and bitten and chewed in a hundred different places. Disgusting! thought Joanna, and then, through the wall of concentration she was still maintaining, she caught the tail end of a thought from Cormac: the Giant Miller is too afraid of them to do anything. They—and the Piper— mean something unendurable to him.

The Miller's great bulk was twitching and jerking, and blood was seeping through his clothes. But the rats were avid. They jostled for places and they scuttled about their victim and bared their teeth at one another, and all the time there was the gnawing, nibbling, *sucking* sound.

And then, at length, there was a choking cough, like dead dry twigs being rattled in a dark place, and the Miller drew a long bubbling breath and lay still. As the rats became quiescent, Joanna glimpsed what she had been trying hard not to see: the crater-like wounds, the gaping jagged hole that had been the Miller's throat, the deep dark bloodied sockets that had been his eyes, and the gleam of white bone . . . liver and kidneys . . . raw stringlike muscles . . . She shuddered and gulped, and looked away, and as she did so, the young man with the pipes ceased playing.

Cormac moved forward very cautiously, and Joanna thought that he was trying to absorb the young man's scent, and that he was puzzled by it. Why? Because it was an alien scent? Or— and this was rather worrying—because there was no scent there?

At length, Cormac said, "Who and what are you?"

The young man smiled and his face changed. Joanna and Cormac relaxed for the first time in many hours.

"I am a being from the Giant's nightmares," he said, and his voice was low and blurred with amusement, so that the other two thought he might be rather fun to know.

"Is that why he was so afraid?"

"Yes. I am the god of fear, but I am the god of many other things as well," said the young man, and Joanna, her mind reaching into the almost-lost lore of her own world, said, half disbelieving, "Pan?"

"I have answered to that name," said the young man gravely and then laughed and slipped from his bench seat and held out a hand to each of them. "My name has been given to your word for great fear, but I am known for many other things. I answer to many names and I have lived many lives, and I have my place in all the creeds and all the legends of the world."

"Are you from the past?" said Cormac cautiously, for his own sorcerers had occasionally been able to summon shadowy figures from the long-ago.

"I am from both the past and the future," said the young man, "for I can travel through the Time Curtain at will, and I have appeared in many different centuries. I am ageless and timeless, and I am possessed of all the virtues and most of the sins." He leaned closer and his eyes slanted. "Fear I am, and Lust. Anger I am and Despair." He smiled, and the sly glint vanished. "But I am also Love and Gaiety and Wine, and I am also Laughter and Revelry. I am sometimes known as the god of music, but also I am the shepherd boy who dwells in the forests and the fields, and lures victims with music so sweet it would melt your soul to hear it." He looked at them, and Joanna thought: it is impossible the number of times his face changes. "Once," said the young man, "I was a Thracian poet called Orpheus, and in that incarnation, I made music so beautiful and so precious that I came within a batswing brush of charming the keepers of the underworld to give me back my lady. For I am jealous of those I own.

"But I am also the Piper, the sinister musician who lives in the Mountains, and who lures into his lair the children of the world.

"In another time—long after your time, Wolfking, and long before yours, Human Child—I shall be a Ratcatcher.

"I shall live in a place called Hamelin, and I shall draw from the city the rats.

"And it is that incarnation that was the Miller's nightmare.

It is as the Piper of Hamelin I have haunted his sleep, and it was as the Piper of Hamelin I appeared to him tonight."

They were all seated together now, the Miller's body stiffening and congealing where it lay, the rats drowsy and replete. Joanna relaxed her hold slightly on the cloak's power, and the young man said sharply, "Do not let me go, Human Child. If you wish to talk a little longer," and Joanna frowned and summoned up her willpower again.

Cormac said, "Are you then bound to obey the cloak's command?"

"I am compelled. While its enchantment calls to me, I am constrained to answer."

"Will you stay and talk with us? Just for a short while?"

"I must do so if you wish it. Whoever wears the Nightcloak of Dierdriu may summon the creatures of nightmares." He leaned forward and there was a light and a gleam in his eyes that made Joanna jump and think: he is very beautiful, but I believe he is quite soulless. The young man said softly and slyly, "Perhaps you also may one day find yourself bound to answer the Nightcloak's summoning, Wolfking."

"I?"

"But yes," said the young man, sitting back and regarding Cormac with malicious amusement. "You are part man, part wolf. There may be a time when such a creature will play a part in the folklore and the legend of the day." He smiled, and again it was the "what fools these mortals be" smile. "You will see," said Pan.

Cormac frowned, but said, "Why was the Miller so afraid? Why did he allow the rats to overpower him so easily?"

"He knew what had happened," said Pan. "He knew of the Piper, for the legend has echoed back in time as well as forward. He knew that one day I would walk through the streets of Hamelin, calling to the rats." Again he leaned forward, so that the flickering candlelight illuminated his features. "All Millers are afraid of rats, for rats are the greatest of all threats to them. Have you never seen oats houses built on stilts so that the rats cannot get in and infest the flour bins? And the Miller of Muileann knew that once the rats had answered my music, once they had fallen into line behind me as I walked through Hamelin, I must bring them *somewhere*." The smile was gentler this time, but still Joanna shivered. "He has dreamt of this night for longer than you can imagine," said Pan. "He has dreamt that I would lead the rats of Hamelin through the Time Curtain, and that between us we would destroy him. He has woken afraid and trembling that I will appear and ruin his Mill, and once his Mill is ruined, he is at the Erl-King's mercy. And even I," said Pan thoughtfully, "would hesitate to provoke the Erl-King. But you see? That is why he was so easily over-powered. It was not the rats who killed him but his own frenzied fear."

"Pan-ic," said Joanna, suddenly understanding, and the young man smiled approvingly.

"Of course," he stood up and looked down on them. "You have a journey."

"Yes."

He turned to Joanna. "Will you let me go now, Human Child?"

"Yes."

"You may see me again," said Pan. "Perhaps not in these lives, but in others. I am to be found in all the centuries. Sometimes you will have to look hard, in order to recognise me, but be assured I will be there."

"Lust and Fear and Greed," said Joanna, and Pan touched her face lightly.

"Yes."

"Did you—forgive me—but did you walk abroad in the days when the Apocalypse burned the world?" She thought she ought not really to have asked, and she could not imagine what the answer might be.

But Pan declined to answer the question. He smiled and touched her face again and said, "I am also the god of Laughter and Music and Wine. And there has always been room for both sides of me, only that in some centuries men allow Lust and Greed to cloud their minds and their judgments. Remember that I am also the god of Love."

And then Joanna let go of the cloak's power, and she and Cormac were alone in the dungeon.

NOTHING HAD EVER tasted so good as the cold night air outside Morrigan's house.

"Night again," observed Dubhgall lugubriously, and Gormgall laughed.

"Your temper is not spoilt by your incarceration, friend."

"It doesn't do to take too optimistic a view of anything," said Dubhgall stubbornly, and Cormac said, "Oh dear," and winked at Joanna. Dubhgall said it was all very well to be cheerful and cut capers and cock snooks, and thumb noses at the Miller and the Morrigna. "But what I say, Your Majesty, is that we aren't out of the woods yet. Not in a pig's eye, we aren't!"

"But Gallan—" started Joanna, and Dubhgall said, "Always supposing we reach it," and Gormgall said, "Why shouldn't we reach it?"

"There's no knowing," said Dubhgall darkly. "But there's mountains to cross yet, and we all know what kind of creatures live in mountains."

"I don't," said Joanna and Gormgall said soothingly, "Nothing so very terrible, my lady."

"And then there's the forest," went on Dubhgall. "Mark my words, Sire, we've got a fair way to go yet."

Cormac laughed and clapped Dubhgall on the back. "For the time being," he said, "we are free and we have come safely through Muileann, and that in itself is something to be thankful for. Onwards to Gallan now, to Cait Fian's house."

"At least it'll be warm there," put in Gormgall.

"And there'll be decent food to eat," said Joanna.

"If we don't get eaten first," muttered Dubhgall, but he said it quietly so that no one heard.

CHAPTER ELEVEN

FLYNN AND AMAIRGEN had been wined and dined and fêted. They had been talked to, and they had been sung to—"And sung *at*," said Flynn—and now their minds were filled to a dizzying point with the beauty and the colour and the brilliance of the Sun Chamber.

They were both very tired. Even so, thought Flynn, I am at home here. I am in my rightful place. And he looked with renewed interest at these people who should have been alien but were not, and at these sights which should have been unfamiliar, but which were very familiar and very comfortable. *I belong here.* And then he thought—if Joanna was here with me I believe I should know a truly perfect contentment. And despite the tiredness, despite the aching fatigue, he whipped up his mind to remain alert, for it was not to be thought of that he should miss any opportunity to find out if Joanna had found her way to Tara. I dare not relax for the briefest instant, thought Flynn.

Eochaid Bres had been regally welcoming, and Bricriu, whom Amairgen thought must be some kind of chamberlain, had been cautiously welcoming. The woman had eyed Flynn and the scholars had been drawn to Amairgen, and Sean the Storyteller had staged an impromptu entertainment about two travellers passing through strange and exotic lands to reach the Plain of Delight. "Merely a little thing that came to me as we sat at supper, Your Majesty," he said with a self-deprecatory air, but later on, when Flynn asked if that had been true, Sean had said at once, "No, of course not. You didn't truly think it was, did you? *Did* you? Well, I put it to you, could anyone have staged all that on the inspiration of the moment? I keep a half a dozen or so things all ready and rehearsed, you never know what might be needed. I'm supposed to provide the King's entertainment; well, that's throwing roses at it, because the King isn't at all easy to entertain, he's a terrible old way of missing all the humour, although it'd be the Miller's cages for me if anyone heard me say it. Still, he'll never know it wasn't spur of the moment stuff, and I shan't tell him. I certainly shan't tell Bricriu the Fox."

Bricriu, the King's chamberlain, had been as smooth as oil to them; he had led them to seats at the High Table, and called for fresh food and flagons of wine to be brought. "I shall be incapable if I drink all that," thought Flynn, half horrified, half delighted, but he drank it all the same, and was not in the least incapable.

Bricriu had engaged them in conversation, while Eochaid Bres looked on and nodded from time to time. As if, thought Flynn, he does so to show he understands what we are talking about.

"And," said Bricriu, "when you are rested, you must tell us of your travels, for we shall be very interested," and Eochaid Bres nodded solemnly. Flynn and Amairgen shared a sudden thought: if we told them the truth they would certainly not believe us!

They partook cautiously of the food, which was like nothing either of them had ever tasted before. "But it is all very good," said Flynn hungrily, reaching out his hand, and Sean the Storyteller said, awed, "You're not having another helping, are you?" and was frowned at by the King, who knew that it was ill-bred to comment on a guest's appetite, but who was rather pleased to see Flynn eating so heartily, because it meant that Eochaid Bres could help himself to another plateful of pork pudding without anyone really noticing. He was very fond of pork pudding, for all that Bricriu said it made you liverish. Eochaid was not liverish in the least, or not very much anyway.

After they had eaten, it seemed to be expected that they should move from the table and mingle with the Court. Flynn looked about him and thought: if I am careful, I may be able to fall into conversation with some of the younger ones. They will surely know if Joanna has been here. Won't they? And he remembered Joanna's curious blend of great fragility and immense strength, and thought that even here, even surrounded by these strange and exotic creatures, Joanna would stand out. Yes, certainly if she had been here they would remember her. He looked warily to where some of the younger ones were foregathering and smiling at him in a welcoming way, and then moved to accept the chair that was being indicated, and to take the wine that was being offered.

At the back of his mind, a spurt of humour arose, so that he wondered whether, if he did find out about Joanna, he would be sufficiently sober to make any sense of the information. He wondered how Amairgen was faring, and saw that he had fallen quite naturally into discourse with the Councillors. How strange, thought Flynn, that he gravitates so easily into the company of leaders. Or is it?

Amairgen was talking to the Councillors quite naturally and relaxedly, finding them courteous and interesting, and rather scholarly. He chose his words with care, because he wanted to find out more about this place, and he listened with genuine interest to what they had to say. Once or twice he wondered how Flynn was getting on, and smiled inwardly to see that several of the ladies were already grouped about him. The boy had caused a strong ripple in this rather rarefied atmosphere; Amairgen had seen the females sit up and eye one another, and the lady they called Mab had been watching Flynn ever since they had arrived. Amairgen wondered if Flynn was aware of his attractiveness, and then thought he was not. He thought that it was probably part of Flynn's charm, and he began to be very curious indeed about Joanna. Flynn would obviously brave all of the dangers in the world for Joanna, and so Amairgen thought that she must surely be something very exceptional. He was pleased for Flynn, because he was beginning to think that Flynn, also, might be something very exceptional. *Because he is Finn of the* Fiana *returned?* said the depths of his mind. And then, no—because he is himself! Amairgen smiled and turned back to his own table.

The Councillors were informative; they were charmed to tell this polite, rather grave, stranger about Tara and about their customs. Wasn't it the grandest thing in the world to be able to talk for a while without watching every word you said, and wasn't it altogether great to indulge in a bit of harmless nostalgia. It crossed the minds of a couple of them that Amairgen might be one of Eochaid Bres's spies; it certainly crossed the minds of several more that he might be one of Bricriu's, for there was no knowing what complexities of intrigue the Fox might stoop to. But they dismissed these suspicions fairly quickly. Some of them possessed a smattering of the Samhailt, although naturally no one would have admitted to it under Eochaid Bres's rule, and they all, within the first five minutes of meeting him, knew that Amairgen was no spy.

They told him about Tara, how it had been raised from the rock, and how it had been the finest Court ever to come into the western world. They told him about Dierdriu of the Nightcloak, and how she had bargained with the sorcerers and the magicians to make the Sun Chamber.

"And the sorcerers," they said, sadly, "although they always swear allegiance to whoever occupies the High Throne, have their own loyalties."

"The Wolfking could hold their loyalty," said one of the younger ones, and was instantly shushed.

They told, as well, about Ireland's great heroes, of Niall of the Nine Hostages, and they talked, in hushed voices, about the terrible Prison of Hostages, and the Star of the Poets. They related the marvellous legend of Nuadu Airgetlam of the Silver Arm, who had fought the great Battle of Mag Tuired; and they told about the cauldron of the god Dagda, which, if you could find it, ensured that no company, however large, would go unsatisfied. They talked about the Battle for the Trees between Dierdriu and the Morrigna, and about the Beltane revels, which would begin in a few days, and which Amairgen and his companion must surely stay for.

They told, as well, about the Fál, the great stone penis on the Hill of Tara, which cried aloud under the hand of Ireland's true destined King.

"Ah, a fine sight it is to see the Ceremony of the Fál," said the eldest Councillor, rather wistfully.

"You have seen it for yourself?" inquired Amairgen, fascinated.

"Indeed I have, and a grand sight it was," said the Councillor, whose name was Bolg. "The High King Cormac it was; the great Wolfking, although of course," said Bolg rather uneasily, "of course, he was not the rightful King, as we all know

now." He sent a wary look to where Eochaid Bres was seated, and several of the others glanced over their shoulders and murmured their agreement.

"Even so," said Bolg reminiscently, "that was a fine old ceremony, the day he was made King." He nodded to himself, and Amairgen waited. "All gathered on the Hill of Tara we were," said Bolg, his eyes faraway. "All waiting. Someone had persuaded the *sidh* to come—"

"Someone had paid them to come, more like," put in one of the younger Councillors.

"They're as greedy as goblins, the *sidh*," explained another.

"Well, however it was," said Bolg, "the *sidh* were there, just out of sight of course, as they always are, and as we know, it is virtual death and certain madness to look on them anyway, so no one ever does. But they were there all the same, melting in and out of the hillside, just a smudge of cold blue and ice green, but their music was all about us."

"You'd forgive the *sidh* a lot for their music," said the youngest Councillor.

"You'd almost forgive them their wantonness," put in another.

"Not entirely," said the first, rather disapprovingly.

"Anyway, their music was there," said Bolg firmly, "and all the Court was there."

"And the Wolves, don't forget the wolves," said the Councillor who had disapproved of the *sidh*.

"I'm not forgetting them," said Bolg crossly. "Of course I'm not." He turned back to Amairgen. "The Wolves were there, ranged on the far side of the hill. Quiet they were, but very watchful. We were all a bit wary to tell you the truth, for there's never any knowing which way a wolf will jump, and there was only His Majesty had any control over them."

"Do lower your voice, Bolg," said the youngest Councillor. "Unless of course you want Eochaid Bres or Bricriu to hear."

"I'm telling a history," said Bolg with dignity. "I'm telling a history, and this gentleman is our honoured guest, and if he's polite enough to listen, I'm polite enough to tell him. And if that's treason," said Bolg with sudden spirit, "then it's time and more that I left Tara and His Majesty found himself a new Chief Councillor. I am Chief Councillor," he explained to Amairgen anxiously. "It's quite a responsibility."

"I'm sure it is. Do please go on."

"Well, we all stood waiting—it was a windy day I recall and I was glad I'd put my woollen underwear on. These younger ones don't understand the things a cold wind does to a man," he added confidentially, "but I'd put it on and I was glad of it.

"So, we all stood waiting, and there was the music, cold and somehow passionate—"

"Like the *sidh* themselves," said the youngest Councillor. "Yes, isn't there a saying they'd freeze a man's balls off before he'd time to—"

"We were all waiting," said Bolg rather loudly. "The music was all around us, for of course the *sidh* were ever true servants of the Wolfline. There's a legend that when Cormac was born they sang him into the world.

"And so there was the music, and there was the Court, and the Wolves, all waiting, and there was the anticipation. So tremendous it was, that you could very nearly see it. You could have reached out and sliced through it and seen it part before you. And at the centre was the Fál, rearing up out of the ground like a—well, we all know what it's like and no call for vulgarity." He glared at the Councillor who had said the *sidh* would freeze a man's balls off, and the Councillor squirmed and looked discomfited.

"The Fál was glowing," said Bolt. "It glowed and it gave off a kind of strength. We could all feel the magic radiating from it. We could all feel that it was waiting as well.

"And then, just as we were all thinking we couldn't bear it a moment longer, that if the King didn't come soon something would snap and break and we should all die, over the horizon he came. Cormac of the Wolves. The Prince of Tara. Plainly dressed he was—well, he never cared overmuch what he wore, and time and again he'd come into Council looking more like a tinker than a Prince of the Bloodline—but even so, every person present fell to his knees, and the Wolves bowed their heads. Authority, you see. He had it in fullest measure; you obeyed him unquestioningly.

"Cormac stood watching us, outlined against the sky, his cloak billowing out behind him, his hair ruffled by the wind, and colour whipped across his cheekbones. For a moment there was silence, and then Cormac said, 'Well gentlemen, shall we begin?' Because," said Bolg seriously, "of course it's

a purely *masculine* affair when a King touches the Fál. They
don't let the women go. It upsets the magic."

"What about Dierdriu?" said the Councillor who had liked
the *sidh*'s music. "Dierdriu went to a Ceremony."

"*And* touched the Fál," said another, and several people
hooted rather derisively.

"Dierdriu hid herself to watch the Ceremony of the Fál
when her father was presented to the Stone," said the first one.
"And the legend is that the Fál wouldn't answer to her father,
and there was great consternation, nobody knew what to do."

"It had never happened before," put in another.

"*Or* since," said a third.

"No, we've never had a High Queen since Dierdriu," said
the first Councillor, who was rather finding himself the centre
of attention. "But they say that as everyone stood around, trying to think what should be done, Dierdriu came out of hiding,
and said that the Fál would accept *her*, and they must present
her to it, and if it didn't answer her, she'd go into exile at
Scáthach forever."

"Did it answer to her?" said Amairgen.

"What? Oh yes," said Bolg. "Oh yes, they say it cried aloud
for nine days and nine nights. They counted. Dear me, they all
talked about it for years afterwards, it's one of our finest legends, you know, although it was a very long time ago. Probably it was a couple of centuries. My word, it's a good story,
though." He leaned forward confidentially. "And they do say,"
he said in a whisper, "they do say it was a remarkable sight to
see her kneeling down clasping the Fál. Of course, she would
only be quite young at the same time, and I expect she
wouldn't understand the *significance* of the Fál, that is . . . hum
. . . its shape."

He looked worried, and a few people sniggered, and one
said that if half the tales told about Dierdriu were true the
chances were she'd have understood it all too well, and somebody else said that if a *quarter* of the tales were true, she'd
have enjoyed it, never mind understanding it, and Bolg
frowned.

"It's a serious and solemn ritual," he said repressively. "And
whatever else you may say about Cormac, you couldn't say
he didn't perform the ritual properly and with full respect."
He turned back to Amairgen.

"Cormac made no ceremony," the Councillor said, "he never did, not of anything, but his presence was ceremony in itself if you know what I mean. He walked to the Stone and lifted his hands above his head. And the music grew stronger and the Wolves growled low in their throats in that restless way they have, and the fur on their necks lifted.

"And then Cormac grasped the Stone."

Bolg stopped and Amairgen leaned forward.

"And? What happened?"

"It was the most marvellous sound I ever heard," whispered Bolg. "The Stone cried, it actually shrieked aloud, so that the sound echoed and spun all about us. On and on it went until you felt it had entered into your head. And then there was a humming sound, and a noise like wings beating on the air, thousands upon thousands of wings, and Cormac just stood there, his expression so serious that for a moment I hardly recognised him, for he'd been a wild boy, and it was rare to see him so grave-faced. And the noise went on and on and no one could hear or think or speak, and no one really wanted to hear or think or speak. We all wanted to drown in the sounds and we all wanted to lay our lives down for Cormac to show how much we loved him.

"On and on it went, until you thought you'd die of pure delight, for it was a sound so—so comforting. So safe. It said: all is well for I am with you, and it said: you are in my hands and I will never fail you. Several people cried openly, well I did myself, for it was an emotional moment," said Bolg. "And at last, when Cormac finally let go of the Stone, there was a great sighing and a sense of loss so keen you felt that something had died.

"And then," said Bolg matter-of-factly, lifting his goblet of wine, "and then, you know we all went back to Tara and held a great feast, and I believe the King got drunker than anyone had ever seen him, and the stories they tell about that night— well I wouldn't repeat them even if I knew any of them which I don't. But they say there's never been a night so wild inside these walls. Oh, he was a reckless one."

Amairgen said, "And the—the present King? Eochaid Bres? What of his ritual with the Fál? Was that as awe-inspiring?"

"Well there it is," said Bolg, his eyes sliding away, and the other Councillors muttered and shuffled their feet. "There's been no Ceremony of the Stone at all since Eochaid came to the throne."

"Not the merest whisper of one," said another.

"They say the King doesn't like the old traditions," said a third.

"He certainly doesn't like the Stone of Fál," put in a fourth, and then looked terrified.

"It's not for us to judge," said Bolg firmly. "If Eochaid Bres wants to change the old ways, then it's his right and his privilege as High King. We mustn't question him." And he reached for his wine again.

Amairgen, sensing their withdrawal, said quickly, "You are being very courteous to the stranger in your midst, gentlemen, and I find your customs fascinating. I hope we may talk some more." And then, encouraged by their evident pleasure at his words, said carefully, "It is clear that you are accustomed to travellers and that you always give them hospitality."

"As it happens," said Bolg slowly, "we have few travellers to Tara."

"Ah. But those you have are clearly welcome," said Amairgen. "For is not this a great place of pilgrimage?"

"Once," said one of the older Councillors wistfully, "once it was."

"Once, all the poets and the musicians and the ballad-makers flocked to Tara."

"Once, it was known as the most brilliant Court in the western world."

"Men would travel the high seas to come here."

"In the days of—"

"Oh hush," said Bolg worriedly, and once more glanced furtively over his shoulder.

"In the days of . . . ?" said Amairgen, lifting his brows, but Bolg said firmly, "We have talked of Cormac quite enough. It is a long time ago. Old men's gossip, I fear. Tell me, sir, do you play chess at all?"

FLYNN WAS BOTH fascinated and repelled by the lady who had sought him out after supper was over. He thought, incredulously: I believe she is attempting to seduce me, and was rather astonished to feel warmth between his legs at the idea. But she is more than twice my age! cried his horrified mind. Was she forty? Forty-two? More? Oh yes. Never mind, said his body, and he found himself leaning nearer to her to hear her speak, for her voice was low and musical, and Flynn wondered, not for the first time, why people were not more aware of the voice as a sexual attraction.

Mab was watching him, and Flynn thought that he had not been mistaken, she was luring him, and he was at once plunged into hideous doubt, for he had thought himself bound to Joanna, and he had thought himself immune to all others as a result. Yes, Mab was easily twice his age, he could see the fine lines at the corners of her eyes, he could see that her neck—traitorous area!—was dry and crepey looking.

Mab laughed. She said, "Yes, I am quite twice your age, and probably more. Does it matter?"

"You heard my thoughts? But is that not forbidden?" said Flynn, alarmed all over again, and remembering that in this odd new world there might exist spies and traps and treasons of all kinds. "I was told it was quite forbidden," he said firmly, because if you had to declare for one side or the other, you might as well declare for the reigning King. However stupid and ill-fitted for the job he was. And there went another treasonable thought!

She caught it at once, of course. She narrowed her eyes thoughtfully and said, "The Samhailt *is* forbidden, for my son the King does not possess it. A question of good manners, you understand? What the King does not have, no other should have either. It makes for awkwardness sometimes. But," a shrug, a spreading of the slender hands, "to forbid a thing does not necessarily kill it. We both possess the Samhailt, you and I." And there again was the intimacy, the suggestion that they shared—that they might in the future share—something exciting and unusual and pleasurable. "In any case," said Mab, "I am not bound by any law my son may choose to make."

"But—forgive me, madam," said Flynn, who had never in his life addressed a lady as madam, but who, chameleon-like, had caught the modes and the manners of these people, "forgive me, but he *is* the High King."

Mab laughed, and Flynn, fascinated and just very slightly enchanted, thought that her laugh was like no one else's he had ever heard. And with the detached, humorous side of his mind, thought: I believe she is trying to seduce me. Shall I let her?

And grinned inwardly, because he was rather intrigued by Mab, and he was certainly attracted by her. And forgive me, Joanna, my darling lovely girl, but never forget that anything I might do in this lady's bed tonight or tomorrow, or any tomorrow after that, can ever touch my feelings for you.

"Eochaid Bres is the King because I put him there, Flynn," Mab said. "He stays the High King because I keep him there." Amusement lit her eyes, and Flynn smiled into them, and thought: yes, I was not wrong. Well, madam, if that is what you want, I find I am not at all averse. And saw by the blaze in her eyes that she had heard his thought. But he only said, "You were ambitious for your son? That is very admirable."

"Not at all," said Mab and although her voice was cool, her eyes were afire with excitement. "Oh, not at all, Flynn." She reached for his hand and held it between her own for a moment. "I was ambitious for myself," said Mab. "And also I was filled with a great desire for vengeance against the man who occupied the High Throne." She leaned forward, and Flynn caught the warm sandalwood scent of her body. "I was dealt a very great insult," said Mab, and her eyes were distant now. "He was eighteen, Flynn, and I was—" the smile was mischievous suddenly, "let us say I was considerably older than eighteen." And Flynn smiled, because it had not mattered how old Mab had been then, and it did not matter how old she was now.

Mab smiled, and said, "It is quite impossible to describe the man who was High King, Flynn. You would have to know him for yourself. But in those days he was wild and wolvish and arrogant. He may have altered now, although it is only seven years, and I do not know. But then, he was . . . so remarkable." She fell silent, and Flynn thought: Cormac! Of course she is talking about Cormac.

"Of course I am," said Mab. "But he paid me a supreme discourtesy, you see. I discovered that he had—flouted one of our most Sacred Laws—that of the Bloodline Enchantment." And, as Flynn looked up questioningly, she said, "No, I cannot say any more. Only that the Bloodline—the Six Ancient Families—are bound by stringent laws if the Lines are to continue. The creation of a Bloodline is so bound about by enchantment and by careful and reasoned decisions, that it is dangerous to step outside those laws.

"Cormac stepped outside them, Flynn. I was the only one who knew, and I have never told anyone of it. But I exiled him. I led the revolution that sent him to Scáthach all those years ago. I deprived him of the one thing I knew mattered to him more than anything else, Flynn . . .

"I deprived him of Tara."

EOCHAID BRES HAD enjoyed his evening. He had danced with the wife of the lesser chieftain once or twice—well all right, four times if you wanted to keep tally like a money-lender—and everyone had nodded and smiled and several of the sterner Councillors had looked disapproving, and Eochaid Bres had felt he had acquitted himself rather well. People liked a King they could disapprove of a bit. Of course, everyone remembered Eochaid's cousin Cormac on these occasions, because Cormac had been quite incorrigible where the ladies of the Court had been concerned. Eochaid dared say that Cormac would have taken the chieftain's wife to bed with him, which was rather shocking. The chieftain would probably not have minded either, which was even more shocking. Wives were not things, pawns to be loaned here and there on a whim. For a moment Eochaid dwelled rather glumly on the thought of wives, because High Kings were expected to marry and beget children to carry on the line. He knew that. He knew how it was done as well; in fact he had tried it once or twice, although he had not really cared for it very much. Still, if custom had dictated that Eochaid Bres should have taken the chieftain's wife off to bed that night, he would probably have done it. Custom had not dictated, not unless you counted Cormac's customs, which Eochaid naturally did not, and Eochaid and the lady had parted circumspectly after four dances. It was probably as well that they had, because Eochaid, after an evening spent in the Sun Chamber's glare, always felt a bit queasy, and it would not have done to have been sick with a lady present. The story would have flown round the Court, these things always did, and before he knew where he was, Sean the Storyteller would have written a ballad and everyone would have sung it just out of Eochaid's hearing, and there would have been sneery jokes being bandied back and forth. It would have been altogether mortifying, and Mother would have wrung her hands and indulged in a tantrum and talked about donating her life's blood. Bricriu would have said, Oh dear, Your Majesty, how very unfortunate, and talked about royal dignity.

"Bother royal dignity and bother being High King," said Eochaid crossly, donning his nightcap and clambering into his bed.

Cormac had not given a tinker's curse for dignity. He had held competitions with his courtiers to see how many women they could each bed in the course of a night, and had set up Sean the Storyteller to keep a tally. Eochaid had heard the final count, and he had not believed it, although he had not said so, because it might have given people an erroneous idea about him. And then you had to allow for exaggeration as well.

Cormac had been wilder than anyone Eochaid had ever known. Eochaid had never forgotten the night of Cormac's Ritual of Fál; the ceremonious embracing of the great Stone which was supposed to shriek aloud for the destined King. A lot of nonsense, of course, and Eochaid was not going to resurrect such an archaic custom.

"I shouldn't if I were you," Bricriu had said, a knowing glint in his eyes. "You never quite know how these things may turn out, Sire."

Cormac had gone through with it, of course, and people had become very wrought up and wept on each other's shoulders, and talked about honour and the One True Line and dying for the King, and it had all been very emotional and sloppy.

But Eochaid had crept downstairs and hidden behind a rood screen later that night; he had been twelve at the time and curious. Cormac and the young men of the Court had been wildly gloriously drunk; they had been bawdy and boisterous and flown with the wine they had drunk. After the ladies had retired, Sean the Storyteller had sung quite the rudest song Eochaid had ever heard. Even now, it made his ears turn bright red to think about it. But Cormac and the young men had laughed and cheered and joined in the chorus, and Cait Fian of Gallan had written two more verses, and everyone had cheered all over again and several people had got up to demonstrate the more explicit parts of Sean's song.

Before they retired, Cormac had challenged them to a new kind of contest.

"Who can fill the pots at twenty paces!" he had shouted,

jumping on to the long banqueting table and unbuttoning his breeches. "Come now, gentlemen, for you've all taken enough wine to have overflowing bladders by now! A contest! Twenty paces, and a gold piece for each pace for the winner!"

As Eochaid had watched, there had been a laughing stampede and they'd all leapt into line, disgusting, obscene, all eager for the prize. There'd been ribaldry and teasing for one of them who had been suffering the concentrated attentions of a lady for most of the evening, and was in a state of natural arousal or as near as made no difference.

"An upright courtier!" cried Cormac gleefully. "Conaire, you're out of the race, for you'll never manage more than two drops in that condition!"

And the curious thing, to Eochaid the incomprehensible thing, was that on the very next day, those young men who had stood with the King, pissing into pots placed in a row, had fallen into respectful silence when he entered the Council Chamber, and later had ridden submissively behind him as he rode out at the head of his armies to some ceremony or other. What of royal dignity there!

It was all too much for Eochaid to grapple with, especially at this hour, especially after an entire evening in the Sun Chamber. He would have to send for a marigold draught or a glass of cold wine to settle his stomach.

"Be bothered to being High King!" said Eochaid Bres crossly and went in search of medicament.

BRICRIU WAS COMPOSING himself for sleep as well but, unlike the King (if you could think of Mab's boy as King, which Bricriu found difficult), had not been so easily able to banish his worries. It was all very well for Mab to smile and shrug and say Eochaid was young, he could be moulded—yes, and then go off to eye with greedy delight the dark-haired young traveller! Eochaid was not so young as all that; in fact Bricriu thought he had been born middle-aged, and he was certainly not as mouldable as Mab seemed to think. Mab said Eochaid was a puppet King, a figurehead; that it was she and Bricriu who ruled, but Bricriu was becoming uneasy. Eochaid was rather more than a puppet of late; he was developing a will of his own. You had only to look at the way he had growled at them all tonight, and at how he had gone off dancing and carousing with the chieftain's lady. Quite out of character that had been, and if Eochaid could do one thing out of character he could do others. Only look, as well, at how he had broken Bricriu's careful policy of refusing entrance to strangers and invited in the two young men who had come to the West Gate. Bricriu looked at this very carefully indeed, and did not like it. Eochaid seemed to be developing a streak of independence, if not of downright rebelliousness, and the one was as bad as the other. It would not do for Eochaid to start making his own laws; Bricriu did not know what matters were coming to when Kings thought they could do that. No, Eochaid must be got firmly back on the path that Bricriu intended him to tread, and they could all relax again. He had not spent those weeks and months consulting with the sorcerers for nothing. He had certainly not taken part in those long and incomprehensible rituals—and some of them had been disgusting!—just to see Ireland snatched from his grasp by a stupid obstinate puppet. Bricriu was going to make Ireland the most powerful country in the world; he was going to send out armies to conquer all the other civilised nations, and once they had been conquered, Ireland would rule the world. And Bricriu would rule Ireland. It was a heady thought.

It would happen as well, Bricriu had determined on that, and he had sought out the most powerful of the sorcerers to make sure of it. The armies that he would send out from Tara would be victorious because they would have the sorcerers at their beck and call, and wars waged using sorcery were nearly always successful.

He had had to make use of the Dark Sorcerers, of course, but he thought you could not have everything. The battles would, as a result, be really rather gruesome at times, but since the battles would not be in Ireland, Bricriu was not disposed to worry over much.

He sighed contentedly, and was glad, rather than otherwise, that he had not summoned any of the Court ladies to his bed tonight. Really, when you came down to it, there was nothing as satisfying as the thrill of power. And Bricriu was going to be very powerful indeed.

Mab should not stand in his way; Mab had an unexpected habit of showing squeamishness at times, Bricriu had noticed it more than once. She thought that captives ought to be treated with respect, and she had wanted him to post sentries at all the borders between here and Muileann; "In case of attack from the Miller's people," she had said. Bricriu had not cared if the Miller's people had attacked and taken off the entire Court, just so long as he himself was left safe. You could replace courtiers. You could not replace Bricriu.

Eochaid Bres should not stand in his way either. He could not be removed, of course, for they needed someone with a vein of royal blood in him, even if it was only a thin trickle. But he would certainly have to be distracted. Perhaps the boy should be married. It would occupy his mind if nothing else. Kings so easily became bored, and everyone knew what happened when Kings were bored; they squabbled and had petty disputes with their chieftains—which was apt to be expensive—or they took to womanising or drinking—which was apt to be injurious to their health. Bricriu did not want Eochaid either bankrupt or poxed, or not until he had found an acceptable replacement for him at any rate. And of course, a High King ought to be married. Bricriu ran his mind over several likely candidates for Eochaid's consideration, but this one was too old, and that one too ill-favoured, and a third too nearly related to the Wolfline. They could not have a Princess of Tara who could not bear children, and they did not want one who was so ugly she would have to wear a bag over her head on State occasions, and they certainly dare not risk one who might owe allegiance to the exiled Cormac. There were enough spies at Tara as it was.

Spies.

The little niggling worry about the two strangers slid into the forefront of Bricriu's mind and he gave it at last his full attention. Just supposing that the two young men, the one fair, the other dark, had come from an enemy? Supposing they had come from Cormac himself? Bricriu had known Cormac as a boy; he had known Cormac's father as well, and he knew that Scáthach, grim ugly fortress, would not keep Cormac imprisoned for long. He would break out and muster an army, and it was no comfort to ask what kind of an army the exiled King could gather, because Bricriu knew very well that Cait Fian and the people of the Morne Mountains would ride out under Cormac's standard. And Cait Fian was not an enemy to be regarded lightly. With Cait Fian on his side, Cormac would put up a very good fight to regain his lost Kingdom, and there was always the chance he might win. Bricriu had done all he could to guard Tara against such assault; he had bound the Bright Palace with as many enchantments as he had been able to buy—although his thrifty soul had been very much shocked at the greediness of the sorcerers—and Tara was very nearly impregnable.

But it was not absolutely impregnable . . .

The Girdle of Gold had long since been lost to the High Kings of course; he knew that. And Tara's sorcerers had never ceased to search for it—or so they would have you believe. "Ever since the Lady Dierdriu's day," they always said, their faces bland.

Bricriu did not entirely trust the sorcerers, although he did not say so directly. They were automatically bound to the one who ruled from Tara, of course; they always swore an Oath at a coronation, and it was all very impressive. But in reality they were as venal as the next man; they knew how to swear an Oath and avoid looking you in the eye, and they certainly knew how to find loopholes in an Oath as well.

And so when the sorcerers told him they continually searched for the Girdle of Gold so that it might be restored to Tara, Bricriu was inclined to be very sceptical indeed. He thought the sorcerers knew very well where the Girdle of Gold was. With the Erl-King?

"We did not say that," said the wily sorcerers. "But your honour knows that no enchantment can be used simultaneously by two different people." And they avoided Bricriu's eyes again, so that Bricriu thought: aha! So the Erl-King *has* commandeered the Girdle for his Citadal, has he? It was not so very surprising if you thought about it. It was not surprising at all if you took into account that the sorcerers—some of them anyway—were probably in the pay of the Erl-King, never mind if they had sworn a thousand Oaths and a million Allegiances.

But Bricriu was annoyed. Without the Girdle of Gold, Tara was vulnerable. Enemies could get in, spies could slip through.

Spies.

Bricriu thought: what would I do if I were Cormac? And back came the answer: send spies into Tara! He considered the idea, and thought it was very likely indeed that Cormac would do just that. It was what anyone would do, thought Bricriu, whose mind worked crablike, and who could not have conceived in a hundred years of Cormac's forthright swashbuckling methods. Cormac, in fact, had never once thought about spies, about the backstairs way of regaining his kingdom, but still—he'll send in spies, thought Bricriu. He'll do that before he does anything else. Spies to find out the number of guards and sentinels; to count the hours of the nightwatches and learn the times of sentry changes. Spies carefully disguised!

Cormac would not know that travellers were no longer welcome at Tara. He would assume that all travellers were made as welcome as he himself had made them, and he would think that a pair of pilgrims would blend easily into any one of the evenings in the Sun Chamber.

The two young travellers who had arrived tonight were exactly the sort of people Cormac would consort with. They bore his stamp, Bricriu had seen that at once. The dark-haired one had a good deal of Cormac's recklessness about him, you had only to look at him to see it.

Bricriu pondered the matter, and thought that no mistakes must be made. The only thing to do with spies was to kill them as quickly and efficiently as possible before they could get back to their master. The travellers must be dispatched as soon as he could manage it; they must certainly not be allowed to find out anything about the Palace's fortifications.

A public execution? Make an example of them? No, it was not to be thought of. To do that would make public the fact that the spies had managed to gain entry in the first place. It would make Tara sound an easy target for the raff and skaff of the world, any one of whose rulers would be very pleased to possess the Bright Palace. It would certainly make it sound a cheap conquest for Cormac and the armies he would be trying to raise. People could not be allowed to know that Cormac's spies had penetrated so far. What was to be done?

They would have to be killed of course, but in such a way that no one would guess the truth. Bricriu considered the matter and thought he would ask the *sidh* for help. It would mean going down into the Sorcery Chambers, which he did not much care for—well, nobody did if the truth was told—but the *sidh* would have to be properly summoned. They would not be far away in any case, for they were never far from Tara. They served the High Kings in their fashion, but they served Bricriu

as well. A very neat little bargain had been struck when
Eochaid Bres had been put on the throne; the *sidh* had helped
Bricriu quite considerably then, and perhaps it was time to
send them a little offering. These bargains were a two-sided arrangement in any case, and Bricriu was really quite pleased to
think he could reciprocate. The fact that the disposal of one of
the young men would be to his advantage did not come into
the thing. He would call up the *sidh* and they would certainly
take one of the spies.

What about the other one? The *sidh* would only ever take
one human at a time; they were greedy but they only concentrated on one victim at a time. What, then, of the one they did
not take? Bricriu tiptoed through the halls, holding his night
candle aloft, and as he turned the curve in the stair, the candle
throwing huge fantastic shapes on the walls, a plan so simple
and so satisfactory slid into his mind that he stood stock-still
for a moment and the candle flickered wildly and almost went
out. Bricriu shielded it at once with his hand, for he had no
mind to be left down here in the dark. He would much prefer
not to have gone down to the Sorcery Chambers in the dark to
begin with, but it could not be helped, he could not risk being
seen, and anyway, enchantments always worked better at night.

But the plan—oh yes, it was beautifully simple, and it would
work, because the simplest plans were always the best. He
smiled to himself as he made his way down the gilt stairway.

Beltane. In just over a week it would be Beltane. Bonfires
and revels and all means of feastings. Rituals, for Tara with its
links with the ancient lore, held closely to most of the old rituals. It held very closely to one ritual in particular.

The Beltane Fire. The great mound of wood on the Plain of
the Fál, lit with great ceremony by the High King at the Purple
Hour, danced round by the Court. And on the summit of the
fire . . .

The Druids had continued the custom when everyone else
had long since abandoned it. They kept their secrets and ceremonies, and even the wiliest of the sorcerers had never found
out their rituals. The Druids were wise, rather eccentric, but
entirely harmless. But on the night of Beltane they worshipped
very old gods indeed; some of them so old that their names
were lost to the rest of the world, and their powers old before
men could communicate with one another.

Every Beltane night, the Druids brought to the Plain of the Fál a rather awesome and slightly grisly practice. The wooden giant. The great rearing Wicker Man, frequently thirty or forty feet in height, cunningly constructed from thin wood and grass, so perfect, so nearly human, that if you had not known it to be a dead thing, a soulless creature of bracken and tree and twig, you might have thought a nightmare had come alive.

The Druids brought it every year, trundling it in silent procession to the Plain, pulling it right up to the fire where it would be burned. It was divided into sections, little hinged compartments that opened and latched shut, and which, once closed, were remarkably difficult to open again. "One of our secrets," said the Druids courteously, but Bricriu had always believed that some minor sorcery was used in the sealing of the compartments. The Druids had their secrets. In each compartment were live things; pigs, geese, lambs; frequently pigeons and doves. The Wicker Man's legs would hold the smaller creatures; the stomach and ribcage housed the larger ones. Inside the head, where the brain would have been in a live man, were traditionally put crabs and lobster to represent the sea creatures.

And at the height of the Purple Hour, when the revelries were at their wildest, the Wicker Man with all his prisoners was consigned to the great Beltane Fire, and every single creature inside the wicker cages was burned alive.

The higher the fire the greater the rewards . . . the more numerous the sacrifice, the better the fertility of the land . . .

It was many years since the Druids had penned a human sacrifice in the Wicker Man's trunk, although Bricriu knew it had once been regarded as a punishment for those convicted of serious crimes. But neither Cormac nor his father had cared for the custom; Cormac had said that burning to death was unnecessarily brutal no matter the crime, and Bricriu believed he had even ordered some kind of draught to be prepared for the condemned animals and birds. The Druids had protested; they had said that blood and flesh and bone must shriek aloud for the sacrifice to be effective; deep and abiding agonies must be endured by the victims to ensure fertility to the land in the coming year. But Cormac had overruled them, for Cormac had always been able to handle the Druids.

The Druids would be very pleased to be given a human sacrifice this year; they would probably swear a strong Allegiance to Eochaid Bres, which meant to Bricriu. They would be extremely discreet about it all as well, for whatever else they might be, they were people of the highest integrity.

Bricriu smiled as he made his way down to the Sorcery Chambers. Yes, it would work.

One to the *sidh* to be dealt with in the dreadful fashion the *sidh* dealt with all their victims. The other to the Druids for burning on the Beltane Fire.

It was a very good plan.

SEAN THE STORYTELLER thought the evening had gone very well. And hadn't it proved that you had always to be on the alert, always prepared for all kinds of occurrences? It did not do to be caught napping, and Sean had not been caught napping when the travellers had arrived. A nice little entertainment all ready and waiting, and very appropriate too. It had been a surprise to them all when the King had given permission for the travellers to be brought up, for he was as inhospitable as a hedgehog as a rule. But of course, he was King only in name, they all knew that. It was Bricriu the Fox who ruled.

But there the travellers had been, and there the King had been, and there the entertainment had been. The King had certainly not suspected that Sean had not made it up on the spot. It was not so very difficult to fool the lions a little.

It was very nearly impossible to fool Bricriu, of course. The Fox had looked at Sean rather sardonically when the announcement had been made, and Mab of course would have known straight off that the ballad and its staging bore the marks of a carefully rehearsed piece. Didn't Mab know all about playacting anyway, for didn't she spend half her time doing just that, only that no one except Sean had ever realised it. Sean grinned and made himself more comfortable in the large old bed. He could tell a tale or two about Mab if he cared to! More than a tale or two!

Still, who couldn't?

IN HER SILK hung bedchamber, Mab was not thinking about the evening or about Sean's entertainment, or about Bricriu or Eochaid Bres. She was drowsy and warm, and she was thinking about how soon she would have Flynn in her bed.

Tonight would have been much too soon, although the boy would almost certainly have come if she had beckoned. But it would put an edge on both their appetites to linger a little, to eye one another, to brush hands and thighs, to exchange smiles. Just as she had done with the young Cormac all those years ago.

Remarkable how she still thought about him, even after he had hurt and humiliated her.

Flynn would not humiliate her as Cormac had. He would not be allowed to. Yes, it would be amusing to plan Flynn's seduction. He was slender and he was very nearly slight in build, but there was a steely strength to him for all that. Like Cormac. Cormac had been slim and narrow-hipped, but no one had ever thought for a moment that Cormac could not best any man in any fight. For a moment, when Flynn had walked into the Sun Chamber tonight, Mab had thought it was Cormac who stood there. The Wolfking returned . . .

She frowned and pulled the bedcovers about her. Cormac was at Scáthach, Cormac deserved to be at Scáthach. He had been vanquished and banished, and there was an end to it.

Beltane would be the right time to seduce Flynn. Beltane was the night when passions ran high and blood ran hot, and people were aroused by the fires and the giant Wicker Man. The heat and the firelight and the screaming of the burning animals let loose frantic passions in people; Mab had seen it so many times. It was a remarkable sight to watch the wooden giant ablaze against the night sky, to hear the screams of the dying animals. It aroused some curious passions in the watchers. Mab had stood back sometimes and watched them all roused to frenzy, so that they fell on those who stood nearest to them, tearing off clothing, unable to wait for privacy, doing it there on the grass in full view of everyone.

Fornication and sodomy were commonplace at Beltane. Bestiality as well, for if the men could not get a woman, a sheep or a pig would do. When you were desperate, they said, you never noticed the difference. If it came to that, where was the difference anyway?

In the dark, Mab's lips curved in a smile.

Beltane.

CHAPTER TWELVE

JOHN GRADY AND Brian Muldooney, estimable and respectable gentlemen of stout hearts if scant imagination, were cold and tired and hungry. They were also befuddled by their surroundings, although Grady said that wasn't it simply that they'd taken a wrong turning in the dark, and Muldooney thought for sure they'd fallen down a well into an underground maze and come out the other side.

"But," said Grady pointing, "we are not so very far from Tugaim. See, there, surely is the Gealtacht. The House of Mutants."

Muldooney shivered and wished they had thought to bring warm coats with them, and was inclined to be disinterested in the Gealtacht.

"But it is a landmark," said Grady rather irritably. "We may see from it where we are, for there is certainly not another such building in Tugaim."

Muldooney said he'd never known the Gealtacht had a bridge crossing over to it.

"Nor did I. Or that it was so big." The two men, accustomed all their lives to the smallish, sparsish dwellings which had been built since Devastation, stared in awe at the crouching lowering shape ahead of them. At length, John Grady, who knew that all parties should have a leader, and who did not forget that he was an Elder of Tugaim, said, "Well it cannot be anywhere other than the Gealtacht. And I believe the landscape to be familiar now I look." Now that he did look, he could see the wasteful frivolous orchard that Michael O'Connor was so proud of, a shocking sight it was as well, and it stretching half

across the countryside, taking up land that would have been
better given over to hay and wheat and good sturdy root vegetables. John Grady had not realised quite how far the
O'Connor orchards did stretch in fact, and he was very surprised to see that they seemed to stretch a very long way indeed. Of course, everything looked different at night.

"Of course everything looks different at night," he said, and
Muldooney, who seldom, if ever, went out after dark, but liked
to tell what you could do of an afternoon, grunted. Exactly like
one of his pigs! thought Grady disgustedly, and stalked off
ahead, so that Muldooney thought wasn't Grady the
Landgrabber an intolerant one, and him with a walk like one
of his own chickens.

"Will we make for the Gealtacht?" he asked, puffing a bit as
he struggled to keep pace with Grady. "Will we be going right
up to the house?" he said, and quelled a shudder, for he knew
as well as anyone the grisly tales told about the Gealtacht, and
he thought that the poor creatures inside it were better off
alone. No sight for a pig farmer to witness. No sight for anyone to witness, really.

"I think we should," said Grady, who liked as little as
Muldooney the thought of the inhabitants of the House of Mutants, but who was not going to leave any corner unsearched
in his quest for his erring daughter.

"We'll go on up," he said, pleased to have a definite plan,
and Muldooney, relieved to be told what to do, wanted to
know had Grady ever been this way before. To himself he
thought the man had a very familiar way about the handling of
all this. If Muldooney had not known better than to even think
it, he might even have said that Grady knew the path to the
Gealtacht very well indeed.

John said, "I have been here, but not for a very long time."
And pulled down his brows because when you were an Elder,
you had sometimes to perform disagreeable tasks, and one of
those was the incarcerating of children inside the Gealtacht.
People were inclined to be ridiculously sentimental when it
came to children, and John had sometimes had to be quite
firm. You could not possibly have Mutants running wild all
over Tugaim (or anywhere else of course), mingling with normal folk and breeding. He was glad to think he had never been
guilty of neglect in his duties.

And so although he thought he knew the road to the Gealtacht quite well, he found, rather to his surprise, that it was not quite as he remembered it. Of course, it had been a good many years since he had been called in to arbitrate over the question of putting away a Mutant child. Truth to tell, he was feeling the smallest bit uneasy out here in the dark with orchards that had doubled, if not trebled in size overnight, and paths and roads that were familiar and yet not familiar at all. He had begun to have the feeling that something very peculiar indeed had happened—something to do with those lights earlier on, was it?—and he was very glad to think he was not possessed of a ridiculous imagination, or he might start thinking all kinds of things. They would go up to the Gealtacht, he was an Elder of Tugaim and it was not the first time he had been here. The chances were that they would find Joanna, because it was just the sort of place that Flynn O'Connor would bring her to. John had even heard them once discussing the Mutants as if the creatures were no different to everyone else. Absolutely ridiculous! Still, walking cautiously through the darkness now, John was aware of uneasiness, because the place seemed so very different by night, and he was glad all over again that he did not possess anything so frivolous as imagination.

Muldooney did not possess any imagination either; he was not thinking anything other than how grand it would be just to sit down and eat a hearty meal. A plateful of roast chicken would be very nice. He was very partial to roast chicken, the skin nicely crisped and served up with well-mashed potatoes and a few early peas. It seemed a long time since they'd eaten.

Neither of the men paid any attention to the small, curiously shaped shadow that detached itself from the trees and fell in behind them.

Portan, keeping far enough behind the two men to remain hidden, spared a thought for Flynn and Amairgen when they returned in the morning. Would she be able to get back to the dry snug little cave she had made for herself? She thought she would. It was unthinkable that she should not be there waiting for them. But it was important to keep track of these two, it was important to see where they went and what they did, and overhear what they said if that was possible. They were enemies, both of them, Portan knew that. She had smelled them for enemies back in Tugaim, and she smelled them for enemies now. They would harm Amairgen and her beloved Flynn, and if there was any way of preventing that, Portan would prevent it. She thought she would follow them for a while and see where they went, and then she would go back to the dry snug cave and wait for morning.

She pulled Flynn's cloak about her, and padded silently on down the dark tree-lined road.

Muldooney said, "There's something following us."

Something? John Grady frowned.

"I tell you I hear it!" And so would you, thought Muldooney, if you were not so puffed up with your own pomposity.

"I think you are imagining it, my friend."

Muldooney was rather affronted by such an accusation, for didn't a man leave all that kind of nonsense behind him when he farmed pigs. Pigs left no time for imagination, not that he'd had any to begin with he was glad to say. They told how the Letheans had had imagination, and look where the Letheans had ended. No thank you. Muldooney would stick to his pigs, and be thankful that he had not such a handicap as an imagination. Even so . . .

"There *is* something," he said, and slowed his pace a little nodding to the other man to do the same.

And then Grady heard it as well. Soft padding footsteps. Furtive footsteps. Someone—something?—coming up quietly behind them in the dark. He hesitated, seeing the looming bulk of the darkened fortress ahead, and he shivered a little, for even if you had no imagination, you could not but be aware of the tales that hung about that place. Supposing . . .

Common sense reasserted itself. He said, very softly, "Keep on walking. And then when we get round that curve in the road, hide in the trees. We can pounce on it then. But be prepared. For it may bite and it may be very strong. They are, I believe." Some long-buried streak of cruelty made him add, "If it is a Mutant it may have claws." And he felt a rather surprising spurt of satisfaction as Muldooney's face paled. "You know what they say about that place," said John Grady, nodding in the direction of the dark castle. "Ready?"

Muldooney was not really ready, and he was not really interested in capturing whatever it was that had been following them, Mutant or otherwise. He thought they could have just

gone quietly on and he thought they could very well have ig-
nored whatever had been following them. No sense in courting
trouble! But Grady the Landgrabber was out for a fight and
Muldooney was not the man to be found wanting. It never did
to run away from a fight, people talked about you if you
did. He could see it already, the way they'd talk. Brian Muldooney? they'd say with a smirk. Oh, he's no use in a fight.
Runs away. Yellow as a dead fish. Couldn't even keep the
Grady girl after he'd been conjoined to her. And the next thing
would be that people would be buying their pigs from Fingal
O'Dulihan. So Muldooney set his jaw pugnaciously and stumbled after Grady into the shelter of the forest fringe, and hoped
that the creature, whatever it was, did not bite very hard.

Portan did not bite; she did not even struggle very much.
She was totally unprepared for the attack, and in any case, she
had no defences against this kind of violence. Sexual abuse she
knew about and could endure; neglect and loneliness she also
understood. But the sudden swoop on a darkened road, the coat
over her head, the blow that sent her reeling and dizzy, were
so alien to her that she was easily overcome.

John Grady straightened up from tieing his coat about
Portan and found that the encounter had excited him. Remarkable. A Lethean emotion he dared say, and not something to be
admitted to. He looked at Portan, helpless at their feet, and felt
a warm arousal.

"A Mutant," he said, his voice carefully colourless. "An escaped Mutant. My friend, this is a very great piece of luck for
us."

"What do we do with it?" Muldooney had not caught the
rippling excitement that had coursed through John Grady's
body, but he had caught something, and he was rather disgusted. There flickered in his mind the suspicion that Grady
the Landgrabber had actually enjoyed the encounter, and he
was genuinely appalled. Muldooney could not kill one of his
own pigs, and had to send for Fingal O'Dulihan to do it for
him, and even then had to retire to the scullery while it was
being done. He sent Grady a sideways glance and saw that the
man was flushed and that there was a hard glitter in his eyes.
"What do we do now?" he said, and hoped the answer would
be one he could comfortably cope with.

"Why," said John Grady slowly and with a lick of pleasure, "why, we take it back to where it came from."

"Up there?"

"Of course," said Grady smiling. "They'll be so pleased with us to have it back, that they'll soon tell us if Joanna and the O'Connor boy are hiding up there."

FLYNN AND AMAIRGEN stepped out through the door of the bedchamber they had been allotted and moved cautiously and stealthily down the starlit halls.

Flynn said wonderingly, "Even like this, in the deepest hours of the night, it is not entirely dark." And then, with a sudden note of firmness, "Where shall we search first?"

"I think it will be a fruitless search," said Amairgen slowly. "I do not think Joanna is here."

Flynn did not think it either. He thought that if she had been he would surely have known. He would have sensed it. *You could not be near to me, my love, and I not know it.* But he thought that he would tear the walls down and take Tara apart section by section if there was any chance of it providing the tiniest clue to Joanna's whereabouts. He had not calculated how long she had been in the Deep Past now, and he thought that if he did he might very well begin to lose his hold on sanity. Joanna was somewhere in this beautiful, cruel, faintly sinister Ireland, and they must find her.

"We *must* search," he said and Amairgen nodded at once and, not for the first time, Flynn blessed all the gods he had ever heard of that Amairgen had accompanied him through the Time Curtain. Without Amairgen, this would have been intolerable.

Amairgen was uneasy. He had sensed that travellers were not welcome at Tara any longer, and he had found it disturbing that they had been admitted at all. The High King had not worried him, for he had seen at once that Eochaid Bres was a straw man, a puppet figurehead, and he thought the strings were probably pulled by Bricriu. He had enjoyed his discussion with Bolg and the Councillors, but he had felt very strongly the dislike and distrust of Bricriu as they sat at supper. That one is suspicious of us, thought Amairgen, and I believe he would not hesitate to harm us. As they walked slowly through the deserted corridors and peered into dimly lit chambers, he began to be aware of something dark and ancient and powerful uncoiling itself far below them.

Flynn said softly, "It is natural you should feel that," and Amairgen jumped, because he had forgotten the Samhailt's power, and he had forgotten Flynn's remarkable possession of it. A faint far-off warmth touched him; he thought that however often he had yearned to make this journey by himself, he had been fortunate indeed to finally make it with Flynn.

Aloud, he said, "You feel it also? The—the darkness?"

"Yes. I think it is that we are directly over the Sorcery Chambers now."

"You cannot know that."

"I do know it. The Sorcery Chambers go deep into the earth. They are a labyrinth, stretching for miles, each one deeper than the last. The deeper you go the stronger the magic." He looked at Amairgen very steadily, and something gleamed in his eyes, so that Amairgen knew that it could no longer be Flynn O'Connor who stood with him, but must be the mighty warrior, Finn of the *Fiana*, from the far-off days of the High Queen Dierdriu.

"This way," said Flynn, turning at an intersection without hesitating, and Amairgen, following, thought: yes, he does know. Because he has been here before. When he was Finn, and when he was Dierdriu's lover.

Flynn said very quietly, "I should like to see her again, Amairgen," and Amairgen jumped and felt the hairs rise on the back of his neck, because it was no longer Flynn's voice, it was a softer, deeper voice now, the cadences different, slower. Delight laced with fear touched him, and he thought he must be very careful not to say anything that would upset the fragile thread that bound Finn to Flynn. He must certainly not do anything to dispel the brief fusing of the two men. And then he thought: but how do I know that it is only a brief fusing, and the horror ran all over him.

Flynn's voice said with amusement, "It is entirely safe, my friend," and Amairgen looked up, startled, and thought: yes, but *which of them is speaking to me?* and remembered that in all of the old stories, Finn of the *Fiana* had been powerful and sometimes merciless, and also that he had sometimes resorted to sorcery to gain his own way.

But Flynn smiled, and it was the old, familiar smile, and

Amairgen relaxed. When Flynn said, "Through here now," Amairgen followed without the slightest pause.

Flynn had no consciousness of leading them. He was distantly aware of that other presence and of Finn's strength and his memories, but he was moving without thought and he was certainly acting without quite knowing why. When Amairgen asked, "Where are we going?," Flynn said at once, "To the Rock. To the very core of Tara," and led them onwards, down stairs and through dimly lit corridors, until the rich marble galleries and the crystal windows began to be left behind, and the floor beneath their feet became rough-hewn rock, and the stairs were hacked from granite.

Down, down to the Rock on which Tara was built . . . Yes, and back, back to the days when Dierdriu charmed the sorcerers into raising the Bright Palace from the Wilderness, and when her constant companion was the great head of the Fiana . . .

There was no sense of separateness between himself and Finn now; there was a single effortless fusing . . . I believe Amairgen is right, he thought; I believe that I truly was once Finn, and that he is now within me . . .

They were within the massive foundations now, and all about them were great rocks, rearing and towering above them, faintly luminous with their own light. "And it is the light that permeates the whole of Tara," said Flynn, and again Amairgen caught the unfamiliar cadences in his voice, and thought: yes, he speaks with sureness. *He was there when it happened.* And he shivered, for there was a sense of incalculable age about this place, and there was an oppressive weight of centuries all about them. Their footsteps echoed on the hard rock floor, and from somewhere close by came the faint steady dripping of water.

Flynn's eyes were shining with a hard clear light now, and Amairgen had to move faster to keep pace with him, for it would be beyond bearing to become lost down here. He was beginning to hope very strenuously that Flynn knew where they were going, but the thought had barely formed as they turned an intersection, and saw ahead a dark, still, underground lake.

Directly in front of them, catching the uncertain light, gleaming gently with the unearthly phosphorescence down here, was the gold-on-rock tracery that had been created by Tara's sorcerers in the first days.

Amairgen stood very still and felt his skin prickle with fear and delight, for he knew they were seeing something rare and precious and so entirely beautiful that it was almost painful. He said, very softly, "Dierdriu?" and Flynn, his eyes fixed on the carved rock, said at once, "Dierdriu? No. That is Joanna."

"No PORTRAIT EVER did Dierdriu justice," said Flynn, as they walked slowly from the underground cavern. "Artists came from every corner of the world, but not one of them ever managed to capture her. The strength and the fragility. The eyes that saw things others did not see. Mischief and authority and integrity all rolled up together. The delight she took in everything and anything. Nothing was ever too trivial for her, and nothing was too great for her to shoulder either. When she lived, Ireland was great, and when she died, a part of Ireland died with her. Forgive me, but I cannot look on that carving without remembering it all."

Amairgen, choosing his every word now, terrified lest he disturb the delicate balance that existed between Flynn and the long-ago Finn, said, "The etching we saw? The gold carving on the rock—"

"That is Dierdriu," said Flynn. "It was created by her own sorcerers who loved her and who served her and who would have died for her. But also it is Joanna, Amairgen. When you meet her, you will understand."

For Joanna is the High Queen returned . . .

The thought formed in both men's minds, and Flynn spoke, "It is an ancient belief."

"That Dierdriu will return?"

"Oh yes. Dierdriu never really died," and for a moment, an expression of infinite happiness passed over his face. "Dierdriu never died," said Flynn again, and this time there was complete conviction in his tone. "That was the legend and that is the belief."

"You are sure of it?"

"I remember it," said Flynn. "And I believe it is why Joanna has been brought back to her people, Amairgen. The High Queen has awakened. Until I stood here again," said Flynn, "until I remembered, properly remembered, I did not realise it.

But it is what has happened. It was no accident that Joanna came through the Time Curtain. She was taken. Something was waiting for her, and that something has her now." He frowned. "It was always prophesied," said Flynn, "that in times of great trouble, Dierdriu would return." He looked at Amairgen. "I remember it all so well," said Flynn, and again there was the other presence looking out of his eyes. "Dierdriu has awakened in Joanna, and so Joanna has been brought back."

Amairgen said, "But Dierdriu would not harm Joanna?"

"Oh no," said Flynn, but there was suddenly a note of doubt in his voice.

"And if someone is using Joanna, then for the moment she must be safe." Amairgen touched Flynn's arm. "Flynn, you must believe that."

"Yes," said Flynn. "Yes, for otherwise, it will be unbearable." He looked at Amairgen. "If Joanna is lost to me, I shall stay here. I shall never go back to Tugaim."

They looked at one another. Amairgen said slowly, "But you promised."

"I don't care. If Joanna is dead, then my place is here."

"And mine also," said Amairgen, and felt for the first time, the strong pull of this strange place that ought to have been unfamiliar, and yet was not unfamiliar in the least. He thought he, also, had race-memory, and he thought he, also, was beginning to recognise things in this ancient world. Had he, as well as Flynn, once lived here?

Of course you did, Human Traveller . . . of course you did . . .

It came as silvery as the night and as insubstantial as the faint light from the rocks that surrounded them. But both men heard it, and both of them stopped at once. Flynn's hand came out warningly. *Don't move. Keep very still. And as you value your soul and your sanity and your life, don't look.*

From the corners of his eyes, Amairgen saw Flynn lower his head so that he was staring at the floor. Flynn said very softly, "Close your mind to them. And walk very slowly with me towards the door."

Do not leave us, Human Travellers. Stay with us, for we are the most desirable of all companions, and we can give you your hearts' desires . . .

Hearts' desires . . . Flynn's mind leapt, and he thought:

Joanna! And heard with mingled horror and delight the strange cold music he had heard on Tara's Hill with his father. He thought: the *sidh*! And even while his heart rejoiced in the beauty of the music, his mind was sending out warnings. Do not look! Do not listen! For they are the coldest, most inhuman creatures in the world!

But we are so beautiful, Flynn ... To see us would melt your soul and burn out your eyes, but you would count your soul's loss as a small price, and you would never want to use your eyes to look on anything ever again ...

Don't listen! cried Flynn's mind. To look on the *sidh* is madness and death.

At his side, Amairgen said softly, "But it would be almost worth it, just once, just to see—"

Flynn felt as if an icy dash of water had been thrown into his face. He thought: Amairgen is falling into their enchantment! And so strong, so frantic was the thought, so urgent the wish to protect Amairgen, that he almost fancied the thought took physical shape as it formed.

Amairgen said rather unsteadily, "We should not linger," and Flynn heard the cry that Amairgen's mind sent out. Help me! Pull me to safety for I am drowning in their music and I cannot hold out against them much longer. He grasped Amairgen's hand and began to edge them both nearer to the half-open door.

Creep away, Human Travellers, but we will follow you, we will find you ... We will feed on your bodies and on your souls, and you will never again wish to walk in the world of men ...

Flynn said, "This door leads down to the Sun Chamber."

Amairgen, struggling to hold on to something real and ordinary and tangible said, "You are sure?"

"I know it." Again the certainty, the familiarity with the unfamiliar. I know it because I have lived here and I have died here, and I have walked these halls many times.

But you know it as well, Human Traveller ... you are Amairgen the Great Voyager, the one the Cruithin once called the Seafarer, and you once knew Tara so well ... Come to us now, Seafarer, for we have sung to you on countless nights as you journeyed across the dark seas of the world ... you have heard our music and you have glimpsed our reflections in the oceans' mirror, and you have longed to follow us ...

Amairgen said in a low angry voice, "No. I won't. You must let me go—"

There was a ripple of amusement and both men saw, on the outer rim of their vision, the blur of blue and green.

The *sidh* were forming . . .

Follow us, Seafarer, follow us, for we are more beautiful than any human woman could ever be, and we are more loving and more passionate and once inside our caves you will cease to long for the world of Men, and once you have spilled your seed into us you will cease to desire human women . . .

Flynn said loudly, "We are not listening," but he did not move. At his side, Amairgen thought: to succumb to the *sidh* would be the greatest experience a man could ever have.

Yes, yes, Seafarer, the greatest, the most exquisite pleasure in the Seven Worlds of Men . . . once you have seen us and tasted us . . . once you have lain with us in the caves beneath the sea and flown with us in the cities beyond the sky, the world of Men will be forever colourless and drab . . .

The blue and green smoke was all about them, and Flynn kept his eyes resolutely closed. He could feel the cold silky arms all about him, and he could feel his own body responding, despite all his resolve. Even so, he knew it was Amairgen they wanted, and he thought that the pull on Amairgen must be very great indeed. Amairgen could surely not resist. The *sidh* were clustering about them now, their arms felt like thin spring water, straight from a mountain glade, silky and sinless, and so soft it would be the most exquisite pleasure to surrender to them . . .

Come with us to the caves beneath the seas and the cities beyond the skies . . . dance with us across the clouds and drown with us in the waterlight . . . swim with us in the music, for music is a living breathing thing in our world . . . we are the creatures of Pan and it is our task to pour the music into the streams and the rivers of the world, and to lure the dying souls of Men to their Heaven, and to make easy the passing of the Dead . . .

Flynn's eyes were tightly shut, but the smoky blue and green shapes still impinged on his vision. He thought he would have given all he possessed to know that Amairgen was not staring into the light, but he sensed that Amairgen was lost to him. He knew the exact moment when the *sidh* had withdrawn their attention from him and directed their persuasion at Amairgen alone.

Amairgen was indeed lost. The warm languorous scent of the *sidh* was all about him, and his heartbeat had slowed. He thought he was dying, and he thought that perhaps he was already dead.

Not dead, Human Traveller, only at the beginning . . .

He felt the cold silky kiss of the *sidh* and he felt his body so ablaze with longing, and stiff and charged with desire and he thought he knew himself to be lost for all time. His mind was spinning and the queer tuneless music was wrapping itself about him. The longing to look directly at these beautiful inhuman beings was nearly unbearable.

Just for a second . . . if I could just see them for a second . . . if I could just be with them for an hour . . .

For all of your life, Seafarer . . . for once you have given yourself to us, you will be ours for all time . . . let us lead you to our world, let us show you the pleasures of that world, and nothing will matter to you ever again . . .

Amairgen was on fire, he was burning with longing and he began to move into the very centre of the blue and green mists. At his side, Flynn felt icy fear clutch his vitals and he reached out his hand.

"Amairgen?" As he spoke, he heard Amairgen give a low moan, and he felt the last triumphant notes of the *sidh*'s music, and he felt the *sidh*'s withdrawal.

He opened his eyes. The room was empty. The *sidh* had vanished, and Amairgen had vanished with them.

AMAIRGEN HAD NOT been aware of the moment when he passed through the finite barriers that bounded Tara and entered into the infinite world of the *sidh*. He had fought the music and he had fought the sensuous pull of the singing and the sweet strong allure of the blue and green mists, but he had known that the moment when he would surrender was fast approaching. He knew he would go into the bewitchment, and he knew he would go willingly—to save Flynn? said a tiny cynical part of his mind. But he knew that it was not to save Flynn, even though Flynn would escape unscathed. If he surrendered now, it would be because he wanted to, because his body was lulled and fired, and aroused beyond all endurance.

There was a low blurred laugh at his side, and then the *sidh* were pulling him through the boundaries, and all he could see were star-spattered skies—hundreds of them, one for every world that ever lived and ever died, he thought—and there was a whirling impression of silver and of blue and green—the Gates of Paradise, studded with jasper and chalcedony and pearl—where had he read or remembered that? and for a moment he thought the Time Curtain glittered ahead of them, so that he thought: home! I am going home! And felt a wholly unexpected surge of pleasure.

And then lightning cracked and hurt his eyes, and the darkness parted and he was lying on a couch so velvet soft that it was like spring water on his skin, and there was soft green light rippling over the walls, and the floors, and there was such triumph in the *sidh*'s voices now that a tiny pulse of fear sprang up. I am in their world and I am at their mercy, and it is said that no man looks upon the *sidh* and lives, that no man experiences their embraces and keeps his sanity.

But it will be worth the loss of your sanity, Amairgen, and it will be worth the loss of your life ... Let us take your body and let us take your mind, and let us teach you to forget the world and forswear the love of humans for ever ...

Amairgen was beyond all control; his desires had been stirred and his body had been caressed. He lay back and looked at the *sidh* and saw them in their terrible beauty, and his eyes burned at the sight.

"Love me," he said in a whisper, and held out his arms. *"Love me."*

Triumphant blue and green music filled the caves as the *sidh* swarmed over him.

IN THE DEEPEST level of the Sorcery Chambers, Bricriu raised his head and listened. After a moment he smiled. The *sidh* had not let him down. They had taken the one called Amairgen, and Bricriu knew, as all knew, that no man may dwell in the distant land of the *sidh* and keep his soul or his sanity. Amairgen might return, for the *sidh* would cast him out when they had no further use for him, but he would no longer be a threat to Tara or to Bricriu's plans.

That only left Flynn to deal with.

Flynn would die on the Beltane Fire.

CHAPTER THIRTEEN

IF AMAIRGEN HAD been with him, Flynn could have set aside the aching worry for Joanna, and enjoyed, for a little time, the preparations for Beltane. He would have been interested in the traditions and the rituals; in the careful selection of rowan and agaric and woodbine for the fire; in the rule that every fire in the land must be extinguished on the eve of the ceremony.

"For," explained Bolg, who was rather sorry for the young companion of the captured Amairgen, "the only fire that can burn on Beltane is the Sacred Fire. From midnight all other flames will be quenched."

But Flynn was encased in misery and numb with grief, and more alone than he had ever been in his life. He would have liked to be part of it, for the excitement running through the palace was so intense as to be almost tangible.

The people of the Court were friendly and sympathetic; they made him one of them, and included him in their plans for Beltane. Sean the Storyteller kept him a place at his side at mealtimes.

"It's a terrible thing to lose a friend to the *sidh*," he said to Flynn. "Terrible. But there was nothing you could have done to save him. The *sidh* take what they want. Not that that'll make you feel better, I know. Dear me, it'll be a grievous loss, I daresay."

Flynn liked Sean, and tried to question him about other travellers who came to Tara. Did women ever come? And what happened to them? But Sean was vague. It had been different in Cormac's time, he said. Everyone was made welcome then. But Eochaid Bres and Bricriu the Fox did not care for stran-

gers at Court. It was all very depressing. And what about a
flagon of mead while they sat talking?

Flynn drank the mead and talked to the others, but no one
seemed to know anything about lone travellers, and when
Flynn pressed them for the story of Dierdriu, and the legend
that she would one day return, they avoided his eyes and
glanced uneasily to where Bricriu sat at the head of the table.
Better not to say too much about the old ways, they said.
Safer.

"Bricriu doesn't care to hear such talk," said Sean and
reached for the mead again. "I make it a rule to keep such
things out of anything I write," he added. "You don't have to
go looking for trouble."

Flynn found the storyteller's friendship comforting, but the
very next night, Sean had entertained the assembled company
with a newly written lament, all about a young man who had
strayed into the forbidden territories of the *sidh* and been carried off by them, leaving his friends and his loved ones weeping on the shores of the world. It was a sad moving tale but
it was very effective, and Sean told it well, half chanting, half
singing. At the end of each stanza was a general lament, in
which everyone joined.

> "When the Golden Bough bends
> You will hear his lament;
> Cold and lonely and bereft of content.
> He has taken his soul to the Lands of the Sea
> And his life is in pawn to the powers of the *sidh*.

> And his love weeps anon
> And his soul is in bond;
> From the shores of the world he is vanished and gone.
> For they hunted him down through the nights of the World
> And he'll never return to the daylight of Men."

Flynn thought Sean was very talented, but he experienced an
angry grief that Sean, whom he had thought a friend, should
have seized so carelessly and so greedily on Amairgen's trag-
edy, and turned it into an hour's pleasure for the Court. He
looked at the listening faces, and knew a sudden desire for
Tugaim and Joanna. He thought: what am I doing here with

these cruel, charming, entirely heartless people? I have lost
Amairgen, and I am no nearer to finding Joanna.

And there was something else, something so potentially sinister that he had not dared examine it in any further detail.

He had gone, on the morning following Amairgen's capture,
to the West Gate, knowing that Portan would be eagerly waiting for him, finding a great comfort in the knowledge. I have
lost Amairgen—perhaps for good—but at least there is Portan,
dear loyal Portan. At least there is another with me in this
world that I can trust. I am not quite alone, thought Flynn,
walking purposefully through the sunlit halls, thinking how different they looked last night.

He had not thought very much about actually getting out of
Tara; he had supposed vaguely that there would be guards of
some kind who would unlock the gates and let him through.

He had certainly not expected that he would be barred from
leaving.

"Only until Beltane," explained the sentry of the guard, who
felt rather sorry for Flynn, but whose present affluence was all
due to Bricriu. "The King doesn't like anyone to leave until after the ceremonies."

"But I'm not involved in the ceremonies," said Flynn, and
the sentry, who knew Bricriu's little ways, thought: oho, and
that's what you think, poor doomed-to-die spy! Aloud, he said
soothingly, "Very likely you're not, but there's a terrible old
danger about on Beltane."

Flynn said, "But Beltane isn't until tomorrow."

"Not it is, nor it is," said the sentry, who knew what the Fox
wanted of him. He leaned forward. "Surely you know," he
said, "that the *Eve* of Beltane is one of the four nights when
the world of men is considered to be loaned to the Dark Powers." He propped himself up against his box and elaborated.
"In safe keeping for most of the year we are," said the sentry,
"but there's the four nights when the light dims a little, and the
Dark Ones find their way through the chinks in the world's armour."

Chinks? Armour?

"There's some say that it's the sorcerers' task to throw an
armour about the world," said the sentry. "So it is, of course.
But no armour's entirely impenetrable, only the Girdle of
Gold, and, of course, *that* got lost centuries ago. We all know

where it went," said the sentry, "and we all know that we'll never get it back, more's the pity. But there, sorcerers are venal same as the rest of us. They're open to all kinds of bribery, and everyone knows that the Girdle of Gold is the most powerful defence anyone can have. It *ought* to be around Tara—so it was once—well, it ought to be around the world," said the sentry. "But we all know it's not. And so the armour we've got isn't as strong as it might be. Anything can slip through. And on the four *Dark* nights, the Evil Ones find it very easy to do just that." He smiled pityingly at Flynn. "The Eve of Beltane is very vulnerable. His Majesty won't hear of anyone setting foot outside the Palace," said the sentry, who knew very well that His Majesty would not have given a tinker's toss if his entire Court had upped and walked through the West Gate that very minute. "Very particular he is," said the sentry. "Why you might be seized by a demon the minute you went through that door, and a fine thing that would be!"

"Demons?" said Flynn, child of a world where the word had long since ceased to hold any meaning.

"Dancing on the Plain of the Fál," said the sentry without so much as the flicker of an eyelid. "Spreading their net to catch souls for their master."

"Their master?"

"The Erl-King," said the sentry, and quite suddenly felt afraid, because it was one thing to feed a doomed-to-die spy with a nice little tale that would keep him safely under lock and key for the Fox; it was another thing altogether to speak aloud the name of the ancient evil enemy of them all. Still, it had done the trick; the poor young man looked quite pale. Well, the sentry probably looked fairly pale himself, because it was a nasty old feeling it gave a man to even think about the Erl-King. The sentry would rather have Bricriu as master any day, even if he did have a terrible old habit of sending people to the Miller's cages for the smallest of misdemeanours, and summoning up the *sidh* to snatch a man's virility right from between his legs! But: better the Miller or the *sidh* any day than the Erl-King! thought the sentry, and shuddered.

Flynn had not been particularly frightened by the mention of demons—superstitious nonsense, he thought it—but he had listened politely enough.

And then the sentry had spoken that name—the Erl-King—

and such a cold fear had sliced through Flynn that for a moment he had been unable to speak. He felt rather sick and rather weak; he experienced the sudden nauseating pain of wrenching an ankle whilst running, or the wincing of a nerve when a fingernail is scratched slowly across a slate surface.

When the sentry said solicitously, "The King doesn't like any of us to go wandering abroad today," Flynn nodded. And when the man said with genuine apology: "And I daren't open the Gate for you," Flynn said, "No, of course not. It doesn't matter in the very least," and turned away.

Portan would surely wait, he thought, after all, it would only be for another day. This time tomorrow he would walk out freely. Surely she would wait another day, thought Flynn, but his mind was still feeling rather sick at hearing the Erl-King's name, and he was not reasoning as clearly as he might have done. He felt a fresh wave of desolation at Amairgen's loss, for Amairgen would have given him the courage and the strength to see what ought to be done next.

He managed to persuade himself that it was only what Amairgen had called race-memory. I suppose I once faced the Erl-King in battle, he thought. And with the thought came a glimpse of a terrible menace: a dark citadel in a walled city; a great stone banqueting hall and a stone table. Seated in the stone hall was a creature so uncanny, so soulless that it could scarcely be borne. The Erl-King! Again he felt the cold sickness.

Well, he would wait until tomorrow—Beltane—and he would help with their feastings and their revelries, because it would be something to do, but at the height of it all he would simply walk away.

He became one of them, joining in the party at the central open courtyard, helping to gather the wood for the Sacred Fire, even finding a rather pleasant camaraderie there. When Sean the Storyteller said, "We'll have to carry this up to the Plain tomorrow," Flynn at once volunteered to help, thinking that once outside he might seize his chance to get away.

"I'll help," he said eagerly, and Sean replied doubtfully, "Well, it'll be heavy, all this wood. Still, there'll be several of us."

"I'll carry my share," said Flynn. And thought that he could sling it across his shoulders. It would be easier.

He did not know that in so doing he was setting the most pitiable, most exquisite of all execution traditions. He would walk to the place of his execution, and he would be carrying across his back the instrument of his own terrible death.

PORTAN WAS VERY frightened indeed. When the thin-lipped man and the fat, red-faced one had pounced on her, she had been utterly helpless. They had overcome her easily and swiftly, and the thin-lipped one had tied her up quite tightly, so that it was difficult to walk.

She had recognised John Grady almost at once, and there had been a terrible coldness about the recognition. As she half walked and was half dragged along at his side through the dark forest surrounding Tara, she felt herself back in those far-off years when the Elders had searched her family's house, and dragged her out from the tiny cramped cupboard so cunningly built for just that eventuality.

It had been John Grady, the youngest and the most diligent of the Elders, who had found her. Portan could still remember how it had felt to be pulled bodily from the dark suffocating place that she had always believed would represent safety for her. She could remember the expression on John Grady's face when he held her out before the others and the gloating note in his voice when he said, "A Mutant! An accursed deformity! Throw it into the Gealtacht!" And so her father had gone, by night, and left her crying on the threshold of that terrible place. She had forgiven her father, because she had understood, but she had never forgiven John Grady.

She thought that he had enjoyed wielding his power then, and she thought he was enjoying doing so now. He had fashioned a rope from his belt, had tied it about her neck, and there had been the gloating note in his voice that she had never forgotten.

"You won't escape me," he had said. "Do not think you will."

The other one—Muldooney was it?—had stammered and mumbled; he had said, "Steady on now, Grady," and John Grady had said at once, "My dear Muldooney, you must not think I am using violence. Violence is a word which has no place in my vocabulary. I am simply being firm. And I daresay the creature is accustomed to being restrained." He looked down at Portan, who was still crouched on the ground, and a smile touched his lips, and Portan knew, without shadow of a doubt, that he was enjoying his power and his superior strength.

She did not speak. She thought that Grady would not remember her, because he would certainly have dealt with other Mutants since. To him, they would all appear much the same. This was a dreadful thought but it was one that Portan was familiar with. John Grady would not remember the shivering crying creature he had sentenced to incarceration all those years ago.

She had not spoken yet, other than to cry out in a startled voice, and now, her mind working furiously, she thought that if she stayed absolutely quiet, there would be a better chance of escape. If both these men believed her to be witless, they might relax their guard.

Grady said, "You see? It is quite accustomed to being tied." And smiled with a dreadful gentleness again.

Portan was by now very frightened. She thought she was not showing it, and she thought she would be able to continue not to show it. It was very important to fool these two men, and it was particularly important to fool John Grady. Grady was searching for Joanna, Flynn's Joanna, and therefore he would inevitably be searching for Flynn as well. And Portan would have died before she would have divulged the whereabouts of either Flynn or Amairgen to these two men. Padding along quietly at Grady's side, her mind was working furiously, trying to see a way of escape, trying, as well, to see how she might outwit these two and make her way back to where Flynn and Amairgen would be waiting for her. And even like this, even in the dark forest, dragged along by John Grady, the thought of Flynn and Amairgen brought its own comfort and its own strength. They would expect her to be brave and to use her wits and so she would be. She thought she would probably have died for both of them.

When Flynn had smiled at her in the Gealtacht and told her that she had a gentle face, she had known a rush of immense love for him; when Amairgen had taken her hand in the Dutch barn and promised that he would never allow her to be sent back to the Gealtacht, she had known herself bound to both of them. For ever? Yes, of course. Probably she would never be able to do anything to repay either of them for what they had done for her, but she would watch her every chance. To begin

with, she would not let these two men know that she could have
told them where Flynn and Amairgen were had they asked.

And so she padded quietly along, and she was humble and
obedient, and even a little cowed. In fact, she did not need to
pretend about this, for the sight of John Grady, the man who
had caused her to be flung into the House of Mutants, had
struck such fear in her, that she flinched from him.

John Grady smiled and nodded to himself, and thought that
after all it was easy to quench these creatures. You had only to
be firm, to show a little strength. Perhaps the Letheans had
been in the right of it after all. All men equal, but some more
equal than others . . .

Brian Muldooney would not have thought it of Grady the
Landgrabber. No sensitive he, but he had now realised that the
other was enjoying the subduing of the poor deformed soul
they'd found wandering in the forest. Grady was finding a
queer dark pleasure in cowing the creature. Muldooney hoped
that once they reached the Gealtacht the poor thing could be
handed over, and Grady would revert to normality. To be sure,
it was a terrible idea for them to be going up to the Gealtacht
in the first place; Muldooney had never thought to see such an
event in his life. It was to be hoped, as well, that the journey
would not last very much longer, because hadn't they all been
tramping about in this forest for what seemed like hours, and
didn't the grim dark building seem as far away as ever?
Muldooney began to doubt that it was the Gealtacht at all, after
a while. And now and then there was a curious sound all about
them; a kind of mocking laughter, a soft, nearly-out-of-hearing
music. Muldooney did not hold with music—nasty frivolous
time-wasting stuff—but he found himself pausing to listen,
straining to catch the voices inside the music.

*You will never reach Scáthach, Men of the Desolate
Land* . . .

Be blowed to that! thought Muldooney, who was cold and
tired, and who had had quite enough of wandering about in
dark forests. Be blowed to that!

You will see, said the silvery music. *You will see* . . .

THE FEAST OF Beltane Eve was nearly at an end. The Court was
replete, satisfied. In some cases, it was satiated, and in some
cases, it was surfeited.

Sean the Storyteller sighed and leaned back and hoped in the name of all the gods together that no one would call for entertainment. To be sure, couldn't a man have a bit of a rest now and again. He belched delicately, and reached for the wine.

Eochaid Bres had eaten nearly as much as he could, which was not quite as much as he would have liked, but was certainly more than anyone else had eaten. He drank his wine and eyed his Court, and wished that he could have given them some kind of brilliant witty speech, told them to raise their glasses to something or other—oh yes, of course, to Beltane on the morrow—and that they would all have cheered him. But—

"A speech, Your Majesty?" Bricriu had said, lifting his brows. "Dear me, how enterprising of you. Well, Sire, I can certainly get one of the lesser *ollam* to pen something; Sean has been at the wine tonight, although of course if you have a preference for his work . . . ?"

Eochaid Bres had grunted and waved Bricriu into dismissal, because he had not wanted any of the *ollam* to write his speech for him, and he had certainly not wanted Sean to do so. Not that Sean would be very much affected by the wine, of course. He never was. Only look at the really shocking exhibition he made of himself on High Feast Days when the young girls were brought up to Tara to pleasure the visiting chieftains! Eochaid wondered that Sean was not more careful of his dignity and he the chief *ollam*, and no chicken either! Sean would in fact have written a very good speech for Eochaid to deliver; the only thing wrong with it would have been that every person present would have known it was Sean's. Eochaid glowered into his stewed hare, and said that Bricriu need not bother, it had only been a passing idea.

Bricriu had enjoyed the feast. A little indigestion afterwards perhaps, but nothing he could not cope with. He thought he might very well send for one of the ladies of the Court tonight; there was no denying that a bit of lovemaking put a grand edge on a man's appetite, and he was looking forward to ridding the Court of Flynn next day.

The Druids had been calmly pleased at his offer; human sacrifice, they had said seriously, could not be matched and Ireland would have a richer year for it. And of course the poor young man would acquire instant merit with Dagda and the other gods, and be taken at once to the place beneath the Roof of the Ocean, which was all any of them ever aspired to anyway. They had gone away, mentally rubbing their hands, yet physically unmoved.

Bricriu thought he was managing things rather well. Yes, he would certainly send for one of the ladies tonight. Which one should it be? He stretched back in his chair and curled the fingers of one hand about the stem of his wine glass, studying the females.

The rest of the Court, in their varying ways, were relaxing, fighting off a slight sleepiness—weighing up the merits of taking a couple of partners to bed against the benefits of an uninterrupted night's sleep. The morrow would bring Beltane, the Sacred Fire and the Wicker Man of the Druids. Beltane Night was always a lively one, and it would not do to be found wanting. The older gentlemen thought that a quiet night's repose would the better armour them for the exigencies of Beltane, while the younger ones thought after all didn't you need to keep your muscles in good working order? It didn't do to let a muscle—any muscle—fall into disuse. Everyone knew the terrible stories of people who'd not exercised themselves in anyone's bed for positively weeks, and then been quite incapable on Beltane Night! It was not exactly obligatory, but it was expected. A matter of honour, you might say.

It was certainly a matter of honour for the Queen to take a lover on Beltane, of course, and speculation as to the identity of this year's victim ran high. Although, as Sean pointed out, to use the term "victim" was to be rather unkind.

"Sacrifice?" said someone, not altogether jokingly, and Sean scowled and took himself to a corner of the room, there to plot an entirely new kind of entertainment, in which all of the insolent young men of the Court received their just deserts.

At one end of the great banqueting table, Conaire of the Eagles was surreptitiously taking bets as to who was going to be sharing Mab's bed that night; watched—beknownst to him—by Bricriu, who knew very well that Conaire's true allegiance lay with Cormac, and knew, as well, that Conaire was astute enough to hide this. Bricriu was not so occupied with the thought of a bed partner for his own bed that he could not be fully alert to a spot of intrigue. He would not have objected to swapping the bedding for the intrigue if he had to. He would, in fact, prefer the intrigue, because the bed thing, though pleasant enough, aggravated his indigestion.

Conaire's party was generating a good deal of noise over some of the bets that were being placed. Several people had made quite sensible, quite possible nominations for Mab's choice, but in the main the young men, by now flown with wine and with the anticipation of tomorrow's feastings, were egging each other on, each bet more outrageous than the last.

Finally, one of them announced that it was an impossible task Conaire had set them, for didn't they all know that the only qualification needed to get into the Queen's bed was the ability to keep it up all night, and at that rate, surely any one of them here present might be a candidate.

There was a sudden silence.

Well, mightn't they? demanded the speaker, suddenly horribly conscious that he had gone out on a limb.

Well as to that, said the young men, of course anyone could keep it up all night, but there were those among them who happened to know, rather particularly, that Mab actually required a few other qualities in her lovers.

Really? said several people, leaning forward and preparing to do battle. What sort of qualities?

Wit. Physical beauty, of course.

Oh, of course, said a number of scoffing voices.

Well, said the first speaker, determined now to brazen it out, the Queen would not want a positive monster on her pillow, that might be quite safely assumed. To which several dissidents said: rubbish! the Queen would sleep with a gargoyle if she wanted to. As long as he could keep it up all night, of course.

Conaire, who had a good deal in common with the exiled Cormac (and was, in fact, some kind of fifth cousin once removed) now entered into the spirit of the thing, and, eyes alight, said with mischief that sure now anyone who had access to the Sorcery Chambers knew how to keep it up all night—how else did old Bolg and the Fox manage? and a shout of laughter went up, causing several of the older courtiers to turn round in their chairs and survey Conaire's party with a blend of annoyance and envy.

"The Queen's eye is on our newcomer," said Conaire with finality, and threw his coins on to the table. "You'll see. He's the type Mab has always had a yen for. Don't any of you see

a resemblance?" Conaire was suddenly serious, and the young
men, who did see a resemblance, who had seen it the minute
Flynn walked in, lowered their eyes and looked furtively to
where Eochaid Bres sat, and hoped he was not listening.

But when Mab stood up and held out an imperious hand to
Flynn, they grinned and nudged one another, and pushed the
pile of coins to Conaire's place.

"Wit," said Conaire solemnly. "And physical beauty. Didn't
I tell you?"

"I hope he can keep it up all night," was the rejoinder.

MAB'S BEDCHAMBER WAS like the centre of a rose, soft pink and
gold and sweetly perfumed, and Flynn, unused to such splendour, and bewitched by Tara anyway, paused on the threshold
and drew in his breath.

Mab, watching, said softly, "Well, Flynn?"

"It is quite the most beautiful room I have ever seen," said
Flynn, and turning to her, took her hands, "Forgive me, but I
am unused—in my home we have not these splendours." And
he smiled into her eyes, so that Mab remembered a long-ago
night when a young man of Flynn's age had smiled in just that
way. And then had hurt her more than any man, and betrayed
her and violated everything she believed in. Anger rose in her,
but with it a long-buried desire. He is so like Cormac . . .

"Come to bed," she said.

IN FLYNN'S WORLD, the world that followed Devastation, the
men and women who had survived had made a set of rules and
a set of morals that was as different as it was possible to be
from the lusty greedy sleep-anywhere ways of the Letheans.
They could not perhaps be blamed for it; they had seen their
world burn almost to nothing, and stunned and homeless, they
had had to set about the rebuilding of a civilization whose val-
ues had succeeded in destroying it.

There should be no more immorality, said those dauntless
men and women who crawled up out of the ruins; there should
be no more preoccupation with the gratifying of the senses and
there certainly should be no bedding together without some
kind of indissoluble commitment. They searched their memories, and came up with the old Bible word "fornication." There
should be no fornication, said the survivors grimly, and, to give

them credit, there was not. Bedding together was a necessary duty, it was not something to be deliberately sought. It was certainly not something to be enjoyed, particularly by ladies, who would find it repulsive. It was something that had to be done, because this sparse new world must have all the brave new inhabitants it could get, and even the Letheans had not found a way of producing children by any other method. But just as the long-dead Victorian age had had its nonconformists, so did this new post-Devastation world.

Flynn was a nonconformist. He knew the rules, and on the surface he kept them. But in the world of post-Devastation, as in the world of the Victorians, it was not difficult to find out places where pleasure might be taken. And Flynn, in company with other kindred spirits, had not infrequently visited the houses once called brothels or seraglios. He had enjoyed his share of drinking in the wine shops, and then of indulging other senses with the ladies who ran the wine shops, and who were not averse to pleasuring blue-eyed, black-haired young gentlemen who had the charm of the devil . . .

Even faced with a lady who had slept with more lovers than she could remember, Flynn grinned and knew himself perfectly capable of meeting her demands.

And if, at some deeply buried and most secret part of his mind, it occurred to him that in this way he might find out more about Joanna, he managed to keep that thought hidden, and he managed, as well, to quench the memory of Joanna lying alongside him on that last night in Tugaim . . . He did not precisely think: by doing this, I may learn more about this place and these people, but it occurred to him that it was a way of becoming closer to Tara's inhabitants. Much closer.

And so he folded away the sweet precious thoughts of Joanna, whom nothing and no one could ever replace for him, and smiled at Mab, and bent forward to trace the delicate line of her jaw, and saw that she was smiling back at him. He moved his hand lower and slid the silk gown from her shoulders.

When Mab said softly, "Come to bed, Flynn," Flynn said at once, "With every pleasure in the world."

And went.

* * *

CONAIRE AND HIS coterie would have given a good deal to know how the newcomer fared in the Queen's bed. "Even though," said Conaire firmly, "we are none of us given to prurience, I trust." He looked rather hard at Sean the Storyteller when he said this, and Sean instantly said he was not, to be sure he was not, and retired to chew over the idea of a poem based on a rejected suitor spying through the keyhole of his lady's bedchamber as she disported with her new lover.

But Conaire and the young men would not have been normal if they had not briefly wondered how matters went between Mab and Flynn. They were certainly sufficiently human to remember the suggestion made earlier, that the only qualification needed to enter Mab's bed was the ability to keep it up all night.

In that, at least, Flynn's abilities would not have disappointed them.

FLYNN AND MAB breakfasted together in her bedchamber, with the morning sun streaming in to turn the honey transparent and make the warm, fresh bread glisten.

Flynn looked at his companion as she sat carelessly dressed, her hair tousled, her hands cupped about the huge breakfast bowl of mead, as she drank from it hungrily. He recalled the uses those hands had been put to during the night, and involuntarily grinned.

Without looking up, Mab said, "You did not object to any one of them," and Flynn jumped, and thought it was rather disconcerting to have all your thoughts read.

"Not all," said Mab and reached for the honey.

"You can read some but not others?" This was interesting, because Flynn had never entirely understood about the Samhailt. He had never understood how it was that some thoughts could be heard or sensed or felt, and some could not.

Mab said, "Those of us who possess the Samhailt also possess the Ancient Code of Honour which charges us to use it without discourtesy." She looked at him very straightly. "I *could* hear your innermost thoughts if I wished it, but it is forbidden for me to do that."

Flynn said cautiously, "But is it not sometimes tempting—" and at once Mab silenced him with a shake of her head.

"No, for that would be to entirely dishonour the Ancient

Code." She regarded him, her head slightly on one side. "No one who has been given the Samhailt would be guilty of misusing it, Flynn."

"Forgive me, but—you cannot be sure of that—"

"I am sure," said Mab. "The Samhailt is *never* bestowed on one who would treat it so wantonly." The smile deepened and became mischievous. "I have been called a wanton sometimes," said Mab, "but I would never use the Samhailt so." She reached out and took his hand. "None of us would," she said. And then, looking at him again with that unblinking slant-eyed stare, "Would you?" said Mab, and without thinking, Flynn said, "No of course not," and Mab smiled and withdrew her hand, and reached for the honey again.

Flynn studied her thoughtfully. "You are a very strong lady," he said.

"Here at Court? Yes, for the King is my son."

"But even if he were not," said Flynn, "you would still be so. You have authority. You would always stand out in a crowd."

"Yes," said Mab, and Flynn noticed that she did not protest or try to have the compliment embroidered. She would stand out in a crowd, he knew it and so did she, and she did not see any reason to be shy or modest or coy. On an impulse, he asked, "Why have you never stayed with one man?" and thought that in any case what kind of man could possibly keep this remarkable beautiful strong woman for longer than a few nights.

Mab said, "They would tell you—in the Sun Chamber, or on my own estates in the north—that I am any man's for the asking."

"That," said Flynn, "is not entirely true."

"No. And that is perceptive of you." They looked at one another, and after a moment, Mab said slowly, "You are rather a remarkable young man, Flynn. I think I only met your like once before in my life." She took his hand again, and Flynn held his breath, for he sensed she was about to talk to him in a way she did not often do. And despite his impatience to find out about Joanna, and despite the nagging worry, he was fascinated by Mab. She is no longer a young woman, he thought, she is certainly more than twice my age—yes, easily—but she still outshines everyone here at Tara.

Mab said slowly, "There was once someone . . ."

"Your—the King's father?"

"Oh no," said Mab. "Oh no, for that was a union of political advantage, nothing more. I was given to him so that my father could increase his lands. He accepted me so that I might bring to his line the coveted Lionblood. He was a pure-bred human, you see."

"Oh. Yes, of course." Flynn wondered why he had not realised that it was from Mab that Eochaid Bres had inherited the lion strain. It was there, quite plainly. The unblinking green eyes, the sinuous strength. The grace and the curve of her hands. And last night, she was almost purring beneath my hands, he thought, and smiled inwardly, and wondered was it overly vain to be pleased at having made a woman purr. At an even deeper level, he wondered had it been entirely from a wish to know more about Tara that he had gone to Mab's bed . . . Perhaps not, thought Flynn, incurably honest. No, perhaps not. Let us admit that I was a little bit bewitched, and let us certainly admit that I was fascinated . . . Yes, for sure lady, you bewitched me and you fascinated me. But you did not have it all your own way, thought Flynn, watching Mab over the breakfast table. And he smiled, and thought that whatever might happen to them in the future, and however much he was Joanna's, and would always be Joanna's, he would never quite forget Mab.

He thought that the last thought had surfaced, for Mab picked it up, and took his hand and smiled back at him, and said, "But I should not want you to forget, Flynn. That is how it should be. No regrets and no bitternesses. Good memories. In loving you should always give a little of yourself away, and you should always take a little part of the one you have loved." And then, with sudden vulnerability, "Did you love me last night, Flynn?"

"Yes."

Mab smiled and leaned back, and the feline look touched her face briefly. "And I you," she said softly, and the hand that held his flexed a little, as if to show its strength. "You will have a good place in my memories, Flynn."

"And you in mine, Mab," and he smiled again, and began to wonder whether he ought not to take her again, like this, across the breakfast table with the honey sticky on the platters and the butter melting, and the breadcrumbs everywhere . . .

And then Mab said, "It is strange you should ask about Eochaid's father, for I have not thought of him for years," and Flynn felt her mood shift, and knew that he would not, after all, reach for her, and that what had been between them would remain sweet and precious, but would never happen again. He thought: she is about to tell me something about this place, and at once his mind came sharply into focus, and the longing to find Joanna became a physical pain. He leaned forward and looked at Mab very intently, and thought that if he could somehow draw the thoughts from her mind and use them to help him rescue Joanna, he would do so without the least heed to the Code that charged possessors of the Samhailt to use it honourably. Be damned to that if it would find Joanna! thought Flynn, and studied Mab and waited. But although he opened his mind to its fullest extent, and although he could almost feel the Samhailt spinning and quivering between them, he could get nothing from her other than a velvety blackness. Because she had veiled her thoughts from him? Yes, probably.

Mab said in a distant voice, "Eochaid's father was a cypher, no more. I did not love him, and he did not love me. But I was the youngest of my line; I was a princess of the Beastline, and I must be given in marriage where it was expedient." She paused, and the three-cornered smile lifted her lips. "I did not love him," she said softly, "but I think I have compensated for that since." Mab smiled, and Flynn smiled with her, and concentrated every shred of his strength on drawing from her whatever she would tell him.

"It was not time for my House to mate with the Beasts, for the rules governing that are very strict indeed. And it is rarely more often than every fourth or fifth generation that the Ritual is invoked." She looked at Flynn, seated opposite to her with the morning sun streaming in, and remembered another young man who had also loved her gently and strongly and excitingly, and who had sat with her like this, drinking mead and spreading butter and honey on bread, and touching her hand. Not Flynn, but someone who had been wild and wolfish; someone whose coronation she had come to Court to attend all those years ago . . . And if I half close my eyes, I can still see him—the Prince of Tara—arrogant and unruly, but so precious to me . . . Something hot and hurting rose up in her throat, and for the first time for many years she allowed memory its head.

She had no longer been a young woman when she came to Court for the coronation of the wild young Prince. She had been—thirty-five? Perhaps a little more. No longer very young. Certainly beyond the age for dazzlement by a callow youth.

Except that Cormac had never been callow.

The minute she saw him, she had known. That one for me. There had been too many years between them of course—and those years have been strongly lived, she had thought—but even so, she had wanted him.

The difference in their ages had not mattered. It had never mattered. It had certainly not counted with them on those nights—endless, exciting, frustrating—when they had circled one another, warily sizing each other up. All through the coronation ceremonies and the revels and the long, noisy, colourful feastings, they had watched one another, and the Samhailt had quivered almost continuously between them, and they had both known how it would end.

"I knew I should have him. I knew I must have him. It was like a sickness, an enchantment." She leaned forward, her face intent. "And for the first time in my life, I was jealous of the pretty pink and white children who came to Court looking for a husband. I was envious to the point of insanity of the girls who were paraded as suitable wives for him. I!" She made a fist of one hand and struck her breast angrily. "I, who had been called the Intoxicating One! Who had once boasted that while I lived there should never be a King crowned in Ireland but he had lain with me." A pause. "They thought that a good joke, the young men. They said it would become part of the coronation ritual. I did not care. I was imperious and selfish and I did not care what anyone said of me." Her voice changed. "But I wanted Cormac," she said softly. "I wanted him more than any man ever before or ever since." She leaned back and reached for the mead again. "And of course, I got him."

"Of course," said Flynn, and smiled, and Mab smiled as well.

"Yes, you understand, don't you? He could not help himself. He was wild for me; he was beyond reason and beyond logic and I believe he would have done anything in the world to have me. I was—well, let us say fifteen years—his senior but he did not care. He would have sacked cities and toppled empires to have me. And when we finally faced each other with all the barriers down . . ." Again the shrug. "Oh, it was like a star exploding. Like a forest fire. Like a whirlpool." She fell silent, and Flynn waited.

"We stayed together in my rooms," said Mab. "Time had ceased to exist for us, and the rest of the world had become meaningless. There was nothing for either of us but each other, and there was no world except the world we had found. Food was brought to us, and wine, but in truth we ate little and we drank even less. We were drunk on each other, and we needed no false intoxicants. We were helpless and mindless, and we had forgotten that any other world existed." She paused again, and Flynn, lost in her story, thought: when she talks like this I can almost see him. Cormac of the Wolves. The High King.

"He was one of the most remarkable looking people you might ever see," said Mab softly, and Flynn knew she had heard his thoughts again. "Dark and slender, but with such strength and with such authority. Patrician and elegant, also, for he came of an old and honourable line, but wild and arrogant and just a little dangerous." She smiled. "Yes, he was always just a little dangerous. There was always something there—an aura, a flavour—that made you remember he had Wolfblood in his veins. Teeth and claws where other men were soft. But he could be gentle when you least expected it. That was one of his strengths, of course. Weak men do not dare to be gentle.

"When Cormac entered a room, everyone else appeared colourless. He was alive, he was sizzling with vitality. He was more alive than anyone I have ever known. His Court adored him; they would do anything for him, and they obeyed him unquestioningly. Once I accused him of employing the sorcerers' arts, but he only laughed at me and said, 'There is no sorcery but that which is in the mind, and there is no enchantment but the enchantment of the senses.' " Again there was the pause, the inward-looking expression, and Flynn sat motionless, fascinated and admiring, but just a little jealous as well.

She caught that at once, of course. Stretching out a hand to him Mab said, "You do not need to be jealous, Flynn. It is only that you have stirred up memories for me. You are so like him . . . I had thought the memories all safely dead you see. I had certainly thought them firmly buried. But here they are, tumbling out into the light. If you had not so reminded me ... You have many of his qualities; strength and gentleness all rolled up together. And arrogance." She studied him. "Yes, the arrogance is there," said Mab. "You are of the same mould, you and Cormac."

Flynn did not speak, but he had heard the thoughts behind Mab's carefully selected words, and he had heard the sudden fear of a woman no longer young, seeing old age approach, alarmed by it. He thought: she knows that to relive the loves of youth is an old woman's pastime. To see the features of a loved one in the face of another is surely the failing of the aged.

Pity stirred in him for this beautiful aging woman, and he clamped down the emotion at once, for it was not to be thought of that Mab should know of this feeling.

He believed she had not sensed it; he thought she was still lost in the past, living again the days of the Wolfking's reign.

"Go on," he said at length. "Tell me." And remembering how she had earlier seemed to convey her own feelings through her skin, he took her hand between his and felt the skin velvet-smooth.

"The world at last intruded," said Mab, speaking in a low faraway voice. "We had thought we had escaped it, but of course we had not. No one ever does. And he was the King; there were responsibilities and duties. There were Council Chambers to attend and delegations to receive. There were ceremonies and courtesies and processions, and the King must be at the centre of them all.

"He did not mind, you understand. He had been bred to be King and these things were a part of his life. He did not question them and I never once saw him impatient with them."

She fell silent, and Flynn said tentatively, "You said he dealt you a—a discourtesy. An insult. A blow of some kind."

"Yes," said Mab and smiled again, but this time it was a cat smile, a lion smile, and Flynn felt as if delicately sharpened claws had been drawn down along his spine. He shivered.

"Oh yes, he dealt me an insult," said Mab softly, and now there was a lick of pleasure in her voice, so that Flynn thought for all her apparent vulnerability and for all her charm, here

was a very formidable opponent: I must be careful not to make
an enemy of this one ...

"But I dealt him a greater blow," said Mab leaning forward,
her eyes flaring with triumph. "I dealt him the greatest blow he
could ever suffer, Flynn. I deposed him and exiled him and set
up my son in his place. For that he will never forgive me." She
sat back and nodded, and there again, startlingly, was the age-
ing, memory-ridden, rather pitiable creature Flynn had
glimpsed earlier.

He said gently, "Tell me what Cormac did. Will you?"

Mab said, "I have never told anyone," and looked suddenly
uncertain.

"It would not matter. I am not of Tara. I am a traveller, a
wayfarer. And I shall soon be gone." Her hand moved uncertainly in his.

"Yes," said Mab softly, "yes, you will soon be gone, Flynn.
They come and they go, the young men. It is so long ..."

"Tell me," said Flynn, softly, insistently, and at length, Mab
lifted her head and looked at him.

She said slowly, "He violated the most sacred, most ancient
of all our laws. The intermingling of the blood of the humans
and the beasts.

"He lay with the she-wolves one night in the forest, and for
that I can never forgive him."

IT WAS AS real to her as if it had only just happened. Another
sign of encroaching age? Yes, of course, but she would disre-
gard it. She could ignore it a little longer. She was still the Intoxicating One; she could still get any man she wanted, and the
Court still took and made bets over her lovers. *While I can still
maintain the legend I am safe. I can cheat age a little longer
yet.*

But none of the young men she had slept with since had
stirred her in the way that Cormac had done; none of them had
touched her heart and her soul, though many of them had possessed her body.

None of them had ever dispelled Cormac's memory. Could
Flynn have done? She looked at him and thought: *oh yes, I believe Flynn might just have done. He has the recklessness and
the dark arrogance, and oh yes,* thought Mab, *Flynn might just
have done. If only it had not been too late, if only I had never*

loved Cormac . . . She had loved Cormac fiercely and wildly, and of course it had been wholly wrong. She had been born too early, or he had been born too late. But she had thought, all those years ago, that it did not matter; they could have toppled the conventions and ruled Ireland together.

And Ireland would have become truly great.

She had even thought of the children she would give him; she had seen them all so clearly in her mind, then and since, and there had been nights—many of them—when she had wept for those lost, never-to-be, little ones.

In the end, she had hated him as violently as she had loved him, and her hatred had kept her alive. For at least I have lived and at least I have loved! she had thought.

Coming out of the warm, silk-hung, rose bedchamber into the world had been like coming out of a warm drowsy-scented bath. She had been a little confused by the harsh noisy world, a little dizzy, like a man faced with strong sunlight after many hours in a dim quiet cell.

The real world, the world of the Court, had broken through at last; Cormac had torn himself from her side with promises and vows to return.

"A night—two at the most—and then I will be back." A swift grin. "Hone your appetite my lady." And then he was gone with the casualness and the absence of ceremony that characterised him. She had stood at the narrow curtained window of her rooms, watching him ride out of Tara to some minor ceremony or other, attendants in line behind him, the small covey of Wolves, without which he never travelled, bringing up the rear. She had never seen him without at least two Wolves at his heels.

He had lifted his hand to her window in a salute, and she had smiled, and pride had swept through her, nearly overwhelming her with its intensity. He is mine. And in two nights he will return.

But the silk-hung bedchamber had become stifling in its emptiness; the fire still burned in the hearth, but it burned for no one, and she remembered how it had danced across the ceiling for them, only the night before, enclosing them in a firelit cave. Outside the window, the Purple Hour was at its deepest now; unbearable for her because she was alone: "For I had sat on the window seat of my room with the night scents drifting in, and I had heard the nightbirds sing the Evening Song, and I had loved it because he was there with me."

Towards the evening of the second day, she had gone walking in the forest, uncaring of the dangers that lurked there, knowing herself equal to most forms of attack.

"The Lionblood was not as pronounced in me as in the men of my family, but it was there. I could have given a good account of myself. Physical attack did not bother me. And sorcery could be fought with more sorcery.

"I had my own sorcerers, and I knew enough to protect myself from the spells of my enemies."

The Purple Hour was creeping over the land, and the forest was an enchanted place at that time of day. She had moved silently among the trees, now and again fancying she could hear them waking—"Although that is something we all fancy at the Purple Hour, and of course they never do wake"—enjoying the deepening shadows. All about her, the forest was coming alive; there were stealthy patterings of feet, and the soft beating of wings on the air. There were glimpses of small woodland creatures that did not venture out by day.

And then she had come out on to the edge of a clearing and there he had been. "As if I had after all captured a wandering spell and conjured him up for my eyes to feast on."

She had felt a huge and surprised joy invade her body and she had made as if to run towards him. And then she had stopped.

For Cormac was not alone.

"THE RULES GOVERNING the joining of animals with humans are very strict," said Mab. "For the balance that must be maintained is a very delicate one. To allow human blood and animal blood to mingle at the wrong generation is not only disastrous, but dangerous. A generation too soon and monsters are brought forth; a generation too late, and the strain can be lost altogether. Both of these have happened, Flynn. Families have been reduced to the plain unalloyed human blood by misjudging the time for the Ritual of the Bloodline; also, dreadful deformities have been created by invoking the Ritual too soon. Hideous creatures who must be incarcerated for their own safety and for the sake of common pity. You look surprised, Flynn. We are a cruel race, but we are not entirely merciless."

"No. It was not that. Please go on." But Flynn was surprised; he was shocked and rather sickened, but he thought: so after all nothing changes so very much.

Mab said, "Despite the risks, every High King must possess a vein of beastblood within him, for Tara can never be ruled by the humans, otherwise it will die."

"How do you know that?"

"We all know it. A terrible and powerful sorceress once placed a curse on the Royal line, and the curse can only be kept at bay by never having a pure-bred human on the throne. Always there must be a vein of beastblood. That is the bedrock of all our religions and all our beliefs, and the first High Queen, Dierdriu, appointed the Twelve Judges of the Bloodline. Dierdriu was a pure human, but she knew that the only way to protect Tara from the sorceress's curse was to ensure that a human never occupied the Sun Chamber.

"The Sorcerers of Tara created the Enchantment of the Bloodline—the Six Ancient Royal Houses—so that the curse should be kept forever at bay," said Mab. "They say it was the night that Tara's history really began, the night of that first Ritual of the Bloodline. They say that the land was so filled with enchantment and strong magic, that if you had by some means been able to look down on Ireland from the skies, you would have seen it thrumming and shimmering wrapped about in its own mysticism, wreathed in spells and alive and alight with bewitchment."

She paused, and Flynn said, "Go on."

"The sorcerers brought the Enchantment straight from their Looms by torchlit procession across Tara's Hill," said Mab. "Past the Fál on the Hill's summit; through the forests and into the clearing where, so it is said, Ireland's heart lies.

"It would have been the Purple Hour, for that is the time of the day when magic is abroad, and they would have wanted to harness the Purple Hour's own natural forces. They met in the clearing, and the Six Families were there, probably wearing ceremonial robes, although we cannot be sure—the legends vary. But it would have been a solemn and an awesome sight, I think."

She fell silent again, and Flynn waited.

"There has never been a night in Ireland's history to equal

that, I think," said Mab, "although when the Ritual is invoked now, it is very impressive indeed."

"You have seen it?"

"Once. Yes, once, when it was decreed that the Eagleline should be strengthened." Mab looked at Flynn. "Dierdriu created the Panel of Judges, so that the weakness or strength of the Bloodline could be properly controlled. The Judges are taken from the wisest and the most honourable of our people; to be one of the Twelve is a hereditary appointment, and the line has been unbroken since Dierdriu's time. Every family who possesses the Bloodline of the Beasts must appear before the Judges each time a child is born, so that the Bloodline can be constantly measured. If the Judges decide that the Blood is weakening, they may order the Ritual.

"Or sometimes," said Mab, "a new Bloodline is created. Perhaps the family's head has rendered the High King a service, or perhaps a son has distinguished himself in battle. Then the High King may confer the Bloodline. That is the highest honour we have, and it is greatly prized, though seldom bestowed. That is why we have several Houses that we term a lesser nobility. And when the Bloodline is bestowed, the family is permitted to choose its own emblem—that is the Beastline with which it will be joined. The Ritual is performed then, always in the same place. For magic lingers," said Mab seriously. "Once an enchantment has been performed in a particular place, then the enchantment never quite fades. That is why it is always the clearing which is called Ireland's heart. It is a place so permeated with magic that it is forbidden to pure humans. But you will know this," said Mab looking at Flynn.

And Flynn, remembering nearly too late that he was supposed to be a part of this world, said, "Yes, of course I know it. Go on."

"Only the immediate family may attend, although it is also permitted that the Six Ancient Houses can send a representative. There is a procession by torchlight, and the air is heavy and scented. We do not see the Enchantment, for the sorcerers are jealous of their secrets, and rightly so. It would not do for such things to be abused. And so the Enchantment is woven in secret, and brought to the clearing, and the Ritual takes place. But only the Judges may decide. And only the Judges may decide whether it is a girl who will receive the beast seed and

give birth, or whether it is a man who will give his seed to the
beast. Unplanned lying with the beasts is forbidden, for to do
so might result in the birth of those pitiable mutilations which
we know of from our historians and our scholars. It is one of
our strictest laws, and to flout it is punishable by mutilation
and exile."

Flynn said, "And that night in the forest—"

"Yes," said Mab, and her hand came out to his. "Yes,
Cormac violated the law and flouted the most sacred of all our
beliefs." She stared at the past again, and then after a moment
began to speak, unwillingly at first, and then faster, the words
pouring from her as if she was at last able to purge her mind
of the bitter memories.

THE LIGHT HAD almost gone when she reached the clearing, but
it had not entirely gone. It was possible to recognise the features of a loved one. It was certainly possible to see the clearing for the hallowed place of Ritual: the place that in
Dierdriu's time had been called Ireland's heart.

It was also possible to identify the low lean outlines of the
creatures there with him. And he had rarely been without at
least two in attendance at any given time . . .

Cormac was standing in the clearing, clad only in a pair of
breeches. His arms and shoulders and his feet were bare, and
there was a look on his face that Mab had never seen before.

"Hungry. Inhuman. Bestial. He looked as if he might rip
open an enemy with his bare hands and exult in the blood. He
was more wolfish than I have ever seen him before or since.
He was so alien; it was as if another being was possessing
him. And to see him there like that, in that place . . ."

She had been afraid, but she had stayed where she was, hidden by the trees and by the approaching night, unable to leave.

"I could feel the magic stirring all about us, and I did not
know what forces might be abroad. But I had to see. I had to
see if I could understand."

The Wolves had sensed the change in him, of course. Mab
had only before seen them obedient and docile with him. Now
they treated him as one of themselves, rolling in the grass at
his feet, jumping up to lick his face. As Mab watched, Cormac
had knelt and pulled one of the she-wolves close and licked

her face in return, and a shiver of pure delight had gone through the animal.

They leapt at him and pushed him on to the ground, rolling over with him on the forest floor, fur and teeth and skin all blurred together, so that it was impossible to tell which was the human and which the wolves.

The male wolves were panting, their tongues hanging out of their muzzles, their bodies sexually aroused. Fear and horror had gripped her, for she had known what was about to happen.

"I could not have prevented it. He was more wolf than man by now; perhaps he was all wolf. He would have torn out my throat and the wolves would have finished off what he left."

She had stayed where she was, unable to move, and unable to look away, and she had seen everything.

Cormac had raised himself to a kneeling position, thighs apart on the ground. He had pulled the nearer of the she-wolves to him with one hand, while the other hand had gone to the fastenings of his breeches. At length, he knelt naked and aroused on the forest floor, his hair black and curling, damp with sweat, his eyes slanting, and a faint mist of perspiration on his skin.

"And he was so beautiful. I cannot begin to tell you how strange and strong and beautiful he looked. I could only stare. I had never seen him like this. My people are of lion blood, and the men of my family—occasionally the women—are strong and handsome and noble. And I have stayed at Gallan with Cait Fian who is of the Wild Panther line, and I have dined with the gentle shy Gazelle people of the west coast, and with the shaggy friendly White Bear clan of the northern islands. And I was at the Ritual of the Bloodline when the Eagleline was strengthened and the clearing shivered and spun with the immense power of the sorcerers' Enchantment.

"But I have never seen anything so beautiful and so out of the world as that sight in the forest."

Cormac mounted the she-wolf easily and naturally, and as Mab watched, he drove into her again and again, the muscles of this thighs rippling, his eyes bright and dark with passion. She had seen the momentum of his desire approach; she had heard him groan and she had seen the she-wolf shiver in ecstasy.

Cormac laughed and pushed the creature from him playfully

and affectionately, and the wolf turned and licked his face. He ruffled the fur on her neck and lay back on the forest floor, as relaxed and as casual as he was in his great Palace of Tara.

The wolves were lying watching him, forming a half-circle about him, their eyes bright and hopeful, their ears pricked. Cormac had laughed again, and emitted a mock groan, and Mab had known that the wolves were waiting for him to take another of their females. He would take them all, one after the other, and then he would come to the rose silk bedchamber, flushed and exhilarated from his encounter with the wolves, excited and buoyed up. *I have lain with the wolves and now I will lie with a human.*

"I could not do it," said Mab. "I could not allow him in my bed then, or ever again. I could understand why he had done what he had—he was part wolf—but I could not forgive him for breaking the most sacred of all Tara's laws. He, the High King! I knew I could never forgive him."

"And so you drove him out?" said Flynn, very softly.

"I deposed him," she said, staring straight ahead as if Flynn was no longer there. "I turned him from my bed—he thought I was simply tired of him—and then I gathered about me the plotters of the Court and the intriguers, and the men and women who would do anything, and serve any master, for power. I led the Great Rebellion against the Wolfline, and I exiled Cormac to the terrible Fortress of Shadow, and I saw my son crowned as High King. I did not tell anyone what I had seen; I allowed Cormac to believe that I had used my knowledge of him to launch the Rebellion and lead the people against him. I never told Cormac's people that their beloved Wolfking had violated the ancient law of the Bloodline.

"But I saw to it that he was punished in the way the Twelve Judges would have punished him. I saw him taken from Tara by his own armies and flung into the wilderness to live or die as he chose.

"But," said Mab, "I have never been happy since that day."

A REMARKABLE LADY. Flynn wandered through the Palace, his mind half on Mab's story, half on his own. *Shall I escape today?* And thought how absurd it was to use such a word. *As if I was a prisoner!* he thought, and immediately wished he had not used the word "prisoner" either.

The Court was seething with activity and excitement, and anticipation ran through the great high-ceilinged halls like a white-hot flame. Flynn was made one with it all, he was welcomed into the various groups and hailed as a friend. "As if," he thought, "I have been here for years."

He was helping Sean the Storyteller and Conaire to stack the woodbine and the rowan for the journey to the Plain of the Fál later that afternoon, when Bricriu, his lips smiling thinly, his eyes expressionless, approached him.

"I wonder now, would you join my party later tonight for the journey to the Plain, Flynn?"

Flynn was rather flattered; "I should be honoured, Sir."

"Only a few of us, you understand. But we like to make Beltane something of an occasion. It is all superstition of course; everyone knows that. But the ceremonies are impressive, and I should enjoy explaining them to you. These things are always so much more interesting if viewed with the proper knowledge, do you think?"

"Oh yes," said Flynn.

"Then I will look for you later," said Bricriu. And then, as if struck by a thought: "You will not forget to carry the woodbine, will you?"

"No," said Flynn. "I shall bring it to the Plain."

"Yes," said Bricriu. "I think you had better."

PORTAN KNEW THAT they were never going to reach the dark stone fortress that swam in and out of the mists, always near, never quite within striking distance.

The place was not, of course, the Gealtacht as Grady and Muldooney seemed to imagine. Portan did not know what it was, although she felt it was a place of suffering of some kind. But it did not matter, for they would not be permitted to reach it.

They were lost in the forest, and they were blundering in circles. Portan knew this quite definitely, and she could not understand why her captors did not know it. It was something to do with the cold, rather beautiful music, and with the voices that sang from inside the music.

You will never reach Scáthach, Men of the Desolate World . . .

They would never reach Scáthach; they would roam for ever in the dark forest.

Until we possess your bodies, until we eat your souls, Men of the Black Desolation . . .

The voices wanted these two men, and Portan shivered in sudden fear, for there was such cold mercilessness in the voices. But she could spare no pity for her captors, for her mind was wholly on Flynn. Flynn was in some terrible danger; he was with enemies, men who wished him great harm. Portan knew this quite certainly now. She did not possess the Samhailt, although she understood about it, but she possessed something, and it was the something that made her lift her head and listen to the night and think: I must reach Flynn.

And then John Grady spoke: "Hush. There is someone quite close by."

"Following us?"

That was the other man, the one who had a large coarse face with the features crammed into the centre of it, and clumsy stupid hands and a slow mind. Even so, Portan preferred him to John Grady.

Grady said, "No. Not following us. But quite near. It may be someone who knows the forest. Someone who can lead us out."

Out of the Forest of Bondage . . . But this is the way Travellers, this is the way . . . over hill, over dale, through bush, through briar . . . this is the way . . .

John Grady said very loudly, "It would be a grand thing to find someone who knew the way out of this place."

And Muldooney, equally loudly, said, "To be sure it would."

John Grady knew, as all sensible men knew, that it was madness to go wandering about in a forest after dark; even so, they had somehow got themselves into this situation—he blamed Muldooney most severely for that—and must perforce get themselves out again. It would do no harm to ask for help. To himself, he thought that wasn't it the worst possible luck to be landed with an idiot like Brian Muldooney who couldn't find his way across lands that should have been as familiar to him as his own pig farm! He began to wish they had never embarked on this ridiculous chase.

Muldooney thought that wasn't it the worst luck in the world to have trusted Grady the Landgrabber, and then find the

man had no more sense of direction than a chicken with its
head chopped off. They'd been tramping about in this horrible
dark forest for hours now; and where the forest had come
from, Muldooney had no more idea than he had of how to fly
in the air! It was a place the like of which he'd never seen before, not in all the years he'd lived in Tugaim. Of course it was
all Grady's fault, and him an Elder and not allowing a soul to
forget it. Muldooney would have a thing or two to say about
John Grady when they got back to Tugaim. If they got back.
As for the sounds they could hear a little to their left, well, all
Muldooney hoped was that it was not going to turn out to be
some desperado or other set to slit their throats and make off
with their goods. A fine old thing that would be for them both!

And then the trees thinned and the mists swirled, and ahead
of them stood Amairgen, his clothes muddied and torn, his
face chalk white.

And two dark gaping wounds where his eyes had been.

With a low animal moan, Portan tore herself away from
John Grady's surprised and suddenly loosened grip, and
bounded to his side.

Behind her, the mists closed in again, and the laughter of the
sidh echoed triumphantly through the forest.

STRENGTH SWEPT THROUGH Portan now, and with it an immense
confidence. At least I can be of help. At last there is something
I can do to help one of the beloved friends who brought me
out of the Gealtacht. She did not stop to think. "And if I had
stopped," she said afterwards, "I should never have been able
to do what I did." She did not think: I am here in the middle
of a dark forest with a sightless man and two enemies nearby;
she thought: I will lead Amairgen to safety.

She took his arms firmly, saying as she did so, "Amairgen.
Hold on to me."

"Portan?" His voice was the voice of a man who has looked
on despair, and thought never to hear a friend again, and
Portan nearly broke down.

But she said calmly, "I am here. I will lead us to safety."

"I am blind . . . !"

The cry tore at her vitals, but for the moment she must bear
that. They must escape Grady and Muldooney; they must cer-

tainly get away from the beckoning, evil music, and they must find some kind of hiding place.

"Listen Amairgen. Do exactly as I tell you. And trust me."

What hurt so much was his utter dependence on her, and his trust. He waited obediently as she fashioned the makeshift leash Grady had used into a kind of harness, slipping one arm through the loop so that it no longer threatened to strangle her, making him take the other end.

"Now I can lead us out," said Portan, and she turned unhesitatingly in the direction of Tara. She did not know, not for certain, that she was going in the right direction, but once more the *something* that was guiding her was at work. She knew her choice of path to be right.

Behind them, the sounds of Grady and Muldooney were fading; once she caught the mocking laughter of the *sidh*, and once she heard the two men still blundering about in the undergrowth, but then there was nothing. She thought that the creatures of the music were surely luring the two men to some kind of terrible fate, and she felt a deep shudder go through Amairgen.

But he stumbled wherever she led, his face grazed by the low branches that he could not see, and that Portan could not reach to brush aside for him, but following her unquestioningly and blindly. *Blindly.* The knife turned in her stomach again, but she dared not pay it attention; there was no time yet for pity or explanations, there was no time for anything at all, other than flight from Grady and Muldooney . . . and the music.

At length, Portan stopped and looked about. "I think we have lost them, Amairgen. I think we are safe for a while. And we should rest."

"Yes. Thank you." The words were no more than an exhausted breath of sound, and Portan saw that he was at the end of his reserves of strength. She caught him as he fell, half-fainting, on to the ground.

Portan was frightened, but she thought: I must not panic. I am frightened, but I must not panic. Whatever there is to do I must try to do it, and one thing at a time. Make him more comfortable. Yes, and warm. Flynn's cloak. Holding on to coping with one thing at a time, she wrapped Flynn's cloak about the unconscious Amairgen, and then scooped a kind of half-hollow in the soft forest floor. Didn't animals sleep that way in the winter? Very well, so would they. And yes, he was a little warmer now, his face no longer had the white waxen look. He would not die, because Portan would not let him. She uncorked the flask of wine that Flynn had left in one of the cloak's deep pockets, and used the strong sweet stuff to moisten one of his handkerchiefs. Gently and carefully, she sponged Amairgen's face clean of blood and dirt, trying not to shudder away from the dark crusted wounds where his eyes had been, and then she was able to sponge there as well with infinite tenderness. For, thought Portan humbly, who am I to flinch from physical mutilation in another? She remembered how Amairgen had never once failed to meet her eyes kindly—often affectionately—and how he and Flynn had always, *always*, treated her as an equal. Portan knew she was not their equal, the years in the Gealtacht had taught her that her kind were no one's equal; but Flynn and Amairgen had never seemed to think about it. She loved them both fiercely for it.

Amairgen moved restlessly under her careful hands, and groaned once or twice. But he did not wake, and Portan, still determined not to be frightened, thought that after all, sleep was healing. He was warmer now, and his breathing was deep and normal. As night drew on, Portan tucked the cloak around the two of them, and curled into a little ball against Amairgen.

She had not thought she would sleep, but she did, deeply and dreamlessly, and when she woke, a faint pink-tinted dawn was beginning.

Portan's spirits lifted a little; after all they had survived the night in the forest; after all they were still alive. And they would find Flynn—they must find Flynn, for it was not to be thought of that Flynn should be lost to them. She would not think it, even for a moment. Flynn would be somewhere near, quite safe. Amairgen would tell her what had happened. Pain sliced through her at the memory of Amairgen's terrible mutilation, and with it a great tenderness. And—*let me help him,* she thought. Oh please, please, let me be able to help him.

At her side, Amairgen stirred, and Portan was at once fully awake, holding his hands in hers, reassuring him, because it would be the most terrible, most pitiable circumstance to wake to the knowledge of blindness, to know, afresh, that you were for ever in the dark . . .

"You are here with me," said Portan, willing her voice to be calm and confident. "You are quite safe, Amairgen."

And I shall not let anything harm you . . .

He turned his head, as if seeking the light, and Portan saw the knowledge of his blindness return to him, as she had known it would. He flinched from it, like a man who has lifted his face for a caress and received instead a harsh blow. The weight of his sightlessness descended on him, and Portan, aching with the pity of it, wanted to reach out and take him in her arms.

But she did not dare, and she thought that anyway she must not overwhelm him, and so she said, in a gentle, conversational voice, "It is early morning. Only a little past dawn, I think. Do you hear the birds? Beautiful. And I should think we are quite near to Tara."

Amairgen said, in a voice of agony, "Portan, I am blind. I am eyeless. I tore out my eyes in the Caves of the *sidh* so that I should no longer have to look at those creatures. I saved my soul and I saved my sanity, but I am blind. I shall never see again!" Portan, hardly knowing what she did, knelt at his side and wrapped her arms about him, so that his poor mutilated face was against her breast, and then murmured words she had once heard, long ago, before John Grady caused her to be thrown into the Gealtacht. She thought she would die from the sheer strength of love and pity. She had been in an agony of worry about Flynn, but for the moment Flynn had ceased to exist for her.

Amairgen had no defences. He clung to Portan, his body wracked with great dry sobs, for a man with no eyes cannot weep, and he felt every one of her thoughts as vividly as if they had been laid out for him, and he was humbled at the strength of her devotion. But his agony was still too raw and his despair was still too complete; he could take little comfort from Portan's love.

The darkness frightened him, for he had never imagined such an utter lack of light. Blackness, impenetrable, had descended about him like a thick stifling curtain. A towering wall had risen up between him and the entire world, and he was suffocating and terrified. He felt as if great chasms were opening at his feet, so that he could never take a step forward again, and he felt as if huge threatening creatures were rearing

up before him. He clung to Portan, unable to speak, barely able
to think, afraid and lost and in the grip of black and bitter despair.

I have saved my soul and my sanity, but at what price?

The price had been too high and he would never again take
his place in the world. He thought: better if I were to die now,
here. But even as he thought it, a spark of rebellion lit within
him. Half to himself, he said, "I am so afraid . . ." and he felt
the strong reassuring hands hold him more firmly. When he
said, "Please—don't leave me," there was at once a strong
sweet sense of loving and of concern, and at once the
response—"Never!" For the first time since the *sidh* had flung
him from their caves, sightless and useless and impotent, he felt
a faint far-off comfort. At least I am safe. At least I am with
one I can trust. I am for ever in the dark and I shall never, from
now on, see anything again other than the black wall, but after
all I am safe. I am sane and my soul is still my own.

A tiny cruel voice that he did not recognise, said: *ah, but
what does it profit a man if he gains his soul but suffers the
loss of his sight?* and he gave it scant attention, frowning as he
did so. But he was already calmer; he lay back, with Portan
still holding him against her, and he felt again the clarity of her
thoughts. *I am here with you, Amairgen. I will never leave you.
You are not alone.*

Not alone. He had the blessing of human companionship.
He had the knowledge of her strength and he could hear her
thoughts flowing gently to him and back again. He knew it
was the Samhailt working within him, but he found himself
wondering a little at the intensity and the purity of it.

*What does it profit a man to gain his soul but suffer the loss
of his sight?*

*A great profit if he also gains the ancient and Mystical
Samhailt of the One True Bloodline of Ireland.*

He had always known himself to possess a thin vein of the
Samhailt, but he had known it to be a frail, tenuous thing, diluted by countless centuries of out-breeding, frayed by use and
by misuse, for his ancestors had doubted its powers and dis-
trusted its meaning. The Letheans had not understood something that could not be seen or measured or analysed, and the
Samhailt, possessed by Amairgen's distant ancestors, had been

worn to the thinnest of thin slivers by the time it came down to him.

Now it had doubled and re-doubled and grown until it was alive and joyful, flooding his entire body with its strength and its purity, so clear and vivid that for a time he forgot he could no longer see.

For I can hear and I can feel and I can taste. I can hear the forest sounds and I can taste the light—yes, just past dawn, pink and lavender and so utterly beautiful a man could cry for it. I can hear the thoughts of all the living creatures soaking in through my skin. Remarkable. He lay for a long time, Portan's cheek against his, their hands still firmly clasped, and he began to savour and explore this new strength. He felt that he was at the centre of a great rainbow, where the colours and the senses and the feelings of the entire world were his for the asking and there for the taking.

And I can drink the colours and I can taste the senses and I can hear the feelings. There is another world that I never once guessed existed, and I am about to enter into it. The door is opening, and it is a door I never knew was there. Beyond it is a world so full of light and beauty that it can hardly be borne. I do not see it, but I am made free of it. I am entering into a secret and most wonderful place.

So this was the price he had to pay for saving his soul and his sanity. This was the wonderful price he had paid for dwelling in the Caves of the *sidh*, for looking on their awesome beauty and for knowing their slender silky bodies, and for feeling his seed drain into them, over and over, until he was fainting and unconscious. He had felt them pull at his soul, he had felt his soul's response, and he had sprung away from them, clawing at his eyes, feeling blood pour out over his fingers, seeing the world begin to whirl and spin in dizzying iridescent colours before the curtain fell and the wall rose up.

But I have pushed aside the curtain, and I have climbed the wall, thought Amairgen, and I believe I shall eventually find some kind of place in the world again. I shall certainly find peace again.

Deep within him, although he only partly knew it, was the spark that had lit Flynn, and deep within him was his own race-memory, that of the shadowy figure of the first Amairgen the Traveller. If the spirit of the great warrior Finn of the *Fiana* had woken in Flynn, so now did that of the courageous Explorer wake in his namesake. As Amairgen lay quietly in the forest, wrapped in Portan's arms, he felt the soul of his dauntless ancestor stir strongly, and he thought: am I to allow this to quench me?

He would not allow it, and he knew that he would one day overcome it. He would tear down the curtain and he would climb the wall, and he would enter fully into this rich new world where sight did not count, but where colours were something to drink and light was something to soak through your skin, and where sounds and feelings could be scooped up and allowed to run through your hands like thin sand.

Amairgen the Traveller would not have allowed blindness to daunt him, and neither would his descendant.

Chapter Fourteen

Excitement was running through the Palace like a forest fire. Tara thrummed with anticipation and hummed with preparation for the evening's ritual, and was so vividly alive that it seemed almost to possess its own heartbeats. It seemed to the younger members of the Court that if you stood still and were very quiet, you might hear it, beat-beating away quietly at the very centre. Several of the more fanciful members of the Court thought that if you could somehow fly over the Palace, from east to west and then from north to south, you would see Tara as a glowing living breathing thing; a golden heart, the gently pulsating soul of all Ireland. Several more, rather taken with this imaginative vision, wanted to ask Conaire to call up the Eagles and ask them to fly a few chosen observers over the turrets, but when it came to it, nobody quite had the courage. It sounded rather too much like making vulgar use of Conaire's relatives. Also, as Sean the Storyteller pointed out, you could never altogether trust an eagle. They were apt to be bad-tempered, said Sean. They'd gobble you up in two bites if the mood took them—snap! with their beaks, and there you'd be, dead as last week's dinner. And while flying over Tara on an eagle's back might sound very poetic and very exciting (and would make a grand base for a new poem as well), it would not be very comfortable, leave aside safe. Well, it would not be at all safe, really. There'd be nothing to cling on to for one thing, only feathers, because you could hardly expect an eagle to submit itself to the indignity of a saddle and harness, as if it was of no more account than a plain horse. Anyone who believed that hadn't the wits he'd been born with! Had they all of them forgotten the terrible time they'd had when Conaire's family had had the Bloodline conferred on them, and chosen the eagles (eagles! of all creatures) as their emblem? Had they indeed? Well, to be sure, Sean had not, and it hadn't been so very long ago, either, there was no call for the younger ones to grin and poke each other and furtively count up the years. Conaire's great uncle Ailill it had been, and nobody had been quite sure why the honour had been conferred, although several people had pointed out at the time that Ailill had been extremely friendly with Mab. But, of course, who hadn't been extremely friendly with Mab at one time or another? Sean himself could tell a tale or two if anyone cared to ask.

Anyway, there'd been the greatest old tussle anyone had ever seen, said Sean, well away by now, with the sorcerers at it all night trying to strengthen the original Enchantment and bring the eagles to a properly docile state, because nobody had ever envisaged a ritual conjoining with eagles, and a good many people thought that Ailill had done it just to be mischievous. But the sorcerers had done their best, although they'd had to go down into the very deepest of the Sorcery Chambers—and they all knew what that meant!—and Sean and Phineas the Gatekeeper had suffered two bitten fingers and a bruised kneecap apiece from the Ritual, not that either of them had especially wanted to play such an intimate part in the ceremony, only that somebody had to hold the eagle down. It had all been very harrowing, said Sean, and if anyone cared to call up an eagle and politely ask could they take a ride on its back, Sean for one was going to be conveniently not there!

So the project was reluctantly abandoned, although it was felt to have been a good idea. But it would be too discourteous to the Eagles, said the Court sententiously, although Conaire, who never missed much of what went on, grinned and said it was more likely they were all of them afraid of falling off. "No guts," said Conaire, who would have called up the entire winged population of Ireland if it would have created some frivolity at Eochaid Bres's ponderous Court.

And so the eagles were left to their solitary splendour, although three of the livelier spirits of the Court—Conaire among them—climbed to the top of the trees on Tara's western boundaries, to see how the Palace was looking. They returned flushed and excited, reporting that it had been nearly as good as flying over on an eagle's back, and they told anyone who would listen that Tara was as bright from above as it was from below, and it was going to be a great shame later on when all the lights were doused and the final Ritual of the Scared Fire on the Plain of the Fál commenced. Tara was brighter than a thousand Sacred Fires, they said rather daringly, and it was never seen to better advantage than when seen from the very topmost branches of the trees.

"But they received a reprimand from the King later on," said Sean. "Silly young cubs, didn't they realise that until the trees are woken, they're forbidden to all of us? I'd have thought Conaire at least would have known," said Sean. "I heard the King was extremely displeased with them, and on the whole the eagles would have been safer."

None of these comparatively minor setbacks deterred anyone from enjoying the day, for wasn't Beltane the greatest night of the year, and didn't they all, every one of them, look forward to it for weeks? A grand feast it was, and plenty of fun for everyone.

Bolg pointed out, in Eochaid Bres's favour, that you had to say he did keep up the good old traditions. He was keeping to them for Beltane, and Bolg was pleased, because once you lost touch with a tradition all kinds of slipshod slapdash behaviour crept in. But the Sacred Fire was to be lit with proper attention to ritual, and the Druids would burn the Wicker Man—Bolg did not care overmuch for that part of the proceedings because of the poor trapped animals—and a little later today they would all of them go in procession through the Palace to ensure that every light was quenched. You could not have any form of light burning that might quarrel with the Sacred Fire on the Plain. Everyone knew that.

They'd all gather about the Beltane Fire, and the virgins would leap through it, always supposing an adequate number of virgins could be found, because say what you liked, you needed at least a dozen to make a proper ceremony. It was to be hoped a dozen could be found. It was getting more and more difficult. Still, it had been very nearly impossible in Cormac's day, at least you could not say that for Eochaid Bres. Sean the Storyteller had probably rounded up a dozen. And the Druids would make their procession across the Plain, just as they did every year, chanting their strange song which was not quite a song but not quite a chant either, and which was in the forgotten tongue of the Ancient Ireland, and so old that not even the Cruithin, who still spoke pure Gael sometimes, could understand it. Bolg thought it was a tongue that men had used before they came to be civilised, but the Druids kept their secrets, and no one had ever been able to decipher the Beltane Chant, although many had tried. Cormac's father, who had been rather scholarly (when he was not chasing women), had said it was in a tongue so ancient that it had never been written down, and that it had been old when men were still walking on all fours and living in caves, but Bricriu, who had friends among the sorcerers, had once said it was one of the sorcerers' tongues.

And then, partway through the day, a rumour began—no one knew quite where or how—that the Wicker Man would hold a human sacrifice this year. There was consternation in the Palace, and people began to whisper together in little groups. It was years since a human sacrifice had been offered at Beltane, or at any other feast, and no one cared for the idea. Certainly the Wolfkings had outlawed the practice; Cormac's great-grandfather had banned it. Several people thought it had been even earlier than that. Nobody quite knew whether to believe the rumour, and everyone began to exchange views.

Bolg and the Councillors were inclined to disbelieve the rumour. "For," said Bolg, "we don't have that sort of thing any longer."

"Sheer superstition," put in another.

"And *messy*," added a third.

"I wonder at His Majesty even considering it, I do really," said Bolg, worried.

"You don't need to watch if you're squeamish," said the Councillor who had called human sacrifice superstitious.

"You don't even need to come out to the Plain," said the one who had called it messy.

But Bolg thought he had better be present; the King might need his guidance, he said. After all, he was His Majesty's senior Councillor he said, rather grandly, and the other Councillors at once said of course, and to be sure he was, no one had intended to suggest otherwise. To themselves they thought that the old boy was beginning to show signs of age; hadn't he appeared in Council only the other day with his breeches unfastened, and didn't he take hours to nibble over a problem, when the rest of them had reached a solution long since? They remembered that he came of the Beaverline, and beavers, of course, were staunch and loyal and tenacious, but they were a bit slow. Bolg was getting a bit slow, said the Councillors, and took themselves off to hold an unofficial conference as to who might be groomed to be successor.

Bolg went off to unpack his winter underwear, which he had lain away with a few sprigs of lavender. It might be cold up on the Plain tonight; you could never tell what the weather might decide to do.

He was very upset at the suggestion of human sacrifice on the Beltane Fire, and after he had dressed he went about the Court trying to find out as much as he could, which was not very much because nobody else seemed to know very much either.

But he persevered, because he thought it was his duty to do so, and he listened in to other people's conversations so that he was told, quite politely, to go away, and he joined groups of gossipers, and was told, not quite so politely, to stop eavesdropping. Conaire became very cross when Bolg skulked outside his room, and asked hadn't he anything better to do than disrupt them all, just as they were preparing for a bit of a feast; spreading gloomy rumours and upsetting people. Bolg, upset himself, replied rather more sharply than perhaps he meant. One thing led to another rather speedily, because although Conaire was not in the least bad-tempered as the eagles were reputed to be, he was certainly quick-tempered and he fired up at once. Tempers became frayed and old feuds were disinterred. Bolg remembered that he had never cared much for Conaire's great uncle Ailill, who had beaten him to the bedpost with Mab twenty years earlier, and he recalled that he had always considered the Eagleline jumped-up second-generation aristocracy anyway. They all of them knew, said Bolg rather tartly, where the family had got its honours.

"And where would that be?" said Conaire angrily, snapping his brows together.

"In the Queen Mother's bed!" said Bolg and turned away crossly.

Conaire then had to be restrained by Sean the Storyteller from issuing a challenge to Bolg there and then, and was with difficulty persuaded to apologise to Bolg, who at once shook hands and said that to be sure words had been spoken hastily, and he hadn't meant any disrespect, not a bit of it, it was only that he was worried and upset by this talk of human sacrifice, and he did not want it to get to the King's ears. And Conaire, who was hot-tempered, but basically kindly, said at once that the entire thing had been his fault, and he hadn't meant to say that Bolg's Bloodline was diluted out of all use and that the Beavers were of no help to anyone in a battle.

"Roaring snobs the pair of them," said Sean crossly, and stumped away to his own room, to remind himself that a man was better by far to have plain honest human blood in his veins without any of that Ritual Conjoining nonsense. Sean would by far rather deal with plain untampered-with humans and would not have thanked you for being offered a Bloodline. The fact that it had never been offered did not weigh; he would not have accepted it, or not without careful consideration anyway.

He set himself to pen a few suitable lines about the feuding of the humans and the Bloodline clans, which he thought might go down rather well in the village, although he would not be able to recite it at Court where a good half of the people were of the Bloodline.

Once or twice it occurred to him to wonder where the young traveller he had found so companionable had disappeared to . . .

THE PROCESSION TO quench all the lights in Tara began exactly one hour before the Purple Time. It was tradition to do it that way, said the Court; there was a grand sense of comfort about tradition. No one wanted it any different.

The procession was to be led by Phineas the Gatekeeper, whose duty it was, properly speaking, to safeguard the Palace, and who had therefore long been appointed to lead the procession. Every light in Tara must be quenched, no single flame or candle must be left burning in case it interfered with the Sacred Fire on the Plain of the Fál. Everyone remembered the shocking year when the King's own bedchamber had been missed and the Sacred Fire would not properly ignite, and the Druids insisted on combing the entire Palace until they found the renegade light. Phineas did not very much like being put in charge of the proceedings as a result, but Bolg had told him they had all occasionally to do things they did not care for, and anyway if Phineas refused, there were plenty to take his place. Phineas, who rather enjoyed his position as Gatekeeper, and who had built up a very cosy little nest for himself over the years, acquiesced glumly.

The procession would end with the High King, and Eochaid Bres was no more enthusiastic about this than was Phineas about leading it. He thought that to bring up the rear of such an important cavalcade was not very dignified, and anyway he had not lived in Tara for nearly long enough to know all its rooms. Supposing they missed one or two again?

"Oh that won't matter, Sire," said Bricriu smoothly. "We always do, and nobody really minds except the Druids, and what the Druids don't know can't hurt them. The whole thing is purely symbolic in any case."

Eochaid thought that if it had not been for everything to do with Beltane being so inflexibly rooted in tradition, he would have cancelled the entire ceremony. He did not say this, because it might have given people odd ideas about him, but he thought that it was not going to be particularly entertaining to traipse through Tara singing the Beltane Chant, which nobody ever knew properly anyway and which people always spoiled by singing the wrong notes in the solemn parts and succumbing to unseemly mirth. It was going to be even less entertaining to have to stand around on the draughty Plain while the Druids conferred about the proper arrangement of the agaric and woodbine and rowan, and the imprisoned sacrifices set up an ear-splitting wailing. Still, it would look bad to say any of this, and so Eochaid donned his warmest robes and assumed an air of benevolent tolerance (he practised this in his looking glass until he got it just right) and then he went down to the central marble hall where the Court awaited him.

They were all there, of course. All the servants, dressed in their best and looking excited; all the footmen and the chambermaids and the cooks and the scullions. The *ollam* in their bird-feather cloaks, carefully assembled into order by Sean; and the *filid*, bright-eyed and gregarious. Eochaid thought suspiciously that several of the *filid* were a little too bright-eyed and a little too gregarious, and supposed they had been drinking poteen down in the village. Standing smartly correct were the King's Own Guard and the Captains and the sentinels, and close by were the ladies of the Court, cloaked and hooded, but doubtless silk-clad underneath, because everyone knew how Beltane would end. Mab stood a little apart, and Eochaid thought crossly that she was eyeing the King's Guard, and then thought that it was probably a bit unfair of him, because it would have been truer to say that the Guard were eyeing Mab.

The families of the Bloodline stood together, as tradition required, a little apart from the rest, and Eochaid paused and looked at them, because grouped like that, ceremoniously clad, there was a strength and an inhuman beauty about them. Conaire of the Eagles. Bolg of the Beavers. Bricriu of the Foxes, looking just the smallest bit out of breath as if he had only just arrived. And the others: a cousin of Cait Fian of the Wild Panthers, there to represent the people of Gallan; CuChulainn of the Chariot Horses; Oscar of the Deer. The twins, Midir and Etain of the White Swans. A tiny voice in Eochaid's head said, "And Cormac of the Wolves?" He frowned, remembered about looking benevolently tolerant, and then descended the stair.

There was the usual friendly scuffle for places, and the usual argument about the correct sequence of the procession, and which rooms should be visited in which order. The Councillors wanted to begin at the top and work down, but the servants—whom Eochaid considered were forgetting their place today—were all for starting in the sculleries and moving up to the grand bedchambers.

Conaire, who had spent the afternoon in company with a few friends and a puncheon or two of wine, was in favour of dealing with the bedchambers before anywhere else. "Naturally," said Bricriu sarcastically, but Sean the Storyteller, who had been so busy calming down Conaire and Bolg earlier that he had missed the midday meal, wanted to visit the sculleries before anywhere else. They might find any number of lights left irreligiously burning there, he said cunningly. To which Conaire, no respecter of a man's stomach, retorted: rubbish, didn't they all of them know it was the leftover venison Sean was interested in, and him as fat as seven pigs. Sean, who was not in the least fat, but who was regretting having missed the venison, scowled and said: well of course, when it came to it, it was His Majesty's decision anyway.

Several of the older Councillors shuffled uncomfortably and hoped that the stool rooms could be visited before they set out for the Plain because they'd been standing about for an hour as it was.

Eventually, Eochaid, who wished people would not continually look to him to make decisions, said that he could not see that the order mattered, but they would start at the top and work downwards. To himself he thought the sooner they got it all over with the better, but the Councillors nodded and looked pleased, and told each other how good it was to see the King keeping to the old ways. To start at the top and work downwards, dousing lights as you went, was how it was always done. Nobody mentioned the never-to-be-forgotten Beltane when Cormac, Conaire, and Cait Fian had paid a number of the village girls to hide in the main bedchambers, one to each room, and lie invitingly on the bed, quite naked, with lighted candles stuck in the most extraordinary parts of their anatomy for the Court to ceremonially quench. At least they might be sure that nothing like that would greet them any longer, said the older members of the Court, and did not listen when the younger ones said it was a shame.

And so the Court walked in solemn procession through the great Palace, dousing every light that was found, chanting one of the old traditional songs. Eochaid Bres sang as well, in his deep rumbling baritone, forgetting the second verse and coming in with the chorus at the wrong time, and being shushed by people at the front who did not realise that it was the King.

"His Majesty's got it wrong again," said Bolg sighing, and then turned to frown at Conaire who had started up a rival and rather rude version of the Chant, written by Sean many years ago under the influence of wine and the Wolfking. Eochaid continued quite happily with singing the wrong verse, but as he was at the back, it did not matter too much, and anyway it covered up Conaire's rude version.

As the last light was quenched (the little back scullery it had been, where vegetables were prepared) and Phineas closed the great West Gate with a flourish and a clanking of keys, Eochaid Bres thought that really it had all gone off quite well. Everyone had turned up, which was something to be thankful for, because you got years when people skulked off to the village to drink poteen, which was insulting, or went off to join

the Druids' procession, which was confusing for everyone else.
Say what you liked, it was a bit of an insult to the High King
when people did either of those things.

But everyone was here tonight, thought Eochaid, pleased
with his Court, grateful to his mother who was demurely
garbed and appeared to be behaving quite well. Of course she
had lured the young traveller to her bed last night. Eochaid
would rather not have known about it, but it was not the sort
of thing that could be kept secret at Tara, and in any case, he
had heard two of the sentries talking about it earlier on. Probably she was tired after such a night; she was getting on a bit
after all. And probably he was tired as well. Eochaid knew the
tales they told about his mother; he did not altogether believe
them, but he thought that if even half of them were true, the
young man ought to be good only for lying down quietly in a
darkened room somewhere. It was all that Eochaid Bres would
have been good for after that sort of a night. Anyway, the traveller Flynn did not seem to be anywhere in the procession.
Doubtless he was not far away.

FLYNN WAS NOT precisely frightened, but he was becoming
worried. Bricriu had been perfectly courteous, he had even
been a little obsequious, which Flynn did not care for, but the
invitation had been framed in a flattering way.

"Some of the pre-rituals," said Bricriu. "You will not have
witnessed them before, for they are unique to Tara. But for a
man of perception, they are extremely interesting. It would be
a pity for you to miss them. And the Druids are a fascinating
people. I have particularly requested permission to take you to
their settlement before the procession sets out from Tara." He
smiled, and for a second, the unmistakable fox's mask showed
on his face. "Once penetrated," said Bricriu, "the Druidic settlement often yields up many things."

Flynn's interest was at once caught; he thought it would be
churlish to refuse such a polite and pleasant invitation, and
he was rather curious about the Druids and the Beltane rituals.
He thought as well that once outside the Palace he might be
able to find Portan; perhaps the Druids might even be able to
tell him a little more about the *sidh*. Flynn could not believe
and refused to believe that there was no escape from them. He
thought that if he once accepted that Amairgen was lost for

good, he would surely be in despair. It occurred to him to wonder whether he was being foolish, whether he was clinging to
false hope, but he thought he could not bear to count
Amairgen as lost.

And so he went with Bricriu, just the two of them walking
sedately out of Tara. Flynn was reassured; he thought, outside
at last! and was ashamed of his earlier suspicions. Of course he
had not been kept prisoner by these charming clever people.
Of course he had been free to go at any time he chose. The
guards had not turned a hair as they walked through the West
Gate; the one who had explained to Flynn about it being dangerous to leave the Palace on Beltane Eve, even gave them
some kind of salute, which Bricriu returned.

They made not directly for the Plain, but for some kind of
village set a little apart from everything else, surrounded by a
fold of hillside. "For," said Bricriu, "the Druids greatly value
their privacy."

It was a longer walk than Flynn had expected. "It will take
perhaps half an hour," said Bricriu. "That will not concern
you?"

"Not in the least," said Flynn, and Bricriu sighed and remembered that the boy had spent the night in Mab's bed, and
wished he also could contemplate the walk to the Druids' settlement without blanching.

It felt strange to Flynn and somehow lonely to be crossing
terrain which was both familiar and alien. He knew a great
feeling of recognition as they skirted the hill which led to the
Plain of the Fál; he wondered whether it could really be possible that this was the place he had known as Tara's Hill.
Would the land not have altered beyond recognition? But he
thought that it was in truth the Tara's Hill he had known, and
he felt a twinge of fear, for surely it was against nature to be
straddling two worlds in this way? He knew an ache for the
much-loved farmhouse with the latticed windows and the low
ceilings and the scent of old seasoned beams and polished oak
floors, and he thought with anguish that he had lost Amairgen
and he had lost Portan, and he was no nearer to finding
Joanna. A wave of helplessness washed over him, and he
thought: what am I doing here, waiting for the commencement
of some pagan ritual that was long forgotten before I was
born? What am I doing on a long-dead hillside with this sly

half-human creature who is looking at me from the corners of
his eyes in a way that I do not trust. He remembered again
Bricriu's ancestry—Bricriu the Fox—and he remembered that
foxes were artful, cunning, out for themselves. Should he brush
off Bricriu's hand, which had been laid across his arm earlier
as if Bricriu needed assistance across the hillside? Assistance
my boots! thought Flynn. He's making sure I don't run away!
Shall I make a run for it? I could be free, out of his sight into
the forest.

Yes, and then what? And then nothing. It would be much
better to stay, thought Flynn, although he was not entirely sure
of this. But the Druids were ahead of them, and the Druids
were learned men who knew the world's secrets. They might
be able to help him.

I shall stay long enough to meet them, thought Flynn, but on
another level, his mind was furiously working out plans for an
escape.

And then they crested the fold of the hillside which protected the Druids' settlement, and at the sight that met his eyes
Flynn forgot all other considerations.

IT WAS TOLD by later ages, that the ancient and learned Druids
of Ireland were no better than eccentric poets, dilettante sorcerers, bands of men who eschewed the world for varying reasons, or elected to live apart from the rest of the community.
Certainly, their activities were surrounded by a cloak of the utmost secrecy, and equally certainly, no one had ever dared of-
fend them, although it is possible, and even probable, that they
themselves offended many.

Flynn did not know anything about them, other than odd
snippets and tag-ends of conversation he had picked up during
his brief sojourn inside the Bright Palace. But he had received
the vague impression that they were rather scholarly, rather absentminded people; unsocial rather than anti-social, given to
studying ancient, slightly ephemeral matters. He had thought of
them as visionaries of some kind, concerned with incorporeal
things. This, of course, was precisely what Bricriu, his plans
laid, had wished him to think.

The Druids of Tara, under the Wolfkings and later under the
first Lionking, were, in fact, very much concerned with corpo-
real things. They were very much concerned with Flynn.

It was not immediately apparent. As Flynn and Bricriu crested the little ridge of hill and walked slowly down to the huddle of stone buildings, they were accorded a quiet, courteous welcome. There was no reason for Flynn to suddenly remember Phineas the Gatekeeper's warning when he and Amairgen had first entered Tara: "Quite polite he'll be," Phineas had said. "The Lions are always polite before they eat you."

Were the Druids also polite before they ate you? This is absolutely ridiculous said Flynn to himself, but still that little core of unease persisted, and he looked about him for some means of escape.

It was difficult to see where escape might lie. The settlement consisted of low, rather austere houses, four-square and small-windowed; entirely undecorated and unadorned, as if the Druids sought only to shelter themselves from the worst of the elements, and had no time for and no interest in making their abodes attractive. There was a central area which was clearly used for communal fire, and there was some kind of temple set a little way up the hillside, with stone pillars and archways and a great marble altar. I won't look at the altar, thought Flynn, but he did look at it.

With a feeling of *déjà vu* he remembered another night in another world, when he had been welcomed into the centre of a group of hooded and cloaked men on a dark hillside. But the Keepers of the Secret had been friendly; the Druids of Tara seemed friendly enough, but their eyes were calculating, watchful, as if they might be thinking: oh yes, this one will suit our purpose very nicely.

Behind them, dominating the settlement, was the immense figure of the Wicker Man. "A particularly good creation this year," said one of them, and Flynn, his senses by now abnormally alert, fastened upon the word "creation", and remembered all the stories of all the brilliant insane people down the ages who believed themselves to have created human life. Just supposing . . .

And then the Druid said, rather dismissively, "Of course, the imprisoned animals give it a spurious air of life," and Flynn relaxed. He stood for a moment, looking at the Wicker Man, thinking that he had known what to expect—everyone at the Court had described it to him—but thinking as well that none

of the descriptions had conveyed the sheer size or the menace
of the Wicker Man. It had been fashioned in exquisite and loving detail; eyes, lips, nipples, fingernails, genitals. It was at
least forty feet in height and Flynn, disturbed and disoriented,
found it easy to think that it might at any moment lift its great
feet, open its blank eyes, and begin striding across the dark
hillside to the Plain of the Fál, crushing the woodland creatures
beneath as it went. The animals imprisoned inside it were trying to escape; Flynn could hear the scrabbling of claws and the
beating of wings; there was a continual bleating and whining
and fluttering. He was sickened; to humanely kill another living creature so that you might survive, was to Flynn under-
standable, even desirable. His world had survived by doing
that. But to throw at least a dozen living, breathing creatures
into the centre of a roaring fire was a thing that left him feeling nauseated. Did these people, these apparently cultivated
and learned men, truly believe that burning alive animals and
birds would ensure a good harvest? They are savages, thought
Flynn in horror. I am alone on a dark hillside with a group of
murderous savages!

There was a movement behind him and he turned sharply.
But—"It is our good friend Bricriu," said the Druid, who had
spoken earlier. "He is returning to the Palace to play his part
in the procession."

"Then perhaps I should return with him," said Flynn, his
heart beginning to beat uncomfortably fast.

"Oh no," said the Druid softly. "You will play your part in
your own procession, Flynn."

Although Flynn possessed the ancient and magical Samhailt,
and although it had strengthened and grown in him since he
had broken through the Time Curtain, now it was another, far
older instinct that awoke in him. That extra sense that the first
men of all had possessed, the sense that warns when danger is
near, became fiercely alive in Flynn now: these people are going to kill me!

"Yes," said the Druid calmly. "Yes, we are going to kill you.
You are surprised that I know your thoughts? You should not
be, you have the Samhailt yourself. And it is one of the tenets
of our faith. The present High King in his wisdom has outlawed it, but to forbid a thing does not unmake it. Out here we
have polished and honed the Samhailt to a very fine degree in-

deed. You cannot conceal your thoughts from us, Flynn." He looked at Flynn searchingly, and rather kindly, and Flynn, transfixed, thought: he quite likes me. He is going to kill me, but even so, he rather likes me. He is quite sorry about it.

"I am afraid it is necessary," said the Druid. "The Wicker Man must have a human sacrifice. If it can be contrived, that is. And you have been—"

"Sold to you?"

"Let us say passed into our keeping as a suitable sacrifice," said the Druid. "You should not mind. It is an honorable death. And I would be glad of your forgiveness first."

Flynn nearly laughed out loud and then was horrified. But he had heard the old stories of the rulers who existed long before the Letheans, who had not scrupled to execute their enemies, summarily and very publicly. And always, the executioner had asked the victim's pardon first. Will you forgive me for cutting off your head, for strangling you on a gibbet, for tearing out your entrails? They had devised some grisly deaths, those people. Were they any worse than the one I am about to face? To be cast, alive and well, into the heart of a huge bonfire. To feel skin scorch, bones crack. To hear the sizzling of your own hair and eyes, and to smell your flesh roasting . . . Oh please don't let me be sick, not in front of them all.

He was not sick but he was unable to speak. He was certainly unable to turn and run. And even if he had, there were thirty—forty—of them to overtake him.

There was no escape as the Druids closed in and bound him neatly and efficiently. They kept him firmly in their grasp, this stranger, this traveller, this credible fool who had walked trustingly and unsuspectingly at the Fox's side, and who had entered, of his own volition, into their hands. A fragment of an old song which Sean had been singing at the Palace a night or two back slid into Flynn's mind.

"O never go walking at Beltane at dusk
In company of one whom you think not to trust.
For the Druids are out and they're looking for souls,
They'll cut out your heart and they'll roast it.

O never go walking on the Plain after dark
On Beltane when the Fires are a-burning;

For the Druids will find you and bind you up tight
And feed you to the Wicker Man to keep the Fire
burning."

But I went walking! cried Flynn, in silent anguish. I went walking on Beltane, and now the Druids have bound me! God help me, they will feed me into the Wicker Man and I shall burn alive.

He was hoisted shoulder high by four of the Druids and carried quite gently to where the Wicker Man waited.

IT WAS DARK inside the Wicker Man and very cramped. Flynn could smell the frightened animals above and below him. He thought that they knew what was going to happen; they sensed it, poor creatures.

He was about halfway up the framework, in its ribcage. "In its heart," said the Druids, nodding with satisfaction. He was at least twenty feet from the ground, and it was a dizzying, disembodied feeling; Flynn had the impression that his compartment was suspended in midair.

The wicker cage was tightly shut. "And there is a minor spell," said the Druid who had talked to Flynn. "You will not be able to escape."

Even so, Flynn had torn his hands to ribbons and broken his nails trying to get out.

And then, far below him, the Druids formed into single file, and took up small burning torches, so that Flynn could see them quite clearly. There was a sudden jolt as the ropes of the cart that held the Wicker Man were pulled tight, and then, without warning, the Druids' procession began, the Wicker Man lurching across the dark countryside on the little wheeled cart, the torches casting huge fantastic shadows on the quiet hillside. The outline of the Wicker Man stretched out ahead of the procession, and ahead of them, Flynn could see Tara's Hill with the Palace procession moving at the same speed. They were converging on the Plain. The dark bulk of the Beltane Fire was clearly visible, and Flynn clutched helplessly at the wicker framework that imprisoned him. He stared at the unlit Beltane Fire. I helped to build that. I carried woodbine, sweet scented and warm, and rich red rowan and agaric. I built up my own funeral pyre. He closed his eyes against the sickening lurching of the Wicker Man, and tried to will himself back through the Time Curtain, back to the safe rather dull world of Tugaim and the comfortable familiar farmhouse.

But I cannot leave without Joanna! he thought, and then remembered that he would soon be beyond helping Joanna anyway. He thought he was certainly going to die, and he thought as well that he would have given anything in the world—his five senses, anything—for a last sight of her. If he could be sure that she was safe somewhere ... if he could be sure that she had not been killed in some grisly pagan sacrifice as he was shortly going to be killed ... He could not be sure. He could indeed believe with ease that Joanna was already dead, that she had been a helpless victim of Druids, of half-humans or wild forest creatures. Then I might as well die also, thought Flynn.

The Druids had begun a strange monotonous chant, neither quite singing nor quite chanting, and from the Plain came an answering chant. From the depths of his despair, Flynn heard it, and in hearing, felt something lift within him. He was transfixed by the dreadful inevitability of his death, but a part of him was beginning to be mesmerised by the chant now. He remembered Amairgen's words about despair: *accidie* he had called it, and how it had once been known as the ultimate sin; the total and complete abandonment of all hope. At least, thought Flynn, I am not counted dead until I am in the heart of the flames, and managed to repress a sick shudder. A tiny green shoot of hope sprang up. Was it at all possible that he could escape? Even now, even so close to the Plain that he could make out the moving figures below him. Was there some hope of escape there? Would Sean or Conaire or Mab help him? He thought they would not; he thought they were probably accustomed to the idea of human sacrifice, and he thought that salvation, if salvation existed, would not come from the Plain ... It would come from Flynn himself.

The strange, strong chant was reaching corners of his mind he had not known existed; it was casting light on the shadowed areas of his soul. He listened and opened his mind to it, and thought it sounded like a form of question and answer. Interrogation and response. From the depths of his memory—his or someone else's—he sought and found the word "catechism." This was some kind of catechism. If he could understand the language they were using, he would understand what was going on. In his by-now wildly abnormal state, it began to seem to Flynn that if he could decipher this ancient, strangely pure speech, he would also decipher the shackles of the spell that sealed him within the wicker cage. He closed his eyes and his hands curled about the wooden bars, and he listened with every fibre of his body, with every nerve-ending raw as the Druids' procession approached the Plain of the Fál.

CHAPTER FIFTEEN

IF IT HAD not been for Portan, Amairgen would not have survived. It was nothing to do with despair or pain, although he had travelled both these emotions since the *sidh* cast him out.

It was simply a matter of practicality. He could not have found his way through the forest. Although one day very soon, I might, he thought. For the moment, however, even with his hearing becoming more finely tuned with every hour, even with the Samhailt flooding his body in great rainbow waves, he could not have kept to the woodland paths. He certainly could not have found food or water.

But Portan was untiring and sure-footed and watchful. She held his arm and guided him; she kept to the path, even when it was overgrown and very nearly impossible to find, and she talked as they went along, telling him about the wildlife and the forest greenery, trying to make him see it with her, certainly helping him to hear it.

"So beautiful, Amairgen. I had never thought to see such things. The sunlight pouring in from overhead, making patterns on the forest floor. Great clumps of wild flowers. And the greens. So many different shades of green."

Amairgen said softly, "Forty shades of green. A very old song, Portan. How lovely to know it did not lie."

"Many more than forty," said Portan.

They stopped from time to time. "For," said Portan, "we shall do no good to anyone if we reach Tara exhausted and fainting from hunger." At midday, with the sun high above the trees, dappling the leaves, and the wild dog rose scenting the entire forest, they found a small clear stream. "Water,

Amairgen. That is very good. And I think there are fish of some kind. Yes, several of them. If I am very nimble . . ."

She was very nimble indeed, and within ten minutes four smallish but plump fish lay on a large, dry dockleaf.

"And I believe we can make a fire," said Portan. "For Flynn left some tinders in his cloak—yes, here! Do I just move the tinder across the dull strip, Amairgen?"

"You do, my dear." Amairgen knew another wave of gratitude. He thought: she is endeavouring to make me feel necessary, she is seeking my help. But he thought that perhaps Portan did need his help, perhaps she had truly never used a tinder box before, and he was glad to be able to explain. Portan listened carefully, and presently managed to get a small fire burning, a cautious arrangement of twigs and leaves. The fish grilled gently at the ends of pointed sticks.

"And they smell good, don't they, Amairgen? They are rather small, but they are quite plump. I do not know what you would call them."

"Trout?" said Amairgen, and at once Portan was overwhelmed with the memories of a life that had existed before the Gealtacht. Long drowsy afternoons, herself as a small child, safe and protected. Father returning from a fishing trip, smiling and triumphant. The unmistakable scent of freshly caught trout being toasted before the fire. Mother had always plucked fresh parsley and chopped it, and Portan had been allowed to help. It was like looking back through a long dark tunnel and remembering that once, at the very beginning, there had been sunlight.

When Amairgen said in a practical tone, "Portan, if we had any parsley we would have a feast indeed," Portan jumped, because quite suddenly he was there with her, he was in the memory with her, and the sunlight, after all, was still here.

The parsley was there, growing quite near, in thick feathery clumps. Portan gathered it and cut it into tiny sprigs with Amairgen's knife, and touched Amairgen's hand and said, "A feast indeed," and thought that it was surely strange to feel so very happy in such a very unhappy situation, but felt happy all the same. And: *I am bringing him back,* she thought. He is returning to the real world. She leaned back and watched Amairgen, and ate the fish, and felt delight stir within her. Yes, I shall bring him back.

But there was still the agony of not knowing about Flynn, and when Portan said, "Amairgen, what of Flynn?" unease stirred the quiet content of the forest.

Amairgen leaned back against the bole of a tree, and thought: she is one of the most remarkable people I have ever known. I must let her know she can still depend on me, he thought; we must rescue Flynn, and Portan cannot do it alone. She must know that I can still guide her. For the first time in several hours, he felt his mind focus on something other than his own loss. When he said, "I left Flynn inside the Bright Palace," it was the voice of the Amairgen who had brought them through the Time Curtain, and Portan heard it and rejoiced.

"I feel that he is in danger," said Amairgen, and Portan said slowly, "Yes," for she, also, felt that Flynn was in some way threatened.

"You do not possess the Samhailt, my dear," said Amairgen's voice, suddenly, "but I think you possess something very like it."

"He is in danger," said Portan in a low voice. "Amairgen, is he still inside the Bright Palace?"

"I don't know. But that is where we must start." And then— "Can you lead the way?"

"Of course."

And Tara, the Shining Citadel, with its own iridescence, was easy enough to see even by night when it was safe to travel. Portan thought it was a beacon, a lodestar, drawing all who saw it into its glowing depths. Perhaps one day I shall be able to see it properly, she thought. But she only said, "It is getting dark now. Almost twilight. I think we shall not be seen by anyone."

The trees had thinned out now, and they were looking across the plain. Amairgen had known for some time that the Purple Hour had fallen, he could smell it and he could feel the velvet chill of the night air. He could taste the new scents of the night forest waking all about them.

And colours are something to drink, and light is something that soaks through your skin, and sounds and feelings can be scooped up and allowed to run through your hands like thin sand . . .

At his side, Portan gasped, and her hand came out to his,

and Amairgen said at once, "What is it? What has happened?" And waited and felt puzzlement and unease from her.

"I am not sure." Tara was a blaze of colour. Beautiful. "I have never seen anything so truly lovely, ever, Amairgen. And then—" Portan hesitated, and then went on. "It is beginning to dim. Little by little, the light draining from it. As if a great hand came out from the sky and doused it. As if something quenched its light."

At her side, Amairgen said softly, *"Light Ethereal, first of things, quintessence pure."*

"What is that?"

"I am not sure. Something once written or forgotten or dreamed."

"By someone dead?"

"Or someone not yet born. It does not matter." But with the vagrant memory, had come another: *I feel and seek the light I cannot see.* Anguish threatened to overwhelm him again, but Amairgen put it from him angrily, because there was no time now to think of what had happened. Flynn was somewhere inside the darkening Tara, and Flynn was threatened, and they must somehow save him.

At length, Portan said softly, "It is entirely in darkness now. I can barely see Tara, only I know it is there."

And I shall never see it again, but I also know it is there, thought Amairgen. And then another memory stirred, and he said, "Of course. It is Beltane. Portan, they have put out the lights for Beltane. They are lighting the Sacred Fire, and every light in Ireland must be doused, so that the Sacred Fire of the Druids is the only one to burn."

"Oh I did not know about that." Portan stayed where she was, watching the dark countryside.

Presently she said, "I can see a row of lights. On the—I think you would say the western side of the Palace. To the left. Bobbing pinpoints of light. A procession of some kind would it be?"

"The Beltane revelries," said Amairgen softly. "So the Fires did, after all, burn at Tara. Do you know, that is something that scholars down the ages have argued over. How extraordinary. Can you see anything that looks like a bonfire, my dear?"

Portan's heart sang within her at the "my dear," but she only said, "There is something. It is difficult to make out, but I think it *is* a fire. Not yet lit. And there are two separate processions now, both making their way towards the fire. They have torches—yes, I can see the figures now in the firelight. There are a great many people, Amairgen."

"Converging on the Plain of the Fál," said Amairgen in a whisper. "Remarkable." And then, tilting his head, "Portan, listen. Do you hear?"

"Something. But so faintly. I am sorry," said Portan, apologetically. "What is it?"

"The Sacred Chant of the Druids," said Amairgen. "It must be. The Lost Tongue of the Cruithin. Question and answer. Interrogation and response.

" 'We have the Wicker Man.'
" 'Do you have the Human?'
" 'We have the Human.'
" 'Is he ready for the Sacred Fire?'
" 'He is ready.' "

In the silence that followed, Portan grasped Amairgen's hand. Both knew in that moment that it was Flynn who was the human sacrifice. It was Flynn who was going to be offered up on the Beltane Fire.

QUESTION AND ANSWER. Demand and acquiescence. Flynn began to hear the pattern of the Druids' Chant, he began to feel the unfamiliar cadences soak in through his skin and he began to see a shape, a form, a logic.

And I have heard this one before . . .

There was no time to give any attention to the brief tug of memory; nevertheless, Flynn was strongly aware of it and it heartened him. Finn of the *Fiana*, if ever you existed, and if ever I existed in you, then help me now.

There was no response, but in the dark places of Flynn's mind something stirred, and for the briefest of instants there was a tumble of images; a bright hillside with a clear blue sky and a young dark-haired man seated astride a great black stallion, leading a battle charge . . . the scent and the heat of half a dozen victories . . . crusades to the wild and desolate northern islands in a great carved ship with a wolf's head at the prow and the water beneath like glass . . . riding through the trees with the evening sun dappling the forest floor . . . And then the last, the most vivid image of all: a gathering like this one, the Plain of the Fál, with the Court and the Druids and the shape of the Wicker Man rearing against the night sky, packed tight with mewling victims . . .

Mental strength swept through Flynn and with it a huge unstoppable confidence. *I know the Ancient Druidic Chant.* I have heard it before and I have played a part in the ceremony. Once I could understand it, and now I shall understand it again.

He bent his mind to a concentration so absolute, that everything else was blotted out, so that he no longer saw the measured procession far below him, or the bobbing lights, or the threatening phallic shape of the unlit fire. He no longer felt the jolting of the journey as the Wicker Man was towed across the last stretch of terrain. He was Finn of the *Fiana* once more, and he was invoking all of the race-memories and all of the knowledge of that warrior.

The chant was becoming a tangible thing to Flynn now; through his half-closed eyes he could see it forming on the night air; a thin glittering silver cord, reaching out from the Druids to the High King's party and back again, not quite real, but not quite a vision. He thought: I have it. I have the Chant. All I must do is take hold of it with my mind. I must wrap my mind about that silver cord.

A silver cord. A silver chain that binds . . . a girdle to encircle the earth . . . I will put a girdle about the world . . . shackles of darkness and death . . .

Flynn shook his head impatiently. The images were wrong, they were too new, too closely aligned to a transient world. The Chant was older by far, it belonged to the far past, when men had talked with gods, and when gods had walked the earth. If he was to wrap his mind about it and hold it and fathom it, he must go farther back, farther back to the dawn of the world, when the land was dew-spattered and wreathed in mist, and then back even farther, into the great darkness that had existed before the dawn . . .

I am Dagda, the god of fire and life and I am a jealous god . . .

Flynn's eyes flew open and knowledge and understanding flooded him in brilliant painful waves.

I brought you out of the darkness of ignorance and out of the time of famine . . .

Great lights were exploding in Flynn's brain, and silently he formed the words that came next.

You shall have no other gods but me. I shall send my curses and vengeance upon the seed of those that do not serve me.

And then a pause, a break in the harshness.

But I shall give my bounty to those that love me, and to those that render me sacrifice.

Excitement was beating against Flynn's consciousness. *Nearly there*, I am nearly there. The silver cord thickened and took on substance.

Great and powerful Dagda, father god of all the gods, look on these your servants. Grant to them your bounty that they may live in plenty and in fruitfulness. Show unto them your mercy that they may be free from all want.

And again the change of pace, the feeling of indrawn breath, of strengths being mustered. And hard on the heels of that, the command, ringing out across the Plain.

Fall down and worship your god!

Again the silence, again the thrumming of the cord. Sweat was dripping into Flynn's eyes; he must keep hold of this tenuous thing, he must understand not just the commands but their responses.

Again it came. *Fall down and worship your god!*

Nothing. A silence. Flynn was beyond movement, beyond thought now. The moment lengthened. He thought in terror: I am losing it.

A third time came the command. *FALL DOWN AND WORSHIP YOUR GOD!*

And at last, blessedly, from the Plain, the response.

We worship our god. Flynn thought: of *course*, the magical three. Of course the question must be put three times. How could I have forgotten.

The dialogue came swiftly now, tumbling out, but Flynn had reached down into race-memory, until he was Finn of the *Fiana* again, participating in the Druids' ceremonies. He whispered the responses with the High King and the Court now.

Let us render up the Sacrifice
And let it be done as it was at the beginning of Time.
Dagda, look mercifully upon thy servants.
That render to thee homage.
Send to us the fruits of the earth.

And for ever make us free of want.

Dagda hear our prayer.

And let our offering rise up to thee.

As they ascended the hillside, Flynn's thoughts were racing ahead. There would be a moment in the ceremony—he knew it quite surely now—when the Druids would be asked: *Do you have the Sacrifice?* And the Druids must make the prescribed answer: *We have the Sacrifice.*

Understanding opened up. Flynn knew with an absolute and unshakeable certainty that the question and that answer was the heart and the core and the pivot of the Beltane Ceremony. Once the Druids had admitted to having ready the sacrifice—no matter whether it was human or animal or both—then the enchantment would leap forward and the Sacred Flame would kindle and Flynn would be lost.

Do you have the Sacrifice?

If a denial was given, the spells would splinter and Flynn would be safe.

PORTAN MOVED STEALTHILY up the hillside, hidden from the circle of people, more frightened than she had ever been in her life.

Amairgen had taken her face between his hands before she left him in the cover of the trees; he had said, "Portan, you must send me your thoughts. All the time. You must not for an instant lose me."

Portan said, "But I do not possess—"

"It does not matter. I have it in sufficient strength for us both now. Listen. Close your eyes and listen." And he had stood very still, a faraway look on his face, and Portan had obediently closed her eyes; after a moment she had felt his thoughts flowing effortlessly into her mind. Clear, undiluted. Encouragement. Love. And strength. You can do it, my dear. And then: I cannot go with you for I should hinder you, but you can rescue Flynn.

"I will be with you all of the way," said Amairgen, and then hesitated. "My dear, if there was any other way—"

But there was no other way, and Amairgen cupped her face in his hands and kissed her.

The kiss helped, but what helped more was the measure of Amairgen's confidence. He trusts me to rescue Flynn, thought

Portan, her heart beating fast. We both know there is nothing else to be done, but still he trusts me. Can I do it? Oh, but I must. Amairgen, are you there? She waited and at once came the response. I am with you, my dear.

Even so, it was the most difficult thing she had ever done to go up the dark hillside, keeping low and close to the ground to where the Court stood assembled, a waiting circle about the unlit fire, single flaring torches giving life, unnatural and weird, to the shadowy figures.

Portan paused once and looked at them, seeing as Flynn and Amairgen had both seen, the faint but unmistakable signs of the Bloodline. Not quite animal, but not entirely human. I suppose I should find them frightening, thought Portan, but I do not . . . I feel a kinship with them.

That is why you do not find them frightening, Portan.

Of course. I never thought of that. Portan glanced across to the people of the Court again.

The Druids were coming over the brow of the hill now, their hooded figures outlined against the sky, and with them came the immense figure of the Wicker Man. Portan's heart almost misgave her; she crouched in the bracken looking up at the figure, and saw in the flickering twilight the scurrying frightened animals behind the cages. Flynn was somewhere there.

The Druids had come to a stop now; they stood motionless, their heads bowed, facing the Court across the fire. The priests and the supplicants.

Oh yes, came Amairgen's thoughts. Oh yes, that is how all ceremonies were carried out. One to command and one to obey.

In another minute, Portan would have to move from the friendly darkness and skirt the edges of the circle of light. She would have to swarm up the outside of the Wicker Man and find Flynn and let him out.

> *But not yet, my dear. Wait until the fire is lit.*
> *I think that will be too late.*
> *Then wait until the Chant begins again.*
> *Amairgen I cannot do it—*
> *You must!*

* * *

SHE MUST DO it, of course she must. She gulped and took a few breaths of air.

Two of the Druids had stepped forward now, they were making ready to fire the bonfire in four separate places. Orange and red flames leapt into the air, and a movement went through the watchers. Portan moved, a silent shadow, darting round to where the Druids stood, and waited in the deep shadow cast by the Wicker Man's legs. In another minute they would begin the Chant again—Amairgen had said so—and the sounds would muffle any sounds she might make.

There was a moment of the deepest silence and then the Chief Druid stepped forward and held out both his hands, palms upwards.

"Dagda hear our pleas,
"And let our sacrifice rise unto thee."

In Portan's mind exploded a single command: Now! and she reached up to grasp the lower rungs that formed the Wicker Man's legs, pulling herself upwards, thinking she must not look down, trying to concentrate on sending out her thoughts to Amairgen.

I am climbing, Amairgen . . . I am swarming up the outside of the frame and it is a strange and sinister experience . . . but I am going up and up, one hand over the next, and I am reaching the knees . . .

The knees were jointed, incredibly lifelike, and Portan repressed a shudder, because it was very easy indeed to think that the knees would suddenly shiver with life, that the legs would lift and stride forward. She thought: I am climbing the body of a giant, and if he looks down on me from his great height with his carved wooden implacable face, he will brush me off as if I was a fly.

An effigy, Portan. A man of wood and straw. No more.

Below her, the Court and the Druids were taking their places as if for the climax of the ceremonies; there was a tremendous sense of excitement rising up from the Plain, an immense feeling of anticipation. Something is going to happen, thought Portan, grimly clinging on, hauling herself up farther; something is going to happen. Oh please let me reach Flynn before they begin their ceremonies again.

Every muscle was protesting now; even so, thought Portan, determined not to give in, even so, I am better equipped for this than an ordinary person. The extra arms which were not quite arms, but not quite legs, helped her to pull herself upwards; the jointed half-hands half-feet enabled her to cling to the wicker bars. I am aching all over and the pain is becoming intolerable, but there is not so very much farther to go.

She caught a thought from Amairgen—Can you see Flynn? and she paused, her eyes searching the interior of the giant, trying not to wince from the sight of the caged creatures.

Not yet. There are all kinds of birds and animals, but I cannot see Flynn. And yet I know he is here. The Samhailt was flooding her mind now, and she through Amairgen's perception could feel Flynn's closeness as strongly as she had ever felt anything in her life. Flynn was here, he was imprisoned inside this great and terrible effigy and Portan would soon reach him. The knowledge lent her fresh strength, and she went up and up, hand over hand, finding footholds in the hinged doors, clinging to the rough wickerwork, barely feeling and certainly not caring about the myriad of splinters that were penetrating her hands and arms and feet, ignoring the rough dry wood that was scraping her body in a dozen different places.

Go on my dear, go on Portan.

She was beginning to feel dizzy with being so high up, and she knew she must not look down, not for an instant. But with that thought: I must not look down—came the overwhelming urge to do so. The world swung and far below she glimpsed the fire and she saw that the congregation had formed a circle about the fire, and that two of the Druids had stepped forward and were holding aloft two flaming torches. At any moment they would begin the terrible culmination of the ceremony . . . A low murmur was stirring the watchers and Portan gulped and shivered and pressed her face into the sharp rough wood, sick and dizzy. Night wind cooled the sweat on her face and on her limbs, and she felt the intense excitement of the congregation as if it was a tangible thing.

But I am surely not far from Flynn now. Amairgen, I am surely nearly there.

He will be in the heart. Go for the heart.

Portan was about a third of the way up; she thought she was just clear of the thighs and just over the jutting hip bone. It was fairly important to keep on this side, to keep in the deep shadow away from the firelight, but she thought she would probably not really be seen from the ground. Inside the giant, the captured animals were a seething mass of frightened life; the Wicker Man's entire frame was moving and pulsating, and Portan thought they would not be able to tell that she was outside of the giant instead of inside it.

As she inched her way under the ribcage and on up to the heart cavity, all noise from the Plain ceased quite suddenly, and Portan froze.

The Druids circled the fire and the flames seemed to respond, flaring into the dark night sky, orange and red and yellow. The scent of smoke filled Portan's nostrils. On the ground, the Druids moved towards the Wicker Man, and Portan grasped the jutting ribcage and began to haul, hand over hand, the last few feet towards the heart.

And then the Druids began to chant again.

IT WAS WHAT Flynn, motionless inside the heart, had been waiting for. The renewal of the Chant. The final imperious question.

Do you have the Sacrifice?

It rang out clearly and terribly across the Plain, and a tidal wave of emotion washed over the congregation. Wait, thought Flynn, wait for the second and then the third. Remember the mystical three, remember that they will send out the question three times.

The second cry rang out, and the crowd surged closer to the fire. *Do you have the Sacrifice?* Flynn tensed, waiting, feeling his muscles cramp and leap. He must answer the third demand, he must break the enchantment before the crowd gave the answer, his timing of the ancient reply must be absolute . . .

The third time the question rang out. *Do you have the Sacrifice?*

There was another of those moments of such utter and profound silence that Flynn thought the world had stopped.

And then—"No!" cried Flynn in the secret Lost Language that once he had known as well as he knew his name. "No! We have not your Sacrifice!"

The compartment fell open of its own accord, and Flynn saw Portan clinging to the wicker frame immediately below, her eyes huge and smudged with fear and exhaustion.

They half fell, half climbed down the Wicker Man, sliding

and tumbling and skidding, their hands scorched and raw, their minds racing with the need to escape quickly, quickly.

Both of them were strongly aware of Amairgen urging them on; hurry, oh hurry, you are in such danger, you are surrounded by such anger, the Druids are furious with you and they will be merciless . . . They will fling you wholesale into the heart of the fire if they catch you . . .

Flynn and Portan knew it, for both could feel the immense dull red waves of fury from the Druids and the thin waves of puzzlement from the people of the Court. Even so, in the midst of the shouts and upheaval, delight burst in Flynn to hear Amairgen again and to know him somehow safe.

This is no time for sentiment, Flynn. Reserve your energies for escape.

Flynn thought that if he could spare the time for amusement, he would be very amused indeed, for the thought was so characteristic of Amairgen.

They had reached the ground now, and Flynn drew Portan into the lee of the giant's feet. The congregation was in tumult; the Druids were searching the undergrowth, swishing angrily at the grass and the low bushes with lighted torches, here and there setting up small fires that burned up into the dry night with a sharp acrid tang. Flynn thought that the Court was bewildered rather than anything else; they had been engrossed in the ceremony and in the ancient ritual of question and answer, and they had thought, if they thought about it at all, that the sacrifices were only those of animals. Unpleasant but bearable. Despite his panic and the urgency to get himself and Portan away, Flynn felt a rush of gratitude. He had thought some of the Court his friends; he had certainly thought them kindly disposed towards him, and he was glad to see that most of them had not been aware of the fact that the Wicker Man had held a human sacrifice. He caught sight of Mab standing a little apart, and for a moment something deep within him stirred, so that he wanted to go to her and take her hand and say: come with us. Come into the forest and the darkness away from these strange half-human people who think little of live sacrifice and who deal in death and treachery. And then he remembered that Mab herself was not entirely human—Lionblood! said his mind warningly—and the moment passed, and he took Portan's hand and smiled down at her encouragingly and saw with anguish how white and frightened she was, and how her hands were streaked with blood and how the skin was torn and blistered.

Portan looked back and an infinitely sweet smile spread over her face. "Flynn," she said. "Oh Flynn."

Flynn grinned and tightened his hold. "Now," he said. "Are you ready to run? Then to the forest, my dear!"

SAFELY IN THE depths of the forest, sufficiently far from the enraged Druids to begin to feel out of their reach, and concealed by the closely growing trees, Flynn looked at his two companions. His composure broke at last. Tears poured down his face as he embraced Amairgen and for a moment he was unable to speak.

Amairgen, very much moved, but as always more in control than the volatile Flynn, said, "You thought never to see me again, Flynn. I am quite aware of your thoughts. I do beg you to be less emotional." But he smiled as he said this, and his hands held Flynn's tightly.

Flynn said in a whisper, "What did they do to you?"

"It is a good tale," said Amairgen levelly. "And one day I will tell you the whole. But not now." He laid his hand on Flynn's shoulder, and Flynn, only partly understanding, clasped the hand. One day Amairgen would tell of what happened in the dim Caves of the *sidh*, but it would not be until the memory had dimmed, and it would certainly not be until he had accepted his sightlessness a little more fully.

Flynn bent to where Portan sat curled up, watching them both, her eyes shining with happiness.

"Oh my dear," he said gently, and with such love that Portan thought her heart would surely burst with sheer joy. She had saved Flynn, just as she had saved Amairgen, and surely, surely, there could be no greater happiness than this. If she could just keep this moment as it was now; if she could cup it in her hands and keep it forever, so that one day, in some future that might not hold Flynn or Amairgen, she could unfold the memory and re-live it and think: oh yes, that was the day I knew pure happiness.

Flynn took her hands and kissed them. "Poor grazed hands," he said. "All for my sake. Portan, I do not deserve what you did, but I shall never forget it."

Portan said, rather unsteadily, "I have only repaid what you and Amairgen did for me when you rescued me from the Gealtacht. I am glad to do it, Flynn." And thought that after all the danger and the anguish had been almost worthwhile. For they are both here safe, they are both with me, and we shall go on together now, and find Flynn's Joanna. And although once there would have been a tiny secret pain at the knowledge of Flynn's devotion to Joanna, Portan could accept this now.

Because there is Amairgen? said a tiny part of her mind. Because Amairgen needs you and called you "my dear" and kissed you before you went out on to the Plain? Well, perhaps. Perhaps it is that he needs me, and perhaps it is a little more than that. She smiled, and thought how truly wonderful it was to be able to do so again, and curled back into her position against the tree, and listened to their plans.

Flynn was saying, "Truly, Amairgen, I do not believe that Joanna was ever inside Tara. Certainly she was never anywhere near to the Druids' settlement, for they would have—" He stopped.

Amairgen said gently, "They would have saved her for the sacrifice tonight, as well as you. Yes, of course they would, Flynn."

"Therefore," said Flynn, "it is possible that she is safe somewhere." And looked at them both, so that in the dim light Portan saw the pleading in his eyes, and searched for the words to reassure him.

"It is possible," she said at length, "that she has fallen in with some—some quite ordinary people, and is being looked after."

"That is true," said Amairgen, listening. "For there are surely many perfectly ordinary people here. Cruithin and others."

"Yes." Flynn found this was easily believable; he thought that Portan and Amairgen were both sensible, logical people, and their reasoning was probably sound. He rather hoped that he was not believing them only because he wanted to believe it, and put this thought from him. Of course Joanna was safe somewhere. Of course they were going to find her. Anything else was intolerable. And although he knew they were all tired and battered, he was aching to be on the move again, and his mind was racing on ahead, planning where their search should be next, watching the sky for signs of dawn, and knowing that there were hours yet before the first streaks of light would appear.

But when Amairgen tentatively suggested that they might travel by night quite safely, Flynn said at once, "No, it is more important that we rest tonight and conserve our strength." And put his hand on Amairgen's, to thank him for his suggestion.

Amairgen said, "Even so, Flynn, the Druids will continue to search for you. They will be angry at being made fools of, and they will certainly be angry at having their Sacred Ritual ruined."

Flynn glanced to where the light of the Beltane Fire still glowed, and Amairgen, sensing the movement, said, "Are we sufficiently far from the Plain to be safe for a time?"

Flynn hesitated, for he did not really think they were far enough to be safe, but Portan said, "Oh yes, we will be safe here." And pointed to the thick undergrowth surrounding them. "We should surely hear anyone coming through the forest, you see." And then, to Amairgen, "We are entirely safe," she said, and Amairgen nodded, satisfied, and leaned back as if to sleep.

For Flynn, sleep was very nearly impossible. He could not close his mind to what might be ahead of them, and he could not shut out the images of Joanna, lost and frightened, alone somewhere. They were entirely at the mercy of this alien land, and although he had not looked at their food supplies, he knew they must be dwindling. What would happen when their stores ran out? Could they hunt the forest creatures? An involuntary smile touched Flynn's lips, for he had a fleeting image of himself riding out at the head of the *Fiana*, spearing the wild creatures, stringing them over a spit, directing his men on hunts for the famous white boar of Tara ... I could do it, thought Flynn, lying wakeful in the dark forest. I could certainly do it. But I could not do it alone. And he glanced to Amairgen and Portan, and his throat was harsh with unshed tears for Amairgen. And Portan, although she would do anything and go anywhere— although she was quite tremendously courageous—had not the strength they needed. Mentally she was stronger than anyone Flynn had ever known—I believe she is stronger than I am, he thought—but physically she was the frailest. He could not depend on her in a hunt or a fight. But the spirit of the great Finn was more awake in him than it had ever been, and despite it all, he knew a sense of hope and a confidence. They would survive and they would find Joanna. He turned over and tried to calm his mind for sleep.

Close by, Amairgen was as much awake as Flynn, and more concerned for their plight than he had allowed his companions to see. He thought their chances of surviving were slim, but then he thought that their chances of surviving this far had been slim anyway, and yet here they were. He tried to take heart from this, but he found that his heart was heavy within him; he knew he would hinder them on their journey, and the black depression hovered again. But like Flynn, he tried to compose his mind for rest, because if they were to embark on a journey in the morning, they had to be properly rested. And so he tried to shut out the doubts, and he fell to listening to the night rustlings of the forest, able by now to identify the different levels of sound, fascinated by the vividness and the clarity of his perceptions.

And then he heard a different sound.

Human sounds.

People coming stealthily through the forest towards them.

THE THREE TRAVELLERS were at once wide awake; Flynn and Portan both reached for Amairgen's hands. Between them flashed the thought that if they should have to run, if the people coming through the forest should prove to be hostile, at least they could pull Amairgen between them and guide him.

I do not need guiding, nor do I need my hands held. I may have lost my sight, but my wits are still there, and my other senses are becoming more acute than you can imagine.

Flynn and Portan both heard his thoughts; Flynn because of the Samhailt (and how incredibly potent that was becoming, he thought!); Portan because she possessed that something that was not quite the Samhailt, and also because she was coming to understand Amairgen and to know his thoughts and feelings. Now, as they crouched together in the clearing, she felt Amairgen's courage and strength again, as she had felt it before going out on to the Plain of the Fál to rescue Flynn.

Flynn was a little ahead of them. He said softly, "Do not move. Let us wait and see who this is."

"Enemies?" said Portan, shivering.

"No," said Flynn, his head tilted to one side, listening. "No, I do not think they have the approach of enemies."

"Nor," said Amairgen quietly, "do they have the scent of enemies."

The footsteps were nearer now, and Flynn thought there were four or five sets of people—perhaps even six. Despite his words to the others, and despite Amairgen's agreement, he felt a trickle of fear.

Through the trees, came Conaire of the Eagles. He stopped when he saw the three travellers, and held up his hand as if to halt others who followed him. Just behind Conaire was Sean the Storyteller, and behind him were several people that Flynn recognised as belonging to the Ancient Houses of the Bloodline. CuChulainn of the Chariot Horses, tall and strongly muscled and with flashing eyes. Oscar of the Deer, quiet and slender and gentle, with large velvety eyes and a thoughtful, rather scholarly air. And the twins, Midir and Etain of the White Swans; Etain so like her brother and nearly always being dressed like him that it was frequently difficult to tell them apart.

Flynn stood up and waited, because they certainly could not run from this group; they would be caught and captured with ease. CuChulainn's great strength would fell them at a blow, and Oscar's fleetfooted speed would outpace them.

No need to run, came Amairgen's thought. They mean us no harm.

"Indeed we do not," said Conaire, stepping forward. "We mean you no harm at all." He looked at them very intently. "And if you are Eochaid Bres's enemies, then you are our friends." He stayed where he was, but his eyes went from one to another of them, and Flynn, understanding, waited and met Conaire's golden stare calmly.

At length, Amairgen said, "You see? We are harmless."

"Yes," said Conaire, "so you are." And the three travellers felt the golden eyes withdraw from their minds.

"Will you tell us why you thought we might be Eochaid Bres's enemies?" Flynn said and Amairgen and Portan both knew he had deliberately not referred to Eochaid as the King. Amairgen, a little removed from them all, felt the shadowy figure of Finn hover over them, and remembered that for all his skill and tactics in battle, Finn had also been known as a great diplomat and a mediator.

Conaire seemed to feel it as well, for he was watching Flynn with a rather unexpected expression. When he said, "May we sit down? We have been walking for many miles . . ." the three friends caught the note of deference in his voice.

Flynn said, "Please do sit . . . all of you." And took up a stance against a tree, arms folded, looking at them all.

Conaire said, "Flynn—Bricriu the Fox sold you to the Druids."

"Yes."

"To be imprisoned inside the Wicker Man and given to the Sacred Fire is the traditional fate for traitors," said Oscar softly.

"The Fox believed you a traitor," said Conaire. "An enemy of Eochaid's. Are you?"

Flynn said, "How did you know I was inside the Wicker Man?"

"We didn't, not to begin with. But we saw you escape."

"Ah," Flynn grinned ruefully. "And I thought we had been so stealthy."

Conaire said, "Oh you were. But some of us have the eyesight of our Bloodline."

"Oh yes, of course," said Flynn, and remembered about eagles, and looked at Conaire with renewed interest.

Conaire said, "If you are a traitor to Eochaid Bres, then it is quite probable that you are a friend to the True King."

The True King . . . For a moment something shivered in the quiet dark forest. Of course, thought Amairgen. Cormac of the Wolves. And so they are a rebellion, they are renegades from Eochaid's Court. Well, I suppose it is all right . . . And waited to see how Flynn would handle this, and felt a great surge of confidence that Flynn would handle it with consummate ease.

Oscar of the Deer began, "Flynn, you know the Ancient Tongue."

"A very little."

"Better than any of us," said Oscar.

"We know enough to reply to the ceremony," explained Conaire. "But none of us would know how to break the Druids' spell. *Are* you a spy, Flynn?"

"No," said Flynn. "Well, not the sort you mean."

"Oh. That's a pity. We had thought . . . but you have no allegiance to Eochaid Bres? You have not taken the Oath?"

"No," said Flynn with perfect truth. "And indeed, my friends and I know little of your—politics."

There was a puzzled silence, and Flynn realised that the word was strange to them. He realised, with surprise, that it was quite strange to him as well. A Lethe word, of course. Aloud, he said, "I mean your—your struggles for power. Your wars and quarrels. The—structure of your governing."

Amairgen leaned forward. "My friends and I would always support true justice," he said. "And Eochaid Bres is a usurper, I think?"

"He is," said Conaire grimly. He looked at Flynn. "And after tonight—after we saw for ourselves how he and his—his *jackal* Bricriu were hand in glove with the Druids—"

CuChulainn broke in. "Excuse me, Conaire, but that's not very complimentary to the jackals. I have a cousin—"

"I'm sorry to hear that," said Conaire coldly.

"An unfortunate marriage," said CuChulainn. "Of course, we don't admit to the connection. And we *never* have anything to do with that side of the family."

"Well we all have relations we don't like admitting to," said one of the twins kindly.

"But," said the other, "you can hardly compare Bricriu's emblem with the jackals."

"Yes you can," said the first one. "We don't want the jackals on our side—saving your presence, CuChulainn."

Oscar said that every family had its black sheep.

"Well we don't want *those* either," said someone else. "Useless in a fight, sheep—black, white, or piebald."

Flynn felt that the conversation was getting out of hand.

Conaire said rather crossly, "The jackals don't owe allegiance to anyone. They're for themselves, we all know that. Don't any of you remember what happened in the Battle for the Trees?" He turned back to Flynn. "People forget," he said.

"Well yes."

"The thing is," said Conaire, "the thing is, that Cormac would never have sanctioned human sacrifice on the Beltane Fire."

"Or anywhere else for that matter," said Oscar.

"He enjoyed a fight, of course," said CuChulainn.

"Oh yes, I didn't mean to imply—"

"But they were *fair* fights," said one of the twins—Flynn thought it was Midir.

"And so," said Conaire, "when we realised that Eochaid Bres had permitted human sacrifice—"

"*Appeared* to permit it, that is," put in Oscar. "We shouldn't judge. He may have known nothing about it."

"He doesn't know very much about anything," said Etain scornfully. "And Bricriu is a wily old Fox."

"When we realised what had happened," said Conaire, raising his voice, "we were all extremely angry."

"We were fighting mad," said CuChulainn, his eyes flashing.

"We saw that the Pretender couldn't be tolerated any longer," said Conaire. "And so we got together—that is, those of us that belong to the Ancient Bloodline—and we decided that he must be got rid of."

Flynn said, "Yes, I see. Can it be done?"

"Eochaid Bres got rid of the Wolfking," said Etain.

"No, that's not quite right," said Oscar. "Eochaid Bres's *supporters* got rid of him."

"It amounts to the same thing," said Etain.

"So," said Flynn, surveying them, "you six form a—what? A splinter group?"

"A rebellion," said Conaire, and grinned.

"A small band of warriors," said Midir.

"Not so very small," put in his sister firmly.

"You see, we can all call up our Blood Creatures if we have to," explained Oscar.

"And a very formidable army that would give us," said CuChulainn in his rich strong voice. "More than sufficient to crush the usurper and his—"

"Jackals," said Etain.

"Of course, *I'm* not really part of all this," said Sean the Storyteller, who had not spoken until now. He leaned forward anxiously. "I'm only here to report what happens. That's my job. I'm the Court's official *ollam*. I shall be quite impartial about everything, you know. If there's a battle, I shan't say that one side was better than the other. I shall only say what happens.

"You can't have a battle without a proper record," he added to Flynn in an aside, and Flynn nodded.

"We have a duty to our descendants," explained Sean seriously. "So I can't be for one side or the other. I shan't do any fighting either. You do know that?" he said, turning to Conaire. "I did make it clear?"

"You've been making it clear ever since we left Tara," groaned Conaire.

"We'll station you safely out of the way," said Oscar.

"Only you'll have to make sure you don't get *in* the way," said the warlike CuChulainn firmly.

"Well, so long as you know," said Sean.

"So you see," said Conaire, "we thought we should search you all out, because we thought that if you were spying on Eochaid Bres, you must be for the Wolfking. We even thought," said Conaire, with a rather wistful note in his voice, "that he might have sent you."

"Oh no," said Flynn. "No, he didn't send me."

"Ah." A ripple of something that Flynn guessed to be disappointment stirred in the clearing.

And then CuChulainn said, rather ominously, "Are we to understand that you are *not* for the Wolfking?" and at once Amairgen cut in.

"My friends," he said, "none of us know very much about the—the rebellion when Eochaid Bres was put on the throne. Although we are of Ireland, we live many days' journey from its centre. But as Flynn says, we would ever be on the side of true justice."

"A diplomat's answer," murmured Oscar.

"But quite fair," said Midir.

"We thought you would join us," said Conaire, and now he was looking at Flynn, and Flynn knew that it was not Flynn O'Connor that Conaire and the others wanted, but the mighty and powerful Finn of the *Fiana*. And he felt a sudden surge of excitement at the idea of riding out to a battle, of liberating the exiled Wolfking. He thought that it was the shadow of Finn again, his other self, but even so, it was there and he had to give it momentary attention. He thought, as well, that before they threw in their lot with these people, they must be sure that they were doing what was right. And then he thought that above all, beyond everything, he must be sure that it would help them to find Joanna.

Conaire was watching Flynn as though trying to fathom him. "We hoped you would come with us to Scáthach," he said. "To free the Wolfking and then to ride to Gallan to seek Cait Fian's aid."

"Cait Fian will be with us at once," said Etain.

"Yes, of course, you've always had a soft spot for Cait Fian," said Midir, grinning.

"Who hasn't?" said Etain, and winked at Portan.

Conaire said to Flynn, "*Will* you come? We need all the help we can get." And again Flynn had the impression that Conaire was not seeing only Flynn O'Connor, but someone who had once ridden at the head of victorious armies, and someone who had never been defeated, and who had been the finest and the most dazzling warrior in all Ireland's history.

He said slowly, "I believe we will come," and at once felt an approval and a confidence from Amairgen. *Better by far to be with these people who know the roads, and who know how to hunt and provide food, than to struggle by ourselves.*

Flynn thought: at least we shall be going *somewhere*. At least we shall be meeting people who may have seen Joanna.

"Yes. We will be glad to join you," he said and Conaire smiled and took Flynn's hand and then Amairgen's.

"I knew you were not the Fox's supporters," he said.

"And if you *are*," said CuChulainn sternly, "you will be dealt with as all traitors are dealt with."

"Don't be silly," said Oscar. "Flynn's been inside the Wicker Man once already on the Fox's account. He won't risk going there again on somebody else's."

"No!" said Flynn.

"In any case," said Conaire, "why wouldn't they be with us?"

"Flynn spent a night with Mab," remarked Midir uncertainly.

"Who hasn't spent a night with Mab?" said Etain, and grinned at Flynn who looked startled. "Oh, it was all over the Bright Palace the next morning," she said.

"It always is," said Sean gloomily.

"Nothing you would need to feel ashamed about," said Etain

with another of her rather saucy, rather attractive winks at Flynn.

"My sister has no idea of the behaviour expected of ladies," Midir said. He looked at Flynn, as though he, too, was weighing him up. "But she's very useful in battle," as if anxious to establish Etain's credentials.

"I'm extremely useful," said Etain, who was wearing breeches and a leather jerkin, and had pale shaggy caplike hair, exactly the same length as her brother's.

Flynn came to sit on the forest floor, at the centre of the little group, and saw at once how they all turned to him.

"Tell me your plans," he said. "Is it to Scáthach you go?"

"Yes," said CuChulainn firmly. "To liberate the Wolfking!" And looked round rather truculently, as if daring anyone to disagree with this.

"But that," said Midir, "is always supposing the Wolfking hasn't already liberated himself."

"None of us have ever really believed that Scáthach would hold him for long," said Etain. "You don't put a wolf in a mousetrap like Scáthach."

"I suppose you'd have broken the enchantments and been bounding out in the first week," said Midir.

"Yes," said Etain. "I would. *Easily.*"

"He'd have had to find a pure-bred human to do so," put in Oscar, and at once something sprang to attention inside Flynn. But then Oscar said thoughtfully, "Although of course, there are any number of those."

"And we all know Cormac's way with people," added Conaire.

"Oh, he'll be out of Scáthach long since," said Etain. "You see if I'm not right."

"I always said it was a mistake to put him there in the first place," remarked Sean. "I told Eochaid Bres at the time; you'll regret this, I said. Cormac's clever; he'll find a way to dissolve the enchantment, because it never was a very strong one, you know. Or so I was told. You're making a mistake, Sire, I said to Eochaid. But of course he didn't listen to me."

"No one ever does," said the twins in unison, and went off into peals of giggles, so that Sean glared.

"You'll pardon the riff-raff we've brought," said Conaire to the three travellers.

"Brought us!" squealed the twins indignantly. "Didn't we come of our own accord! And you'll be very glad of the swans when the battle begins!"

"Behave yourselves," said Conaire, and the twins grinned, and relapsed into silence.

"We ought to go first to Scáthach in any case," said Conaire, "Flynn, don't you agree? Because even if Cormac *has* broken the enchantment that the sorcerers wove to keep him in exile, we might pick up some clues as to where he is."

Sean said solemnly that you could not, anyway, liberate someone without first finding them. "Of course, he might be halfway to anywhere by now," he observed, which, as Oscar pointed out, was not being very helpful.

Conaire said loudly, "We'll go to Scáthach, providing no one has any sensible objections?" And looked very hard at Sean, who said hastily, "Oh, not the merest smidgeon of one," and fell to contemplating the forest floor.

"And then we'll go to Gallan," said Conaire. "And if you two gentlemen and the lady—forgive me, but we've not been properly introduced—"

"Forgive *me*," said Flynn, horrified that he had not included Portan in any of this. "This is Portan." And he carefully named each of the Bloodline, and saw that Portan had blushed, but that she was taking the hands that were held out to her, and he noticed that the newcomers were greeting her politely and interestedly, and was thankful, but not surprised.

Portan, smiling and trying to remember the names of all these strange, friendly people, saw, and was astonished to see, that not one of the Bloodline seemed to find her odd or deformed. And then, with a burst of joy, she realised that to them she was neither. In fact, Oscar, with his gentle, clever smile, came to sit beside her, and asked about her emblem, and how long it had been since it was conferred, and how far back the Ritual had been.

Portan had only the dimmest idea of what he meant, but she had listened to Amairgen and Flynn last night, talking of Tara, and she had grasped a little of the concept of the Bloodline families. She said cautiously, "I am not sure. My—my family and I have never been close."

And Oscar, who understood about quarrels and divided dynasties, said at once, "Ah. It is always a great pity when that happens. But clearly you are a member of a distinctive family, and that is always something to be proud of."

"Yes," said Portan, and Oscar, who liked history and legends and ancestries, and who found nearly everybody interesting, stayed where he was, talking to Portan of the Six Ancient Houses of Ireland, and of the Families of the Lesser Nobility.

Conaire and CuChulainn were explaining to Flynn and Amairgen about the journey.

"First to Scáthach to free the Wolfking," said Conaire.

"A night's journey," said CuChulainn.

"More like two," put in Sean, who was listening.

"Well it depends how fast you go."

"And once we have Cormac with us, we shall invoke the Mindsong and the creatures of the Bloodlines will answer."

"I beg your pardon," said Flynn, "but will they? I mean, do they *have* to?"

They stared at him.

"Yes, of course," said Conaire at length.

"They cannot help it," said Midir.

"They are bound by the Ritual," said CuChulainn. "And it is an extremely strong enchantment."

"It had to be," said Conaire, and the others nodded.

"I see," said Flynn.

"They will all obey," said CuChulainn. "Conaire's Eagles, and my Chariot Horses, and Oscar's Deer—"

"The twins' White Swans," said Oscar.

"And Cormac's Wolves," said Conaire. "Don't forget them."

"Oh yes, the Wolves will come. I thought that went without saying," said CuChulainn.

"They're probably with him in any case," said Conaire. "Cormac never moves without at least a dozen or so of the creatures," he added, and Flynn thought: *oh dear.*

"But they'll be more or less tame," said Conaire, picking this up without any difficulty. "Cormac knows how to control them." I hope he does, Flynn thought.

"And then we'll be off to Gallan and Cait Fian's people," said Conaire.

"And *then* we shall join battle with the usurper," added CuChulainn contentedly.

"The Wolfking will reign again."

"And won't the fur fly," said Sean.

"It's a long journey of course," said Conaire.

"But we know the roads," said Etain.

"We've brought food," said Oscar.

"But not very much," said Sean.

"No, but we can shoot things as we go."

"And build fires to cook."

"Find streams."

"Scáthach and then Gallan!" cried CuChulainn.

"Scáthach and then Gallan!" cried the others, and Flynn and Amairgen both felt as if it was a living thing, the delight and the excitement that surged through the forest.

CHAPTER SIXTEEN

EOCHAID BRES WAS in the nearest thing to a bad temper he ever got. He was quite well known for his placidity; he thought that if you had to say anything about him, you would say he was placid. Even-tempered. Tranquil. Yes, that was a good word. He was tranquil. He dared say it was a restful change for the Court to have a placid and even-tempered and tranquil High King . . . particularly after Cormac. The last thing Cormac had been was placid, but Eochaid Bres thought it was a useful thing to be if you were a High King.

He was not at all placid now. He was angry, and he thought he might deal out a few punishments—not the Miller's cages, of course, he did not want to be thought barbaric, and anyway, it would give him nightmares or indigestion or both—but punishments of a kind.

He was certainly not going to be made to look silly by those wicked sly Druids who had quite obviously tried to smuggle in a human sacrifice for the Beltane Fire. The smuggling had been quite skilfully done as well, you had to admit that. Eochaid Bres did admit it. What he did not admit was that it had been the right thing to do, because human sacrifice had been forbidden at Tara for as long as anyone could remember. It was archaic and messy. It was also unnecessary, not that that came into it, but everyone knew these days that human sacrifice made absolutely no difference at all to the yield of the land. Animal sacrifice did not make any difference either, but you could not abolish all of the old traditions in one go, and anyway, everyone knew that the animals did not suffer very much. Also, they provided a rather appetising scent as they

burned, and if you were watchful, you could sometimes extricate a nice leg bone of lamb, or those thin, rather juicy rib
chops of young pigs. Eochaid Bres was very fond of roast pig,
although it did not do to admit to the raff and skaff of the
Court that the High King went about prodding the embers of
the Beltane Fire, just to gorge himself on the remains of the
Druids' sacrifices! He could imagine the comments! But, still,
there was no denying that meat roasted at the heart of a Sacred
Fire on a crisp early spring night tasted very good indeed.
Eochaid had not, naturally, dwelled very long on the kind of
pickings that might have been gleaned had Flynn not escaped
so timely from the Wicker Man, because he did not believe in
dwelling on unpleasantness. But he was very glad indeed that
he had not been faced with the ignominy of discovering that he
had not eaten roast pig or roast lamb at all, but rather roast human. It would have given him a few sleepless nights. It would
most certainly have given him indigestion.

He had not, in the beginning, quite understood what had
happened when the ritual question about the sacrifice had been
put.

Do you have the Sacrifice? They had all chanted, just as
they had done every year, and the Druids had to say, *Yes, we
have the Sacrifice.* It was what always happened. Eochaid did
not properly understand the words, of course—well he dared
say that nobody understood them any longer—but he knew
that was what was being said.

Do you have the Sacrifice?
Yes, we have the Sacrifice.

Three times it had to be said, because the Druids said that
to say a thing three times gave it immense power. The Chief
Druid had explained this to Eochaid very solemnly on the day
of his coronation, and Eochaid, just jokingly, had said he
hoped that if he asked for his dinner three times it would give
him a powerful good dinner, but the Chief Druid had not seen
the joke, and nobody had laughed, and Eochaid had felt silly.
Of course, Druids never had any sense of humour, everybody
knew that.

Do you have the Sacrifice? There it had been, the third time,
and everyone, Eochaid Bres as well, had drawn breath to give
the reply.

Only the reply had never been given. They had been fore-

stalled. Before anyone could speak, a voice had come ringing
from within the Wicker Man, speaking in the Ancient Tongue,
and the next minute, the Plain of the Fál had been thrown into
utter chaos, as the Wicker Man seemed to fall apart where he
stood, and all of the caged animals came tumbling and scurrying out and down, and ran into the forest, tripping people up,
barking and bleating and clucking and flapping their wings,
and making the night quite hideous.

Eochaid had not, at first, known where the voice had come
from. He had been, truth to tell, rather overawed, because he
had thought it might have been the voice of Dagda himself, the
father-god of all the gods, and he had wondered how he ought
best to reply, because as far as he knew, there was no recorded
instance of Dagda having spoken to a High King for centuries
upon centuries. He had been very much flattered and had
thought he would go down in Tara's history as the King who
had called to earth the mighty father-god.

But then Mother and Bricriu had explained that it was not
Dagda who had spoken, only a wicked spy who had somehow
been concealed inside the Wicker Man, and who had known
the Druids' Ancient Tongue, and had known how to break the
spell of the Wicker Man.

Of course, Eochaid had said at once that he had seen
through the trick; he had not really believed the voice to come
from Dagda at all. He had asked how the spy could have got
into the Wicker Man, and Bricriu had said sadly, "Well, Your
Majesty, I am afraid he must have been put there," and
Eochaid had said, "As a sacrifice?" rather sharply, and Bricriu
had said that after all, Sire, it was the punishment for spies.

This was extremely worrying, because Eochaid had not
known they had had a spy in their midst. He hoped he had
not said anything amiss in the spy's presence.

"I am sure you could not have done, Sire," said Bricriu
soothingly.

Even so, it was disconcerting to find that spies were being
uncovered at Court and sent to justice willy-nilly without the
King being aware of it. Eochaid thought it ill became his dignity to be treated in such a way; he thought he should have
been consulted. He certainly thought he should have been told.

He sent Bricriu off to summon the Councillors to an Extraordinary Meeting in the Star of the Poets, and once assembled, demanded a full explanation of them.

"But Your Majesty, none of us knew anything about it," said Bolg, huffing and puffing a bit, because he had just been coming from the stool room on the upper floors when the King issued the summons, and he had arrived at a fast trot, a bit out of breath, a bit dishevelled, his thoughts as disordered as his dress.

Several heads nodded in agreement; nobody, it seemed, had known anything about the spy.

"And if we had known," said Bolg, beginning to recover his wind, "we would have put a stop to it. We certainly don't want human sacrifice at Tara again." He shuddered, and the Councillors all shuddered with him and looked shocked, and said indeed they did not, to be sure it was the very last thing they wanted. Eochaid Bres stormed out of the Star of the Poets, which was an insult to the Ancestral Chamber of all the High Kings, but which was comforting to Eochaid Bres's injured dignity, and told Bricriu that if there was one thing he could not bear, it was a pack of sybarites telling him lies.

"I think Your Majesty means sycophants," said Bricriu, and Eochaid lost his temper in earnest then, and stamped his foot and threw his best official gold chain on to the floor, and said they none of them treated him with the respect he deserved, and things would have to change.

The Court seemed somewhat depleted when they gathered in the Sun Chamber that evening—"Sleeping off the excesses of Beltane, Your Majesty," said Bricriu soothingly.

It was a fairly safe guess that one or two of the Court had found excesses somewhere. Conaire of the Eagles would be sure to; Eochaid was not surprised to see Conaire's chair empty tonight. He was not particularly surprised to see that CuChulainn was not here either, because CuChulainn was inclined to be a bit wild as well. Eochaid had never quite trusted that family. Too fond of making war, Bricriu had once said, but Eochaid thought that CuChulainn's family were quite fond of winning wars as well, and they had a disconcerting habit of throwing in their lot with the side most likely to ride to victory. He hoped that Conaire and CuChulainn had not gone off to start up a silly rebellion somewhere.

The twins, Midir and Etain, were missing tonight as well,

which was probably the gods' mercy, because they were apt to get a bit out of hand. Etain was fond of teasing the young men (well, the old men as well—there had once been a most unpleasant incident with Bricriu) and it sometimes caused unpleasantness with Mother.

"Jealousy," said the Court, and told each other how Etain's mother, Fuamnach, had once challenged Mab as the greatest beauty at Tara. "Plain jealousy," they said, but Eochaid thought that Mother had no need to be jealous of anyone, and certainly had no need to be jealous of a pale pointy-faced creature like Etain. A few of the men held that Etain was unusually beautiful and possessed of a certain, rather wayward charm—Cait Fian was believed to have had his eye on her for a year or more—but Eochaid had never been able to see anything in her.

He was not especially unhappy to see the twins absent tonight, but he was very sorry not to see Oscar of the Wild Deer. Oscar would certainly not be sleeping off any excesses, because so far as anyone knew, Oscar never indulged in any. Also, he could be relied upon to soothe over any awkwardnesses that might occur in the course of an evening, not that Eochaid classed this business of sacrificing a spy on the Beltane Fire as awkward precisely, but there would be bound to be talk, and Oscar would have been tactful and discreet. Eochaid was very sorry not to see him in his usual place; he was even sorrier not to see Sean the Storyteller.

"Overeaten himself again no doubt," said Bricriu when Eochaid asked where Sean might be. "Disgraceful in a man of his standing," said Bricriu. "And at his time of life." Eochaid, who had also overeaten himself, but did not see what age or standing had to do with it, grunted and reached for a dish of spiced woodcock, and felt abandoned by his friends, and beleaguered by his enemies, and wondered, not for the first time, whether the game was worth the candle.

BRICRIU WONDERED SO as well. It was all very well when the King did as he was told, but of late, he had not done at all as he was told; he had developed a habit of asking the wrong questions, and it would not do. You could not have Kings thinking they could rule, otherwise you ended up with a despot which was bad for the people. You could not have the people ruling either, because then you ended up with chaos, which was bad for everybody. Ideally the Councillors ruled, but absolutely ideally Bricriu ruled the Councillors. With a little—a very little—help from Mab. She thought she ruled completely, of course, and Bricriu was not going to disillusion her. She knew too much about Bricriu himself for any chances to be taken.

Bricriu had known at once that it had been Flynn who had broken the Druids' enchantment, and he had been stunned, because nobody, not even the High King, knew the Druids' Ancient Tongue these days. Everyone knew the words of the Ritual, of course; the question and answer part of the ceremonies, but nobody really knew what the words meant any more, because the Druids were extremely jealous of their traditions.

But Flynn had known. Flynn had known the Ancient Tongue sufficiently well to use the Ritual Denial, and that was something whose origin was so old, that Bricriu thought even the Druids did not fully understand it. Flynn had understood it though. He had broken the Wicker Man's spell and set himself free. The Druids had been angry, but Bricriu had been angrier still. He had been very nearly beside himself when he had realised that not only had Flynn slipped from his grasp, he had taken half the Bloodline with him.

A rebellion! A new assault on Tara, only this time it would be Bricriu who was under attack. It was one thing to ride against the Bright Palace from outside, with the armies streaming out behind you and the Lion pennants fluttering in the breeze; it was quite another to be the one who was within besieged Tara. Bricriu had a sudden, highly disturbing vision of himself (and the others, of course) trapped inside Tara, fighting off Eochaid Bres's ill-wishers, besieged and starving and beaten. It was something that could not be allowed to happen on any count. He took another look at the vision, and thought he saw, very clearly, the Wolf emblem on those pennants.

He dare not risk it. Was there any likelihood that it might happen? Although it was not pleasant to examine distressing things closely, Bricriu now examined the very unpleasant possibility of a new rebellion, and was forced to admit that it was more than a possibility; it was a probability. And given that particular group of people, it was very nearly a certainty.

Flynn was the lodestar, of course; he was the leader, and they would all follow. Bricriu admitted, albeit unwillingly, that the boy had that singular blend of recklessness and charm and intelligence that made for leaders. Odd how you never mistook it. Cormac had possessed it as well, of course, which was one of the reasons why Cormac had been removed; the Court never paid any attention to anyone else when Cormac was at Tara.

Conaire of the Eagles possessed it as well; not in quite such strength, but still he possessed it and it had to be reckoned with. He would be a good person to have in a rebellion, and his eagles would be remarkably good creatures to have as allies. Bricriu shuddered as he thought of those cruel merciless talons and beaks, and those massive wings swooping down on an enemy. Yes, it was quite easy to see Flynn and Conaire together; Bricriu could well visualise them throwing in their lot with someone like Cait Fian of Gallan, attempting to set Cormac on the High Throne again, even, perhaps, succeeding. They were insolent reckless young men who would fight for any cause they considered worthy, and it was really a very great pity they were on Cormac's side. They were arrogant swaggering cubs who made far too much of their youth and their virility, thought Bricriu, steaming himself into a high rage. It would be very pleasant indeed to see those three young men—four if you counted Cormac himself—with their thick glossy hair thinning and dry, and their clear bright eyes watery and dim, and their strong firm bodies withered and feeble. Well, there were such spells. He touched the knowledge in his mind with satisfaction. More ways than one of defeating an enemy.

The others who had gone to Flynn would be useful to him as well. CuChulainn was a great brutish creature, of course, all muscle and flashing eyes, but he had at his back the great and fearsome Chariot Horses, and anyone who had ever seen the Chariot Horses galloping across the plains and the fields of Ireland would know they were creatures to be reckoned with. CuChulainn's family had always liked to style themselves the champions of the High Kings, which Bricriu thought presumptuous. He remembered about the spell again—loss of hair and teeth was it? And softening of the wits. CuChulainn should be taught a lesson.

Midir and Etain should be taught lessons as well. Bricriu had never cared for the twins overmuch, not since he had made a certain behind-the-hand suggestion to Etain, which she had rejected with such coarseness that Bricriu had been deeply offended. He had not minded the rejection itself—goodness, of course he had not!—but he had thought Etain's exact wording of it quite unnecessarily vulgar. Also, if Etain did not want to receive such propositions, she should not flaunt herself so blatantly. Of course the family had no real breeding; they were only fourth generation aristocracy, if they were not third. A very new Bloodline indeed. In fact, Bricriu could remember the twins' mother, twenty-five years earlier, giving herself airs and trying to rival Mab. Now that he thought about it, Etain's mother had rejected a very similar proposition from Bricriu in very nearly the same words as Etain. What was in the meat came out in the gravy, and the twins were no particular loss.

Oscar of the Wild Deer might, at first look, seem not to be a particular loss either, but Oscar was clever. He was so clever that he had by now probably mapped out an entire plan of campaign for the rebellion, and he was so shrewd that he would have persuaded them all to adopt it. Yes, the rebellion needed planners as well as leaders and fighters.

It was really a very alarming combination. Individually, those five—six if you counted Flynn, which Bricriu would certainly do—were not especially dangerous. But together with the might of their respective Bloodlines behind them, they posed a very grave threat. It could not be risked, and Bricriu would not risk it. The army that those six could summon would be formidable, but Bricriu could summon another army that would be more formidable still.

You did not meet force with force; you met it with sorcery.

Descending to the Sorcery Chambers of Tara was like passing through many layers of its life. It was like cutting down and down, through each level of the Palace's history, so that you could see all of the different ages, and you could sense all of the different levels of the High Kings and Queens, all the way from Dierdriu of the Nightcloak to the present day.

Down and down you went. Through the low-roofed passages with the flaring wall sconces placed at intersections; down the narrow twisting stairways with huge walls all about you; with low arched doors leading off them. Bricriu had once heard it said that the doors were gateways to Tara's past, and if you could find the key you could open the doors and step back into those lost Golden Ages—of Dierdriu, and Niall of the Nine Hostages, and Nuadu Airgetlam of the Silver Arm:

magical times. And now they had Eochaid Bres who could not
spend above an hour in the Sun Chamber without getting a
headache from its glare.

The awesome thing about descending to the Sorcery Chambers was the way in which the past crowded in. You hardly
needed keys to unlock the doors; all you had to do was to
stand very still and shut your eyes, and let the entire history of
the Bright Palace soak in through your skin. Bricriu was not
especially fanciful, but he never failed to be aware of the sheer
weight of age that permeated these walls; these underground
chambers were Tara's soul and its memory and its heartbeat. It
was not fanciful to think you could feel the emotions and the
fears and the hopes that had been captured and held by the sorcerers.

You caught fleeting images as well if you watched for them;
nothing very clear, and sometimes things that were meaningless to you. But Bricriu had twice seen the dazzling weave of
the protective spell that had been sent out with what were
known as the Crusade Wars, fought by the followers of the
god-idol Crom Croich, whose mortal body was of pure living
gold, and who ate the warm, still-beating hearts of his victims.
He had seen the great armies of the Fomoire and their leader,
the son of Goll the One-Eyed. Once he had glimpsed the spell
that had driven out the marauding Mag Tuired—a heavy dark
enchantment that had been, laced with crimson and gold, not
ugly, in fact rather beautiful, but menacing and smothering so
that you felt as if the light had all been blotted out, and a great
weight descended on to you making it difficult to breathe.

Once he had glimpsed something that was made of pure
light; rose and gold and the colour of a summer dawn; glistening with cobwebs and warm with a strong heady perfume. He
had put up his hand to shield his eyes at once, for he had
known it to be the Final Great Enchantment, the spell that carries men to the Place beneath the Roof of the Ocean; the Lure
of the Old Gods, more beautiful and more complete than anything the *sidh* could spin. He had backed from it at once, but
the vision had sobered him, for he had not realised that Death
walked these corridors.

*Death is Life, and Life is Death, Inquirer, and all must meet
the Old Gods and their Lure eventually.*

You did not see the sorcerers until they were ready for you

to see them. They did not much like being seen—Bricriu
thought it was probably because they thought it preserved their
sense of mystery, while in fact the only thing that remained a
mystery about the sorcerers was who they truly served.

"They serve the High King of course," Eochaid Bres had
said firmly when Bricriu had once voiced this doubt.

Bricriu knew perfectly well that the sorcerers these days
would serve anyone who would pay them well enough.
Eochaid, very much shocked, had said no, this was entirely
wrong, and Bricriu must not think like that. "They have all
taken the Oath," he had said, as if that settled the matter, but
Bricriu knew perfectly well that a few words spoken on the
Plain of the Fál did not automatically ensure allegiance to the
High King, and any words spoken by the sorcerers did not automatically ensure anything at all.

It had been different in Dierdriu's day, of course. People had
known where they were then. The sorcerers had served Dierdriu faithfully and well. Bricriu quite accepted that. They had
sworn allegiance to her in the days when oaths meant loyalty
and not something quite different. They had done everything
she had ever asked. They still took the Oath, of course—and
made quite a performance of it as well!—but if they were any
more loyal than Bricriu was, it would be a matter for comment. Bricriu was not loyal, of course, because sensible people
were not any longer; you knew which side your bread was but-
tered and that was all there was to it. Bricriu would swear
oaths to any manner of people if it would help him rule Ireland
on his own account. By the same token, the sorcerers would
swear allegiance to anyone as well, if it would pay them sufficiently. They were as greedy as goblins, sorcerers. They were
wily as well, but Bricriu could be wilier still. He would be
very wily now.

He made his way through the passages, holding his single
candle aloft, knowing that eventually he would come to the
high-ceilinged Supplicants' Chamber—the place that lay at the
centre of these subterranean passages, where the sorcerers
came out to meet those who asked their help.

Bricriu hated to ask anyone for help, but still, the sorcerers
were there, they lived and worked and had their great Looms
where they weaved their spells beneath the Bright Palace, and

you might as well make use of the means to hand. In any case, the sorcerers lived well enough off the High King.

The Supplicants' Chamber was hewn from the rock—Dierdriu's Rock, some called it, and told how the Queen had sat on the Rock and thrown back her head to the sky, and let the wind lift her rippling black hair, and how it was here she had bargained with the sorcerers to raise the Bright Palace for her, and build the great Sun Chamber.

Superstition, of course. Bricriu did not believe a word of it. And yet, and yet . . .

And yet, there was the remarkable portrait of the woman they said had been Dierdriu, etched in gold into the rockface; the one they said would one day return. *"If the Darkness of the Necromancers should ever dim the Bright Palace . . . I shall return."*

For some reason, it always made Bricriu feel uncomfortable to remember that legend. The High Queen returning . . .

Still, even for an unfanciful man, there was something uncomfortable about the Sorcerers' Chamber. It was steeped in magic and soaked in history, and whether you believed the legend of Dierdriu or whether you did not, it was easy to imagine that Dierdriu's shade might walk these halls now and then.

The Central Chamber was lined with marble and porphyry; there were great soaring pillars of alabaster which reared up into the dim vaults far above. The floor was patterned with the symbols of all the gods, with Dagda the father-god at the centre.

Bricriu approached the great oval table, thus shaped so that no one sorcerer would ever sit at its head, and no one at its foot, and snuffed his candle. The sorcerers were believed not to like direct light very much, and in any case, all light that was necessary came from the Rock; a faint bluish glow that lit Dierdriu's gold-etched image to eerie life. Bricriu felt uncomfortable all over again. He did not believe in the legend of the High Queen returning, because no sensible person *did* believe it, but it still made him feel a bit odd to be down here and see it like this.

The sorcerers would make him wait, they always did. But in the end they would come. Not all of them, but enough, and the bargaining would commence. They were greedy, but they would do what Bricriu wanted, because Bricriu would pay.

They would not necessarily do it for Eochaid Bres, or even for Mab, but they would do it for Bricriu for the money.

And so Bricriu settled himself to wait, and presently the sorcerers appeared, almost seeming to materialise in the shadows, not there one moment and then suddenly there the next, so that you could not see how they arrived. It was a trick, of course, and if Bricriu had known how it was done he would not have been so impressed. He did not know how it was done.

The sorcerers wore plain dark cloaks with deep hoods that shadowed their faces. Bricriu knew that these were their Outer World garments; the clothes they wore when they had to meet with people of the Court, or when they went out into what they called the Outer World on some quest or other. Once there, they liked to mingle with ordinary people—but of course you could always tell a sorcerer by looking at his eyes. Deep. Dark. Brooding. It was said that every sorcerer possessed a wardrobe of dazzling robes, some of them woven of spells, others of light, yet others of living breathing colours, but they never appeared in these robes other than to one another.

Their manners were exquisite. They were exquisite now, to Bricriu, as they seated themselves at the table, and indicated to Bricriu that he should take the Supplicants' Chair which faced the table.

That was the part he disliked. To stand before these clever unfathomable men, and ask for their help. To know himself inferior to those who had spent numberless years immersed in study and the pursuit of the forces hidden from the rest of the world. To feel himself a lesser creature than these dark hooded beings who lived in scholarly seclusion, but who knew the secret longings in men's souls, and who understood the ancient laws of the necromancers and the wizards and the Druids. But he took the chair and waited, hands folded, and presently, one of the sorcerers spoke.

"You disturb our work once more, Creature of the Fox and Vixen. What do you want?"

"Your help," said Bricriu. "Tara is threatened by enemies." He waited, and saw the tiniest flicker of consternation go round the table.

"That is distressing." A pause. "Tell us how you believe we may help you."

Bricriu said, "Tara should be rendered safe from attack. The Girdle of Gold—"

"Unobtainable," said the sorcerer, his eyes at once frosty. "As you know."

"The Erl-King has it?"

"I did not say that," said the sorcerer, and Bricriu thought: so the Erl-King *does* have it! And they know it, of course. I wonder did they get it for him?

"We are sworn to serve the High King," said the sorcerer blandly, and Bricriu knew that his thought had been heard. He remembered that although the Samhailt had been outlawed at Court, down here the sorcerers had their own laws. He remembered, too, that the Oath of Allegiance was not what it had once been, and that sorcerers were not what they had once been either. He thought that the sorcerers of Tara were perfectly capable of dealing with the Erl-King if it suited their pockets, but he clamped this thought down at once, because it would not have done for it to have been picked up.

The sorcerer said, rather coldly, "You may request another enchantment, and if it is in our power, we will agree to weave it."

At a price, of course. There was always a price.

"I wish you to weave a spell that will render Tara invincible," Bricriu said and hoped that they would not know that it was Cormac he wanted to render Tara invincible from.

The sorcerer regarded him thoughtfully, and it struck Bricriu that the sorcerer's eyes were exactly the colour of cold, still lake-water.

"You know the rules," said the sorcerer. "You must name the enchantment you require."

Bricriu, hedging, said, "I am not well versed in sorcery."

"The Book of the Academy of Necromancers is available to all. The enchantments of the world are written on its pages. Our Looms are able to spin everything in the Book."

Bricriu knew, and the sorcerers knew, that to read in the Book of the Academy required immense understanding and also great purity of purpose. He knew, as well, that those who turn the pages of that ancient vellum book with the live illustrations and the coloured incantations, and do so without a pure heart and a clean conscience, risk being cast into the Prison of Hostages, from which no man ever emerges. He did not say this, of course, but he knew that the sorcerers knew he had never dared to go near the Book of the Academy. Even so, he did not waver; he looked directly at the sorcerer and said, "A great army is being mustered against Tara."

"Yes?" The faintest question.

"A strong army," said Bricriu firmly. "We shall not be able to defeat it with our own Guard."

"Well?"

"If we had on our side those who do not rely on strength alone, those who have at their fingertips the old magics of the Dark Ireland—"

"War by sorcery is a nasty business," said the sorcerer, and an uneasy ripple went round the oval table. Bricriu thought: they are a little afraid, but I think they are more afraid of losing the Sorcery Chambers of Tara. And remembered that the Silver Looms on which the enchantments were spun were said to be at their most powerful when they were housed beneath the Bright Palace. No, for sure, the sorcerers would not want to find themselves cast out of Tara. Emboldened by this thought, he leaned forward and said, "We dare not permit this invasion."

"It would be—inopportune," said the sorcerer, and Bricriu caught the faintest of nods from several of the other shadowy figures.

"If we had the Dark Powers on our side—on the side of Tara—perhaps even inside the Palace walls . . ."

A sudden and rather terrible silence descended on the sorcerers, and a great stillness fell about them. Bricriu thought: of course they know what I am going to say. But he said it all the same.

He moved closer to the oval table so that the light fell across him, and although he did not realise it, in that moment, the fox's mask of his forebears, cruel and sly and calculating, fell across his face.

"We must summon the Morrigna."

CHAPTER SEVENTEEN

THE JOURNEY TO Gallan, through the Morne Mountains, was not nearly as arduous as Joanna had feared.

"You're getting your second wind, my lady," said Gormgall approvingly.

"Or you're beyond caring," muttered Dubhgall, but Joanna laughed and thought that this new strength and this feeling of being more alive than ever before, came as much from the cold clean mountain air and from the majestic tranquillity of the mountains themselves, as from anything else.

"Yes, they're very tranquil, these mountains," said Dubhgall in the manner of one humouring a child.

"Calming," said Joanna firmly.

"Very likely," agreed Dubhgall. "Of course, it's as likely to be the magic up here as anything else."

Cormac, who had been rather quiet since their escape from the Morrigna, said, "But the magic of the Morne Mountains is the purest of all the magics."

"Well that's what they say," said Dubhgall.

"Of course it is."

"We'll hope so," said Dubhgall. "But we all know that there're sorcerers in these mountains, and they're a greedy breed, sorcerers. There's no knowing whose pay they might be in," said Dubhgall. "Nor there's no knowing if someone's got here before us."

"Who?"

"The Erl-King," said Dubhgall, and a rather terrible silence fell. Joanna, who was a little ahead of the others, caught sight of three large-winged, very black birds sitting on a jutting rock, and just for a moment, the sun seemed to slip behind a cloud.

Gormgall looked round and said in a whisper, "But that can't be so."

Cormac gave himself a little shake and said, "Of course it isn't so. The Erl-King's powers have never stretched this far."

"So they say, Your Majesty. How do we know that isn't just a rumour put about by the Erl-King himself, just to lull us all into a false sense of security?"

"Well," said Cormac, "I never heard that the Sorcerers of the Morne Mountains were other than extremely loyal to my family. In fact, it was those very sorcerers who worked harder than any to try to regain the Girdle of Gold for us."

"Yes, you never *heard* they were other than loyal, Sire, but that isn't to say they were," said Dubhgall, and having thus unburdened himself of this opinion now assumed a more cheerful mien. "It's my belief," he said confidingly, "that it'll be as well for us not to trust anyone we meet in these mountains, human or otherwise. And I never trust sorcerers of any description," said Dubhgall, chewing reflectively on his portion of stew which Joanna had cooked from the rabbits that Gormgall had snared earlier.

"And anyway, we aren't going into the mountains yet. We're going on to Gallan. Goodness gracious me," said Gormgall rather crossly, "I should hope that His Majesty knows better than to venture into the mountain halls with only the four of us! We need at least half an army before we even think of it," said Gormgall.

"Armies don't worry sorcerers," said Dubhgall.

"No, but Cait Fian can muster a remarkably strong force," said Gormgall. "And what's more, he'll know the gossip. If anyone knows what goes on in this part of the country, it's Cait Fian. That's begging Your Majesty's pardon for seeming to speak ill of his cousin," added Gormgall, who never, no matter what the occasion, forgot what was due to the High King and his near family. "But Cait Fian always *does* know what's afoot," he added in an aside to Joanna, and Joanna, who had been rather dreading meeting the Mountain sorcerers (meeting *any* sorcerers) heaved a sigh of relief to think that they were going directly to Gallan.

"Of course," said Dubhgall, just as everyone was beginning

to relax, and Joanna was thinking they might after all reach Gallan, "of course, you don't need to go *into* the Mountain Halls to meet the sorcerers. I daresay they're prowling about all over the mountainside. We shall very likely meet one tomorrow," he added, and, rather pleased at having imparted this sober note to the party, composed himself for a night's slumber, and then kept everyone awake by snoring enthusiastically, until Cormac kicked him out of his fur rug.

But in fact nothing occurred to cause any disquiet to the four travellers as they went deeper into the mountains. At times Joanna thought the Nightcloak stirred and whispered, and once or twice they saw the black carrion crows—"Are they following us?" asked Gormgall once.

"Are we following *them*?" said Dubhgall.

Joanna shivered and said, "Oh *don't*."

"I only meant it could be a trap," said Dubhgall, but he looked chastened.

"Even so," said Joanna to Cormac later that night, "I believe the cloak is protecting us."

"From traps and sorcerers?"

"From something," said Joanna, and Cormac looked at her.

"One day, Human Child," he said softly, "one day, I shall take you down to the Sorcery Chambers of Tara; to the great central chamber which is called the Supplicants' Chamber and I shall show you the rock that Tara stands on. It is called Dierdriu's Rock, and on it is the great Queen's likeness, etched in gold by the people who served her, who loved her, and who wept for a year and a day when she died. It has never faded, and it has never weathered." He paused. "We will see it together, you and I, Joanna, but for you it will be like looking in a mirror."

Joanna was frightened and delighted. She said, "Am I then so like her?"

"Not to start with," said Cormac, studying her. "Not when you came into Scáthach, when the Wolves escorted you across the great Bridge to my place of exile. But you are a little more like her each day. You know her thoughts and you speak with her tongue." He smiled. "Even I have not the old pure Gael that she had," said Cormac. "But you have it. You challenged Morrigan with it in Muileann. Dierdriu is you and you are her," and a shiver of the purest excitement spiralled under Joanna's ribs as he spoke.

But—Yes, of course she is part of me, she thought. The High Queen returned ... How else did I know how to challenge Morrigan? And how else did I have the strength to endure the things Morrigan did to me? I shall never be able to forget it, thought Joanna shuddering, but I did endure it. And a cold sickness twisted her stomach at the memory of that night in Morrigan's chamber, and Cormac took her hand. Joanna thought: he knows what happened up there in that dark evil-smelling room. He will never ask me and I will never tell him, but all the same, he knows.

"Of course I know," said Cormac. "It is in your eyes and in your heart. I hear the echoes." He looked at her, suddenly and disconcertingly more wolf than human, certainly more mystical than she had ever seen him. "You will forget it," said Cormac, his eyes hard and slanting and golden. "Memory is arranged in layers. The topmost layer is vulnerable. It is open to the air. But it is quickly laid over with other memories. You are overlaying it now, Joanna. You are burying the memories of Morrigan and Muileann with new layers. Your pleasure in these mountains. Your anticipation of Gallan." He smiled suddenly. "Cait Fian will fight me for you," he said, "but he shall not have you, Joanna."

Walking on through the purple-misted Morne Mountains, listening to Gormgall and Dubhgall reminiscing about their last visit to Gallan—"The year before the usurper's rebellion it was."—"*Two* years before," said Dubhgall—Joanna did indeed begin to forget.

"Of course you do," said Cormac, his eyes golden and slanting, but soft this time, making love to her on the grassy mountainside in the shelter of a half-cave. Joanna had protested; she had said, "Gormgall and Dubhgall are within hearing," but it only excited Cormac more. Joanna lay back and saw, outside the cave, the sky and the mountain peaks, and vivid splashes of colour from the mountain ash and the gentians. She thought: he is right. I am forgetting.

"Of course you are," said Cormac and bent over her.

"It's all very well," said Joanna at length, "but how am I to face Gormgall and Dubhgall when we rejoin them? They will know what we've been doing."

For answer, Cormac laughed and pushed her back on the grass.

"Again?" said Joanna, half joking, half not. And, "So soon?" she said.

"Girl dear, did you think me a weakling? A rabbit? A beaver? A—"

"Rabbits are extremely virile."

"So they are. And one of the Beaver line was once my staunchest and truest Councillor," said Cormac, and Joanna thought: damn! Now I have reminded him of his lost kingdom.

"I do not need reminding," said Cormac softly. "It is always with me." He touched her face. "But one day soon, I shall regain it, and then we will look upon Dierdriu's likeness, you and I."

It was embarrassing, but not as embarrassing as Joanna had thought, to rejoin Gormgall and Dubhgall after these interludes.

It is true that once Dubhgall said, "I expect you'll be hungry for your supper now, Sire," and it is true that Gormgall every night paced out a discreet distance between his and Cormac and Joanna's makeshift beds, but these things could be accepted with a small degree of equanimity.

She thought of the journey—later when she was able to look back on it—as a kind of intermission. She certainly thought of it as a time of renewal and refreshment.

"My feet often blistered from walking so far each day," she would say, "for of course, we had had to leave the horses with the Cruithin and the Wolves far beyond Muileann. And I used to worry every day about whether we would hunt down that night's supper. But I do not recall being other than deeply happy on that journey."

And blisters could be soothed with Gormgall's pots of ointments—"All brought along specially, my lady, for I knew how it would be"—and if there was ever a night when they had no supper, Joanna did not remember it.

There was food a-plenty in the mountains; rabbits and hares which they snared and made into savoury stews with handfuls of herbs: wild thyme and sorrel and lemon balm, and the pungent wild garlic that grew on the roadside. And there were leaping fish in the mountain streams that could be caught and grilled over their camp fires and eaten hot and fresh. There were berries of a kind Joanna had never seen.

"Delicious raw," said Gormgall, picking them, "but even more delicious if we just cook them gently for a few minutes with honey and a drop of His Majesty's mead. I knew we'd be glad of all these provisions, Sire. I said so at the time."

"They're a bit cumbersome to carry," said Dubhgall, but he had two helpings of the berry and mead concoction which, as Gormgall had promised, was very good indeed.

"It's a pity we didn't bring the berries from the Sleeping Trees," said Gormgall as they sat back replete and rested.

"It's a pity you threw them away on the Muileann borders," remembered Dubhgall.

"They went rotten," said Gormgall.

"Waste of time gathering them then," said Dubhgall.

Once they managed to kill a wild pig, and Cormac made Joanna retire while he and the others skinned and gutted it.

"For," said Gormgall, sharpening his knife, "you don't want to see what it is you're eating, my lady. Not but what we shan't all enjoy it, and I'll gather a few apples and slice them up in the pot. There's nothing so grand as a touch of apple in with roast pig."

On the fourth day, as they began to descend the mountain path and Cormac was shading his eyes and peering into the distance, Dubhgall shot with his longbow two pigeons, which he said he would make into a pie.

"Pigeon pie," he said. "Although I'm bound to say that there isn't much meat on a pigeon, Your Majesty. You need at least six to make it anything like enough."

"Enough for a good supper tonight, though," said Cormac.

Dubhgall said, "Ah, but what about tomorrow, Sire?" and Cormac laughed and pointed.

"Look my friends! The Mountain Palace of Cait Fian! Gallan! Tomorrow night we shall dine in the company of the Wild Panther people!"

And there, towards the east, wreathed in clouds of mist was Gallan and the ice-blue Mountain Palace.

As they started down the mountain path, three carrion crows circled above them . . .

IN THE DARKEST, deepest Sorcery Chamber, Bricriu sat again in the Supplicants' Chair and looked at the sorcerers ranged about the oval table.

"You have done what I asked?"

"We have. The Three Sisters are following the Wolfking and his servants. They are keeping watch on them."

"Ah." An expression of the utmost satisfaction passed over Bricriu's face. Then—"Have they killed them yet?" he asked.

"No." The sorcerer regarded Bricriu. "That is *their* price, Son of the Vixen. They will fight on your side against the armies of Cormac, and of Conaire of the Eagles, and Cait Fian of the Wild Panthers. They will use sorcery and necromancy to win . . . But the Wolfking and his Lady they will keep for their own purposes."

Bricriu said, "The Morrigna want Cormac?"

"Not for themselves," said the sorcerer. "For their master.

"They will feed the Wolfking and his Lady to the Erl-King. There is no escape for them."

CHAPTER EIGHTEEN

BRIAN MULDOONEY, RESPECTABLE pig farmer and a person of some standing in Tugaim, was very nearly at a loss. He thought wasn't it all too bad of John Grady to lead them on this ridiculous wild chase through the night, and he wished, and had been wishing for some time, that he had not come. The girl, Joanna, pretty little dear, was certainly a loss to Muldooney's farm, but not so much that she could not be replaced. As good fish in the sea as ever came out of it!

And now here they were in the middle of a dark old forest, which might be anywhere at all, but which seemed to lead absolutely nowhere, and there was nothing to help them get out but the cold eerie music.

Muldooney did not trust the music. He did not, in fact, trust music at all—senseless frivolous stuff. He certainly did not trust this odd tuneless singing that crept nearer and nearer and then backed away. It was all very well for John Grady to put his head up and listen, and say wouldn't they follow it; Brian Muldooney knew that the music was in some way wrong. He sought for words to explain this to Grady, but he had never been a great one for the explaining, and he failed to find the words. Well, looked at sensibly, there were no words. It was just *wrong*. It made you think of upsetting things. It made you think of pain . . . misery . . . hunger and thirst and dark and loneliness.

Yes, Men of the Desolation, we are hunger and we are thirst . . .

It made you think of endless dark seas and yawning chasms

369

and bottomless wells where water drip-dripped echoingly for
ever . . .

*Oh yes, we are endless, Men of the Desolation, and we are
timeless . . . we are at home in the dark oceans of the world,
and in the underground caverns, and in the water caves of our
ancestors . . .*

And it was *cold*. It was so cold that you felt icy lumps form
at the pit of your stomach, and you felt your bones ache, and
a great solid knot of coldness form behind your breastbone.

*Cold we are, Men of the Desolate World . . . for we have no
human blood in us . . . but once you have seen us, once you
have descended to our caves, you will never want human
warmth again . . .*

It had seemed very sensible to just stop and take a bit of a
rest in the tavern they finally came to. John Grady said, "Ah!
A road at last!" and bounded forward, but Muldooney followed more slowly, because he did not trust roads and taverns
that appeared so conveniently out of nowhere; very likely it
would be a trap of some kind, he said knowledgeably, and
John Grady, who was tired of wandering about in the dark with
this idiot, and who wanted to get closer to the music, said
sharply, "Don't be absurd, man." And then, "What sort of a
trap?"

Well, as to that, Muldooney would not like to say. He had
heard tell of such places, he said darkly; wicked sinful houses
set on lonely roads to trap weary travellers, luring them inside
where all manner of decadent practices went on.

John Grady said, "But it's just a tavern. Look at it!"

Muldooney did look at it, and a poorish sort of place it
looked, half set into a rock as it was, and with a kind of greenish growth half obscuring it. He thought that anything might
lurk in there, although he did not say this, because of being
called absurd again. Muldooney was not a man to invite insults. He said, rather loudly, that the place did appear to be a
tavern, to be sure it did, not that he had ever actually been inside such a place. He had too much consideration for the
teachings of the Survivors, he said rather piously; hadn't they
taught how the Letheans' taverns had been wicked places, full
of laxity and greed, and very likely even—fornication. He said
this last word in a whisper, because it was not the sort of word
a man liked to use, not even to Grady the Landgrabber. Espe-

cially not to Grady the Landgrabber. Anyway, he said, if you believed only a quarter of the stories about the Letheans' drinking places, your toes would curl in your boots. To himself, he thought that the place had the same sort of *wrongness* about it that the music had. Also, he'd heard tell that you had to spend good money in such places, and that, although he was not of course a mean man, was a great old consideration.

Still, there was Grady, dead set on going in after the music, and Muldooney was not going to be left standing out here at the mercy of the cold dark night. Very likely it would do no harm to just go inside for a rest and a bit of a warm. He was also just the smallest bit curious to see what such a place might look like. And so he agreed that after all they'd just take a look inside, and then they'd be on their way again. He thought privately, that if there was any paying out to do, Grady could do it for the both of them, for wasn't he known as a well-heeled man in Tugaim, and him an Elder to boot! Plain pig farmers had not the means to be flinging good coins about in taverns. He would tell Grady so if he had to. Muldooney was not the man to jib at speaking his mind.

John Grady, staring at the half-covered, half-cave place, said in an odd, vague voice: "We might meet someone inside who would direct us on our way again," and Muldooney at once saw the sense of this. *What* way, he did not quite know, but he had heard that people were apt to be very friendly in taverns. Even so, John Grady hesitated.

The lighted windows of the low dwelling were rather inviting, and the place itself was intriguingly and attractively set into the rock face. There were warm savoury scents and there was an air of welcome. Every fibre of him wanted to step inside and follow the music to its source.

But he hesitated, because it accorded ill with his position as an Elder of Tugaim to go inside such a place, but even so . . .

Even so, surely his credit was sufficient for just this one visit? And there was the point that a man had a duty to know what went on in the world; how else should he guide sinners away from sin? Unaware that this worthy-sounding but possibly specious reasoning had been used by generations of gentlemen (and one or two ladies) who knew it their duty to guide fellow creatures away from sin but had sometimes been found doing so in some very questionable places, John Grady now moved forward.

The doorway—they were surprised not to see a proper wooden door—was low and curved and quite narrow. Both men had to duck their heads to go through, and Muldooney, who was a bit bulky (all of it good solid muscle, of course) had to turn sideways. He beat down the sudden impression that he was descending beneath the ocean, and thought had you ever seen the likes of that Grady, as keen to get inside as a bull to a cow! And him an Elder! Muldooney might be a good many things, but one of the things he was not was a hypocrite.

Once inside it was not quite as they had expected. It was also very quiet. It was ominously quiet, in fact. There was a waiting, a sense of unseen eyes, unseen minds, unseen hands ready to reach out and draw the humans farther inside.

Yes, yes, farther in, Human Travellers, come farther in . . . farther in and farther down . . . down into the caves beneath the sea . . .

Muldooney and Grady stopped and looked about them.

"This is extremely odd," said John Grady, and Muldooney agreed at once, because it was odd, it was surely the oddest thing out of the many odd things that had been happening of late. Where was the music? Where were the people? John Grady looked for the people and listened for the music, because he knew that taverns were heavily frequented. Muldooney looked for ladies of a certain reputation, because he knew that they were always to be found in taverns. He had never, of course, seen a whore, but he dared say he would recognise one if he did. To a person of perception these things were always apparent.

They were standing in a low cavernlike place, with waterlight rippling on the walls, and a faint bluish greenish light seeping in from somewhere. There was the muffled sound of water somewhere—the ocean! thought Muldooney, and was startled into fear, because wouldn't it be a terrible thing altogether to be trapped down here if the ocean came rushing in.

The oceans are our friends, Human Travellers . . . come inside and you will see . . . And then, as if in completion of a formula: *You are expected.*

Neither man recognised the words which had once been almost ritualistic in the telling of fairy stories in the Lethe world.

Neither man recognised the words, but both men recognised *something* ... a threat? a menace? A whole unsuspected *dark* world yawned, a world where shadowy caves housed nameless evil, where silky voices invited the traveller to come inside, even where a place was laid ready at the table and a bed prepared ... where the Lost Traveller was "expected" ...

There had been no door, but both men had the impression of a huge door, iron-clad, steel-studded, clanging to behind them.

And now we are locked in with whatever inhabits these caves, and the ocean is above us, and the waterlight is all about us, and it is cold and dank and we are being drawn towards a forgotten world ... Muldooney felt horror prickle his skin; he knew they were shut in with a *something*. John Grady, by now more deeply under the *sidh*'s spell than his companion, thought: I am getting closer to it.

Both of them moved forward, Muldooney warily, though he did not see what else was to be done, for they could not go back—could they?—and it would not do to stand stock-still like a brace of idiots. And so they moved a little nearer to the soft light, a little nearer to the music's heart.

Come farther in, Human Travellers ...

The waterlight rippled and stirred all about them, and there was a gentle lapping sound. The floor beneath their feet was damp and cold, and as they moved, a scattering of objects crunched and snapped with a brittle splintering twiglike sound.

The Bones of Men, Human Travellers ... cast up by the seas ... but not until we have sucked them dry of their marrow, and not until we have taken their senses and their souls and woven them into our music ... The music you hear is the music made from Men's souls, Travellers, and from their eyes and their hearing and their speech ... What shall we take from you, Human Travellers ... ?

A cascade of cold triumphant laughter echoed round the cave ...

Brian Muldooney, honest, practical pig farmer, knew by this time that there was something quite dreadfully wrong with the cave. Wouldn't it be as plain as a cowpat to anyone other than Grady the Landgrabber? But Grady was plunging off ahead, and so Muldooney followed, because you could not let a fellow man go off alone into a dark cave with queer lights and the strangest old feel to it. And anyway, Muldooney did not want to be left out here by himself.

John Grady said, in a rather odd voice, "It has a strange atmosphere to it, this place," and Muldooney thought that if he never heard another understatement in his life, at least he'd heard one now, because couldn't you feel the evil of the cave soaking into your bones, and couldn't you smell the danger as strongly as if it was an uncleaned pigsty. This was odd, because he had always prided himself on being down-to-earth, a great one for the practicalities of life. Wasn't he known in Tugaim—yes, and a bit farther afield as well!—as the most practical pigman between Galway and the Boyne!

But he knew that the caves, like the music, were wrong. They were very wrong indeed. Even so, when Grady said, "I suppose it won't hurt to just see what lies ahead," Muldooney said it would not hurt a bit, to be sure it would not, and thought that Grady looked as if he was a man in a trance. He ventured the suggestion that they were not, after all, in a tavern, and John Grady said quite sharply, "Of course we are not in a tavern! Don't be a fool, man." Muldooney thought this unnecessarily harsh. Any person of sense could see it was not a tavern, it was no more a tavern than Muldooney was a tinker's donkey. It was a nasty dark cold tunnel they were walking along, full of echoing whispered laughter and billowing shadows; full of an odd tuneless music that froze a man's blood in his veins, and set him thinking of those dark oceans again, and those endless chasms into which a man might tumble, down and down, until he came to the centre of the ocean and was trapped there forever.

"But," said Grady, in a whisper, "think of what you would see if that should happen," and Muldooney jumped and stared, because it had seemed, just for a second or two, as if Grady, actually John Grady the Landgrabber, had known what he, Muldooney, had been thinking.

John said softly, "I do know. I can hear and I can sense everything down here." And then, "Listen," he said, and put out a hand to grab Muldooney's arm, so sharply that Muldooney thought he would very likely display a bruise for days.

The whispers seemed closer now. They echoed and reverberated about the cave roof.

Closer now, Human Travellers . . . and your senses are

*sharpening . . . you can hear and you can see and you can feel
with heightened perception, with greater clarity than ever you
thought possible in your bleak, faraway world . . . we are hon-
ing your senses, Travellers, for we do not take what is not of
the best . . . we shall take your souls and your senses for our
music . . . so come nearer and see us for we are lovelier than
anything you have ever dreamed of . . .*

"Down here," said Grady with a purposeful air, and
Muldooney thought would you just look at the cheek of the
man, taking them into something that would probably turn out
to be very nasty indeed. And a terrible thing it would be to get
lost down here. A man might easily wander about for longer
than bore thinking of. A man might certainly lose his wits
down here.

*Yes, yes, you will lose your wits and you will lose your soul
for we are fishers of souls, we are greedy for your bodies and
your souls, Men of the Desolate World . . . we send many a
Human from these caves into a dark hopeless world . . . we
can take your sight, your speech, your hearing . . . it is all one
to us which we have, but it is what makes the music, and it is
what makes our beauty, for beauty feeds on pain . . .*

Grady said, still in the same soft wondering tone, "I have
never heard anything so truly lovely in my life," and paused
and then moved forward again, Muldooney panting along after
him, for wasn't the man all but running now. When John said
impatiently, "Do keep up, Muldooney," Muldooney opened his
mouth to protest, and then closed it again, because you had to
keep all your energies reserved for the chase, in a situation of
this kind. It would not do to get lost down here.

*Lost without a soul, Human Travellers . . . without sanity . . .
for what is the difference between soul and sanity . . .*

"No difference," whispered John Grady, his eyes fixed to
the pinpoints of light ahead of them. "Oh, no difference at all."
The laughter echoed all about them again, and Muldooney received the eerie impression of snakelike blue and green arms
reaching out to them. Like writhing smoke, like ice-cold fire.
Really, this was a very strange place, and if this *should* turn
out to be a tavern after all, then all that Brian Muldooney
would say was that taverns were not what he had been led to
believe.

They were walking along some kind of low-ceilinged passage now, with Grady always leading. Muldooney thought they were winding even farther downwards, and the lapping of the ocean was all about them. It was to be hoped that there would be no fissures anywhere in the rocky walls of the passage. It was to be hoped, as well, that neither of them slipped on the wet slippery rock floor. A turned ankle would be a very awkward thing to have down here. You had to be practical. Probably, of course, there would be a great old letdown at the end of all this.

"Oh no," said Grady. "Oh no, Brian, you will see," and Muldooney felt the hairs stand on end on the back of his neck, because no one, *no one*, and especially not John Grady the Landgrabber, ever called him Brian. Something very peculiar was happening to both of them and it was especially happening to John Grady. Still, thought Muldooney—who was not fanciful but who was beginning to be frightened—still, I'd better stay with him.

The tunnel widened into a stone chamber, and Muldooney thought they must be near to some kind of river, because a soft waterlight rippled on the walls. There was the faint far-off sound of water lapping gently on a shore.

You are beneath the oceans, Human Travellers . . . you are in the water caves of the sidh *. . .*

It would be better for Muldooney not to be seen. Muldooney was not the man to run away, of course, but even so, it would be better not to be seen. He would just conceal himself somewhere and wait for Grady to come to his senses again, when they could go peacefully home (couldn't they?) and all would be normal again.

And so he crouched down into a shadowy corner and began to feel chilled and afraid, and hoped there was not going to be any violence, and watched John Grady walk into the centre of the light. And although the light made your eyes ache, after a while it began to seem to Muldooney that there were shapes inside the light . . . figures . . . thin sensuous creatures with round, hard, sleek heads like seals, and slender silky bodies, and arms and hands that curled and beckoned like blue-green flames on the hearth fire on a frost-ridden night.

They were not quite human, those shapes, but nor were they quite inhuman either, and Muldooney could not decide if that made it better or worse.

*We are not human at all, Men of the Desolate World . . . we
have no human blood in us, only the music of the Old Gods
and only the hunger of our lusts . . .*

Grady was at the very centre of the light now, and the *sidh*
were all about him, tying him with thin silver cords, spreading
his body out, the arms and legs outflung. The cords were tight;
Muldooney could see them cutting into the man's flesh.

*We must have you safe, Human Traveller, we must not allow
you to escape us . . . None do escape us . . .*

Sanity was returning to John Grady's eyes now, and with it,
fear.

"Let me go."

Laughter filled the cavern, and the waterlight rippled and
danced on the ancient stone walls.

*There is no escape, Traveller, you are ours for all time . . .
You are ours until we tire of you, until we have sucked you
dry . . .*

Grady struggled and the cords bit tighter. Beads of blood
flecked his skin. Muldooney thought: should I try to free him?
But what about those blue and green creatures?

The *sidh* were clustered about Grady, peeling off his clothes,
their tendril hands and fingers caressing his skin. Muldooney
saw that despite his fear, Grady was reacting to the caressing
hands; the man was becoming aroused. Really, wasn't it a terrible shocking thing to crouch here and witness a fellow man
be given a stalk like an autumn crocus, even if it was only
John Grady?

The *sidh* were swarming all over Grady now, liquid and
formless at one moment, nearly but not quite human the next.
Muldooney thought it must be like feeling thin water pour over
your body. Beautiful. But he thanked all the gods he believed
in that it was Grady out there and not him.

The *sidh* were lying across Grady now, four and five and six
of them all together, and Grady was beginning to breathe a bit
faster.

*You cannot escape us, you must stay here and love us until
your loins are empty and aching, and until your mind is spinning . . . you cannot leave us without bequeathing to us one of
your five senses . . .*

Muldooney was genuinely sickened at what happened next,
and honestly horrified to find himself powerless to help. He

had been really rather fascinated by the sight of the *sidh* pouring over Grady's naked body; he had watched, unable to look away, while the blue and green fire licked the man's body from head to heels, until Grady was all but enveloped by the icy flames.

Give us your seed, Human, for there is nothing we like so well as the warm seed of a human spilling over us . . .

As Muldooney watched, Grady's body arched and jerked, and semen spurted between his legs, so that the *sidh* moaned in triumph and writhed.

More, Human, we want more . . .

They closed in on him again, reaching their smoky hands for him, insinuating their slender boneless bodies against him.

In the hours that followed, the *sidh* worked most cruelly and most pitilessly on John Grady, and Muldooney, cramped and cold in his corner, saw everything.

To begin with, it was rather beautiful in a cold sinister way; the sight of the cave creatures, ever changing, never constant, was something he thought he could watch for ever.

But the *sidh* allowed their victim no mercy, and Muldooney began to feel rather sick after a while. Grady was brought again and again to abrupt and painful orgasm.

John Grady let out a dreadful cry—"No more! Please . . . I am dry." And Muldooney's own thighs tightened in involuntary sympathy. Once Grady broke a hand free of the thin silver cords and clutched his groin protectively, but the *sidh*'s hands whipped out, and pinned his arm down again.

More, Human, more . . . we will have your blood and your marrow and your juices, and when we have done, you will leave us your soul . . .

Grady was moaning and sobbing. "I am empty. I am dry. Leave me be . . ." But the *sidh* were darting all over him, icy tongues of blue flame; they were bathing him in an eerie blue fire, and if it had not been so terrible, it would have been breathtaking.

And then: *Turn him over . . . we will wring you dry, Human, we will take every drop you have . . .*

They turned him on to his face, spreading his thighs apart. *Wider . . . wider . . . we shall pleasure you in the ways of men with men . . .*

Muldooney choked, "Oh God," and saw the snaking boneless hands reach between Grady's buttocks.

And, incredibly, Grady hardened again.

There was a great exultant cry: *Not dry! Not empty! Give us more, Human* . . .

But Grady was barely conscious now; as the *sidh* turned him on to his back again.

We will have one last thing from you . . . we will take one last offering . . . we are fishers of souls and we are fishers of senses, and if we do not capture your soul, we will take one of your senses . . . to feed our music and to feed our beauty, Human Traveller . . . One of the senses . . . we will take one of the senses . . . which shall it be? . . . sight, speech, hearing, taste, touch . . . Which? Which? . . . eyes, ears, nose, fingers, tongue . . .

A pause. Then:

TONGUE! Speech! We will take your speech, Human, and we will pour it into our music and the world's music will be the richer for it . . . you will never speak again, Human . . . you will never be able to tell of what happened to you in the caves beneath the sea . . . you will never speak again . . .

The blue and green fire reached up to his face and smokelike, ethereal fingers that felt like steel clamped about his jaw. He felt his mouth forced wider and wider, and he strained back, feeling his eyes bolting from his head.

What were they going to do to him?

And then the hands were reaching down into his mouth, down and down into his throat, so that he choked and retched and jerked away. But the fingers held his jaws wide apart, and he could not resist.

He felt something in his throat tighten and strain, and then pain exploded inside his mouth, and agony tore apart his throat, a dreadful, raw, open agony that sent his mind spinning.

His mouth was a huge wound, filling up with thick blood that ran down his throat and spilled from his lips, making him gag and vomit.

The *sidh* released him at last, and he sagged on to the floor, vomiting blood and saliva, pain throbbing inside his mouth, his control stretched to its ultimate.

Blood dribbled in great clotted strings from his mouth, and he thought: *they have torn out my tongue.*

The thin thread of his control snapped, and a merciful darkness descended on the tortured plains of his mind.

MULDOONEY FLATTERED HIMSELF that he was not often found at a loss—ah, you had to look a long way before you could match Muldooney—but he was completely at a loss now.

They were standing on the road again, and he was clutching John Grady's arm, poor mutilated soul, and trying to think what they had better do next.

The dreadful thing was that he had seen it all so clearly, in fact he had seen it a great deal more clearly than he had cared for. But there had been no help for it; crouched in his corner, he had seen the *sidh* hold open Grady's mouth wide, so wide it must have hurt his jaw intolerably; he had seen the blue and green sinuous arms dart into Grady's mouth, and he had seen and, more terrible, *heard* tendons tear and skin rip. There had been a truly sickening glutinous sound as Grady's tongue had been torn from his head, and there had been a kind of unwilling sucking sound.

For a moment he had thought that the cave creatures were now going to turn their attentions to him, and he had crouched motionless in his corner, unable to turn and run, quite unable to think of how he might defend himself. And there had been John Grady, lying in his own blood and vomit, a nasty sight if ever there was one, but Muldooney was not the man to leave a fellow creature alone in a place like this. It was not something you did.

But the *sidh* had faded, dim blue and green forms, dissolving into early morning mist, dissolving into the rocks, so that you wondered if you had in truth seen them.

Oh, you have seen us . . . you may see us again, for we are in the oceans of all the worlds, and we are in the music of all the ages, and in every century we fish for souls for our music . . .

And now here they were, on a dark road that might go anywhere or nowhere, and Muldooney had not the remotest idea of what had happened. He admitted, if only to himself, that they were quite hopelessly lost, and he certainly admitted that they had quite clearly strayed rather a long way from Tugaim. If it would not be fanciful, he would almost have begun to think they had somehow got themselves into one of those ancient legends that people sometimes told of. Muldooney knew that people spoke well of legend-telling, but when you were a pig farmer you did not have very much time for that.

He considered the matter carefully, because it was as plain as a pig's bottom that John Grady was not going to be of any help, and he rather thought that he would do well to concentrate on practicalities. This made him feel better than he had expected, because hadn't he always been the great one for the practicalities? People often said so. Ah, Muldooney the pig farmer's the man for the practicalities, they said. It was entirely true.

The first thing to do was to decide about Grady, poor tormented soul. There he was, as witless as a chicken, and it the middle of the night! Muldooney knew that a number of people might call pigs witless, but pigs were solid sensible creatures. They were predictable. Whoever heard of a pig that went running about the yard like a banshee after its head had been cut off! There was never a pig yet born who would be so ridiculous, but anyone who had seen a newly decapitated chicken knew precisely what to expect! Witless!

John Grady, who had kept chickens, was witless now. He was wild-eyed and empty-eyed, and he was floundering all over the road, not seeming to recognise Muldooney or their whereabouts, although to be fair, Muldooney did not recognise their whereabouts either, only he knew it was certainly not Tugaim any longer. But there were the practicalities to be thought of before anything else, and there was Grady reeling and grunting. If anyone came along and saw him, it was sure that there would be a vacant seat on the Council of Tugaim's Elders! Of course, Muldooney himself would not be at all averse to just stepping into place. Not if he was asked in the proper manner, he would not be. And then he remembered that no one could come along from Tugaim, because Tugaim had somehow inexplicably vanished.

Blood and spittle dribbled from Grady's mouth, and he kept emitting animal grunts of pain. Every now and then, he spat, rather sickeningly, and Muldooney, who was inclined to be a bit squeamish, tried very hard to repress a twist of nausea, because to be sure, the poor man could not help it. The pity was that there was nothing at all that Muldooney could do. It was not even possible to give the tormented soul a cup of water to rinse his poor wounded mouth. Muldooney felt helpless, and began to feel angry with himself for feeling like that, because surely there was something he could think of. Wasn't there?

If only someone would come along . . .

And then, entirely without warning, someone did come along. Just as Muldooney was thinking that perhaps after all they were in the middle of some kind of nightmare, and trying to calculate what ought to be done, a light appeared, a little way off, and Muldooney felt the most enormous relief he had ever known in his life. It would be altogether grand if it was someone they knew, but anyone would be welcome really. At least the burden could be shared. Muldooney, who had rather thought he liked a bit of solitude—because say what you would, most people were empty-headed chatterers—thought it would be altogether grand to share this problem with another human being.

He sat down and took John Grady's hand in his because you had to give the man some bit of comfort, and watched the bobbing light draw nearer. He thought it was probably a lantern, being carried by someone, and he was certainly more thankful to see it than he had ever been to see anything in his life.

The lantern was held by a lady, rather tall and pale, cloaked and hooded, and apparently prepared to be extremely helpful.

Muldooney, remembering his manners, got to his feet, and made haste to explain. A shocking accident, he said . . . His poor friend hurt and bewildered . . . And the both of them hopelessly lost.

At the back of his mind, there flickered the vague hope that the lady might be able to point them in the direction of Tugaim, but when he suggested this, she only said, in rather an odd voice, "Tugaim? Dear me, I have never heard of it. I fear you are quite *hopelessly* lost, my friend."

And then she lifted the lantern aloft and studied the two of them for a moment. A rather satisfied smile curved her lips. "But if you will allow it, I will help you," she said. "I am abroad very late, and should be glad of some company. My house is not very far distant. If you will come there, you will see that a welcome is always kept for travellers.

"And my two sisters will be *so* pleased to see you."

* * *

IT SEEMED TO Joanna that the carrion crows got nearer all the time.

"That's nonsense," said Gormgall, but Dubhgall said it was not nonsense at all.

"Her Ladyship *knows*," he said.

"Yes I think she does," said Cormac.

Joanna did know. She knew that every time they saw the birds the sun slipped behind a cloud and a chill settled on the mountain. She could feel the Nightcloak stirring uneasily.

"Spies?" said Cormac.

"Something much worse," said Joanna and shivered.

Cormac took her hand. "We are nearly at Gallan," he said. "Cait Fian's Mountain Palace—"

"I don't think we're going to reach it," broke in Joanna, her face white and strained. "I don't think we're going to be allowed to reach it."

As they rounded a curve in the path, there was the sound of laughter, and a dreadful, dry, rattling-bone noise.

"Indeed you will not reach it, my dears," said a voice, and there, barring the way, was Morrigan, with Scald-Crow and Macha behind her.

There was no point running—"Even if there was anywhere to run to," thought Joanna wildly. The Morrigna would catch them, they would easily outpace them; Macha's army of monsters would fall on them and claw them back; Scald-Crow would turn into some loathsome *thing* that would pull them into Morrigan's waiting arms.

At her side, Gormgall said, "The cloak—use the cloak!"

Joanna gave an angry sob: "I cannot! 'Never twice against the same enemy!' And the Nightcloak was used in Morrigan's house in Muileann!"

"Against the Miller!" said Dubhgall. "Try it!"

But the cloak was dead, as Joanna had known it would be.

"Of course it is," said Morrigan, coming forward—Joanna saw the white Bonds of the Hag form and reach out to trap them. "The High Queen knows that her cloak may not be used twice against the same enemy. You destroyed that oafish fool the Miller with it, and since he acted under my direction, it was as if you had used it against me, *Your Majesty*." She reached out and snatched the Nightcloak from Joanna's shoulders.

"You cannot wear it!" yelled Cormac.

"Watch me," said Morrigan, swirling the cloak over her shoulders.

Behind her, Scald-Crow let out a wail and jumped up and down. "I wanted it! You promised! Let me have it!"

"Silence, Sister, or I will allow Macha to send the Hags to devour you!"

Macha grinned and lifted her arms as if to summon them at once, making Scald-Crow droop her lip . . . and droop it and droop it, until she became one enormous drooling *lip*, slimy and glistening with saliva.

The four travellers were bound tightly now, and Joanna wondered how she could have forgotten the horrid stickiness of the Bonds.

"You will have plenty of time to re-acquaint yourself with them," said Morrigan, standing close to her, and Joanna thought that her saurian look was more pronounced than she had remembered it. Morrigan seemed to tower over them, easily eight feet high, and Scald-Crow spiralled up from her lip shape and became an overripe corpse, with juices bursting through the skin. Joanna shivered and looked away.

Morrigan walked round the group, in a slow thoughtful circle. At length, she said softly, "And so we face each other again, my friends." She looked at Cormac. "A pleasure to see you all once more."

"Where are you taking us?" asked Cormac.

"You will join my other prisoners," said Morrigan. "A little something I gathered up for my Master. He will enjoy them, but not half as much as he will enjoy you, Wolfking . . . the choicest morsel of all. I shall serve you to the Erl-King on a jewelled platter, and we will sup your blood and dine off your flesh."

Silver platters and golden goblets . . . of course there was never any escape, not really. How foolish of us to imagine otherwise, Joanna thought.

"Foolish indeed," said Morrigan, and the snake-tongue flickered. "You are all my prisoners once more; you are bound by the Bonds of the Hag, and you are going to the Erl-King's Citadel.

"And this time there will be no escape!"

CHAPTER NINETEEN

An air of dark menace hung over the Erl-King's Citadel and over the little straggling township that had grown up around it. We do not choose to live here, the people of the walled city seemed to say, but we know no other life. We have to live. Our families have to eat.

They all knew the tales, and all of the legends about the Erl-King. They knew about the silver platters and the golden goblets—were not their silversmiths and their craftsmen kept busy by the fashioning of them? They knew about the great vaulted sculleries below the Citadel where the ovens were set with massive brick buttresses, and where the fires were kept burning for days sometimes, and the pots were left simmering for nights on end.

For human fat takes a long time to burn down, and human bones take a long time to dissolve . . .

"Light the fires and heat the pots . . ."

They knew better than anyone the truth of all the stories whispered about the Gentleman; they preferred to call him that, they said, their eyes sliding away. They knew about the windowless cells cut into the rock, and the cages in the bowels of the Citadel, cold dank dungeons where prisoners might languish for years. Except that prisoners did not live very long at all in the Gentleman's cages. They were brought up to the Banqueting Chamber each evening for the Gentleman's pleasure. The Hall was always lit by wall sconces—human fat slowly boiled down on the brick ovens made the Gentleman's candles—and there would be knives, pincers, needles. It was whispered how the Gentleman sometimes gouged out his vic-

tims' eyes and ate them; how he ordered thin slices of flesh to
be cut from their arms and then forced that flesh down the
poor creatures' throats; how he slit their throats and drank the
fresh warm blood direct from their veins as they died.

It made them feel less than men to know themselves powerless to help the poor wretched victims. But we have to live!
they cried despairingly. Our families have to eat!

And it was rare for the Gentleman to seek his prey in the
Walled City itself. He went farther afield, sending his hunchback servant to scour the countryside on the black sledge
pulled by jackals; or he extended hospitality to the Three Sisters of Muileann.

The Master needed them, said the townspeople. He needed
their craftsmen and their artisans. Boys and young men—never
young girls—were sent to the Citadel to work, and good honest work it was as well. The Citadel needed constant maintenance; it needed carpenters and stonemasons and scullions.
The Gentleman kept his own sentinels and guards and chariot
horses. Chariot horses had to be cared for and cleaned and fed;
sentinels and guards had to be fed as well. They had their own
kitchens, a little apart from the Citadel; it was no shame to
cook for the Gentleman's guards, and it could be rather useful
as well, because there was frequently a surplus of food, which
could be taken down into the town. You could feed a family
very well indeed on the leftovers of the guards; sides of ham,
barely cut into, a dish of brawn, roasted meats of all kinds. A
family could live very comfortably in the shadow of the Citadel. And on the nights when the Gentleman drove out of the
Walled City, his hunchback whipping up the team of jackals, a
sense of freedom so great gripped the entire town that all manner of revelries went on.

And so it was not so difficult to turn a blind eye and a deaf
ear on the nights when frightened screams pierced the quiet, or
when running footsteps rang out in the cobbled streets. They
were used to it, said the townspeople, huddling together in
their little houses. None of our concern, they said when the
handcarts came rumbling through the streets under cover of
darkness. None of our concern; lock the doors and shutter the
windows and do not, on any account, hear if the knock falls on
the door . . .

For although the Gentleman did not as a rule take his prey

from the Walled City, there were nights when the countryside was in the grip of winter; when the jackal sled could not get through the city gates, and when the frozen highways and the moonless nights permitted of no journeying in or out.

On those nights, the hunchback would come loping down into the town, just as dusk was creeping through the streets, dragging the handcart, his lumpish swart face avid and searching, and full of ugly mirth.

My Master has the hunger upon him tonight!

And someone will be devoured ...

It was whispered that the hunchback also had hungers; that he rutted with young boys and forced young girls to pleasure him in unnatural ways; that his Master turned over to him the drained corpses of the victims, so that he might relieve his lusts on the lifeless mutilations.

It was better not to know. It was better not to listen for the hunchback's shuffling gait.

And if the next morning, the town's ditches ran with reddened water, it was nobody's concern—even if somebody's child, somebody's sister, or wife, or love was missing. It was no one's concern but their own; griefs skinned over in time, ditches could be cleared.

Silver platters could be polished and golden goblets could be cleaned.

Flight was impossible; rebellion was not to be considered. There was not a one of them who had not, at times, dreamed of marching in torchlit procession up the hill, and razing to the ground the towering evil fortress; there was not a one who would not have liked to drive the Gentleman's own torture weapons into his black heart, but there was not a one who did not know it to be impossible. You did not need particularly good eyesight to catch daily glimpses, daily reminders of the tremendous Girdle of Gold that circled the Walled City; you did not have to be possessed of especially quick wits to know that the Girdle of Gold, the most marvellous enchantment ever created, rendered the Gentleman forever safe from enemies. It circles the Gentleman's fortress and his town—and it circles us as well, thought the townspeople. We are shut in with him. And while he has the Girdle, no one can get into the Walled City without him knowing. Nor could anyone get out of the Walled City without having the jackals on his trail. You would not get ten leagues, said the people. The hunchback would whip up his sled and you would be caught and taken to the Gentleman's stone Banqueting Chamber.

And then?

Better not to think about it, said the townspeople, and went diligently and unseeingly about their daily business.

They were accustomed to the Gentleman's prisoners being brought into the Walled City by the handcarts, and at such times they knew what was expected of them. And although it was not in their natures to cheer the miserable captives, they knew that the hunchback would be on the watch with his sly darting eyes, that he would mark—and mark *out*—anyone not seen to cheer. To displease the hunchback was almost as dangerous as to displease the Gentleman himself, for it was the hunchback—and sometimes the Three Sisters—who kept the Gentleman's dungeons filled, kept his ovens stocked.

And so it was prudent to line the streets when the handcarts came rumbling through the Walled City on their way to the Citadel. It was sensible and wise to jeer and poke fun at the poor wretched creatures who lay bound and terrified in the carts. Not to do so might earn you a place in the cart yourself, and then who would look after your wife and your children? And so the townspeople learned how to jeer and mock, and how to humiliate the already humiliated prisoners. They learned to sing the Goblin Song of Muileann.

> Light the fires and heat the pots,
> Sizzle the fat in the waiting vats.
> Mince and stew and roast and batter,
> Pour the juice in the Erl-King's platter.

They learned to exult in the Gentleman's powers.

THE FOUR PRISONERS brought in by the Sisters reached the Walled City midway through a bright afternoon, the Girdle of Gold strong and iridescent above the City walls, sunlight sending diamond sparks from the windows of the houses—too beautiful a day to go to your death. Far too beautiful a day on which to know yourself bound for the silver platters and the golden goblets.

A second cart followed, containing two men roped and

bound, but the townspeople did not spare them a second glance once they had seen the figure in the first cart.

Proud. Defiant. Pale and ragged and travel-stained, but with his head held high and his golden eyes inspecting his tormentors insolently. *Mock me only at your peril!*

The crowd fell silent, briefly puzzled, for although the prisoner was familiar, no one quite recognised him.

And then quite suddenly, everyone recognised him and everyone knew him.

The Wolfking. Cormac mac Airt. Cormac Starrog, the great High King of all Ireland, who had ruled from the Bright Palace of Tara, and who had been exiled by his cousin. The One True High King.

And in the power of the Gentleman!

They would have *liked* to show him their loyalty, and they would certainly have *liked* to show him their sympathy. *They did not dare do either.* The hunchback was scanning the crowds gleefully, the leather whip laid beside him. *A fine prize for my Master! Exult with me!*

In the second cart which held the two no-account prisoners—one plump and rather pig-faced, the other a bit witless-looking—also rode the Morrigna, all three of them, triumphant and evil. Morrigan's reptilian eyes darted hither and thither. *See what I have snared for my Master! See the choice morsel I have brought him!*

The lady at the Wolfking's side was slender and pale, and extremely composed. She was not Cormac's queen, for they all knew that he had no queen. But she was regal, she was dignified. The people of the Walled City were not accustomed to seeing the Gentleman's prisoners so composed and so arrogant seeming. Even the two servants—Cruithin by the look of them—were glaring and scowling and entirely unquenched.

But the townspeople cheered and called out insults, and chanted the Goblins' Song, because it was death, and a bad death at that, to do otherwise. As the carts rumbled through the City and on up the hill to the Citadel, they dispersed and went to their homes, because it would be dangerous to be seen discussing the prisoners. But all knew that the ovens would be firing, and all knew that the Gentleman would be licking his lips over the prize brought to him by Morrigan and her Sisters. He would taunt and torture the Wolfking and his lady for a very long time tonight.

But in the end, there would be the silver platters and there would be the golden goblets.

The Wolfking and his lady and their two servants would be eaten by the Gentleman . . . they would not necessarily be dead when he started.

FLYNN WOULD NOT have believed it possible to be so instantly and so thoroughly at one with a group of people he scarcely knew, but so it was. From that first night with Conaire and the others, there had sprung up a deep sense of comradeship, the underlying feeling that these were his own people. By the time they came to the Morne Mountains, the feeling of homecoming was so strong that he thought he could have believed that he had never really lived anywhere else.

There had been one rather bad moment, on the second day of their journey, when they had crossed a part of the mountain range and seen from a distance the Walled City of the Erl-King.

"Dangerous," said Conaire, shaking his head. "We ought not to have come so close."

"Why did we?"

"It's the best route to Scáthach," said Oscar, but Flynn saw how they all looked uncertainly towards the Walled City far below them, surrounded by ridges of mountain. He followed Conaire's pointing hand to the cluster of buildings at the foot of the dark Citadel.

"The Erl-King's township," said Conaire in a rather subdued voice. "Poor creatures."

"Can they not escape?" said Flynn, and the nobles of the Bloodline looked at him in surprise.

"No one ever escapes from the Erl-King," said Conaire.

"People are born and die in the City," said Midir, and Flynn saw him turn pale.

"No one ever really grows old there though," put in Sean.

"That's a terrible thing to say," said CuChulainn.

"It's true though."

"I'd break out," said CuChulainn, planning at once. "I'd muster an army and I'd lead it against the Erl-King."

"They haven't the spirit any longer, poor creatures," said

Oscar sadly, his eyes on the far-off City. "They are crushed and quenched and utterly terrified. Do let's leave here."

But Flynn stayed where he was, looking down on the Walled City of the Erl-King, seeing how the little buildings huddled together, seeing the dark menacing shape of the Citadel, set a little apart from the township. He felt a sick dread at the sight and shuddered, because Joanna might be anywhere in this sinister world, she might even be inside the Walled City and at the Erl-King's mercy.

"I felt," he said to Amairgen afterwards, "as if I ought to be down there."

"Joanna?"

"Oh dear God, I hope not," said Flynn. And then with a little shake, "No, of course not. Out of all the places she might be, why should she be there?"

"There is no reason at all," said Amairgen, but he had heard behind Flynn's words the sudden fear, and he thought: I believe Flynn *does* think she is there. And although he stretched his mind to its utmost, and although he used the Samhailt to its outermost limits, he could feel nothing other than a nebulous darkness, and a formless evil.

And then Conaire said, "Flynn, look. Over to the east. Gallan. Cait Fian's Mountain Palace," and pointed. Flynn saw, in the distance, pale spires and blue turrets, wreathed in cloud.

"The most beautiful place in Ireland," said Etain, and for the first time, there was a softness in her voice.

They turned in the direction of Scáthach at last. "It isn't as far as it looks," Conaire said, rather anxiously. "And we can go through the mountains."

"It's too close to the Erl-King for my comfort," said Sean in a cross mutter.

"But anywhere in these mountains is close to the Erl-King," said Oscar, with the patient air of one who has explained this a good many times already. "But so long as you go by daylight—"

"And keep a *very* sharp look-out," put in Midir.

"Yes, so long as you do that, you ought to be safe," finished Oscar.

But Flynn left the Walled City behind with reluctance. "It was irrational," he said to Amairgen and Portan later, "but I could not help it."

"They understand," said Portan, nodding to the others. "I think they will help us, Flynn."

"Oh yes," said Flynn.

"They are our people," said Portan, softly. "But you knew that, in any case." She smiled. "I am glad you told them who we really are."

Flynn had told them the truth about himself, Portan, and Amairgen on the first night, as they had made camp, and sat together round the fire.

They had listened attentively and absorbedly. "And Flynn told the tale well," Portan said later to Amairgen.

"Flynn is Irish," said Amairgen, and smiled. "We are a nation of storytellers, my dear."

Conaire and the others had been fascinated. They had sat for a very long while—"into the night," said Portan, who was coming to love the gentle scented nights of this ancient land—and they had wanted to know everything about the world that Flynn and his companions had come from.

"It is so interesting," said Oscar. "I wish so much that I could travel though a time curtain."

CuChulainn had wanted to know about the Apocalypse. "Didn't your people fight him?" he said, and Flynn tried to explain that the Apocalypse, when it came, had been so vast and so invincible, that it had burned the world and nearly destroyed mankind.

"There were no possible defences," said Flynn.

"I'd have thought of one or two," said CuChulainn. "I'd have fought."

Sean had been so taken with the notion of people from the future, that he had taken himself off into the forest to write an account of the entire thing, "for posterity," he said seriously, and had become so absorbed in his task, that he nearly missed the supper that Etain and Midir had cooked, and had to be searched for, and CuChulainn, who had gone to help find him, had tripped over a trailing ivy creeper and fallen headlong into a bed of nettles.

"Dock leaves," said Midir. "Go and find some."

"Be thankful you fell headfirst instead of the other way about," said Sean.

"Stop making such a fuss," said Etain. "Come and have

some supper. Flynn is going to tell us some more about his world."

But Flynn found himself curiously reticent. He sat eating the supper, which was rabbit stew, and very good indeed, and said that they would find it a rather bleak, rather barren world.

"And I never fitted there," he said.

"None of us did," said Portan rather wistfully, and Flynn thought: but at least Portan is at home now. And knew that of the three of them, it was Portan who must certainly never return to Tugaim.

Conaire and the others had been helpful and interested and very sympathetic about Flynn's quest to find Joanna. "We do not pry," Conaire said seriously, "not ever, for to do so would be to violate the Ancient Code of the Samhaill. But we understand, Flynn."

Oscar said, "And if we can, we will help you find Joanna."

Flynn found it odd, but unexpectedly comforting to hear Joanna's name spoken like this, normally and naturally. These people had never met Joanna, but they would help him to find her. Quite suddenly, he felt confident; in some way, just to speak of her, to share the doubts and the plans like this, made her strongly alive. Of course they would find her. Of course she would be safe.

And then Oscar, whom Flynn had noticed appeared to possess the Samhaill more strongly than the rest, said thoughtfully, "She might be at Scáthach," and everyone sat up startled, and CuChulainn upset his plate of stew.

"Why?" said Midir.

"Well," said Oscar thoughtfully, "it is only an idea, you understand . . ." and paused, frowning, so that Flynn had to restrain himself from shouting at Oscar to continue. It was Portan, who was discovering a cautious friendship with Oscar, who said, "Would you tell us, please?"

"Well," said Oscar again, "I am thinking of the Enchantment that binds the Wolfking to Scáthach," and looked at them.

Conaire said slowly, "Cormac is held in Scáthach by the Enchantment woven at the time of the Great Rebellion. What did they call it?—the Enchantment of Captivity wasn't it?"

"Scáthach was never a prison of locks and bars," put in Etain.

"No, which is why, when anyone is sent into exile, the Enchantment of Captivity has to be woven."

"You wouldn't keep the Wolfking bound for very long, not even with that," said CuChulainn, but he said it rather uncertainly.

Oscar said, "But they did keep him. They bound him with the Enchantment, and they threw him into Scáthach." He leaned forward, eager to make them understand, his eyes bright in the fireglow. "Don't you remember it?" he said. "The terrible spell woven by the sorcerers under Eochaid Bres's bidding—"

"Under Bricriu the Fox's bidding," Etain broke in, and everyone nodded in agreement.

"That was a dreadful day," said Conaire. "You could feel the weight of the Enchantment everywhere you went." He looked at Flynn and the other two. "They had thrown Cormac into the dungeons," he said. "We all knew he was there. But until the Enchantment was woven, they dared not let him out."

"He'd have been at their throats in an instant," said CuChulainn. "Wouldn't he just!"

"The Enchantment was like a—like a massive dark heaviness," said Conaire. "We all knew what was happening, and none of us could do anything about it."

"I didn't look," said Sean.

"You wrote a good enough ballad about it afterwards, though," said Midir.

"That was for posterity," said Sean, injured.

"I went away and got drunk," said CuChulainn. "I don't care who knows it."

"And a fat lot of good *that* was," said Etain scornfully.

"I talked to the sorcerers," said Oscar, his eyes faraway now.

"Oh that wouldn't do any good. We all know that the sorcerers only work for those who pay the highest," said Conaire at once.

"They're supposed to be solely in the service of whoever occupies the High Throne," said Etain.

"Only we all know that they're not," added Midir.

"Well anyway," said Oscar, "I did talk to them, and they let slip one very interesting thing about that Enchantment." He looked round at the listening faces. "Don't any of you remember the ancient belief?" he said. "No, I can see you don't. Nor did I, until one of the sorcerers mentioned it, purely by accident. And he oughtn't to have done, you could see at once that the others were very angry with him."

"*He'll* be for the Miller's cages," said CuChulainn with relish. And then, with an apologetic look, "I don't like sorcerers," he said.

"Who does? Go on, Oscar."

"It's the ancient belief that a pure-bred Human can sometimes break the Enchantment of Captivity," said Oscar thoughtfully. "Surely you remember it? *'Open locks, to the Human's hand . . .'* It's a very old belief," he said. "I don't know how true it is, of course."

"There's no use in a belief if it doesn't work," began Sean.

But Conaire interrupted, "No, but Oscar's right. I'd forgotten that myself."

Open locks, to the Human's hand . . .

"It has to be the right kind of Human, though," said Oscar.

"Why haven't we remembered this before?" demanded Sean.

"I'll bet Cormac's remembered it," said Etain. "You see. I said Scáthach wouldn't hold him."

"Of course Cormac's remembered it," said CuChulainn. "The first Wolfkings believed in that very strongly. Don't you remember the old saying that only the Humans were the Kingmakers? Cormac will have been laying traps for Humans ever since he was thrown into Scáthach. And if he *hasn't*," he said severely, "then he isn't fit to return to Tara." And he sat back and regarded them all.

"CuChulainn's right," said Midir. "If you were Cormac, and held by the Enchantment of Captivity, what would you do?"

"Fight," said CuChulainn promptly.

"Rubbish," said Etain. "You can't fight an enchantment with muscle."

"Don't be silly, CuChulainn," said Oscar, but he smiled as he said it.

"You'd set a trap for a Human," said Conaire thoughtfully. "Of course you would." He looked at Flynn. "Cormac would try everything to break the Captivity Spell," he said. "He would make sure that the Wolves—and probably the *sidh*—

would lure every Human who ever came near to Scáthach inside."

Midir wanted to know if Cormac would trust the *sidh*.

"Yes, because the *sidh* are actually quite loyal to the Wolfkings," put in Sean. "They always come up to the gates of Tara and sing whenever a Prince is born. Don't you remember?" And then, as everyone looked blank, "Well," said Sean rather quickly, "of course, I was only a child myself when Cormac was born. But everyone knows the story of the *sidh* singing him into the world."

"But surely, Cormac would not have had to wait until now to find a—a Human?" asked Amairgen.

"How long has he been at Scáthach?" asked Flynn, and the others muttered and calculated, and at length, Conaire said, "Five or six years."

"That is a very long time," said Amairgen gently.

"Yes, but Scáthach is dreadfully remote," said Oscar. "And it has to be a—a particular kind of Human."

"What kind?"

"Well," said Oscar, "it is only a small part of the legend, and I don't know that I would give much credence to it—"

"Don't prevaricate," said Etain.

"I wasn't," said Oscar, "it is only that it sounds rather . . ." He frowned. "The legend says it has to be a direct descendant of the Royal Line.

"It has to be one with the blood of the first High Queen of all in her veins."

FEELING SICK FROM the jolting of the cart, and from the hunchback's pinches and fingerings, Joanna thought: finally and at last, we are all inside the Erl-King's Citadel. She watched as the drawbridge was lowered, and then, because she could not bear the feeling that they were going into a dark tunnel, she turned to look at the two prisoners in the other cart.

Muldooney had borne up rather well. He was pale and rather belligerent-looking; Joanna vaguely remembered that he had struck out quite hard at the guard. But he did not seem very frightened by any of it.

"The confidence of ignorance," Cormac had said, and as Joanna looked inquiringly at him, "He has not the slightest idea of who the Erl-King is, or what is ahead."

Joanna looked back at Muldooney as the carts rattled over the drawbridge, and finally, with a deep reluctance that made her feel ashamed, she looked at the other man.

"Is there nothing we can do for him?" she had asked Cormac earlier.

"We will see."

But Joanna had known, as Cormac and the Cruithin had known, that the *sidh*'s victims were always beyond human help. There would be nothing at all that any of them could do for John Grady. Joanna, her throat aching with unshed tears, thought it was unlikely that the Elders of Tugaim would recognise the shattered figure in the cart. John's hair was lank and matted, his eyes stared blankly ahead of him, and there was a low shambling look to him.

"Animal," said Cormac after a glance. "Unintelligent animal. It is often the way with the *sidh*'s victims. They take away something which can never be replaced."

"The soul?" Joanna said hesitantly.

"They are called Fishers of Souls," said Cormac. "But he sold you to the man called Muldooney. Where is the difference?"

"There is a difference," said Joanna. "It is different in our world."

"Is it?" said Cormac. As they crossed to the walled courtyard inside the Citadel, his hand closed about hers.

The great iron gates clanged to behind them, and panic gripped Joanna ... Lost. We are utterly lost. We are in the hands of one of the most evil beings ever known. We are in the power of the Erl-King. Tara is lost to us, and we shall die slowly and painfully.

And when we are dead, he will eat us.

I can't bear it, thought Joanna, and in the next moment, knew that of course she must bear it. I won't despair, she thought determinedly, I will not. We are not counted dead until all is done, and I will not believe that all is yet done. A thin, rather uncertain vein of confidence trickled into her, and she clutched at it and held it, because it was a good thing to hold on to in this terrible place, and anyway, there was nothing else. But they were not dead until all was done.

They were surrounded by guards the minute the carts jolted to a halt. "Do not let these ones escape!" cried Morrigan, her cape whipped about her like bats' wings in the wind. She stood watching as they were pulled from the carts by the guards.

"Well, Your Majesty?" she said, smiling the snake-smile. "I bid you welcome to my Master's house." And then, to the guards, "Take them below.

"We shall meet at supper, Sire," she said to Cormac. And then, looking to where Joanna stood, "And there will be a very *particular* welcome waiting for you, madam."

They were pulled and pushed by the guards into a dark narrow doorway with an iron grille in the door.

"The Gentleman's *special* apartments," said the guard with a leer, and Cormac snarled and rounded on him, lunging and clawing at his face, drawing blood. The guard jumped back and clapped a hand to his face.

The hunchback was at his side at once, his whip snaking out. "Mind that one," he said. "Vicious. Half wolf. My Master likes wolfmeat." He moved ahead of them with his quick lurching step, rattling a great bunch of keys, and the prisoners were forced along by the guards.

The passages were narrow and low-ceilinged, and so sharply angled that at times it seemed as if they were about to walk into solid rock. The walls had the faint bloom of damp, and a constant drip of water from somewhere. Joanna shivered, because the sound conjured up vast dark caverns with great still pools of black water . . . there was something very sinister about large masses of stagnant water.

They were thrust into a single cell which had been hollowed into the rock, so that it had three solid stone walls and one of iron. The water sounded louder here, and there was an echo.

Cormac fought as they pushed him into the cell, and Gormgall and Dubhgall struggled; even Muldooney, who was by now frightened, but who was not going to be thought a coward by such company, managed to land a good square punch on one of the guard's jaws. The man retreated and eyed Muldooney unpleasantly.

"You'll regret having done that, son of the Pigline," he said, and Muldooney, flown with his show of bravery, made a rude noise at the guard.

To be sure, this was a very strange situation they were all in, but Muldooney would not be the man to be found wanting. He had been quite surprised to see Joanna again, and he had an uncomfortable suspicion that he had not acquitted himself perhaps as well as he might have done that afternoon in the farmhouse bedroom. He thought to himself that it behoved him to appear in a good light to Joanna, and he was certainly not going to allow the other three men to find him at a loss. He had not the slightest idea of where they all were, but he supposed that someone would tell him at some point. For a moment he toyed with the idea of asking, but it would not do to admit his ignorance, and anyway, everyone else seemed to know. Muldooney would bide his time and listen very carefully, and probably he would quite soon find out what was going on. Ah, they all of them thought him dull-witted, but he was cannier than any of them realised. He sat down in a corner and waited to see what came next.

Cormac had been standing by the bars, and now he said to the hunchback in an imperious tone, "You! Come here!" and Joanna, who was nearby, thought that even like this, beaten and captured and under certain sentence of death, he was unquestionably the High King.

The hunchback regarded him, and then came lurching back. "Well, wolf?"

"Something to sit on for the lady, if you please," said Cormac, and stared at the hunchback unblinkingly. For a moment, Joanna's heart leapt; she thought the hunchback flinched beneath that hard golden stare, and hope bounded up in her. Then the hunchback grinned, and beckoned to the gaolers and pointed.

"He wants something for his *lady* to sit on!" said the hunchback derisively, and looked closely at the guards, almost, thought Joanna, as if he was waiting for their reaction; certainly as if he was saying: well you scum? Haven't I made a joke? Then laugh with me!

There was a split second of silence, as the gaolers seemed to search for the requisite response. Then it came.

"Something to sit on?" said one. "We'll give her something to sit on."

"I know what I'd like to give her to sit on," said the other, eyeing Joanna. "And it wouldn't be a chair, neither."

Cormac said frostily, "She is frailer than the rest of us. A chair, of your mercy."

"Oh, a *chair*!" said the gaolers. "And of our mercy! She'll sit on the floor like the rest of you!"

They picked up their lanterns and began to move away down the passage, and Muldooney got up to frown because Joanna had been looking at him and it was always a good idea to spring to a lady's defence. He remembered how he had punched the gaoler, and began to feel quite pleased with himself.

The hunchback lingered, staring at the prisoners, and inspecting John Grady who was slumped against the far wall.

"Him. What's the matter with him?"

"He's witless," said Gormgall shortly.

"No concern of yours," added Dubhgall.

"Witless, is he? Best thing for him in here then," said the hunchback. "You'll all be joining him before the night's over." He leered at them again, and then shuffled off, taking the remaining light with him, the lantern throwing weird fantastic shadows on to the rock face as he went.

For a long time, nobody in the narrow cell spoke. Muldooney was just summoning up the courage to ask did any of them know exactly where this place was, when Gormgall said, practically: "Has anyone any means of making a light of some kind?" and Muldooney was quite glad he had not asked, because it seemed as if nobody else was wondering where they were. He remembered that he had decided to listen and bide his time.

The silence that followed Gormgall's question about a light was rather dreadful, because they were all suddenly aware of the dark. Dubhgall said in an aside to Joanna that it was probably not as bad for Cormac as for the rest of them, because wolves had some nightsight, but Joanna did not feel any better for knowing this.

Nobody appeared to have any method of making a light, and Joanna had just begun to wish Gormgall had not made the suggestion, when Muldooney suddenly said, "I have a tinder box," and Cormac said crisply, "Excellent."

Muldooney turned beet red with pleasure, and thought he was not acquitting himself so ill. He might not know just where they were, but he had stuck up for Joanna when the gaolers had been so rude (well, he had frowned at them anyway), he'd punched one of them quite hard, and now he was able to provide everyone with some kind of light. He fired the tinders carefully, and bunched together a piece of old sacking and some straw so that it made a rough but serviceable torch, and Gormgall stuck it into an ancient wall bracket. There was a bad moment when they feared the straw to be too damp to burn, but after a moment it caught and flared up, shedding a welcome light on them.

Dubhgall was just wondering could they tunnel their way out, and inspecting the floor to see how solid it was, when Cormac said, in what both the Cruithin recognised as his battle tones—"My friends! We must hold a Council of War!" Everyone sat up a little straighter, and Muldooney thought wasn't it a grand thing to find you had a leader amongst you, and got up to make a second torch, so that they'd all see the clearer, and also so that everyone would remember his contribution with the first one.

Gormgall and Dubhgall exchanged looks, each thinking: His Majesty's in fighting mood again, and Joanna leaned forward, clasping her hands about her bent knees, and hoped they would be able to think of something effective.

Cormac fixed each one of them with a penetrating look, and despite her fear, Joanna felt herself responding. There must be a way out. Surely they would find it.

Cormac said, "We are in the bowels of the most terrible fortress ever known," and Muldooney nodded wisely to show that he had known this all along. "We are in the power of a creature who has at his beck some of the strongest necromancers in all Ireland, and we must consider, one by one, the ways we may use to outwit him." He looked at them again, and Joanna suddenly understood that Cormac was deliberately and calculatedly making them think; he was making them turn their minds and their energies to forming a plan. He was rallying them.

"Well? Surely each of you can come up with a suggestion?" said Cormac. "Or am I served by creatures of no imagination! Gormgall, let us hear from you first. Speak man!"

Gormgall looked unhappy. "Well, Your Majesty," he said and stopped, and Cormac frowned. "Well, Your Majesty," said Gormgall a little louder, "normally I'd say create a diversion and then, just as you've got the other side properly confused, nip out under cover of it all." He looked a bit doubtful. "I know it isn't brilliant," he said.

"No matter, it is a thing to consider. We might incorporate it into a larger plan. Dubhgall?"

"I say tunnel, Sire," said Dubhgall, pointing to the hard-packed earth of the cell floor. "We mightn't get out, but we'd get somewhere, and that somewhere might be a place we could hide in for a time."

"Yes. And—Muldooney?" Cormac eyed the man with a blend of curiosity and amusement, as if he had never encountered his like before, and Joanna thought: oh my, I believe that Cormac is actually enjoying this, and at once caught the flare of a thought from him.

Enjoyment is not the right word, my dear. But I am alive again; I am face-to-face with the real enemy at last! I may lose my life before the night is out, but I shall at least be fighting for all I hold dear! He smiled at her, and Joanna smiled back.

"Muldooney," said Cormac in a decisive tone. "We should have met under happier circumstances, but here we are, and we will be glad of your ideas for escape."

Muldooney was, truth to tell, rather awed by Cormac. He had grasped by now that Cormac was some kind of King, and although he was not accustomed to such things, he was glad to know that he was not the man to be intimidated. Ideas about nobility and about titles were Lethean of course; Muldooney would certainly not be dazzled by them. Even so, Cormac was like no one he had ever encountered, and Muldooney found himself deferring. He did not exactly tug his forelock, but he spoke very respectfully indeed. To himself he thought that if he could come up with a plan that Cormac approved, it would be a very good thing. And then he remembered about impressing Joanna as well, and he began to think that it would really be a rather good thing to stand well in the sight of these two. When at length he spoke, he found himself doing so clearly and simply.

He was a man of limited imagination, he explained, tucking down his chins. And there was no good pretending he had ideas and plans, because he did not. This was not quite what he had set out to say, but he saw the look of approval in Cormac's eyes, and he saw Joanna smiling at him, and he thought that after all, you could not beat truth. There was the thing; to tell the truth and be honest.

He did not quite say that with the provision of a light for them all, he had expended his reserves, but he implied it, and everyone present privately agreed with it. Gormgall, in fact, considered that His Majesty was wasting his time on this fat, rather stupid person, but he was too polite to say so. Dubhgall, who would not have considered politeness, thought it as well, but did not say it because it might have started a fight, which was the last thing they wanted, and anyway they hadn't the room.

Muldooney, after losing himself in a welter of opening sentences and circumlocutions, finally said they should negotiate terms. It was what was always done, he said. Hadn't they any of them heard of all the wars where leaders had done that? You negotiated terms, said Muldooney, beginning to think the expression had a good sound to it.

Nobody, with the exception of Joanna, knew what he was talking about. But Cormac thanked him with such exquisite courtesy that both the Cruithin instantly thought: well, at least His Majesty has this fool's measure!

Then Cormac said, "Joanna?" and Joanna felt her heart lurch, because she knew at once that Cormac wanted her to come up with the solution.

"Nobody ever escapes from the Erl-King's Citadel," she began, and quite suddenly, she knew what Cormac wanted.

CHAPTER TWENTY

THE PLAN HAD slid into Cormac's mind whole and complete, its edges neatly trimmed, its surfaces planed smooth. He thought it was not the most watertight of plans, but he thought it might work. Energy coursed through his body, for he had spoken truly when he sent Joanna the thought: I am alive again!

He felt more alive than he had through the dreary years at Scáthach; he knew that the greatest battle of his reign lay ahead, for the Erl-King was Tara's oldest and strongest adversary. He was not afraid, for he had in his veins the blood of the High Kings, and he would meet death if he must. But he would not meet it passively, and he would put up the wildest fight the Citadel had ever seen. And the fight would begin with the plan.

Joanna, the dear brave child, had seen it as well, of course, he knew that, she had picked up his thoughts easily and clearly. It was from Joanna that it must come. Only she, of them all, had the right. He fixed his eyes on her face and willed her to speak.

Joanna took a deep breath. She said, "I do not think we can beat the Erl-King and the Morrigna by human tricks, or by human strength either." And unwittingly, used the words of Bricriu the Fox. "We must fight sorcery with more sorcery."

"Sorcery to beat sorcery," said Gormgall, and nodded. "Sound reasoning, my lady. Go on."

"We cannot get help from outside," said Joanna.

Gormgall said, "Forgive me for interrupting, but Sire, the Samhailt—"

"—cannot get through the Girdle of Gold," said Cormac.

"Ah. Forgive me, but has Your Majesty actually tried—?"

"Yes," said Cormac in what was very nearly a growl.

"Forgive *me*," said Gormgall again. "It's only that it would have been grand to think of the Wolves streaming into the Citadel."

"Forgive me," said Cormac, and his hand briefly touched Gormgall's shoulder. "But to see the Girdle of Gold like this—in the hands of Dierdriu's great enemy—"

"Yes, it's a bad thing," said Gormgall solemnly. "And of course, her ladyship's right; we cannot expect any help from outside." He looked back at Joanna expectantly.

"And," said Joanna, "since the only way to fight sorcery is with more sorcery ..." She paused and looked at them all, "we must get the Nightcloak from Morrigan."

Gormgall said slowly, "But it has already been used against Morrigan."

"Yes. Or against her creature—the Miller, which apparently amounts to the same thing." Joanna leaned forward, her face serious. "But if we used it against the Erl-King ..."

They all looked at one another, and Muldooney adopted an air of concentration. At length, Dubhgall said, "But would it work against him? Would it be strong enough?"

"And," said Gormgall, "how would we get it away from Morrigan?"

Joanna said, "I don't know if it would be strong enough to defeat the Erl-King. I don't know what it would call up."

"The nightmares of the victims," said Gormgall slowly.

"Yes. A terrible thing," said Joanna, who was trying very hard not to think of what sort of creature might be expected to strike fear into the Erl-King.

Cormac said softly, "Pan was not terrible."

"No," said Joanna, looking up. "Nor he was."

"But the cloak must first be got back," said Gormgall.

Joanna, speaking rapidly, not looking at any of them now, said, "When we are taken to the Banqueting Chamber, the Erl-King's attention, and Morrigan's also, will be on the Wolfking and on me ... That's not vanity," said Joanna, anxious to explain, "it's a statement of fact. Morrigan wants to avenge herself on me because of what I did to her in Muileann. We know that. And both of them have always wanted the King. We know that as well.

"I don't think they will kill us straight away," said Joanna, looking and feeling rather sick. "I think there will be—well, preliminaries. It won't be very nice, but we shall have to—to do the best we can.

"Now—they will keep an eye on the rest of you, of course. That's you Gormgall and you Dubhgall, and Muldooney and on—my father. But probably not such a close eye. So it will be up to one of you to create a diversion of some kind, so that while their attention is distracted, I can take the cloak."

There was a thoughtful silence.

Gormgall said, "I don't see how we could do it, my lady."

"You yourself suggested a diversion of some kind, Gormgall."

"Yes, but not—" Gormgall looked round uneasily, and then, lowering his voice, "not in the Banqueting Chamber itself!"

"But it's the only place where we can be sure Morrigan will be present."

"That's true," put in Dubhgall. "She'd never miss seeing her great enemies defeated and humiliated. If only we could be sure she'll have the Nightcloak with her."

"I think she will," said Joanna. "I think she will want to use every weapon she can to taunt us."

Gormgall said, "Can she actually use the cloak as a—well, to call anything up?"

"No," said Cormac. "Only a pure-bred human can do that. And we know how strongly the cloak responds to Joanna."

Gormgall said, "But what kind of diversion—I'm sorry Sire, but I don't think it will work. The very minute one of us steps out of line, he'd be whipped straight back."

"Not," said Joanna, "if the person creating the diversion was not in possession of his sanity."

This time the silence lasted longer. They stared at her.

Then Dubhgall said, in a low voice, "But your ladyship, begging your pardon, but—he'd never do it. He wouldn't understand what was wanted." He stole a glance at the blank staring eyes; John Grady had barely moved since they were put in the cell, he had grunted once or twice, but he had stayed lying slumped against the cell wall. "It wouldn't work," said Dubhgall.

"He's right," said Muldooney, unexpectedly speaking out. "The poor man couldn't be made to understand." Muldooney had followed the conversation carefully; he had not said very much, because he had not been able to think of anything to say, and he had been told that a still tongue meant a wise head. He had only dimly grasped the business of this cloak they all seemed to set so much store by, but he had certainly grasped Joanna's idea about creating a diversion, and he thought it a sound one. But he agreed with Dubhgall, and although he dared say it was not his place to speak out, speak out he had. You had to have the courage of your convictions sometimes. And it was a remarkable thing, but when he *had* spoken out, voicing his agreement with Dubhgall, in a firm voice, they had all turned to look at him, and they had listened and nodded their agreement. Muldooney was not very used to people according him this degree of attention, and it occurred to him that it was rather pleasant. And although it would be too much to say that it lent him confidence (because there was never a Muldooney born yet who lacked confidence, of course), he found himself able to join in the discussion that followed and to feel that he was a part of it all.

Joanna said, very calmly, "But I did not mean him to do it. Of course he could not. One of you must pretend to be witless."

"But," said Gormgall, "that would mean there'd be *two*. And the guards and Morrigan and the hunchback all know that when they brought us here there was only one."

"Yes," said Joanna, and looked at them all very steadily. "We cannot trust him to carry out our plan, and so one of you must take his place.

"And since, as Gormgall says, we cannot have two idiots, then the real one will have to die.

"We shall have to kill him."

Cormac thought that if he had never loved Joanna before, he loved her in that moment, her little face white, her eyes huge and fearless, her voice steady. But Cormac could feel, as the others could not, that she was burning up inside with horror, and he could feel that every nerve in her body was alive with pain. Even so, he thought, she understands that if we are all to live, then one must die.

If they all died, Tara would be within the Erl-King's grasp at last . . .

Cormac looked at Joanna and remembered the old word "kingship," and the new one "statecraft." She has both, he thought, and remembered again the old stories and the old beliefs in Dierdriu: The High Queen would return when her people were in their darkest hour . . .

Joanna said, "It is the only way, you know," and there was a silence, while each of them absorbed the plan, and each of them saw that it was indeed the only way.

Gormgall said, "Who is to take his place as the—the witless one?" and they all looked at one another.

And then, quite without warning, entirely without anyone suspecting, Muldooney said, "I will."

And Joanna leaned forward and took his hands, "Oh will you? Will you really?" and Muldooney turned beet red and patted her hands, and tried not to hear Dubhgall who had snorted disgustedly.

In fact, Brian Muldooney, respectable, unimaginative pig-farmer, was becoming genuinely appalled at the mess they were all in. He had by now grasped that they had all fallen into the hands of a very evil being, and he quite saw that Joanna's plan was their only chance of escape. As for playing the fool a bit when the time came, well, they might all of them find it hard to believe, but Muldooney could cut a bit of a caper with the best. Ah, Muldooney might not be one of your fine handsome gentlemen (although there were those who had considered him not so dusty in his time!) but when a bit of the fool-playing was needed, Muldooney was your man! He squared his shoulders in manly fashion and cracked his knuckle joints a few times, just to show them all how formidable he was, until Dubhgall said, "That's a terrible sick-making sound. Is it some kind of affliction you have?"

They discussed the plan from all angles, and Muldooney was careful not to miss a thing, because it was best to know what was expected of you on these occasions; and finally, Joanna said, "I cannot see any other way. I wish I could." And her eyes went to the figure in the corner.

They had made some further attempt to bathe Grady's poor wounded mouth, although there had not been very much they could do.

"But I have a lotion that will soothe it," said Gormgall.

"If he'll take it," said Dubhgall.

Grady would not take it. He had lapsed into a kind of stupor, but when Gormgall tried to sponge his mouth and Joanna held his hands down, he backed away, glaring at them with such maniacal fury in his eyes, that they stopped. He was a pitiable sight by this time. His hair was lank and matted—"And somehow greyed," said Joanna—and his clothes were muddied and bloodied, and really rather sordid.

"We are all muddied and bloodied, of course," said Gormgall always sympathetic.

"There's a difference," said Dubhgall.

But the greatest and the worst difference was in Grady's face. Joanna, who could hardly bear it, thought it was as if his features had collapsed in on themselves, as if his bones had all been extracted along with his power of speech. His eyes were dull and staring, except for the brief occasions when they became filled with a mindless fury. It was this that tore Joanna apart with pity and revulsion. She thought she might have coped with the pity, but to recognise the revulsion was barely endurable. Several times she tried to talk to him, searching for a flicker of recognition, but there was nothing. John Grady simply sat dribbling and staring at nothing, soiling himself where he sat, utterly beyond their reach.

"He is gone," said Cormac when Joanna wept on his chest. "Human Child, he is for ever in the dark, and he is for ever lost to the world of men. We will make an end to his suffering, and his death will help Ireland."

Joanna said, "Yes, of course. Forgive me. And I hold by my plan." She sat up and wiped her eyes, and everyone tried not to look, although Dubhgall blew his nose rather loudly. Gormgall and Muldooney both assumed an air of hopefulness, and Muldooney had the mien of one who carries a weighty responsibility. A feeling of optimism pervaded the cell. "Although," murmured Gormgall to Dubhgall, "there's the actual disposing of the poor man to be done."

Cormac, who heard him, said at once, "That is not the least bit difficult. There is a pressure spot on the neck. A few seconds only. Quick and clean. He will never know." He looked at them rather haughtily. "And only a High King may decide when to take a life," he said, and Gormgall and Dubhgall both backed off.

Cormac turned to Joanna. "All right?" he said gently.

Joanna gulped and said, "Yes. All right," and Cormac moved swiftly to where Grady sat, and reached out his hands.

CHAPTER TWENTY-ONE

FLYNN AND THE others stood on the ridge of rock that led across the chasm and stared ahead of them.

"Scáthach," said Conaire softly. "The Fortress of Shadow."

"Ireland's place of exile," said Oscar, from behind him.

"And," put in Sean, "it looks deserted."

"It *is* deserted," said Etain. "I *told* you."

Scáthach was very deserted indeed. They walked warily through the echoing chambers and halls, and peered into the empty galleries, and heard their footsteps echoing rather forlornly in the huge old fortress, and tried not to remember that the Wolfking had lived here for five long years after he had been cast out of Tara.

"Unbearable," said CuChulàinn.

"He did bear it, though," said Conaire.

"Did he?" said Etain.

But the signs of departure were there, and the signs of recent occupancy were there as well. Oscar laid his hand against the chimney breasts—"Warm," he said. "My friends, it is not so long since fires were kindled here."

And Sean, descending to the kitchens—"By instinct," said Conaire—reported that the bread in the crocks was still fresh, and that honey and cheese and milk were all there. "And the side of a nice piece of pork as well," he said, and CuChulainn looked hopeful, and said he did not see why they should not spend a night's rest here.

But at length, they stood facing one another in the dim sunken hall that Joanna had entered, and when Conaire said

softly, "He has broken the Enchantment," a great delight flared
between them.

Flynn, watching, standing between Amairgen and Portan,
thought: yes, but *how* has he broken it? *"Open locks, to the
Human's hand . . . "?* Oh Joanna, my love, were you here?
And did you in truth dissolve the Enchantment? He closed his
eyes, and for a moment, Joanna was with him, so that he could
hear her laughing and see her eyes narrowed against the sun,
and he could smell the clean hair and the sweetness. An ache
of longing rose up in him, but he listened to their plans, and
agreed quite calmly with CuChulainn that they might as well
rest inside Scáthach before going on.

Conaire said, "Yes, we could certainly start for Gallan in the
morning. We could be quite comfortable here," and Sean and
CuChulainn went off to see about the food and discuss could
they find any apples to go with the pork.

Flynn, seeing Portan lead Amairgen to a fireside seat and
then turn to mend the fire, felt suddenly and sharply lonely. He
thought: I believe Joanna *was* here, and the wish to have her
with him, to share this strange, beautiful, cruel world with her,
was so overpowering, that for a moment he felt he could not
go on. And then confidence came rushing back, and with it
strength: I will find her if I have to tear Ireland apart with my
bare hands! and he was able to sit with Amairgen and discuss
the journey, and speculate on what might be ahead.

After supper, which CuChulainn and Sean prepared between
them—"And very good it was as well," said Oscar, who believed in praising people as often as you could—they sat together to discuss their plans.

"Gallan," said Conaire firmly, and the twins nodded in
agreement. "At daybreak," said Conaire. "Because it's a long
journey we'll have."

"And," put in Sean, "it means going through Muileann."

A sudden silence fell. Finally, Oscar said, "We could go
round Muileann."

"Could we? How could we?"

"Where's a map? Hadn't the Wolfking ever a map in this
forsaken place? What? Oh, a map room. Well," said Oscar,
"I'm rather surprised to find such a thing in Scáthach. I'll wager that Eochaid Bres and Bricriu didn't know about it when
they brought the King out here."

"Eochaid Bres and Bricriu don't know everything," said Midir.

"They only think they do," put in Etain.

"Yes, but are the maps any use?" said CuChulainn.

"Let's find out," said Flynn, and nearly the entire party got up and tramped off through the castle, making, said Sean, a great to-do and raising a good deal of quite unnecessary noise.

"Of course, it all comes of bringing CuChulainn and those unruly twins," he explained to Amairgen who was sitting in the sunken hall, with Portan nearby. "They're the King's men, you understand," added Sean, "and they'll be very useful in the battle, well, so will all the creatures of the Bloodline. You wouldn't believe the havoc that the Swans can cause, and of course, as we all know, there's not many that can hold back a stampeding team of Chariot Horses.

"But they're so *noisy*," said Sean, lifting his head complainingly, as the rest of the party stamped about overhead, punctuating their search for the map room with cries of "Who's got the key?" and "Don't trip over that bearskin," and "While we're at it, let's raid the wine cellars."

"They're so *loud*," said Sean. "They have to be off doing things. Finding things. It's very tiring."

"I'm sure it must be. Tell me, is Gallan a great journey off?"

"Well I have to say it is," said Sean.

Amairgen said rather wistfully, "I should like to have seen it. Is it as beautiful as they say?"

"Yes," said Sean. Portan reached out for Amairgen's hand.

"You will see it," she said softly. "For *I* shall see it for you," and Amairgen smiled, and returned the pressure of her hand, and Sean, who was not, of course, the smallest bit sentimental, had to blow his nose rather violently, and interpose a question about the world Amairgen and Portan came from.

"Not," he said earnestly, "that I'd pry."

"Of course not," said Portan politely.

"No, but I have to be always on the alert for new ideas," said Sean seriously. "You never know what mightn't be useful."

Portan said, "You would not like our world, Sean. It is cruel and harsh and—rather bleak." And she leaned back against the warm brick of the chimney breast and smiled at Sean, and Sean smiled back.

The others, in the meantime, had finally discovered the map room. "And a fine gloomy old place it is," said CuChulainn, disgustedly surveying it. "I don't suppose the Wolfking entered it from one year's end to the next."

"I don't suppose he knew it was here," retorted Etain.

"Well now we're here, let's see what we have," said Flynn, turning his attention to the maps they had unrolled on the table, and to the quarrel that was now being happily waged.

The twins and CuChulainn were all for going openly through Muileann. "Never mind the Miller," said Etain, "we can deal with a dozen Millers," but Oscar was inclined to opt for a discreet journey across the plains.

"We'd be more noticeable crossing the plains," objected CuChulainn.

"Not if we went by night," said Oscar, and a sudden silence fell. To journey across the countryside in the bright clear day, hailing chance-met fellow travellers, taking meals in the high noon, was one thing; they were all used to that. They rather enjoyed it. But to go by night, secretly and furtively, not able to see an enemy creeping up behind you, well, that was another thing entirely. They looked at one another, and several of them remembered that the Morrigna were said to scour the countryside for victims by night, and several more remembered that in all the old stories, the Erl-King walked abroad after nightfall.

Flynn, holding on to patience, said, "But which is the quickest route?" and they all turned to look at him, and Oscar, the most perceptive of all these very perceptive creatures, said, "Flynn, we had almost forgotten—" and Etain came to sit beside Flynn and said, "But we had not really forgotten."

Flynn said, "I suppose it does not really matter where I go, because she might be anywhere," and hoped this did not sound as desolate as it felt.

Oscar said thoughtfully, "But, you know, I don't think that's entirely so," and Flynn looked up.

" *'Open locks, to the Human's hand,'* " said Oscar softly.

"Then you *do* think she is with Cormac?"

Oscar said, "Cormac escaped from Scáthach *somehow*."

"And," said Conaire thoughtfully, "he escaped quite recently."

"So he did," said CuChulainn, and they all looked hopefully at Flynn.

"Could Joanna have broken the Enchantment?" said Flynn, but even as he said it, he was remembering the etched gold of the portrait deep beneath Tara.

Dierdriu, the High Queen who would one day return . . .

"Why not?" said Conaire lightly, and Flynn thought: yes, after all, why not?

"And," said Conaire, "if Joanna is truly with Cormac, then we are almost certainly going in their footsteps at daybreak."

"We are following them," said Midir, and Flynn looked at them, and felt again the strange sense of comradeship, and thought: yes, I was right. They do understand. And with an effort turned his attention to the maps again.

Oscar was explaining carefully that they would not be going anywhere near to the Erl-King's Citadel. "You see?" he said, spreading out the map and setting weights on it because it had been rolled up so tightly for so many years that it kept springing back. "Here is Gallan." He indicated the jagged mountain range. "And here is the Erl-King's Walled City. There's at least two days' journey between the two."

"I've often wondered," said Conaire, "how Cait Fian has managed to live so close to the Erl-King and escape him."

"Cait Fian's got nine lives," said Midir and grinned.

"He's got good sorcerers," scoffed Etain.

"Well you should know."

"Everyone knows," said Etain. "And anyway, there's the mountains, very nearly encircling Gallan. You hardly need sorcerers to protect you with those. They'd be nearly as good as the Girdle of Gold. All Cait Fian has to do is station the Panthers at the mountain passes to keep an eye out for intruders."

"But supposing an intruder killed the sentry Panthers?" said CuChulainn.

Conaire said, "Have you ever tried to kill a Panther?"

CuChulainn said, "Oh. Oh yes, of course."

"You've got to catch it first," put in Midir.

"And Cait Fian would only send out the best," added Conaire.

"Cait Fian only has the best anyway," said Etain.

Flynn said, "Aren't we wandering from the point?" He could see with surprising clarity that the best route to Gallan was around the Muileann Valley and through the Morne Mountains, and he thought that Cormac would certainly have taken that route. But although he wanted to throw the maps back into the cupboard and set out for Gallan there and then, he knew that without the others, he would be at the mercy of this unknown, wild land.

But once you would not have been, said his inner voice and although the longing to be up and off and find Joanna was still gnawing at him, he felt a sudden surge of excitement. Because I made this journey once before perhaps? Because I planned this route in another life and in another world and in another time? Yes, perhaps. And, *Joanna, my darling girl,* he thought, *if I cannot find you, then for sure the great Finn can.* With the thought came the confidence again. Yes, she is here, and yes I am going to find her. *Finn will not let her be lost.*

Finn of the Fiana *and the High Queen Dierdriu* ... The thought sprang unbidden, and Flynn frowned, because there was something there, something he ought to remember ... And then memory shifted and fell into place, and he remembered that only a direct descendant of the Royal line could break the Enchantment of Captivity, and he remembered that someone, somehow had certainly broken it, and then memory moved again, and he was standing in the chambers that ran beneath Tara, staring at the carved face on the Rock.

Dierdriu, and yet Joanna ... He thought: but of course Cormac has her, and of course she is safe, and it was as if a great calming hand had laid itself on his mind. It will be all right. I shall find her.

Oscar was saying, "Well, Flynn? What do you say? Do we travel to Gallan by night?" and Flynn discovered that they were all looking at him expectantly. He started to say, "but you know this terrain far better than I do," and he looked at the map again, and saw the clarity of the route they ought to take, and saw that after all he knew the terrain very well indeed and knew that this was the way he must lead them.

But he said only, "Shall we vote on it?" and then had to explain what he meant, because the concept was entirely new to them.

"But it's rather a good idea," said Conaire, fascinated, and

Flynn, watching, thought they were exactly like children some-times.

They voted. "To go sensibly and stealthily by night," said Oscar.

"Or boldly and openly by day," said CuChulainn, and Flynn counted hands carefully.

Oscar, of course, voted for his plan. "Of course he did," said CuChulainn.

CuChulainn wanted to travel in the day. "Let's let them know we are coming," he said, striking the table with his fist, setting the maps slithering, and dislodging the weights that Conaire had set on the Gallan/Muileann map, so that one fell on Midir's foot, and Conaire lost the road through the moun-tains altogether.

CuChulainn apologised to Midir at once. "Even so, I still say we march by day," he said. "Are we warriors, or are we mice?"

"We're pretty useless warriors with bruised toes," said Midir crossly, nursing his foot.

Both the twins opted for going by night in the end. "Safer," said Midir, and after some thought, Conaire agreed with them.

"I'm sorry," said Flynn to CuChulainn. "You're outvoted."

"Oh, that's all right," said CuChulainn. "I daresay you all know best. I'm a warrior, you see," he explained to Flynn af-terwards. "Nothing more. I don't pretend to be clever like Os-car, or far-seeing like Conaire, or even amusing like the twins. But I'll fight as well as anyone when we get to the battle," he said anxiously, and Flynn was rather touched. He thought that CuChulainn was perhaps not overbright, but he was loyal and true and trustworthy.

"Oh, he's as stupid as an ox," said Sean, who received the news of their nocturnal journey with philosophical calm. "Be-cause I'm not here to fight anyway, if you recall," he said.

Even so, Sean was doubtful about the wisdom of night travel, although he thought it might make a rather good poem. " 'The King's Armies by Night'—yes, that's got a goodish ring to it. Fetch me something to write on, somebody."

"Fetch it yourself," said Etain, but Flynn noticed that she got up and went in search of the thin woven sheets that were used for writing.

"He'll be like this all the time," said Conaire to Flynn.

"Writing everything down. Still, we do want an account of the battle, of course."

"Of course," said Flynn, who was not, truth to tell, thinking very much about the battle at all, and who now remembered that a very fearsome battle certainly lay ahead, and that he might not find Joanna until after it was all over.

"Yes, but you cannot get out of the battle," said Amairgen later that night. "It is something you must be a part of, I think." He tilted his head to one side, and, not for the first time, Flynn received the eerie impression of sight where there could not be sight. "You are Finn of the *Fiana* again," said Amairgen. "He has woken in you in earnest now, and he will spur you on. You will not be able to deny him, Flynn." He took Flynn's arm. "I think you will fight for the Wolfking again, Flynn, just as you did for Dierdriu all those centuries ago. I think you will be compelled to do so by Finn, for if Ireland is not restored to the rightful High King, a terrible and ancient evil will envelop the land."

The Erl-King . . .

"You are right. I wish you were not." Flynn knew that even while he was rent apart with anxiety for Joanna and aching with longing to see her and know her safe, still the thought of the battle that must surely be ahead of them was exciting him.

Amairgen said, "I wish I could be there with you," and Flynn felt as if something had fallen away inside him.

"But you will surely be with us—"

"You cannot possibly take me," Amairgen said gently, and Flynn felt the anguish and the burden of Amairgen's blindness descend upon his own shoulders for a moment. He saw Amairgen's hand come out, and he saw Portan take it, and he thought: they are very close now, these two, and felt the sharp loneliness for Joanna again. Aloud, he said, "But I can't go off with these people and leave you," and at once saw the absurdity of this, because Conaire and the others were friends, he knew them and he trusted them entirely. He was at home with them. Even so, "I can't leave you," he said.

Portan leaned forward. "Flynn, there is nothing that Amairgen or I can contribute to this venture," she said, and then, releasing her hand from Amairgen's, stood up and took Flynn's arm. "Come with me," said Portan, and led him out through the massive iron doors of Scáthach, so that they were standing looking out across the valley. Flynn drew in a deep breath, and felt the sweet night air fill his lungs, and felt, as well, an immense calm.

At his side, Portan said softly, "You see it, don't you? You feel it. No longer a place of desolation." She stood close to him, staring out across the valley, to the blaze of lights that was Tara. "I think that for many years it was a terrible place. I think that for Cormac it was."

"Five years," said Flynn.

"Perhaps a little more. And there are places of immense despair," said Portan. "I have walked through Scáthach, and I have felt them, Flynn. It is like—like falling into an icy cold blankness. There are—I do not have the words to explain—but there are patches of the most immense sadness. As if Cormac's anguish and his loneliness has soaked into the walls, and as if some of that loneliness still lingers: I recognise it for what it is," said Portan in a very low voice, and Flynn turned to watch her.

"Was it so very bad?" he said gently. "In that place?" And thought that of course it had been so very bad, and of course it would never be possible to understand.

"It was more terrible than ever you could imagine," said Portan, "but always there was hope. Always there was the dream of being rescued, and of a life beyond. Sharing. Working. Being a part of a community. *Accepted.* Oh Flynn," said Portan, her eyes bright with joy, "you cannot know what it has meant to me to be accepted by these people." She smiled at him. "Here is the dream, Flynn," said Portan softly. "Here, with these people. I am no longer repellent, or even very different." She looked out across the valley again. "I believe we will stay here, Amairgen and I, I believe we could dissolve the sadness in this place and sweep away the desolation. Already there is a feeling of happiness here. Have you not felt that?" Flynn, who had felt something but not the whole, nodded and understood.

"What should you do?"

Portan said, "Amairgen is clever, you see. He is a scholar. A thinker. People would come, just to talk with him."

"Yes," said Flynn. "Oh yes, they would."

"And I could be his sight," said Portan, and again there was the delight in her voice and in her eyes. "I could write his thoughts and his philosophies and all his learning, so that they could be shared. I could be *useful*," cried Portan, and Flynn smiled, and blinked rather hard, because there was such sheer undiluted joy in her voice, and such unshadowed gratitude in her eyes.

"But before we can think of such things, you have to find Joanna." Flynn knew that however far behind he might have to leave Portan and Amairgen in the journey ahead, they would yet be with him in their thoughts. Strength. Yes, they would give him strength.

When he said softly, "Think of me, Portan. Through what lies ahead of me." Portan took his hand and looked at him for a long moment.

"You will never be entirely absent from my thoughts for all of my life, Flynn," said Portan. "And when you leave for your own world, I shall set aside a part of each day to think of you." Again the smile, shyer this time. "You will never cease to be a part of me," said Portan.

THEY SET OUT at dusk the next day—"A good time for a new venture," said Conaire.

Flynn, who had seen the dawn rise in Tugaim many times, was very nearly speechless at the sight of the pink and grey light pouring down over the Morne Mountains, etching fingers of colour across the terrain ahead of them.

"Wait until we are in the mountains themselves," said Oscar. "For there, as nowhere else in Ireland, in the world perhaps, one may wake with the dawn and feel the colours and the scents and the sights of each new day." He glanced at Flynn. "From the Morne Mountains, you may stand in the dawnlight and see nothing but pure new light reaching out to bathe the entire country. And you may know that in one direction there is nothing between you and the very top of the world, where the great travellers say are ice sheets and glaciers and snow-covered lands."

Even so, Flynn was rather silent, for it had been very hard indeed to bid farewell to Amairgen and Portan, and go off into the unknown.

"But you went into the unknown when you went through the Time Curtain," said Amairgen.

"You were with me," said Flynn.

Conaire and the others understood about Flynn's sadness, of course. CuChulainn said, "It is very hard to go into a battle leaving friends behind," and Flynn felt again the sense of belonging. He thought that after all this was his place in the world.

They talked as they went along, telling Flynn all the grand old legends of Ireland, and all the stories of the High Kings and Queens, back to Dierdriu. Flynn was interested in it all; he was especially interested in Dierdriu, and he listened absorbedly, occasionally recognising a snippet of legend, or a fragment of folklore.

Conaire told stories of how the Court had been in the years of Cormac's reign; "A marvellous, brilliant place," he said. "It drew all of the gifted artists and the music makers and the ballad singers. People would travel across the Northern Seas just to come to Tara."

"And they would always be sure of a welcome," said Oscar, rather bitterly.

"Oh yes, for no one was ever turned away," said Conaire.

As they left Scáthach farther behind and the Morne Mountains began to loom nearer, CuChulainn told them stories of Ireland's most splendid battles; the Second Battle of Mag Tuired, fought between the Tuatha, who were the people of the mother-god Danann, and the marauding Fomoire, led by Cichol Gricenchos, son of Goll the One-Eyed and by his monstrous mother Lot, whose bloated lips were in her breasts, and who had four eyes in her back and the strength of twenty men in her arms. He told, as well, of the famous Battle for the Trees, which had been fought between the Morrigna and the armies of Dierdriu. "And which," said CuChulainn, "was won by neither side, for the Trees fell into a great sleep from which it is said they will never wake."

"They would surrender to neither side you see," said Oscar softly, "neither side could claim victory, and so the Battle for the Trees is still known as Ireland's great unwon war."

"And ever since," put in Midir who had been listening, "the Morrigna have never ceased to seek out Dierdriu's descendants and try to destroy them."

At that, Sean launched into the Lay of Dierdriu, and everyone joined in the chorus, and CuChulainn became rather emotional when they reached the part about Dierdriu promising to return, and had to be given a drink from Conaire's flask, retiring to the back of the procession to blow his nose and recover.

Sean became quite militant as they sighted the forest surrounding Muileann, and composed a stirring march about the Wolfking's armies going into war, and everyone learned it that night as they ate their supper round the fire, and sang it the next morning. As CuChulainn said, it had a grand swing to it, and you could march better with a rousing song to cheer you on.

"It makes us sound a much larger army than we really are," said Midir when they had sung it through twice, and CuChulainn had finally got the words of the last verse right.

"We won't be small when we call up the Bloodlines," said Etain.

They made camp each dawn and ate very well it seemed to Flynn, who was not accustomed to this way of life. But there were wild animals to be shot or trapped—"Not our own creatures, of course," said Oscar.

And Flynn said, "Of course not."

As they passed through the forest, there was fruit which gave Flynn a sudden sharp jolt of homesickness for Tugaim and the orchards, there were pigeons and some kind of wild pheasant. It was all very amicable, and more than once, Flynn found himself enjoying the easy camaraderie.

Ahead of them was the forest screening Muileann. "Although Muileann is on the floor of the valley," said Oscar, "we would go through the forest to come out directly above the township, and then we would go down into the valley if we were going through Muileann itself. As it is . . ." he paused and they waited. "As it is," said Oscar, "we can skirt the forest, and wait until nightfall. Then we will go across the sides of the valley. Beyond that are the Morne Mountains, and beyond them Gallan."

Even so, they could see Muileann as they went cautiously through the trees, and Flynn felt a tightness in his chest at the sight. The township was so dark and so filled with shadows, that he found himself thinking that anything might lurk down there, and he found that he was extremely glad they had agreed to Oscar's plan to cross the plain and avoid the town. He was just thinking that they ought to be considering making camp for the day while the trees still sheltered them, when Conaire, who was in the lead and who saw better than any of them, stopped and said sharply: "There's something moving in those bushes," and at once everyone froze.

Lying on the bracken between Etain and Oscar, Flynn saw for the first time the unmistakable signs that these people had indeed the blood of the beasts in their veins. It was in the way that Conaire stood looking into the forest, not narrowing his eyes at all, but looking straight into the glare of the setting sun. And it was in the alert stillness of Oscar and the twins, and in the sudden tensing of CuChulainn's powerful muscles. Flynn felt rather useless beside them; if something threatening was lurking in the forest he would not be of very much help. But he tightened his grip on the sword he had borrowed from Conaire, and he kept very still and presently there was another scuffling, and Flynn saw Conaire spring forward and pounce, and heard a yell of indignation.

"Well!" said a cross voice from the bushes. "If that's how you treat the Wolfking's supporters, Conaire of the Eagles, all I can say is it's not surprising we're all forever fighting!"

The bushes rustled irritably and Conaire let out a shout of laughter and said, "By Dagda and all the gods, if it isn't one of the Wolfking's Cruithin servants!" and a great sigh of relief went through the watchers, because, as Sean said to Flynn, anything might have been hiding in the bushes.

"There's all manner of nasty things bound to be abroad in this vicinity," said Sean, brushing himself free of bracken. "I wonder we've got this far, I do really. I said it was a mistake to come this way in the first place."

Conaire marched the Cruithin servant into the clearing grinning hugely, and beckoning to the others to come out.

"It's Domnall," he said, "who went with His Majesty to Scáthach."

"Along with the other *faithful* servants of the Wolfking," said Domnall with a nasty look at Conaire, and Flynn hoped they were not going to have animosity among their own people.

"Oh I shouldn't think so," said Sean, who had been listening. "But I daresay Domnall's annoyed with Conaire, well, you can't blame him; have you ever looked at Conaire's hands? Oh they're just like talons. Eagles, you see. He wouldn't mean it, but I expect he's given poor Domnall a fine set of bruises. And

of course, the Cruithin have always considered themselves the
High Kings' chosen followers. Well to be fair, so they are.
Only they like to remind you of it."

Conaire seemed to be treating Domnall cautiously however;
he invited him to be seated, and waited to hear more of the
Wolfking.

"And we know he's not at Scáthach any longer," said Midir,
"because we've been there."

"Oh, he's not been at Scáthach for many a night now," said
Domnall. "Didn't you know that? *Didn't* you? I thought everyone knew. Oh yes, the Enchantment's wound up and he's free.
Well, nobody expected Scáthach to hold him for long in the
first place."

"Just as I said," put in Sean pleased. "Didn't I say just
that?" And he retired to his hillock again, to just note a few
ideas for "The Wolfking's Escape" which would go down very
nicely at the celebrations when Cormac returned to Tara. After
they had routed Eochaid Bres and the Fox.

Flynn, unable to help himself, leaned forward and said,
"Had he anyone with him when he left?" and waited, and
thought: I cannot bear it, this is the worst yet, for if Domnall
says that Cormac was alone, then I am once more without
hope. And he fixed his eyes on the small, slightly gnarled figure of Domnall and waited.

Domnall said caustically, "Did you ever know the Wolfking
to be without a woman?" and a murmur of rather uneasy
laughter went round, but Flynn knew such a rush of thankfulness that he barely noticed.

"I didn't actually see her," said Domnall before Flynn could
say anything. "I don't think any of us did, because the King
kept her in his own quarters."

Flynn said carefully, "Was she the one who broke the Enchantment?"

Domnall, appearing to understand, said, " 'Open locks, to
the Human's hand,' do you mean?" And, as Flynn nodded,
"Well," said Domnall, considering this, "I believe that the feeling was that she *was* the one, although of course I could no
more swear to that than I could fly to the moon." He eyed
Flynn thoughtfully, "Would it be a matter of some concern to
you?" And when Flynn said, "Yes it would," Domnall nodded,
"I see." Everyone wondered what it was that he saw.

"Whoever she was," said Domnall, looking at Flynn rather fixedly, "Cormac was treating her extremely well." And he regarded Flynn with his head on one side like an alert sparrow, and nodded and smiled, and Flynn nodded and smiled back, and thought that if only Cormac had kept Joanna safe and if only he had looked after her in this cruel, beautiful world, then he, Flynn, would happily fight to the death for the Wolfking.

Domnall sat cross-legged in the circle of people, and began to explain what had been happening. "We all of us went to Scáthach in the beginning," he said. "Of course we did. Aren't we the chosen race of the High Kings?"

Sean said in an aside to Flynn, "See what I mean?" and was ordered by Conaire to be quiet or leave.

"Leave for where?" demanded Sean, for once belligerent.

"Muileann or the Walled City of the Erl-King!" said Conaire crossly, and Sean scowled and muttered into his notes that they'd never had this discourtesy under the Wolfking, and it all came of Eochaid Bres's slipshod, slapdash Court.

"I knew how it would be the very minute that the Fox started plotting," he said. "But nobody listened to me. Well, don't blame *me* if Ireland falls into the hands of something very nasty indeed."

Oscar said, rather loudly, "Domnall, do tell us what happened at Scáthach. Is the King with you?" and Flynn felt a ripple of delighted anticipation go through the others.

"He is not," said Domnall, "not but what we haven't followed him all the way from Scáthach here, and that's been no picnic I can tell you, not in a bull's foot it hasn't. Although it has to be said that Scáthach was no picnic either," he added, "not but what we didn't all go willingly." He glared at Conaire. "There wasn't a one of us who'd have stood for being under Eochaid Bres's rule," said Domnall, "and there wasn't a one of us who'd have stood for being under the Fox's rule either. Anyone who knows anything knows that Eochaid Bres is ruled by Bricriu."

"And Bricriu is ruled by the Queen Mother," murmured Oscar.

"Is he now? Is he indeed?" said Domnall interested. "Of course, I wouldn't be knowing about that. I left with the True King. Which," he added, "if your honours will pardon me for saying, is more than any of you did."

Conaire, rather red in the face, said, "But we've come to find the True King and restore him."

"You've taken your time about it," said Domnall.

Sean remarked to no one in particular: "He's right you know. We have. Not that it's any business of those Cruithin, but you'll never tell them that."

"I don't think—"

"Arrogant," said Sean, shaking his head. "Comes of having served the High Kings for so long. It's bound to rub off a bit. I daresay it can't be helped."

"Sean," said Conaire ominously, "I freely admit that you are a gifted *ollam* and an excellent fellow, and I wish you nothing but good, but if you do not keep quiet till we hear what Domnall has to say, I shall drop you over the cliff face."

"Sorry I'm sure," said Sean, hunching one shoulder.

Flynn said, in a voice he had never heard himself use before, "This is quite enough of such childish nonsense. Both of you will please behave like sensible people and remember the purpose of this journey," and Conaire and Sean and Domnall all fell over themselves to apologise.

"Well," said Domnall with a pleased look to where Flynn sat, "there isn't much more to tell. We all came with His Majesty from Scáthach, and we stayed here, camped out in the forest while the King and his lady went on to Gallan with Gormgall and Dubhgall."

"Yes, of course, he'd never leave those two behind," said Conaire, and everyone nodded.

"They were going to go through Muileann," said Domnall. "Well, it's the most direct route to Gallan of course, we all know that. And they were going to ask Cait Fian for his aid, and then come back here with the people of Gallan and the panthers. A grand army that would have given us," said Domnall, "and we'd have ridden against Tara and Eochaid Bres right away.

"But," said Domnall, jabbing a finger into midair the better to make his point, "they haven't returned. And there's been time and to spare for them to have reached Gallan and got back. Well, your honours, not to mince words, we're all getting very worried. We're all saying to ourselves—supposing something's happened to them? And to tell you the tale with no bark on it, there's one or two of us who're saying—supposing the Giant Miller's caught them? Now that," said Domnall severely, "would be a very bad thing, indeed it would."

There was a rather worried silence. At length, CuChulainn said, "They might have reached Gallan."

"Then where's Cait Fian and the Panthers?" demanded Domnall.

"They might have been delayed in Gallan," said CuChulainn rather doubtfully, and at his side, Oscar snorted in disgust.

"Cait Fian was never delayed if there was a fight in the offing," he said.

"And he'd ride out for Cormac at an hour's notice," added Etain.

"Well," said Domnall, "we—that is all the Cruithin—think that the King must have fallen into the hands of the Miller. Or even—" he hesitated and glanced over his shoulder, and everyone else did the same. "Or even," said Domnall drawing a little closer, "the Morrigna or the Erl-King."

A sudden silence fell on the little group, and Flynn had the impression that the forest had grown momentarily darker.

"Well it's what we think," said Domnall rather defiantly, "for they say that Morrigan and her sisters have been seen in these parts, and we all know that the Erl-King's Citadel is within two days' march of Muileann. We've been holding a Council of War," said Domnall, "that is those of us who understand about war, for it's no use leaving it to the youngsters. They're all for riding full pelt down into Muileann and brandishing swords and crying death to the Miller and confusion to the Morrigna. And that won't do," said Domnall. "Only you can't tell them. They're all for fighting first and thinking afterwards, and we all know that isn't the way to win a war. You've got to fight sorcery with more sorcery, always supposing you can get it, and always supposing you can afford it as well, because good sorcery's very expensive nowadays. Well, wasn't it always. But then you'd all know more about that sort of thing than I would," he added, "having been at Tara for so many years."

"It isn't—"

"With Eochaid Bres and the Fox," said Domnall pointedly.

Conaire threatened, "If I have to suffer any more jibes, son of servants—"

Flynn said, "Oh Conaire, do please stop it. If we are to

make any kind of rescue attempt we've got to band together. And Domnall, a little more tolerance from you, if you please." And he wondered whether this could possibly be himself, Flynn O'Connor, speaking with such authority. Lethe arrogance, thought Flynn, and then grinned to himself, because weren't the Letheans many centuries in the future?

But the Lethe arrogance worked at once. Conaire and Domnall apologised all over again, and Conaire asked, very politely, if Domnall would continue.

"There isn't much more to tell," said Domnall. "We—that is the older ones—had been trying to work out a plan to get into Muileann without being seen so that we could spy out the land, when one of the sentries came running to say they'd got wind of your presence—well, of the presence of something lurking in the forest. Something that was being a bit furtive. And so—"

"We're not furtive!" Midir put in.

"And we certainly don't lurk," said Etain.

"Well, we were being stealthy," said Conaire. "Let's say that."

Domnall said, "Yes, let's say that." Everyone wondered how long this new peaceable mood was going to last. Sean shook his head and remarked to anyone who might be listening that the Cruithin and the families of the Bloodline never had got on.

"A chancy blend," he said. "Very chancy. You won't change the feuding of centuries in half an hour. Well, it's nothing to do with me." And he wondered could you stage a mock feud as part of an evening's entertainment, with the Cruithin on one side, and the Bloodline on the other.

"Well, I came to investigate," said Domnall. "To find out who you were. That's meaning no disrespect, of course."

"Of course not."

"And here I am."

"So you are. Tell me," said Conaire, "how large is the camp?"

"If you don't count the Wolves, there's about thirty of us," said Domnall.

"Oh I think we should count the Wolves," said Conaire, and looked at the others. "Don't you?"

"Useful things in a fight, Wolves," agreed CuChulainn, and

the twins and Oscar nodded. Flynn hoped he did not look as worried as he felt, and wished that he had not heard Sean muttering that wolves were all very well so long as somebody could control them.

"Of course, we're having a bit of trouble controlling them," said Domnall, and Sean groaned. "They get a bit unruly when the King isn't there, and nobody else can really do anything with them."

"Nobody ever could," said Oscar.

"All the more reason to set out soon to find him," put in Midir.

Domnall, who had been studying them all one by one, said suddenly, "I suppose you *are* going to join us, sirs?" and at once they all looked to Flynn.

"Flynn? What's your opinion?" asked Conaire and Flynn thought: oh dear, here we go again.

Aloud he said, carefully, "I think we must join them, don't you? That's if Domnall is sure his people will accept us."

"The more the merrier," said Domnall mournfully.

"It'll mean a greater chance of being seen when we cross the plain to Gallan," said Oscar.

"I know that," said Flynn. "But it'll mean a better army when we join with Cait Fian's people."

From his hillock, Sean said to himself, "Wolves and Panthers together. Oh *dear*."

"The greater the army, the better our chances of restoring the Wolfking," remarked Midir.

"Not that there's any doubts about us doing that," said Etain.

"No, but we might as well make it as sure as we can."

"The Wolves form a whole battalion in themselves as well," said Conaire.

Sean said, "Yes, so long as somebody can control them."

"Oh, we'll have Cormac with us by then," said Etain. "Won't we?" And then, as nobody replied, "*Won't* we?" she said again.

"I hope so," said Oscar. "In any case, we can't go without the Wolves."

"No," said CuChulainn firmly, "for when we ride triumphantly into Tara with the King, we must certainly have the Wolves of Tara with us."

* * *

FLYNN WAS RATHER glad that CuChulainn had painted that bright and optimistic picture, for without it he thought he might very well have fallen victim to despair. He had begun to be more than cautiously hopeful that the lady with Cormac *was* Joanna, and he had begun to think, as well, that if this was so, his only chance of finding her was to fight for Cormac's restoration and rout the usurpers. Once or twice he found himself wondering whether he was in truth on the right side. I suppose Cormac *is* the rightful King, he thought. I suppose I *am* on the right side. But he did not let these thoughts surface, for he knew that the Cruithin, Conaire, and the others would deal very sharply with a traitor. And then he remembered the delight that showed on their faces when anyone mentioned Cormac, and he remembered (and found it a thought to hold on to) that Domnall had said that whoever Cormac's lady was, she was being treated very well. He thought, afterwards, that it was this that helped him to remain in control, and it was certainly this that enabled him to plan Cormac's return and the defeat of Eochaid Bres and Bricriu. "Without that hope," he said later, "I should not have cared who sat in the Sun Chamber. I certainly should not have cared whether Cormac lived or died. But if he had Joanna then I did care." And then—"But that was before I knew Cormac," he said, and smiled.

He found the Cruithin to be likeable, interesting, and thoroughly loyal. He talked to them rather a lot in the days that followed, but in all cases the story was the same. The King had certainly had a lady with him—to be sure when had he not?—but they none of them had seen very much of her. Yes, she was thought to be young and beautiful, although wasn't this the way of it with His Majesty? Yes, said one of them, they had all believed that she had dissolved the Enchantment of Captivity, although of course you could never be sure about these things, because enchantments were tricky things to be sure they were. And what about another little drop of mead?

Flynn liked the way the Cruithin referred to Cormac with indulgence and respect blended; he thought that every one of them would fight to the death for Cormac, and never think of showing him less than the respect that was his right. Equally, he thought they all knew the King's weaknesses and failings. It made this exiled High King much more real to Flynn, and the fact that Cormac had weaknesses made him very much more likeable as well. Do we love others because of their faults or in spite of them? wondered Flynn, and smiled, and thought that Cormac's people at any rate loved Cormac for his weaknesses. He began to be curious about Cormac, and he began to hope that they would find him and restore him for his own sake.

He began to look forward to that triumphant march into Tara with the Wolves, and he began, as well, to wonder about Gallan and Cait Fian.

CHAPTER TWENTY-TWO

THE WALLED CITY of the Erl-King was silent tonight. The Citadel was ablaze with light, but down in the streets, the people double-locked their doors and shuttered their windows and huddled round their firesides. It was no night to be abroad, for already the whisper had gone round.

The Gentleman has the hunger on him tonight . . .

There were four new prisoners in the dungeons, but even the great Wolfking and his lady would not slake the Gentleman's hunger and his thirst tonight. Tara, the Shining Palace, the great and wonderful heart of all Ireland was at last within the Gentleman's reach, and his hunger would be great. He would be thirsting for the blood of humans, and the warm young flesh of boys and girls. A terrible night lay ahead of the people of the Walled City, and when the night was behind them, the cold dawn would show the town ditches running with the blood of the poor wretched creatures who had slaked the Gentleman's hunger and quenched his thirst.

Someone will be quaffed tonight . . .

The hunchback had come down into the town a short while ago, the wheels of his cart clattering over the cobbled streets. They had all heard the sounds, but they had pretended not to. They had pretended, too, not to hear the frantic footsteps running across the cobblestones, followed closely by the hunchback's dragging gait.

"My Master has the hunger on him tonight . . ."

Screams had pierced the quiet streets, and then had been replaced by a quiet, hopeless sobbing. The sound of despair. The townspeople recognised it of course, and wished, as always, that they did not. Somebody's son, somebody's daughter or sister. Presently the cart had jolted its way back up the hill, the poor abandoned victims bound and gagged on the floor, destined for the Gentleman's stone Banqueting Chamber, destined for the silver platters and the golden goblets. The townspeople knew because they had lived through it all before.

THE MOMENT THE Erl-King entered the Citadel, Joanna and Cormac and the two Cruithin felt as if a dark cloud had descended. Cormac sprang up, his hands curling about the bars of the cell, staring upwards.

"He is here. He has come."

"The Erl-King?"

"Yes. I can feel him," said Cormac. "Can't you? Be very still."

Joanna stood very still and closed her eyes, and said in a whisper, "Yes. He is here. An immense power. A gaping chasm. A nothingness." She shivered.

Gormgall noticing, said, "Would you take Grady's coat, my lady?"

"After all, he's no further use for it," added Muldooney who liked to include himself in any act of chivalry that was going, even though, as Dubhgall had pointed out earlier, the exact meaning of the word had had to be explained to him. "Grady won't be needing his coat any longer," said Muldooney, and Gormgall and Dubhgall glared at him.

"Remember, son of the pigs, that Grady was my lady's father," said Gormgall.

"And respect her grief," said Dubhgall.

Well, if it was grief they were to be talking of, Muldooney knew all about that. Hadn't he tried to comfort the pretty little dear when she'd sobbed fit to break apart after Cormac had snuffed out John Grady's life? Hadn't she cast herself upon his body, crying pitiously as he lay lifeless and cooling in the corner of the cell? A terrible thing it was, and Muldooney had felt a lump come to his own throat. But Cormac had waved Muldooney aside in the most high-handed manner you could imagine, just when he had been going to go over and calm the poor dear creature. Muldooney did not know what things were coming to when a man could not comfort his officially conjoined partner. Nor did he care overmuch for the tone of

Gormgall's voice, for wasn't it Muldooney who was going to be the saviour of the entire party in a while? He knew just what he was going to do, because he and Gormgall and Dubhgall had tried out a few gestures and movements suitable to a witless person, and he thought he would manage it really rather well. Dubhgall, always tart, had commented that to be sure, didn't he take to it with a great naturalness, but Gormgall had said, "Oh hush," and Muldooney had pretended not to hear. Still, they'd worked out a grand set of actions and little by-plays for when they got up to the Banqueting Hall. Gormgall had said to Dubhgall that it was going to be fine, and Dubhgall said sourly that he hoped it was, because their lives all depended on it being fine. There'd been a plan made and an agreement reached, and they'd all shaken hands on it, even Cormac. Joanna had kissed Muldooney on the cheek, her eyes bright, and said, "Oh I *knew* you would not let us down!"

The cell door was flung open and the grinning figure of the hunchback stood in the opening, with eight guards behind him.

The prisoners stood up, and Cormac said, "Is it time? Are we to meet your master, serf?" and the hunchback grinned and cracked his whip.

"You are," he said. "Upstairs with you all. And quickly, my Master does not like to be kept waiting. And tonight he has a guest." He loped across to where Joanna was standing, and looked her up and down. "Nice," he said approvingly. "My Master will enjoy you, my dear." He chuckled with a low bubbling sound. "I shall enjoy you as well," he said, "for my Master allows me his victims when he has done with them." His face swam nearer, pock-marked and swart. "Something for you to look forward to when you are strapped down to the Table," he said, and reached out his hand.

At once Cormac slammed him against the cell wall, his hands reaching for the hunchback's throat, and for a moment Joanna truly thought he would tear the hunchback's throat out while the guards stood helpless. But the guards suddenly moved as if pulled by a string; they dragged Cormac away, and the hunchback, fingering his throat, spat venomously, "Chain the wolf. He's dangerous."

Cormac backed into a corner of the cell, snarling and lashing out, and Joanna caught a glimpse of his face, and thought: he is all wolf. There is no human blood in him at all at this moment. And then caught the tail-end of a thought: *all part of the plan, Human Child. If I can make them think me more dangerous than they had believed, they will keep their attention on me all the more. And all the more chance for the rest of you to get back the Nightcloak* . . .

The guards advanced cautiously, trying to surround him, and Cormac's eyes gleamed red. He bounded across the cell and leapt on the nearest guard, his face a wolf's mask of bloodlust and ferocity. The guard went down, and Cormac fastened his teeth into the man's throat, tearing and clawing.

Gormgall, who was being held by two men shouted, "Sire! No! There are too many of them!" and as he spoke, the guard gave a choking retching sound, and blood spurted out on to the cell floor. The guard sagged and his head fell back, eyes glazing. Cormac snarled again and stood back, and turned to deal with the others.

The hunchback was hopping up and down in blind rage, the leather-tipped whip cracking out across the tiny cell. "Seize him! Chain him!" he screamed. "Or are you a pack of spineless cowards that my Master keeps to serve him! Seize the wolf!" The whip snaked out, laying open one of the guards' faces, and the man flinched.

The guards had recovered themselves now; they drew their swords and advanced, and for a moment there was confusion and struggling and the sound of blows.

Cormac fought with every ounce of energy. He clawed and bit and growled and Joanna and the others, unable to move for their captors' firm hands and the hunchback's whip, held their breath. But as Gormgall had known, there were too many of them—the chains clanked coldly on the stone floor, and Cormac was fastened, his hands behind his back, his feet shackled, the blood of his victim still spattering his shirt.

To Joanna it was dreadful to see him like this—chained and defeated—but Gormgall's hand closed on hers, and she saw in the dim light, the glint that still showed in Cormac's eyes, and she felt a tremendous uplifting of courage. We are fighting to the last ditch. We have a plan to defeat the adversary. And you are not counted dead until all is done.

They left the guard lying in his blood, and were half pushed, half dragged out into the low-ceilinged rock passage.

"Watch the wolf," said the captain, "or he'll have your throat and your lungs all over the floor."

"Nothing new for this place," said another, but the prisoners noticed he'd said it quietly.

As they were taken out, Gormgall said to the captain, "You have seen that one of our party is dead?"

"Yes." The captain glanced round, and then said softly, "Merciful. You understand my meaning, friend?"

"Yes," said Gormgall.

"Nothing to be done," said the captain, and then, in a louder voice, "Go along with you. Don't tarry. The Gentleman does not care to be kept waiting. Keep the wolf ahead. No tricks."

They filed out, with Cormac held firmly, and the hunchback leading, carrying the lantern aloft. Muldooney was at the rear. In fact, he was beginning to feel just the smallest bit excited about what lay ahead. Gormgall had spoken truly when he had said softly that Muldooney was in the grip of a confidence born of ignorance, for Brian Muldooney, stolid solid pig farmer of little or no imagination, could not begin to comprehend the smallest part of what lay ahead. He thought, if he thought about it at all, that they were being held captive by some minor tyrant, and he had long since settled with himself that they would all be allowed to go free, because anything else was unthinkable. Muldooney's world did not allow for evil, and it certainly did not allow for sorcery. He thought they would all very likely be free before the night was over, and wouldn't there be a grand tale to be told then! He had a major part to play in it all, and he was going to play it very well. Ah, they should see that Muldooney was not so no-account as they all seemed to think! On this cheering note, he loped off along the corridor in the opposite direction to the others, and assumed the idiot-stare he had practised in the cell, rolling his eyes and emitting a few grunts.

The guard caught him at once. "Ho!" said the captain. "Another escapee! Into line with you now!"

"He's the witless one," said one of the others. "A bit wanting up here," and tapped his head significantly.

"Is he now? Well, see he stays with the rest." He eyed Muldooney who grinned vacantly and blubbered his lips. "At least he doesn't understand what's ahead of him," said the captain, unknowingly hitting the truth square on.

"The wolf knows," said the other guard. "Keep your eye on it."

The guards kept a very careful eye on all of the prisoners as they conveyed them through the narrow passages. It would not do to let a single one of the Gentleman's prisoners escape. They all of them had wives and children down in the village. They escorted the five prisoners through the Citadel and up to the stone Banqueting Hall of the Erl-King.

THE GREAT IRON doors of the Banqueting Hall clanged to, shutting them in, and for a moment, pure and undiluted panic threatened to overwhelm Joanna. She felt her senses swim and her vision blur, and she tried very hard not to faint. She must be alert to regain her cloak. It was their only chance. Gormgall and Dubhgall came to stand on each side of her, and Joanna was grateful for their presence. Cormac was nearby, half sitting, half kneeling on the floor, his eyes like burning coals, his hands curved dangerously. The guards were standing very close to him, but Joanna could see that he was so heavily chained that he could not break free. It was up to her. Muldooney had gone wandering off, uncaring or unnoticing of the guards, swinging his arms in vaguely simian fashion, mumbling to himself, his eyes vacant. Occasionally, he pulled at his lower lip; and when the doors were bolted and barred behind them, he seemed not to hear, but stood lost in contemplation of an apparently blank spot on the stone floor. Joanna felt a rush of gratitude, because truly, had any of them suspected that Muldooney would be able to put up such a grand show? She glanced at the guards, and saw them look at Muldooney with a kind of shrugging tolerance.

And then at last she looked about her, and her confidence ebbed away completely, and a cold and deadly fear took possession of her.

The stone Banqueting Hall and the Stone Table of the Erl-King had been written about and sung about down the ages. It had formed the base for every dark legend and every malevolent fable ever recounted, and it had figured for centuries in Ireland's folklore as the ultimate place of fear and despair and pain, and the strongest evil ever known.

Cormac, seeing it with an unwished-for clarity, knew at once that the legends had not lied, and that the songs and the tales had told the truth. This was the place of fear and pain and despair; if he closed his eyes, he could feel the immense suffocating weight of all the suffering that had taken place here.

The two Cruithin, nearly as sensitive to atmosphere as their King, felt it as well, and both of them turned pale. Close by, Joanna, child of that brave new world where places such as this had no meaning and, indeed, no name any longer, knew a terrible sense of recognition. So this is the place of the nightmares, and this is the place that we all, in our innermost souls, fear.

Only Muldooney, blessed with that lack of imagination which had been carefully bred in the survivors of Devastation, saw and felt nothing especially sinister, other than that the candles up here smelt rancid and that it was rather dark and narrow. But Muldooney was by now well caught up in the task allotted to him, and he was by this time only concerned with telling the tale of an idiot, full of sound and vacuity, signifying nothing but a profound witlessness. Muldooney it would be who would save the day! He lumbered back over to the corner, and bent over to study the blank spot on the floor with intense concentration.

The Banqueting Hall was not as large as Joanna had expected; it was a rather narrow chamber with small windows set very high up, which admitted little light. The walls were rough and scarred and they gave the Hall the stifling appearance of a massive coffin. Here and there, crimson hangings brushed the stonework, and the floor was bare.

At the far side, stood two waist-high, oblong tables, hollowed out in the middle, and fitted with thick strong leather straps. Culverts ran down each side and out to a central drainage outlet.

For the golden goblets will be filled to overflowing tonight . . .

At the head of the room, directly facing them, was the Stone Table, set with highly polished cutlery and with plates and chalices . . . Golden goblets and silver platters . . . Before the Table was a small brazier with a glowing fire burning, giving off a pungent unfamiliar scent.

All the better to flavour you with, my dear . . .

Behind the Stone Table was a flight of stairs, framed by crimson curtains that half concealed a shadowy archway. A miasma of darkness seemed to hang in the archway, like heavy black smoke, and then, as they looked, they saw the figure that stood on the steps, as still as if it was carved from stone.

The Erl-King.

Joanna, who was nearest, felt horror flood her body, because the candles were very bright just there. She could see him quite clearly, and she could not believe that her eyes were not playing some malevolent trick on her, because she had thought that the Erl-King would at least have the semblance of a human, she had thought he would be in some way a man, but he was not, he was not . . .

He was not human in the least, he was the most dreadful being she had ever seen.

He was an insect, a monster with a man's narrow-waisted body, and huge black fly's head.

The moment lengthened and Joanna shook her head, but the figure on the steps did not change.

CHAPTER TWENTY-THREE

THE ERL-KING wore black, some kind of soft material that might have been velvet, and that was moulded to fit him tightly. His body was frail-looking—no spine! thought Joanna, and shuddered—and his arms were thin with pale clawlike hands. He wore a great ruby ring on one finger. Even so, thought Joanna, even so, they are human hands and they are human arms, and therefore he must have human blood in him somewhere.

But his head was not human at all. It was disproportionately large for his body, and it was the head of a fly, bloated, magnified, swollen to a hundred, a thousand times the size of any ordinary fly. There were the enormous, slightly protruding, shiny black eyes taking up most of the face; there was the pointed black mandible, the fly's jaw. An insect, thought Joanna, repelled. Oh dear god, a crawling, spiny-skulled insect. An insect that walks upright and eats men. This is far worse than anything I had imagined.

The Erl-King stood watching them for what seemed to be a very long time, the terrible head turned sideways a little, so that the unblinking eyes could survey them better.

All the better to see you, my dear . . .

All about them, the Citadel seemed suspended in a waiting silence, and the weight of all the years and pain and helpless torment that the chamber had witnessed seemed to descend about them.

Morrigan sat at the head of the Stone Table, her eyes as unblinking as those of the creature on the steps, and Joanna saw with a rush of gratitude that the Nightcloak was flung over the

440

back of Morrigan's chair. She thought: oh thank you! Thank you! My father's death is justified this far at any rate.

They stood helpless as the Erl-King continued to inspect them, Cormac still half sitting on the floor, a wolf crouched and ready to spring; Muldooney standing a little apart, twisting at his lower lip and making bubble-blowing sounds, every few minutes shambling back to study the same spot on the floor, and bending over to stare at it.

The burning coals in the brazier settled with a little hissing sound, and at last the Erl-King moved, walking down the steps towards them with a jerky uncoordinated gait, as if his body was gristly and ill-designed for walking upright. Joanna wished she had not had that thought about insects having no spine. Morrigan leaned forward, her eyes slitted with anticipation, a beautiful, cruel snake-smile on her lips. Joanna's courage almost failed. Even if she got the cloak away from Morrigan, how could it possibly be strong enough to defeat these two? They would fail and they would die, and Tara would be in the power of the Erl-King, and Ireland would be forever lost.

The Erl-King said, "You are welcome to my Citadel, Your Majesties," and the prisoners jumped, for it was not the harsh ugly voice they had all expected, but a soft caressing voice; a gentle velvet voice, belonging to a creature who understands about poetry and music, and enjoys good wine, and talks with scholars and philosophers. Cormac, of them all, knew the name given to the Erl-King by the people of the Walled City, and he understood for the first time why, in his own domain, the Erl-King was called the Gentleman.

"We meet at last, High King," said the Erl-King, studying Cormac intently. "You have eluded me for a very long time, just as your ancestors did. But I think I am not unknown to you."

Cormac snarled and tried to spring forward, but the chains held fast. The hunchback and two of the guards moved at once, alert to a possible attack, but the Erl-King waved them back and went on studying Cormac.

"That was unwise and useless, High King. You must know I am protected."

"With the Girdle of Gold," said Cormac. "My family's gift from the sorcerers. I did not know that stolen enchantments were so potent."

"It was not stolen," said the Erl-King, quite calmly and seriously, as if they were discussing a minor matter. "I bought it
from the sorcerers. A price was named and paid." He regarded
Cormac unblinkingly. "Did you really believe your sorcerers to
be incorruptible, Cormac," said the Erl-King. "Then you are
trusting indeed. You are certainly unfitted to be High King. Enchantments are available to all, Cormac. The Solemn Oath is
worthless." Unbelievably, the fly's jaw stretched in an approx-
imation of a smile. "I expended many years in obtaining the
Girdle of Gold," said the Erl-King softly. "And you will never
get it back."

"We shall see. The battle is not yet won."

The Erl-King smiled again as if he found Cormac's threats
amusing. He passed on to Gormgall and Dubhgall. "Servants,"
he said dismissively. "But they will serve for an hour's pleasure. And the High King will writhe to see the uses I shall put
them to." He ran his eyes over the two Cruithin thoughtfully.
"Well enough," he said, and then looked to where Muldooney
was seated by himself, legs asprawl, engrossed in an inspection
of his toes. "The mindless hold no interest for me," said the
Erl-King.

"You prefer to have your victims fully able to understand
what is being done to them?" said Cormac smoothly, and the
Erl-King looked at him for a long moment, his huge black
eyes unreadable. At length, he spoke.

"Everything you have ever heard about me is true, Cormac.
Every story, every legend, every tale told round a night fire by
stupid men and women is true. Presently you shall see it all for
yourself. And let us have no mistake about it, Cormac of the
Wolves; you are my prisoner and you are my victim, and I
shall do with you what I wish." A glitter lit his eyes. "I have
waited a very long time for tonight," said the Erl-King, "I shall
savour it." He turned to where Morrigan sat quietly listening.
"My mistress and I will savour it together," he said, and incredibly there was a sexual flavour to his tone now.

Morrigan smiled the snake-smile and said very softly, "I
have sent my Sisters away, Master." And then, to Cormac and
Joanna, "They are greedy, you see. And I do not wish to *share*
you." Again there was the sly reptile smile, and when she said
share, Morrigan opened her lips, and the forked tongue flick-

ered. "They will return when I call to them," said Morrigan. "But for tonight, you are both my Master's and mine."

Cormac said scoffingly, "Golden goblets and silver platters?"

The Erl-King said, "Exactly, High King. And more . . ." He appeared to dismiss Cormac and moved on to where Joanna stood. The black eyes glittered.

"Madam," said the Erl-King, in a tone of deep satisfaction. "We have waited a long time for this, you and I." He looked at her closely. "When Morrigan told me, I did not at first believe her. Dierdriu of the Nightcloak, the High Queen returned. But you were always ridiculously sentimental, my dear. You were always chivalrous. So you have come back to save your people from me, have you?" Again the dreadful smile. "You are too late, Dierdriu," said the Erl-King, "for I have Ireland within my grasp, and all your puny enchantments and all your *pure* magic will avail you naught." He leaned closer, and Joanna stood very still. "The last battle, Dierdriu," he said, "and already you are inside my Citadel, and already you are locked within my Banqueting Chamber."

Joanna said very steadily, "It was a long time ago that we met, sir. But I do not forget any of it."

"Nor I, my dear." The eyes flickered again, and the lascivious note crept into the beautiful voice again. "Do you recall the vow I made, Dierdriu?"

"Let us say I have forgotten it."

A smile lifted the bony jaw again. "I vowed that one day I should defeat you, Dierdriu, and that when I did so, you would be forced to serve me as a woman." His eyes raked her body. "And so you shall, my dear, so you shall. After the blood of your friends has aroused me to the highest pitch of human excitement, I shall have other appetites to satisfy. I think you have already experienced the caresses of Morrigan. I think you did not much care for them. Shall we see what happens when you are in my bed, Dierdriu? Shall we see how you respond when you are lying beneath me? I am an expert in every level of torture ever thought of, or dreamed of, or hoped for, Dierdriu. Before this night is over, you will be begging me to kill you. You may yet see the dawn break, but it will be a terrible dawn."

Joanna said very loudly, "If you touch me, I shall kill you," and the Erl-King laughed, a low, blurred sound of mirth.

"You would not even manage to lift your hand to strike me," he said. "For I am bound by your own Enchantment, the magical Girdle of Gold you yourself coaxed the sorcerers to weave. How ironic, how beautifully and superbly ironic, that it should now be that very Enchantment that protects me from you." He regarded her. "While I possess that, nothing can harm me." He moved away with graceless gait, and seated himself at the stone banqueting table.

"Commence," he said to the hunchback, "for I grow weary with waiting. And I have waited a very long time."

As the hunchback went to the door, Morrigan moved eagerly to the brazier and lifted a shallow copper cooking pot on to the heat.

To THE HORRIFIED prisoners, none of whom had ever watched or even heard of a theatrical performance, the most chilling part of what followed was the organised manner of it all, the sheer systematic smoothness. Every person who played a part in the Erl-King's terrible banquet knew exactly what he had to do; every person did what he must quickly and efficiently, and with practised ease. Joanna remembered an old Lethe word: orchestrated, and she thought that the banquet was orchestrated. A ritual often repeated. Practised until it was perfect. Terrible. To begin with she thought she would be sick, and then she thought she would faint. But she did neither; she remained quietly where she had been put by the guards, and she saw, with absolute clarity, all that took place.

The hunchback and the guards had brought in two prisoners that none of them had seen until now. Fellow captives in the narrow rock-lined cells? Yes, probably. Cormac, who knew a little more than the others about the Erl-King's ways, thought the boys had probably been captured earlier that day by the hunchback, and brought up to the Citadel.

The boys were very young. They were white-faced and trembling, but the elder of the two was putting up a heartbreaking show of bravery, eyeing the Erl-King with defiance, pushing away the restraining hands of the guards.

The Erl-King said softly, "So you will defy us, will you, my dears? I wonder how you will behave when we have you on the tables, little defiant ones?" The boy's head came up, and Joanna, aching with pity for them both, saw their eyes dart to the hollowed-out centres of the two high tables. She thought that the boys were a bit dazzled and bewildered by the candlelit chamber, and she thought they had the not-quite-focussed look of people who have been kept captive in a dark place. They were blinking and flinching from the candlelight, and for some reason this roused a fierce anger in Joanna. She thought: but they are children! And remembered what Cormac had said at the very beginning. *The Erl-King eats the children.* Anger flooded her body and with it strength, and she tensed to spring at Morrigan and wrest the Nightcloak from her. But even as she drew breath to move, Morrigan leaned back and drew the cloak about her, tying the cords beneath her chin, and Joanna leaned back, because it would clearly be impossible to get the Nightcloak while Morrigan was wearing it.

But she cannot wear it for long, Joanna . . . remember . . . ? Only a pure-bred Human can use the Cloak, and only a pure-bred Human can wear it for any length of time . . . be watchful . . .

Morrigan said suddenly, "Tie the prisoners tighter. The Wolfking is known for his chivalry, and the others may make some absurd attempt at a rescue." She smiled the snake-smile. "My Master does not care to be interrupted while he is being pleasured," said Morrigan softly. And then, as the guards moved, "Leave the High Queen," and her forked tongue flickered. "My Master will wish her to be left free for she will not be going to the Table yet. We may both wish her left whole."

The other guards were dragging the boys to the two tables, and as their eyes adjusted to the light, the younger one seemed to become fully aware. He began to scream, dreadful trapped-hare screams, pleading and struggling as they dragged him across the floor. Joanna saw that his nails were scrabbling at the stones, trying to find something to hold on to, but the guards had him by his legs, and they pulled him with ease to the tables, his nails tearing from his fingers as he was taken.

The Erl-King seemed to rouse. His great black eyes glittered, and he sat up a little straighter, watching the boy. Morrigan glanced at him and then said, "That one for the knife. The other one will watch." And, turning to the five prisoners, "You will watch also. It will prepare you for what is ahead." She raised the knife, lying by the brazier, and honed it on a rough whetstone, smiling as she did so. "There is nothing my Master likes so well as the warm fresh meat of a young boy," said Morrigan softly.

The guards had strapped the first boy down, and as Morrigan stood over him, seeming to tower to a great height, the boy, his eyes bolting from his head, sagged, his head rolling in unconsciousness.

"Weakling," said Morrigan, and lifted the knife.

"A weakling indeed," said the Erl-King, watching, his head rested on his hand. "But commence. Position the other one so that he can see what is done."

Morrigan stood back and the guards adjusted the leather straps. "Secure?"

"Quite secure, Mistress."

"Then," said Morrigan, "we shall commence." She turned her head to look at the Erl-King.

"Now!" exclaimed the Erl-King and Morrigan lifted the bright sharp knife.

To begin with there was no sound, and then little by little, they became aware that there *was* a sound. The gentle cutting of flesh, the parting of muscle and the ripping open of tendons and skin. A ripping fraying sound. A snipping sound. Bits of flesh and lumps of skin.

Once Morrigan said, "His skin is like a peach in full bloom. A pity I could not have had the use of him for a night or two." A little later she said, "Tender, Master. He will serve us well. Turn up the heat, you," and the hunchback lolloped across the room and flung more wood and strongly scented herbs into the brazier.

Morrigan was calm and unhurried, and even graceful about her gruesome work. Once the boy seemed to revive a little, his head lifting, a deep moan breaking from his lips, and Morrigan stood back and waited, and the Erl-King tilted his head. Then—"Dead," said Morrigan contemptuously. "A weakling indeed. Shall I go on with him?"

"Go on," said the Erl-King.

Morrigan bent over again, her long hair falling across her face. She was slicing into thicker flesh now; upper thighs and lower soft belly, fleshy arms. Blood had bubbled and spurted over and spilled into the deep channels at the sides of the tables. The hunchback moved quickly, placing golden chalices to catch it.

Golden goblets for human blood ... So it is true, thought the prisoners, and the Erl-King turned his head and smiled.

"Yes, my poor victims, it is true."

The blood was running sluggishly now, and there was the stench of it in the room, and a taste like tin on the air. Morrigan lifted the raw slices of pale flesh and transferred them to the waiting copper pan, and then placed it over the heat. She turned back to the boy, cutting again, gouging into the stomach. The inner organs began to spill out. Liver, lungs, kidneys ... a layer of rich yellow fat just beneath the skin ... the glimpse of raw stringy muscle and the whiteness of ribs ...

The smell of the sizzling flesh cooking was filling the stone chamber now. Incredibly, the smell was barely indistinguishable from the smell of roasting pork, and to Joanna's horror, a pang of involuntary hunger twisted her stomach, to be followed by an abrupt nausea.

The Erl-King stood up and leaned forward. "The feast!" he said in a high excited voice. "The feast! Quickly!" and Morrigan began transferring the slices of cooked flesh to the silver plates.

Silver platters for human bones ...

The Erl-King fell upon the pale meat, holding up each piece and inspecting it before conveying it to his mouth. Rivulets of warm fat ran down his jaws and his body quivered. Once he looked towards Cormac and said, "Your turn before long, Wolfking," and Cormac snarled and turned away. Joanna, who had been waiting for Morrigan to discard the Nightcloak, thought they must surely try to save the second boy, but Cormac threw out a warning at once.

You will never get the cloak while Morrigan is wearing it ...

With the thought, Joanna saw Morrigan shift uneasily, and put up a hand to loosen the cloak's fastenings. Hope welled up inside her, and she thought that of course Cormac was right, and of course Morrigan would not be able to bear wearing it for very much longer. If only the Nightcloak was strong enough ...

The Erl-King was hunting amongst the litter of plates, almost sniffing at them, as if to ensure that no morsel of edible meat remained. Once he lifted the golden chalice and they saw it stain his jowls with red. A film of yellowish grease covered the silver plates now, and shreds of the pale meat lay cooling.

The Erl-King lifted his head from the feast at last, and looked at the second prisoner, and a smile widened his jaw.

"My appetites are fully aroused now," he said softly. And then, to the guards, "Is he fast?"

"Well fast, Master."

"I should not like him to escape," said the Erl-King. "You know what will happen to you if he escapes."

The man blenched, but said firmly, "He is quite secure, Master."

The second boy was screaming again, and straining against the wide leather straps. His eyes were starting from his head in terror, and he was crying for mercy. Joanna, held tightly by the guards, found herself crying, tears streaming down her cheeks, and Gormgall's hand came down on her arm.

"You can do nothing, my lady. And this one will be quick."

"How do you know?" said Joanna, in an agonised whisper.

"I know what is going to happen. In all of the stories—" Gormgall stopped and said in a very low voice. "But I did not until now believe any of those old tales."

Dubhgall was the nearest to the table where the second boy was being strapped down, and as the boy writhed and cried for mercy, and as the Erl-King stood up, he gave a sudden wrench to the men who held him, and in one swift movement, was at the table, tugging at the leather straps, his hands frantic. Joanna's heart bounded—was this the moment?—and once again she braced herself to spring at Morrigan.

But in an instant, Morrigan was there, towering over Dubhgall, the cloak hissing into its silken folds about her ankles, her eyes glittering darkly.

"Fool!" said Morrigan contemptuously. "You must know that once on my Master's Tables, no one ever escapes. Did you really think you could rescue him—and escape my Master's wrath?"

"Begging your pardon, Mistress," said Dubhgall with his own voice brimful of contempt, "but I thought at least I'd try. As for the wrath of the creature you serve—well, it seems to me that we're all at the whim of his fancy anyway. One more or one less shred of wrath won't make so much difference."

He glared at the Erl-King as he said this, and the Erl-King inclined his head in a gesture that was very nearly courteous.

"Will it not make any difference, servant?" He leaned closer, and Dubhgall flinched. "There are many levels of pain and there are many heights to which agony may aspire, and before this night is over, I promise you that you will all have aspired to the very greatest heights." The black eyes moved down over Dubhgall's body. "And now I shall ensure that you shall have special treatment." He nodded to the guards, but Dubhgall had already been taken and held by three of them. "I think we will carve you as we did the first one," said the Erl-King in his beautiful corrupt voice. "And we shall make it very slow, servant, so that you do not miss savouring one second of pure pain." He considered Dubhgall, his head on one side. "And we will begin with your *hands*," said the Erl-King, "for there is nothing so tasty as a little braised hand. Your friends will perhaps share the dish with me?" He looked at them and smiled. "But yes, yes you will," said the Erl-King. "You will help me to eat your friend, even if every mouthful has to be forced into your unwilling throats." He smiled again and then looked at the guards. Something unreadable flared in his eyes.

"Which of you let the servant go? Ah, you was it? How foolish. Take him below." And then, as the guard was led out, "Secure the others," he said. "You know what will happen if you let another one break free."

The guards twisted the prisoners' arms high up behind their backs, and Joanna's heart sank, for there was no hope of any of them breaking free. Only Muldooney continued to roam aimlessly about the room.

The Erl-King approached the second table slowly, his head on one side, considering his victim. The boy looked up at him, and Joanna saw his lips frame yet another plea.

"Let . . . me . . . go . . ."

If the Erl-King heard, he gave no sign. He moved nearer and then made a sudden pouncing movement, leaping on to the table and straddling the helpless boy, so that he was crouching over him.

The hard fly's jaw quivered and the Erl-King began to salivate copiously, the thick fluid running out of his mouth and down on to the boy. Joanna shuddered and bit her lip.

The Erl-King crouched lower, the pointed shiny mandible

quivering. The thin curved claw-hands came out to fasten on to the boy's shoulders, and Joanna saw the blood spring to the surface. The boy screamed again, a dreadful abandoned hopeless, helpless sound, and then the Erl-King lowered his fly's head and buried his maw in the boy's stomach. A liquid sucking sound filled the chamber.

Gormgall said in a strangled voice, "He's eating him. He's eating through his stomach."

Joanna said in a low voice. "This is terrible. Can't we do something . . ."

But each of them was held firmly by the guards, and each of them knew that their only hope was the Nightcloak. And Morrigan was still wearing it.

Blood was seeping into the gulleys of the second table and trickling down into the drainage outlet, and the hunchback again placed the golden goblets to catch the flow.

The boy had not screamed again, but they could see that his lower lip was bitten through, and Joanna remembered—and wished she had not—the Lethe accounts of ancient religious martyrs who had taken vows of silence under torture, but who had screamed through the nose.

The Erl-King resettled on the boy's body, and as he lifted his head, they saw that his jaws were bloodied and smeared.

"This one is soon done also," said the Erl-King, and now the beautiful voice was thick and clotted.

"Already dead, Master?"

"Cooling," said the Erl-King, and moved from the table. "Remove him. Sluice down the floors." He reseated himself at the banqueting table, as the hunchback emptied buckets of water, sending the blood and the thick fluids gushing down and out through the drains.

The Erl-King was studying the five prisoners now, the blood-stained mandible seeming to smile.

"My hunger is upon me," he said, and Joanna realised that the voice had returned to its soft, caressing tone. He glanced across to Muldooney, and away again, and the four prisoners thought it was as if he had considered Muldooney and then dismissed him.

"The witless hold no interest for me," said the Erl-King, "although my hunchback may like him to toy with for an hour or two." The black eyes slewed round to the others. "And the

High King and his Lady shall be kept whole until I have had my fill of them," he said, and his voice held a note of immense pleasure. "But the insolent servant shall be dealt with now." He nodded to the guards. "The Table," he said. "Do it."

Dubhgall was dragged to the centre of the room, and then lifted, struggling, on to the Table which had held the first victim. Morrigan moved to the brazier and placed a small copper pan on the heat, throwing in a handful of scented herbs. "For my Master likes his flesh to be spiced."

Gormgall said defiantly, "It is strange to see you doing servants' work, Morrigan," and she turned to look at him as if she had only just discovered that he was there.

"This would normally be my sisters' task, son of peasants," she said. "But for tonight, I do not care to share anything." She smiled. "And when you, in your turn, receive my undivided attentions, and those of my Master, you will understand a little better." The narrow eyes smiled. "They are useful, but for tonight they will do my bidding and we shall not be troubled by their petty squabbles and their conceits."

The hunchback was laying out a selection of knives and saws, and Joanna began to hope very strenuously that Dubhgall would faint before it began.

The Erl-King turned to look at her, as if he had caught the thought, and said, "We shall keep him conscious, madam," and Joanna thought wildly: he heard me! But he cannot possess the Samhailt! He cannot!

The Erl-King said softly, "Not the Samhailt, my dear. But something much more effective," and Joanna saw Cormac become very tense.

"When I came out of the North, in the days when Tara was still only a barren rock," the Erl-King said, "I, also, had my sorcerers and my necromancers. You were not the only one to harness the old magic, Dierdriu, I was there, also. But you know this." He studied her. "And my sorcerers created for me not the Samhailt with its absurd restrictions and its *honour*," the word was dragged out sneeringly, "but something much deeper and stronger and infinitely preferable." He paused, and Joanna heard Cormac draw in his breath sharply, as if he knew what was coming.

"They created for me the Stróicim Inchinn," said the Erl-King, and Cormac and the two Cruithin gasped. The Erl-King glanced at Cormac. "Yes, you know of it," he said. "Of course you do." And then, to Joanna, "Roughly translated, the Stróicim Inchinn means to tear into the brain," he said. "I can do that, Dierdriu. I can tear into your thoughts, as if I were clawing apart your mind. You can hide nothing from me, for if I care to, I can see your every thought." The smile was genuinely amused now. "A valuable gift, my dear," said the Erl-King. "But then you always knew me to be a formidable enemy, I think? The Stróicim Inchinn is one of the darkest and most powerful enchantments of the mind ever created."

"It is also," said Cormac, unexpectedly austere, "totally and absolutely forbidden. By any rule and by any creed and by any academy of sorcerers or necromancers."

"I do not concern myself with your puny rules, High King," said the Erl-King. "I can claw my way into your thoughts, and I can know your mind's most secret recesses." He leaned forward. "You can hide nothing from me, Cormac," he said. "Nothing."

Dubhgall's arm was bared and manacled, and between them, the hunchback and Morrigan selected knives. Then the hunchback lifted the first of the knives, and sliced down on Dubhgall's forearm. Skin parted and blood seeped out and dripped on to the floor. Dubhgall moaned and sagged, and at once, the Erl-King turned his great black stare on to him. Straight away Dubhgall revived, and let out a deep moan, and Joanna knew that the insect-eyes had penetrated to Dubhgall's brain, and that the Erl-King had called up the terrible Stróicim Inchinn.

The Forbidden Enchantment of the Necromancers . . .

Of course, Human Child . . . Did I not tell you? I can keep you all alive to the point of death and beyond . . .

Aloud, the Erl-King said, "Since I came out of the North, Dierdriu, I have used the Stróicim Inchinn—oh, many times. I can call corpses out of the earth with it. Would you like to see my Army of Corpses, Dierdriu? It is the work of moments to summon them, and they are the most terrible sight you could ever see. Their bones are rotting and their skins hang from their skeletons, and their flesh is putrefying, for they have all long since died.

"But I can summon them with the Stróicim Inchinn, and I

can force them to do my bidding. They are my army, Dierdriu, and they have fought for me, not once, but many times."

Joanna said, "The Battle for the Trees—"

The Erl-King said, "Of course. Do you remember that, madam? How we fought, and how your sorcerers sent the Trees into their sleep by means of the *Draiocht Suan*." There was a faintly contemptuous note in the velvet voice now. "A minor sorcery," said the Erl-King.

"And yet one which preserved the Trees from your destructive wrath," said Joanna calmly.

"The Trees are still lost to you, madam."

"They will waken when I call to them."

The Erl-King and Joanna looked at one another, then—"Do you remember, Dierdriu," he said softly, "how I called up my Army of Corpses to fight in that battle?"

"Yes."

"Do you remember the pity and the terror and the stench of death and decay they brought with them?"

"Oh yes," said Joanna. "Oh yes, I remember that."

And you shall suffer as you never thought possible for that. You shall suffer a thousand times more than the poor wretches you keep bound to you, their minds and their souls chained to their rotting bodies.

"Wait and see," said Joanna, and the Erl-King smiled.

"Perhaps, Dierdriu," he said, "perhaps that will be the end I shall decree for you and the Wolfking this time. A fitting end, I think." He looked at Cormac. "Something for you to contemplate while you are eating your servant."

The hunchback was parting the gaping cut on Dubhgall's arm, and Dubhgall was moaning. "Slowly," said Morrigan, "for we do not wish to miss any of the pleasure of this, Master."

"Slow indeed," said the Erl-King, returning to his seat at the table.

No one dared to speak, although Cormac was snarling softly, and the chains that held him slithered to and fro on the stone floor as he tried to break free. To their right, Muldooney had gone shuffling off by himself, and seemed to be inspecting the stonework of the walls with minute attention, stroking the stones with a finger and licking the finger interestedly. But Joanna thought he glanced back at Morrigan, and saw that he knew that with Morrigan still wearing the cloak, their slender plan had no chance of working. If only she would remove it . . .

The Erl-King had returned to the banqueting table, and was sitting watching them all. He indicated for a goblet to be placed beneath the table where Dubhgall lay, and at once Morrigan obeyed. Blood seeped through into the goblet.

The hunchback had cut all round the thick fleshy forearm now, and he reached for a smaller pointed knife. Dubhgall was struggling and crying out, but the manacles held. Strips of flesh were pared from his arm and Morrigan laid them in the small pan over the brazier. The stench of cooking flesh once again filled the chamber.

Dubhgall's hand and lower arm were now only attached to his body by bone, gleaming white where all the flesh had been neatly cut away. Joanna and the others could see raw red muscle and shreds of skin.

The hunchback chuckled and bent to pick up the golden goblet, by now full to the brim with Dubhgall's blood. He handed it to the creature at the banqueting table, and waited as it was tasted. Blood ran from the Erl-King's jaw, and as he lowered the chalice he said, "A good temperature. *Warm.* But continue."

The hunchback reached for the saw.

With the sawing of Dubhgall's bone, Joanna's control broke. She managed not to actually sob, but her face twisted, and tears streamed down her cheeks. She tried to look away, but at once the luminous eyes of the Erl-King drew her back.

"You must share in everything, madam," said the soft voice.

Dubhgall was screaming now, hopeless anguished cries, and the rasp of the saw filled the chamber . . . the hunchback took his time . . . There was a dreadful smell of heat as the friction of the saw built up, steel teeth on solid bone . . . A kind of whitish dust flew and Joanna, who had seen trees sawed, and logs cut, more times than she could remember, knew it for bone-dust.

Blood was congealing on the floor now, and the hunchback left off sawing to sluice down the floor. Water, red-streaked, ran down into the culverts and out through the drains once more.

Dubhgall's hand was severed altogether now, and he was

free. He was panting and jerking, his face the colour of pale marble. Morrigan took his raw flesh and once more peeled thin slices from it. The pan sizzled and the herbs gave out their pungent scent . . .

For what seemed to be a very long time, the only sound in the narrow chamber was the sizzling of Dubhgall's pale flesh.

At last, Morrigan said, "Ready, Master." And to the hunchback, "Bind the Cruithin's wound. We will need him again." She carried the pan to the banqueting table, and began to distribute the flesh on to the silver platters.

"I should not dream of eating this feast alone," said the Erl-King. "Bring the prisoners to the table, if you please." And then, to the prisoners themselves, "I think you would not wish me to display such discourtesy as to partake of a meal without inviting you to join me."

Cormac said contemptuously, "The *Gentleman*."

The Erl-King at once replied, "I am well named, High King. When I brought the Dark Necromancers out of the North, they were uneducated fools. They were greedy, but they were quite unable to think or to plan. They were coarse, graceless. Uncouth." He made an unexpectedly fastidious gesture with one hand. "Distasteful to me," he said. And then, to Morrigan, "I am so glad you forbade your oafish sisters their presence here tonight, madam."

"Their presence would have disgusted you, Master," said Morrigan, "their manners are repulsive." She beckoned in peremptory fashion to the hunchback before dismissing him, and the prisoners were forced into chairs around the table. Before each of them was placed a platter which bore several strips of flesh, lightly cooked only, still oozing blood and juices, like a very lightly grilled steak. There was the scent of animal flesh, a slightly sweetish odour.

Joanna thought: but this is impossible. I can't eat Dubhgall. And she looked imploringly at Cormac. Cormac at once lowered his head, and Joanna thought: of course, the Erl-King can hear our thoughts. He can tear into our minds with the Stróicim Inchinn. It was a dreadful thought, but to Joanna, more terrible, was the Stróicim's close kinship to the Samhailt, the ancient and sacred Mindsong bestowed on the Bloodline of Ireland.

But the Stróicim Inchinn was ever the other side of the coin, my dear . . .

The thought slid into Joanna's mind unbidden, and she glanced involuntarily to where the Erl-King sat. Had that been the Stróicim, or something else?

For every Enchantment ever woven by the sorcerers who serve the High Kings, there must always be its dark counterpart . . . or have you forgotten that?

Dierdriu! breathed Joanna, and at once was the ruffle of sweetness and the gentle strength that was Dierdriu. I can bear it, thought Joanna. She is still with me, and I am still with her, and I can bear it. But she kept her eyes lowered as Cormac was doing, for although it seemed almost impossible to cheat the Stróicim Inchinn, eyes could be a window and a chink into the mind. Perhaps if we are very careful and very watchful, we may blur the Stróicim, thought Joanna, and looked down at the plate again. At her side, quite deliberately, Cormac picked up the small knife set out, and after a moment, Gormgall did the same.

The Erl-King said, "Not hungry, madam? Perhaps you need a little assistance," and Joanna remembered how he had threatened to force the flesh into their throats. She looked back at the platter, and thought: perhaps if I think of it as ordinary anonymous meat it will not be so bad. And it cannot *hurt* Dubhgall any more than he has been hurt already. Perhaps it will not be so bad . . .

But it was. It was the most terrible thing she had ever had to do in her life. To begin with she tried to take very tiny mouthfuls, but that was no good because it only prolonged the ordeal. After that, she cut great lumps and swallowed them down whole, but they stuck in her throat, so that she coughed and gagged. And even then, every shred, every sliver seemed to lodge between her teeth, so that she had to work it loose with her tongue.

Cormac ate savagely, as if he did not care, disdaining the small bone-handled knife at his place, tearing at the flesh with his hands and his teeth. The Erl-King said, "You are not so civilised as I had supposed, Your Majesty," and Cormac growled and threw the flesh across the table at him. The guards moved, and Joanna, thought: *this* is the moment. Oh please let Morrigan discard the cloak. *Now*, when they are all looking at Cormac.

Morrigan flung the Nightcloak over the back of her chair. Cormac half rose in his seat, and at the far end of the chamber, Muldooney broke into a mad little dance, humming to himself, circling the room, looking, thought Joanna wildly, like a great lumbering bear. Cormac was tearing at his chains now, overturning the chair he had been sitting on, and Muldooney danced farther away, blubbering his lips and twitching his face rather horridly. Joanna thought: I must either move in one great leap before they realise what is happening, or I must go inch by inch, stealthily and slowly. Which should it be? What would Cormac do? At once came the answer: Cormac would never do anything by stealth in his life. Then nor will I, thought Joanna, and strength poured into her, so that she felt huge, invincible, unstoppable.

She moved then, a sudden whirl of colour and flying hair and blazing eyes, and she was across the chamber, the Nightcloak was in her grasp, and great bolts of light were sparking from it. Joanna swung it about her shoulders and lifted her arms and cried aloud: "Dierdriu! Help us! Send the nightmares! Help us!" And then felt a great tremor go through the chamber.

Joanna was frightened and exhilarated and yet still filled with immense power. We are in the greatest possible danger, but we are also engaging in the greatest battle this Ireland has ever known, she thought. We are confronting the Erl-King, Tara's oldest and strongest enemy. We are trying to defeat an ancient and very terrible evil. She stood rooted to the spot, and felt the power of the High Queen stream through her, and as she did so, the Erl-King suddenly turned his head.

In the shadows, something was moving . . .

They saw it all in the same instant. Something began to take form. Something that had eight legs and a great bloated body. Something whose eyes were at the top of its body, and whose gristly jointed legs could move at an astonishing rate.

Araneida Arachnida.

A giant spider.

The five prisoners backed away at once, Gormgall dragging the injured, just conscious Dubhgall, and as they did so, the

Erl-King began to scream, and they saw Morrigan stretch out a hand and fling a spear of white light at the spider.

Joanna heard herself laugh, "Oh no Morrigan, you cannot destroy this by your incantations. This is your Master's nightmare, and all know that the nightmares of others do not respond to sorcery."

The great spider had remained motionless in the corner, its huge body swelling. It became gross, bloated, a monstrous black crouching thing, a nightmare . . .

The Erl-King's nightmare . . .

The spider was six feet across now, it was eight, ten . . . perhaps more. Joanna, speechless with horror, thought that the spider's body must be all of twelve feet across. The legs were great sinewy protrusions, as thick as tree trunks, steely strong and bristling with the spider's coarse black hair. A man's neck or his spine would snap like a twig in the grasp of the creature's legs . . .

The short-sighted eyes on the top of the spider's body were swivelling towards every corner, as if they searched for something in particular. They were bulbous and almost blind, but there was a terrible intelligence in the jellylike mass. It can barely see, thought Joanna, but it can *smell*. It can smell that there is fear in here, and it scents that there is something in this chamber that it will savour.

Morrigan was chanting and walking in a circle about the spider, but Joanna and the others saw, with a great upsurge of hope, that the Erl-King was backing away.

He is frightened! thought Joanna, and felt a burst of confidence so great that she thought she could have slain the Erl-King with her bare hands. In the same moment, there was a blaze of Mindsong from Cormac.

Yes, he is frightened! And there is nothing to be afraid of except his own fear!

The fear of a fly for a spider.

And the Stróicim Inchinn? cried Joanna's own mind warningly. There was a ripple of delight from Cormac.

"Look at him!" cried Cormac aloud. "He can no more summon the Stróicim at this moment than he can move." And indeed, the Erl-King was helpless against the wall of his own Banqueting Chamber, his eyes never leaving the menacing bulk of the spider.

The spider was moving now, a sudden scuttling movement, and they knew that it had picked up the Erl-King's terror-filled scent. It will smell its way to him, thought Joanna, horrified, and moved closer to Cormac. On the other side, Gormgall was holding the half-conscious Dubhgall, and across the room Muldooney stood irresolute, and then began to tiptoe round the perimeter of the chamber towards the others. Joanna at once held out a hand to him, because after all he had done, it was not to be thought of that Muldooney should not be with them.

In the flickering light, they saw silken threads begin to emerge from the spider's body, and Joanna knew that it had begun spinning its sticky prey-trapping web.

The Erl-King had seen it as well. He retreated further into his corner and quite suddenly began to scream at Morrigan, a dreadful high-pitched whinnying sound that made Joanna's teeth wince.

"Forget your spells, fool! Kill it! *Kill it!*"

Morrigan was chanting frantically now, pointing her long boneless fingers at the spider. Shafts of light pierced the dark stone chamber, and bounced off the spider's fibrous skin.

"KILL IT!" screamed the Erl-King again. "Fish filth! Useless snake filth! Hack it to pieces! Let us roast it over the braziers! You! Guards! Rend the creature apart and throw the pieces on to the streets of my City! Or must I summon my Army of Corpses to make you!"

The guards moved uncertainly, and one of them made as if to draw his sword. The spider darted at him, and clamped one of its gristly legs about his waist, lifting him, and then dashing him to the ground. There was a sickening, crunching sound, and the guard lay still, his head at an unnatural angle, his spine broken.

The Erl-King was still shrieking, hurling threats, screaming to Morrigan to destroy the spider, but Morrigan was sounding frantic now, and the Erl-King was standing with his back to the wall, one hand held out before him to ward off the spider's attack. The guards were huddled together, by now as frightened of the giant spider as they were of the Erl-King, and it was clear to Joanna and the others that the guards would not do anything. Muldooney and Gormgall rushed to bar the doors of the stone chamber, and the Erl-King, rallying briefly, screamed at them. "Fools! Locked doors will not keep my armies out! I shall call them up, the rotting corpses and the carrion. You will have the stench of graveyard filth for ever in your nostrils! You will see at close quarters the worms that feed on men's flesh, and you will see how fat and bloated those worms are with their skins bursting with the juices of the dead flesh they feed on! They will crawl all over you, and you will be taken into the embrace of rotting arms and you will be covered in graveyard mould and smothered with the kisses of putrefying lips!"

He paused, to draw in a sobbing breath, and Cormac, his eyes never leaving the great spider, said, "Empty threats, I think. He is disabled by his own terror." He nodded to Gormgall and Muldooney, who made haste to shoot the bolts of the door, Muldooney reaching for the topmost ones, because wasn't a bit of height needed for such a job.

The silken threads were lengthening now, they were sliding across the floor, leaving sticky snail trails in their wake. From the corner of her eye, Joanna saw Gormgall begin to inch his way to where Morrigan stood, still chanting useless spells.

The web strands had reached the Erl-King now. Three of the strands whipped round his body, and three more took his legs. As they watched, he was lifted, a struggling squirming prisoner, and drawn nearer to the great spider.

Morrigan began to scream imprecations now, calling on the Dark Ireland to come to her aid, calling to the necromancers and the Black Enchanters; calling on the first sorcerers who had created the terrible Stróicim Inchinn.

"Useless, Morrigan!" cried Cormac, and the undiluted delight and the pure confidence in his voice was like fresh rainwater, like a spring dawn, to Joanna and the others. "You are beaten, you are bested. Dierdriu has triumphed!"

Begone adversary . . .

"My sisters will feed on your blood for this, Wolfking!" cried Morrigan. "They will make you suffer their hag embraces and their greedy love-making! You will see, Wolfking! You will see!"

"Look to your master!" cried Cormac. "Oh, Morrigan, look to the terrible Erl-King who has held the people of the Walled City in fear and terror ever since he came out of the North! Caught and held by a giant spider! Spitted on the end of a nightmare!"

The rudimentary lips of the spider's food canal were gaping open now. *All the better to eat you with* ... As the lipless mouth opened wider, there was a terrible sucking, lip-smacking sound, and a wet gobbling noise that made Joanna feel quite dreadfully sick.

The Erl-King was fighting every inch of the way, but he was being slowly and inexorably drawn closer to the gaping hole in the spider's body.

"Kill it!" screamed the Erl-King, beside himself with fury and terror, and Joanna suddenly saw that he was no longer a dark and sinister figure, he was no longer the powerful and evil Gentleman of the Walled City; he was a struggling writhing puny creature, spineless, but made up of tiny brittle bones which were beginning to snap and crunch in the spider's steely grip. When the Erl-King screamed again to the guards to kill the spider, to cut its web and free him, Joanna felt only a rather distant revulsion, as if none of this could really have very much to do with her.

The guards had not moved, and quite suddenly the five friends realised that the guards were waiting for the Erl-King to die. For then they, also, would be free ...

Cormac reached for the bunch of keys that would unlock his chains, and the guard, meeting Cormac's eyes steadily, handed them to him. "Is he dying, Sire?"

"He is dying," said Cormac and began to unlock the chains.

"Praise the gods," said the man quite quietly, but very fervently. "Then we shall be free of him at last."

The spider's maw was gaping wide now, and the Erl-King was being drawn against the creature's body. There was a liquid swallowing sound, and Dubhgall turned away and vomited violently on to the floor. Joanna's own stomach lurched, for the spider was doing to the Erl-King exactly what the Erl-King had done to the young boy earlier; it was sucking the juices from his body while he lived. They heard the small frail bones snap. In moments, the Erl-King would be flung, dried out and shrivelled and most mercifully dead at last, on to the stone floor.

As they watched, rivulets of not-quite transparent fluid spattered the stone flags beneath the spider.

Gormgall had not been sick, he had not even felt sick. He had inched his way slowly and stealthily to where Morrigan stood near to the brazier, and as he did so, Muldooney reached for the dead guard's sword and passed it to him. Muldooney had not the stomach for killing, but he would not scruple to help someone else, not when it was a creature like this terrible woman, who was probably not a woman at all.

Gormgall grasped the sword, and moved nearer to Morrigan. He heard behind him the dreadful sucking feeding sounds of the spider, and he heard as well the fading cries of the Erl-King. Nearly dead, thought Gormgall. But there is still this one. How near are her sisters? Are they back in the house at Muileann? If so, then she may be less strong, thought Gormgall. And although he had no idea whether Morrigan needed the Morrigna to work her evil sorcery, he thought there would never be another opportunity like this again. And with that thought, came another: she could not banish the spider! Hope surged up in him, and he edged nearer.

As the Erl-King sagged and a driblet of thick smeary liquid stained the floor beneath him, Gormgall lifted the sword and brought it point-down on Morrigan's skull.

Her head burst open as if Gormgall had halved a ripe melon, and white fishblood and grey matter spurted. Morrigan fell to her knees and Cormac, who was frantically unlocking the padlock of his chains, shouted, "Harder, Gormgall! Again!" And as Gormgall struck again, Cormac cried, "For Ireland!"

"And for you, Sire!" said Gormgall very quietly, but very fervently, and took a firmer hold upon the sword.

Morrigan had fallen in a blind boneless heap and was squirming on the floor, not quite dead. As Gormgall began to lift the sword again, Morrigan raised her hand and pointed at Gormgall. "My sisters will avenge—" And then Gormgall brought the sword flashing down again, this time severing what remained of the creature's head from her body. As skin and flesh and muscle parted, he turned very white, but there was a determined look in his eyes, and the others did not doubt that he would strike her again if it was necessary.

"And now," said Cormac, turning to the guards, "is there any man who will try his strength against us? Or," he said, his eyes blazing with triumph, "have I adjudged you all correctly? Will you ride out with your King and rid Tara of the usurpers?"

"Sire," said the captain, falling to his knees, "you must

know that now we are free of that creature's malevolence, we will follow you into hell itself."

THE WOLFKING'S COMPANY lay spent and exhausted in the chamber, uncaring of the congealing body of Morrigan, barely noticing the shrivelled thing that had been the Erl-King.

Joanna thought: we are safe—safe! And was conscious of an immense inner peace.

They fashioned a more comfortable dressing for Dubhgall's arm, and Gormgall produced his flask. Dubhgall, who was white about the lips and clearly in a good deal of pain, drank gratefully, and managed to say, "As well fight for Your Majesty with one hand as with two."

Cormac smiled and gripped Dubhgall's sound arm. "Quite as well, my friend," and was turning to say something to the guards, when Gormgall sat up.

"Listen, Sire. Can you hear it?"

Joanna, who was more tired than she could ever remember being, was just framing the thought that she could not bear anything else to happen, when Muldooney, who had got up to open the door of the stone chamber, said, "It sounds like cheering. Some kind of celebrating."

"It's the people of the Walled City," said Gormgall, his face alight. "They have heard that the creature is dead. Sire, you must come out and speak to them."

Cormac looked very tired indeed, and Joanna thought he must be more tired than any of them. But he did not hesitate; he at once stood up and said, "Of course. Come—all of us." He led the way down to the great stone hall with the massive iron-studded doors that opened directly on to the drawbridge. Gormgall went to the winch, and Muldooney stepped up to help, because wasn't a bit of good solid muscle needed for a job like this? Slowly and protestingly, the great gates folded back and light poured into the Erl-King's dark Citadel, blinding them and sending dust motes dancing in and out of the rays of blue-tinged light.

"Twilight," said Cormac softly. "The Purple Hour."

The others fell back, and Cormac moved forward into the soft blue light that was pouring in through the doors, and stood there, a solitary figure, silhouetted against the night. Far below him were little pinpoints of moving light, a torchlit procession, and as the cheering grew in intensity and as the shouts of gladness and wild joy floated up to the Citadel, Cormac stood, framed in the great gateway, waiting for the liberated people of the Erl-King's city to start the ascent to the Citadel.

No one quite knew how the news of the Gentleman's death reached the town, and no one, to begin with, believed it. Wouldn't that be just a rumour, a malicious tale, probably put about by the Gentleman's faithful hunchback, just to see how they'd all behave. The Gentleman had the habit of testing his people's loyalty now and then.

But the rumour persisted, and people began to gather in little groups, furtively at first, and then more boldly. Several of the Gentleman's guard were seen walking through the town, not on the Gentleman's business, but so far as anyone could see, with the intention of spreading the good news.

For the Gentleman was in truth dead. He was lying in his own Banqueting Hall, destroyed for ever by the great Wolfking and his lady. Morrigan lay with him, felled by a blow from one of the Wolfking's loyal Cruithin servants.

At first they could not take it in. They dared not take it in, for hadn't the Gentleman been there as long as anyone knew, one of the terrible band of Dark Sorcerers who had come out of the cold Northern Wastes to feed on Ireland? Wasn't the Gentleman immortal?

But lights were flaring from the Citadel now; not the thick dull lights that meant the Gentleman's candles of human fat, but joyful clear yellow lights that meant good honest tallow or wax candles and wall torches of applewood and bright log fires. And there was a feeling in the dusk as well; a fresh clean scent, as if rain had fallen on a hot summer's day, or a fresh rose-and-gold dawn had appeared over the mountains.

The townspeople gathered in small groups, and the groups joined, quite naturally and easily with other small groups, until they were no longer small groups, but quite large ones. People came running out of their houses asking, "What has happened? Is it true?" And, "Dare we believe it?" because although everyone wanted quite desperately to believe it, no one yet dared. Because the Gentleman had his ways . . .

And then one, bolder than the rest, spoke out and said wouldn't they prove the story one way or the other between them? and a rather uncertain cry of assent went up.

"Lights!" cried someone. "Fetch up the lights! As many as we can manage, for it's nearly dusk," and in the searching for the blazing torches, nearly everyone remembered the old hopeless dream of a torchlit procession up to the Citadel to destroy the evil Lord who lived there, and nearly everyone thought wouldn't it be a strange old thing if that procession was actually to happen now, the dream come true, only the Gentleman not being there at the end of it.

As they began to walk up the hill, someone at the back of the line began to cheer, a bit raggedly at first, and then with more assurance, and the sound was taken up by those at the centre, and then by the leaders.

The sound grew in volume, for the people of the Walled City were finding their voices again, and finding as well a rich fountain of joy, that had been almost but not entirely quenched, bubbling over into the light again.

When Cormac stepped out into the huge high open gateway of the Erl-King's Citadel, the townspeople of the nameless city of the Erl-King surged forward, cheering and shouting, and as Cormac stood there, a light rain began to fall, blurring the brave little torches, beating down on the uncovered heads of the people of the town. He saw them through a mist, and he tasted salt mingled in with the rain on his cheeks, and he thought: if I have done nothing else for Ireland, at least I have freed these poor souls from this unbearable weight of evil.

And as he held up both his hands in a gesture that was both supplication and pledge, a great shout went through the people.

"The Erl-King is dead!"

And then, from the heart of the crowd, "Long live the Wolfking!"

Cormac stood before them, his head bowed in silent acceptance, as the cleansing rain continued to fall.

CHAPTER TWENTY-FOUR

FLYNN WAS NOT quite sure how he came to be riding out at the head of them all when they came through the mountains and looked down on Gallan, but at the head he undoubtedly was. He thought it had happened quite simply and naturally; he certainly had not sought it. And then, because he possessed a strong streak of self-honesty, he thought with some amusement: yes, but I could not have borne to have fallen into any kind of subordinate position.

Because you are anxious to lead them forward so that you may find Joanna? said a voice within him.

Yes, certainly it was that, although he was beginning, in some curious and inexplicable fashion, to feel very much closer to Joanna now. *The danger she was in has passed . . .* There was no value in trying to explain how he knew this, but he did know it. Somewhere, somehow, Joanna was safe. They would find her.

And so, although he wanted to reach Gallan and he wanted to waste no time in finding Cormac, who might very well be with Joanna, he thought there was more to it.

I am Finn of the Fiana *again, and there is a battle ahead of us, and I know how it must be fought, and I know where it must be fought and if only, IF ONLY, they will give me my head, I know we can win . . .*

Lethe arrogance, said the old, coolly amused Flynn, but, plain fact, said the small strong voice deep inside him. Finn had not won battles by holding back or being modest, and his descendant would not either.

Descendant? Of course I am his descendant, thought Flynn,

riding along at Conaire's side. How else should I know so many things. How else should I recognise the terrain, and have this aching sense of homecoming. Why else would I be already laying out the battle plan; choosing the ground, deploying the White Swans to the east and the Chariot Horses to the fore. And if only Joanna can ride out with me, then the two worlds will have been spanned at last.

The High Queen returned, Dierdriu fighting for Tara again, with the armies of Finn at her back ... The High Queen and the head of the *Fiana* together again ...

The two worlds, past and future, converging at last, and fusing naturally and gently.

Gallan lay below them, circled by the Mountains—"A marvellous protection, of course," murmured Sean—Cait Fian's palace was set into the side of the mountain itself.

As Flynn sighted it, he gasped, for he had somehow not expected such cool, elegant beauty. He had certainly not expected it to rival Tara.

"Well, not quite," said Conaire. "But it is very lovely."

"And it's perfectly proper for it to be nearly as good as Tara," put in Sean. "Because Cait Fian is nearly as powerful as the High King."

"A sort of second-in-command," said Midir.

"Only it doesn't do to remind Bricriu of it," grinned Etain.

The Mountain Palace of Cait Fian was a pale, graceful edifice, turreted and delicately carved; ice-on-blue and gently glistening. Flynn thought that a light frosting of snow lay on its highest spires, and then he was not sure. Mist wreathed the towers and the pinnacles, and Flynn thought it would be easy to imagine the mist to be cloud. It was a palace of the skies, and although it did not blaze and flame as Tara blazed and flamed, still it was coldly and regally beautiful.

They saw the Panthers as they approached the pillared gates—gleaming sleek black creatures who watched their approach disdainfully. At the rear, the Wolves growled and bunched together, and Sean and Domnall both said together, "Oh *dear*." The Panthers blinked their hard green eyes, but Flynn and Conaire, who were at the head, saw two of them unfold and go padding off.

"To tell Cait Fian we are here," murmured Conaire. "He has them very well trained."

"A pity the King's Wolves aren't half as well trained," said Sean in a not-quite-whisper.

Conaire said, "Oh do hush."

Several Cruithin servants came running out to welcome them, and took the horses. "*And* the wolves," said Sean with relish.

Conaire said, "You see? *Efficient*."

"Our master will receive you when you have washed the dust of your journey off," said one of the Cruithin, and Sean poked Flynn and said, "Cait Fian can't abide dust or dirt."

Flynn, who had just been thinking how much he would welcome a civilised wash and fresh clothes, said rather sharply, "Well, why should he? When you are in Rome, Sean, you must behave as a Roman."

Sean, who had never heard such expression, said, *"What?"* and Flynn had to explain.

"Which," he said to Oscar later, "all took time when I wanted to talk to Cait Fian's Cruithin."

The rooms they were shown to were furnished with velvet-covered couches and silk-cushioned beds.

"Oh for a day's sleep!" cried Midir, stretching.

"Weakling," said CuChulainn. "To the bath house with us both!"

"Yes, for we can't appear before Cait Fian dusty," reiterated Oscar seriously, and Flynn began to be rather curious about their host.

But he washed in the warm water brought to him, and donned the clean linen shirt laid out, and lay down to order his thoughts before being summoned.

THE MOUNTAIN HALL of Cait Fian was large and airy, and everywhere there was the faint ice-on-blue light. Flynn wondered if it was something to do with the actual substance of the walls—weren't they half into the mountain?—and he remembered the pale misty light of the Morne Mountains which he had often seen from Tugaim. In here it was almost as if the mountain light had been trapped and harnessed and redirected. Pure light, thought Flynn, fascinated and charmed in quite a different way to the way in which he had been fascinated and charmed by the Sun Chamber. A great hearth had been hewn into the rock, and a fire burned up, sending out a gentle musk-scented essence. Flynn thought that if a fire could possibly be described as cool, then this one could be so described. The floor beneath them was of pale solid rock, polished until it gleamed, smooth and very nearly glass-like, touched with the same ice-blue as the outer walls of the palace. Thick pale skin rugs were strewn on the floor and Flynn was just thinking that this was one of the most beautiful rooms he had ever seen, when a curtain at the far end drew back and their host appeared.

Cait Fian was far more obviously of animal blood than anyone Flynn had yet met. His hair was pure black and silky, and his eyes were a bright clear green. His ears were set very high on his skull, and they were pointed and covered with silky fur, and his mouth was wide and curving, the upper lip short like a cat's. As he moved to greet them, Flynn saw that his feet were bare, the soles padded like an animal's.

At Flynn's side, Sean said out of the corner of his mouth, "Whatever you do, don't look surprised. It's a very ancient and very strong Bloodline. Nearly as ancient as the Wolfline."

Flynn, trying not to stare, said, "I've never seen anyone quite like him."

Sean said, "Wait until you meet Cormac himself."

Cait Fian greeted them all with exquisite courtesy, exchanging ribald greetings with Conaire, entering into bluff discourse with CuChulainn, but inquiring of Oscar the precise route they had followed.

"All things to all men," muttered Sean to Flynn. "He always knows what to say. It's just a knack, of course."

"Of course," said Flynn, fascinated.

"Easily acquired if you care to bother," said Sean.

"Oh yes."

"I wish I had it," said Sean wistfully.

Cait Fian was greeting the twins now, and the green eyes were surveying Etain with unconcealed interest. Flynn, waiting his turn to be presented, thought they made a striking couple.

"Yes, it's generally thought they'll wed," said Sean. "Quite suitable of course, because the White Swans are *very* good family. A touch flighty perhaps, but Cait Fian is more than equal to that. Here we are. You don't need to bow. He's only a Prince, not a High King. And even *then* you don't need to bow."

Flynn found himself greeted with immaculate politeness and a shrewd green stare.

"A traveller," said Cait Fian at length. "Dear me, this is *very* interesting. I *do* like to hear about journeys, because if you cannot always be travelling *yourself*—so *exhausting* and so time-consuming—hearing about other people's is nearly as good, don't you think? Of course, people say it is just living vicariously, but I *never* bother about what people say." He took Flynn's hand and smiled a cat-smile. "Flynn you must sit next to me at supper," said Cait Fian, and then, "Ah Sean, is it you? *What* an age it has been. I shall want to know *everything* that has been happening at Court—*everything*, and you must omit *nothing*.

"Do come along into supper, my children. Etain, you are to sit beside me, with Flynn."

The meal, which was served in a small room just off the coolly beautiful main hall, was very good. "And very *lavish*," said Sean, pleased.

They began with plovers' eggs and rocs' eggs served on a bed of dark moss, and Cait Fian leaned across the table and said to Conaire in a whisper, "*Not* relatives, Conaire dear one, I should not dream of behaving so *tastelessly* as to serve anything that could be misconstrued. Plovers and rocs, and you would not give *credence* to the trouble my people go to to secure them." He prodded the dish. "But plovers and rocs and nothing more, cousin, unless of course a pigeon's egg has slipped in, for I would not like to actually take an *oath* that is has not."

After the eggs, which Flynn had never encountered, but which he enjoyed, there was a preponderance of fish.

"*Quite* fresh," said Cait Fian, taking a minute portion from several different platters. "Do allow me to guide you, Flynn. *Here* is a type of lake fish which I am sure you will—Yes, Sean, there *are* lakes in the mountains, and if you do not believe me I can convince you by *dropping* you in one—Well, that is the lake fish. And *here* is, dear me, can it be Twilight Fish? Ullgall, have we Twilight Fi—Ah, *have* we? *Really?* Ah, caught in the Candle Mountain, yes that would account for it so early in the . . . Well, my dears, it is apparently Twilight Fish and *rather* a delicacy at this time of the year, as you know. Etain, you must let me slice a portion for you. And the veriest *morsel* of sorrel to go with it? Now *this* is salmonidae—*very* good. And ingot fish. Flynn, you will like this . . .

"Will somebody please refill Conaire's goblet for him, for we all know he cannot *survive* without *frequent* draughts of wine. CuChulainn, my precious, did you *know* your sleeve was trailing in the turbot? It *cannot* be by design . . ."

There were dishes of what Flynn thought might be chicken or perhaps rabbit, braised in some kind of sauce, and there were small dishes of rich sweet honey. Cait Fian ate daintily, licking his fingers after each few mouthfuls, and Flynn grinned to himself and remembered about being in Rome all over again.

"And there should be honey for each place," said Cait Fian, "for I *always* finish a meal with a dish of honey. Ah yes, I see that Ullgall has not disgraced us. Oscar, there is no need *what-soever* to think you have to be *dainty*, we are not in the Sun Chamber now. And it is *impossible* to *eat* warm honey. *Drink* it, my dear ones, dish to lips. Allow me to demonstrate, Etain." He slipped a practised arm about Etain's shoulders as he said this, and winked at Flynn, as he did so, and the wink said: do not be fooled by my apparent softness and by my sheathed claws, Flynn. And Flynn, who had not been in the least fooled, grinned and lifted his honey, which was warm and buttery and wholly delicious, to his mouth.

"Well," said Cait Fian, returning to his own dish of honey, "so we are to re-establish my cousin Cormac at Tara, are we?"

"We hope so," said Conaire, "will you help us?"

"Oh I should think so," said Cait Fian lightly. "Yes, I do think I should." He leaned over to Flynn. "I *do* enjoy a fight," he said confidentially. "And of course, there is *nothing* I would not do for Cormac. Really, my dears, Eochaid Bres ought to have been removed *long* before this, but there is so much *to* a war, isn't there? And of course, to begin with, Eochaid and Bricriu guarded Tara so fiercely that not even a *gnat* could have breached the defences." He placed his empty honey dish down on the table, cleaned his fingers again thoughtfully, and reached for a second dish. "Do tell me," he said, "Sean, you will be sure to know. All those years in Scáthach . . . I suppose they have not—ah—*affected* Cormac at all?"

Sean said, rather blankly, "Not so far as I know."

Conaire chuckled and said, "No, cousin, they have not. Cormac has *not* lost his sanity."

"I am *very* glad to hear it," said Cait Fian seriously, "because I really could not countenance the restoration of a mad King on the throne—oh no, it would not do *at all*."

"It wouldn't be the first time we've had—"

"Sean, if you bear us the *smallest* goodwill, *not* Lugalla the Fifth," said Cait Fian plaintively. And then, to Flynn, "One of our more *unfortunate* High Kings, you understand."

"Cormac," said Conaire firmly, "has retained all his wits."

"I am delighted to hear it," said Cait Fian. "Even so—exile! And at Scáthach!" He shuddered, and addressed himself to his honey. "Of course, I could have told him that the very *minute* he tangled with Mab—" His eyes suddenly slewed round to where Flynn was trying to look noncommittal. "Of course," said Cait Fian, "it's always a great *compliment* to be one of Mab's lovers."

"Ah. Really?"

"Only the best of us," said Cait Fian and sent Flynn another of his winks. "But as for Cormac—yes, there is no question but that he must be reinstated. He's very wild, you know." He paused and went through the same procedure of licking the honey and then cleaning his fingers afterwards. "But he's by far the finest High King Ireland has had since Dierdriu."

"*Is* he?" said Flynn, who did not really think he had thrown in his lot with the wrong side, but was glad to have his judgment approved.

"Oh without a doubt," said Cait Fian, still sorting out his honey. "I daresay I ought to have done something about it *well* before this, but there never seems time. But now here you all are, *beautifully* organised—I do admire efficiency—and it is high time that we gave Eochaid Bres and the Fox the beating they deserve." He stood up and they all followed suit. "And now," said Cait Fian, "if we are to hold a Council of War— dear me, *what* fun, I *shall* enjoy it—do let us move to a more comfortable room. I like to be comfortable," he added to Flynn. "Etain, my child, allow me to show you the way. Do you know, you are rather more beautiful than I had remembered . . ."

THE MORE COMFORTABLE room turned out to be a kind of library with books ranged round the walls, and deep soft chairs covered in thick fur. Skin rugs lay on the floor, and a fire burned. Someone—Ullgall?—had set out pitchers of wine and mead, and tall glasses, and there were dishes of glazed fruits and crystallized ginger.

Etain threw herself down in a chair by the blazing fire, and said, "Oh, it is *so* good to be here again."

Cait Fian smiled at her, and said in a voice that was very nearly a purr, "You should perhaps consider staying for a long time."

Etain said, "Perhaps I should," and Sean's ears twitched, because if this was not a Declaration, it was very close to one, and Declarations meant Betrothals, and Betrothals meant Marriages, and all three meant ceremonies with properly written entertainments. Sean thought it would not hurt to just earmark a few preliminary ideas. Swans and Panthers. Yes, you could do quite a lot with that.

Oscar had moved to the serried rows of books, and Cait Fian said with a pleased smile, "I do like people to admire my books. And I have a *rather* good copy of the Book of the Academy of Necromancers. Ullgall reads it to me," he added, his expression as bland as buttermilk, "for we all know the requirements. 'Only the purest of heart'—I daresay the wretched thing would *frizzle* if I approached it. But I do believe in knowing what the sorcerers are up to.

"Now, you must all of you seat yourselves *wherever* you like, and CuChulainn, *would* you just put a few more logs on the—Ah yes, that is the way. *Best* mountain ash, I never have anything else on my fires, but they are *not* Sleeping Trees, I am *very* strict about the Tree Laws." He curled himself into one of the chairs, and smiled. "And so," said Cait Fian in his velvet voice, "you must tell me *everything* about your plans."

He listened attentively to the campaign outlined by Oscar and Flynn, and at the end he was ruthlessly and charmingly efficient. He wanted to know the precise number of people in their small army. "And," said Sean later, "he barely batted a whisker when we told him."

"I know it doesn't sound many," said Conaire, rather worriedly when they had counted up three times and reached the same dismal total each time.

"I freely admit it does *not*," agreed Cait Fian with the utmost politeness.

"Yes, but we shall each call up our Bloodline creatures."

"Well I do think you will have to. Let me see. Chariot Horses and Deer and Eagles, and dearest Etain's and Midir's White Swans."

"And the Wolves," put in Sean. "Don't forget the Wolves."

"I wish I could forget them," said Cait Fian with a shudder. "My kitchens have been a *battleground* since they arrived. I love Cormac *devotedly* and I will spare no effort to help him regain his throne, but I do wish he would train those creatures. However, to our plans. The Mindsong ought really to go out tonight, children."

"So soon?" said Conaire, rather startled, and the others looked up.

"*Too* exhausting for you all I know," said Cait Fian. "I do sympathise. But I do *not* think we can leave it any longer. We do *not* know where Cormac is, and if the Miller has him—or worse—every hour makes a difference."

"He's right," put in CuChulainn.

"Precious one, I am always right," said Cait Fian, and sent Flynn another of his conspiratorial winks. "And once we have the Bloodline creatures with us, I think we should leave for Tara at first light. After," he said, with a thoughtful look at Etain, "after we have spent a *restful* night here."

"Do we journey all together?" inquired Flynn.

"Oh I think we should," said Cait Fian.

Conaire said, "If we are together it will be easier to repel any enemies we might encounter."

"Enemies?" said Sean suspiciously. "What sort of enemies? I'm not here to do any repelling. You do *know* that, don't you? You haven't forgotten?

"I made it perfectly clear," said Sean to Cait Fian, who was looking amused, "that I would *not* do any fighting. I'm a man of peace," he said with an air of dignity, "and I'm an *ollam*, and if there's any idea of me actually *fighting*—"

"Unruffle yourself, Sean, my poor unloved peacemaker. You shall brandish the pen rather than the sword—dear me, how *poetic* that sounds. Do you suppose that in time to come it will be quoted as a *philosophy*? If that should happen, I do hope that you at least will remember that I said it first." And then, to the indignant Sean, "You see," said Cait Fian, "we are not very far from the Walled City of the Erl-King, and Conaire, with his *admirable* logic, thinks we may encounter one or two of his creatures."

"I hope not," said Oscar, and Flynn noticed that even Cu-Chulainn looked thoughtful.

"The Gentleman has his spies," said Cait Fian, "well, don't we all. But *his* spies are *very* nasty people. And then, of course, we must pass near to Muileann, and I have to tell you that the Morrigna and I are *not* on very good terms these days." He sat back and smiled the cat-smile.

Conaire grinned, "More wars, cousin?"

"My life is one perpetual *sacrifice* to war," said Cait Fian cosily. "The tales I could tell . . . But yes, we had a small battle last year—the merest skirmish really, but still . . ."

"We didn't hear about it," said CuChulainn interested.

"Dear one, it was a courtyard brawl and nothing more," said Cait Fian. "Even Morrigan did not bother to attend."

"I bet you did," said Midir, grinning.

"Well I do *not* like to miss these things," said Cait Fian. "And I had a new cloak—silver trimmed, *very* becoming—which reminds me of our apparel for this war for Cormac; *do* let us choose really *bold* colours, I *do* like a battle to be colourful . . ." He smiled and resettled himself in his chair. "But as for last year's little matter, oh, it was only Macha and one or two of her nasty little followers."

"Followers?" said Flynn.

"Hags and crones," said Etain. "Cait Fian eats them for breakfast and spits out the bones."

"Yes, there *were* some hags," said Cait Fian. "And I recall seeing two banshees which was unusual for that time of year. But it was all very *trivial* and we beat them *quite* easily. Sean, my love, if you must compose one of your delightful ballads about it, I do ask you to do so later."

"Quite right," said CuChulainn looking round. "This is a Council of War." He glowered at Sean who had been making some furtive notes, and Sean shuffled his jottings together rather huffily and said, "Oh excuse me for breathing."

Oscar had been scanning the shelves for maps. "Beautifully catalogued," he said afterwards, and now produced one which showed the entire Manor of Tara and the surrounding countryside. Cait Fian helped him to unroll it and spread it out on the floor at their feet, curling himself neatly at one corner. "Tara," he said, tapping the map's centre. "And *here* is the Forest of Darkness. Just fringing the Plain of the Fál."

Flynn said, without thinking, "And of course, we must make our camp on the Plain," and Cait Fian shot him an admiring look.

"So we should," he said.

"It's very near to the Druids' Settlement," said Conaire.

CuChulainn grinned, and said, "Flynn's been there once. He won't risk it again," and Cait Fian sat back and stared at Flynn.

"No! Flynn, have you really? Oh you must tell me *all* about it. Everything. I have *always* wanted to get inside the Druids' Settlement, and I've *never* managed it."

Sean said, "As a matter of fact, I did just dash off a bit of a Lament—" and was instantly shouted down.

"*Not* during a Council of War," said CuChulainn firmly.

"But perhaps afterwards," said Oscar kindly. Sean retired to a corner of the room to study Cait Fian's books, and could be heard muttering that they none of them had any romance in their souls, and he wished he had not come.

"I knew how it would be," he said, and began ferociously to read *The Conjoining of Men with Beasts: A Manual*.

Flynn was studying the maps, his eyes narrowed. "Once we are on the Plain," he said, "we shall have to divide our strengths. The Eagles and the White Swans ought to mount an attack from the air, and while they prepare to do that, we should use the Chariot Horses and the Deer as decoys." He frowned and went on studying the map, and the others looked at him respectfully.

Cait Fian said to Oscar, "Is that all right? The Deer won't mind being used as decoys? CuChulainn? What about the Chariot Horses?"

"It's a good idea," said Oscar, nodding.

"So long as we can be in on the fighting later," said CuChulainn firmly.

"Oh any amount of it, I should think. Flynn?"

"Oh we'll all be in it," said Flynn, but he sounded rather absentminded now, and although he was hearing the voices of the others, and although he was vaguely aware of being in Cait Fian's warm comfortable room and of drinking Cait Fian's really excellent wine, his mind had flown ahead, and he was on the Plain of the Fál, preparing to sweep Cormac's armies down to the finest victory ever known in Ireland's history.

Cait Fian said in his soft cosy voice, "And so the *splendid* Horses and the *beautiful* Deer will come galloping down the hill to the west boundary, Flynn? Ah, yes of course the west boundary. Hoofs and teeths and all manner of *noise* and of course creating a *very good* diversion. Then what?"

"Then," said Flynn, his eyes alight, "*then* the Eagles and the Swans swoop on to the battlements, and *then* we go in through the East Gate."

"Oh!" said Cait Fian. "Dear me, yes, how *very* astute. The East Gate is *never* properly sentried." He rearranged himself, curling his feet up neatly. "Do we see any flaws, any of us?"

They all thought about it carefully, and Sean, who was trying to listen, dropped *The Conjoining of Men with Beasts*, and made everyone jump.

At length, Conaire said cautiously, "Flynn, that's a very good plan."

"Simple enough to work," said Oscar, smiling at Flynn.

"Will we trust the Wolves to be quiet?" demanded CuChulainn.

Midir said, "But we'll have Cormac with us by then."

Everyone said, "Oh yes, of course," and began to study the map again, and to listen to Flynn who was by now charting the journey they would make to the Plain.

Etain said loudly, "I hope we *will* have Cormac with us," and Conaire at once wanted to know what she meant.

"Has it not occurred to you," said Etain, sitting back in her chair, quite as graceful in her own way as their host, "that we've decided to summon an army, and we've mapped out a battle plan under Flynn's guidance, and worked out how to depose Eochaid Bres, and restore Cormac, but we haven't actually *got* Cormac. We don't even know where he is."

"He might be safe somewhere," said Conaire hopefully.

"But he might be a prisoner," said Midir. "We are so close to Muileann and the Miller."

"He might be dead," said CuChulainn, and at once looked horrified.

"I'm sure I should have heard if he was," said Cait Fian. "These things do get about out here, you know. People gossip so." But he sounded just a little doubtful.

Conaire stood up and walked to the window and back. "Listen," he said, striking his fist on the table. "If Cormac were dead, then surely it would be up to us to avenge his death. Yes?"

"Yes! Yes!" cried several voices.

"And the best way to do that, is to give the usurper his just deserts," said Conaire.

"Quite right!" shouted CuChulainn.

"Absolutely!" said Midir.

Conaire said, "If Cormac is dead, no one will mourn him more deeply than I will. You all know that." He looked at them with his golden eagle's eyes sternly, and they all nodded.

CuChulainn said rather emotionally, "Oh he can't be dead. Let's not think about it."

"If he is dead," said Conaire in a hard voice, "the least we can do for his memory is to restore his throne to the rightful heir. It's what he would want. Depose the usurper and his jackals and bring Tara back to glory! I say we remove Eochaid Bres and Bricriu no matter what!"

"Hear hear!" cried several voices excitedly, and CuChulainn thumped the table in delight: "By Dagda, he's in the right of it!" he cried. "To war and the sooner the better! Death to all pretenders!"

"Death to all pretenders!" shouted his listeners eagerly, and Conaire grabbed his glass of wine and raised it challengingly.

"To Scáthach with them!" cried Midir.

"Remove them!" broke in Oscar.

"Send them to the Miller's cages!" shouted the twins.

"Feed them to Morrigan!" put in CuChulainn.

"But," said Flynn, "who are you going to put in Eochaid Bres's place if Cormac is dead?"

There was a rather appalled silence. Then Etain said in a practical voice, "Who's next in the succession?"

Cait Fian at once said, "Don't anybody look at me!"

"You're his cousin," said Midir.

"You're a Prince of Ireland," added Oscar.

"*And* you'd make a good job of it," suggested CuChulainn hopefully.

"But I don't want the throne," said Cait Fian horrified. "No, no, this won't do at all. See now, my grandfather and Cormac's were only second cousins. There must be a nearer heir. Who was the old man's first cousin?"

"Ailill of the Eagles, wasn't it?" said Oscar. "Then Conaire—"

"Oh no!" said Conaire, quite as appalled as Cait Fian. "No, you can't bring *my* family into this at all. It's the *old* lineage we want. Look now, if we go back to Cormac's *grand-mother*—"

"But you can't go through the female line," said CuChulainn.

"Why not?" said Etain.

"We never have," said CuChulainn.

Etain, a martial glint in her eyes, said, "What about Dierdriu?"

CuChulainn said, "Oh. Oh yes."

Flynn started to explain to Oscar about the Lethe Salic law he'd read about, and Sean, who was getting interested again, came over to listen.

Conaire and Cait Fian were arguing over the precise degree of relationship between their grandfathers—"First cousins," said Conaire, but *"Second,"* said Cait Fian. "And very likely even third." Midir was sketching out a genealogical tree on the back of the Muileann map, helped by CuChulainn. Neither of them heard the door swing open, but without warning, a cool amused voice suddenly said, "Fighting over my Throne before I'm dead, gentlemen?" and they turned at once.

Conaire cried, "Your Majesty! Cormac!" and every person in the room fell to his knees; each of them placed his right hand on his heart in the symbolic ancient Oath of Allegiance which every High King of Ireland may command, but which none has never compelled.

Flynn, on his knees with the rest of them, saw the pure and undiluted joy in all their faces, and saw, as well, something he could only afterwards describe as an immense faith. It was as if they were all saying: he is with us: now everything will be all right. It was the most extraordinary demonstration of pure unswerving trust he had ever witnessed.

And then Flynn saw who stood just behind Cormac, and a tremendous happiness welled up inside him.

* * *

THAT FIRST SIGHT of Joanna, travel-stained and dishevelled, her eyes smudged with tiredness, affected the others remarkably. Where there had been delight and instant obedience at the sight of Cormac, now there was something that was very nearly awe at the sight of Joanna. They fell silent as she walked into the room, and from where he stood, Conaire said softly, and in a voice of extreme reverence, "Dierdriu."

Oscar who was next to Conaire, said in a whisper, "The Portrait on the Rock. The High Queen returned."

Flynn, staring, quite suddenly saw not Joanna, his Joanna that he knew from Tugaim, but someone quite different.

Someone whose features were indeed carved into the ancient Rock deep beneath the Bright Palace, and in whose eyes shone a light that he had never seen anywhere in anyone's eyes before, and in whose face was such strength and beauty and humour, that for a moment his sight misted over.

The High Queen returned and the head of the Fiana *with her again* . . . the two worlds, past and future fusing at last . . .

He turned to look at the others, and saw such deep and unswerving love in their expressions, and such delight and gratitude, for the first time, he understood fully and completely. Joanna was in truth the High Queen of Tara returned, and her people would follow her to the ends of the world . . .

"I DON'T UNDERSTAND any of it," said Flynn, facing his love at last in the bedchamber he had earlier washed in.

"I don't think any of us understand it," said Joanna, watching him, and thinking: how could I have forgotten? How could I have forgotten the way his eyes slant up at the corners when he smiles, or the way his hair falls over his forehead when he talks, or the way his mouth curves . . . Seduced by a half-wolf and an ancient enchantment? Not quite. Perhaps I was not altogether to blame.

"We have not much time."

"My dear love," said Flynn, unable to take his eyes from her. And then, hungrily, "Oh Joanna, come here—"

His mouth tasted as she remembered it, and his body was hard and firm and *right*. She thought: *this* is what was meant. *This* is who I am meant for. Even so . . .

"Flynn, you must not. Not yet." She traced the lines of his face with her fingers. "It would be cruel of me to desert

Cormac until he is back at Tara. I cannot do it—and he would know."

Flynn said slowly, "The Samhailt—"

"Yes, you understand," said Joanna thankfully. "And I owe him so much. My life and my sanity—oh there is so much. I must stay until he has regained the throne."

"The High Queen returned," said Flynn.

"It is what they believe. And you cannot know how courageous he has been ... Flynn I must ride against Eochaid Bres with him." Her hand came out and Flynn took it. "But I think you must be there as well."

Dierdriu, the first High Queen of all Ireland, with Finn of the Fiana at her side ...

They looked at one another, and then Joanna tilted her head, listening.

"Can you hear it?" she said softly, and Flynn heard—felt—the low sensual beckoning note begin to thrum through the palace.

"What is it?"

"The Mindsong. The Samhailt. They are calling up the Beasts of the Bloodline."

Flynn moved to the window. "Can we watch?"

"Yes I think so. I saw it at Scáthach, when Cormac called up the Wolves. It is rather awesome and a bit frightening, but it's safe enough up here."

They stood hand in hand at the window and watched as Conaire and Oscar and CuChulainn and the twins stood motionless, heads lifted a little, eyes half closed. Cormac stood a little way off, watching.

"He will not go any nearer," said Joanna in a whisper. "To do so might distract them."

The low humming strengthened, and Joanna felt again the urge she had felt at Scáthach; to run helter-skelter through the forests and the fields and the hills in pursuit of the call, to answer the command that was being sent out, to follow the beckoning until you could follow it no more. Her blood stirred and her senses tingled, and she felt Flynn's hand tighten in hers and knew that he felt it also and understood. It suddenly seemed tremendously and achingly right that she and Flynn should stand together like this, hand-locked, listening to this ancient summoning, and wave upon wave of happiness flooded her body. She thought that it was too wonderful a feeling to be broken by words, and she hoped—and then was sure—that Flynn would know this, and would remain silent.

Flynn could not have spoken, even if he had not sensed Joanna's deep need for silence. His entire body and mind and every sense he possessed was concentrated on the Mindsong; he thought, as he had thought that night on the Plain, inside the Wicker Man: I know this. I have heard this before. Once I stood on a high hilltop with someone close by, and heard the first ever Mindsong. I was there when the first people of the Bloodline sent out their call to the Beasts. A new enchantment, for it had only just been created. I heard it then and I am hearing it again, and it is one of the strongest and strangest enchantments ever known to the World of Men.

The Beasts were streaming down the mountainside now, the Chariot Horses and the Wild Deer, sleek and powerful, fleet of foot and beautiful to watch. The air was dark with the immense and cruelly beautiful Eagles and the White Swans, their wings beating on the night sky until the whole countryside was filled with the sound. The mountain became a blur of gold and white, feathers and fur and hoofs and wings, and Joanna and Flynn watched until night fell and they could see no more.

CHAPTER TWENTY-FIVE

OF ALL THE great battles of Ancient Ireland, none holds greater pride of place than the famous Battle of the Wolfking. It is that battle that the poets have written of down the ages, and that the ballad-makers have sung of, and the storytellers recounted over and over. It is of that battle that the great scholar, Amairgen the Blind, speaks in the beautiful stirring "Battle of the Wolf."

It was the first battle where beasts and humans and princes and servants joined together to drive back the might of the dreadful army raised by Bricriu to defend Eochaid Bres, and by Macha and Scald-Crow to avenge their dead sister, and for that reason, it is sometimes known as the People's Battle. Among the different tribes and different people who took part in it, each has their own tale to tell, and these have been woven into the many strands of folklore which make up Ireland's rich heritage.

The people of Cormacston—once the nameless Walled City of the Erl-King—feel that it is especially their battle, "For," they were to say, "had we not joined with the King after he slew the Gentleman, his armies would not have been so strong." And they tell how it was the men of their city who rode behind the King in the famous charge on the Palace of Tara.

The Cruithin know this to be somewhat exaggerated, but they let it lie; as Gormgall, in rather garrulous old age was to say, it did no one any harm, and the poor souls of Cormacston had had little enough pleasure in their lives. And the Cruithin consoled themselves that it was *their* people who had really won the day; without their knowledge of the terrain and without their stolid solid fighting, the outcome might well have been different.

Conaire and the people of the Bloodline did not in the least mind the Cruithin thinking this; as Oscar pointed out, the Cruithin were loyal and staunch, and they had served Cormac's family faithfully and well. Let them have their share of the glory. But of course, without the Beasts, without the Eagles and the Chariot Horses and the Wild Deer and the twins' White Swans and the Panthers of Gallan, Cormac's army would have been on the thinnish side. Anyone who had fought in the battle—and it was remarkable the people who later tried to claim that they had been there—would have seen how the Beasts had swung the tide and ensured the victory.

Brian Muldooney, respectable citizen and sometime pig farmer, would not have dreamed of contradicting one of these beliefs; you did not contradict other people because it was extremely discourteous. But people of sense knew that it was sometimes the very smallest things that could sweep an army to victory, and it was a solid fact that if Muldooney had not gone plunging across the Plain in pursuit of his horse, from which he had become temporarily parted, then the final sweeping charge might have taken a slightly different route, and the outcome would probably have been startlingly different. The human factor, there was the thing. The Muldooneys were very big on the human factor. It would not, however, do to say this aloud, or not very often anyway.

THEY HAD REACHED the Plain of the Fál as dawn was lightening the skies, and Flynn had stood a little apart, surveying the terrain, seeing how the Plain's height gave them the advantage, seeing as well how they might encircle Tara with their armies.

The entire landscape was as familiar to him as if he had lived in it for years, and the sense of being on his own ground again was piercingly sweet.

At his side, Amairgen said gently, "But of course it is familiar. You are Finn of the *Fiana* again, and you are aching to lead them all against the enemies of Ireland."

"Am I?" said Flynn, who did not really doubt this, but who found it just the smallest bit frightening now and again.

"You know it," said Amairgen, and smiled, and Portan, who was never far from Amairgen's side, smiled as well, because it was so wonderful to see Flynn like this, wearing the Wolfking's colours and taking command of the armies as simply and as easily as if—"As if he has never been away," said Amairgen afterwards, and Portan said, "Yes. Just that." And thought that Flynn would surely win this battle, and there would be a tremendous victory and they would all of them be safely inside the Bright Palace before nightfall.

When Amairgen said, "Are you afraid of what is ahead?" Portan at once said, "Oh no, for Flynn cannot fail. Joanna cannot fail." And looked to where Joanna was standing with Cormac, dressed in dark breeches and a cambric shirt and leather boots, with the Nightcloak slung lightly about her shoulders.

Portan had been a little shy of Joanna, because surely any lady whom Flynn loved so very much must be extraordinary. Joanna would be lovely and kind of course, Portan had always known that, but would she perhaps be unapproachable? Portan, listening round-eyed to the stories of Dierdriu, and the High Queen's return, and of how Joanna was in some inexplicable way Dierdriu reborn, had thought that it might be difficult to meet Joanna.

"She is—very lovely," said Oscar when Portan asked what Joanna was like.

"Strong and gentle and intelligent," said Conaire.

"A leader," said CuChulainn, who had been very pleased to discover Joanna, and who had in fact enjoyed a long talk with her about some of the old battles. "Well read in our history," he added.

The twins said that she was fun: "If there is amusement to be found in a situation, she will find it," said Etain.

Portan, putting all of this together, had tried to form some kind of image of Flynn's Joanna, of the girl for whom they had all come so far, and for whose sake they had endured so much. And then, in the end, it had not been in the least bit difficult to meet her. Joanna had smiled and held out her hands, and said, "Oh Portan, Flynn has told me so much!" And she had taken Portan in her arms, and hugged her, and they had both cried together for happiness and a little for fear of the battle.

"And perhaps," said Portan, "for relief. For we had both known so many dangers."

And then it had struck them both that it was slightly absurd to be crying when there was so much to be pleased about, and they had laughed, and Joanna had produced her handkerchief to mop up with, and they had talked together and liked one another very much, and it had all been easy and warm and natural. And, "I wish there was time to know you better," Joanna had said.

"Will there not be?"

"I do not think so," said Joanna. "I think we will not be permitted to remain here." And a wistfulness filled her voice, so that Portan said shyly, "Shall you mind very much?"

"I think it will break my heart," said Joanna simply, and then smiled again. "But I do not think this is my place. After the battle . . ." For a moment her eyes were sad, and then she seemed to give herself a small shake, for she smiled again, and said, "No matter. Let me see if we can drive out the usurper and his jackals," and Portan thought, but did not say, that Joanna and Flynn were both talking in the distinctive, slightly formal way of Cormac's people.

"Yes, they are taking up the mantle of their alter egos," said Amairgen thoughtfully, for he, also, had been feeling and sensing and hearing the change. "They are no longer Flynn O'Connor and Joanna Grady."

"Finn of the *Fiana* and the High Queen Dierdriu?" said Portan hesitantly.

Amairgen said, "Oh yes. They are no longer aware of it happening, but it *has* happened."

Behind Flynn and Joanna, the others were sorting themselves out. "Staking out our bits of territory," was how Sean put it. Sean had found himself a spot three quarters of the way down the hillside. He could see *very* nearly everything from there he said, surveying the landscape carefully. He would not be able to see whoever it was who stole in quietly through the eastern gate, but you could not have everything.

"Cait Fian and a few of the Panthers are to do that," said Flynn, and Sean had said, oh well, in that case, there was no difficulty at *all* because Cait Fian would certainly tell him about it all afterwards. "And if you make sure to keep well to the *left* when you gallop down the hill," he said to CuChulainn seriously, "I shall be able to see *all* the battle charge."

CuChulainn wanted to ban Sean from the field altogether at that, but Conaire said, rather impatiently, that CuChulainn would be as pleased as any of them to have a proper account of the battle when it was all over, and that Sean ought to be given every facility. At which CuChulainn took himself off to marshall his Chariot Horses, who were getting restless, and grumbled to Oscar, who was deploying the Deer, that he did not know what fighting was coming to.

Dubhgall had been put in charge of sounding the battle cry, and had been given the golden bugle with which to do so. He had been extremely pleased about this, because it was a very great honour, and he had practised assiduously all the way to the Plain.

"It upsets the Swans," said Gormgall to Domnall and Cait Fian's Ullgall, "but nobody liked to stop him. And a battle cry has to be right, of course. You can't ride into battle on an off-key battle call."

Muldooney, who admitted to not having a note of music in his head had remarked that it came to something when a man could not get his proper rest, because Dubhgall got up a half-hour early each morning to practise. In fact, Muldooney had been so pleased to be given a tiny detachment of his own to lead, that he would not really have dreamed of complaining in earnest. Muldooney was not the man to make war, of course, but it had been explained to him how usurpers sat inside Cormac's Palace, and how it was absolutely necessary to rout them. Justice, there was the thing. Ah, the Muldooneys were strong on justice, well, they were strong on everything that was right, of course. And so Muldooney had drilled his small platoon very carefully, and had beamed when Flynn, inspecting them, said crisply, "Excellent, Muldooney. We shall look to you to play a decisive part in what is ahead."

Which was no more than was right, because the Muldooneys were the ones when it came to victory.

"And actually," said Flynn later, "it has to be said that he managed very nicely."

As everyone had foreseen, the Wolves and the Panthers fought—"Several times," said Oscar, who had been called in to part the combatants—and one Wolf had its tail bitten and had to be bandaged by Portan, and two Panthers suffered chewed ears.

But when they all assembled on the Plain of the Fál, over-

looking Tara, a great hush fell on them, and a sense of friendship and of oneness seemed to bind them together.

Flynn, at Cormac's side, felt it as if it was a huge surge of
warmth, and a strength so tremendous enveloped him that for
a moment he thought he would be overpowered by it. He
thought that Cormac felt it as well, for just for a brief instant,
Cormac seemed to hesitate, and Flynn turned to look, because
it was not to be believed that Cormac should ever be at a loss.
And then he saw that Cormac was looking at the assembled armies with an expression of infinite love, and that his eyes held
the look of a man who has been wandering in the dark for
many years and has suddenly come into Paradise. Flynn felt
the pity of Cormac's exiled years slam into the base of his
throat, and in that moment he forgave Cormac everything that
Cormac had ever done with Joanna, and although he knew he
would never quite forget the nights that Joanna and Cormac
had spent together, he knew at the same time that he might understand. He reined in his horse, and stayed where he was, motionless, waiting for Cormac to give the signal to charge.

Joanna had seen Cormac's hesitation as well, and like Flynn,
had understood. She thought: this is almost more than he can
bear. It is this that kept him alive and kept him hopeful through
the terrible years inside Scáthach. It was the knowledge that
one day, one day he might be able to lead his armies against
the creatures who drove him out. Tears sprang to her eyes, and
she dashed them away, and thought: after all, I think *this* is
how I shall remember him. Like this. Proud and reckless and
with such a belief in what he is about to do. With such a burning fervour for his people and such an unshakeable courage.
The Wolfking returning . . .

Cormac had not been fully aware of Flynn and Joanna's
thoughts, but he had been aware of a sharing and an understanding, and it had heartened him.

But he had stood alone and apart for a brief moment, so that
he could savour to the full the pure happiness of it all. For
him, it was the culmination of every hope and of every lonely
dream of Scáthach. He wanted to take hold of the moment and
cup it between his hands and keep it safe. He wanted to taste
it and enjoy it, and he wanted to remember it, so that in years
to come, he could return to it, and think: oh yes. *That* was the
moment when I knew pure happiness.

Pure happiness. Now, on the Plain of the Fál, with Joanna close by, with Flynn heading the army, with the Cruithin and the creatures of the Bloodline. With faithful friends who have stayed with me, he thought, and with new friends who have trusted me. With people who have endured danger and hardship for my sake. *This* is the moment. Take hold of it and capture it and never ever let go of it, for there will never be another to equal it.

He turned to the waiting Flynn, and Flynn met his eyes steadily. Cormac thought: by every rule, Flynn of them all ought to hate me. For what I did to Joanna, for the enchantment I spun about her that drove him from her mind, he ought to hate me. And then Flynn smiled, and Cormac saw that Flynn did not hate him in the least, that Flynn understood.

And understanding, is surely the greatest and the most generous of all the gifts . . .

After all, thought Cormac, this is Flynn's battle as much as it is mine. And quite deliberately, he drew his own horse back a little and made a gesture to Flynn, as if to say over to you.

Delight flared in Flynn's eyes, and he bowed his head slightly in acknowledgement. As he turned to lift a hand to bring the armies to attention, Cormac saw that it was no longer the young man who had forced through the Time Curtain in search of his lost love, but the mighty warrior who had once been known and revered and honoured throughout Ireland.

Finn of the *Fiana* . . . And he will fight for me to the death, thought Cormac.

Flynn brought down his hand and a great shiver of excitement went through the waiting ranks.

FROM WHERE SHE WAS, Joanna, could see the stealthy descent of Cait Fian and the Panthers to the East Gate. For a moment she lost them, for the sun was in her eyes, and spears of brightness were glinting on the helmets and the armour. And then she picked them out again, sleek and graceful, the Panthers' bodies flowing gracefully down the hillside, Cait Fian at their head.

"Wait," said Flynn, "let him reach the Gate. Etain?"

"Almost there."

"Conaire?"

"Approaching hard."

Flynn turned to Oscar and CuChulainn. "Are we ready for the charge?"

"Ready!"

"And eager!"

Flynn turned back, and then Etain gave the signal which meant that Cait Fian had reached the East Gate of Tara. Flynn looked to where Dubhgall was poised and nodded, and Dubhgall lifted the golden bugle to his lips, and the stirring notes of the call to arms rang over the Plain, filling the air and echoing through the forest down to the Bright Palace.

"To arms!" cried Flynn, and at once, the Chariot Horses and the Wild Deer with CuChulainn and Oscar at their head streamed down the hillside. The bugle was still sounding, clear and rousing, and the armies were cheering from the Plain, and Flynn felt as if he was being filled up with excitement and energy. The turf was flying beneath the horses' hooves now, and the whole Plain was shuddering with the force of the first battle charge.

Flynn turned to watch, narrowing his eyes against the light, and thought that it was a good clean charge. "As good as ever I saw or led," he thought, and then grinned.

But it *was* a good charge. It was swift and sure, and Oscar and CuChulainn were at the West Gate within minutes. Through the smoke and the noise of the thudding hooves, and the cheering of Cormac's armies from above them, they could hear now the alarm being raised inside the Palace.

"Tara is under attack!"

"Close the West Gate!"

Just what we want! thought Flynn, jubilant. The West Gate! And while their energies are directed on to that, Cait Fian will be stealing in through the East Gate. Let them deploy every single creature in the place to the West Gate, and we shall win! he thought.

They could all hear the shouts from Tara now, and they could sense the panic and the chaos that seethed within.

"The Palace is being besieged! Haul up the drawbridge!"

"To your posts everyone! Under attack!"

"To the West Gate!"

And then, quite clearly, through the heat and the thundering hooves, "Repel the invaders!"

"And kill their leaders!"

Flynn glanced involuntarily to where Cormac stood, and thought that a hardness had come into Cormac's eyes. But Cormac did not flinch; he stayed where he was, and he looked to Flynn, waiting for Flynn's command. Flynn saw for the first time, the greatness and the incredible strength of Cormac. Cormac would put himself under Flynn's command for the duration of the battle, and anything that Flynn demanded, he would do. I cannot possibly fail him, thought Flynn, I *cannot*. And without warning there came into his mind an old Lethe saying—what was it? Something about loving those with whom you are sharing a great danger. He thought he loved Cormac in that moment, and he thought that whatever happened to them in the future, he would never quite forget how Cormac trusted him.

CuChulainn and Oscar seemed to have reached the West Gate now, and Oscar was flinging burning torches at the barred Gates. As they spurred their horses on again and again, Eochaid Bres's guards appeared on the battlements. The sun glinted, and then there was a sizzling of arrows flying through the air; Oscar half fell, a hand clapped to his shoulder, a burning pain where the arrow had sliced into his flesh. Flynn half started forward, and then checked, for Oscar had risen and was struggling to get into the lee of the castle wall. Flynn saw CuChulainn go running to help him, and heard CuChulainn cry, "Forward! Beneath the castle walls!" and begin to drag the injured and dazed Oscar across the ground.

Flynn, watching, had just begun to frame the thought that CuChulainn was providing a sitting target for the archers on the battlements, when he saw CuChulainn cry and then stagger. As he stood, helpless on the Plain, CuChulainn fell back, and Flynn saw a trickle of dark blood come from his mouth, and then gush from his chest.

Oscar stood for a moment, as if unable to take in what had happened, and then he half ran, half dragged himself into the lee of the castle, and fell against the wall.

Close to Flynn, Joanna gasped and made as if to start forward, but Flynn held up a hand to halt her, for they could not, even to aid the wounded Oscar, depart from the plan they had so carefully mapped out. Cait Fian would be inside the Palace now, he would be making his cautious way through the great halls to the Sun Chamber. Would they have discovered him yet? Surely they would not, for surely they were all at the West Gate, fighting off the attack?

CuChulainn lay where he had fallen, and Flynn knew from the angle of his head that he was certainly dead. He felt a leaden pain at the thought, and dared not remember how CuChulainn had sung the marching song with them when they marched to Gallan, and how he had forgotten the words of the last verse, and had to be reminded. He dared not think, either, of how CuChulainn had related stories of Ireland's greatest battles, and of how CuChulainn had always been brave and amiable and entirely loyal.

"*Don't* think it," said Cormac softly, at Flynn's side. "Think it after the battle—we will all think it then, and we will all mourn. But for now look ahead, Flynn."

And Flynn, knowing that Cormac was right, turned to where Oscar was still slumped against the wall, but saw, with immense relief that he was managing to rally the Chariot Horses.

Cormac said, "The Horses will not respond to Oscar so well, but they will obey. Oscar will manage."

Oscar would manage, even though he must be within yards of CuChulainn's dead body. He would manage because the battle could not be lost, and it certainly could not be lost for the sake of CuChulainn who had loved war, and who had died fighting for his beloved King . . .

Flynn turned to the hillside and lifted his hand to the twins and Conaire, and at once there was an answering signal, and almost immediately the air was filled with sweeping Eagles and Swans, and there was a great beating of wings on the air as the huge birds swooped down on to Tara's battlements, flying into the faces of Eochaid Bres's guards, darting for their victims' eyes and bringing their massive wings down on their victims' shoulders.

From his position by the Palace wall, Oscar, dizzy with loss of blood and the heat of the charge, sick at the death of CuChulainn, leaned against the old stone walls, and felt the warmth of the ancient bricks.

"Spiked, by the gods!" he whispered thankfully. "Now then Cormac!" And heard once again the bugle call sound the advance.

Flynn nodded to Cormac, and turned to face the waiting armies. The Wolf pennants fluttered in the breeze, and the horses pawed the ground. Anticipation raced through the ranks, like a wind ruffling the surface of a cornfield.

"TO ARMS!" cried Flynn again, and the last battle charge began.

JOANNA WAS AWARE of nothing other than the wind in her face as they went down the hillside in a single concerted sweep, of her hair streaming wildly out behind her, of the heat and the smoke from the bombarded West Gate, and the furious excitement and the exhilaration of the moment. A fierce joy filled her, and she glanced back over her shoulder as they galloped down and down towards the Bright Palace. She was very nearly at the head of the charge, with Cormac to her left, and Flynn to her right.

Flynn . . .

There was nothing in his face but the purest concentration; there was certainly very little of the Flynn that Joanna had known in Tugaim. And yet, the man ahead of her *was* recognisable, and infinitely dear, and Joanna was able to think: Finn! and to remember other battles, exactly like this one, and to remember as well that *of course* this was how it felt to be swept along by the mighty warrior head of the *Fiana*, with whole armies thudding down the hillside after you. This was how it felt to ride in a great glorious victory charge, crying death and destruction to Tara's enemies. *This* is what I remember! cried Joanna silently. *This* is what I understand!

Dierdriu and Finn, together again . . . fighting for Ireland once more . . .

And we are going to do it! thought Joanna exultantly. We shall win. Down the hillside, across the last stretch. A single clean sweep to victory. And the Wolfking will be restored.

But even as her mind was shaping the thought, she felt the ground begin to heave and shift beneath them, and the horses began to rear and whinny with fear.

Through the smoke and the heat, coming towards them, appeared Macha and Scald-Crow with the Erl-King's ugly hunchback at their side. From where she had halted, reining in her horse, Joanna heard Macha's bubbling throaty laugh, and saw Scald-Crow spin and blur and assume several different but equally gruesome forms. Joanna gasped and turned to Cormac, and for a moment, memory shimmered between them:

Morrigan's house, where we were so nearly slaughtered by the Giant Miller, and where we were saved by Pan and his strange beckoning music, and his ability to move in and out and through Time ... And then Joanna, like Flynn had, remembered the old adage that you always love those with whom you share a danger, and she knew that she had in truth loved Cormac, and that a part of her would always love him.

Because of what we shared? Or something else? I do not think I shall ever really know, thought Joanna.

But her eyes had gone automatically to Flynn, and as they waited, they saw him galloping hard across the remaining ground, finally bringing his horse up within feet of the three creatures who stood grinning and gesturing.

Flynn was genuinely appalled at the sight of Morrigan's two sisters. He thought he had never seen them, and then he thought that after all, he knew them very well.

Yes, my dears, we have faced one another before, very like this. And I was the victor that time, and shall be so again!

Macha was holding out her fat white arms, and the ground was cracking and shivering and a great chasm was opening up, cutting off the charging armies. The horses baulked and showed the whites of their eyes, and Flynn stood up in the saddle to urge them on.

"Onwards! Over the ravine!" he shouted. "Before it opens any more! ONWARDS!"

Cormac and Joanna were riding hard at the chasm, spurring on their mounts, but the others were struggling to hold their horses and everywhere people were being thrown to the ground, as the earth continued to shudder and as the ravine widened. Flynn saw Gormgall tumble and go spinning across the undulating earth, and Muldooney fell off his horse and went helter skelter down the hillside, landing headfirst in a muddy ditch. A quiver of amusement touched Flynn's mind, and he thought: Muldooney going arse over breakfast-time down the hill! But he bit the amusement down, as he saw Muldooney extricate himself from the ditch, and brush himself down, and go plunging off to capture his horse again.

The Cruithin contingent were rallying, Gormgall running to remount, and through the confusion, Flynn thought he saw Domnall and Ullgall re-forming the others.

The chasm was twenty feet across now, a great gaping

abyss, and it was so deep that it might very well have been bottomless.

Cormac, bringing his horse alongside Joanna, reached out and took her hand. "Use the cloak!" he cried. "Joanna, use the Nightcloak!"

Joanna cried, "But what is it? What is she doing?"

"She is summoning her monsters from the abyss," said Cormac, his eyes never leaving the squat, repulsive figure of Macha, who was grinning at them. "And when she has done that, she will call up the Erl-King's Army of Corpses."

"But the Erl-King is dead!" cried Joanna.

"His Army will still walk," said Cormac. "They will walk for Macha and Scald-Crow, for those two have a little of the necromancers' powers. They can summon the Army of Corpses."

Joanna shuddered, and Cormac turned to look at her. "Use the Nightcloak!" he said again, his tone peremptory, his eyes flashing.

"No!" said Joanna, and met his eyes squarely and fearlessly and at once, anger flared in Cormac's eyes.

"Do it!"

"No," said Joanna again, more quietly. "For if I use it now, then I cannot use it later in the battle." And then, in anguish, "And there may be a greater need."

"But if you think that, you may never use it! Joanna, do it!"

"No!" said Joanna, and now it was Dierdriu's tone and Dierdriu's imperious voice. "You cannot command me!" said Joanna, and through the smoke and the noise, saw Cormac's face soften suddenly.

"I never could," he said gently, and turned again to where Flynn was galloping hard along the ravine, trying to gauge its depth, trying to find a chink in Macha's dark enchantment.

Clouds of smoke and heat were belching out from the chasm now, but Cormac's armies had rallied. The unmounted Cruithin, with the people of Cormacston, had already gathered at the brink of the chasm, arrows on the strings of their bows, ready aimed at whatever might arise from the depths; farther along, the Wolves were tense, ready to pounce. Their eyes were showing red, and their expressions were hungry, and Joanna thought: yes, they are hungry for whatever is going to come out of that ravine. They are hungry for the blood of their Master's enemies . . .

And then from out of the black abyss, pouring outwards, pouring *upwards*, spewed forth the ancient malevolence that Cormac's ancestors had striven to keep out of Tara, and that Bricriu had tried to invite back. The Dark Ireland. The evil underside of the land: twisted and stunted and corrupt, greedy and unwholesome and soulless.

The hags and the banshees and the crones; the harpies with their female heads and greedy taloned bird-bodies; the wraiths who crawled up out of the slime of graveyards to feast on fresh corpses; the giants and the ogres and with them the dread Cyclops, each with a single red eye in the centre of its forehead—the misshapen beings who were the results of forbidden conjoining, half human and half beast, but so dreadfully blended that they were travesties made up out of skin and pelts and claws and teeth and eyes.

Morrigan's goblin men were there as well, bony-fingered and sharp-featured and red-eyed, swarming across the Plain, dancing and jeering and gesturing obscenely to where Cormac's armies stood helpless.

And then, "Look there!" cried Cormac. "The Dark Bloodline!" And a shudder of horror went through the watchers.

From Tara's northern boundaries, from out of the shadow of Tara itself far below them, Bricriu came riding, leading the Dark Bloodline. The vermin and the parasites and the beasts of prey, ugly and warped and greedy, but with a thin trickle of human blood and with the enchanted ancestry bestowed on the beasts by Dierdriu's sorcerers.

The people of the Weasels and the Giant Rats came; the Spider clan—created by a malevolent necromancer in the days of Niall of the Nine Hostages—tiny and venomous and possessing a sly human cunning; the Vultures and the Jackals and the scaly-skinned Lizard people.

From his commanding position at the head of the chasm, Cormac felt his blood chill. He stood, eyes narrowed, watching the dreadful beings that Bricriu was leading out of Tara, and he thought: so these are the terrible creatures who are the other side of the Ancient Bloodline. These are the creatures who make up the dark underside of my land. And he remembered again the old belief that for every enchantment ever spun, there must always be an opposite.

Bricriu led the creatures of the Dark Bloodline across the Plain to the West Gate where the Chariot Horses and the Deer were still attacking the gates of the Bright Palace. As they neared the massive West Gate, Oscar's forces seemed to rear and shy away, and Joanna, watching, thought that the Deer and the Chariot Horses were very much afraid.

"But they will fight, nonetheless," said Cormac softly.

"Will they?"

"Look now," said Cormac, nodding to the scene below them.

The Deer had recovered and were charging forward, heads lowered, and the Chariot Horses were bunching together for a single concerted onslaught.

"And they cannot be beaten for speed," said Cormac.

As they watched, a solitary figure detached itself from Bricriu's armies, and went riding hard across the terrain, crouched low over its mount. Joanna felt Cormac tense, and from within the Cruithin ranks, a low angry murmur reached them.

"Mab."

As Joanna shaded her eyes to see, the cloaked figure went at full gallop across the Plain, hair whipped into dark smoke by the wind, the turf flying.

"Escaping," said someone from the Cruithin army—Joanna thought it was Domnall—and then another voice said, "Do we train our archers on her, Sire?"

Cormac turned a look of such black fury on to the speaker, that the owner of the voice trembled and shook in his boots, and began to think he might have done better to have thrown himself into Macha's ravine.

Cormac said frostily, "It is not in keeping with a High King's honour to fire at a defenceless woman. It is certainly not for the Ancient Nobility of Ireland to fire arrows on one another. Let her be."

Gormgall, who never was intimidated by the King, said, "But Sire, she may escape."

Cormac said, "She will not." And Gormgall remarked to Muldooney, who happened to be next to him, that say what you liked, Cormac was sometimes foolishly chivalrous.

Muldooney nodded sagely, and said that this was very true indeed, and wouldn't Gormgall look at the likes of those creatures being brought up below them.

"Nasty," said Gormgall. "I hope we don't have to join battle with *those!*"

Muldooney hoped so as well.

Flynn had ridden farther down to where the ravine wound its way into the forest, and he was encouraging Conaire and the twins, who were stationed a little way off. Joanna thought that the air was thick with the Samhailt now. Once or twice, she almost fancied she could actually see it; shafts of pure white light, splitting the air.

Conaire and the twins were responding to Flynn; they were sending the Eagles and the Swans swooping on to the Vultures and the small long-tailed Lizard people, to tear and maim. The Eagles caught up the Lizard people in their talons, and carried them into the centre of the chasm, dropping them into its gaping mouth. The Swans flew at the Cyclops, pecking at the angry red eyes, sending the Cyclops blinded and screaming into chaos, driving them backwards over the edge of the ravine, so that they tottered on the brink, and then hurtled below, their screams piercing the air as they fell.

And then Flynn turned to look to where Cormac waited, and for a moment Joanna actually *saw* the Samhailt flash between the two of them; a dazzling spear of the purest brilliance she had ever seen, so that for a moment she was completely blinded.

And then she watched Cormac nod, and turn his horse about, and go galloping along the side of the chasm to where the Panthers waited, half crouched; couchant cats, their tails lashing furiously, their eyes slitted and as green and as hard as bits of glass. Joanna held her breath for surely Cormac could not control them . . . ?

"It's all right, Your Majesty," said Dubhgall to her from where he was seated quietly nearby.

"Will he control them?"

"Yes," said Dubhgall. "Watch . . ."

Cormac had ridden straight into the centre of the Panthers, and at once Cait Fian's creatures began moving, swift and sleek and sure. Joanna could not quite see what they were doing, but she thought that some kind of rope bridge had been fashioned.

"They are going to bridge the chasm," said Dubhgall, and now Joanna saw that this was exactly what they were doing.

Two of the Panthers had leapt across the chasm at its narrowest point, in a single fluid movement, the ends of the rope bridge held in their mouths. Several more followed them, their sleek bodies pouring across effortlessly. The first two secured the rough but serviceable rope bridge by means of winding it round and round a tree trunk, while the others fell upon the Weasels and the Jackals.

The Plain begin to ring with the screams of the victims, and blood and gore spattered the ground, and still the Panthers kept on, savaging and tearing and clawing.

Scald-Crow changed shape so fast it was impossible to identify most of the things she became. She was a giant club that bludgeoned Cormac's creatures to death, and she was a sharp bright sword that hacked limbs and heads. She was a whirling scimitar from the East, and a two-headed axe, and an iron-tipped nine-tailed whip. Everywhere was the fighting of creatures who were neither quite human nor wholly animal, and who used both animal and human methods of attack. They used claws and teeth and talons, but they used fists and swords and clubs as well.

Joanna, knowing that very soon now she *must* use the Nightcloak, saw a scaly Lizard-man, who walked upright but possessed a lizard's head and reptile eyes and a long slithery tail, smash a Panther's head to splinters, chuckling as he did so. And at once, the goblin men were there, singing the song of Muileann, slitting the Panther's fur and skinning it, until there was only a wet, near-formless mass of red raw flesh, and stringy muscle and bone and grinning white skull.

"Skins for the floors, boys, skins for the floors. That's the way. And into the fire with the meat, boys. Over the edge." They rolled and pulled and dragged the skinned Panther, until they toppled it into the abyss, and Joanna saw a tongue of flame belch upwards, and smelled the odour of roasting meat.

"Burning up nicely," said the goblin men, rubbing their hands together. "Frizzling away. Where's another one?"

They lined up close to the rope bridge and stood waiting, grinning and beckoning. "Over you come, my dears, over you come! That's the way. And down you'll go, my dears, down you'll go! Skin them and burn them and there'll be rugs for the floors, boys, and flesh for the fire. But what do we do with the hides? There's nothing so fine as a human skin beneath your feet of a cold winter's night. Over you come, my dears, and we'll have your hides!"

Flynn at once stopped the Panthers in their headlong flight, for although the Panthers were snarling and lashing their tails, and although they would certainly have leapt at the throats of the goblins, there were far too many of the goblins and other creatures for them to have had much effect. The Dark Armies were infinitely more powerful, and there were too many of them . . .

He stood looking at Macha and Scald-Crow and the hunchback and the goblin men, and he remembered all the things that Joanna had told him about Morrigan, and the things she had suffered. A tremendous anger surged up inside him, and he leapt from his horse, and began to run straight at the rope bridge. He would stalk these miserable, wicked, jeering creatures and smash them to pulp. He would tear their hearts from their bodies and fling them into the ravine. He bound on to the rope bridge, holding his sword aloft, and stood midway along, suspended across the chasm, the bridge swaying a little beneath him, his eyes brilliant, and his hair whipped into disarray.

"Well?" cried Flynn, brandishing his sword. "Well, my little men? Shall not a one of you try his strength against me? Which of you will fight me?" He moved closer now. "Come now, for there are so many of you and only one of me! A challenge!" He began to walk across the rope bridge, deliberately and slowly, and the goblin men hesitated, and glanced at one another from the corners of their slanting red eyes.

"Flesh for the fire?" said Flynn tauntingly, and took several steps nearer. And now the goblin men did back away, there was no doubt about it. Joanna stood very still, because at any minute they might spring, and at any minute one of the lizard creatures might easily leap on Flynn and hurl him into the depths of the chasm. And then the dreadful thick oily smoke would billow out and the flames would shoot upwards, and Flynn would be flesh for the fire and skin for the floor, and if

that should happen, there would be nothing ever again anywhere . . .

"Joanna, the Nightcloak!" cried Cormac, but still Joanna
hesitated. And yet—what could be more precious than Flynn?
cried her mind in silent anguish. What could be more needful
than to save Flynn?

And at once the answer: *to save Ireland!*

I cannot do it for Flynn alone! thought Joanna in agony. It
must be to the good of all of us! But she grasped a fold of the
cloak and felt its response at once, and felt a distant comfort.

Flynn was barely conscious of danger. He was filled with
energy and strength; he thought he could have fought the Dark
Armies single-handed and won, and he saw with exultation,
the goblin men's retreat.

"Flesh for the fire!" cried Flynn, advancing on them. "Come
now, who is to prove that! Who is to stop me from taking Tara
back for the rightful High King!"

"We shall," said a soft, throaty, chuckling voice close by,
and Flynn turned to see Macha, and Scald-Crow close behind
her, grinning horribly and assuming the form of a great bloated
worm with soft pulsating skin and blind white stalks for eyes.

"I shall spit you like so much roasting meat, madam," said
Flynn, and Scald-Crow laughed and turned at once into the
semblance of a half-cooked side of meat, one side succulent
and pink, the other rotten, a mass of weaving maggots.

"We shall stop you," said Macha again, and as she spoke,
the hunchback came scuttling out of the smoke and Flynn
stopped dead in his tracks, for shambling in the hunchback's
wake were beings more terrible even than those he had yet
seen.

Rotting skeletons; decaying corpses with flesh still clinging
to their bones; eyeless skulls with grinning lipless mouths and
tattered blackened skin; flesh oozing with corruption and swollen with graveyard gasses: the Erl-King's Army of Corpses.

Flynn made to lunge forward, but the corpses were moving
against him, and the stench rose up to meet him, filling his
nostrils, so that nausea threatened to overpower him, and for a
moment he put up his hand to shield his senses from the sight
and the stench.

Macha said, "Yes, Flynn. The Erl-King's Army of Corpses.
Waiting to be called. Waiting to devour those who killed their

Master." She moved nearer. "Did you really think your puny Wolfking and his lady could slay the Erl-King and our beloved sister, and *live*?"

"Wait until you have felt the embrace of the corpses," said Scald-Crow, grinning. "Wait until they have clasped you to their rotting bodies, and wait until the filth of them has oozed and run out over your skin."

"Wait until they are swarming all over you," said Macha. The hunchback was grinning and plying his whip, and Flynn saw, with a kind of pitying horror, the skeletons cringe and put up their fleshless hands to protect themselves. He thought that he had never seen anything so truly dreadful and so pitiable. "I could not look away," he was to say afterwards. "I was horrified and sickened and repulsed beyond anything I had ever known. But I could not look away."

The corpses were closing in—In another minute they will have reached me, thought Flynn. I shall have to retreat . . . Surely to stand in the face of these creatures is more than any one can endure . . .

But behind him were the High King's armies, and behind him was Joanna. If I once submit to them, they will be over the ravine and on to Cormac's armies, he thought. They will fasten on to the bodies of our people. Disgust filled him, but, I will *not* let them do it, he thought. I will stand and fight them, one by one, and they will *have* to defeat me. If I retreat now, thought Flynn, I shall have let in the Dark Armies, and then we are all lost and Ireland is lost and Tara is forever beyond our reach.

He took a firmer grip on his sword, and stood on the precariously swaying rope bridge watching the terrible Army of Corpses driven nearer by the hunchback. He saw that Macha and Scald-Crow were advancing. To go forward would be suicide, and to go back . . . To go back is defeat, thought Flynn. To go back is to betray Cormac.

He stood firm, and saw Macha throw back her head, laugh and stretch out a hand, and at once the heat began to glow again from the abyss. Heat rises, thought Flynn wildly. Heat rises, and when the heat reaches the rope bridge it will burn.

Within minutes, he might be cast into the abyss, and when that happened, the Dark Ireland would swarm and fall upon

Cormac's armies, and the true Ireland would be once and forever lost.

But at least, thought Flynn, I shall die fighting.

JOANNA HAD BARELY been aware of the moment when Flynn leapt forward to challenge Macha, Scald-Crow, and the hunchback. Her whole attention was concentrated on the Nightcloak, and on whether it could help them. Could it? Supposing she called on it and found it impotent? This was a terrifying notion, and Joanna banished it at once.

And the Nightcloak never has been impotent, my dear . . .

But the cloak had been used against Morrigan, and the Erl-King already; what if that counted, and what if it meant it had no power against Morrigan's sisters and against the Erl-King's hunchback? What if, thought Joanna, it is not strong enough?

It was the most awful thought. And the trouble is, thought Joanna, the trouble is, that once you have thought a thing, it is there with you. She knew—of course she did—that the Nightcloak would be strong and that it would call down the nightmares of her enemies. But still, "what if," thought Joanna.

To call on the cloak and find it useless against the enemy would be the most crushing blow of all. Joanna thought she could not bear it, and she thought that if there was another escape, another way to aid Flynn, then she would use it.

And then she turned her head slightly and found that she was looking straight at the forest. Deep within her mind, something stirred . . .

MOVING WITHIN THE Sleeping Trees was a curious and rather unsettling experience. Joanna was no longer sure why she was here, or why she had come running from the battlefield but as she came into the dimness of the forest, she suddenly felt no sense of doubt. This was right, this was what had to be done.

She thought that Dierdriu was with her more strongly and more completely than ever before, and she had the sensation of hands pulling her deeper and deeper into the forest.

Where to? Where am I going? There was a ruffle of sweetness and amusement and courage that was Dierdriu, and Joanna stood very still and said aloud: "Of course! We are going to wake the Sleeping Trees!"

A ripple of amusement stirred the air. *What else?* said Dierdriu.

How?

You will see, my dear . . .

That is all very well, thought Joanna, that is all very well indeed, but what must I do! I don't know what I must do! And despite the danger for Flynn—oh please let Flynn be safe!—despite all the urgency, there was amusement at what she was doing. Hadn't there been old songs—Lethe or earlier?—about people talking to trees? Was one supposed to stand in the clearing and say politely, "Please wake up"? Well, this is quite certainly ridiculous! thought Joanna, standing beneath the trees and surveying them. Because *I don't* know what to say, and I definitely don't know what to do, and I am not at all sure that to wake an entire forest of trees is going to be very helpful or even particularly safe . . .

And then from the far side of the clearing, on the outer rim of her vision, she caught a blur of movement, and she turned sharply, narrowing her eyes.

A flash of scarlet, a glimpse of horns . . . three-cornered features . . . It was possible, of course, for one's eyes to deceive one—but I believe I am seeing him truly, thought Joanna. Pan, the shepherd god, the god of music and love and wine, moving quietly in between the trees.

A great joy filled Joanna, and she cried aloud with delight and went running forward.

He was sitting cross-legged beneath a tree, the silver pipes held to his lips, and his hair clustering in tight little curls about his beautiful narrow skull. There was the faint translucency to his skin that Joanna remembered, and there was the wisdom and the knowledge and the mischief in his eyes that she had seen before.

Pan smiled, and Joanna saw that it was the "what fools these mortals be" smile, but saw as well that he was watching her with affection.

Joanna said, rather breathlessly, "The trees—"

"Waken them," said Pan.

"How?"

Pan smiled again. "Human Child, you are very stupid."

"But I *don't* know how!" said Joanna loudly and rather crossly. "Tell me."

"They will waken for you if you want them to strongly enough," said Pan. "Have you not yet learned that you may have anything you want, if only you want it sufficiently." He tilted his head to one side, regarding her, "The Trees will almost certainly turn the tide of the battle," he said.

And then Cormac will be restored and Ireland will be safe . . .

"I do want it," said Joanna. And then, as Pan continued to look at her, with his eyes full of gentleness and humour and wisdom, "Help me," said Joanna.

Pan looked at her thoughtfully, and after a moment, he said, "Did I not tell you that I should be here when you least expected it?" And then, without pausing, he said, "And since you have sufficient faith, Human Child, I think I may help you."

He lifted the silver pipes to his lips and began to play.

The awakening was so slow and so gradual that it was very nearly imperceptible. But the Trees were waking; there was no question about it, their branches were moving and their leaves were sighing in the wind, and Joanna thought that to stand here like this and see them and hear them and feel them waken was the most beautiful thing in the world.

And there was the music, Pan's music. Joanna thought that even the Mindsong, the great Beckoning that Cormac had sent out at Scáthach could not equal this. It was light and elusive and faint, icicle-on-glass, frost against a windowpane.

When Pan stopped, Joanna felt as if something had died, but then he took her hand and smiled at her, and said very gently, "The Trees are with us, Joanna."

"So they are," she whispered.

The massive wave of life broke through the Forest of Darkness, and the Trees began to surge forward towards the battle that was raging.

As they moved, the Dark Armies faltered, and then fell back, and Cormac turned and stared, and felt something so intense and so tender clutch his heart that tears sprang to his eyes.

The Forest was alive; it was a huge dark seething mass, rushing over the hillside. Cormac could see Joanna amongst the Trees, her hair flying in the wind, the Nightcloak streaming out behind her. For a moment he thought there was someone with her—slender and slight and faintly alien—and then he was not sure. But he could see the half-faces of the Trees now, he could see the nearly recognisable features, and he thought that the Trees had the faces of an ancient and implacable vengeance. They are going to crush the enemy, thought Cormac. They are merciless and rather terrible, and I think I am a little afraid of them.

But he knew that Joanna had awakened them, and then he thought: No! Not Joanna! *Dierdriu!* And then he wondered was there really any difference?

Flynn had moved back from the rope bridge: "In retreat," he said later, but, "No!" said Cormac. "You had held them back for long enough for the Trees to come to life again. You had won your battle, Flynn!"

Flynn stood watching the onset of life among the Trees, hearing the rushing sound as they crossed the Plain; a great susurration of leaves and branches and boughs. He caught, as Cormac had, a glimpse of the Trees' inner spirits, and he knew that the old legends had not, after all, lied. Here were the dryads and the naiads and the tree-nymphs, beautiful and solemn and wise.

Cormac moved at last; he made a sweeping movement with one hand, and shouted, "Back! Back all of you! Out of their path! Let them go on, let them destroy the Dark Armies!" and the Cruithin and the Bloodline and the people of Cormacston at once tumbled over each other to be out of the way of the Trees. Muldooney, who had been standing with his mouth open, fell over his feet and tumbled into a ditch again, and had to be pulled out by Dubhgall.

Flynn, who was standing with Cormac now, said softly:

> " 'I will not be afraid of death and bane
> Till Birnam Forest come to Dunsinane.' "

And frowned, for the words were unfamiliar—and yet I know them for a fragment of the future and of the past, he thought.

The Trees had reached the chasm, and the roots and great solid trunks bridged it with ease. As the Dark Armies fell back, the Trees were upon them, crushing and rending, the slender birchlike tree-spirits fully emerged now, pouring out on to the enemy, fastening on to the hags and the harpies and the wraiths, subduing them with ease and flinging them into the chasm.

A strong straight beech had stretched across the ravine and, for a moment, they saw its spirit hovering, red-gold and supple and strong.

"Come across, Sire!" cried the tree-spirit, in what Joanna afterwards thought of as a warm woodsy voice that made you think of pine-scented forests and burning apple logs and the clean smell of sawdust in a workshop. "Come across, Son of the Wolves, and rout the filth!"

Cormac's armies rallied, and as Flynn moved forward, Dubhgall sounded the attack. Flynn looked at Cormac and smiled, and Cormac said, "Proceed, if you will," and Flynn began to walk across the chasm, hideous now with the bodies of victims. Tongues of flame shot upwards from time to time.

"They have touched the earth's core," said the birch naiad, "and for all who are flung into the Pit, there will be no rescue."

Flynn stood on the other side of the yawning abyss, and waited, and Cormac led the armies across. At once the Wolves and the Beasts fell upon the Dark Bloodline, biting and savaging; the Trees seized on what remained of Macha's creatures, breaking the spines of the harpies and crushing the grey malevolent hags. The fire from the abyss roared upwards, and the Plain was lit to red and orange life, a seething mass of fighting humans and animals.

At length, the Trees turned their attention to the Erl-King's Army of Corpses, and a sudden gentleness descended on them. A great oak, who seemed to lead the others, moved, and they saw the oak-naiad, ancient and wise and with the domed forehead of a thinker and a scholar.

The naiad spoke. "Into the Abyss with you also. But you will find release." He moved, and several slender, rather beautiful silver birches moved with him, and the Corpses turned about and walked submissively over the edge, their hands held palms upwards in the age-old gesture of supplication and submission, their sightless eyes lifted to the skies.

A profound silence fell upon the Plain . . .

The Trees stood in a half-circle about Cormac, their boughs bent in obeisance, for a long time. Nobody broke the silence, for, as Sean said afterwards, what was there to say? And all knew that the High King must be the first to address the awakened Trees.

Cormac made no ceremony. "He never did," said Sean, who would have enjoyed a bit of pomp now and again.

"He doesn't need to," rejoined Dubhgall.

Cormac simply looked at the Trees, and after a long while, nodded his head. "You are timely come," he said. "Without you, the battle would have been lost," and the formal, rather archaic words suited the occasion very well.

The oak said, "We owe you obeisance, Cormac, and we are your most loyal servants," and Cormac smiled.

"I welcome your awakening," he said, and again the words had the ring of ritual about them.

"Well, it is a sort of ritual," said Sean to Gormgall. "For the Trees have their own language."

The oak bowed again, his trunk nearly but not quite recognisable as a face, but the ancient wise form of the naiad still just discernible. "It is the Lady Dierdriu who called to us," said the naiad. "Only she could awaken us, for it was she who sent us into the Enchanted Slumber in order that we should not fall into the power of the Evil One of the Walled City."

And he turned to where Joanna stood quietly watching, and made again the deep bow.

CAIT FIAN HAD taken the Sun Chamber and its occupants with such speed and with such ease that, as Sean later said, it was very nearly insulting to Bricriu's army.

It was particularly insulting to Eochaid Bres, who had been told about the invasion, but had not paid very much attention to it.

"A small matter, Sire," Bricriu had said. "Your House Guard will deal with it quite easily."

The House Guard had not dealt with it easily, in fact they had not dealt with it at all. Cormac's supporters rampaged through the Palace in the wake of Cait Fian and the Panthers, and from all that Eochaid Bres could hear through the closed door of the Sun Chamber, the Panthers were having a high old time. He had chosen the Sun Chamber as a refuge—"*Not,*" he had said to Bricriu, "to *hide* from the attack, you understand"—and Bricriu had said, "Of *course* not," and had gone off to issue orders to somebody somewhere. Eochaid had let him get on with it, because an invasion of Tara was not something he had been prepared for.

"We're none of us ever prepared for anything here," said Phineas the Gatekeeper, drawing up the West Gate as he was told. But he cast a hopeful eye to the Plain and Cormac's armies, because wouldn't it be altogether grand to see the Wolfking come rampaging back!

Eochaid sat in the Sun Chamber by himself, and thought rather pettishly that it was too bad of them all to leave him like this, with no word of what was going on. Anything might be happening out there. Cait Fian and his terrible Panthers might have murdered every living soul in the Palace, and be now lying in wait for Eochaid himself. He supposed he ought to just go out to take a look, but he was not so curious that he was going to risk meeting up with the Panthers. One had to be realistic. And he was the King—or so far as he knew he was, because all manner of revolutions might have taken place by this time. Still, Kings had duties, and one of those duties was to preserve themselves. Eochaid decided to preserve himself by remaining safely in the Sun Chamber until it was safe to go out.

He was just thinking that it all seemed very quiet, and wondering could he find himself a bite of supper, when Cait Fian, with half a dozen Panthers at his heels, opened the door and stood smiling in at him.

Eochaid Bres, who knew that you had to be practical when the opposing forces were stronger than you were, said simply:

"I surrender."

CHAPTER TWENTY-SIX

THE TRIUMPHAL RE-ENTRY of the great Wolfking into Tara and the restoration of the legendary Wolfline to the Bright Palace is told in loving and lyrical detail by Amairgen the Blind in his famous epic poem, "The Road to the High Throne."

From it, scholars and historians of a later age have re-created with ease the immense pageantry and the spectacles which surrounded the exiled King's return, and from it they have been able to understand, in part at least, the overwhelming joy that the people expressed on that day.

It was a day for singing and dancing and laughter; it was a day for exulting and for thanking the gods for Cormac's return. It was a day to obtain, by whatever means were to hand, a place near to Tara's West Gate, for it was there that the High King would make the ceremonious re-entry.

The excitement began at dawn, although older people said with tolerant good humour that in some quarters it began even sooner. Certainly a great many people did not go to bed on the night before the King's re-entry, and equally certainly a great many more did not go to bed on the night after it either, or at least not to their own beds, which amounted to nearly the same thing.

The streets were lined with people, and the music and the feasting began long before the King's procession could be expected. None of it mattered in the least, for weren't they all so delighted that they could keep up the celebrating all day? While there was music to be played and wine to be drunk, it would not matter if the King did not appear until the Purple Hour.

And then the first notes of the King's musicians were heard, away to the west, and everyone craned his neck and jostled for a better position, and several people straightened the tubs of flowers, and everyone began cheering, for weren't they going to give the Wolfking the finest old welcome that ever a High King of Ireland was given! Long reign to His Majesty and death to all usurpers!

And then, quite suddenly, he was there, riding quietly at the head of his armies and the leaders of the great Bloodlines of Ireland, and so calm and so unassuming was he, and yet so entirely and so absolutely a King, that for a moment a great hush fell on the crowds as he came into the City. And then every person present, quite without warning, surely without realising, placed his hand on his heart in the ancient symbolic Oath of Allegiance; the Oath that Eochaid Bres had tried to make compulsory but had never managed to.

The people rose in a single solid movement then, and cheering, wild and uninhibited, broke out. Cormac looked at them all and lifted his hand in a gesture that was completely lacking in ceremony, but that was a ceremony in itself, and thought: *this* is surely the equal of that moment I knew on the Plain of the Fál? Isn't it? I ought to be feeling proud and strong and great, he thought, and wondered a little that he felt only rather humble and strangely empty. He thought that perhaps it was because the moment of purest happiness had already occurred, and that you could not have two moments like that, not in one lifetime, and certainly not within a few days of each other.

But he knew that the emptiness and the unaccustomed humility sprang from something much deeper and much more complex.

I have come so close to losing Ireland to the Dark Forces, that it is possible that I shall never feel safe again.

He looked at the wildly cheering people and at the bright eyes and the laughing lips and the waving hands, and thought: oh, my poor people, will you ever know how close the Ancient Evil came to us? And will you ever forgive me for so nearly losing Tara forever?

They would forgive him, of course, because they loved him—he had never understood quite why, but he knew that they did. Because he came of the old unbroken Royal line? Did they love him in spite of his faults, or because of them?

A smile touched his lips at that, because for sure the people knew those faults.

They would love him and cheer him, and they would tell tales of him, long into the night; they would recount the great Wolfking's triumphant return to the Bright Palace. Cormac smiled, because the tales would lose nothing in the telling. They would form a few more strands in the folklore of Ireland.

He glanced behind him to where Amairgen was riding quietly in the procession, with Portan at his side. Amairgen would certainly write something splendid and moving and lyrical about today, thought Cormac. He would conjure up the marvellous magical moments, and he would create songs and poems that would live long after him. They would all be created in his head, and Portan would write them all down and so they would be preserved. Cormac, who could remember the dazzling Court of his own father, and the later, lively Court he himself had presided over, thought that it was true that great scholars and poets were nearly always linked in history with the Kings they had served. He would not use the word "serve" in relation to Amairgen, for Amairgen would call no man master, but he thought that in years to come, people would remember that Amairgen had lived in the reign of the Wolfking. Would Amairgen stay at Scáthach? wondered Cormac, and although the memory of his lonely hopeless years inside Scáthach still made him flinch, he thought that Amairgen and Portan would no doubt turn the grim fortress into something warm and welcoming and sunlit.

Joanna and Flynn rode directly behind Cormac, and Joanna knew a deep happiness.

"I felt a fraud," said Flynn afterwards, but Joanna knew that he had been very much moved.

"And you?" said Flynn.

"I had come home," said Joanna very quietly.

The Cruithin had enjoyed the procession, although Gormgall had nearly wept at the King's refusal to have any ceremony.

"The plainest of breeches," he said. "And all he would wear in the way of regalia was the thin gold circlet of Niall of the Nine Hostages!"

"And even that he took off the minute he got inside the Palace," put in Dubhgall.

The Bloodline had ridden directly behind Flynn, solemn and

correct, richly garbed. At the head of them, Cait Fian led CuChulainn's favourite black mare, caparisoned in the colours of CuChulainn's line. Sean had written a lament, "The Riderless Horse," and there was going to be a proper ceremony of remembrance later on, so that they could all render the proper homage to CuChulainn.

"I wish I hadn't been so impatient with him before we went into battle," said Conaire.

"He'd understand," said Oscar.

"I know he would. That's not the point," said Conaire.

Etain had been at Cait Fian's side, which had momentarily distracted Sean from CuChulainn's riderless horse. "There'll be a Declaration there before long," he said. "And very nice too."

Muldooney, bringing up the rear, had found it all rather overwhelming. He knew about Cormac being a king—Dubhgall had explained it to him—but he had not really visualised the homage and the delight of Cormac's people when their King returned to them. He had certainly never envisaged anything like Tara, because nothing like Tara had ever come his way. He found it, truth to tell, a bit overpowering, and the radiance gave him something of a headache. Still, wasn't this what they had all fought for—Muldooney had surely not been lacking in courage when it came to the battle!—and wouldn't they all enjoy it to the full. He joined in the cheers as Cormac rode in through the West Gate, and was later very much delighted to be given an important place at table when they all sat down to a grand feast.

"But you were a part of it as much as any of us," said Gormgall, and Muldooney said that this was very true indeed, and would there be a bite more of roast boar, since all that riding in processions and cheering gave a man a fine healthy appetite.

Seated at the great table in the marble Banqueting Hall Cormac looked across at Joanna and smiled. "Do you recognise it, lady?" he said softly, and Joanna looked about her, at the colours and the light and the dazzling brilliant Court. There was music and laughter and the rich scents of foodstuffs, and the exotic perfumes of the people of the Court. Joanna sat back and looked at it all, and for some reason, Pan's words came back to her.

"I am Love and Gaiety and Wine and Laughter and Revelry.

And although you will sometimes have to look hard to find me, remember that I *am* to be found in every world and in every century."

I do not see him, thought Joanna, but I believe he is here, all the same. Just as he was there to rescue us from the Miller, and just as he woke the Trees with his beautiful eerie music.

Cormac was watching her. He said, "It is yours, you know—this place."

Medchuarta . . . the heart and the soul and the centre of Tara. Did I coax this from the sorcerers? wondered Joanna. Did I once live here and did I once die here, and did I rule creatures like this, half human, and unpredictable and wild? In another life and in another world . . .

She said carefully, "I think it is no longer mine, Cormac. I think it is yours now."

For my task is accomplished, and I must go home . . .

The thought came quick like a knife, and—surely this is my home! cried Joanna silently. But she smiled, and said, "Let us talk of other things for tonight."

And for a few tomorrows as well, for I cannot yet bear to think of leaving.

CORMAC WALKED INTO the Sun Chamber and drew a deep breath. *Now* I am home. *Now* I am once more in the place I was born to. *Medchuarta*. The heart and the soul and the core. He sat on the great gilded throne—the throne that had once belonged to Dierdriu of the Nightcloak and to the great Nuadu Airgetlam, and to Niall of the Nine Hostages. Yes, I am home.

He waited for the despair and the agonies and the shackles of the years of his exile to fall away; for, thought Cormac, surely this is the place where all will be healed and where all will have been worthwhile.

But the shackles were still there, like a faint bruise on his mind, and he thought that after all the road back to Tara had been a long and arduous one. Too many losses. Too much pain.

And I should never have succeeded if Joanna had not been with me.

He shook himself as if to clear the images, and moved to the door. The guards sprang to attention at once, and Cormac smiled inwardly. Have I missed this? This instant, unthinking obedience? But he knew that he had missed it; it was everything he had been bred to and it was everything that he had grown accustomed to. I do not demand it, neither do I compel it, but still it is there for me, no matter.

The guards were waiting, looking at him with respect and interest, and at length, Cormac said, "Tell them to bring up the prisoner."

"Yes, Your Majesty." The captain hesitated. "Alone, Sire?"

Cormac said, "Quite alone. I do not think I shall be in any danger."

But all of his senses were alert as he resumed his seat; he thought that there was not truly any danger, but he knew, within himself, that there was danger of a sort. He had loved Mab to the edge of madness; he had been willing to outface them all and place her by his side.

And together we would have made Ireland great.

Would they? He was no longer the helplessly romantic boy; he was no longer the young man who had loved Mab and believed that he could outface the world for her sake. And you were greedy, Mab! cried his mind. Once you could have shared it all with me; once I would have given you half my kingdom.

But you wanted it all, my dear. You wanted the power and the glory, and once you had it, you would have found it empty, for the power is the power of a straw man, and the glory is only the reflection of Tara itself.

The power and the glory do not work, Mab, unless the people love you.

And then, as he heard the footsteps approach, panic seized him. He thought: it has been so long. How shall I bear it if she has aged and greyed? How shall I stand it if she is defeated and cowed? He knew that his own soldiers had captured her very quickly indeed; that mad headlong flight had availed her nothing, as Cormac had known it would. He knew that she had not resisted; only that she had submitted to them with arrogance and disdain, they had not even had to chain her.

And I could not have borne to have seen her chained and defeated.

A low laugh spilled into the room. "Oh Cormac," said Mab softly, "how could you think I would ever be defeated or cowed?" And she stood looking at him from the door.

Cormac stayed where he was—*For I am the Wolfking returned, madam, and I am the High King of all Ireland, and I will have from you the homage I can command!*

He watched her and saw that she was as beautiful as he remembered, and as desirable as he remembered. And saw, as well, with infinite relief, that he no longer wanted her: because *I have loved Joanna since then? Yes, perhaps. And perhaps, after all, it was never intended that Mab and I should be together.*

A great gentleness filled him, but he did not yet know it for the gentleness of a still-young man towards an older woman he has ceased to desire. *And she is changed,* said his mind. *She is not aged—impossible!—but the fires do not burn quite so fiercely as they once did.*

At length, he said, "Are you older and wiser, Mab?"

The reply came promptly. "Neither, Sire."

He smiled. "I am glad. Never change, my dear. I should wish to remember you as always young and forever headstrong."

Fear showed in her eyes. "I am to be executed?"

"No."

"Ah. It is the traditional punishment . . ."

"Yes. And Bricriu will receive it. But after what we were to one another . . ." This time the pause was painful. Cormac said in a low voice, "I cannot send you out to die, Mab. But I must send you away."

This time the silence was much longer, but Cormac waited, watching her. Finally Mab said, "So. It is to be exile."

"It will be a luxurious exile, my dear."

"Better than the one I condemned you to?"

"Infinitely better," said Cormac.

"You are generous, Sire," said Mab, her tone bitter.

Cormac, feeling her pain, said, "Mab, I have no choice! You led the rebellion that deposed me and you instigated it!" He moved from the throne and began to pace the Sun Chamber restlessly. "You placed your son on my throne, and for that I should pronounce the High Execution over you!" He stopped and looked at her. "Only I cannot do it, Mab," he said in a voice of extreme tenderness. "We missed each other in time, my dear, and now, for Ireland's sake, you must leave Tara."

"What of Eochaid Bres?"

"He may go with you."

She drew in a sharp breath. "Not the High Execution?"

"No."

She studied him. "They will say you are mad."

"They have said it more than once in the past."

"Am I to be placed under any restraint?"

"No. You are banished and Eochaid Bres with you. But I make no stipulations."

A smile curved her lips. "Oh Cormac," she said softly, "you may live to wish you had made the pronouncement of Execution after all. How do you know I shall not ride against you again? How do you know I shall not try to take your throne from you a second time?"

Cormac looked at her, and without warning, a flame kindled in his eyes. "I don't know it," he said softly. "Would you do it, Mab? Find some poor ambitious wretch, as you did with Bricriu, and set up a Pretender again? Plunge Ireland into intrigues and civil war again?" He studied her thoughtfully. "Admit it Mab, just between us. Admit that I am the rightful High King."

Mab said, "Between us, Cormac, in the privacy of the Sun Chamber, I admit it. Because of what we once were to one another, I admit your right to the Ancient Throne.

"But I shall never admit it in private again, Cormac. I shall defy you in public and challenge your right to Tara."

"And," said Cormac, watching her, "raise an army against me again?"

The smile widened. "Wait and see, High King," said Mab. "Wait and see."

BUT IF CORMAC had missed Mab in time—by ten years? fifteen?—by how much had he missed Joanna? By centuries and by millennia, and by whole worlds, said his mind. For Joanna did not belong in his world, nor he in hers. Losing Joanna now would be the cruellest wrench of them all, but he knew that he would summon the sorcerers to pull aside the Time Curtain, and Joanna and Flynn would go back to their strange, harsh world.

And I shall be left here with nothing.

You have Tara, said his mind.

But it will be empty if Joanna is not there with me.

Or would it? Something at the back of his mind moved forward into the light—and in the light, waited for his consideration. An idea? An intuition? Or something stronger?

The wolf-smile touched his lips.

JOANNA SAID, "I cannot bear to leave. Cormac, I *cannot*."

"But you will do so. My dear, you must."

Task accomplished . . . there it was again, an unwanted thought.

Cormac looked at her, and thought: oh my love, if only you did not have to go. If only I could keep you here with me. But aloud he said, "You will return with Flynn."

Flynn . . . Delight rose in Joanna's heart. Flynn and the old stone farmhouse . . . She would walk the hillsides of Tugaim with Flynn, and there would be memories everywhere. There would be the Glowing Lands, and she would look at them and know that just beyond them, on the other side of the sheet of light, lay this ancient enchanted land. Yes, she would be able to feel that Cormac was not so very far away, after all.

And so when Cormac said again, more firmly this time, "You *will* go back, Joanna," she gave a deep sigh and said, "Yes."

"It is your place, Human Child," said Cormac, and Joanna, in sudden agony, thought: he is withdrawing from me. He no longer has use for me, for I have helped him to regain his throne.

He felt the thought at once, of course, and reached for her hand. "No," he said. "Never that. But for you—and Flynn—to be out of your own time for too long is dangerous. I cannot explain—perhaps the sorcerers can—but it is very wrong to tamper with time, Joanna. And perhaps there are things in your own world that you must do. Things that await you. Things you are meant to complete there." He looked at her, his head on one side, and Joanna felt all over again the strange wild beauty that had beckoned to her at Scáthach.

She said, "To leave you—after all that has been between us—" and Cormac smiled at her very gently.

"Listen," he said, "we will roll up the memories, Human Child, and we will store away what we have had, because it can never really be lost to us. And one day, a little way in the future, we will be able to unwrap our memories and lay them out. What we have had will not die because we shall not let it. I shall unwrap the memories of you, not once, but many times in the years ahead, and every memory will be sweet-scented and wholly precious. And in time, I shall be able to enjoy the memories without pain and with deep happiness." He took her face in his hands. "I shall never regret any of it Joanna," said Cormac, "and you will never be truly gone from my mind."

Joanna leaned against him and felt tears on her cheeks, but she did not think they were her tears.

"And also," said Cormac very softly, "also, for you it will be easier. For you will have the child."

And then, as Joanna started, and drew back, "Won't you?" said Cormac.

Joanna said, "When did you guess?"

"Am I right?"

"Yes," said Joanna in a whisper.

FLYNN SAT OPPOSITE to Amairgen and Portan in the firelit hall of Scáthach and saw how the leaping flames lit Amairgen's face to gentle radiance. He thought that for Amairgen this was home now; this was his place.

But isn't it my place also? Have I not, also, come home? With the winning of the battle and restoring of Cormac, undreamed-of memories had come alive for Flynn. When Amairgen had said to him, "You are Finn of the *Fiana* again," he had not fully believed it; now he did believe it. Now he knew himself alive and charged with an energy and a confidence so great that he felt he could ransack cities and storm citadels and ride out at the head of great armies.

As I did once before in another life and in another world . . .

The words hovered unspoken, but Flynn saw Amairgen's head come up and he saw the sudden awareness in the tilt of Amairgen's whole body. He thought: something has struck a very deep chord in him, and when Amairgen spoke, he knew he had been right.

"Finn of the *Fiana* returned. Yes I feel it in you more strongly now than ever before." He leaned forward and without warning, a soft faint far-off wind stirred the quiet of Scáthach's stone hall. Flynn felt the hairs rise on the back of his neck, and for a moment the figure of the great warrior Finn was there with them, whipcord-strong, tall and slender and

straight. Dierdriu's champion, the High King's paladin. Fighter
and lover and scholar and leader. *And how do I know all that
about him?* But he did know it, and he heard echoing down the
centuries the cries of victory and the sounds of the immense
armies of Tara riding out under Finn's command.

Flynn blinked and the fire burned up and the figure blurred
and then was gone. Flynn was shaken, but he turned to
Amairgen, still seated quietly in his corner.

"Yes it was real," said Amairgen without moving. "I saw it
also, Flynn, not with my outer vision, but with an inner one.
And I could not call into being that which had never had ex-
istence."

Flynn said, "You called up—"

Amairgen leaned forward and touched Flynn's forehead.
"Finn was your ancestor, Flynn. His blood is still in you, and
his memories are still in your heart. I drew on those memories." He fell silent, and Flynn felt the strength of him and the
emotions and the love flow outwards. When Amairgen spoke,
Flynn already knew what he was going to say.

"Do you remember," said Amairgen, "the night we agreed
to go through the Time Curtain, you and I?"

"Yes," said Flynn, and he thought: *I remember, and nothing, not wild horses, would have stopped me going in after Joanna* . . . And he remembered, as well, the moonlight and the
mystery of the night, the aching loneliness for Joanna gone beyond their reach.

"You placed yourself under my authority then, Flynn. You
are still under it."

Flynn did not speak.

"I am still the Leader of the Great Council of the Keepers,"
said Amairgen, "and as such I may expect from you obedience." He smiled. "And that, my dear, goes uneasily with you,
I think. Finn of the *Fiana* would not bow to the authority of
another, and neither will you." He leaned back in his chair.
"We vowed to return, you and I."

Unless death or mutilation should prevent us . . . The words
formed themselves on to the silence, and Flynn waited. He
thought: but I cannot go back. I belong here.

And with that thought, came another: you must go back.
You promised.

Even though I made that promise in another world, and in another life?

Even then.

But I did not know how it would be! cried Flynn in silent anguish. I did not know what I would find here! Surely a promise made under such circumstances—

But a promise is a promise, said his mind sternly. You do not qualify a promise. You do not say, "I promise, but only if this does not happen or that." You do not promise and then discover extenuating circumstances when the time comes to make the promise good. It is all or nothing.

Amairgen said softly, "We both promised, Flynn. To return unless death or mutilation should intervene." Not by the smallest gesture did Amairgen draw attention to his blindness, but Flynn felt it as never before; he felt the terrible weight of Amairgen's eternal sightlessness descend about his shoulders, and he thought: after all, it might have been me the *sidh* took that night. It is his burden, but it is a burden that I might so easily have had to shoulder. And then—perhaps I can shoulder a little of it, thought Flynn. If I return to Tugaim and the Keepers, I am fulfilling our promise. I am making it possible for him to remain here. Where he belongs. Amairgen the Traveller, the Voyager, come to rest . . .

There was something else as well. Amairgen could have no easy place in Tugaim now. He would be unable to make any contribution to the world that was the Apocalypse's legacy to mankind and that was the Letheans' bequest to their descendants. But perhaps I am being harsh to them, thought Flynn. Perhaps they, also, discovered extenuating circumstances.

In Tugaim, Amairgen would be useless. Perhaps he would be a burden. An intolerable thought. Flynn could not allow it to happen. As for Portan—his mind flinched away from the memory of Portan's life inside the Gealtacht. Certainly, whatever happened to the rest of them, Portan must stay here. At Scáthach? Yes, why not? Flynn remembered the night that Portan had talked to him, and he remembered as well that Portan had talked of dissolving the sadness and the despair that Scáthach held within its walls. Seated here, like this, he could feel that it was happening already. The patches of desolation are fading, thought Flynn, and they are being replaced by peace and tranquillity, and by a calm, quiet happiness. Portan's long-ago dream of a little community where she could work and be useful and accepted, would happen. Scáthach would become a part of Cormac's world and of Cormac's kingdom; Amairgen and Portan would be welcomed at Tara, they would be sought out by the men and women of the Court who liked to discuss philosophy and travel and the teachings of the great scholars of the world as they had hoped. Flynn thought that Joanna had unlocked the Enchantment of Captivity that had held Cormac, but in doing so, she had also unlocked something else. She had let the sunlight into Scáthach, so that in years to come it would no longer be known as the Fortress of Shadow, but something quite different. He thought it would happen. Amairgen would make it happen, and Portan would help him.

And so I must go back. Because I promised, and the promise has to be all or nothing. And because I am whole and well, and he is not . . .

None of it needed to be said. Yet when Amairgen touched Flynn's hand and said, "You understand, Flynn," Flynn bowed his head . . . Amairgen said softly, "You must go back through the Time Curtain, Flynn. You and Joanna. Cormac's sorcerers will help you."

Because you do not qualify a promise. And after all, thought Flynn, perhaps I owe it to the Keepers as well. And he remembered the silent watchers on Tara's Hill, cloaked and faceless, and yet genuinely friendly—a brotherhood—curiously comforting. He remembered, as well, how those unknown men had guarded the Secret of the Time Curtain for several centuries, quietly and staunchly, never once attempting to break the vow, never once attempting to go back into the Deep Past. Yes, for sure he owed it to the Keepers to return.

As if a decision had been reached, Amairgen said, "Yes, you must return to the Keepers, Flynn," and as he spoke, Flynn felt the quality of his voice change. In the flickering light, Amairgen lifted the hand that still wore the ornate ring, the Leader's symbol of office, and Flynn saw it catch the light.

Amairgen said, "You remember this also, Flynn? That the office of Leader is a hereditary one?"

"Yes."

The cool heavy gold of the ring brushed Flynn's hand, and

as it did so, something as yet unidentified and certainly uniden-
tifiable stirred deep within him.

"I have no son," said Amairgen, and Flynn felt panic disturb
the surface of his mind. He thought: No. Oh no! I don't want
this!

Or do I? He remembered again the other-world feeling of
Tara's Hill, and he remembered the faint elusive music that
haunted the place. Had he not foreseen this when he stood on
the Hill that night? When he made that vow to go through the
Time Curtain to find Joanna and then return? And with the
vow had there not been something else?

And you no more qualified a vow than you did a promise.

Amairgen's fingers closed about his wrist, and Flynn felt the
steady flow of the other man's thoughts. For a breathspace,
panic welled up in him again, and then beneath it came something much deeper and stronger. Acceptance of an old old authority? Yes, perhaps. He heard again the out-of-hearing music
and he saw again the out-of-sight shapes. The *sidh* guarding
the Gateway to the Deep Past? Probably. So after all this Ireland is not so very far away from that other one. And with that
thought came another:

*Imagine being a part of a Secret so immense, so magical
that only a few people in the course of the entire world will
ever know of it. And imagine, as well, being a Guardian of that
Secret, knowing the Secret from within.*

Wouldn't that be the most exhilarating experience of all?
said his mind, and despite himself, Flynn felt a thrill of anticipation.

When Amairgen said again, "I have no son," Flynn felt excitement well up inside him.

Hereditary Leader of the Council of Keepers ... Guiding
the Brotherhood, ruling them, safeguarding the Secret from the
rest of the world. All that, knowing more than any of them
the great truth of the Time Curtain. And in time handing on the
ancient symbolic gold ring to his own son ...

His son and Joanna's ... Flynn would welcome the child
that Joanna would bear, and he would love it for her sake and
for the memory of Cormac as well. But there would be other
children, and delight opened up within him at the thought.

When Amairgen said, "Well? Will you do it, Flynn? Return
with Joanna and lead in my stead?" Flynn bowed his head

again, and this time there was genuine submission in the gesture.

In the silence that followed, he felt Amairgen's hand close about his.

So AFTER ALL, there was to be no reneging on the promise he had made. After all they would return, himself and Joanna.

And the child with them.

Flynn examined the idea of the child, Cormac's child, born out of strong magic and Cormac's enchantment.

"He wanted me with him," said Joanna. "He needed me to release him from Scáthach."

Open locks, to the Human's hand . . .

"I was fascinated and bewitched," said Joanna, and then, in answer to the question Flynn would not have asked, "And a part of me did love him, Flynn. But it was the part that was once Dierdriu, I think." She regarded him steadily. "There will always be the memory," she said. "But you do not need to mind about it."

For I was always yours, my love . . .

"You knew that I was," said Joanna, and grinned, and said, "As much as you were mine, even on that night inside Tara with Mab."

Flynn grinned back at her, and thought: yes, she understands, just as I do. And remembered that he, also, had been a little bewitched, and a little fascinated, and that he, in his turn, would always have the memory of a wild, unprincipled lady who was not quite human, and who loved well, if not always wisely. Aloud, he said thoughtfully, "I do not think she will be in exile for ever that one."

"Cormac will not let her be for ever in exile," said Joanna.

"Because he once loved her?" said Flynn, who thought he could understand Cormac in this.

Joanna said, "No. Because he does not love her any more."

"Of course," Flynn said and remembered that Cormac would be left with nothing at all of Joanna, that the child would be going with them. He thought he could easily accept the idea of Cormac's son, and he thought that Cormac would always be a little with them.

But for Cormac it would not be so easy.

* * *

THEY WERE TOGETHER a great deal, Joanna and Cormac, in the weeks and then the months that followed, for the sorcerers consulted by Cormac and by Amairgen had been wary of allowing Joanna to journey back through the Time Curtain before her child was born.

"Not meet," they said. "For the unborn soul to journey in such a way would be unwise."

"Downright dangerous," said one of them firmly. "Her Majesty should remain here until after the birth, Sire."

It was a curious restless time; "Although," Joanna was to say afterwards, "it was a peaceful time as well. A healing time after the battles and the dangers."

Flynn hunted and fished and rode with Conaire and the others, and talked long and deep into the nights with Amairgen and Portan. "Acquiring a little of their wisdom," he said. "A very little."

They all attended the wedding ceremonies of Etain and Cait Fian at Gallan—"So beautiful," said Joanna, gazing around her. "I should have been sorry to miss this. And it is one more memory to take back."

The wedding was splendid, and the feasting went on for days. "Of course it did," said Conaire.

"It was *very* lavish," said Oscar, and, "I have to say," added Conaire, "that Sean excelled himself over the entertainments."

"He prepared for them long enough," said Midir, who seemed to be voicing the thoughts of them all.

But in the main, they were alone together, Joanna and Cormac, walking in the forests that surrounded Tara, and over the hills and through the meadows. "Talk to me," said Cormac. "Enough to last me for a lifetime. Leave me as much as you can, Joanna. Make me know you so well that I shall never forget you. Let me store you in my mind, so that when you are back in your own world, I can unravel the memories and spread them at my feet. I shall never see you again in this life, Joanna." He grasped her hands. "Give me *memories*," cried Cormac, his eyes hard and slanting and golden, and Joanna could feel that he was being wrenched apart with longing.

Cormac had closed his mind to her, for it was not to be thought of that she should see his agony. But he knew that she did see it, and he knew that she shared in it.

He wanted to say, "Leave me something, Joanna. I shall

bear losing you if I can have something of you to remember. I shall never see you again in this life, my dear sweet brave girl, but I shall bear it because I must."

Joanna was crying. She reached up to take his face between her hands. "Cormac, you will have other women."

Oh yes, my dear, and often ... A smile lifted his lips, and Joanna managed a smile in return. The moment lengthened, and Cormac thought: if I asked her now, truly asked her, would she stay with me?

He drew in breath to speak, and then Joanna gasped and bent over.

AFTERWARDS, SHE WAS to think that it was entirely natural and somehow very right that the birth should happen there, only the two of them amongst the ancient trees.

She had staggered and almost fallen with that first tearing-apart pain, and Cormac had supported her as far as the grassy bank beneath a huge oak tree. She thought she had gasped out a plea for help; she certainly had expected him to go running towards the Palace to summon some of the women.

"But there was no time," she said later. "And Cormac was all the help I needed."

There had been a tremendous feeling of excitement and anticipation all about them. "As if," Joanna said later, "the trees knew that something momentous was about to happen and as if they were helping me."

She had felt, as never before, Cormac's strength, and there had been a great serenity from the listening trees; "And that was all I needed."

Cormac's thoughts had surrounded her then: be calm. There is no pain. This is as it was meant to be, my dear. *And I am here with you.*

Cormac's child, born within sight of Tara, born beneath the ancient trees that Joanna alone had woken from their long sleep ...

The birthpain had suddenly become something to be beaten, something to thrust back into the shadows so that it should not interfere with the excitement and the anticipation of the moment.

"And I was tremendously excited," said Joanna.

She remembered that the survivors of Devastation had given

birth almost like this, amidst smoking ruins, in tunnels and caves, and she had drawn great comfort from the knowledge.

"And the trees were there," she said again. "Weren't they?"

"Yes," said Cormac. "For you had woken them. Do you think they would not have helped you?"

There had been the warm woodsy scents of the forest and there had been the softness of the pine needles at her back like a carpet, and the pain had been easy to bear. Sunlight had filtered in through the branches above them, and at last Joanna felt a final wrenching, as if her body was being torn apart, and there had been the warm, living, breathing child between her thighs. And then there had been the pain again, sharper this time, deeper, and Cormac's hands closed about her, and then Cormac had said in an odd unfamiliar voice: "Twins!" and Joanna heard the mingled cries of two babies.

Twins. A boy and a girl.

FLYNN STOOD AT the very centre of the light that was pouring into the Sun Chamber.

"Dawn," said Amairgen. "The rebirth. The renewal. A traditional time for new beginnings. And the time of day when the Leadership has always been handed on." He smiled. "I cannot give you the full ceremony, Flynn, since for that we need the full Council. But we will do our best."

"The trappings don't matter," said Flynn.

But the trappings were there all the same. They were in the watchful faces of the courtiers, all of whom had gathered to witness the ceremony. "And it was *not*," said Sean afterwards, busy with an entirely new ballad, "it was not just vulgar curiosity."

"I was curious," said Midir. "I don't mind who knows it."

"It was extremely interesting," said Oscar.

As the sun rose slowly over the horizon, the clear new light began to spill into the Sun Chamber, so that prisms of colour danced off the walls and irradiated the great Throne of Niall of the Nine Hostages. Several of the watchers saw Amairgen turn his face to feel the warmth of the new day, and Sean, who would not have admitted to being the smallest bit sentimental, even under threat of extreme torture, had to wipe away a tear. "Nor," said Conaire, "was he the only one. Amairgen could feel the light but we all of us knew he would never see it again. A terrible thing for him to bear."

"But his loss will be Tara's gain," Oscar had said quietly, for already Amairgen was becoming known and revered.

Joanna stood with the others, fascinated and intrigued. "For," she said sadly, "this is perhaps the last time we shall all be together in this way. This is the beginning of our return to Tugaim."

"Shall you mind so much?" Conaire asked.

"Yes," said Joanna softly, "yes I shall mind."

Cormac stood a little apart from them, watching the ceremony, his face unreadable. Joanna thought that he was already distancing himself from them, and felt again the ache of loss. The twins lay nearby, with Portan at their side. They were warmly wrapped and lightly covered, and Joanna glanced at them. Was it only imagination that made her think that the girl—dark-haired and pointed-faced—was fascinated by the patterns of the light? And was it only imagination to think that the boy—golden-eyed and patrician-featured—was more interested in the ceremony and the people?

Ridiculous of course, for they were only a few weeks old, but—"Remember that they are not wholly Human," Oscar had said to her. "There will be differences." Joanna thought that already she could see those differences.

Flynn was still at the exact centre of the dawnlight, he was becoming bathed in the pure colour, and as they waited, the sun came wholly into sight, a great glistening globe of fire and light and life. Delight burst in Joanna's heart and she saw Flynn turn slowly and reach out both his hands to Amairgen. Amairgen moved forward and Flynn took the other man's hands in his. Something flashed between them, and those of the Court who possessed the Samhailt saw with deep contentment the slender white light.

Amairgen said very clearly, "Flynn O'Connor. Son of Michael, son of Liam, son of Patrick, son of Seamus, son of Donal, the First Keeper of the O'Connors. To you, by right of my Ancient Office and by right of the powers vested in me by my own ancestor, I vouchsafe the Ring of the Leader of the Council. You will sit at its head, and to you the Brotherhood of the Keepers will swear allegiance. To you falls the weight and honour of guarding the Secret of the Glowing Lands. Do you accept this?"

Flynn said in a low voice, "I accept it."

"And will you promise to keep the Secret from the world at all costs?"

"I promise it."

"Will you promise, also, never to use the knowledge of the Secret for your own purposes, and will you promise never to travel again beyond the Time Curtain into the Deep Past, unless it should be to rescue another?"

A pause. Flynn thought: well, I knew it would be said. And of course I must promise. But he took a moment to reply, and as he paused, he felt a great calm and a great strength descend on him. A stillness fell on the Sun Chamber, and to the watching Court, it was as if a great calming hand had been laid on him. Portan, never taking her eyes from his face, thought that for an instant the light of the great Finn of the *Fiana* shone in his eyes, but she could never afterwards be sure. Conaire, who was nearest, saw the expression in Flynn's eyes change and thought: he is accepting this strange unknown leadership. With all of his being he is accepting it. And perhaps because his perception of the Samhailt was a little sharper and a little more finely honed than that of the others, he saw the light about Flynn's head become momentarily tinged with a pure clear blue, and he thought: authority. And knew the light for the sorcerers' ancient mystical symbol of leadership.

Flynn was aware only of a great peace like a thick dark cloak. He felt as if a warm sweet breath had ruffled across his mind, and then he thought that it was more as if he had come from a darkened forest into a warm bright room and been welcomed by people he loved and by people who loved him. When he finally answered Amairgen, he did so with a confidence he had not until now felt.

"I accept!"

Amairgen slid the heavy gold ring on to Flynn's finger, and Flynn felt his mind and his heart accept. And then, as a movement from the corner of the Sun Chamber caught his eye, he glanced up to see both the twins watching him unblinkingly. Something that was mischievous and reckless stirred in Flynn, so that he shook off the solemnity of the ceremony, and found, as he was always to find, amusement in the situation, in any situation.

He regarded Joanna's twins thoughtfully, and he thought: well, I have promised not to return to Tara, and I will keep my promise. But I would not count on what those two might do!

CORMAC SAT ALONE in the Sun Chamber, watching purple shadows steal across the floor. Twilight. A time for lovers. And yet I am alone.

He need not have been. There were more than sufficient young women in the Court, any one of whom would gladly have come to him. His lips curved in a smile. Quite soon, perhaps, my dears, but for the moment, for tonight, and for a few tomorrows as well, I shall be alone.

He would not feel this way for ever, of course. He would soon be scanning the Court, selecting the ones that pleased him, wooing them with courtesy and mockery and mischief, taking them off to his bedchamber. And everyone would smile and say that the Wolfking had not changed so very much.

But for a little while, I prefer to be alone with my memories of Joanna . . .

The shadows had deepened when the door was pushed open, and he looked up, startled, for he had been thinking of her, and imagining her, and for a moment he thought the light was playing tricks. The Purple Hour, when strong magic was abroad . . .

But it was Joanna in truth, smiling rather hesitantly, a little unsure of her welcome, standing in the doorway, not moving.

As Cormac stood up, he saw what Joanna held in her arms and a sudden hope flared up inside him.

And then Joanna walked across the room and held out her burden to him.

It was their daughter.

Cormac could not speak. An intense and painful happiness was unfolding inside him, and he thought: of course! Not Mab's daughter, *Joanna*'s. Joanna's daughter to be here with me, to be reared in the ancient wonderful tradition of High Queen. Joanna's daughter to inherit the legacy of Tara. Joanna's daughter—and mine.

Together we will make Ireland great.

It would happen. Delight was exploding inside him now, and

at last he felt slide from him the despairs and the frustrations and the feeling of: is this all? He had felt his victory a hollow one, because he had known that Joanna would not be there to share it with him. Now he saw that it was not hollow, it was filled to brimming point with promise and happiness and love.

Joanna's daughter and mine.

Joanna shed no tears, but he knew that she was crying inside. But she handed the child to him and stood back, as if, thought Cormac, she is deliberately severing the link between them. And she will have the boy . . . An ache rose in him for the boy also, for the son he would never know, but he quenched it at once. If she will leave me this, if she will leave me our daughter, I shall bear it. I shall bear losing her because I shall not be losing her at all. I shall see Joanna every day in the child, and she will be doubly precious to me because of it.

He was alight and alive with happiness now, and laying the child down—and yes, her eyes were watching the light, fascinated and aware—he took Joanna's hands in his.

Joanna said, "I am hardly bearing this, Cormac, but there is no help for it. There is nothing else to do." She looked down, and Cormac felt her whole body wracked with longing. "I shall know nothing of her!" cried Joanna in sudden anguish. "I shall share in nothing of her life!"

"Then take her with you," said Cormac. "Go now, through the Time Curtain. With Flynn and the boy."

Joanna said in a low voice, "No. Tara is hers as much as it is yours." And lifted her head and looked at him.

Cormac stood, unable to speak, Joanna's hands still in his. And then, without warning, an idea slid into his mind.

"Listen," he said. "There may be a way."

THEY STOOD TOGETHER, Joanna and Flynn, hands tightly clasped, the child—Cormac's son—held firmly between them. Ahead of them were the sorcerers, and behind the sorcerers lay the darkling forests. And somewhere within the forests . . .

"We will do our utmost," the sorcerers had said. "But we cannot promise."

Behind the sorcerers was the entire Court, all of them lined up, waiting to bid a farewell. And it is the last farewell, thought Joanna. It is scarcely to be borne. If only I can keep a tight hold on control. If only I do not cry. She thought she would not cry, and she thought she would manage if she could keep thinking about the things that were ahead; Flynn and the boy, and the life she would have with Flynn in the square white farmhouse. Oh yes, those were things to hold on to, because those things were real and solid and good and enduring.

And yet, and yet . . .

"But I shall do it," said Joanna to Flynn. "I shall bid them all farewell."

"You cannot omit a single ceremony."

"I know."

Certainly the people of the Court and the Cruithin were gathered before them with a look of eager expectation, and despite her resolve, Joanna very nearly panicked. I cannot do it! Can I? And then, with a sudden squaring of her shoulders: of course I can!

The Bloodline came first; Conaire and Oscar and Midir and Etain, with Cait Fian at Etain's side. "I shall never forget any of you," said Joanna, and now she felt the tears begin to gather, and thought that after all it was going to be as difficult as she had thought.

The Councillors were next, with Bolg nodding solemnly, because he liked a bit of ceremony, telling the others that you should always be prepared to learn about new things. The Councillors would all be very interested in the enchantment that had been specially woven for this occasion. Bolg said, and the others agreed, that new enchantments were a good thing. You could not have too many. Progress, that was the thing, declared Bolg, and the Councillors nodded and said wasn't that the truth?

Muldooney stood with the others, waiting to say a last goodbye to Joanna. He had thought that there might be just a touch of awkwardness between them, and he had prepared a bit of a speech, nothing very much really, only a few words, wishing Joanna well and Flynn of course. He had spent quite a long time over this, and he had shown it to Sean, because Sean had the way with words, Sean had been enthusiastic about it. "Don't change a word of it," he had said, and Muldooney had beamed, and then had said anxiously couldn't it be improved on at all? and Sean had said, very vehemently, that it could not be improved on *in the very least bit*, and

Muldooney had thought that a fine thing for a person like Sean to say.

And then, in the end, there was no need for the speech, because Joanna had hugged Muldooney, genuinely and warmly, and thanked him for being such a true friend, and Flynn had shaken his hand, and Muldooney had had to mop his brow and blow his nose, and wonder after all if he shouldn't be returning to Tugaim? But the sorcerers had been explicit about this also.

"Only Joanna and Flynn and the boy," they had said firmly. "We can only weave the enchantment for three."

And of course if it was a question of enchantments, Muldooney was the one to be agreeable. You could not tamper with enchantments. Anyone knew that. And when you came to think it over, this was not such a bad place to be living. Muldooney had surveyed the terrain with an experienced eye, because the Muldooneys knew about these things, and had seen that you could, if you were careful, start up a very nice little farm of your own here. Pigs and wild boar and some geese. He'd had a word with the King's cooks, and it seemed that there would be a grand living to be made from supplying the Royal Kitchens. Ah, Muldooney was the man to be making the most of any opportunity that offered itself! They'd all of them see how prosperous he'd become, and they'd be astonished at what he would make of the bit of land that Cormac had made over to him and the nice snug house that went with it. He'd visit Amairgen and Portan from time to time, and Gormgall and Dubhgall had said they would be sure to come to stay. And so, although he would be very sorry indeed to bid farewell to Joanna and Flynn and the little one, Muldooney felt that he was not going to be acquitting himself so ill in this rather odd, but not at all unfriendly land.

Sean was there, of course, well to the fore, his eyes bright, drinking in everything. He had already composed a lengthy ballad, and they had all promised that later on that night, they would all attend a banquet in the Sun Chamber, and Sean would sing the ballad, and they would tell again the marvellous stirring tale of Cormac's escape and the final battle, and the slaying of the Morrigna and the Erl-King and the defeat of the Dark Ireland.

"In case," said Oscar caustically, "there is anyone left in Ireland who has not yet heard it."

But they would all be thinking of Joanna and Flynn, said Sean earnestly, pressing a copy of the ballad into Flynn's hands. They must be sure that they would all be thinking of them.

Joanna and Flynn had reached Amairgen and Portan now, both of them quietly waiting their turn.

Joanna thought: I believe this is the worst yet. I barely know them, and yet I feel as if I am going to lose something very precious and infinitely dear. She bent to embrace Portan. "And I wish there had been more time for us," she said.

Portan smiled, although she, too, was crying. "Love Flynn very much for me," she said, and Joanna, understanding, said at once, "Yes. Yes, I will."

When Flynn moved forward, they saw that he was beyond words.

And then, he also, embraced them both, and everyone watching knew that there were no words possible, and that anything Flynn said would have been inadequate.

Portan was crying, but she was smiling too. She took Flynn's hands and said softly, "Flynn, I am going to be so very happy here," and Flynn managed to smile.

Then Amairgen reached for Flynn's hands also, and said very gently, "Flynn, you will be in my thoughts for a part of every day for all of my life," and Flynn remembered that this was what Portan had said to him at Scáthach before the battle, and he thought: after all, what could be a better parting sentiment?

You will be in my thoughts for a part of each day . . .

What better memory to take with them.

And now they turned at last to where Cormac stood, a little apart. Joanna thought: the Wolfking alone. Is *that* how I shall remember him? And then she looked across at him and saw that he carried their baby girl in his arms, and she saw that he was smiling at her. A mist clouded her vision, but she blinked it away. When she looked again, he was still there, the wind lifting his dark hair a little, his eyes glowing, and quite suddenly, Joanna knew that it would be all right. And I shall remember all of the good things about him. The way he could make love and the way he was strong and gentle and generous. And quite suddenly, the dying words of Dierdriu slid into her mind.

"I shall be with you in the good things of life. In the things you love. In the woodsmoke of a twilight fire, and in the moonlight over the Morne Mountains, and in the golden sunrise. You will hear me laughing in the Purple Hour, for that is the most magical time of all. I shall be in the wine you drink, and when you hold feasts, I shall be among you still. You will never quite lose me."

"You will never quite lose me," said Cormac very softly.

Joanna tightened her hold on the child in her arms, and said, as if completing some kind of ritual: "And you will be in my thoughts for a part of each day." And to herself, thought: after all he will be with me, I shall see him in the boy. I think it will be all right.

The sorcerers were coming to meet them, drawing them into the forest now, hurrying them forward, and Joanna felt excitement and apprehension flare up, and felt Flynn's hand tighten on hers.

Here we go . . .

And then the great glittering Time Curtain was stretching out ahead of them, filling the horizon, and they were being drawn towards it, and Joanna had just time to think: Cormac's magic was always strong, and then they were in the light and they were in the scents and the sounds, and Time was closing all about them, and it was going to be all right, it was going to be all right . . .

EPILOGUE

THE HILLSIDES OF Tugaim were calm and untroubled and in a curious way welcoming. Flynn and Joanna walked slowly up to the summit of Tara's Hill and stood looking down.

Below them, they could trace the paths they had taken; the Dark Forest of the Sleeping Trees; the Plain of the Fál; the narrow path that had led to Gallan and the cool fires of Cait Fian's Mountain Palace. Fragments and snippets of history; the thin sheet of the Time Curtain that separated all the worlds just out of sight now.

The Glowing Lands . . .

"They are still there," said Flynn softly. "We could go back."

"Yes." But Joanna knew they would not. And they both knew as well that the Glowing Lands would cool and dim, and the Gateway would eventually re-seal. "We shall not return," she had said to the sorcerers as they stood on the edge of the light. "We shall never come here again."

"Never is a very big word, Human Child," the oldest of the sorcerers had said. "One day you may look across a valley and hear the echoes of our world. We are still here, Human Child, in our world as you are in yours, for Time is simultaneous."

Time is simultaneous . . .

Joanna stood on Tara's Hill, Flynn by her side, and thought: I could almost believe it.

And then Flynn said, "Down here . . ." and moved forward.

"Are you sure?"

"Yes. Look. The hillside is virtually unchanged." He smiled

at her. "Not by flood or fire or Devastation. Not by the passing of the centuries.

"And Oscar's eye for terrain was very good."

Joanna said uncertainly, "They would not fail us—"

"No." But Flynn's voice held a note of uncertainty, for how could they be sure. So many centuries . . .

Yes, but Time is simultaneous . . .

But the small cave in the hillside was still as Flynn had remembered, and they burrowed their way inside.

Joanna's throat closed with the dust and her heart was thudding erratically. She thought: of course they would not have failed us; they *promised*.

But that was centuries ago . . .

The little cave was thick with the accreted dust and dirt of decades and the light was poor. They moved cautiously forward, both of them experiencing a strong feeling of recognition, neither of them daring to hope.

Flynn said, "We may have to dig."

"Yes. We knew that."

But the digging did not take very long, for the spot had been chosen carefully and well. Sheltered by a jutting overhang of rock, protected by a solid wall of the hillside, time had barely touched the narrow recess. There, a few feet beneath the cave floor, was the cache chosen by them with so much care and so much searching before they came back through the Time Curtain.

"A month ago?" said Joanna.

"Or a thousand years."

"Would they have had the box specially made?"

"Yes. It's solid gold," said Flynn, and grinned. "That must have cost Cormac a pretty penny."

But gold would have been the only substance that could have withstood the centuries. Even though Time is simultaneous? Even then.

Open it! cried Joanna silently, for I cannot bear it. But Flynn was already prising open the beautifully crafted box.

He glanced at Joanna. "Airtight," he said. "I think we can be hopeful, acushla."

The box opened with very little persuasion, and the thin linen sheets they remembered so clearly lay carefully packed beneath, exactly as Amairgen and Portan must have placed them. A month ago? A thousand years? Joanna sat in the dim narrow cave that they had spent weeks searching for until Flynn and Oscar were both sure that they had found a cave that Flynn remembered from Tugaim and the future they were about to return to.

A cave that had survived from that world to this . . .

For a moment, that other world closed about them again, and Joanna felt tears sting her eyes.

And then Flynn lifted the contents of the box out, and said very gently, "Joanna. Look." And fell silent as they stared at what lay in the casket.

A tress of hair. Pure black and even in the dark cave gleaming like a raven's wing. A small engraving—a pure profile etched on silver. Tip-tilted cheekbones and mischievous eyes.

At the bottom of the casket were more linen sheets, thin and rather brittle, but preserved by the gold of the box. The writing—Portan's clear firm hand—was easily readable, worlds after it had been written.

"The Chronicles of the Great Wolfking of Tara, Cormac mac Airt."

And underneath—

"And of his only daughter, Dierdriu."